Elizabeth Elgin is the bestselling novelist of *All the Sweet Promises* and *Whisper on the Wind*. She served in the WRNS during the Second World War and met her husband on board a submarine depot ship. A keen gardener, she has two daughters and five grandsons and lives in a lovely Roman village near York.

By the same author

Whistle in the Dark
The House in Abercomby Square
The Manchester Affair
Shadow of Dark Water
Mistress of Luke's Folly
The Rose Hedge
All the Sweet Promises
Whisper on the Wind

Writing as Kate Kirby

Footsteps of a Stuart
Echo of a Stuart
Scapegoat for a Stuart

ELIZABETH ELGIN

I'll Bring You Buttercups

Grafton
An Imprint of HarperCollins*Publishers*

Grafton
An Imprint of HarperCollins*Publishers*
77–85 Fulham Palace Road,
Hammersmith, London W6 8JB

Published by Grafton 1993
9 8 7 6 5 4 3 2 1

ISBN 0 586 21696 0

Set in Times

Printed in England by Clays Ltd, St Ives plc

To my father Herbert Wardley
whose book this is

1

1913

Alice Hawthorn had never been so happy, and not in her seventeen years past nor surely in the seventeen to come could she be this happy again.

To London! She was going to London by railway train; rushing and thundering through six counties to a city which was to her only a far-away fairy tale. Not that she didn't know all there was to know about that city. Miss Julia had spoken often of the parks and the genteel folk who strolled through them, and the shops – streets and streets of them – and theatres and music halls and squares of townhouses. Oh, and people *everywhere* and the King and Queen reigning over half the world!

She wriggled deeper into the feathers of the mattress and pulled the blankets high over her ears. She was so happy she was afraid, for sure as anything could Fate snatch back her happiness. Fate always had, ever since she could remember. That was why she had hurried to tell it to the rooks, for not until she had told it, shared it, could this happiness be safely hers to keep. It was important the rooks should know. Rooks kept confidences and held secrets safe. You told them all: of birthings and dying, of sorrow and joy and hopes and fears. You always told them.

Rooks, it's Alice here. She had stood, eyes closed, beneath the tallest tree in the wood, leaning against the trunk as though to link herself to the black birds that nested in it and wheeled and cawed above it. *You know me. I'm sewing-maid at Rowangarth and I'm to go to London with Miss Julia and I'm that excited I shall burst if I don't tell someone . . .*

She had almost gone on to tell them about Tom Dwerryhouse but had decided against it, though heaven only knew why. Tom and Alice. Even their names seemed to fit; sounded so right together that it sent a glow of contentment from the tip of her nose to the tips of her toes. Tom, the under-keeper with whom she was walking out – well, almost walking out. Tom who was tall and twenty-two and had fair hair and blue eyes and a smile that completely transformed a face inclined to seriousness.

She was glad he was clean-shaven, because when he kissed her – and one day very soon now he would – she didn't want it to be spoiled. Cousin Reuben had a moustache and he'd kissed her cheek the day he visited Aunt Bella with whom she once lived. She couldn't have been more than eight at the time, but the memory of that prickly kiss lived on through the years. Reuben wasn't really her cousin, though she called him that out of politeness, and because he was old.

She smiled, closing her eyes. She'd been on her way to Reuben's cottage the day she met Tom – and all because of a lovable, lolloping dog who'd caused more trouble in the few months he'd been at Rowangarth than two dogs in two lifetimes.

'Off you go, boy,' she had whispered, slipping his lead, smiling as he hurtled into the green deeps of the wood, and hardly had she placed a hand on Reuben's garden gate when she heard a roar so enraged that the whole of Rowangarth must have heard it, too.

'Drat you, dog, you great daft animal! There'll not be a game-bird left in this wood!' The man who strode towards her carried a shotgun over his right arm, his other hand firmly grasping the collar of a bewildered spaniel. 'Does this creature belong to you?'

'N-no, but he's with me.' Alice gazed up into eyes deep with anger. 'He belongs to Mr Giles and he isn't a creature. He's called Morgan and what's more he's got every right to run where he pleases,' she ended, breathlessly defiant.

This was *him*, it had to be: the new under-keeper whose coming not two weeks ago had sent housemaids and kitchenmaids for miles around into a tizzy of delight; the man who had been so oh'd and ah'd over at table that Mrs Shaw had been obliged to tell them to stop their foolish talk, and if he were as tall and broad and good to look at as they made out, didn't it stand to reason he'd be married, or at the very least promised?

'That animal runs where I say he can, and where I've got pheasants sitting on eggs, he isn't welcome. There won't be a bird to show for it come October if he frightens the hens off the nests. And Morgan? What sort of a name is that for a dog, will you tell me?'

'It's the name Mr Giles chose.' Alice tilted her chin. And this was Mr Giles's wood, like all the woods on the estate, or his as made no matter with his elder brother away in India. 'And what's more, I think Morgan suits him!'

'So it does. A daft name for a daft dog, and likely you aren't responsible for an animal not your own. But I've bother enough with hawks and magpies taking chicks and eggs: I can do well without that animal adding to my troubles. Now do you understand me, miss?'

'But I *always* walk him here.' Her mouth drooped at the corners.

'Not any more you can't, so best keep him near the house; trees enough for him there. Or you could let him run in the big meadow – if he isn't afraid of cows, that is.'

He threw back his head and his laugh showed white, even teeth, and made her want to laugh with him. But she refused to give him the pleasure, for even though there was no denying that all she had heard whispered about him was true – he *was* as handsome as the devil – she tilted her chin still higher, for the new keeper was bossy and full of his own importance. Taking the lead from her pocket she murmured, 'Come on home, Morgan.' They wouldn't stay where they weren't welcome. She would call on Reuben tomorrow and, anyway, it was almost time for tea.

Servants' tea at Rowangarth, when the big brown pot was set beside the kitchen range to warm and Mrs Shaw presided over bread and jam and fruit cake, was a happy time; the kitchen a haven of laughter and warmth where Alice Hawthorn could forget this slight.

'Bid you good day,' she had murmured in her most ladylike voice, deliberately refraining from using his name, though she knew it to be Tom Dwerryhouse. Everyone had known it; even the servants over at the Place.

Now she poked her nose out of the blankets to let go a sigh of relief, grateful that her hoity-toity behaviour hadn't frightened Tom off for good. And well it might have, she admitted, had it not been for Morgan and his disorderly ways, for to Tom a dog so undisciplined was a challenge, a creature to be taught its place. And she had to admit that no dog she'd ever known was as tiresome and unbiddable as a spaniel called Morgan – and no dog so lovable. She would miss him when she went to London.

'London,' she whispered into the darkness. So far away that the journey could take hours and hours and they would have to eat luncheon on the train from a picnic basket, Miss Julia said. And when they arrived at King's Cross station it would be she, Alice, who would call a porter with a raising of her forefinger and the slightest inclination of her head and instruct him to procure a cab for them. He would place their luggage on his trolley – Miss Julia would have three cases at least, as well as a hatbox and a travelling bag – and wheel it

10

to the cab rank. Already Alice had been well-schooled by Miss Clitherow, the tall, thin housekeeper whose back was as straight as a ramrod and who carried her head so high that when she looked at anyone it seemed she was looking down her nose at them. The housekeeper, if she consented to let a body get to know her, was a kind, lonely woman who was neither below stairs nor above and had long since learned that to keep herself to herself was by far the best solution.

Yet she had taken to Alice, right from the day the nervous girl of almost fourteen had presented herself in her ill-fitting clothes and too-big boots for the close scrutiny of Rowangarth's housekeeper; had found the girl's innocence and candour pleasant after some of the pert, badly spoken young women she had interviewed. Without hesitation she had given the position of under-housemaid to the brown-eyed child who came without references but with a glowing report of her docility from the aunt who had brought her up and from Reuben Pickering, head keeper at Rowangarth, related to the girl through a niece, once removed. And though she was never to know it, it had been on Miss Clitherow's recommendation that she was accompanying her employer's daughter to London, and the well-instructed Alice knew exactly how a lady's maid behaved; exactly how much money she should carry in her coat pocket and how much to tip – if the service had been good, that was. Because a lady like Miss Julia never called a porter or a cab, or stooped to ask the cabman how much, Miss Clitherow stressed, let alone proffered a tip. It was why a lady never travelled without a maidservant or chaperon. It was why, Alice exulted, she was going to London in two days' time and, even though it would part her from Tom for almost a fortnight, she wouldn't have missed it for all the tea in China or, to be fair to Rowangarth, in India!

'To the mews off Montpelier Place,' she would tell

11

the cab driver in a softly spoken, genteel way; to the Knightsbridge home of Miss Anne Lavinia Sutton, maiden aunt to Robert, Giles and Julia, elder sister of the late Sir John of Rowangarth, God rest him, who had gone to his Maker before his time and at great speed: at fifty-eight miles an hour, to be fatally exact.

Alice closed her eyes, willing herself to sleep. Tomorrow she must be up early, for there was unfinished work in the sewing-room; buttons to sew on Lady Helen's tea gown – fifteen of them – and heaven only knew how many darts and tucks her dinner dress needed.

Poor Lady Helen. It would make her sad to wear that long, full gown in lavender slipper-satin. Alice was prepared to bet she would have gone anywhere at all in it rather than to Pendenys Place. After all the long months in mourning for her husband, must she not be dreading this first public engagement for three years, Alice brooded. Wouldn't it have been better had she been able to accept some other, kinder ending to her years of black drapes and widow's weeds, for Pendenys was not the friendliest of houses to visit, even at the best of times.

But the Suttons of Pendenys Place were kin to the Suttons of Rowangarth, and it was to kin that a woman turned when her mourning had run its course and she was able to step back into society again – even kin she disliked.

'Lady Helen has lost weight,' Miss Clitherow remarked to Alice only the week before as together they shook out and pressed the morning dresses and tea dresses and dinner dresses and ball gowns put away for the period of milady's mourning. There would be a lot of work to be done before her sewing-maid went flitting off to London, she suggested pointedly, or where would her ladyship be, after so long in nothing but dreary black and purple? And Alice had fervently agreed and made

12

a mental promise that Lady Helen's clothes would all be seen to in good time, for she cared deeply for the mistress of Rowangarth, would always be grateful for the stroke of good fortune that landed her with the Rowangarth Suttons and not the Suttons of Pendenys Place. To have been in service at Pendenys, with the ill-tempered Mrs Clementina and the need always to be on the lookout for young Mr Elliot who thought all servants fair game, would have been unthinkable. She wondered why Lady Helen did not employ her own personal maid; why she preferred the aid of the housekeeper to help her dress and herself, the sewing-maid, to look after her clothes when Mrs Sutton of Pendenys had a lady's maid from France to keep her clothes immaculate and even to style her hair.

Alice sighed, and thought instead of the lace-trimmed, blue-flowered tea gown and the pernickety sewing-on of fifteen shanked buttons in mother-of-pearl. And so fiddling a job was it that she was soundly asleep by the time she had bitten off the cotton attaching button number three.

'I heard it whispered,' said Mrs Shaw, who stood on a three-legged stool in the servants' sitting-room, 'that you and Tom Dwerryhouse are walking out.' She had been longing to ask the question, but had refrained from asking it in public since it was obvious the lass wanted it kept a secret.

'Not walking out exactly,' Alice whispered from the swinging folds of Mrs Shaw's hem. 'But he does seem to have taken Morgan in hand: sits when he's told, that dog does now, and comes when I call him – or most times he does. And you can't say it isn't an improvement, and not before time, either.'

Alice didn't usually sew for Rowangarth staff, it being understood that when she had attended to the needs of her ladyship and Miss Julia, any spare time was spent repairing household linen. But Lady Helen was taking her afternoon rest, Miss Clitherow was away to town on Rowangarth business, and Miss Julia was out bicycling, so no one would be any the wiser if Alice spent a little time pinning up the hem of Cook's newly acquired skirt. And it was, remarked Mrs Shaw, an ill-wind that blew nobody any good because here she was, the recipient of a quality skirt, passed on by a friend in service in Norwich as a direct result of the sinking of the SS *Titanic* and the late owner of the skirt having no further use for it, so to speak. And more bounty to come. A good winter coat, Mrs Shaw had been promised, and anything else the poor unfortunate lady's executors thought fit to dispose of.

'He's a well set-up young fellow, yon gamekeeper,' Mrs Shaw pressed.

'Yes, and he likes dogs. Even sees good in Morgan.' Alice was not to be drawn. 'Can make him do anything. Now me – still sets me at defiance, sometimes. Fairly laughs at me – aye, and at Mr Giles, too. Turn round a little to your left . . .'

'Was Mr Giles that found him – the dog, I mean. By the side of the road, wasn't it?'

'It was, Mrs Shaw, and in a terrible state, all battered and bleeding. Wrapped the poor thing in his jacket and carried him to the village, to the veterinary. Vet said the dog had been whipped something cruel, and neglected too, and it looked as if he'd run away or been abandoned. Best put the poor creature to sleep, he said.

'But there were no bones broken, so Mr Giles brought him back to Rowangarth and him and Reuben got him on his feet again, between them.'

'Aye. And a nuisance he's been ever since, the spoiled animal,' the cook sniffed. 'For ever knocking things over; always in the kitchen, begging for scraps. And when I go to chase him back upstairs he looks at me with those big eyes. Well, what's a body to do, will you tell me?'

'Just like Mr Giles to bring him here, though. He don't like animals suffering.' Alice removed pins from her mouth. 'Don't like it when the shooting season starts. Not a one for killing, not really – well, that's what Cousin Reuben said. A waste of two keepers Rowangarth is, though it might have been better if Mr Robert had been here. You can step down now, Mrs Shaw . . .'

She gave her hand to the small, plump cook, who said that now the pinning was done she could see to the sewing herself and thanks for her trouble.

'No trouble, Mrs Shaw. And if your friend at Norwich sends you anything else, I'll be glad to help alter them. But tell me about Mr Robert? Why didn't he stay at Rowangarth after his father died? Why did he go back to India when her ladyship needed him here?'

'Mr Robert? *Sir* Robert it is now, him having inherited. And as to why he came home from India after Sir John got himself killed and saw to everything and got all the legal side settled then took himself off again with indecent haste leaving his poor mother with the burden of running the estate . . .' She inhaled deeply, not only having said too much for the likes of a cook, but had run out of breath in the saying of it, '. . . beats me,' she finished.

'But there's Mr Giles here, to see to things.' Alice liked Mr Giles. It was one of the reasons she took Morgan for a run every day.

'Happen there is, and I'm not saying that Mr Giles isn't good and kind and it isn't his fault he's got his head in a book from morning till night.

'It's his brother, though, who should be here, seeing to his inheritance and not bothering with that tea plantation, or whatever it is they call it.'

'A tea *garden*, Miss Clitherow says it is, and it's tea

15

that keeps this house on its feet,' Alice reminded. Tea came every year from Assam; two large chests stamped *Premier Sutton* and the quality of it unbelievably fine.

'Yes, and a tea garden that could well be looked after by a manager and not by the owner, my girl,' came the pink-cheeked retort. 'But it's my belief –'

'Yes, Mrs Shaw?' Alice whispered, saucer-eyed.

'It's my belief there's more to it than tea. More to it than meets the eye.' Nodding, she tapped her nose with her forefinger.

'A woman?'

'A woman. Or a lady. Can't be sure. But one he's fond of, or why did he go back to India when his duty's here, now that Sir John is dead and gone? Why doesn't he marry her and bring her back here as his wife, eh?'

'You don't think she's a married lady!'

'A married *woman*,' corrected Mrs Shaw from the doorway, 'and if you ever repeat a word of what I've just said –'

'Not a word. Not one word, Mrs Shaw. And I'll be off, now, to give Morgan his run.' And maybe see Tom, and perhaps discover where he would be working tonight, for gamekeepers worked all hours, especially when there were pheasants and partridges to see to, and poachers to look out for. 'See you at teatime, Mrs Shaw.'

Oooh! Young Sir Robert and a married woman! And him in love with her, or so it would seem. But it was easy to fall in love, Alice acknowledged, thinking about Tom and how far they'd come since that first stormy meeting. Very easy indeed.

Reuben Pickering spooned sugar into the mug of tea then handed it to the young man who sat opposite at the fireside. He was pleased enough with the underling who had recently come to Rowangarth and who, if he behaved himself, would one day be given the position of

16

head keeper. When he, Reuben, had presided over his last shoot, that was, and snared his last rabbit and shot his last magpie, and gone to live in one of the almshouses on the edge of the estate; in the tiny houses where all Rowangarth servants ended their days, were they of a mind to. And when that day came, young Dwerryhouse would leave the bothy where he lived and come to this very cottage with his wife, like as not – a thought that prompted him to say, 'Kitchen talk has it that you and young Alice are walking out.'

'Then talk has got it wrong, Reuben.'

'So when you meet her this afternoon it'll be by accident and not by design? Trifling with the lass, are you then?'

'Trifling? No. But what do you know –' He stopped, eyebrow quizzing.

'Know that whenever she brings that dog of Mr Giles's along the woodland path you always seem to be there, checking nests or just plain hanging about!'

'It's the only way I can see her,' Tom coloured. 'She's like a dandelion seed, is Alice Hawthorn. You think you've got her, then puff, she's away. But I didn't know there'd been talk, for there's nothing to tell,' he shrugged.

'Didn't hear it from gossip – not exactly,' Reuben chuckled. Hadn't he seen the pair of them; seen them often? It hadn't been all that difficult. A gamekeeper learns quickly to move like the shadow of a passing cloud; learns to drift in and out of sunlight dapples and to tread carefully and soft-like, so that neither beasts nor poachers know he's there, watching or waiting or following. 'Fond of the lass are you, Tom?'

'That I am, though I've held my tongue. Wouldn't do to tell her. I've a feeling she's a lass that might be easily frightened off.'

'So you haven't even kissed her?'

'That I have not!' The head jerked up and blue eyes blazed, staring into Reuben's paler ones, growing dim with age. Though it was more fool him, Tom silently admitted, for Alice's mouth was made for kissing, her tiny waist for cuddling, and that pretty, pert nose made him want her all the more when she tilted it, all hoity-toity.

'Then best you get a move on, or you'll be beaten to it.' By the son of Rowangarth's head gardener for one, who was serving out his time at Pendenys Place, or by the young red-haired coachman for another. 'Well, if you've got decent and gentlemanly intentions towards her, that is,' he added solemnly, him being related to Alice in a roundabout way and therefore responsible for her because of it.

'You think I don't know it? But I can't seem to make any headway. She's a fey one.'

'So are all lasses. They play you along like a fish on a line till they're ready to pull you in. Unless,' said Reuben, placing a log on the fire, 'you show her you mean business.'

'And how am I to do that? She tells me nothing; doesn't even talk about her family nor where she comes from; no, nor even if she has a young man back home. Won't give me a straight answer.'

'Nor will she, Tom. She has no family – save for me and my niece Bella. It was Bella took on the rearing of Alice when she was nobbut a bairn – and did it with bad grace, an' all. Many's the time that woman nearly packed the lass off to the workhouse. Well, stood to reason, didn't it; another mouth to feed on nothing but charity. Had her for seven years and begrudged every mouthful the bairn ate. Mean, my niece is.'

'Poor little Alice,' Tom said softly. 'To lose her folk, and her so young . . .'

'Younger than you think. Only a babe of two when her mam died, so her father left her with his mother and went off to be a soldier, the barmpot, and got himself killed at

18

Ladysmith. And the old granny didn't last long after that, neither, so Alice was farmed out again.'

'An orphan at three,' Tom frowned. 'She's never known a childhood.' Not like his own. Not a growing-up secure in the care of parents and a brother and two sisters to fight and squabble with and stand solid against the rest of the world with. 'Never known anything, really, but charity.'

'Aye, and charity that's given grudging is a cold thing, and as soon as the lass was old enough she came here, into service. The only good thing that woman did for Alice was getting me to speak for her to Miss Clitherow, or she might have ended up with the wrong Suttons; might have gone to that martinet over at Pendenys Place. And heaven help any lass that ends up there – especially one that's bonny to look at. The *Place* Suttons have no breeding, see? Brass, yes; background, no. Not the *right* background, any road.' Like all servants who were fortunate enough to end up with a family of quality, Reuben was a snob, and looked down on the Suttons at the Place.

'Now the Suttons here at Rowangarth – the *Garth* Suttons – have breeding. Goes back hundreds of years. Pedigree. That's what counts.' Reuben knew all about pedigree, from gun dogs upwards. 'So be sure to give Pendenys as wide a berth as you can, lad, for even their head keeper is crooked as they come and feathering his nest.'

'But she's all right now?' Tom didn't care about the Pendenys Suttons. All he wanted was to talk about Alice Hawthorn who had scarcely been out of his thoughts since the afternoon he met her. 'Alice seems happy enough at Rowangarth.'

'Oh my word, yes. A different young lady, these days. And done well for herself. Her mother was a dressmaker, so I'm told, and Alice seems to have inherited her skills.

She's sewing-maid, now, and answers to nobody but Miss Clitherow – and Lady Helen, of course. And her's going to London, maiding Miss Julia.' To London, and her not eighteen till June. All that way away when most folk never strayed beyond the Riding, let alone set foot outside of Yorkshire. 'Ah, well,' he consulted his pocket-watch, checking it with the ponderously ticking mantel-clock, 'if you've finished your sup of tea we'd best get on with the rounds. You take the woodland and I'll see to the rearing field.'

'Right, Mr Pickering.' Tom jumped instantly to his feet, giving the older man his full title, which was only polite once in a while. 'There's still a few nests not hatched out yet.'

Nests? Reuben chuckled, eyeing the fast disappearing back, when Alice and that Morgan dog should be walking the woodland? Always did, wet or dry, before servants' tea. And to be hoped when the lad met her he talked about summat more interesting than dogs and the weather, or he'd lose her, sure as eggs was eggs, he would. And Reuben didn't want that to happen, for he'd found a lot of good in young Dwerryhouse and he was more than fond of the lass who took the edge off his loneliness and was ever willing to sew on a patch, or a button or two, for an old widower. To have her settled with Tom would please him greatly.

'Sure as eggs is eggs,' he muttered, pulling on his hat.

Helen, Lady Sutton, sighed deeply and gazed at the lavender dinner dress draped carefully over the bed; at the matching satin shoes, the white silk stockings and the garters laid beside them. She did not want to wear those clothes, for when she had bathed and had her hair pinned and finished the time-consuming ritual of dressing, she would be going to dinner at Pendenys Place and she did not like Pendenys, nor anything about it, nor care overmuch for anyone who lived there – except Edward, that was.

'Why the frown, Mother?' Julia Sutton slammed shut the door behind her. 'I told you not to wear the lavender, didn't I? You're out of mourning now and lavender and mauve and purple are mourning colours and you shouldn't –'

'Julia! When will you learn to knock on a bedroom door and please, don't ever *tell* your mother anything! And what do you expect me to wear, newly out of black? Red, should it be, like a music hall soubrette?'

'Blue would have been lovely. Pa always liked you in blue.'

'Your papa is no longer here,' she whispered, her voice sharp-edged with remembered grief.

'No, darling. Sorry.' Julia brushed the pale cheek with gentle lips. 'And the lavender is perfectly acceptable, come to think of it, for a visit to Pendenys. Shall you wear your pearls?'

'I think not.' She didn't want to wear the pearl choker tonight; not her husband's wedding gift. 'Just the ear-drops, and flowers. They're in the pantry now, keeping fresh.'

Flowers. She would be wearing Pa's flowers, Julia frowned; she should have known it. Her mother had carried orchids as a bride, and thereafter Pa had ordered the cream-coloured beauties to be grown in the orchid house at Rowangarth. No one was to pick them without milady's permission, and no one was ever to wear them but her ladyship. A dashing declaration of love it had been, for though their marriage was arranged, they had loved deeply, too. And she, Julia Sutton, would marry for love or not at all. One day she would find the right man, and at the first meeting of their eyes he would know it and she would know it and . . .

'Darling Mama.' She hurried to where her mother sat, dropping to the floor at her feet, resting a cheek on her lap. 'I know how awful it will be for you without Pa, this coming out into the world again. But Giles will be with

21

you tonight. And I think she meant to be kind, asking you over there when she knew the time was right.'

'*She*, Julia?' The voice held a hint of reproof.

'Aunt Clementina, I mean, only I do so dislike calling her Aunt. It means she's *really* family . . .'

'Which she *is*,' Helen Sutton sighed.

'Well, Uncle Edward married her, I suppose, though the poor old love had to, him being –'

'No one *has* to do anything. How many times have I told you that?'

'Then when you say I must marry, can I remind you of what you just said?'

'I merely meant that Edward married her of his own free will.'

'And for her money . . .'

'Married Clementina Elliot of his own free will, Julia, and what else was he to do? What else is a second son whose expectations are nil to do?'

'Hm. I suppose Giles will have to do the same, poor pet – marry for money, I mean.'

'Your brother, I hope, will eventually love where money lies. It would be to his advantage were his wife to have some means of her own.'

'I don't think Giles will ever marry,' Julia shrugged. 'It's a pity he can't go to Cambridge. He'd be happy, there. Why must he stay here, just because Robert is too selfish to –'

'Julia! You mustn't speak of your brother in that way.' Helen Sutton rose swiftly to her feet and strode to the window. Mention of her eldest son always agitated her – and the secrecy he wrapped around himself; his selfishness in returning to India.

'Why mustn't I?' She was at her mother's side in an instant. 'You know he should have stayed here after Pa died. Why should Giles have all the bother of Rowangarth when it won't ever be his? Why can't Robert come home and marry and do what's expected of him? *Why?* Will you tell me?'

'Because your brother is his own master. Because he's a grown man and –'

'Then why doesn't he act like one? He's needed here, now, but he's oceans away, growing tea.'

'Tea keeps Rowangarth going – and besides, Robert loves India.' They were on dangerous ground and her daughter, Helen Sutton was forced to acknowledge, was altogether too blunt for her own good. 'And I don't wish to talk about Robert.'

'No. Nor his love for India – though I'll bet anything you like that isn't what her name is!'

'Julia! I will not –' Her voice trailed away into despair and she covered her face with her hands as if to block out the conversation.

'Mama! I'm sorry. You know I didn't mean to hurt you. And I know it's just three years since Pa went and I shouldn't be talking like this because you're the dearest mother anyone could wish for. You know I didn't mean what I said.'

'I know you didn't. But could we talk about tonight instead? Could I tell you how much I'd rather stay home – how much I'd rather do *anything* than accept Clemmy Sutton's hospitality.' Her lavish, ostentatious hospitality; her patronizing of the Garth Suttons, who were poor compared to the Suttons of Pendenys. Why did they irritate her so when it was obvious to anyone that jealousy was at the root of Clementina's discontent; because not all the money in the Riding could buy the one thing she – and yes, her father, too – coveted above all else and would never, could never possess.

She had come to Edward Sutton, that only child of an Ironmaster, with nothing to commend her but her father's riches, knowing she was tolerated but not accepted by the county society into which she had married. Her father

23

was in trade – it was as simple as that, and Clementina was considered to be as vulgar as the house her father's money had built. An obscenity in stone and slate was Pendenys Place; a flat-roofed, castellated building that had set out to be a gentleman's house and ended up believing itself a castle, so much pride and defiance had gone into it. For old Nathan Elliot's imagination had run wild when he built his daughter's house, and the architect, being young and ambitious and extremely poor, had not gainsaid his patron.

Pendenys boasted a butler, a housekeeper, two footmen and many servants, most of them young and poorly paid. It stood out like a great grey scab on the beautiful countryside, the only thing to commend it being that it could not be seen from the windows of Rowangarth.

Pendenys Place stood brash on a hilltop, a defiant monument to the pride of a self-made man, lashed by wind and rain and still not one iota mellowed by them.

Helen Sutton signed, becoming aware that her daughter's eyes regarded her with an openness she had come to expect, a frankness that was a part of her.

'Is something wrong?' She drew her fingers across her cheek. 'A smut?'

'No, dearest. Whilst you were miles away, thinking, I was thinking how beautiful you are and wondering why I'm not in the least bit like you.' Why she had not inherited the fineness of her mother's bones, her clear blue eyes, her thick, corn-yellow hair.

'Not like me? And you aren't like your father, either. I think you favour your aunt Sutton, child. You have her independence and her courage. But don't grow into an old maid like she is, because you have your own special beauty, though you won't admit it.

'Why do you freeze men out, Julia? Because you do, you know. Sometimes I think you go out of your way to do it.'

'I know I do. But it's only because the right man hasn't come along yet, and you did say, you and Pa, that you'd never interfere and let me marry where I wished. And I shall know him, when we meet. I'll know him at once, so don't worry about me. Let's talk about tonight, shall we, and Aunt Clemmy and her awful Elliot?'

'Must we?' Helen Sutton shuddered. She intensely disliked her brother-in-law's elder son; wondered why a stop hadn't been put to his extravagant ways, his drinking and his women. And especially to his whoring.

Blushing, she checked herself at once. She had allowed herself to think a word no lady should even know. But whoring – and there was no other word for it – and Elliot Sutton were synonymous, and she would rather her daughter entered a convent than marry a man with so dreadful a reputation. 'Must we talk about Clementina and her everlasting complaining about the cost of servants and the amount they eat?'

'Perhaps not.'

'Nor about her son who is no better than – than he ought to be.'

'Elliot . . . I suppose you can't entirely blame him for being as he is.' Julia Sutton was nothing if not fair. 'After all, his father spends his time buying books and reading books. I think Uncle Edward loves learning better than he loves his son, and you can't, as Mrs Shaw is always saying, make a silk purse out of a sow's ear. Elliot can't ever be a gentleman with a mother like Aunt Clemmy. She's common!'

'That is unfair! And Mrs Shaw shouldn't say things like that,' Helen gasped, though her eyes were bright with mischief and her lips struggled against a smile. And hadn't her John always said that a man could choose his friends, but his relations he was stuck with and must make the best of.

So tonight she would try her best to be kind to Clemmy

and her eldest son. She would wear her almost-out-of-mourning gown because it would be expected of her, and she would take the arm of her younger son for support and wear John's orchids with love.

Tomorrow it would be all over, and she could pick up the threads of her shattered life and face the world alone. And tomorrow, too, she would wave a smiling goodbye to Julia and Hawthorn and do nothing that would cast the least sadness on their great adventure.

'Let's talk about London,' she smiled.

'So what's this, Alice Hawthorn? You dog-walking again tonight, an' all?' The young keeper's face so reflected his pleasure that he even forgot to reprimand her for bringing a dog to the rearing field, where coops and runs for game chicks stood in orderly rows. 'Thought Mr Giles usually gave him his late-night run?' He bent to pat Morgan's head and fondle his ears and the spaniel whimpered with delight and wagged his tail so furiously that his rump wagged with it. 'Gone out, has he?'

'Gone out with her ladyship, and Miss Julia's away into Holdenby for supper at the vicarage, so Cook said staff could eat cold tonight and I wasn't needed to help out.' She finished, aware she was blushing furiously on account of her being here, because Reuben had told her when she passed his gate that Tom was in the rearing field shutting up the coops for the night, and that if she hurried she might just catch him there.

'Don't know what you mean,' she'd said, all airy-fairy as she strolled past, but she had run like the wind the moment she was out of sight of the cottage, desperate to see him. They were leaving for London early tomorrow morning, and if she didn't see him tonight, she had thought despairingly, she didn't know how she would live out fourteen days away from him.

'There now. That's the last of them done.' He placed a

26

board against the slats of the coop, leaning a brick against it. 'I'll walk you back, if you'd like.'

'You don't have to, Tom . . .'

'No trouble. It's on my way to the bothy.' He smiled again. 'Come on now, Morgan. Keep to heel,' he said in the stern voice he kept for the dog, nodding his satisfaction as the spaniel did exactly as it was told. 'So Lady Helen is visiting? Gone to Pendenys, so the coachman told me'

'Mm. Sad for her, isn't it, without Sir John? And she looked so beautiful tonight. We all stood in the hall to see her go – and so she'd know we wished her well, poor lady.

'There was Cook and Tilda from the kitchen, and Bess. And Mary who waits at table, and me. And Miss Clitherow gave her a hand downstairs. That frock has a bit of a train on it, so she had to walk very straight, and careful.' And proud, Alice thought, with her lovely head held high. 'She smiled when she saw us, Tom, and we all gave her a curtsey, though she don't ever expect it.' Not like one she could mention who – though she wasn't a lady and never would be, Cook said – had her servants bobbing up and down like corks in a bucket.

'Not a lot of staff at Rowangarth,' Tom offered his hand at the woodland stile. 'Not for a gentleman's house, I mean.'

'Happen not, but we manage. After all, Sir Robert's in India, Miss Julia's no trouble at all and Mr Giles is as often as not shut up in the library. And with her ladyship being so long in mourning and her not going out or receiving callers or giving parties – well, we haven't been overworked, exactly.'

'Do you remember what it was like at Rowangarth, Alice, before Sir John was killed? I reckon there'd be some fine old shoots, here on the estate?'

Alice didn't know about the shooting, she said, but she remembered one or two parties.

'They'd just had their silver wedding when the master was taken. My, there was half the Riding at that do. But I'd only been here a couple of months, then the house went into mourning when Sir John was killed.'

'A motor accident, wasn't it?'

'Aye, and all the fault of King Edward and his speeding.' All because the King had driven at *sixty* miles an hour, would you believe, along the Brighton road. After that, every motor owner had donned cap and gloves and goggles and tried his damnedest to do the same. But the Prince of Wales – they'd hardly got used to calling him King when he died – had waited so long to get his throne, Cook said, that he lived life fast and furious as if he'd known he'd get less than ten years out of his crowning. 'Sir John tried to drive faster than the King, you see, and skidded at a bend, and –'

'And that's why her ladyship won't have a motor,' Tom finished, matter-of-factly.

'That's why. And Mr Giles and Miss Julia both able to drive and desperate for motors of their own and not daring to buy one. Miss Sutton in London has a motor – it's at Aunt Sutton's house we'll be staying when we're in London. Oh, who'd have thought it? Someone like me maiding Miss Julia!'

'And what do you mean by that?'

'Well, someone – *ordinary*.'

'But you aren't ordinary, Alice Hawthorn.' He stopped, resting his hands on her shoulders, turning her to face him. 'You're *extraordinary* pretty, to my way of thinking.'

'*Pretty?*' Her eyes met his and she felt trapped and excited and peculiar, all at the same time. 'Oh, but I'm not! If you'd wanted to see what pretty is, you should have seen her ladyship tonight. So lovely she was, and all shining in satin. And no jewels at all, 'cept for her earrings. And her orchids, Tom; her own special orchids,

28

all creamy-white, same as she carried to her wedding to Sir John.

'They were special between them, those orchids. Oh, mustn't it have been wonderful, them loving like that – and romantic, to be given orchids. But listen to me going all soft. No one will ever give me orchids,' she sighed.

'Happen not, pretty girl, but it isn't all women are suited to orchids, and you are one of them. You, lass, are more in keeping with –' he bent to pluck some of the flowers that grew wild in the grass at their feet, smiling as he tilted her chin – 'to these. You're a buttercup girl, Alice. All fresh and shining you are, so hold yourself still so I can see if you like butter.' He held one of the flowers to her throat and smiled at the golden glow that shone from the whiteness of her skin. 'Oh, aye, you're a buttercup girl, and no mistake.'

'I am?' She closed her eyes because his mouth was only a kiss away and she had wanted so long for him to kiss her.

'That you are. Let them keep their fine flowers, Alice. I'll give you buttercups, my lovely lass, and they'll be more special between us than the rarest orchid that ever grew.'

He touched her lips gently with his own and fire and ice ran through and left her shaking and afraid to open her eyes lest he should see what shone there. And when he gathered her to him it was like a homecoming, and she lifted her arms and wrapped them gently around his neck because it was the only way she knew to tell him that she would like to be kissed again.

'You're my girl, aren't you, Alice?'

He had never expected it would be like this; never thought he would feel tenderness for her along with his wanting, nor once imagined he would feel like throttling with his own hands any man who threatened to harm her innocence.

'I'm your girl, Tom . . .'

'So we're walking out steady, now, and you'll sit by me in church?'

'When I'm back from London.'

'Then look at me, and tell me so.'

'Tom?' All at once it was easy and she looked smiling into his eyes and whispered, 'I'm your girl, Tom Dwerryhouse, and I love you. There now, does that suit you?'

'It does, sweetheart. It suits me very nicely.' His eyes loved her as he handed her the buttercups. 'Very nicely indeed.'

She closed her eyes again and sighed tremulously. In her lonely youth she had longed for this; yearned to be close to someone, and special. Not so long ago she had been so happy about London she had told the rooks she was fit to burst of it, but this was different. This was even better than happiness. Tonight, Tom had kissed her, and she was loved.

2

London seethed and shimmered and sang with magic: nothing but houses in streets and terraces and squares; trees in May leaf and parks pink and white with blossom; elegant ladies and elegant shops; costermongers yelling their fruit for sale; motors honking, and cab drivers shaking their whips at motors for frightening their horses and oh, just *everything*.

'I said you'd like London, didn't I, Hawthorn?'

'Oh, *yes*.' She did, now that she had become as off-hand about it as Miss Julia; used to the size and the speed and the sound of it and learned to keep out of the way of motor drivers and cab drivers, all determined to run her over. Already they had window-gazed and walked in Hyde Park and St James's Park and visited Westminster Abbey and stood, shaking with excitement, at the gates of Buckingham Palace – though not so much as a glimpse of the King and Queen had there been. And now they sat, feet aching from the London pavements, in the kitchen of Aunt Sutton's tiny, tucked-away house, eating sandwiches and drinking tea and discussing where to go tonight.

'We mustn't waste money on theatres and things, Hawthorn. A lot of London is free, if you know where to go. Soon we shall take a trip on the Underground, but tonight we must try to find a meeting.'

'A meeting, miss?' Alice frowned, all the while thinking fearfully of trains that hurtled through dark tubes dug deep beneath London.

'You *know* what kind of meeting.'

She knew, but like riding on a tube train, Alice was determined not to think too much about it, though it wasn't any use ignoring the fact that Miss Julia was looking for a political meeting – a Votes-for-Women meeting – and if Lady Helen ever got to hear about it there'd be no end of a to-do.

'Take care of my daughter, Hawthorn. Don't let her lead you a dance,' she'd said as they left Rowangarth, but when Alice thought about it, there wasn't a lot a sewing-maid could do if her young mistress was set on going to one of those meetings; nothing, save go along with her because that, really, was why she was in London. But downright ridiculous it was, and a waste of time, because what would a woman do with a vote, even supposing she got one? At least that was what Cook wanted to know when they talked, one teatime, about the suffragettes who'd been sent to prison for causing an affray and had straight away refused all food. And the prison warders were compelled to force-feed them – for their own good – which couldn't have been very pleasant, Alice remembered thinking.

'Force-feed,' Tilda scathingly remarked. 'Isn't nobody can make you eat if you don't let your throat swallow.'

'Happen not. But they force a tube down your throat,' Cook had retorted, red-cheeked, 'then they pour slops down it, so you'd be *forced* to eat. Force-feed, see? That's what they mean by it.'

'Meeting, miss?' Alice closed her mind to the horror. 'One of Mrs Pankhurst's meetings? I don't think her ladyship would like that, nor Miss Sutton.'

'But my mother isn't here, nor Aunt Sutton.'

No. Nor Miss Sutton's maid, either. Indeed, they were alone in this house – apart from the cleaning woman who came mornings. It was unheard of, Alice brooded. Lady Helen would never have allowed the London trip had she known her sister-in-law's live-in maid would be away in Bristol for a family wedding, and staying on there for a holiday.

'I don't know why Miss Sutton didn't think to mention it to her ladyship – about us being here on our own, I mean.'

'Nor do I,' Julia grinned, 'but I'm glad she *thought* she'd mentioned it.' Always forgetful, her father's elder sister – when it suited her, that was. 'And you aren't going to mention it when we get back home, are you, Hawthorn?'

Alice said she wasn't, though she didn't like being a party to deceiving Lady Helen. Suffragette meetings were illegal now; had been since last year when there'd been terrible trouble over breaking windows and knocking off policemen's helmets and the forced feeding in prison. But Miss Julia was set on going, though if they ran away quickly when the police arrived, then surely no one need be any the wiser.

'If we were to find one of those meetings, miss, you wouldn't do anything awful, would you?'

'Of course I wouldn't. I just want to be there, that's all. Oh, isn't it nice doing exactly as we please and no one at all to boss us about?'

Alice had to agree that it was. It was better than nice, in fact, because Miss Julia was no end of a good sport who, since they'd been in London, had treated her almost like an equal. And wasn't she being stupid, Alice asked of her conscience, to start making a to-do about a meeting that might never come about when she was having such a fine time?

Where was the wrong in one forbidden gathering when Miss Julia hadn't so far done anything awful, like meeting a young man or going without a gentleman escort to a music hall, even though she had the spunk to do either had she been of a mind to. Miss Julia had more about her than her brother Giles, who was quiet and bookish. Julia Sutton, it had more than once been remarked upon, should have been born a lad, so much devilment had she in her.

'*Exactly* as we please? We won't be looking for trouble, will we? Well, I *am* responsible for you and –'

'You? Responsible for *me*? Oh, Hawthorn, you're only a child!'

'I'm eighteen!' Well she would be, come June.

'And I will be twenty-one soon, so it is I who must look after *you*.'

She was right, Alice conceded silently. Not only was Julia Sutton older but she was wiser, too, if you thought how far afield she had been: to Switzerland and France and to London ever so many times; whilst she, Alice Hawthorn, had never set foot outside the Riding until now.

But she *was* here: just to think how it would be when she got back, with everyone demanding to know what London was like, and gasping and exclaiming when she told them about sitting in a ladies-only first-class compartment, and riding through the crowded London streets to the house of Miss Anne Lavinia Sutton, so near to Hyde Park you could see the tops of the trees from your bedroom window. Indeed, the whole of Holdenby village would be curious about it. The comings and going of the Garth Suttons and the Place Suttons provided a fair proportion of Holdenby gossip – not to mention the goings-on of Mr Elliot Sutton.

What a journey it had been: such speed, and the two of them eating luncheon as the rest of the world rushed past the window of their compartment. It was only the second time Alice had been on a railway train, the first time so long ago that she couldn't recall it at all and had had to take Aunt Bella's word for it. So she wasn't going to say anything about them being alone in Miss Sutton's house, nor about trying to find a Votes-for-Women meeting, because these two weeks in London would stay with her for the rest of her life and be brought out fresh and bright when she was old to be lived through again. And the things she would have to tell Tom!

She smiled to remember that night – the buttercup night – and the yellow flowers which now lay carefully wrapped in tissue paper and placed inside her Bible at her favourite place. Luke, Chapter Two: *And she brought forth her firstborn son, and wrapped him in swaddling clothes, and laid him in a manger; because there was no room for them in the inn* . . . Tom's buttercup, and the Christmas story.

'Hawthorn! What are you brooding about now?'

'I – er – just about what you'll be wearing tonight. Best tell me, miss, so I can give it a brush and a press.'

'Something plain I suppose, and ordinary. Well, I shan't want to look frivolous and uncaring, shall I? Women getting the vote is important – to be taken seriously.'

'And you agree with it, miss – that some women should be given the vote?'

'Not some women – *all* women over twenty-one. And not *given* it. It should be theirs by right.'

'Yes, miss. I'll put out the blue costume and the pale blue blouse, then?'

'Whatever you think. And Hawthorn – nothing will happen tonight and, anyway, there mightn't even be a meeting because they don't exactly advertise them now. Wouldn't do to have the police waiting to stop it before it had even started, now would it? So don't look so worried.'

'All right.' There wasn't anything else to say, come to think of it, because tonight something *would* happen, she was sure of it, though whether good or bad or a mixing of both, she couldn't for the life of her tell. But they would be there, the two of them, at Speakers Corner, hoping to find a meeting. And finding trouble, like as not . . .

'Thank you, Mary.' Helen Sutton smiled as the parlourmaid set down a tray bearing afternoon tea.

'Is it muffins?' Her son lifted the plate cover.

'No, it is not. Muffins are consolation for winter, Giles. It's May, now, so it's egg-and-cress sandwiches, I hope. Now pour my tea, won't you? I feel like being spoiled today.'

'What did my sister say in her letter?' Giles Sutton demanded, passing the cup.

'Julia seems to be having a grand time and says that Hawthorn is, too.'

'Dear little Hawthorn. I miss her.'

'Don't you mean that you miss her looking after your dog?'

'Well, I've got to admit that Morgan misses her too, but giving him his outings does get me out, once in a while.'

'I don't know why you spend so much time in that dull old library.'

'I like it there.' He liked the library better than any room in the house: the smell of old books and wax-polished furniture, the slow, soothing tick of the clock, and dust-motes hanging sunlit on the still air. Peace, there, and words for the reading. It was all he ever wanted, come to think of it, except to go to his father's old college at Cambridge. 'But how do you feel, Mother, now that it's all behind you?' He referred, hesitantly, to her period of mourning. 'It's good to see you out of that dreary black.'

'That dreary black was necessary. I wore it for your father, Giles. Not because society demanded I should, but because it suited my mood.'

'You still miss him, don't you, dearest?

'I miss him.' And not so old, yet, that she didn't want him, too, and the comfort of his nearness. 'And I don't know what your father would have thought to both his sons still being unmarried. One son interested only in tea-growing, and the other never so happy as when he's got his nose in a book!'

But they were men, both of them, for all that. It was

36

just that neither had yet decided upon a suitable wife. And at least they didn't flaunt their masculinity like some not so far from this very house. Why, even the other night at Clementina Sutton's dinner party, Elliot hadn't been able to keep his eyes – or his hands, if she hadn't been mistaken – off the parlourmaid who helped at table. She could almost feel sorry for her brother-in-law's wife and the embarrassment their eldest son must cause her.

'Why the sigh, Mother?'

'Nothing, really. Just a sigh. A coincidence, I suppose, that I happened to be thinking about your cousin.'

'Elliot? It's a butcher's daughter now, I believe. And trouble, so I heard.'

'Giles! You mustn't listen to kitchen gossip!'

'Not even when it's true? They were talking about it in the stables. I heard them. The man's a fool. Why can't he do his carrying-on in London, though I suppose he's at it there, too, when it gets too hot for him around here.'

'I think you're right. One of these days, Elliot will find himself in real trouble.'

'Which he'll be promptly bought out of with old Nathan's money.'

'I fear so.' She stirred her tea reflectively. 'What that young man needs is a good whipping, and more's the pity his father doesn't give him one before he's beyond redemption.'

'Don't blame his father. Like me, Uncle Edward was born a second son.'

'And second sons must shift for themselves – I know; though it seems that both you and your uncle would have been better suited to the academic life. For Edward it was a choice of the army or the Church – so the poor man chose Clementina.'

'Aunt Clemmy chose him, don't you mean?' Giles laughed, making his mother wonder why this serious, bookish son of hers didn't laugh more often, and why he didn't marry and give her grandchildren; for it seemed that her other son, whose duty it was to provide an heir, had little intention of doing so in the foreseeable future.

'Must go, dearest,' Giles kissed his mother's cheek with affection, 'and give Morgan his outing. When will Hawthorn be back?'

'Not for a while yet; and Giles,' Helen murmured, eyeing his pocket with mock severity, 'that animal will always be fat if you insist on spoiling him with titbits.'

'Just a macaroon. He's very fond of them.' He grinned, boyishly disarming, which made his mother love him all the more and send up a small prayer of thanks that her younger son at least did not prefer India to the springtime greenness of Rowangarth.

Rowangarth. So dear to her. Built more than three hundred years ago at the time of King James's dissertation on witches and the evils of their craft. Small, by some standards, for the home of a gentleman of ancient title, but built square and solid against the northern weather, and with a rowan tree planted at all four aspects of the house, for witches feared the rowan tree and gave it a wide berth, their early ancestor had reasoned. And should a rowan tree die of age or be uprooted in a high wind, another was always planted in its place. It was still the custom, and thus far the Suttons had prospered, having had no generation without a male heir, so the descent was direct and ever would be, Helen Sutton fervently hoped. And above all else, Rowangarth was a happy place in which to live – which was more than could be said for her brother-in-law's home, if one could call Pendenys Place a home.

'Pendenys,' she murmured, shaking her head. Completed little more than twenty-five years ago, the newness was still on it, with its carefully arranged trees little more than saplings still, and the house proud and cold and loveless. It made her feel sorry for her husband's younger brother, and the need for him to love where money lay. Edward Sutton had not been cut out for clerical orders, and even to think of being a soldier had left him cold with apprehension. So he had married Clementina, daughter of Nathan Elliot, an Ironmaster of prodigious wealth, whose ambitions for his only child were boundless. Thus brass, so local talk insisted, had married breeding, as so often happened these days.

Clementina had come to Edward Sutton possessed of a dowry that built Pendenys Place. The house had been named for Clementina's grandmother, Cornish-born Mary Anne Pendennis who, talk had it, had scrimped and saved and even taken in washing to help fund that first, long-ago Elliot foundry.

Yet Clementina had done her duty by her marriage contract, Helen admitted with scrupulous fairness, and had given Edward three sons in as many years, then straight away closed her bedroom door to him, enabling him to live his own life again, more or less, and return, duty done, to his beloved books. And his wife, secure in her loveless marriage, ruled Pendenys like the martinet she was, doing exactly as she pleased, for it was she who paid the piper.

Helen clucked impatiently, wishing Clementina would mellow just a little, be less belligerent. Clemmy was so insular; could not forgive anyone she deemed better born than herself; still clung unconsciously to her roots and sheltered behind the power her father's money gave her. Defiantly, she had called her first son Elliot, determined her maiden name should not be forgotten; her second-born she named for her father, Nathan, and her third child for her father's father, Albert. Her eldest son wanted for nothing, and coveted only one thing: the knighthood his father had not received, despite the many and bountiful donations made by his mother to Queen Victoria's favourite charities.

39

Now Elliot secretly hoped that pestilence would strike down his Rowangarth cousins Robert and Giles, thus ensuring the baronetcy would pass, eventually, to him. Not, Helen frowned, that she could be *sure* that Elliot thought it, but she was as certain as she could be that he did.

'And her servants,' Helen confided to the vase of lilac reflected in the window-table. 'She screams at her servants, too.'

Clementina harangued her domestic staff as no lady would ever do. Reprimands to servants should be given to the housekeeper to pass on, for a lady never stooped to such behaviour. Not ever, Helen sighed. And now, she supposed, she must return Clementina's kindness – if kindness the recent dinner invitation to Pendenys had been – and ask her to Rowangarth. And since her husband would find an excuse to decline, he being so embarrassed by his wife's loud voice, and since it always left him pained to visit the home he had been born in; it would be Elliot Sutton who would accompany his mother to Rowangarth, and his braying laugh and doubtful jokes would be a discomfort to all, except to his doting mother.

Helen set down her cup. The tea had gone cold and she decided against sending for a fresh pot. The servants would be taking their own tea now, and it wasn't kind to send one of them hurrying to answer her ring.

She sighed again, tears rising to her eyes. Instantly, she blinked them away. 'Oh, John,' she whispered to the empty room, 'I do so miss you, my dearest.'

Alice held the flat-iron an inch from her cheek, satisfying herself it was hot enough, then rubbed it in the tray of powdered bathbrick to clean and polish it, relieved that Miss Julia's blue costume had travelled well, with hardly a crease in it to press out.

She glanced around the kitchen, easily the largest room in the house, at the brown sinkstone and shining brass taps; at the wooden plate rack above it; the red-tiled floor and the white, bright paintwork. All this pretty little house was white. It was the new fashion, Julia said. There was white furniture, too, in the bedrooms, and pots and pots of ferns: aspidistras were completely out of favour, now. It was so different, this light, bright house compared to Rowangarth in the far-away north.

To recall her home – for Rowangarth was her home now, and she wanted never to leave it, except with Tom – brought a pang of longing for the ages-old house that lay gently in a fold of the hills, sheltered and secure.

Rowangarth had been built with mellow stone, pillaged from a roofless priory nearby. It was an early Jacobean house, with mullioned windows and twisted chimneys. Inside there was oak in plenty – wall panels, staircases and uneven floorboards – and rooms built smaller for warmth in winter yet with high, wide windows to let in the summer sun. Rowangarth smelled of wax polish and musty tapestries and wood fires, and of smoke, too, when the wind blew from the south – which wasn't often – hitting Holdenby Pike and gusting down chimneys to send smoke and soot billowing. But mostly the wind blew from the north-east; a fire-whipping wind that sucked smoke from the ancient flues and reddened fires and heated ovens with no bother at all. Rowangarth was a winter house that wrapped itself around those who lived there; Aunt Sutton's house was a bright, summertime house that had once been part of the stables at the back of Montpelier Place. Stables, indeed, and Miss Anne Lavinia Sutton a lady born!

But perhaps it was one of Miss Julia's jokes. You never knew when to believe her and when to take what she said with a pinch of salt, for she was always teasing

41

or laughing, though once she had given up her tomboy ways she would grow into a very beautiful lady. Miss Julia was fair-to-middling now, but mark Cook's words, those beautiful bones of hers would come into their own before so very much longer, and there'd be young men killing themselves for love of her. And when, Cook had plaintively demanded, was the girl going to get herself wed? There was nothing Cook would like better than a wedding at Rowangarth, now milady's mourning was over, with dinner parties beforehand and such a wedding feast that the skill of Rowangarth's Mrs Shaw would be the talk of the Riding for years to come; the yardstick by which all other wedding feasts were measured!

Alice smiled down at the blue jacket, shook it gently, then draped it on a chair-back. Blue of any shade suited Miss Julia; it seemed to shade her grey eyes and make them look larger than ever. Julia Sutton's eyes were beautiful, and her brown hair waved softly so it was a pleasure to dress and hardly ever needed hot tongs.

Alice wondered if she should press her long scarf, for didn't folk say it could be draughty on that Underground railway, and mightn't it be wise if she were to tie down her hat?

She sighed, wishing the trip on the tube train had never been mentioned, though it was safe as houses she was assured, with people riding on the Underground every day of the week. And what Miss Julia said was doubtless correct: that she would be glad that she had done it. It wasn't given to many around Holdenby to ride on a tube train, even though Alice didn't think it natural to burrow beneath a city like moles.

Carefully she carried the costume upstairs, laying it over the bed with the blouse, then took out a clean chemise and drawers and black silk stockings. Later, she would help Miss Julia to dress, pulling and tugging at her corset laces from the back until the girl cried,

'Enough!' and was satisfied with the shape nature had never intended her to be. Corsets, said Julia, were the very devil, and one day women would refuse to wear them, just see if they didn't! It was good, Alice smiled, that the dress of servants was far less bothersome; good that her shape was her own.

Closing the bedroom door she took the narrow, twisting stairs to the attic in which she slept, thinking of the costume in finest grey flannel she had been given.

'Take it, for I'm sick and tired of black and grey!' Julia Sutton had said when her mourning for her father came to an end. Children were luckier than their elders; needed only to shut themselves away in drabness for one year, not three. 'And take this black skirt, if you'd like it, and these white blouses!'

Alice had gratefully accepted such bounty, for were not grey and black the colours servants wore, and mightn't it be fine, now that she and Tom were walking out officially, to have so beautiful a costume to wear for him; to walk proudly at his side in, with pink satin roses on her hat?

Tom. Thomas Dwerryhouse. Her cheeks pinked just to think of him; to think how she missed him and loved him and how very much she wanted him to kiss her. And though she was enjoying every minute of her stay in London, she wouldn't complain when they boarded the train for home. And meantime, there was Miss Julia's shoes to polish, and her own boots too, and a meal to prepare before their evening outing.

Life was all rush and bustle. Life was *wonderful*!

They walked through Hyde Park in the direction of Marble Arch and Speakers Corner, looking like young ladies of quality, Alice thought with delight, with Miss Julia stepping daintily because of her fashionable long hobble skirt, and herself in the grey flannel and a flower-trimmed hat.

'What a beautiful evening, Hawthorn. It's much warmer here than at home.'

It was, Alice had to admit, with none of the northern sharpness in the early night air. It was a perfect evening in every way, because even if they did find a meeting and even if the police got wind of it, they'd just take to their heels and run, wouldn't they, laughing at the fun of it, though sad that it would be one adventure that neither would ever dare speak about when they were back home again. But Rowangarth and parental authority were a long way away, and this was a May evening in London, and they still had a week to run before they must leave it all behind.

She wondered what she would say to Tom after so long apart, and he to her. Maybe, though, there would be no need for words; just a whispered 'Hullo', and she closing her eyes and lifting her chin, the better, the sweeter for him to kiss her. It was, she thought happily, so nice to stroll companionably at Miss Julia's side and daydream of Tom.

The sooner a woman took charge of her own destiny, Julia reasoned silently, the better; though if the men who ruled their lives had anything to do with it, she would wait long and maybe in vain, for even though a woman was now allowed by law to keep her own money when she married, she still belonged to her father in her youth and to her husband in marriage. A woman, she frowned, was allowed no opinions of her own. Politics was men's business.

'I think here will do nicely.' She stopped at a bench on which they could sit and wait and later stand so they might miss nothing of the speakers, if any speakers arrived, that was, and were not discovered by the police – which they almost certainly would be. 'And all this is our own fault, Hawthorn,' she fretted. 'We are our own worst enemies. We come into this world precisely made for the bearing of children, and men take advantage of the fact!'

Women, she reasoned, died too young, worn out by too many pregnancies. 'You must have no more babies,' doctors would warn, but women were never told how, for birth control and the advocating of it was illegal, and those women who campaigned for the vote were still dependent on the indulgence of a government made up entirely of men. And men were afraid that a vote would give women an undue advantage, for weren't there far more women than men? To allow a woman such a weapon would be nothing short of madness; a surrender, some even went so far as to say, to bitch-power.

'And I'll tell you something else, Hawthorn. Until women can have babies *when* they want them, *if* they want them, we'll never get anywhere!'

'Miss! Don't talk like that,' Alice wailed. 'You'll get us locked up. Having babies is what women are for!' Who ever heard of a man having a baby? 'It's what the good God intended us to do!' It was as plain as the nose on your face, and nothing – not even giving a woman two votes – would change it.

'Did He now? Intended us to be wives and providers of heirs. And to scrub and clean, too, and be grateful to some man for putting a ring on our finger? A servant for life, that's what you'll be, and me not so much better!'

'But, Miss Julia, that's what I am. Being a servant is all I've ever known and I – I think I shall like very much being married,' she hesitated. 'I *want* to marry Tom.' She could think of nothing nicer, in fact, than having her own home – her very own home – and being beholden to no one. 'Yes, I *do*.'

'Tom? You haven't got a young man,' Julia gasped. 'Oh, not Dwerryhouse? But, Hawthorn, they're *all* in love with Dwerryhouse!'

'Then I'm the lucky one, aren't I? Because Tom and me are walking out seriously. On the night milady went to Pendenys – that was when he asked me. And I said yes, so those others had better find someone else to be in love with!'

'Oh, my dear, I'm so glad for you, I truly am. You *lucky* girl! Are you really in love? Really and truly, I mean?'

'I don't know, miss, and that's for sure. It's the first time it's happened to me, and the last, I hope. But if being in love makes you feel contented all over, and special, and if the sun comes out every time you see him – even on a rainy day – then yes, I suppose I am.

'Mind, I haven't told anyone, yet. Not even Cousin Reuben. Tom and me can't marry, you see, till Reuben retires. There'll be nowhere for us to live till then. And I'm only eighteen, so that gives me three years to get used to it and to –'

'To be quite sure you're both suited?'

'Yes. Though I know we are. I've never been so sure of anything in my life before.'

'Then I envy you. I would so like to be in love,' Julia sighed. 'Not engaged, or anything. Not something arranged by the families, but a real romance and me knowing, the moment I set eyes on him, that he's the one. And I shall know. The minute I see him, I'll know . . .'

'The minute,' Alice confirmed, yet wondering why, when Miss Julia had been presented at Court, something didn't happen for her then. After all, that's what it was really about. The season in London was really a marriage-market, and the gentry, if they were honest, would be the first to admit it. Most young ladies of Julia Sutton's age and station in life were wedded and bedded by now – aye, and some were with child. 'Hadn't you thought to meet your husband when –'

'When I ought to have done, you mean; when I made

my curtsey to the King and Queen and had my London season?'

'Well – yes . . .'

'Ah, but Hawthorn, at the beginning of my season, Pa was killed and there was an end to my coming-out before it had hardly begun. Mourning for a year for me, and for Aunt Sutton too. And three years in purdah for my mother. Betrothal and marriage just don't arise when a house is in mourning.

'But do you know, those three years haven't been wasted, because they gave me time to think about what I really wanted to do with my life, and one of the things that came out of it was the certain fact that I wanted to choose my husband for myself.'

'Choose your own –' Alice gasped. But the upper classes *never* chose their own husbands!

'Indeed. And what was more, my mother said I might. She even said Pa would have agreed with her, too, because though their marriage was arranged, they'd been in love for ages beforehand, and kept it a secret.'

'Oh, how lovely.' Tears misted Alice's eyes and she felt suddenly closer to her employer's daughter and found herself hoping that she too could know the joy of loving and being loved. 'And maybe you'll meet him, soon. Maybe he might be just around the next corner.'

'The next corner we come to will be Speakers Corner and I'm almost sure that the only men who'll be around there will be policemen and I very much doubt –'

'Look, miss! Over yonder!' Alice pointed excitedly to the roadway and the carriage drawn by two splendid white horses. 'Those horses! There's a wish on a white horse. One for you and one for me. Close your eyes and cross your fingers and wish, *quickly*, afore they're out of sight!'

Foolishly, fervently, they wished, neither confiding in the other, for both knew that a wish shared was a wish

47

wasted, and Alice let go her indrawn breath and opened her eyes and Julia did the same. Then smiling, she said, 'We mustn't tell, Hawthorn.'

'No, we mustn't.' But oh, when Miss Julia met him, let him be tall and broad and handsome and let him be rich enough to keep her in the manner to which she'd been born – *please*?

It seemed there would be no meeting that night; at least, not at Hyde Park Corner, for there was no gathering of waiting women, no banners, no policemen lurking.

'Shall we go back, miss?' Alice murmured with relief. 'Looks as if nothing's going to happen, and if we go home by way of the bandstand, perhaps there'll be music.'

'No, Hawthorn. We must stay just a little longer. Someone might come.'

They sat down again, stubbornly to wait it out, for it stood to sense, didn't it, that forewarned was forearmed, Julia declared. If the police knew *exactly* when a meeting was to be held, they could all the more easily prevent it. The police, she flung, were the instruments of their masters, the Government, and wasn't that government made up entirely of men; men ruling women's lives?

'It's the way of the world,' Alice reasoned forlornly, for she would rather have listened to the band. She was not interested in politics because not for a minute would men even consider giving the vote to women. It would make a woman a man's equal, almost, and men would never stand for that.

A woman carrying a child over her shoulder walked past them and Julia nodded her head in the direction of the pale-faced mother.

'Look at her. Not a lot older than I am, I shouldn't wonder, yet that's her life for the foreseeable future – a baby or a miscarriage every year. And why? Simply because her husband doesn't know any better!'

'But that's what they call nature, Miss Julia. It's the way things are.'

'It needn't be. They don't have to wear themselves out having children they can't afford. If they listened to Doctor Stopes, and people who think like her, it needn't.'

Alice's mouth made an ooh of protest, for she had heard of the young woman who advocated birth control. Disgusting, Cook said it was, and not fit for a young girl's ears and if women didn't want to have babies there was one sure and certain remedy. Let them stay unwed!

'Ooooh, miss, where do you hear of such things?' But that was what came, she supposed, of sending a girl to a boarding school. Julia Sutton wouldn't have been exposed to such free thinking at the Church of England school in Holdenby village.

'Learn? You read, I suppose, and you listen. And if ever you get the chance, you reason calmly and sensibly. And you keep on and on, like the suffragettes are doing, until men take notice of what you say.'

'And is that why you aren't married or spoken for – is it because of the way you think?'

'No, Hawthorn. I want to be married, but only to the right man. And until I meet him I shall go on sticking up for women and –'

'And getting yourself disliked, miss, if you'll pardon me. You don't want to end up a lonely old lady, do you, like Miss Sutton?'

'But my aunt *isn't* lonely and, what's more, she does precisely what she wants. Aunt Sutton thinks more of good food and good horseflesh than about husbands. That's why she's always taking off for the Camargue – it's where the men worship horses and the women are all fine cooks, she says. She'd live there all the time if she could.'

'And does Miss Sutton believe as you do; does she believe women should have the vote and not have babies unless they want them?'

'I really don't know. It's not a subject one discusses with family. But Aunt Sutton is broad-minded and very forward-thinking and I wouldn't mind betting she agrees with everything I say.

'And you mustn't breathe one word at Rowangarth of what I've said tonight – not to *anyone* – nor that we've been looking for a meeting, because it would upset my mother and I wouldn't do that for all the votes in the world. So you promise, Hawthorn, don't you?'

'I promise.' Not one word would she breathe. Ever.

'Good. And it looks as if we might as well give up and come back another night and – oh – *look* . . .'

'Where?' Alice frowned uneasily.

'By the big gate. A woman, and she's selling something,' Julia pointed. 'She's giving out handbills – or is it newspapers?' She was off as fast as her skirt would allow in the direction of the gate and the several women who had appeared from nowhere. 'Come on, Hawthorn. Oh, *damn* this stupid skirt!'

The woman who sold papers was tall and slim, with hair swept back in waves around a high-cheeked face. She asked one penny for the single sheet of print which was headed, to Julia's great joy, *The Suffragette*.

'Thank you,' she gasped, handing over a sixpenny piece and waving away the change. 'And can you tell me where the next meeting will be? Tonight, is it? Will there be any use in waiting?'

'Sorry, my dear, not yet. Not just yet. Not safe, you see . . .' She handed a sheet to the young, pale-faced mother. 'But soon. Perhaps in Trafalgar Square. Maybe on Wednesday.'

She spoke in short, anxious sentences, her eyes swivelling right and left as they were joined by more women.

'Not tonight, ladies,' she called softly. 'They know. They're watching . . .'

They had known and they had watched and waited,

and now they marched purposefully across the road; four constables, headed by a police sergeant riding a black horse.

They advanced on the group of women as though they had expected the paper-seller to be there; held their truncheons at the ready as a warning to all who saw them that they meant to use them.

'Cor! The perlice! Blimey, wouldn't yer just know it!'

'Don't go, ladies!' called a bespectacled woman. 'We're doing nothing wrong. We have every right to buy a news-sheet. Don't let them frighten you,' she urged.

'Miss – let's go?' Alice wanted no truck with the police who could arrest any one of them and march her off to the nearest lock-up to cool her heels in a cell for the night. 'I promised her ladyship I'd look after you and I don't think we should stay.'

'You do what you like, Hawthorn, but *I'm* staying. Like she said, we've every right to be here. It isn't a meeting and I won't be bullied!'

'No, miss, but it looks like a meeting.' Now a score or more women had gathered. 'But if you're set on it, then I'll stay, too.' Alice closed her eyes and swallowed hard. 'But don't say anything, will you, or they'll have just the excuse they want to lock you up.'

'I'll not harass them if they don't harass me,' Julia said quietly. 'But I have every right to be here and so have we all and I'm not going to turn tail and run as if we're up to something!'

'But we *are* up to something – at least we would be, if we could. They know what we're here for.'

What Miss Julia was here for, she mentally corrected, because she, Alice, would rather have been anywhere than gathering in the defence of a woman who sold news-sheets about votes for women.

'They can't *prove* what we're here for, and if we don't make trouble they can do nothing about it. So stay beside

51

me and don't be afraid, Hawthorn. I won't let them hurt you.'

And that might have been the end of it, had they all of them listened to what the sergeant on the black horse had to say and quietly gone home.

'There'll be no meeting tonight,' he'd said, 'so be off to your homes, all of you, and you'll hear no more about it. And you, Davison – pack up those papers and be off, or I'll have you inside again, soon as look at you!'

If they had listened and acted on advice that was sound enough, Alice conceded . . . But they had not. They had stood there, all of them, pretending not to have heard, saying not a word, clutching their news-sheets. It might still have been all right had someone not thrown a cricket ball and knocked off a constable's helmet; a well-aimed, masterful throw that sent it flying, and the constable's dignity with it.

It was all the sergeant needed. A cricket ball was a missile and the throwing of a missile at an officer of the law was an arrestable offence.

'Right! That'll do!' He pointed to the law-breaker who stood, chin set defiantly, as if she wanted to be arrested; because why else, Alice reasoned desperately, should a woman carry a cricket ball if she wasn't set on throwing it at someone?

The sergeant urged forward his horse, scattering the women, followed by truncheon-waving police who grabbed their victim roughly and hurried her off to the horse-drawn cab with windows of darkened glass, ready and waiting but a few yards away, as if they had known – or intended – that there would be arrests.

'Leave her alone!' The challenge had been made and taken up by those set on confrontation; those determined that one of their own should not be taken away without at least some protest.

'Bullies! Take your hands off her!'

'Pick on someone yer own size!'

'Like knockin' women about, do yer?'

The pushing and shoving and shin-kicking began then, and more helmets were sent flying, and such screeching and screaming arose that Alice would have taken to her heels had not Julia been intent upon staying. And not only on staying, but on cat-calling and digging her elbows sharply into any uniform that came her way. Then she really excelled herself. All at once her face went bright pink and she let out a yell of indignation.

'How dare you! How *dare* you strike a lady!' She flung herself in front of the pale-faced young woman who had walked past them only minutes ago. 'You did it deliberately. I saw you. And a child in her arms, too!' She kicked out wildly, her skirt pulled shockingly above her knees.

Miss Julia had taken leave of her senses, yet even then, Alice was to think later, she might have got away with it had not she, who should have been looking after her mistress, suddenly taken leave of her own senses and joined in the affray, giving the policeman an almighty shove from behind, knocking him off balance, sending all fourteen stone of him hurtling at Miss Julia, taking her down with him in a flail of arms and legs.

Alice would always remember the thud as that poor head hit the ground, and she would never forget, not if she lived to be a hundred, the sight of that defenceless face with blood already trickling down it.

'Brute!' Alice shrieked, on her knees in an instant. 'I saw what you did, you great bully! Out of my way and let me see to her,' she flung at a bewildered constable, still sprawled on hands and knees and wondering at the fury directed at him from behind. 'Get a doctor, before she bleeds to death. Go on! Do as you're bid!' How dare he? He'd fallen bang on top of Miss Julia; done it on purpose, and him putting on an expression of innocence. 'Oh, miss, open your eyes?' Alice patted the marble-white cheeks. 'Oh, Lor'. . .'

There was a sudden silence as though neither side had intended it should go this far and realized the folly of it too late.

'I said fetch a doctor!' Alice yelled. 'And give her some air. Don't stand there, gawping!'

'Let me through. And do as the young lady asks. I am a doctor. I'll see to her, and the rest of you be away to your homes – at once!'

And not, if she lived to be a hundred and *one*, Alice thought fervently, would she forget her relief as the young man took off his hat and removed his gloves, then felt with sure, gentle fingers for the pulse at Julia's wrist.

As if they had never been, the women were gone. Only the policemen remained, dusting down their uniforms, retrieving lost helmets, returning truncheons to back pockets.

'Is there any need for you to stay, sergeant?' the doctor asked quietly.

'If you think she's all right, doctor; not badly hurt, I mean?'

'She'll do, but I'd like to get her home and have a look at her. Do you know where she lives?' he asked of Alice.

'Yes, sir. Not far away – the other side of the park.'

'Then if I could have the use of your – er – conveyance, officer, to get her there, I'd be obliged. I take it she isn't under arrest?'

'No. I'm prepared to look the other way this time.'

'And when she comes round,' Alice gasped, 'I'm sure my young lady will be prepared to do the same.'

But it was all her fault, she admitted silently. She shouldn't have pushed the big policeman quite so roughly, even though he'd been a threat to Miss Julia and the young mother. Oh, *what* a mess they were in, and when would Miss Julia open her eyes?

'There now – that's better,' said the strange young man, who shifted and swayed into focus as Julia blinked open her eyes.

'Who? Where . . .'

'You are safely home, ma'am, and I am a doctor.'

'Oh, my head . . .' The room tilted, then righted itself. 'And the blood!'

'It's all right, miss. It's stopped, now.' Alice whisked away the offending bowl and towel. 'You hit you head – knocked yourself out, and the doctor had you brought here – in the *police* van.'

'That poor woman,' Julia fretted. 'They'd no right . . . Was there any trouble?'

'No trouble. I think Miss – er –'

'Sutton,' Julia supplied.

'I think, Miss Sutton, that there was fault on both sides, so there'll be nothing further said about it – this time.'

'And the girl who threw the cricket ball?'

'She scarpered, miss,' Alice breathed. 'Well, with the doctor wanting their carriage for you, there was nothing to cart her off in.'

'Good. I'm glad she knocked his helmet off.'

'Madam! You are completely without shame – but at least you appear to be recovering.'

'Shame? Yes, I suppose I am.' There was a silence as Julia looked, as if for the first time, into the face of her deliverer. Then, grasping the chair arms firmly, she rose unsteadily to her feet. 'I am grateful to you, doctor, though I'm still not sure what happened.'

'Nor I, Miss Sutton, though from a distance you appeared to take a flying leap at a policeman. Luckily I was there, though your injuries appear worse than they

55

really are. The abrasion to your forehead, though slight, bled rather a lot, and you *will* have quite a bruise in the morning. I can well believe that your head aches, too.'

'Aches!' Alice whispered. 'She went down with such a bang I'm surprised it's still in one piece!'

'Well, I think she'll be all right now, with your help, Miss –' He smiled.

'Hawthorn, sir. I'm Miss Julia's maid, and I'll see to her.'

'And you'll call a doctor at once, should Miss Sutton develop a sudden feeling of sickness or coldness or clamminess of the skin. Is there a telephone in the house?'

'There is, sir. But she *will* be all right?'

'I'm almost certain she will. And take a powder if the headache prevents you from sleeping, ma'am.'

'But where will we find you, if –' Julia stammered.

'I'm afraid I'm not on call, Miss Sutton. I'm not in general practice. I work at Bart's. But your local doctor, perhaps . . .'

'I've been a terrible trouble, haven't I?' Julia whispered contritely. 'How can I thank you?'

'By thinking no more about it. I'm only glad I was there in the park to – to get you out of trouble.'

Gravely, he made a small, polite bow; smiling, he left her.

'Do you think he's married?' Julia demanded when Alice had handed him his hat and gloves and bobbed a curtsey before closing the front door behind him.

'Married, miss? The doctor? Whatever put such a thought into your head?'

'I haven't the faintest idea. I think it must be the bump to my forehead. And I don't know why I'm making such a fuss, because I won't ever see him again, will I? He didn't even tell me his name.'

'No, miss, he didn't.'

'Just my luck to meet someone like him, then find he isn't interested,' Julia whispered soberly.

'Well, miss, the way I see it is this. Tonight you were his patient, so it wouldn't have been proper for him to be interested, would it? And he didn't need to tell you his name, because he gave me his card – just in case, he said – before he left. And if you'd like to know it says his name is Andrew MacMalcolm, and if you want my opinion I'd say definitely that he isn't married.'

'*Isn't?*'

'Not a chance. Married men have all their shirt buttons. Doctor MacMalcolm had two of his missing.'

'He did?' A smile lifted the corners of Julia's mouth and a distinct sparkle lit her eyes.

'Oh, yes. A sewing-maid always notices such things.'

'Hawthorn! What a dear, clever person you are. Do you know, I'm really glad you came to London with me. It wouldn't have been half as much fun with Mary or Bess. And I think I'll go to bed now. It's been a funny sort of day, hasn't it, and all at once I'm a little tired. Be a dear, and untie my corset laces? I can manage on my own, if you'll do that for me.'

All at once, Julia wanted to lie quietly in her bed and think about the young doctor and the height of him and the broadness of his shoulders – and those grey, thick-lashed eyes – or were they green? – that laughed, even when he was scolding her.

'I'll do that,' Alice smiled, 'and when you're settled down I'll bring you up a drink of milk. And you won't be cross with me in the morning, will you, when you find you've got a terrible ugly bruise?'

'Of course not. Why should I be?'

'Because it was my fault, really. All of a sudden I didn't see why I shouldn't join in too, and I gave that big policeman such a shove from behind, though if I'd known he'd land slap-bang on top of you I'd never have done it. I wouldn't – honestly.'

'Why, Hawthorn – and you pretending to be such a sober-sides! And I'm not the least bit cross with you.'

'You're not?'

'Honestly. I'd even go so far as to say,' Julia smiled, 'that I wouldn't have missed tonight for anything.'

Nor missed meeting Andrew MacMalcolm and gazing, bewildered, into those wonderful green – or were they grey? – eyes. And wanting, very much, to meet him again.

3

Clementina Sutton's heels tapped angrily across the floor. She had had enough, more than enough. This time Elliot had gone too far! She pulled on the bell handle, then pulled again. She was hurt and humiliated and near to tears. Debasing, it had been, and to hear it in such a way had been nothing less than mortifying.

How often, in the hope of an invitation, had she left her card at the home of Mrs Mounteagle; how many times had she been ignored – *snubbed* – and by a lady related by blood or marriage to half the gentry in the Riding. Yet this morning Mrs Mounteagle had finally acknowledged the existence of the mistress of Pendenys Place and had called, actually called, to a joyful reception.

Yet why had she come? Only to put her down; to humiliate Clementina Sutton. Not only to thrust in the knife of humiliation, but to turn it excruciatingly; to let it be known that Elliot was the subject of gossip of the worst possible kind and that his mother need only visit Creesby to learn the cause of it.

Then Mrs Mounteagle had risen to her feet and left at once. The coveted visit was over in less than four minutes and the lady had indicated, with the absence of even the slightest departing nod from her carriage window, that Clementina Sutton could never again expect to receive another call.

But this was the last time, the very last time she would brush Elliot's affairs under the carpet. She would *not* be cheapened; not in Holdenby nor Creesby, nor *anywhere*! She began to pace the floor, eyes on the door, ears straining for the irritatingly unhurried step in the slate-flagged corridor outside.

Below stairs, in the long, draughty passage where the bellboy spent his days sitting on a stool, the third bell in a row of twenty began its ringing and he was on his feet in an instant, hurrying to the kitchen.

'Three,' he called. 'Number three!' and the under-housemaid sighed, then ran to fetch the butler who had just taken his newspaper to his sitting-room and would bite her head off when she told him the breakfast-room bell was ringing.

It wasn't as if, Clementina reasoned to her reflection in the wall mirror, there was any need for this kind of thing. Not hereabouts, anyway. Granted, young gentlemen always took their pleasures, and her own son was no exception. But not on their own doorstones; not where they were known. Elliot was a fool! Women in London were eager and willing, yet her son chose to pleasure himself not five miles away with the daughter of a butcher!

Her hand hovered over the bell handle, then fell to her side. He was coming, his tread measured, and he would open the door sedately, turn slowly to close it behind him with annoying quietness, then look down his nose and say, as he was saying now, 'Mrs Sutton?'

'What kept you?' she hissed.

'Madam?' Didn't she know a butler walked slowly; must never, ever, lose the dignity that years of butling for the quality – the *quality*, mark you – had bred into him, the dignity that rich Americans would pay good wages for, were he to put himself on offer.

'Fetch me Mr Elliot!'

'I will try to find –'

'*Now*. This instant!'

He closed the door behind him, walking disdainfully, slowly, across the great hall – eighteen measured steps, it always took – to the door of the smoking-room, there to shatter the self-satisfaction of the young buck who would be filling it with the stink of Turkish tobacco.

She'd heard, then, about the butcher's daughter? Did she, he wondered with distinct pleasure, know that the talk had reached Holdenby, too? My, but he'd like to be a fly on the breakfast-room ceiling, though they'd hear, like as not. Mrs Sutton in a fury could be heard the length of the house. Pausing briefly to remove all traces of smugness from his face, he drew a deep breath then opened the double doors with the aplomb of long practice.

'Mrs Sutton asks that you join her in the breakfast-room,' he murmured.

'Oh, God.' Elliot Sutton removed a leg from the chair arm. 'What does she want now?'

'The mistress did not tell me.' *But if I were you, laddie, I'd shift myself.* He opened the doors wider, inclining his head as the young man slouched through them. *And I wouldn't be in your shoes for all the port in the cellar. Oh my word no – not if they threw in the Madeira, too!*

'Well?' demanded Clementina of her son.

'Well *what*?'

'You know damn well, and don't light a cigarette in here,' she warned as his hand strayed to his inside breast-pocket. 'Creesby, that's what. And stand up. I didn't give you permission to sit!'

'Oh – Maudie.' He remained seated.

'*Maudie*! I got told it this morning, and it wouldn't surprise me if half the Riding doesn't know, an' all!'

'Mother!' He sucked air through his teeth, wincing at her directness. 'Keep your voice down. Do you want the servants to hear?'

'*Hear*? I'll wager they know already. Aye, and the best part of Holdenby, as well.' Her cheeks were flushed, her eyes sparked outrage. 'Why can't you take yourself off to London or to Leeds, even? Why must you shame me? This is going to cost me – but you know that, don't you? It cost me plenty for your last brat!'

'*Mother!*' He lifted his eyes to the ceiling. 'Must you talk like a fishwife?' But then, every time Mama got into a rage she reverted to type. 'Or a washerwoman . . .'

'Damn you, boy!' It was the ultimate insult. She lifted her hand and slammed it into his face. 'And where 'ud you be today, eh, if it hadn't been for a washerwoman? Well, you can get out of this one yourself, because I'll take no more of your arrogance! Pay her off out of your own pocket; I'm done with you. Done, I say!'

Tears spilled down her cheeks and not all Elliot's sorries nor back-patting could stop the sobbing that could be heard all the way down the corridor and half-way across the great hall.

In the library, which was so vast that it needed two fireplaces to heat it, Edward Sutton laid down his pen as sounds of the confrontation in the room next door reached him.

Elliot, he sighed. Elliot upsetting his mother again so that the whole house would suffer for a week, at least. Why couldn't Nathan have been their firstborn; that second son who would have made Pendenys a happier place, a home. Nathan was serious like himself, and in his final year at Cambridge; though what would be left for him afterwards but the Church, heaven only knew. But Nathan was a Sutton; Elliot was his mother's son, and it would be to Elliot one day that Pendenys would pass, and Clementina's influence would still be on him from far beyond the grave.

He looked around the ornate room, longing for the library at Rowangarth and the homeliness that once had wrapped him round. Rowangarth was where he'd been born, was still home to him. Pendenys was where he lived out his days.

A slamming door and hurrying footfalls caused him to close his eyes briefly. Elliot was in a rage, and soon Clementina would be here, pouring out her anger, pacing the floor, complaining about '*your* son'. Elliot was always *his* son, Edward smiled thinly, when he was in trouble, and his mother's at all other times.

Well, this morning he would not take the backlash of her temper, be the whipping-boy for Elliot. He would walk to Rowangarth and be invited, hopefully, to lunch with his sister-in-law. Helen would be missing Julia and be glad of his company.

Julia. In London at his sister's house and having the time of her young life, he shouldn't wonder. Julia could have made a fine wife for Elliot, cousin or not, but she did nothing to hide her dislike of his elder son, and who could blame her? Julia, if she married into Pendenys, would be more inclined to Nathan, were she to choose, though that could never be. His second son had nothing to offer but kindness and goodness, and neither of those commendable graces paid bills.

Carefully he opened the long, low window. Like a schoolboy playing truant, he stepped out. Helen and Rowangarth would soothe him. Helen and Rowangarth always did.

Alice jabbed the last pin into the bun at the nape of her neck, then set her starched white cap primly upon it. Her hair, she supposed, was quite nice, though it went its own way at the sides and front and curled where it fancied and never, despite her efforts, where she wanted it to. But this was eight o'clock on a bright spring morning, and the whole of London was beckoning. Smiling, she picked up the tray.

'Mornin', miss,' she called, drawing back the curtains. 'Here's a nice cup of – oh, my goodness!'

'Hawthorn?' Julia's fingers moved reluctantly to her forehead. 'Is it . . . ?'

'It is.' There would be no covering that up with vanishing cream and face powder. 'Your eye, an' all. What on earth do we tell her ladyship?' she whispered, reaching for the hand mirror.

'That I tripped and fell, of course.' Critically, Julia surveyed the bruising.

'With a big fat policeman on top of you?'

'Of course not. Oh, we'll thank of something, and anyway, it might almost be gone by the time we get home.'

'Does your head still ache?' Solicitously, Alice plumped the pillows, then poured tea.

'Only a little. I think, though, that a walk might help clear it. Where did you put the card, Hawthorn?'

'The doctor's card?' Alice took it from her apron pocket. 'You weren't thinking of – well, wouldn't it be better to call Miss Sutton's doctor, if you need one?'

'I don't need a doctor – I *want* one.'

'Doctor MacMalcolm?' Alice swallowed hard.

'Yes. I – well, I want to thank him. He was very kind, last evening,' she murmured, oddly defiant.

Kind? Aye, and tall and handsome, Alice brooded. There had been a glazed look in her eyes last night that wasn't altogether to do with the knock on her head. A look, she mourned, that could spell trouble for Alice Hawthorn.

'Miss Julia – do you think it wise for us to –'

'No. Not at all wise, but I want to see him again. And not us – *me*! Smithfield way, I think he lives.' She reached for her wrap, put on her slippers, then ran downstairs. 'I'll have to check. There's a street map in the desk.' Aunt Sutton had said it might come in useful. 'Yes, I was right. Look, Hawthorn. Little Britain. Quite near St Paul's, and very near the hospital he works in. I can take a motor bus to Newgate Street, walk up King Edward Street, and I'll be there.'

'Miss! We're not going to his lodgings?'

'*I* am going to his lodgings.'

'But Newgate Street – that awful prison . . .'

'Not any more. It's long gone. I'll be perfectly all right. This is London and young women go about alone all the time. It isn't right I should be escorted everywhere – well, not here.'

'But you wouldn't go inside his lodgings?' She was becoming uneasy. You never knew, with Miss Julia. 'Not without me, you wouldn't?'

'Of course I wouldn't. I shall leave my card with his housekeeper – and anyway, he's sure to be at the hospital. My card, that's all – then if he wants to visit he can do so.' And please, *please*, let him want to . . .

'You promise, Miss Julia?'

'Promise. Word of a Sutton.'

'Mm . . .' With that, Alice had to be content. Even though she was expected to take good care of her young mistress, she wasn't her keeper, wasn't her equal. She was the sewing-maid and sewing-maids didn't tell their betters what to do. And she knew how Julia Sutton felt. Hadn't it happened to herself? It had only taken, *Does this creature belong to you?* It was the same the world over, she was forced to admit, be it servants or ladies of quality.

'We-e-ll – maybe just this once, miss . . .'

The air was cool in Brattocks Wood, and smelled headily of green things growing. Edward Sutton breathed deeply. Almost the instant he had set foot on Rowangarth land he had felt more calm.

'Am I welcome?' he smiled as he tapped on the morning-room window. Helen Sutton answered with a smile, and was waiting at the front door to greet him as he walked up the steps.

'My dear.' She held out her hands and offered her cheek for his kiss. 'Come in, do. It's far too late for

65

coffee. Shall we have a sherry, and shall you stay to lunch?'

He lingered his lips on her cheek because, as her brother-in-law, it was his privilege, and because an imp of defiance inside him whispered that Clemmy wouldn't have liked it.

'Now, my dear,' she said when they were settled, 'tell me about it.'

'It shows? How well you know me.'

'And so I should. You are John's brother, and you were here, shy and not a little perplexed, when first I came to Rowangarth. And debating, if I'm not mistaken, the pros and cons of proposing to Clementina Elliot.'

'So long ago. And she accepted me the year Robert was born. I was a father myself not a year after. And now your Robert is a grown man, and –'

'And miles away in India. I had a letter from him this morning, telling me he is well and happy, that the tea garden thrives, and not one word of what I most want to hear – that he'll be bringing his bride home to Rowangarth. And how is Elliot?' They were to talk of family, it seemed.

'Elliot is – Elliot,' he shrugged. 'He'll never change. But you'll know. It's why I'm here, really, to get out of Clemmy's way.' Clemmy always vented her anger on him, especially when it concerned their eldest son. Clemmy disliked the Suttons and all they were, yet fretted that it was Nathan and not Elliot who favoured them most.

'Tell me about young Nathan.' She knew what Edward would say, given the chance, for hadn't Giles told her about the butcher's daughter? 'He'll be coming down, soon. What will he do then, do you think?'

'Holy orders, I imagine. Strange isn't it, that I've sired a saint and a sinner – and a gigolo.'

'Oh, poor Albert! Don't call him that!'

'Then what else should I say, will you tell me, when our youngest goes off with a woman fifteen years older – though he did have the sense to pick a wealthy one and the decency to marry her. But he's a kept man, Helen, though I suppose I'm the last one to talk about being kept.'

'Don't, my dear.' Her eyes showed pity. 'He did what he thought best, I shouldn't wonder. And you do hear from him from time to time. Only last week, Clemmy said there had been a letter from Capetown.'

'Yes, and Auckland before that. And three months ago, one from St Petersburg. The lady must have a liking for travel. But it's Elliot who caused the upset this morning. Somehow Clemmy found out – there was a caller, so maybe that was how. About the girl in Creesby – but I don't have to tell you, do I?'

'No.' Helen studied her glass. 'I'd – heard. Is the girl – I mean, did he get –'

'Get her pregnant? I don't believe so, but nothing Elliot does now would surprise me. And it isn't the first time there's been a scandal. There won't be a father in the county lets his daughter within a mile of him if he carries on like this. He'll end up with a butcher's daughter, just see if he doesn't. You've heard the saying, Helen: from clogs to clogs in three generations – back to Mary Anne Pendennis, it'll be.' Morosely he held out his empty glass. 'Do you mind, m'dear?'

'Don't blame yourself, Edward.' She placed the decanter on the table at his elbow. 'Elliot has been spoiled and we can't expect our children to be as perfect as we are,' she smiled impishly. 'But you aren't alone. I have doubts and worries, too – Robert, you know . . .'

'Trouble with the tea? Nothing wrong, I hope. Last time I asked you seemed to think there'd be a good picking.'

'I was talking about his liking for bachelorhood. I want him home, Edward, not growing tea. And I want him married, and children – sons – about the place.'

'And?'

'And he stays unmarried and won't tell me why. But I think he's taken up with a married woman or someone who isn't suitable, so I don't ask. But why else would he go back to Assam after John died, when his place is here, now, at Rowangarth? And with almost indecent haste, too. Why doesn't he tell me, Edward? Why the secrecy?'

'As you just said – why can't our youngsters be like us.' He reached for her hand and held it gently, briefly. 'But tell me about Julia? She'll be having a fine time in London with Anne Lavinia away in France.'

'She does have Hawthorn with her,' Helen hastened to say. 'I've missed her, but she'll be home soon, full of the things they've seen. I wonder what they're doing now?'

'Oh, my Lor',' Alice muttered to the brass taps she was polishing furiously. 'I didn't ought to have let her go.' 'No, Miss Julia,' she should have said, arms folded defiantly, 'you don't take one step in the direction of that Newgate Street motor bus without me beside you. And don't you *dare* go to his lodgings, even if you don't intend setting a foot over the doorstone, without your maid with you!'

But she hadn't said it. She had stood there, lips set in disapproval as Julia Sutton, hat at an angle to hide the worst of the bruising, set out to find a street called Little Britain and a door with 53A upon it. Lord alone knew what trouble she could land herself in, her being so straightforward in her ways and a believer in votes for women. Only the Lord Himself knew, and for sure He'd never tell. Closing her eyes tightly she prayed fervently,

'Get her back home in one piece, will you? And soon, please, afore she lands herself in more trouble. And if you do, Lord, I swear I'll never let her go out alone again – *not ever*!'

Julia Sutton had stepped off the motor bus, walked the length of King Edward Street and found Little Britain with no trouble at all. Yet it came as a shock to see the street he lodged in, for though 53A was situated above the premises of a stationer and bookbinder, it was a run-down, cheap-looking shop and close by – too close – was an establishment whose sign announced that its owner was the purveyor of sweetbreads and pickled ox-tongues.

Yet the doctor's lodgings were comfortingly near the gates of St Bartholomew's church, and the curtains at his windows were bright and clean. Doubts gone, she lifted the knocker and brought it down firmly, the noise of it echoing hollowly inside, mocking her that she'd been foolish enough ever to hope to find him at home and more foolish still to imagine that anyone who lived in so unfashionable a street could have employed a scrubbing-maid, let alone a housekeeper. And why had she come here – come without thinking – because might not Andrew MacMalcolm be in love with a nurse; might it not even be his wife who opened the door to her, in spite of those missing shirt buttons?

There were footfalls on the stairs – on uncarpeted stairs – then the sound of a bolt being drawn. She ran her tongue round dry lips as the door opened.

He was there as she had hoped, wished, *prayed* he might be, and for a long moment they stood, her eyes raised to his. Then he said, 'Miss Sutton.'

His voice was low, indulgent; his eyes kind. He lifted his hand and laid gentle fingertips to the bruising beneath her eye

'My dear,' he said, smiling softly, 'I hoped you would come . . .'

'So you see, it *was* right. Oh, I had doubts,' Julia murmured huskily as they shared the firelight in the small parlour. 'When I was waiting for the door to be answered I nearly turned and ran. But he was there and he isn't married. Such a relief . . .'

'Relief. Yes.' Alice rose to build coal on the fire. Indeed, she in her turn had never been so relieved as when Miss Julia walked in, none the worse, it had seemed. 'But miss, I've been thinking and I've made up my mind. If you're to go out again, I shall go, too. I promised her ladyship I would see to you, and don't tell me no, because it'll do you no good.'

She had suffered agonies of conscience for almost three hours, and if there was to be a next time, it was best Miss Julia was given fair warning.

'Hawthorn, listen. I *didn't* go into his rooms. He was gentleman enough not to ask me to, because we'd have been alone together. At six tonight he goes on duty – all night – and tomorrow he'll be sleeping till noon.'

He had told her that, walking her slowly back to the motor bus, seeing her safely aboard it, raising his hat as it moved away.

'He's very proper, Hawthorn. He's invited you and me to walk in the park. At two tomorrow. And because you'll be there, it's perfectly all right for me to invite him back to tea.

'So are you satisfied, you straight-laced Hawthorn, or are you going to be stuffy about it and say I can't meet him because we haven't been properly introduced?'

Alice pursed her mouth into a Mrs Shaw button, and frowned sufficiently deeply to make sure that Julia understood she was not giving in easily. Then, carefully considering every word, she murmured, 'I think, just this once, miss, you might accept the invitation, since I'm to be there.'

Though what would happen if Miss Sutton should all of a sudden return to find the two of them drinking tea together and Alice Hawthorn aiding and abetting it, didn't bear thinking about. Or if someone from Holdenby or Creesby or York, even, should chance on them in the park. Oh, the *scandal*!

'Then why are you making such a bossy face? Frowning doesn't suit you.'

'I was just wondering, miss, what would happen if you were seen with him.'

'*Seen?* But who in all London do we know?'

'One of her ladyship's friends, perhaps.' Many of Lady Helen's acquaintances had a house in London. Come to think of it, it was strange that someone as rich as Mrs Clementina hadn't bought one, too. 'Why, you might even run into Mr Elliot,' she added as an afterthought, though in fact it was a distinct possibility, since that young man seemed always to be popping off to London.

'I doubt it. Cousin Elliot won't be walking in Hyde Park, even if he should decide to come to town. He'll be eating and drinking all night and sleeping all day, be sure of that.

'So do we have a fresh cucumber, Hawthorn, and an uncut cake, or must we got out shopping? And don't spoil it for me, please? I do so want to meet him again.'

'Then you're being very forward, if you'll pardon me.' Alice was compelled to say it. 'It isn't for the likes of yourself to go running after a gentleman, no matter how nice he is, or how respectable. But you like him, don't you, miss?'

'I like him,' Julia whispered, her eyes large and bright, her cheeks flushing. 'You like Dwerryhouse – can't you see how it is for me?'

Liked Tom? Loved him, more like. Yes, *loved* him and

wanted, all at once, to hold him close, to lift up her face for his kiss.

'Yes, I can see, and I'll not spoil it for you. But be careful, miss. Please be careful.'

Liked him? Julia Sutton was smitten, that's what. Alice knew the signs, for hadn't it happened exactly the same to herself? Miss Julia had fallen head over heels for a man she knew nothing about, Alice fretted silently, and where it would end was anybody's guess.

'And since you ask, there *is* an uncut cake in a tin in the pantry,' she said in final surrender. 'Hope he likes cherry cake . . .'

4

Julia Sutton had never been in such a tizzy of indecision. What to wear, and why did the hair combed so carefully over her forehead insist on springing back to reveal a bruise so angry that everyone must notice. And not only her forehead, but her eye . . .

'The astrakhan-trimmed costume, Hawthorn?'

'No, miss.' Not fur-trimmed. Not in May.

'The blue, then?'

Alice pursed her lips and shook her head. The blue, hobble-skirted costume brought back memories of a young lady's ankles and knees shamelessly exposed, and made her blush.

'Then *what*?'

'An afternoon dress.' Alice had long ago made up her mind. 'The flowered voile.' So lovely and floaty, with full sleeves. And the pretty pink shoes, perhaps, and the wide-brimmed hat with the flower trim. That was what a young lady wore for a walk in the park with a young man. A *romantic* dress.

'You think so?'

'Oh, *yes*.' A dab of rosewater at her wrists and on her handkerchief, perhaps, and a little face powder to tone down the bruising. 'And if you walk on his left, he'll not even see it – your eye, I mean.'

'It's worse than I thought. Mama's going to want an explanation.'

'She is. So how about the truth?'

'I *couldn't*. She'd never let me out alone again!'

'She won't if you lie to her and get found out. All you have to say is that –'

73

'Is that we were walking in Hyde Park – innocently – and got caught up in a meeting and running away – in my hobble skirt – I tripped and fell and hit my head on a kerbstone.'

'No, miss. We were walking in the park – never mind the *innocently* – and a policeman set about a young woman who did nothing more than buy a news-sheet and you went to help her. And I'll tell her ladyship that a great policeman went his length and took you down with him.'

'And a kind young doctor took me home?'

'That a doctor happened to be passing and came to your assistance,' Alice amended, 'and said you should send for Miss Sutton's doctor, should the need arise.'

'Of course! And it's almost the truth, isn't it?'

'As near as makes no matter.' It wasn't right to tell lies to her ladyship. Not deliberate ones.

'And we needn't mention it was you sent him flying?'

'Best not, miss.'

'You are quite right. Not only would London be out of bounds for me but for you, too. We'd never be able to come here alone again.'

'But I'd never –' Not for a minute had Alice thought to have so fine a jaunt again.

'Never see London again? When we're having such a good time? Oh, but I intend to come as often as Aunt Sutton will allow. Suddenly, I seem to have a fondness for London – and for –' She stopped suddenly, meaningfully.

'For young doctors?' Alice supplied, amazed at her forwardness.

'One *particular* young doctor,' Julia laughed. 'So are you going to be on my side, Hawthorn? Are you going to help me and never, *ever*, say so much as a word about him until I say you can?'

'I'm on your side, miss. I'll never ever tell on you and anyway, it isn't likely you'll ever meet him again, is it?'

'Never again? Oh, Hawthorn!'

She smiled, and all at once the bruises didn't seem to matter, because all at once Julia Sutton was beautiful, just like Mrs Shaw said she would be if only she'd let herself.

'See him again!' Alice gasped. Oh, my Lor'. Miss Julia was in love!

Elliot Sutton left the house by the conservatory door, walking quickly across the croquet lawn, making for the kitchen garden and the birch wood that lay beyond it. He should, he thought viciously, have brought a gun. He felt like blasting at something; felt like killing. But there was no shooting until August – only vermin, and that was for keepers.

Moodily, he kicked at a cobble. He was sick of Holdenby; sick of Mama who held her Ironmaster's money over him, an ever-present threat. But she'd never leave it to Nathan, his holier-than-thou brother, though she'd said, more than once, that she would.

He could never be sure of his mother; never certain when she would open her mouth and let him down. Most times, of course, she carried her corn well, but when angered or defiant, her Pendennis temper showed through and her Pendennis tongue too.

This morning, he thought with savage disdain, she had screeched at him like a fishwife, showing a side to her not all the iron gold in the world had been able to breed out. There was a defiance about her that screamed, 'All right, my fine aristocrats – so you've got the breeding, but *I've* got the brass, and don't ever forget it!'

He was ashamed of her, of his own mother; ashamed of the half of him that came from trade, even though his other half – his Sutton blood – was without equal. It was a pity his father could hardly bear to be in the same room with him, let alone treat him like a son to be proud of, because he, Elliot, was tall and handsome, and charming too, when he needed to be, and could get any woman he wanted with no effort at all. He was rich as well, and would be richer one day, so why did everyone seem to prefer his younger brother? Why did Julia show preference for Nathan when she knew he'd end up a parson, with nothing in his favour but his sick-making goodness?

But Albert had had the right idea. Albert had found himself a well-heeled old woman – and the best of luck to him! His youngest brother had struck it rich, and lived a life of luxury in the best hotels and on the most luxurious liners in the world. Clever young Albert!

Elliot climbed the boundary fence, making for the rising ground and Holdenby Pike. There would be a wind up there, even in May, that would blow away his black mood. Up there he could look down on Pendenys Place and wonder how long before it was his; could wonder, even, what it was like to bed an old woman, for his brother's wife must be well into her forties. Did Albert, on such occasions, close his eyes and think of the money that would one day be his? Come to that, would he, Elliot, have to close his eyes too when he wed the ugly daughter of a penniless peer, and think instead of Maudie's soft, warm lips, her small, round breasts, her eager thighs?

He wished, sometimes, that he belonged to the working class and could marry any Maudie he pleased, but the working classes had to work, it was as simple as that. He would marry fairly soon, he supposed; some simpering, well-bred virgin bitch with more titles to her pedigree than was decent. She might even have one in her own right. Mama would like that; she'd envy it, but still she'd like it.

But there would be no title for Elliot Sutton. That had eluded him. All Mama's money had failed to buy the knighthood she so desperately wanted for her husband – to pass down to her son, of course. The Garth Suttons had

76

that. Cousin Robert, just one year older, had inherited the baronetcy at twenty-four, then hared it back to Assam to his precious tea garden. And even supposing Robert never married, never got a son, then Giles would inherit the title. It would remain at Rowangarth for another three hundred years, like as not. Only if his cousins were to vanish from the face of the earth would his father get lucky.

God! Imagine Mama; Lady Clementina at last! She'd be good for a touch, then; would even forgive him his Maudies, provided he kept them quiet and didn't rock the boat. Yet it would never be, he knew it. The Garth Suttons would hang on to what they had. Though they were nowhere as well-off as the Suttons at the Place, they had the esteem of the entire Riding, which was better than riches.

Temper spent, he flung himself down on the grass, lit a cigarette, then gazed down on Pendenys. He felt badly done by, and bored, misunderstood and miserable. He would go to London, keep out of Mama's way until the edge had worn off her temper. His allowance had just been paid into the bank – where better to spend it?

Or maybe Leeds? Mama had said it, hadn't she? Take yourself off to London, or Leeds even. Maybe she was right. Women were cheaper there, easier to find. The better-class whores frequented the music halls; were always available in the promenade area at the rear of the theatre. Buy one a drink and a deal was struck almost before she'd had time to say, 'Cheers, young squire!'

He would go to Leeds. Now. He could be there before dark if he shifted himself. For once, he'd do *exactly* as he was told.

'You look lovely, Miss Julia.' She did. Really, really beautiful. And not just the long dress nor the pink shoes peeping out beneath it, nor the hat. She was beautiful all over; her eyes, her smile – even the way she walked. And all because of Andrew MacMalcolm.

'You'd better take this.' Alice offered a parasol.

'Oh, no. I won't need a sunshade.'

'You take it. Never know who you might meet. You can always hide behind it if you have to.'

'But why should I hide? You'll be with me, all perfectly correct . . .'

'No, miss. I shall come with you as far as the bandstand and wait with you, till he comes. Then I shall have to excuse myself. There'll be the tea to see to and things to do and I'll expect you –'

'Hawthorn! You *darling*; you absolute love!' She grasped Alice's hands and swung her round in a little dance. 'I promise I'll be good. I *will*.'

'And you'll be back here at half-past three, prompt, for tea,' Alice ordered grimly, ''cos if you aren't, I'll come looking for you, and I mean it!'

'Then I promise we shall be – word of a Sutton. But what if he doesn't come? What if something goes wrong and he's needed at the hospital and we wait and wait . . .'

'Then the bandstand is the best place to be, isn't it, because we can sit there as if we're waiting for the music to begin and nobody'll know that – well – he's –'

'Left me in the lurch.'

'Exactly. But he won't, so take your parasol and let's be off. Don't want him waiting there, thinking *you're* not coming, now do we?'

He was waiting. He was there, looking handsomer than ever, and his smile as he walked to meet them set Julia's heart thudding deliciously.

'Miss Sutton. Miss Hawthorn.' He raised his hat, giving each a small, polite bow, and Alice could see why Julia Sutton had fallen head over heels, because if it hadn't been for Tom she could, quite easily, have done the same.

'Shall we walk, ladies, or shall we listen to the concert? The choice is yours.'

'I thank you, sir, but I find,' Alice said primly, trying to say it as Miss Clitherow would, respectful yet genteel, 'I find I'm not able to accept your kind offer. I – I have things to do, but the kettle will be on,' she looked directly at her employer, an eye to eye gaze that allowed for no misunderstanding, 'at three-thirty, if you're of a mind to take tea.'

'Then I thank you, ma'am.' Andrew MacMalcolm tipped a finger to his hat, his face serious, his eyes bright with merriment. 'And I shall take good care of Miss Sutton and bring her safely home on the dot of half-past three.'

'Thank you, sir. Bid you good day, then.' For no reason she was sure of, but maybe because her warning had been a little too blunt, she bobbed a curtsey which put her back in her place again, and made everything all right.

'Isn't she a dear?' Julia smiled as they watched her walk away.

'You're fond of her, aren't you?'

'Very fond.'

'And she of you, Miss Sutton. It's easy to see.'

'Hawthorn is fond of the whole wide world,' Julia laughed. 'She's in love – walking out seriously.'

'And you? Are you walking out?'

'No. I'm a free spirit, doctor.' *But don't ask me if I'm in love, for I couldn't look at you and say I wasn't.*

'Then shall we listen, or shall we walk?' Gravely he offered his arm. It was the wrong arm, for when she took it, she realized that every time he turned to look at her, her bruised and puffy eye would gaze up at him like a blot on the landscape of her adoration.

'How do you feel today?' He asked it as if he could read her thoughts. 'Is your eye less painful?'

'Almost no pain at all.' She withdrew her hand from

79

the crook of his arm and touched it with anxious fingers. 'But oh, isn't it a sight?'

'I've seen worse,' he smiled, taking her hand, tucking it gently back. 'Much, much worse . . .'

'Oh, Hawthorn.' Eyes closed, Julia swayed back and forth in the kitchen rocker. 'What am I to do? Two days more, then we'll be on our way home. *Two days*, that's all.'

'Did he ask you?' Carefully Alice wrapped the remainder of the cherry cake in greaseproof paper and returned it to the tin. 'To meet him again, I mean.'

'Yes. Tomorrow – same place – but after that there'll only be one day and he hasn't kissed me yet; hasn't even called me Julia and I don't –'

'Hasn't kissed you? Indeed I should think not! For him to try wouldn't be right, and for you to let him would be common – first time, that is. Second time, an' all. My Tom didn't kiss me for ages.'

'But you and Tom had – *have* – all the time in the world, and we haven't. He'll be in London and I'll be miles and miles away and not knowing when we'll meet again; not knowing, even, if we'll be able to write to each other.'

'You can always have his letters sent to me, though there might be talk about them, so I'd have to tell Tom. But why shouldn't you write to each other openly?'

'Because we haven't been properly introduced. What do you think my mother would say? She wouldn't like it at all. Mind,' she frowned, 'when next I go to London I could tell Mama that Aunt Sutton had introduced us and that would make it all right. Aunt Sutton would do it for me, I know she would. But what do I do in the meantime?'

'We'll think of something, though I still think you should tell her ladyship everything – right from the start.'

'And land *you* in bad grace, Hawthorn? No, we'll have

80

to be careful; very careful. And anyway,' she whispered, her face suddenly sad, 'who's to say he'll want to write to me?'

'He'll want to. I know he will. But one day at a time, eh? And you haven't told me where you went nor what you talked about.'

'I know.' And she did so want to talk about him. She wanted to tell the entire Mews that Julia Sutton was in love; climb to the top of Holdenby Pike and shout it out to the whole of the Riding. 'But will you come upstairs and untie me? I feel so jumpy, so anxious, and these corsets are getting tighter and tighter. Be a dear, then I'll put on a wrap and I'll tell you all.'

She let go a sigh of relief as Alice untied the knot and eased open the back lacing of the torturous garment. 'I swear that when we have the vote and can send a lady to Westminster, I shall agitate for an Act to be passed, outlawing corsets. I will!'

'Oh, miss – you and your votes. Now get into your wrap and pop your feet into something more comfortable, then tell me all about it. *All*. Nothing missed out.'

And because she was so besotted, so suddenly, shiningly in love, Julia did just that. In truth there was nothing about their meeting which could be deemed shocking – other than meeting a young man unintroduced and unchaperoned, that was. But oh, the delight of it all: the brilliance of the sun, the most beautiful, sweetly scented flowers she had ever seen or smelled; even the London park-sparrows were the cheekiest, the most endearing little birds in the whole world.

'And Andrew – Doctor MacMalcolm – told me about Scotland, where he was born, and how hard he'd had to work to become a doctor because he did it all on scholarships, Hawthorn, and but for the money an aunt left him, he couldn't even have bought the books he needed, let alone eat.

'His father was a miner, you see; injured at the pit. He suffered a lot before he died. Then his mother took consumption and she died too. There was only his aunt left after that. She wasn't well off, but she gave him her savings. He's very sad she died before he qualified. She would have been so proud of him.'

'Proud. Yes.' And Miss Julia's doctor had no one, no background, except that of a miner's son who had risen by his own efforts.

'He can't afford his own practice, either. Not for years will he be able to – not even buy himself a partnership. But he's a brilliant physician, Hawthorn.'

'He said so?'

'No, of course he didn't. But I know he is. Life's very unfair, isn't it?'

'It is.' Alice offered daisy-printed satin-quilted slippers. Unfairer than she knew, because how was the daughter of a baronet ever to be allowed to marry the son of a man who had dug coal? The world she lived in didn't, *wouldn't*, allow it.

'He was determined to be a doctor – after both his parents had suffered so. And, Hawthorn, he believes that women should have the vote – well, responsible women, that is.'

'Then it couldn't be better, could it?' Alice poured water into the papier mâché bowl kept especially for the washing-up of the best china, adding cold water and flaked soap, concentrating hard on making it into a sud so she might think, uninterrupted. Because what Miss Julia had just told her was what she wanted least to hear. Not that the young doctor wasn't the worthiest of gentlemen, but wouldn't it have been better for all concerned if he'd found himself a nice, genteel nurse to marry? Such a woman would have made a better wife for a young physician on his climb to the top. How could he ever hope to support the daughter of a gentleman? And would he be acceptable, even if he could?

Mind, Mrs Clementina had come from trade, and she had married into the gentry; Alice supposed trade was all right. Anything was all right if it brought money into the family. But the doctor could barely support himself, it seemed, let alone a wife. Doctor MacMalcolm had nothing to commend him at all but ambition and good looks, she sighed. Yet folk didn't choose where to love; not penniless young physicians nor young society ladies, it seemed, and oh, deary me, what had Miss Julia gone and done?

'Hawthorn?' Julia snapped her fingers. 'You were miles away. Thinking about Dwerryhouse, were you?'

'No, miss. If you want the truth I was thinking that Doctor MacMalcolm having no family, so to speak, and having no means yet of supporting a wife, changes things a lot. Once, I thought it would be best if you told her ladyship all, hoping she would understand. But him having nothing, so to speak, even if there's all credit due to him for getting to be a doctor, won't go down well with her ladyship. Now I'm beginning to wish I'd been more firm; hadn't let you –'

'Hawthorn – nothing you could have said or done would have made a scrap of difference. I told you that one day I would meet the man I wanted to marry, and two days ago I met him. And it's all right. Whatever happens, I won't involve you. I'll just have to find a way out of it – or round it, won't I? And I *will*.'

'Then I wish you luck, I really do. Tomorrow, when you meet him, you *will* be careful? You won't make any promises or get any hare-brained schemes into your head, will you?'

'I'll go carefully, I promise you.'

She would have to, she thought, for so much was at stake that one wrong move, one wrong word even, could be the end of it for them both, and that could not, must not, happen. And she would go carefully, because Andrew MacMalcolm was the man she wanted to marry. She had known it yesterday when he opened his door to her, and no one else would do.

Andrew, or no one.

Alice pulled out the oven damper, then gave her full attention to the scones she was baking. She had been unable to get to shop to buy a cake, and since Miss Julia couldn't offer the cherry cake again – to offer a cut-into cake would suggest they were nothing short of poverty-stricken – she had left a note asking the milkman for cream. This afternoon they would eat fresh scones with cream and jam, though to be truthful, neither would notice if she served a slice from yesterday's loaf, gone stale.

Oh, miss, she mourned, sniffing the milk to make sure it was good and sour – only *sour* milk for scones, Mrs Shaw always said – why did you have to go and fall in love? No, that wasn't what she meant, for every woman had the right to fall in love. What she really meant, she supposed, was why had she fallen in love with someone she could never be wed to. Because it wouldn't do; it really wouldn't. Doctoring was the most desirable of professions, but when it didn't come hand in hand with money, then there was nothing more to be said.

It was then, and for the first time, that Alice acknowledged how very fortunate she was. Fortunate to be a nobody, to have nothing, and no one to forbid her marriage to Tom, save an aunt who wouldn't care if she wed the midden-man. And how very fortunate that Tom loved her in spite of the fact that she had nothing; loved her for herself – his buttercup girl.

'Tom,' she whispered to the rolling-pin. 'I'm glad that in two days' time I shall be getting off that train back home.' Glad she'd be taking Morgan for his afternoon walk and that Tom would be there. And he would tilt her chin with his fingertip and bend and kiss her. Tom, her love. Thomas Dwerryhouse, whom one day she would marry. For they could wait. They had all the time in the world – not like Miss Julia and her doctor, because after today they might never meet again.

'It doesn't bear thinking about,' she muttered, flouring the rolling-pin. And who, she demanded with amazement, would ever have thought that the day would dawn when she would pity Julia Sutton. Because she did. She pitied her something awful.

Julia walked slowly, her hand in Andrew MacMalcolm's, speaking little, for there seemed nothing more important than being together. Their talking had been done, their plans made, promises asked and given.

'After today, Andrew,' she had used his name without thinking because it was beautiful to say, 'I won't be able to meet you. Tonight, Aunt Sutton's maid returns from Bristol, and my aunt will make the overnight crossing and be in London before Hawthorn and I leave.'

'So it's goodbye, for a while.'

'For as short a while as I can make it,' she had whispered, knowing she was being forward, yet being so only because there was so little time. 'I shall come back as soon as I can, but I shall tell Aunt Sutton about you and you must leave your card at her house. And I'll beg her to receive you so she can say to my mother that she knows you, and approves.'

'She'll approve, do you think?' He smiled down and she smiled back, without embarrassment. 'She'll take a wee rubber approval stamp and plonk it right in the middle of my forehead and that'll make it all right?'

'No, but it's the way it's got to be, so we must accept it.'

'Why must we,' he asked softly, 'and, come to that, why must it be?'

'Because –' She glanced up quickly, alarmed, but saw no rancour, nothing in his face to warrant her fear. To him, she supposed, it was as simple as being in love, because he was in love, too; she knew it. 'Because – well – that's the way we do it. Being properly introduced, and all that sort of thing.'

'But, Julia, you and I *weren't* introduced, yet here we are, miserable because we're parting, wanting to see each other again, both of us –' He stopped, asking the question with his eyes.

'Both of us knowing we might fall in love?'

'*Have* fallen in love, and against all the rules and conventions. We know all we need to know about each other; that my father dug coal and your father burned it; that I am a good physician and intend to be even better; that you and I met three days ago and knew –'

'Just as my parents knew,' she whispered.

'Aye – that we were right for each other and that we must be back, soon, or your Hawthorn will be glaring at the clock, thinking I've run off with you.'

They had turned then, and retraced their steps, and because she did not at once place her hand back in his, he reached for it, holding it tightly for several seconds before he tucked her arm in his own.

'How old are you, Andrew?' She knew so much about him, yet so little.

'I'll be twenty-six in August.'

'And I shall be twenty-one, soon.'

'Good. That's just right. And did I tell you that you should always wear blue?'

She smiled at him, shaking her head, holding his eyes in a too-long glance. But it didn't matter, because he was making love to her: not the physical love she wanted so much to share with him; but with every look, every touch, every carefully chosen word, he made her love him a little more, and knew it was the same for him.

'When we meet again – if it's still summer – I shall wear this dress for you.'

'It will still be summer, Julia. Soon, I shall have a week's leave of absence. I have no close family to spend it with, so I could well come to –'

'To York!' she supplied, joyously. 'I could meet you there – I'm sure I could. When will it be?'

'In June. The second or third week.'

'And you'll come? You won't change your mind?' Her cheeks flushed hotly, a small, happy pulse beat at her throat. 'I – I couldn't bear it if you didn't.'

'I shall come. Only if my employers at the hospital decide otherwise will I not be there.'

'And you would write and let me know if you couldn't – write to Hawthorn, that is?'

'I would let you know.' They had stopped walking now, because the park gates were only a few steps away and each was reluctant to walk through them.

'Andrew – you *will* try to make Aunt Sutton's acquaintance? You've got to agree it would help?'

'I don't know, lassie. I'd like fine to meet your aunt, but if I don't – well, it wouldn't be the end of the world. Because it's a big world we both live in, though you've seen precious little of it from inside your safe, sedate walls. But nothing can change these last few days. You know it and I know it. There'll be a way,' he said comfortably, confidently. 'We'll find it, between us.'

'Andrew,' she whispered, 'we're almost back and Hawthorn will be hovering and we mightn't get the chance, so –'

'So will you stop your chatter, lovely lassie, for just long enough for me to tell you I love you?'

'I will. Oh, I *will* . . .'

'Mind, I don't know what's come over me,' he said

softly, shaking his head at his own foolishness, 'for I'd got my life all mapped out and everything in its place, and there was no place in it for a wife – not just yet. And now look at me.'

'I'm looking. And I love what I see,' she laughed. 'And we'd better go and eat Hawthorn's scones or she'll have the constabulary out looking for me . . . It *is* true, isn't it? And you *will* come to York?'

'Aye. And I'll leave my card at your aunt's house.'

'Then there isn't any more to be said, is there?' she whispered. 'Except that I wish you would kiss me goodbye, when you leave.'

'I will,' he smiled. 'Be sure, I will . . .'

5

He had kissed her, Julia thought dully, when he left
Aunt Sutton's. When she had begged Hawthorn with her
eyes not to come to the door with them, he had cupped
her face in his hands and laid his lips softly to the bruise
on her forehead. Then he had kissed her mouth, softly,
tenderly, lingering his lips on hers as if claiming them for
his own.

Now this train was taking her from him. With every
minute it was pulling them further apart. Soon they would
reach York, then take the little slow train to Holdenby
where the carriage would be waiting. They would be more
than two hundred miles apart. Half a day apart.

'Don't be sad, miss. We had a lovely time. If you're
sad, her ladyship's going to think the holiday has done
you no good at all. Drink up your wine now.' Aunt Sutton
had given them wine for the journey; sweet, local wine
from the Camargue.

'Come again soon,' she had said heartily. 'Come when
I'm at home, both of you, and I'll show you a London
you'd never have thought existed.'

Both of you, Alice had particularly noted, and it pleased
her because she had liked Aunt Sutton the minute they
met. And she couldn't, Alice thought guiltily, be sad. Not
for a minute, for, wonderful as London had been, soon
she would see Tom, would run to his arms and tell him
how she had missed him – after they had kissed . . .

'I don't believe it happened, Hawthorn; not any of
it.'

'It happened.' Gently Alice laid a fingertip to a bruise,
now shading paler and fading to yellow at the edges.

89

'And miss, remember that night – the two white wishing-horses?' Since the stop at Darlington they were the only occupants of the compartment and to talk was easier. 'A wish each, we had . . .'

'I remember.' The smallest smile tilted the corners of Julia's mouth.

'Well, I can tell you mine now, 'cos it's come true. I wished you could find someone like I'd found Tom – and you did. That very night, you did.'

'Then white-horse wishes must be powerful stuff, because I wished for much the same thing.'

'There now. You should go and tell it to the rooks when we're back, miss. I always tell them. Share your secrets with those old rooks and they'll keep them safe. And you can tell them when you're unhappy, an' all. Don't think they can do a lot about unhappiness, but it helps to tell them.'

'You won't say anything, Hawthorn – not at home, I mean? Not until I've got used to it all – sorted myself out?'

'You know I won't. Not a word. When they're talking about your eye in the kitchen, I shall tell them what we said it would be. And I'll wish like anything I don't get a letter from London, 'cos that would mean he wouldn't be coming on holiday.' And goodness only knew how she'd take it. She'd set her hopes on York, Miss Julia had. 'Oh, can't you tell her ladyship? She'd understand, I know she would, and then there needn't be any lies and always having to watch what we say.'

'I can't, just yet. I couldn't risk a refusal. She could well be angry, you know. I've broken all the rules.'

'Which rules?' There were no rules about falling in love. It happened, and there was nothing anybody could do about it, thanks be.

'*Our* rules. There's a way of doing things for us that's simply got to be, and one of the things you don't do is go against convention. I did. I went sneaking off like a scullery maid to meet him – oh, I'm sorry, Hawthorn, I didn't mean to sound arrogant, I truly didn't. But *I* ran after *him*. I knew exactly what I was doing and I didn't care. No lady does that, does she? You didn't.'

'We-e-ll – not running as such. But I always made sure to take Morgan out reg'lar, before servants' teatime. And once I went as bold as brass to the rearing field, 'cos I knew he'd be there. And I acted all surprised, like, though I'm glad I did it. That was the night he walked me back and asked me to be his girl, so don't take on about what you did, Miss Julia. Men need a helping hand, sometimes, and you didn't have a lot of choice – not with only three days left.

'But your mother is a lovely lady, and you told me, didn't you, that her and Sir John were secretly in love ever before they were matched. She'd understand. She *would*.'

'A young doctor without expectations? Hardly to be compared with Pa.'

'But they were in love,' Alice insisted, 'and love's a powerful thing – stronger than white-horse wishes.'

'No. I can't tell her yet. Wait until Andrew has left his card at Aunt Sutton's. By the time he visits York she might have received him and I can tell Mama more then. But I've got to drop it in bits, sort of. Just a hint here and a word there, so that when it all comes out she'll look back and realize I hadn't been deceitful – well, not *exactly*.'

'But that isn't the way it should be.' Stubbornly, Alice held her ground.

'I know. After that first time in the park I was so excited that I needed everyone to know. I wanted to climb Holdenby Pike and shout it into the wind. But it's gone too far between us and I'm afraid to lose him. So you won't tell? Not even Tom?'

'No one. Cross my heart.'

'Well, then,' Julia drained her glass. 'We'd better get our things together.'

The train was slowing now, and from the window the towers of the Minster could be distantly seen. Soon they would be at Rowangarth, and telling everyone what a fine time they had had – and watching every word they said.

Alice folded the napkins, carefully wrapping them around the glasses, fastening the hamper, mentally checking the hatbox and travelling bag on the rack, remembering there were four cases in the luggage van and a porter to be found to put them on the Holdenby train that left at three o'clock. And Tom, she thought blissfully, was little more than an hour away.

'I wasn't fast, was I, Hawthorn?' Julia asked anxiously as the little stopping train clanked and shuddered out of York station. 'I mean, I wasn't forward or anything? You *do* think Andrew will get in touch? He won't think I've been a bit – well – unladylike . . .'

'No, miss. You weren't unladylike – not a bit; leastways, not when I was there, so don't keep on worrying about it.'

'But I was a little bit – *eager*. I know I ought to have refused, when first he asked me to walk in the park – a lady always should say no, the first time she's asked. And I shouldn't have gone to his lodgings, either. But we didn't have a lot of time . . .'

'Not a lot. Did he kiss you?' Alice demanded, amazed at her daring. 'Was it nice?'

'He did, and it was nicer than nice. He kissed me twice.' Julia closed her eyes, remembering. 'A little one, then one that made me – oh –'

'Feel peculiar all over? I know.' Alice, too, closed her eyes.

'And you're sure he'll come to York to see me?'

'Sure as anyone can be,' Alice comforted. 'And just to be certain, you'd better watch out for another white horse, and let the rooks know about it, an' all. Best to make sure.'

'I will. I *will*.'

There was a warning hoot from the driver as the train swayed over a level crossing and took them on to Rowangarth land, then the hissing of wheels on steel took on a heavier note as the train met the gradient that wound upward through Brattocks Wood.

'Hawthorn, *look!*'

Standing beneath the trees at the edge of the track, a gun dog squatting at his feet, stood the under-keeper. Knowing the time of their train and that it would lose speed at the wood, Tom was waiting to see it pass.

Only a glimpse, but he had been there and Alice knew, in that moment, how much she had missed him; wondered how she could ever have been so foolish as to leave him for a day, let alone two weeks. And then she blushed for shame, because soon she would be with him, and sitting opposite was poor Miss Julia, sad and worried in case she never saw her young man again.

'Oh, miss – you'll see him again. You *will*.'

Giles Sutton looked up, smiling, as Alice peeped round the library door and Morgan, tired of the hearth rug, gave a yelp of delight and skidded across the floor, tail wagging furiously.

'Hawthorn! You're back. I've missed you; we've both missed you!'

'And I've missed you and Morgan and Rowangarth and, oh, *everyone*, even though London was like a fairy story. And I'm come to say I'm sorry that I can't take Morgan for his run, 'cos I haven't finished Miss Julia's unpacking and it's almost teatime. But I'll take him tonight, if that's all right with you, Mr Giles.'

93

'It is, and I'll be grateful, because I'm dining out tonight. Did you have a good time?'

'Oh, *yes*. You wouldn't believe the half of what I saw. There was –' She stopped, cheeks pink. 'But you *would* believe it. You've been before, ever so many times.'

'Too many times. Rowangarth is where I like to be.'

'I know, sir.' She *did* know. It had tingled through her from head to toes, that feeling of homecoming. 'But I'll see that Morgan gets his run tonight, after dinner's over and done with.'

She bent to stroke the spaniel's head and he whimpered softly, reaching to lick her cheek.

'Silly old thing.' She laughed, bobbing a curtsey to Giles Sutton: not that he would expect it, but because it was right for all that, and because she was grateful, perhaps, that he understood her need to find an excuse to be in Brattocks Wood tonight. 'Oh, and Cook says I'm to tell you that Mary has just taken tea up to her ladyship.'

Closing the door behind her she hugged herself tightly. Home, to Rowangarth, and servants' tea at four o'clock and kitchen chatter and plum jam and seed cake. And tonight he would be waiting: Tom, who loved her.

'How on earth did you get that?' Laughing, Giles Sutton contemplated his sister's face.

'Through not minding my own business, I suppose. Does it look awful?'

'Absolutely terrible. How could you have –'

'Your sister *could*, and did. Apparently, there was a fracas in Hyde Park and Julia joined in.'

'Mama! I told you! There was a suffragette selling news-sheets and a young woman – she was so pale and thin, Giles, and had a little one in her arms – well, all she did was buy a news-sheet and a policeman told her to move on – the suffragette, I mean – and he started pushing the young woman.'

'And your sister charged to her aid – and in a hobble skirt, would you believe – and tripped, and hit her head.'

'Yes, and Hawthorn told the policeman off, then demanded he find a doctor –'

'And it just so happened that a doctor was taking a stroll in the park,' Helen Sutton supplied, trying hard not to smile.

'The luck of the Suttons,' Giles grinned.

'He was very kind to me.' Julia's cheeks blazed. 'Told me I wasn't badly hurt and that if I suddenly felt ill I was to call Aunt Sutton's doctor and – and Hawthorn looked after me.' There, now, she hadn't told any lies – not *actual* lies . . . 'And please don't tease, because it did hurt, at the time.'

'Not another word, Sis. And would you mind not eating *all* the sandwiches . . .?'

'Hobble skirts,' said Alice at servants' tea. 'That's what did it, Bess. Miss Julia goes striding out, all angry with that fat policeman I told you about, and forgets you don't stride, exactly, in a hobble skirt. Next thing you know there's the most awful bang –' She paused to collect her thoughts, painstakingly jamming her bread.

'Where?' Bess demanded.

'On her head, of course.'

'Where in London, I mean.'

'Hyde Park, it was. Beautiful, Hyde Park is.' Change the subject, Alice. They've had all they're going to get about that black eye. 'Just beautiful. Like a bit of the country, right in the middle of London.'

'And was there blood?' Tilda demanded, wide-eyed. 'Did she knock herself out cold?'

'She felt a bit groggy, for a time,' Alice admitted reluctantly, 'but luckily there was a doctor handy and he took care of her.'

'Ooh. Was he young and dark and handsome, and –'

'No, Tilda, he was a doctor, that's all, and he said she wasn't badly hurt, though she'd likely have a headache in the morning, and a black eye – which she did.

'Still, Miss Julia knows now not to go telling policemen off in a hobble skirt. We went on the Underground railway, an' all.' Talk about other things. 'Imagine – trains hurtling about, underneath London. You could be walking down Oxford Street, and for all you knew there could be a rushing train beneath your feet.'

'If you ask me, Hyde Park is near where they have meetings. Speakers Corner, I believe they call it,' Mrs Shaw, offered. 'I did once hear there was a raving lunatic there, saying all manner of things about the King – King Edward, God rest him – and as how the monarchy was all lazy and overfed and should be deported to Australia and the money they cost us given to the poor.'

'I believe London folk go to Speakers Corner just for fun,' Alice nodded. 'Seems you can say almost what you want there, and get away with it.'

''Cept if you're one of them suffragette women. Illegal those meetings are now, and so they should be – women making a show of themselves in public. Ought to be ashamed of themselves.'

'Ashamed,' Alice echoed, eyes on her plate. 'But we didn't see any of them. And we didn't see the King nor the Queen, neither, though we saw their palace.'

'What's it like?'

'Big, but not half as nice as Rowangarth – well, not from the front.' Alice held out her plate as Mrs Shaw dispensed seed cake. 'Though I heard it said they've got a garden at the back.'

'You should've put raw steak on that eye,' Tilda grumbled. 'And on her forehead.'

'Was no need to go wasting good beef,' Alice declared firmly. 'Not for a bump, and that's all it was. Gracious me, folk go falling over every minute of the day and it doesn't

96

warrant a fuss. And don't be embarrassing Miss Julia by staring at her, Tilda. Nobody bothered about it in London; never gave her a second glance.'

She wished she wouldn't keep on about Miss Julia's eye. But crafty as a cartload of monkeys, that kitchenmaid was, and all the while letting folk think she was gormless.

'I did see one or two skirts down there just like your new one, Mrs Shaw.' Deftly, Alice changed the subject. 'Very nice, they looked. Ladies were wearing them with a pretty blouse with full sleeves and a brooch at the neck. And a flat straw hat, with ribbons.'

'Hm. Might get myself a bit of material, now you mention it.' Mrs Shaw had a brooch, too, that had been her mother's. 'How many yards for a blouse, Alice, would you say?'

'Two and a half, if you want full sleeves. And as for those hobble skirts – well everybody's wearing them in London. Tight as a sausage skin they are, and ladies having to take little short steps in them, and as for climbing the steps of a motor bus – make you laugh, it would . . .'

'I don't suppose you went to the theatre?' Mrs Shaw indicated with her eyebrows that Alice might be allowed another slice of cake. 'Or the music hall?'

'Sadly, no.' Alice refused more cake. All she wanted was for teatime to be finished and herself putting away Miss Julia's clothes and for the slow-moving minutes to be quickly spent so she might the sooner be with Tom. 'Women – young ladies of Miss Julia's standing, can't go to music halls without a gentleman – not even in London. But a lady can go sight-seeing or shopping with a servant with her, or a companion. Miss Julia went shopping quite a lot. My, but you should see the London shops. Swanky, they are. Great big places you could get yourself lost in, and the windows all set out with dummies with clothes on them; it's an entertainment in itself, is looking at shop windows. I used to stare at those dummies – so lifelike it wouldn't have surprised me if one of them hadn't winked at me.

'But will you be wanting any help tonight, Mrs Shaw? I've almost finished the unpacking and there's nothing in the sewing-room that won't wait till morning.' She rose from the table, asking to be excused. 'If you're short-handed . . .?'

'Nay, lass. You'll be tired after your long journey, and I've only got milady and Miss Julia for dinner tonight, so we'll manage.'

'Then Mr Giles wants me to take Morgan for a run, if that's all right with you.'

'All right with me, but best you mention it to Miss Clitherow.'

'I will,' she whispered through a sigh of relief. 'I'll mention it now.'

Eight o'clock tonight, and she would be hurrying as fast as might be to Brattocks Wood. Or perhaps to the rearing field, or maybe he'd be waiting at the parkland fence? Two whole weeks it had been and oh, how she loved him, needed him. And how very sorry she felt for Miss Julia.

Reuben was digging in his garden when Alice passed.

'Evenin', lass,' he called, jamming his spade into the earth, straightening his back. 'How was London, then?'

'Oh, you'd never believe! Wonderful, that's what!' And wonderful to be back, did you but know it, Cousin Reuben. 'I'll look in tomorrow, and tell you about it.'

'Aye. And if Tom isn't at the coops he'll be doing the rounds in Brattocks . . .'

'Thanks!' She gave him her most rewarding smile without even trying to pretend she wasn't in the least bit interested in the whereabouts of the under-keeper. 'C'mon, Morgan.'

The rearing field was deserted, the coops already shuttered for the night. Alice stood at the gate, calling softly, but there was no answering whistle.

She walked on, slipping the spaniel's lead when they came to the big pasture, watching him bounce off, sniffing, snuffling, yelping happily. At the lane end she climbed the fence, taking the path into Brattocks Wood, calling again as she went, a little apprehensive in the deep, dim greenness.

'Tom? Tom Dwerryhouse?'

She heard his whistle, long and low, and ran to the sound, laughing. He was standing beside the old oak; the one with the propped-up branches people hereabouts said was as old, almost, as Rowangarth. Then she stopped her running and walked slowly, the more to spin out the delicious seconds, watching as he laid his gun on the grass at his feet.

'Tom!' She was in his arms, loving the closeness of him, wondering how she had endured so long away from him.

They held each other tightly, not speaking, glad to be together; touching, loving, their days apart forgotten.

'I missed you, Alice Hawthorn.' His voice was low as he tilted her chin with his forefinger. 'Don't ever leave me again.'

'I won't. I missed you, too.'

'Even among those grand London folk?'

'*Especially* among those London folk,' she whispered, 'because not one of them was you.' She closed her eyes and parted her lips, wanting him to kiss her, but he twined her fingers in his own and tucked her arm in his and walked her deeper into the wood, teasing her, teasing himself, wanting her as much as she wanted him.

'Was it a good holiday, then? Is London all it's cracked up to be?'

'It is, and more. Parks and green places, and people everywhere. And cabs and motors making such a din. And you should see those big shops and oh, the fashions.

Such clothes, Tom, and ladies so elegant with their fine hats and parasols.'

'But you wouldn't live there, Alice? You wouldn't take a position in London and start getting grand ideas? I couldn't imagine you carrying a parasol, giving yourself airs. Not my buttercup girl. I don't want her to change.'

'Nor shall she.' She smiled into his eyes. 'Well, not if you were to tell her you love her, and give her that kiss she's been waiting for,' she said softly, all pretence gone. 'Waiting two weeks for.'

'Then I must do as I'm bid,' he smiled, tilting her chin again. And she remembered how she had dreamed of this moment in that far-away London bed, and when his mouth came down hard on hers, her need of him began as a blush in her cheeks and sliced through her, shivering down to her toes. It was a feeling strange and new, but right, because she knew that what she suddenly felt was not the love of a sewing-maid for her sweetheart, but the pulsating need of a woman – a woman soon to be eighteen – for her man.

Her heart began a slow, sweet thudding and she pressed closer, because it was the only way she knew to still the tiny, wayward pulses that beat out a need only he could satisfy.

'It's been so long,' she murmured, searching again for his lips. 'Kiss me again? Kiss me . . .'

His mouth was rough, his arms claimed her possessively. They kissed as if there would be no tomorrow and this moment was all they would ever have.

'I love you,' he murmured, his voice harsh with need. 'Never for a minute forget you're spoken for.'

'Not ever.' She laid her cheek on his chest, feeling the roughness of his jacket, closing her eyes against a happiness so overwhelming that it made her cling the harder to him, so weak and useless were her legs. 'Never, as long as I live.'

'And we'll be wed, Alice?'

'We'll be wed, and as soon as we are able.' She sent her happiness winging to the tall trees at the far end of the wood; to the black, cawing birds that nested there. Best tell them, tell this happiness to the rooks. Best share their loving – keep it safe from harm. 'Just as soon . . .'

6

Mrs Shaw had floated on a cloud of contentment ever since the invitations had been posted on the day following Julia's departure to London.

Things were getting back to normal. Lady Sutton was giving a dinner party, her first for three years, and though it was to be small and simple, it was a step in the right direction as far as Rowangarth's cook was concerned. Now, once more, she could proclaim her expertise. Before the death of Sir John, her reputation had been without equal, and she had scorned bribes of a superior kitchen, higher wages, and all the scullery maids she could wish for, to remain steadfastly loyal to Rowangarth.

Acceptances were quickly received. All the guests were close friends of Helen Sutton, with the exception of Mrs Clementina and Elliot, though the presence of Edward Sutton would more than compensate for that of his wife and son, and since Judge Mounteagle and his wife would be there, it was reasonable to suppose that the lady's ferocious stare would keep Elliot in his place. Mrs Mounteagle's stare could stop a runaway horse, John once said, so Elliot should present no problem at the table.

Already Mrs Shaw had spent two enjoyable sessions with her ladyship, pencil poised, notebook at the ready. It gratified her that Lady Helen always consulted directly with her cook on such occasions, which briefly elevated her almost to Miss Clitherow's station, and though the dinner party was to be small and simple, none of the joys of planning and conferring and buying-in would be wasted on a cook who had languished unseen and unsung for three unhappy years. Now the menu was finally agreed, and calculating quantities and making timetables occupied her time, for even the most ordinary of dinner parties needed three days, at least, of preparation.

Thick fish soup to start with presented no problem at all, nor the next course of poached whole salmon, served on a bed of green salad and covered, completely, with thin slices of cucumber. A joint of roast beef was child's play to a Yorkshire-born cook, but the sorbet to follow would need ice in plenty in its making, and Miss Clitherow must be reminded to send the coachman to collect half a sackful of it, on the two mornings beforehand, from the fishmonger in Creesby.

Fruit jellies to follow? Lady Sutton had enquired, to which Cook added her own suggestion that Mr Edward fair loved ice-cream and meringue pudding and might not that be offered too?

'Very well, Mrs Shaw, but in that case there will be no ices to follow the savouries, wouldn't you agree? Simple, remember? And could you make your special savoury for the gentlemen? It was always so much appreciated . . .'

Cook purred her pleasure, for even after three years it seemed that her special, secret-recipe savoury was not forgotten.

'You'll see to it, milady, that Miss Clitherow asks Ellen to help wait-on?' Sixteen at table was too much to expect of any parlourmaid, even one of Mary's capabilities.

'She has already done so. Ellen is willing,' came the smiling reply. 'I understand her uniform still fits her nicely so there'll be no problem.'

Ellen was Mary's predecessor, who four years ago had married a local farmer: the housekeeper had been gratified by the pleasure with which the appeal for help was received.

'Of course I'll come, Miss Clitherow. It'll be just like

103

old times again. I'll be there good and early, will I, to help with the silver and the table?' Time away from the demands of two young children and the promise of goodies to take home with her made the prospect of once more working at Rowangarth a pleasant one. 'And now that Lady Sutton is entertaining again, I'll always be willing to give a helping hand – if I'm able,' she had added hastily, so as not to tempt Fate overmuch.

Mrs Shaw left the morning-room, casting her mind back to the huge dinner parties of twenty years ago. Almost indecent, they were, if you considered that the cost of the out-of-season strawberries alone would have fed a family of four for a week. Perhaps it was as well these days that, following the example set by the new King and Queen, entertaining had become simpler and the upper classes less inclined to dig their graves with their knives and forks.

Next Friday's dinner was to be small and simple, but perfect for all that, and the crowning glory of Lady Helen's visit to the kitchens, even before the guests had begun to depart, would make it a day to be dwelt upon for a long time to come. Her ladyship's thanks to all concerned would be sincere, and her suggestion that they should cool themselves by finishing off the remaining ice-cream and sorbets before they melted, would be met with smiles of delight.

Rowangarth, thought Mrs Shaw as she returned to her kitchen, was her home and her pride and may the good Lord preserve it and, if He wouldn't mind, see what He could do about providing an heir, which would please milady no end and maybe help the dear soul to smile a little more often.

'Tilda!' she called to the maid who had taken advantage of her superior's absence. 'Put that love book down this instant!'

There would be no time for reading now. Rowangarth

was coming into its own again, and by the time Friday had come and gone, that silly girl wouldn't know what had hit her! Oh my word, no!

The letter came long before she expected it. Addressed to Miss A. Hawthorn, there were raised eyebrows when it was handed to Alice at servants' breakfast.

'London,' Tilda gloated, eyes on the postmark.

'London,' Alice confirmed primly, with not so much as a blush. 'Miss Sutton's live-in said she would write to me if I was of a mind to get a letter occasionally.' Firmly, she pushed it into her pocket. 'I'll read it later.'

She hoped it wouldn't say that he wasn't coming. Miss Julia would be disappointed – *heartbroken* – if she didn't see him again soon. The letter was from Doctor MacMalcolm, she was sure. What she wasn't so sure about was how she could quickly – and secretly – get it to the lady for whom it was intended.

She cut a slice of bread then, spearing it with her fork, held it to the hot coals of the kitchen range.

'Do you think, Mary,' she murmured, eyes downcast, 'you could give Miss Julia a message when you take breakfast up? Something I've just remembered. Would you tell her that I've run out of blue thread, and can she let me know if she'll be going to York in the near future?'

'Why York?' Tilda demanded. 'You can buy cotton just as easy in Holdenby.'

'Because it's special buttonhole thread,' Alice flung scathingly, dratting the kitchenmaid's nosiness.

'Buttonhole thread, I'm to say?' Mary frowned.

'That's right. From York – or Harrogate. She'll know. And pass the butter please, Tilda, afore my toast gets cold.'

She could have set her clock by Julia Sutton's breathless arrival. Breakfast at eight-thirty, with twenty minutes – give

105

or take the odd few seconds – before she could decently excuse herself. Then half a minute from the morning-room to the sewing-room; a little before nine, it would be.

'Hawthorn?' At eight fifty-two exactly, a pink-cheeked Julia opened the sewing-room door.

'You understood my message, then?' Alice held the envelope between her first and second fingers. 'It came this morning. From him.'

'Andrew!' She snatched the envelope, tearing it open with shaking fingers, pulling out the smaller one inside which bore her name – just *Julia*, written squarely in the very centre in black ink. 'Oh, Hawthorn – what if . . .'

'Read it and see.' She waited, hardly breathing, as the tiny mantel-clock ticked away a long minute, loud in the silence; then Julia lifted her eyes.

'He isn't coming to York mid-June,' she whispered soberly, then her cheeks dimpled and she laughed out loud. 'No! It's to be Harrogate, and he's coming next week! He says he thinks it had better be Harrogate because he wants to visit the Pump Room and the Baths, and find out all he can about the water cures. Well, I suppose a doctor would be –'

'Interested?' Alice nodded. 'Yes.' Though not for the life of her could she ever have been persuaded to drink those curative waters. Tasted something awful, Cook said, and a pint of ale would do more good, to her way of thinking. 'Did he say, miss, why he's coming earlier?'

'No, but does it matter? All I know is that he'll be arriving on Monday, a little before noon, and he wants me to meet him outside the station entrance at two.'

'And can you?'

'I've *got* to.' It was so ridiculous that a grown woman must be escorted everywhere, as if she were incapable even of crossing the road unaided. 'I'll have to think up an excuse to get away – alone, if I can.'

'And will she let you – go by yourself on the train, I mean?,' Alice frowned.

'Why shouldn't I, in a ladies-only compartment? But if she won't allow it, I shall ask her if you can come with me. You can buy your blue thread, then.'

'You know I don't want thread, miss. And if I was you I wouldn't make too many plans, because next week it's the dinner party – had you forgotten?'

'As if I could. Mama's as jumpy as a kitten about it already. Well, she would be. It's three years since she last had people here.'

'Yes. So think, miss. Who's to be spared to go to Harrogate with you? We'll be busy all week, and I'll have to help out in the kitchens, what with all the extra work.'

Silver and table-linen to be brought out and checked after so long out of use; Cook pink-cheeked and indignant and loving every minute of it, from the first menu ideas to the last of the savouries sent up to the servery in the shuddering lift; then she would collapse in the kitchen rocker and fan herself with a tea towel, murmuring, 'My, oh, my . . .'

'Busy? *Everyone?* Then I'll just have to get away on my own.'

Perhaps, Julia thought, the dinner party might be a blessing in disguise. Perhaps Mama would be too taken up with it to argue the rights and wrongs of an unchaperoned trip. Or would she say no, in a voice that meant no?

'I must see her – now!'

She was gone before Alice could offer a word of advice or warning or caution. Blue thread, indeed! It was going to take more than a reel of thread to get them out of this one.

Sighing, she returned to the kitchen, where silver fruit baskets and candlesticks and flower bowls waited to be polished, and knives and forks and spoons and salt cellars and sauce bowls cleaned and rinsed in soapy water, then cleaned again. And Cook fussing over her stockpot, complaining that the fire wasn't drawing properly; that the flues would have to be brushed clean of soot in the morning and Tilda had better not forget it, either!

She had been so looking forward to the dinner party, Alice fretted; to the fuss and bustle and helping in the kitchen and seeing the table decorations and the lovely dresses and eating leftover goodies. It should have been nice to see Rowangarth come to life again, with her ladyship looking lovely and wearing her orchids, but now the letter had come and there was no knowing what Miss Julia would do. The cat would be out of the bag and London out of bounds for all time, if she didn't mind what she said.

'Oh, Lor',' Alice whispered. 'Be careful, miss.'

Julia found her mother in her dressing-room, swishing aside dinner gowns, murmuring, 'No, no, *no*! Oh, it's you, child. There is absolutely nothing to wear and less than a week to go and no time at all to buy new . . .'

'Blue,' Julia pronounced. 'Something blue, it should be.'

But Pa had always liked her in blue, so blue could not be considered. Nor the apricot silk with the draped neckline, because Mama had worn that to Pa's last birthday dinner; nor the green satin, either, because she had been wearing it when they came to tell her that Pa wasn't just late for dinner, but that he wouldn't be home, ever again.

'Blue.' Julia reached for a hanger and removed the cover from the gown. 'Your orchids will look beautiful with this one. And you should have Miss Clitherow make you a chignon so you can wear orchids in your hair, too.'

'Hmm. Did you want something?' Clearly she was in no mood to talk about clothes.

'N-no. Nothing in particular, except perhaps could Hawthorn be spared to come with me to Harrogate on Monday? I'd thought on the noon train – or it would be better if I were to go alone . . .'

'*Alone?* But you never –'

'Mama! Girls go everywhere alone, now. In London it's quite commonplace.'

'But this is not London, Julia. Nor, I imagine, can Hawthorn be spared on Monday – or any other day next week.'

'Yes, I know she's needed to help out downstairs, but I've got a good reason for going on my own. It will be Hawthorn's birthday in two weeks, and she was such a help in London and so kind and thoughtful when I got my bruises, that I'd like to buy some special roses for her hat.

'The ones she's got she made herself out of satin scraps, and I want to buy her some silk ones, and maybe a little matching bud for her jacket lapel – to say thank you, I mean. So it's best she doesn't come with me and I *can* manage alone, I really can. If I'm seen on to the train and met off it when I get back, I can't possibly come to any harm.

'And I'm nearly twenty-one and it *is* 1913, Mama, and women travel alone every day in London on the trams and tube trains, really they do,' she finished breathlessly.

'London has given you ideas, Julia, and yes, I know you're not a child and it's kind of you to think about Hawthorn, but –'

'But I can't go alone and no one can be spared next week to go with me!' Her mouth set stubbornly.

'Then you are wrong. But just this once, I was going to say, if you promise to get the five o'clock train back, I think you might be allowed –'

'Mama! Oh, *thank* you, and I will take care, I will! And Hawthorn wants blue thread and if there's anything you'd like me to get for you . . .'

'There is nothing. But if you find yourself in need of a ladies' room, then do be careful where you go? The tea-shop on the corner of James Street is very respectable.'

'I'll be careful – I truly will. And when women get the vote there'll be an end to chaperoning,' she added, breathlessly triumphant.

'The *vote*, Julia?'

'Sorry, dearest.' Sorry indeed! Hawthorn had said to be careful and she had forgotten. She'd just blurted it out, and now it was said it couldn't be taken back. 'The vote, Mama,' she said soberly, meeting her mother's gaze. 'Women will get it, one day. We will, you know.'

'One day, perhaps. But not just yet. Not for a long, long time. And you are not to talk about such things on Friday night – please?'

'I won't; I promise. I'll be very ladylike and I'll watch my tongue and if it gets too bad for you – missing Pa, I mean – look across at me, and I shall understand.'

Helen Sutton closed her eyes tightly, then smiling just a little too brightly, she whispered, 'The blue it shall be, Julia. I shall wear the blue, on Friday. For your Pa.'

He was waiting outside the station beside the little flower shop, and her feet felt like lead weights, so difficult was it to place one in front of the other. Then the colour Julia had felt drain from her cheeks at the sight of him all at once flooded back, and she began to tremble with relief that he was there.

'You remembered,' he smiled, raising his hat. 'To wear the blue, I mean.'

'I said I would, next time we met – if it was still summer.' Love for him washed over her and stuck in her throat in an exquisite ache. 'And I want so much for you to kiss me.'

'I want to kiss you, too, but not here.' She was more beautiful than he remembered, her eyes larger, more luminous, her voice husky with a recognized need. 'Close to where I am staying, there are gardens. We can walk there . . .' He offered his arm and she slipped her hand into it, worried that someone she knew would see them; wishing with all her heart that they would.

'This seems a prosperous town – what little I have seen of it,' he murmured. 'Fine houses, hotels, gardens . . .'

'Indeed. A physician could do well here.' Briefly she teased him with her eyes. 'Would you ever consider moving north?'

'Most certainly – given the means to buy myself into a town such as this. But I haven't enough saved, yet – it's only right you should know that, darling – so I must stay in London a while longer. By the way, I left my card at your aunt's house, though I haven't received hers in return. So until I do, I can't call on her.'

'Then I think you should leave another,' Julia urged. 'I wrote to her, two days ago, telling her that my bruises were almost gone now, thanks to your skill, so maybe next time you'll be luckier. I do so want her to receive you.'

'*Receive* me? D'you know, lassie, that where I came from there was no card-leaving, no waiting to be asked. In the pit house I grew up in, a neighbour would walk in without fuss and ask was there anything she could do to help – and help we needed, I can tell you that. Or maybe they'd just call for a gossip and a cup of tea – if there was tea to spare, mind, and milk to put in it.

'But I don't hold with all these peculiar customs – leaving cards, then waiting to be asked to call. It's a funny way of going on, to my way of thinking.'

'I know, Andrew, and I don't much care for it myself. But it's the way we do things and – and –'

'And see where it gets you; snubbed or frustrated, or both. And I haven't the time to waste leaving cards. I've thought a lot about us since you left, Julia; I even tried telling myself you were out of my reach, and to forget you.

'I'm stubborn, though. When I get to be a fine physician I shall need a fine wife, so you'll suit me nicely. And there is another thing, far more important. I love you, fine wife or no', so it's right I should ask you to marry me and –'

'Marry you?' She stood stock still, cheeks blazing. 'Right out of nowhere, when you haven't even asked me how my bruises are, you ask me to *marry* you!'

'Your bruises are gone, almost, and your eye is fine. I'd be a poor physician if I couldn't see that with half a glance. No! I have reached the conclusion that time is too short and too precious for the nonsense of card-leaving. I have six days here – few enough, to my way of thinking – so there is no time to waste being socially correct. That is why I've decided to speak with your mother or your brother, or both. And I shall declare my intentions and ask that I might be allowed to write to you and meet you here, or at your Aunt Sutton's house. There now – how does that suit you?' he smiled.

'Andrew! You cannot – *I* cannot –' He could not, must not, do anything so awful! 'It isn't right or proper and you mustn't call! It isn't the way we do things. My mother doesn't even know you exist.'

'Then you shall tell her, tonight, and ask that when I call tomorrow she'll be kind enough to invite me inside. I'm not of a mind to shilly-shally, and I don't approve of hole-in-the-corner affairs between two people who love each other. And do you know, Miss Julia Sutton, how very dear you are, standing there with your mouth wide open?'

'Andrew, dearest love.' Tears brightened her eyes and she blinked them away, matching his smile with her own. 'I don't think I've been so happy in the whole of my life, but it isn't possible for you to call – it truly isn't. There's a way of doing things, and calling uninvited isn't one of them. I'm sorry. But darling, I'll soon be twenty-one and can tell them about us. Then, if they forbid it, I shall run away to London to you and –'

'No, Julia. There'll be no running anywhere! And do you know a short-cut to those gardens, because I need to kiss some sense into you. And don't argue, or ask me to change my mind. I intend gettings things straight before I go back to London, so there's no more to be said! Is that quite, quite clear?'

'It is – oh, it is! But you don't know what you are doing. You *don't*! Are you willing to risk everything just because of your impatience – and your stubborn Scottish principles?'

'Aye,' he said mildly.

'Then you are a fool, Andrew MacMalcolm, and I love you very much.'

'Good. And you'll marry me,' he whispered, 'just as soon as I can afford you?'

'I'll marry you,' she choked, sniffing loudly, wondering why it was happening like this and where it would all end. 'But I can't think why you should want me. I'm very ordinary and inclined to bossiness and I'll never be as beautiful as Mama. I really can't see why –'

'Can't you? Then maybe it's because you aren't standing where I am. And you might as well know that I've loved you right from the start, lying there white-faced and your eyes closed. Even then, I wondered what colour they were . . .'

'Then you meant it, Andrew, that day you opened your door to me and said you'd hoped I would come?'

'I meant it.' Taking her hand, he lingered a kiss in its upturned palm, just as though they were walking in Hyde Park again, where no one knew them. 'I meant it, lassie.'

It was seven o'clock before Julia was able to find Alice alone.

'Hawthorn! At last! Can you come up to the sewing-room? It's important – and oh, such a mess!'

'Miss, it's suppertime and Mrs Shaw's going to glare if I'm late. Can't it wait till after?'

'It can not! And you must tell Cook I waylaid you; say what you want, but I've got to talk to you. It can't wait, because at dinner when Mama and Giles are together, there's something I've got to tell them and you must know about it first because you're involved – indirectly, that is – and I don't want to land you in trouble.'

'What happened in Harrogate?' Alice sighed. She had known something would go wrong, carrying on like that. 'Someone saw you, didn't they?'

'No. Leastways, I don't think so – but I don't care if they did! This is far worse, you see, and far more wonderful. Trouble is, it's all going to come out.' She closed the sewing-room door, then leaned against it dramatically. 'Andrew has asked me to marry him – no, that's not strictly true. Andrew *told* me we were to be married just as soon as he can afford me, but –'

'Miss Julia – that's *lovely*!' Alice closed her eyes rapturously, all at once imagining yards of bridal satin and silk and lace. And creamy-white orchids and a veil so long that –

'Lovely – yes. But listen! Andrew intends coming to the house tomorrow and telling Mama and Giles that he wants their permission to write to me and visit me here and at Aunt Sutton's when I'm in London – if ever I'm allowed to go to London again, that is!'

'Oh, Lordy, miss. You should've told him it isn't done.' Even a servant knew it wasn't done. 'You've got to stop him or the cat'll be out of the bag about London, and I'll be up to the ears in it, an' all.'

'But that's it, Hawthorn. You *won't* be in trouble because I intend telling them what really happened in London. What I *won't* tell them is that Andrew and I

114

met alone. I shall say that you were with us at all times and that it was me who insisted on meeting the doctor and that there was nothing you could have done about it, short of locking me in. So you won't be in any trouble, I promise you. That's why I had to see you so that when I've told Mama you'll be able to confirm that it was all perfectly correct – if she asks you, that is – and that no blame attaches to you.'

'I said so, didn't I, miss; said our sins would find us out. But *marry* him! You said yes, didn't you?' She *must* have said yes.

'Of course I did. But you're the only one who knows, Hawthorn, so you mustn't breathe a word until I've talked to Mama and warned her that a very determined doctor intends presenting himself tomorrow at ten o'clock. And I'll *die* of shame if she doesn't receive him.'

'She will, Miss Julia. She's too much of a lady not to. But I hope it turns out all right for you, and that her ladyship doesn't forbid you ever to go to London again. The doctor's a lovely gentleman, and if I can I'll try to get out for just a few minutes – tell it to the rooks, for you, to make it all right. And thanks for not landing me in trouble. I'm ever so grateful, though it's going to mean we'll both have to tell a few fibs.'

'But it's worth it, Hawthorn. I wish tonight were over and done with, though. I don't want to set Mama at defiance and tell her that if she won't see Andrew and says I must never see him again, I shall marry him anyway, as soon as I'm twenty-one.'

'You wouldn't do that – her ladyship's got worries enough being without Sir John, and your brother away in India. You'll think on, won't you, miss? Wasn't she just like you, once, with a young man she was in love with, and didn't it turn out all right for them? Promise you'll count to ten?'

Oh, Lordy. What a mess it all was. And where would

it end? Because soon it would be out in the open. What would happen then, Alice Hawthorn shuddered to think about!

'Mama,' Julia whispered, when dinner was announced. 'When she has served us, can you ask Mary to leave – *please*?'

'Leave us?' Normally she would have refused such a request, but Helen Sutton heard apprehension in her daughter's voice and saw it in her eyes. 'What is so important that it cannot wait until later?'

'Something that needs to be said to you both, and it can't wait any longer, though I've been wanting to tell you ever since I got back from –'

'From London?' On reflection, she thought, her daughter had not been quite her usual impetuous self, though she had supposed it was due to the quietness of Rowangarth after the flurry and whirl of London.

'No, dearest; from Harrogate. And it isn't,' she hastened, 'anything awful. Just something you and Giles must know. You will, won't you – ask Mary to leave us alone so I can talk to you?'

'If I must.' Helen Sutton slipped her arm through that of her son, frowning as he led her to the dining-room, wondering what had happened between noon and five o'clock to cause such consternation. 'Did you lose your purse? Your ticket?'

'No, Mama.' If only it were that simple. But further talk was impossible, because Giles was drawing out his mother's chair and Mary stood smiling, soup ladle at the ready, and it seemed an age before the joint was carved and plates passed round and her mother was able to say, 'Thank you, Mary. We can manage quite nicely now. Coffee in the conservatory tonight, I think it will be. I'll ring when we are ready for it. And now, if you please, Julia,' she demanded as the door closed quietly,

116

'what is so important that dinner must be disrupted because of it?'

'Well, it's – it's . . .' Julia drew in a steadying breath, the carefully rehearsed words forgotten. 'When I was in London I met a young man – a doctor – and he intends calling on you and Giles tomorrow morning, at about ten.'

There now, she had said it, and in her usual tactless, bull-at-a-gate manner. And oh, please, *please*, Mama, and you too, Giles, don't look so stonily at me.

'I see.' Helen Sutton laid down her knife and fork.

'Well, I'm damned.' Giles's fork remained suspended between plate and mouth. 'Calling, is he?'

'He is. I told – *asked* – him not to, but he's set on it, so you will receive him, Mama? And please listen to what he has to say – sympathetically, I mean.' Her voice trailed into silence and she looked from one to the other, eyes pleading.

'Do I know this young man?'

'No. Nor does Giles.' She refused to tell one more untruth. 'But if you'll let me introduce him to you, and if you'll at least let him stay for coffee, you'll – you'll . . .'

'Perhaps begin to understand why you appear to be so taken with him?'

'Yes, Mama. So can I –'

'Can you get on with it, I hope you mean,' Giles smiled, 'and let Mama and I eat our dinner whilst you tell it, for there's nothing worse than mutton gone cold.'

Then he winked at her and she saw the sympathy she so needed in his eyes, and was grateful that at least her brother was on her side.

'Well,' she whispered. 'I suppose the best place to begin is the beginning and it began when I fell in Hyde Park.'

'And he was the doctor who helped you. Then he must have called on you again?'

'No, Giles. I called on him.' Her eyes were downcast, her fingers plucked nervously at the napkin on her knees. 'He'd left his card and I wanted to thank him. No. Not to thank him, exactly.' Her head lifted and she looked directly into her mother's eyes. 'I wanted to see him again. And nothing happened. He walked me – *us* – back to the motor bus, then asked if we would both like to walk in the park the next day. It was all perfectly proper.'

'It was *not* proper and you know it, or you'd have told me the truth of it long before this, Julia. I thought you were sensible enough to be trusted alone, but it seems you were not. And Hawthorn encouraging you . . .'

'No! It wasn't like that! Hawthorn spoke most strongly against it, even though she was relieved and grateful he was there to help when I hit my head. But I insisted.'

'She's right, Mama. You can't blame Hawthorn,' Giles urged. 'What else was she to do, when Julia had her mind set on it?'

'Very well – I suppose Hawthorn acted as properly as she was able. And how many times, Julia, did you meet this doctor?'

'Twice. And correctly chaperoned.' She closed her eyes for shame at yet another lie, even though it was uttered to protect Hawthorn. 'Then he said he was coming to Harrogate to study the water cures and asked me to meet him there. And I did and now you know it all,' she finished breathlessly.

There was a long, apprehensive silence before Helen Sutton demanded, 'All? Then what foolishness has prompted this man to call on me tomorrow without invitation?'

'His name, Mama, is Andrew MacMalcolm, and he is a doctor,' Julia said quietly, knowing all was lost, yet determined, still, to defend him. 'And he is coming to see you because he wishes to marry me and I,' she rushed on as her mother's eyes opened wide with shock and her brother's knife and fork clattered on to his plate, 'wish to marry him!'

'Stop, at once! I have listened to more than enough for one night. You have deceived me, Julia, and I suggest you go to your room. I would like to speak with your brother alone.'

'No. I'm sorry, Mama, but I won't.' Her voice was less than a whisper now, and trembled on the edge of tears. 'I didn't deceive you today; not wholly. I did buy roses for Hawthorn. But I am almost twenty-one – almost grown up – and will not be sent from the room like a naughty child, nor discussed behind my back.'

'Let her stay, dearest?' Giles pleaded. 'Julia has been truthful, and told you all.'

'Yes! But would she have been so forthcoming had this young man not announced his intention of confronting me in my own home?'

'I think,' said her son levelly, 'that it is I he must confront if he wishes to marry my sister. In Robert's absence, *I* am her legal guardian – for the five remaining months she is a minor, that is.'

'I see. So after November, when she is of age, you will condone such a marriage, simply because you are not prepared to do anything about it, Giles?'

'No, Mother. But at least receive the man. You'll know at once if he is a fortune hunter.'

'Your sister does not have a fortune!'

'A social climber, then?'

'Stop it! Please stop it!' They were talking about her as if she were not there, and Julia had reached the limits of her tolerance. 'And please don't keep calling Andrew *the man*, and *this man*. He is a person, a doctor, and is entitled to your respect. Doctor MacMalcolm. It isn't so difficult to say. He works at St Bartholomew's Hospital and he's saving hard to buy a partnership in general practice.

'And, Mama, before you forbid it out of hand, will you remember that you said I might choose my own husband?' Her eyes were stark with pleading; tears still trembled on every whispered word. 'And will you remember that you and Pa were in love?'

'Your father, Julia, had expectations. Doctor MacMalcolm appears to be without the means, even, to buy a practice.'

'So if my father hadn't been rich, you wouldn't have fallen in love with him?'

'You are being unfair, Julia, and pert, too.' Her voice was softer now, for she could not deny a love that went even beyond the grave. 'I am shocked and at a loss as to what to say. It is unbelievable that you can even consider marriage on so short an acquaintance.'

'Mama, with the greatest respect it is not – and you know it.'

'Julia, Julia – what am I to do with you, say to you?'

Despairingly she closed her eyes. She was eighteen again, and John, love of her life, was signing her dance card, claiming the supper dance and the last dance, and she was looking into his eyes, knowing even then that if she never saw him again after that last waltz, she would remember him for the rest of her life. She had worn blue that night.

'Do, Mama? You must do what you think right, but don't say I must never see Andrew again. I wouldn't want to disobey you or deceive you – but I would, if I had to.'

'Then Doctor MacMalcolm may call,' Helen said wearily, for in truth sitting opposite was the girl she herself had once been. And equally in love. 'Might I be told how he will get here?'

'He'll walk. He'll take the early train to Holdenby and I shall meet him there. I shall cycle over to the station and –'

'Then you had better use the carriage. Let Miss Clitherow know . . .'

'Oh, my *dear*!' Julia pushed back her chair and was at her mother's side, lips brushing her cheek. 'It's all right? You mean it?'

'I mean that it will attract less attention than if you were to walk through the village with him, pushing your bicycle at his side!'

'That's settled, then?' Giles demanded, eyebrows raised. 'We can finish eating?'

'By all means. And Julia, I am sure, is sorry for the commotion. But it is by no means settled,' Helen said firmly. 'It is not settled at all, but for the time being the matter shall be dropped, save to say that I will be receiving at ten in the morning.'

Julia picked up her knife and fork, regarding her plate with dismay. She hadn't lost, exactly, but neither had Andrew been received with the enthusiasm she had hoped for. Her mother's gentleness had proved to be a cover for a sternness seldom seen. In future she would go carefully, think before she spoke, for so very much was at stake. And what was more, she thought mutinously, she would never again eat leg of mutton without extreme distaste, and she hoped with all her heart that Hawthorn was making a better job of it with the rooks than she had done. Because she had made a mess of it, had let Andrew down dreadfully. Tomorrow he would be received politely – too politely – which would make him begin to wonder if it was all worth it.

But she would never give him up. Soon she would be her own mistress, and answerable to no one. And it was Andrew, or no one. She had loved him from the moment they met, and no one else would do.

So sorry, Mama, and you too, Giles, but that's the way it is and nothing will change it. Not ever.

7

The engine rounded the bend, whistling importantly, then came to a stop in a hiss of steam.

'Holdenby!' called the stationmaster as a single passenger alighted; a stranger, stepping down from the third-class carriage at the end of the train, which would be noted and remarked upon, of that Julia Sutton was certain.

Smiling, raising his hat, he walked to where she waited. She acknowledged him with the slightest inclining of her head, holding out her hand which he shook, thanks be, and did not kiss.

'Good morning, doctor.'

'Miss Sutton,' he murmured most properly for the benefit of the ticket clerk who waited at the barrier.

'My mother thought it better we use the carriage,' Julia whispered. 'And my dear, be careful what you say? Anything William hears . . .'

The red-haired coachman was a hard worker and a fine horseman, and for that his weakness for listening and gossiping was tolerated, it being politic, Helen Sutton had long ago decided, to make sure that when he was driving there was nothing for him to listen to and nothing, therefore, to repeat. William, Miss Clitherow declared, wouldn't have lasted the week out at Pendenys, but he was cheerful and willing, and neither drank ale nor wasted his wages on tobacco, so his virtues far outweighed his one vice.

'I've asked William to let us down at the gates so we'll be able to talk.' Julia inclined her head in the direction of the coachman who stood beside the open carriage door, eyeing the visitor, wondering what to make of him. Then he took up the reins and clicked his tongue, ordering the horses to walk on, guiding them carefully out of the station yard, and not until they were on the road did Julia reach for Andrew's hand, to press it briefly. Then she sat straight and correct, saying not one word until Rowangarth gates came into sight and the horses were brought to a halt at the lodge.

'I thought we could walk the rest of the way,' she smiled as the carriage drew away. 'Last night, you see, my mother was a little put out. I told her that you wanted to marry me. I'm sorry, but it just slipped out.'

'Then small wonder she was not well-pleased. And your brother?'

'Giles is on our side, I think. And when I'd reminded Mama she had promised I should marry where I pleased and that she and Pa were so in love, she agreed to be at home to you.'

'There you are, lassie – it's happening again. Your mother *agrees* to receive me. I'll never understand it.'

'I know, and I'm sorry, but there's more, I'm afraid. My mother is *Lady* Sutton. Pa was a baronet, you see.'

'So I'm to remember to call your brother Sir Giles?'

'No. Giles is the younger brother. Robert – the one who grows tea – inherited.'

'Why didn't you tell me this before, Julia?'

'Would it have made any difference?'

'No. And we're wasting time over trivialities,' he smiled, taking her hand. 'We are here, together; I am to meet your family, titled or no, and I look forward to it.'

'Even though Mama might be a little – *aloof*?'

'Even though. I'm very determined when my mind's made up.'

'But you'll go carefully,' she begged, eyes anxious.

'Very carefully. I mind how much is at stake.' He stopped as they rounded the curve in the drive and saw

123

Rowangarth, its windows shining back the morning sun in a sparkle of welcome. 'That's where you live?'

'That's Rowangarth. It's higgledy-piggledy and draughty in winter, and sometimes the fires sulk and the windows rattle when the wind blows, but we love it very much.'

'Aye, I think I'd love it too,' he said softly. 'But what was your reason for not telling me about all this?'

'Because where I live didn't seem important. And it still isn't – not if you don't mind about it, that is.'

'Of course I don't, though I can see I'll have to work even harder if I'm to keep you in the manner you're born to.'

He smiled gently, not one bit put out, once he'd had time to get his breath back. And didn't Andrew MacMalcolm thrive on challenges? Even when they'd laughed and told him that doctoring was out of the reach of a miner's son – all but Aunt Jessie, that was – he had shrugged and carried on. And maybe the folk who lived in the fine house down there were decent enough bodies, in spite of their wealth. He hoped so, for he wanted Julia so much it was like an ache inside him, and he knew he would do anything, agree to any condition they might impose, to keep her.

'Then why are you frowning so?'

'Was I? Truth known, I was thinking about my aunt and wondering what she would have made of all that.' He nodded in the direction of the house. 'My, but she'd have liked fine to poke around and see how grand folk live. The gentry and their houses always fascinated her. She used to wonder how so few people could take up so many rooms.'

'Then I'm sorry she isn't here to see it, though Rowangarth is small compared to Pendenys – that's Uncle Edward's house. Now your aunt would really have enjoyed a poke around there.'

'And what's so peculiar about this Pendenys?'

'Wait until you see it. But it's almost ten and it won't do to keep Mama waiting.' She smiled up at him, serious again. 'And I love you very much. Whatever happens, you'll remember that, won't you?'

Mary opened the front door at their approach. She had been warned by Miss Clitherow that her ladyship would be receiving at ten, and ever since Miss Julia left with the carriage half an hour ago, Mary had hovered between the front hall and the kitchen, all the time wondering who the daughter of the house was to bring back with her. Most times the parlourmaid wouldn't have given it a second thought, but last night she had been excused before dinner was over which meant that her betters wanted to talk privately; and afterwards, when she had taken in the coffee tray, she sensed an atmosphere and wondered what it was she hadn't been meant to hear – and who had been the cause of it.

She supposed at first it was Mr Elliot, for talk still buzzed about the goings-on in Creesby. Indeed, it had been reasonable to suppose just that – reasonable until this morning, that was, when the carriage had been ordered and gone off with Miss Julia in it and she, Mary, had been told there would be a caller.

'Miss.' She bobbed a curtsey, holding out her hand for the visitor's hat and gloves. 'Milady's in the small sitting-room. She said you were to go in.'

Sedately she placed the hat on a table, then, hearing the closing of the sitting-room door, ran like the wind to the kitchens below.

My, but he was handsome! Tall and broad, with lovely eyes; and the smile he'd given her had been fit to charm the birds from the trees.

'There's a young man!' she gasped, flinging open the door. 'Came back in the carriage!' William would know. Someone would have to ask William. 'And he's gone in with Miss Julia to see her ladyship.' And Mr Giles there, too, which was unusual to say the least, since Mr Giles was always in the library, nose in a book, by ten in the morning. 'What's going on, Mrs Shaw?'

Cook did not know, and said so. She only knew that, before so very much longer, her ladyship might well be ringing for a pot of coffee – and that the kettle stood cold and empty in the hearth.

'Set the water to boil, Tilda, just in case,' she murmured, hoping that a summons from above would give Mary the chance to assess the situation in the small sitting-room. 'And the rest of you get on with your work. 'Tisn't for us to bother about what goes on upstairs.'

But tall and good-looking, Mary had said. Had London been the start of it, then? She glanced across at Alice, busy with silver-cleaning, and was met with a look as blank as a high brick wall.

But it *was* London. Cook was so sure she'd have taken bets on it.

'Mama.' Julia cleared her throat nervously and noisily. 'May I present Doctor Andrew MacMalcolm? Andrew –' She turned, shaking in every limb, the easy introduction all at once a jumble of words that refused to leave her lips.

'Lady Sutton,' Andrew murmured, bowing his head, yet all the time unwilling to take his eyes from the beauty of her face. 'How kind of you to receive me.'

'I had little choice, doctor,' she smiled ruefully. 'And since my daughter seems tongue-tied, this is Giles, my younger son, who would really rather be in the library, I must warn you.'

Giles held out his hand. Gravely, firmly, Andrew took it.

'There now,' Helen Sutton murmured. 'Please sit down – you too, Julia.' She indicated the sofa and, gratefully, Julia took her place at Andrew's side, her mouth dry, fingers clasped nervously in her lap. 'Tell me about London, doctor, and how you and my daughter met.'

'In extremely unusual circumstances, I fear. It was lucky I was near when needed. A young lady lay concussed; had tripped and fallen I was told, and I could well believe it when I saw the skirt she was wearing – and I beg your pardon, ma'am, if I make comment on ladies' fashions about which I know nothing.'

'I'm inclined to agree with your observations.' There was unconcealed laughter in the reply. 'About the skirt, I mean. But my daughter's bruises are gone now, and I am grateful to you for your attention. And then, doctor?'

'Then Miss Sutton was generous enough to thank me for my help, and consented to walk in the park with me the following afternoon.'

'And now, my sister tells us you wish to correspond with her and to meet, which we – *I* – find hard to understand on so short an acquaintance.' Giles took up the conversation, wondering if his voice sounded as stern as he meant it to sound, yet all the time admiring the directness of the young man's gaze and his complete ease of manner. 'Might it not, perhaps, be –'

'Sir – I think you have not been fully acquainted with the facts. True, we wish to write to each other and to meet whenever my work allows it. But I want to marry your sister, and would like your permission – and Lady Sutton's blessing – to that end.

'And as for so short an acquaintance – that I cannot deny. But in my profession I must make a decision and hold firm to it, often with no time at all for second thoughts. I made such a decision when first I met Miss Julia, and I have had no reason to change or regret it.'

'Then might I know how you will support my sister?'

'I must admit,' Andrew replied gravely, 'that at first

127

the matter did cause me concern. But I am a competent physician and intend to become a better one. Time is all I need. And I beg you to hear me out with patience, for I think your sister cannot have told you all.

'I am the son of a coal miner. My father was injured in the pit and suffered pain for two years before he died. Those two years affected me greatly. I was unable to help him, you see, then had to watch my mother work herself to a standstill so we might live.'

'But that is dreadful!' Helen Sutton's dismay was genuine. 'Did not the owner of the mine make some restitution?'

'No, ma'am, and we did not expect it.' He spoke without bitterness. 'But after my father died, my mother took consumption from a sick man. She went out nursing, usually night work, so she might have the days free for other things. Apart from a child to tend to, she worked mornings for the wife of the doctor, to pay off the debt of my father's illness.

'She insisted I remain at school, though I was old enough by then to have worked at the pit. But she would have none of it. The only comfort in her death was that at least she lived long enough to know I'd been given a scholarship to medical school.'

'But how did you manage? All those years of study,' Giles murmured, uneasily. 'How did you eat – buy books?'

'I bought secondhand books and ate as little as possible,' Andrew laughed. 'I'd sold up the home, though there was little left by that time. Most of it had gone, piece by piece, over the bad years. But what was left helped, and my mother's sister, my aunt Jessie, gave me her savings, to be paid back when I qualified. I was grateful for her faith and trust. I even had thoughts that, once I could afford decent lodgings, she could come to me: I'd have cared for her for the rest of her life. She died, though, even before I qualified. She was never to know me as a doctor.

But that is why I have no family to offer you – only myself . . .'

'I am so sorry,' Helen whispered, 'and please, if you find it upsetting, there is no need to tell us.'

'Upsetting? No, Lady Sutton, you misunderstand,' Andrew smiled. 'What I have told you is neither to seek praise nor pity. It is merely a fact of my life – my background – that you should know about and, I hope, try to accept.

'The two women who made it possible for me to qualify are beyond my help how, so instead I pay my debt to them in other ways. Apart from my work at the hospital, I hold a twice-weekly surgery at my lodgings; those who cannot afford to pay, I treat without charge. I turn no one away, and it pleases me to think that one day I might diagnose consumption in its early stages and be able to prevent a woman dying as my mother died.'

'Then your beliefs are to your credit, doctor,' Helen said gently. 'I wonder – would you care to take coffee with us?' She pulled on the fireside bell and was amazed by the speed at which it was answered.

'Milady?' Mary stood pink-cheeked in the doorway.

'Will you bring coffee for four – and will you apologize to Cook and tell her there will be one extra for luncheon?'

Unable to conceal her delight, Mary made triumphantly for the kitchen.

'Mama!' Julia cried. 'It's all right? We can be married? Oh, *thank* you!'

'Julia!' As sternly as she was able, Helen Sutton silenced her daughter's excited flow. 'You may *not* be married whilst you are still a minor, and even when you come of age I ask you not to consider yourself engaged to Doctor MacMalcolm.

'What I *am* prepared to agree to is that you may write as often as you please and meet each other here, or at Aunt Sutton's. Then, in a year from now, if you are both

129

of the same mind, we can all discuss the matter further. There, miss – will that suit you, for the time being?'

'Ma'am, it will suit me very well indeed,' Andrew replied warmly, 'and I – *we* – thank you most gratefully. You will not regret the decision you have come to today, I promise you.'

'Dearest Mother.' Julia's voice was low with emotion, and tears, the sweetest, happiest of tears, shone in her eyes. 'Thank you . . .'

It was, as Mrs Shaw said when Mary had carried up the coffee tray and reported in detail on the atmosphere in the small sitting-room, only to be expected. Miss Julia had come back from London an altogether different young woman, and beautiful for all to see.

'London,' said Cook, looking across the table at Alice, silently daring her to deny it. 'London was where it all started, or I'm a Dutchman. Am I right, Alice Hawthorn?'

But Alice merely smiled and went on with her polishing and said never a word, whilst upstairs, as his sister crossed the lawn outside, fingers entwined in Andrew's, Giles Sutton demanded of his mother why she had capitulated so suddenly and completely.

'You surprised me. You almost said yes to their marriage, Mama. Oh, he's likeable enough and makes no bones about his upbringing, which is to his credit,' he shrugged. 'Indeed, I can see why Julia is so besotted. But you, dearest Mother, fell completely under his spell, too. Why, will you tell me?'

'Spell? Tut! Not at all! But yes, I liked him, and his complete honesty won me over. That, and the dedication with which he follows his profession, is to be commended. But, Giles – how am I to explain?'

How could she, even to herself? How, when she had been prepared to stand fast and completely forbid the affair, had she surrendered without protest? How could her son, who had yet to love, understand that even the height of the doctor, the way he held his head, the way he smiled even, had so reminded her of John that it had almost taken her breath away. And how, when he looked at her with eyes neither green nor grey – looked at her with her husband's eyes – she had known, as surely as if John had whispered it in her ear, that this man was right for her daughter.

'I think,' she murmured, 'that his eyes won me over. Didn't you notice them, Giles?'

'No, dearest, I did not,' he offered, mystified.

'There you are, then. You are a man and you'll never understand.'

So he had kissed his mother's cheek and begged she excuse him until lunchtime, and closed the library door behind him still wondering about it.

But Helen Sutton, when she was alone, closed her eyes blissfully and whispered, 'John, my dear, thank you for being with me when I needed you. Thank you, my love.'

'I cannot believe it!' Julia laughed. 'I don't believe that you are here and we are walking in the garden for all to see.'

'Then you'd better, darling girl, for I'm to stay to luncheon, remember – and hoping to be asked again.'

'You will be. Mama liked you; I knew she would – Giles, too . . .'

'Aye. Your brother tried fine to be the stern guardian, and all the time trying to work out what the upset was all about, I shouldn't wonder.'

'Mm. And wanting to get on with his work. He's seeing to the library. Pa neglected it dreadfully, so Giles is trying to get it into some kind of order. Some of the older books need attention, and he's packing them up, ready to send to London for repair. And oh, darling, isn't it a beautiful morning?'

'Aye. And will you smell that air?' He breathed in deeply. 'And look at that view. Do you ever look at it, Julia, or have you seen it so often that you take it for granted?'

'Perhaps I do, darling,' she smiled, looking at it with his eyes; at the last of the sweet-scented narcissi and the first of the summer's roses, climbing the pergola, tangling with honeysuckle and laburnum. And at the delicate spring green of beech leaves and linden leaves, newly uncurled; and a sky, high and wide and blue, with the sun topping Brattocks Wood. 'But I shall look at it differently now, and how I wish you could be here when evening comes. That's when the honeysuckle smells so sweetly. The scent of it is unbelievable. I'll ask that you be invited to dinner before you return, and we'll walk here at dusk and you shall take the smell of it back with you to London, to remind you of me.'

'Silly child.' He gentled her face with his fingertips because he wanted so much to hold her and kiss her. 'Can we walk in the woods, do you think?'

'I think we'd better.' She lifted her eyes to his, loving him, wanting him. 'Because I need to kiss you, too. And don't say you don't want to, because I know you do. Your voice changes when you want me – did you know it? You speak to me with a – a *lover's* voice and it makes me – oh, I don't know . . .'

'You *do* know, Julia, and one day we *will* – only don't make me wait too long?'

'I won't. I promise I won't. And can we please find a place where no one can see us?'

'See us!' he exulted. 'But we are walking out, you and I, and in a year we shall announce our engagement. So let's tell the world about it –' he tilted her chin with his forefinger and laid his lips gently on hers – 'with a kiss.'

It was, said Bess, who had been carrying coal to the library and was passing the window in the front hall when she saw it, so romantic you wouldn't believe it. The way he'd kissed her, chin tilted, and she with her eyes closed, just like in a love book.

'And then she picked a rosebud, and put it in his buttonhole,' she sighed, misty-eyed. 'I stood there and saw her do it and if you don't believe me, then Mary'll tell you when she serves luncheon. You'll see that rosebud, Mary, then you'll know I'm not making it up.'

'Hm,' grunted Tilda, annoyed that kitchenmaids saw nothing, stuck downstairs, whilst Bess and Mary had a better time of it altogether. 'I never said I didn't believe you.' Tilda, who knew everything there was to know about falling in love from books in the penny library, had suspected all along that something was going on, and that Alice knew more about it than she was letting on. 'And what's more, I'll bet you anything you like that Hawthorn knows more'n she'll admit to.'

'*Alice?*' Cook demanded in a voice that commanded obedience.

'I know no more than any of you,' she offered reluctantly, 'and that's –' That's the truth, she'd been going to say, but when she thought about it, when there was one extra for luncheon and Miss Julia getting herself kissed in full view of the entire household . . . 'that's all I can say, except maybe that his name is Andrew MacMalcolm, and he's a doctor, in London. And when Miss Julia fell and hurt herself –'

'It was him!' Tilda supplied triumphantly. 'Him that brought her round and tended her, and saved her life!'

'Him,' Alice confirmed, pink-cheeked. 'And if any one of you breathes so much as a word of what I've told you in the village, then I'll never tell you anything again!'

They said they wouldn't; never a word of it, and demanded of Bess what had happened then – after he'd kissed her, that was, and Miss Julia had picked the rosebud. And Bess said she couldn't rightly say, as they'd climbed the park fence, then, and made hand in hand for the woods.

'The woods,' Mrs Shaw repeated, her mouth screwed up as if she had just swallowed vinegar.

'Ooooh, the woods,' Tilda sighed, closing her eyes in a shudder of purest bliss. 'The *woods* . . .'

'Oh, don't be so silly,' Alice snapped, annoyed she had told them anything at all. 'Where's the wrong in her walking in her own woods, will you tell me, with a guest?'

She wished she could talk to Miss Julia; tell her the cat was out of the bag. And she couldn't wait to see Tom and tell him all about it, from first to last. It was awful, having to help out in the kitchen and not being able to take Morgan for his afternoon run and wanting, so much, to hold Tom, and kiss him – just as Miss Julia and Doctor Andrew were doing now, she fervently hoped.

She closed her eyes and crossed her fingers, wishing that tonight Mr Giles would be too busy to take Morgan out, because if she didn't see Tom soon, she would die. She really would.

'Hawthorn! That is *enough*!'

'Well, if you're set on wearing the green tonight, miss,' Alice gave another determined tug on the corset laces, 'they'll have to be tighter.'

'Ouch! Did you know that Doctor MacMalcolm does not approve of corsets? He says that tight lacing is unnatural and the cause of a lot of ailments in women. He blames them entirely for the vapours.'

'Ooh, miss. You don't talk to him about *corsets*?' My word, but things had come on apace, if they were talking about unmentionables!

'Indeed I do, and he said that two weeks free from corsets would do most women more good than two weeks at the seaside. But aren't we both lucky? You and

Dwerryhouse sharing a pew in church for all to see, and Andrew and me . . .'

'Yes?' Now at last they were getting down to brass tacks.

'We-e-ell, since you were the cause of it – in a round-about way, that is –' How indeed would they have met if Hawthorn hadn't sent the policeman flying? – 'I want you to be the first to know. It's going to be all right!'

'Me, miss – the first? But they *all* know.' Carefully Alice knotted the laces. 'They put two and two together. You were seen in the garden, and that settled it. They'd all been wondering who the caller was, and when Mary came downstairs and told Cook there was one extra for lunch .   .' She shrugged eloquently.

'So did you tell them?'

'N-not exactly. I kept getting looks from Mrs Shaw, but when Bess said she'd seen you and him – well –'

'Kissing?' Julia laughed.

'Yes. That an' all. I had to admit, then, that he was the doctor who'd taken care of your bruises. No more'n that though – honest.'

'Hawthorn, it doesn't matter. It's all right for us to write and to meet, you see, but not to be engaged – not just yet. I've promised Mama we'd wait a year and then, if we are both of the same mind –'

'Which you will be . . .'

'Nothing is more certain! Anyway, in a year we can be properly engaged – isn't it wonderful? And Andrew is invited to visit again, tomorrow, because Mama likes him. I could tell she was going to, right from the start.'

'Yes, miss, and I'm glad. But what am I to tell them downstairs?' Alice pleaded. 'They'll give me no peace till they're told something.'

'Poor Hawthorn. Never mind. Thank you for helping. I can finish dressing myself, now. And you mustn't tell them anything at all, except –' She smiled, then, and her eyes shone and she was all of a sudden so beautiful, Alice thought, that it fair took her breath away. 'Except that tomorrow, when Doctor MacMalcolm visits again, I shall take him downstairs to meet them all.

'And sorry – I'm in such a tizzy that I forgot. Giles said I was to ask if you could possibly find time to give that dog a run tonight – if Mrs Shaw will allow it, that is.'

'I think,' Alice smiled impishly, 'that she will.' Mrs Shaw would be in such a bother of delight when she heard that Miss Julia's young man would be visiting her kitchen, that she would agree to anything. 'And, miss, I'm that happy for you both, and I'll come and unlace you at bedtime,' she added soberly. 'And thanks about Morgan.'

Because Miss Julia, bless her, had arranged it. Miss Julia was a dear, kind young lady who would grow to be like her mother; beautiful, and mindful of those around her, for she *was* beautiful – just like Cook said she would be, and she and the doctor would have beautiful children together and live happily ever after.

She hugged herself with sheer happiness, then ran to the kitchen with her news.

'Off you go, then.' Alice slipped the spaniel's lead at the woodland fence, watching him go, nose down; sniffing, snuffling, scenting rabbit and partridge and hare. Away looking for Tom, she thought fondly, and when he found him he would yelp with delight and shiver all over, from his nose right down to the tip of his furiously wagging tail. Morgan was devoted to Tom and obeyed him, now, without question. But then, Tom had a way with dogs. They liked him. Everyone liked him and she loved him, and maybe around the next turning of the path he would be there and she would run to him and lift her face for his kiss . . .

The evening was warm, but so it should be, for it was almost summer. Tomorrow she would awaken to the first

136

day of June, her birthday month. Eighteen. It sounded almost grown up.

She breathed deeply on air that smelled of honeysuckle and wild, white roses and green things growing. There were no buttercups in the wood. Buttercups grew in meadows, seeking the sun, collecting it, giving it back in a glint of gold. Buttercups were her very own flowers; Tom had said so.

She looked over to her right, where Reuben's chimney puffed creamy woodsmoke. He was building up his fire for the night: Reuben was home, so it was Tom who would be doing the night round. Tom was there, somewhere in the deep greenness, and when Morgan found him he would know, whistling softly as he came to look for her, and oh, how was it possible for one person to have such happiness inside her?

Elliot Sutton walked angrily, head down, hands in pockets. He was wronged, misunderstood. He should have gone to London – anywhere but Leeds. He'd had no luck with the women there and less luck at cards. He'd lost his allowance twice over, paying his hotel bill with the last few sovereigns in his pocket. What was more, his money-grasping mother had refused to make his losses good, reasoning, he shouldn't wonder, that the less he had, the less he could spend on things she disapproved of. Women, for one, and wine, and wagers so ridiculously high as to make the game excitingly worth playing. His mother held fast to her money – she always had – pinching every penny, arguing over a shilling she believed overcharged. Nor could she understand that a gentleman always paid his gambling debts – but then, his mother wasn't a lady.

'Money! You're always short of money!' she had shouted. 'I declare you pour it down the nearest drain the minute you lay hands on it. But you'll get no more from me!'

'Mama,' he said softly, deliberately, 'why must you

always share our business with the servants? Your voice could sell fish in Billingsgate!'

'Damn you, boy!' His remark had struck the raw nerve he'd intended, though he hadn't bargained on the contents of her teacup being flung in his face. 'Get out! Get out of my sight!'

He had left, then, mopping his stinging cheek, because his mother in a rage was a match for any man, and the lash of her tongue was to be avoided. Mama in a fury harked back to her roots and became the embodiment of Mary Anne, his peasant forebear.

He walked without direction, his anger increasing. He needed comfort. He had a good mind to go to Creesby, to Maudie who loved him. In his present mood he'd marry her for two pins, then laugh in his mother's face. But if he married the butcher's daughter, two pins was all he'd be worth.

A pheasant rose clucking in his path. He supposed he was on Rowangarth land, now. No use calling, though. Aunt Helen would be at dinner. But dammit, he *would* go to Creesby, where he'd be welcome. Maudie was always available, always free. He turned about suddenly. He would take the motor and seek Maudie out – and serve his mother right, too. That was when he saw her – one of the Rowangarth servants if he wasn't mistaken – slim and pretty, her waist a hand-span round. Her breasts reminded him of Maudie, and made him forget her at once. Eyes narrowed, he ran his tongue round his lips with pure pleasure.

'Good evening,' he murmured.

'Mr Elliot.' Eyes lowered, Alice moved to pass him, but he sidestepped, and barred her way.

'Please, sir,' she murmured, all at once uneasy, 'if I might –'

'No, you might not. You might do nothing that doesn't please me. Tell me your name, and who you are.'

138

'It's Hawthorn, sir; Alice Hawthorn. I'm sewing-maid at Rowangarth and if you'll excuse me I'm going to meet my friend.'

Small pulses of fear fluttered in her throat. She tried to call out for Tom, but her throat had gone tight and no sound came.

'Your *friend*, Alice Hawthorn? What kind of a friend is it that you slink off to meet behind bushes? And he isn't here, is he, so you'll have to make do with me!'

Laughing, he reached for her, pulling her closer. She smelled whisky on his breath and oh, God! where was Tom?

His mouth groped for hers and she pushed him away. His moustache scrubbed her cheek as he grabbed her hair and held back her head.

'No!' She brought the heel of her boot down on his foot with all her strength.

'Damn you!' He gasped with pain, releasing her. She ran, stumbling, but he caught her again, pulling her to the ground, grunting his pleasure as he straddled her, pulling at her blouse, ripping it open.

'No. No. *No!*' She clawed at his face; pulled her fingernails down his cheek so hard that she felt pain in them. Blood oozed in tiny droplets, then ran in a little rivulet on to his chin, his stark white collar.

'Leave me be!' She rolled away from him, over and over, into a bramble bush. Branches lashed her, thorns clawed at her face, her neck, at her uncovered breasts.

'Bitch!' No more. He'd had enough of her teasing, her refusals. The games were over and he tore at her skirt. 'Please – *don't*!' He was wild-eyed; a madman. He was drunk; he was going to kill her. Terror gave her sudden strength, gave back her voice. 'Tom! Reuben!' she screamed. 'Help me, Tom! Oh, God – *help me*!'

There was a crashing in the undergrowth. Someone, *something*, was coming. With a howl of rage, a wedge of fury hurled itself at her attacker, snapping, snarling, fangs bared, knocking him to the ground.

'Morgan!' She pulled herself to her feet, eyes closed against the flailing, whipping branches. Oh, Tom, where are you?

She began to run; stumbling, sobbing, crying out. There was blood on her face, her hands; her hair fell untidily down her back.

'Lass!' It was Reuben, running down the path to meet her and oh, God, thank you, *thank you*!

Arms folded her, held her. She was safe. He couldn't hurt her now. Sobs took her, shook her.

'Elliot Sutton! He tried to – oh, Reuben . . .'

'There now, lovey. It's all right.' He was making little hushing sounds, stroking her hair. 'Tell me. Tell Reuben, then.'

'Down there!' She pointed along the woodland path. 'Morgan went for him . . .'

'Alice!' It was Tom. Tom running. 'Alice – was it you I heard?' One glance told him. '*Who*, girl? Who did that to you?'

'Down yonder,' Reuben ground. 'Down t'path. And lad, give that thing to me.' He reached for Tom's gun. You didn't let a man white with hatred go seeking revenge with a shotgun in his hand.

'Tell me!' Tom spat.

'Elliot Sutton.' Alice closed her eyes at the shame of it. 'But he'll be gone, now. Leave him!' She needed Tom to hold her, but he was away, hurling curses, murder in his eyes.

He found them, twenty yards down the path; the man crying out, hands shielding his face, the dog gone berserk, its teeth at Elliot Sutton's throat.

'Morgan! Stay!'

The spaniel heard authority in the voice and slunk to do its bidding. Tom reached down to touch its head briefly,

140

then: 'You! Sutton!' His eyes blazed contempt. 'On your feet!'

'Now see here – that animal! If it's yours, you're in trouble.' Bloody, mud-stained, Elliot Sutton rose unsteadily. 'Damned beast went for me – for my throat. Could have killed me . . .'

'Could he, now?' Tom's voice was soft as the fist of iron slammed into the arrogant face, sending the man sprawling again. Then, taking him by the lapels of his coat, Tom pulled him to his feet. 'Could he just? Well, listen to me, Mister-fine-bloody-Elliot. If ever you lay so much as a finger on my young lady again; if you even walk on the same side of the street as her, it won't be a dog you'll have to contend with – it'll be me. And I *will* kill you!'

He flung him away contemptuously to lie sprawled in the brambles, blubbering, threatening. 'My aunt – Lady Sutton – she'll hear about this! And the police! I'll have you dismissed, run off the place. I'll see to it you never work again! My mother'll see to it . . .'

'Go to hell, Sutton!'

Reuben had taken Alice inside, sitting her beside the fire, setting the kettle to boil, telling her it was all right, that Tom would see to it.

She leaned back, eyes closed, moaning softly, her body shaking still. Because it wasn't all right, and if it hadn't been for Morgan . . .

She began to weep again. Morgan had saved her, had turned into a devil. Lazy, lolloping Morgan had been her salvation.

The door latch snapped and Tom stood there, the spaniel at his heels.

'Did he, sweetheart? Did he harm you?' He was at her side, gathering her to him. 'Tell me, if –'

'No, Tom. He tried, but not – not *that*. Morgan came.'

141

'Aye. Morgan. But for that daft dog –' His smile was brief. 'What are we to do, Reuben? Young Sutton can't get away with this. I won't let him!'

'What happened out there?' Reuben demanded. 'Did you catch up with him?'

'I did. The dog had him pinned down, so I called him off . . .'

'And from the look of your knuckles, I'd say that wasn't all.'

'It wasn't.' Tom clenched and unclenched his right fist. 'I hit him. And I told him if he even so much as looked at Alice again, I'd kill him.'

'Tom! You shouldn't have,' Alice moaned. 'Don't you see, he'll do you harm. We'll both be out of work. You can't go hitting the gentry . . .'

'Sweetheart, I just did. And anyone else who tries to harm you will get the same.' His voice was thick with suppressed rage, hatred still flamed in his eyes, and Reuben saw it.

'Now see here, Tom – kettle's just on the boil. Make the lass some tea – with plenty of sugar. Don't leave her, though. Stay with her – you hear me?'

'Why? Where are you off to? Don't get caught up in it, Reuben. Elliot Sutton is *my* business.'

'And Alice is mine, and I'm off to Rowangarth. Miss Clitherow's got to be told about this. She's got her ladyship's ear; she'll know what's to be done.' He clicked his fingers at the spaniel. 'I'll take the dog back. Someone's got to clean him up. And Mr Giles will have to be told, an' all. Now do as I say. Stay with the lass,' he instructed. 'Leave things be, and do nowt till I'm back. And that's an order!'

8

'Well now. This is a fine to-do, and no mistake.' Agnes Clitherow removed her bonnet and cape. 'Those scratches – how did you get them?' she murmured, turning Alice's face to the window.

'*Him*, that's who! What kind of a man would attack a bit of a lass!' The words poured derisively from the young keeper. 'A damn good hiding – that's what he needs!'

'Thank you, Dwerryhouse, you may wait outside. And Reuben, a basin if you please, and a little clean, cold water. Now, miss.' The housekeeper rolled up her sleeves. 'Let's get you cleaned up.'

Taking lint, disinfectant, and a pot of marshmallow salve from her basket, she nodded her thanks to the elderly keeper, indicating with the slightest movement of her head that she wished him too to leave.

'Elliot Sutton, Reuben tells me,' she said without preamble, combining hot and cold water in the basin, adding liquid from the green, glass-stoppered bottle. 'Did he – *harm* you?'

'No, ma'am, though he would have if Morgan hadn't gone for him,' Alice choked, eyes on her tightly knotted fingers. 'I didn't give him cause, I swear I didn't. I tried to run away – that's how I fell into the bramble bush.'

'But there was no – ' The middle-aged spinster paused, searching for words.

'I know what you mean, and no, there wasn't.' Tears filled her eyes again.

'And you'll swear, Hawthorn, it was Elliot Sutton?'

'On the Bible, I will. And Tom hit him hard, he told me, and I scratched his face an' all, so there'll be marks to show for it. But Tom won't get into trouble, will he, because of me?'

'Dwerryhouse, it would seem, acted under provocation. If what Reuben told me is true, there'll be no trouble – not for your Tom, that is – when I've told her ladyship.'

'Milady! Does she have to know?' Alice cried, dismayed. 'I'd prefer it were kept quiet.' Imagine Mrs Shaw's indignation if it all came out. And that wouldn't be the end of it either, because there might be those who'd say she had led him on. It would be his word against hers, and who would believe a servant? 'Please, ma'am, leave it be! Don't tell anyone!'

'Don't tell? Have you seen the state you're in? Clothes torn and your face scratched and swollen. Come along now – off with that blouse and camisole, and let me have a look at you. This might sting a little,' she murmured, wringing out the lint cloth, 'but it won't seem half so bad when we've got you tidied up. Oh, my goodness!' she gasped, dismayed. Dwerryhouse was right, she thought. What kind of a man would do this? 'These cuts need cleaning.'

'They would. He had me on the ground. But I fought him – drew blood – '

'Good for you. And we have no choice but to tell Lady Sutton about this – you realize that, Hawthorn? And Mr Giles, too. I know it'll be an embarrassment,' she hastened on, 'but her ladyship is responsible for those who work for her, and she's going to be very angry, if I'm not mistaken.'

'Not with me!'

'Of course not with you, Hawthorn. Goodness – we all know you better than that. Mind, Dwerryhouse would have done better to have kept a hold on his temper. It isn't for him to take the law into his own hands, though we can all be wise with hindsight.

'There now,' she smiled. 'Feels easier already, doesn't

it? And the marshmallow will help those scratches heal quickly. Now tidy your hair and wrap my cape around you and we'll be off. We'll go in by the front door, I think, and you'd better go to the sewing-room. And if anyone should see you, tell them you slipped on the path and fell into some brambles – that'll take care of the scratches – though how we'll explain away the state your clothes are in, I really don't know.'

'Me neither, ma'am, but thank you,' Alice whispered. 'And I'm sorry you had to be brought into it.' Tears, unstoppable now, ran down her cheeks. 'And what they're all going to think of me, I don't know. It's so – so *shaming* . . .'

'Oh, come now.' The housekeeper offered her a white, lace-edged handkerchief. 'There's no blame attached to you, though I can understand your distress. It isn't the nicest thing to have happened to a young girl.

'But dry your face and try to stop crying, or you'll look a worse sight than ever. Just say as little as possible, if you're asked. As soon as we're back, go to your bedroom and make yourself presentable, then wait in the sewing-room – now is that understood?'

When Agnes Clitherow shepherded Alice outside, Tom was at her side at once.

'All right now, sweetheart? Feeling a bit better? Think I'd best walk you both home, Miss Clitherow. Don't know if *he* might still be hanging about.'

'I thank you, Dwerryhouse, but I'm well able to take care of myself, and Hawthorn, too. And I hope that you'll both be discreet about this. We want no scandal attached to Rowangarth.' Goodness, no. The Place Suttons could provide more than enough for both houses.

'Don't fret,' Reuben was quick to assure her. 'There'll be nowt said. And thanks, miss, for your help.'

'Thanks are not required.' Slowly, carefully, the older

woman drew on her gloves. 'You did right to come to me – now leave it with me; is that understood?'

They said it was and tipped their caps, murmuring a respectful goodnight.

'Night, Reuben – and thanks for all you did,' Alice whispered, clasping the cape tightly around her nakedness. 'And, Tom – will you keep an eye open for Morgan's lead on your way back? I dropped it . . .'

'I'll find it,' he smiled, touching her cheek with gentle fingertips. 'Goodnight, lass, and try not to worry.'

She smiled briefly and said she wouldn't, though it was easier said than done. There would be trouble, especially for Tom, because servants didn't hit their betters and get away with it. And it only seemed like minutes ago, she mourned silently, that she had been so very happy.

'Will you tell me,' Helen Sutton demanded of her housekeeper, 'what is so very urgent that it cannot wait until morning?'

'It's Hawthorn, milady. She was attacked in Brattocks Wood, tonight. These were almost torn off her.'

'Hawthorn? But is she all right? Where is she?' Her eyes were wide with apprehension as she regarded the garments. 'These are ripped to shreds. Someone must have used terrible force. This is awful – *monstrous*! I must see her at once, poor child!'

'With respect, milady – no. There are things I should tell you first. I've sent Hawthorn to the sewing-room. It isn't likely anyone will go up there yet awhile. With dinner just finished, they'll all be busy downstairs.'

'But *attacked*? She wasn't – ?'

'No. She assured me it wasn't – *that*, though it might well have been if the dog hadn't defended her.'

'Dog? Giles's Morgan, you mean?'

'Morgan. According to Reuben, that creature's got

another side to him. If he hadn't been with Hawthorn, it's almost certain we'd be worrying about something very serious indeed. The word that comes to mind, if you'll pardon me, milady, is – '

'Rape?' Helen Sutton supplied, chalk-faced. 'Please sit down, Miss Clitherow. I think you'd better tell me about it – *all*!'

'Elliot!' It had not made pretty hearing. Helen Sutton's jaws clamped tight on her anger. 'How *dare* he? Here, on my land and to one of my household! Is there no stopping him? But he's gone too far this time!' Family or no, her nephew must be confronted, accused. Drawing in her breath, biting back the flow of condemnation, she whispered, 'Has my son been told?'

'Not yet, milady. I came to you first. But I think you should know that the dog is with William. Reuben left him at the stables before he came to me; told them Morgan had got himself in a mess in the woods, and that someone had better clean him up before Mr Giles saw him.'

'And William believed him?'

'That I don't know. William's a gossip, we all know that. If he sets eyes on Hawthorn the state she's in now, he'll put two and two together and come up with worse than the truth. Reuben is fond of the girl, you see. I got the impression he'd like it kept quiet, for her sake; but Dwerryhouse – now he's another matter altogether . . .'

'I know. It's a pity he struck my nephew.'

'But wouldn't you have done the same, in his shoes?' Agnes Clitherow shrugged expressively. 'It's no secret he and Hawthorn are walking out. It surprises me he held on to his temper the way he did, and didn't give the man the leathering he deserves. According to Hawthorn, Elliot Sutton smelled of drink. Sober, he's obnoxious; under the influence he's dangerous, if you ask me!'

But her ladyship hadn't asked her, and the housekeeper

felt her cheeks redden, knowing she had stepped outside the bounds of her position.

'I'm sorry, milady. I beg your pardon – but Hawthorn isn't a flighty one. She didn't deserve to go through an experience like that, and I believe her when she said she gave him no encouragement.'

'Encouragement? When ever did my nephew need that? No. This time he shall be called to answer for his behaviour. His parents must be told.'

'And Hawthorn?' Agnes Clitherow rose to her feet, sensing the interview was over. 'The girl is upset, and sooner or later it's all going to come out. Falling into a bramble bush is one thing, but the bruising is another; she won't be a pretty sight in the morning. And the staff have a right to know, milady; to be warned. It seems no woman is safe from him.'

Frowning, Helen Sutton pursed her lips. Those who lived and worked at Rowangarth were indeed her responsibility – hers and Giles's; they had a right to protection. But Elliot was a Sutton, and because of him the Sutton name would suffer. It was altogether too much!

'I am bound to agree with you, Miss Clitherow, and I suggest you first discuss the matter with Mrs Shaw. It will be up to you both, then, to agree on what the staff is told, and how much. But I beg you to ask them to be discreet for a little while longer. I would like time to discuss this with my son first. That I must speak to Mrs Sutton is without dispute, but I know the staff will keep the matter out of the village for as long as they can – and be kind to Hawthorn, too. The poor young thing. Are you sure there is nothing I can do?'

'Best you shouldn't, milady. Not just yet. She's very embarrassed at the moment. But when I've talked to Cook, I'll tell Mary to take some milk up to her.' Milk and honey. The best soother there was. The housekeeper swore by it. 'Mary's a sensible girl; I'll tell her to see Hawthorn into bed and stay with her for a while.'

'Yes. Perhaps that would be best. And please tell Hawthorn that I hope she'll feel better in the morning. You're *sure* we shouldn't call the doctor?'

'As sure as I can be, milady. No lasting harm was done – it might have been a lot worse. And I'll give Alice one of my herbals to help her sleep.'

Leaving alone, that was what the girl wanted; not being quizzed and prodded by Doctor James, well-meaning though he might be. A bit of sympathy and understanding from her own kind would do more good than physic. And as for Elliot Sutton – well, let his equals deal with him. He was nothing to do with the likes of her, the housekeeper stressed silently, though from the set of her ladyship's mouth, the young buck at Pendenys was in for a real eye-opening – and not before time, either!

'I'll bid you goodnight then, milady.' Respectfully the suddenly weary woman nodded her head. 'You can leave the matter of the servants to me.'

'Thank you.' Helen Sutton rose to her feet, forcing a smile. 'I appreciate all you have done. Will you first call in the library and ask Mr Giles to come and see me as soon as he's able? And goodnight to you, Miss Clitherow.'

'I would like, Julia,' said her mother briskly, 'for you to make haste from the station this morning. No dallying, if you please, when you meet the doctor. I am going to Pendenys and would like to be there before ten.'

'Why, might I ask?' Julia frowned. Ten o'clock was calling time; before ten smacked of urgency. 'You'll be seeing them on Friday night – can't it wait?'

'It can *not* wait and you might not ask, either. What I have to discuss with your aunt is disturbing enough without having to repeat it over breakfast.'

'But she has every right to know,' Giles protested. 'She's

149

in just as much danger from the man as any other woman. And she's bound to find out for herself sooner or later.'

'Danger? Now I insist you tell me, Mama.'

'You'd better tell her, then, for I declare I've had enough of the sordid business already.' Helen Sutton rose to her feet. 'I shall go to my room, or I'll have a headache.'

'What is it; what's going on?' Julia demanded. 'Shall I ring for Miss Clitherow? Would you like to lie down, Mama?'

'No, I thank you. I am well able to take a powder without assistance and I'm sorry if I snapped, but – oh, Giles will tell you. I'll be all right. Don't worry.'

'Don't worry?' Julia flamed when the door closed behind her mother. 'What has upset her so? She looks as if she hasn't slept all night. What *is* going on, Giles? What danger? And from which man?'

'Do you need to ask? Elliot attacked Hawthorn last night in Brattocks. That's why Mama's going to Pendenys.'

'Hawthorn! My, but he's gone too far this time. Is she all right? He didn't *do* anything?'

'No, but it wasn't for want of trying, I understand.'

'My God! Is no one safe from him? He needs whipping.'

'That he got last night. Dwerryhouse knocked him head over heels.'

'Good for Dwerryhouse! But where is Hawthorn? I must go to her.'

'Working in the sewing-room today, I believe.'

'Right!' Damn Elliot Sutton! The man was a menace, though no matter what Mama said, his silly mother would get him out of it – again. 'You should have sent for the constable, Giles. That monster needs locking up!' she called over her shoulder. Locking up till he'd learned sense, and a few good manners!

'Oh, *Hawthorn*!' Gently Julia touched the swollen cheek. 'Not you, too! Goodness! That bruise is almost as bad as

150

mine. You poor girl. I know how it hurts. How dare he do that to you?'

'Elliot Sutton does what he likes hereabouts. It's thanks to Morgan he didn't do worse, though. Morgan went for him like a mad thing. Didn't know the creature had it in him. Had him worried, Morgan did. Pinned him down till Tom got there. But I didn't stop to see any more. Ran for all I was worth . . .'

'Giles told me that Tom hit Elliot?'

'He did, and I hope there'll be no trouble. But Tom was real mad. Could have throttled him, he said.'

'Then more's the pity he didn't. You wouldn't believe that Nathan and Elliot are brothers, they're so unalike.'

'I know, miss. But Tom –' Alice wanted the business of Tom's hasty fist settled. 'I'm worried, see, that he'll be in trouble. Hit Elliot Sutton deliberate, he did. Said he hoped he'd broken his nose. And he might have, for all I know. Tom's a big fellow. He could have hurt him.'

'Hurt him! Wasn't a lot of use hitting him if he didn't, now was it? Anyway, there'll be hell to pay this morning. Mama is going to Pendenys – unannounced – and if I know Mama, Elliot is going to be on the receiving end of her displeasure. She looked furious at breakfast.'

'Oh, I wish she wouldn't,' Alice wailed. 'I don't want there to be any bother. I just want to get on with my work and forget all about it.'

'But it can't be forgotten. Elliot is evil. He always was, and he's got to be stopped. It isn't your fault, Hawthorn. Just be grateful that Morgan flew at him.'

'Yes, miss, and don't let's talk about it any more. I'm that ashamed with all the bother it's causing her ladyship.'

'Then don't be. But I must go now. Mama wants the carriage later, and I'm off to meet Andrew. And he shall come up and look at you – I insist – though what he'll do about that bruise, I don't know. Oh, Hawthorn dear – first me, now you. Whatever next?'

'Whatever next?' Alice whispered when the door had banged behind Julia and her footsteps could no longer be heard. Trouble, was there to be? Trouble for Tom, for herself? Because Mrs Clementina wasn't going to let Elliot be taken to task, nothing was more certain. And under-keepers didn't go punching their betters, neither.

Best for all concerned if her ladyship let it be; forgot about it. Better for her and Tom, that was, though Elliot Sutton would go on doing exactly what he wanted and no lass would be safe from him.

And how safe would it be now in Brattocks? And if she could no longer walk Morgan there, when was she ever to see Tom, except on her half-day off?

Alice blinked back a tear. She would *not* cry; not any more. They would find a way of meeting. And hadn't everybody been so kind and good it had made her feel warm all over? Miss Clitherow had been like an angel of mercy last night, and Cook had sent Tilda up with an eggcupful of brandy, for the shock, and not one question had Tilda asked; not one lurid detail did she demand to know – offering a humbug and the loan of her love book instead.

But, best of all, Bess had peeped around the door to tell her that Tom had left Morgan's lead at the kitchen door, asking anxiously how she was.

'And he said to give you this,' Bess whispered, handing her the flower. 'Said you'd understand . . .'

The flower was there now, in a glass on the window-sill, and she had cried over the buttercup and loved Tom even more; glad she lived at Rowangarth, glad Miss Julia was her friend, yet sad that this morning there would be trouble at Pendenys and hoping with all her heart that Tom never came upon Elliot Sutton in the woods. Lordy, but it was a real worry, and heaven only knew where it would end.

'Tom,' she whispered to the buttercup. 'Take care, lad; don't do anything you'll be sorry for.'

Clementina Sutton stood in the morning-room window, following the progress of the Rowangarth carriage with narrowed eyes. Helen was a punctilious caller, and calling time, it was accepted hereabouts, began at ten o'clock; indeed, not for another quarter of an hour, she calculated, checking the jewelled watch on her lapel with the clock on the overmantel. But she would soon know the cause of the breach in protocol, for her sister-in-law was making all haste to alight.

'My dear.' She smiled with genuine pleasure as the door opened, for in spite of the feeling of inferiority Helen's presence always gave her, Clementina grudgingly admired her, though never, she sighed – not even if she tried until the crack of doom – would she acquire the ease of manner that placed Helen Sutton's pedigree beyond question. Helen could dress in rags and mix with the motley and still be indisputably what she was. A lady.

'Clementina.' Briefly their cheeks touched. 'This is not the happiest of visits,' Helen murmured. 'Indeed, I wish to say what I have come to say as quickly as possible, and beg your indulgence in the saying of it.

'Giles left me in no doubt that he considered it to be his business, and was put out when I insisted it should be myself who told you, but when you have heard me out I'm sure I can safely leave the matter in your own capable hands, and we can bring this to a satisfactory conclusion,' Helen murmured. 'And I apologize for the early call, but what I must say is family and private, so I had little choice. Elliot,' she said without more ado. 'Have you seen him this morning?'

'Why, no – but the boy was out late last evening and doubtless wishes to sleep on. Indeed, he rarely rises before ten . . .'

'Then when you do see him, Clemmy, I warn you that you might be shocked by his appearance. Last night, you see, he made unwelcome advances to one of my maids who was forced to defend herself by scratching his face.'

'Elliot? Unwelcome advances?' Her face registered disbelief. 'I cannot think my son would be interested in a – a *servant*.'

'Then you must take my word for it that he was. What was more, the attack took place on Rowangarth land.'

'*Attack*, you're saying? Oh, come now, Helen, that is a most serious accusation. My son would never – '

'Elliot *did*.' Helen's eyes held those of her brother-in-law's wife. 'He attacked a young girl not yet eighteen. What is more – '

'Now see here!' The mistress of Pendenys rose to her feet, all pretence at gentility gone. She was only too ready to admit to her son's shortcomings, but that was a privilege allowed only to his mother. 'I cannot allow this. You come to my home at an extremely inconvenient time, then accuse my son of pressing his advances upon a servant! Are you sure the little madam hasn't got herself into trouble and now tries to implicate my son? The working classes are full of guile; never miss an opportunity. Elliot is a handsome young man and attractive to the ladies, but never would he stoop so low as you say!'

'Your son, Clemmy, would stoop as low as it suited him to. The girl in question is young and innocent and not for a moment do I suspect she is in any kind of trouble – apart from the distress caused her by Elliot last evening.' Helen Sutton took a deep, calming breath, wondering why she should feel so agitated when she had known all along that Clemmy would spring instantly to her son's defence. 'What is more, his face will carry the marks to prove it, since proof seems to be what you need. He may also be nursing a swollen nose or a blackened eye, or both, for it was my under-keeper's young lady your son attacked!'

'Attacked? I refute it utterly!' Clementina cried. 'And I resent your blacking of his character. If you are seeking a scapegoat, then I suggest you look elsewhere. And if it is true that one of your keepers assaulted my son, please to remember that I can have the law on him; teach the wretch his place!'

'Indeed you can *not*! I will not have scandal attached to Rowangarth, nor will I have my staff placed at risk by your prowling son. And since it seems you are not prepared to do anything about his ungentlemanly behaviour, Clemmy, then I have only this to say. Elliot is not welcome at Rowangarth until he has made a full and unconditional apology to Giles for his behaviour, and given an understanding that it will not happen again to any member of my household. And until that apology has been received, your son must not set foot on Rowangarth land, for I cannot risk the well-being of those in my care. Do you fully understand that?' The steely quiet of her accuser's voice sent fear screaming silently through Clementina Sutton. The Creesby affair had been bad enough, but to be snubbed at Rowangarth was unthinkable.

'I fully understand that you slander Elliot's reputation,' she snapped, 'and he will not set foot on your property until an apology is received by *him* from you!'

'Very well. The arrangement suits me admirably,' Helen breathed, 'though should Elliot have cause to change his mind and walk through my woods again, I want it understood that my keepers will be instructed to treat him as a common poacher, and pepper his backside with leadshot! The choice is entirely Elliot's!'

'*Well!*' Clemmy's voice faltered on the edge of tears, for never before had she seen Helen so angry, so white-faced with outrage. 'I can only say that things have come to a pretty pass between us when my son – my *innocent*

155

son – must be treated like a criminal!' She flung round, her face red and ugly with temper. 'And if your doors are closed to my son, then they are closed to me, too!'

'So be it,' Helen murmured. 'And now I will bid you good morning.'

'I cannot believe this is happening to me, and in my own home, too.' Clementina's wail of torment rose to fresh heights. 'My son slandered, accused, and by his own flesh and blood, too. You and I who have always been close, to be parted by the likes of a servant!'

'The remedy lies in your own hands. Order your son to make a full apology – that is all I ask. That, and an understanding that all members of my household are to be treated with respect by him in the future . . .

'To speak plainly,' Helen sighed, 'had I sent for the constable, my accusation could well have been one of attempted rape. Elliot must count himself lucky that I care for the good name of the Suttons, otherwise it would need more than an apology to get him out of this!'

'*Rape!* You go too far, Helen, even for family! There can be no more said between us save that I will never again accept your hospitality nor set foot in your house.

'And don't be too sure I won't have that keeper of yours up for common assault! We'll see then who does the apologizing. It might well be *me* who sends for the police!'

'Then take my advice, Clemmy; think about it. Wait until the scratches on his face heal and his bruises are gone, otherwise they're going to take some explaining away – even to our amiable constable!' With studied disinterest, Helen Sutton drew on her gloves. 'I will see myself out. Goodbye, my dear.'

'Dearest! What is it?' Giles Sutton offered his arm to the woman who stepped uncertainly from the carriage. 'You are shaking. What happened to upset you so? And why didn't you leave it to me as I said you should?'

'I don't know, and that's a fact.' Wearily she unpinned her hat and removed her gloves. 'And yes, I should have left it to you, Giles, though I thought Clemmy would have listened to reason. Oh, family squabbles are so very distasteful . . .'

'Squabbles? You had words?' Giles guided his mother to a chair, calling over his shoulder for a tray of tea.

'Words? I asked for an apology from Elliot and was told it will not be offered. So I was obliged to tell her that I will not receive her son and that he may not even set foot on Rowangarth land until it is – offered to *you*, Giles,' she sighed. 'Whereupon your aunt said that neither would she come to Rowangarth, either. When will she ever learn that Elliot is heading for trouble if he carries on as he is? That's what upsets me so.'

'Mama dear, Elliot is Uncle Edward's problem, not yours. And what is more, I'll lay odds that he'll turn up this afternoon bearing flowers and chocolates and apologizing charmingly. Because that's what he is – a charmer. And he can't bear it when a woman doesn't fall flat at his feet.'

'Elliot is *not* a charmer. Elliot is selfish and spoiled and a womanizer and where he'll end up is anybody's guess! Don't make excuses for him, Giles. You lean over backwards to find good in everyone, and there is no good at all in that young man. What is more, I as good as said so to his mother. I also told her that Elliot would be treated like a poacher if he's caught in Brattocks Wood again. I said the keepers would pepper his backside.'

'Dearest, you are priceless!' He threw back his head and laughed his delight. 'How Dwerryhouse would welcome the chance to do just that!'

'Oh, dear. I made a mess of it, didn't I?' The smallest smile lifted the corners of her mouth. 'Clemmy is most put out. She swept past me in a fury as I left, taking the stairs two at a time, yelling for Elliot at the top of her voice. I'm only sorry it will make trouble for poor Edward. Thank you, Mary,' she smiled at the parlourmaid who placed a tray at her elbow. 'This is exactly what I need.'

'A message from Miss Julia,' Mary smiled, hand on the door knob. 'She said to tell you that she and the doctor are out walking, but they'll be back in good time for lunch. Will that be all, milady?' she murmured, noting at once the hand that shook as it lifted the pot.

'Thank you, Mary – yes.'

What, wondered the parlourmaid as she closed the door behind her, had happened at Pendenys that her ladyship should come back so agitated? Because William had said she'd left in great haste and never a sign of Mrs Clementina to see her off. William noticed everything.

But it was all on account of that Mr Elliot and what happened in Brattocks. Mary frowned. A bad 'un, that's what he was, who'd come to a sticky end. And what was more, Mrs Shaw would agree with her when she told her how upset her ladyship was.

'Oh dear,' Helen whispered, when they were alone again. 'I shall have to tell Miss Clitherow. She won't like it one bit. And had you thought that, if Elliot doesn't come to dinner, neither will his mother, and no matter what he thinks to the contrary, your Uncle Edward will, through loyalty, be absent too.'

'And shall you mind? At least without Elliot there won't be an atmosphere.'

'Not one jot shall I mind.' She was fortified, now, by the tea and the comfort of her own fireside. 'But had you thought that three refusals will mean we will be sitting thirteen to dinner, and that I mind about very much.'

'Yes. I see . . .' No one ever sat thirteen at table. 'Mind, there *is* a way out of it. Ask Julia's doctor to fill a space. You know you've taken to him, Mama, and it seems pretty serious between the two of them, so you'll have to introduce him to friends sooner or later.'

'What a good idea! He'd have to stay the night, though,' she frowned. 'Do you think he'd mind?'

'Not a bit – and Julia would love it.'

'But what if he has other plans? He might not want to.'

'He'll want to,' Giles grinned. 'Julia will see to that! Problem solved, so drink up your tea and forget about Pendenys. It'll all blow over – just see if it doesn't. Storm in a teacup, that's all.'

'Storm in a teacup,' Helen nodded. But it wouldn't blow over, because Clemmy was proud and she would never give in – not where Elliot was concerned. This morning, in only the space of a few minutes, a deep and wide chasm had opened up between the Garth Suttons and the Place Suttons and she dreaded to think where it might end. 'Soon blow over,' she said with a brightness she far from felt. 'A lot of fuss about nothing, but for all that we'll ask Doctor MacMalcolm to dinner on Friday – to please Julia . . .'

9

'Elliot, damn you, where are you?'

Clementina Sutton took the stairs two at a time, shaking with fury, cursing the stays and petticoats and folds of skirt that impeded her undignified haste. First Mrs Mounteagle, and now her sister-in-law, and all because of Elliot and his stupidity!

'Where are you, boy!' For two pins she would tan his hide as he deserved. She could do much worse for the shame he had heaped upon her! She would be an outcast, the laughing-stock of local society, and far, far worse, she would have to endure the ill-disguised sniggers of her servants who would glory in her humiliation. 'Get out of that bed!'

She opened the door with a force that sent it crashing back on its hinges, then, pulling at the bed-covers, she grasped her son's nightshirt, pulling him, startled, to face her.

'Mama! What the hell . . .'

'Dear God!' She beheld a bloodstained pillow, a face bruised and battered, and a left eye no more than a swollen slit. 'Oh, you fool! You – you – ' She flung herself at him, fists pummelling, rage and mortification giving strength to her blows. In that moment of blind fury she hated him, hated herself, and hated the girl who was the cause of it all. But most of all she hated Helen Sutton and her smug superiority. 'Oh, what has happened to you?' She collapsed, all at once exhausted, over his bed, sobbing, shaking, moaning pitifully. 'What is happening to *me*?'

Arms grasped her, pulled her to her feet. Not knowing where she was, unable almost, to place one foot before the other, she allowed her husband to lead her to the door.

'You, boy! Get out of that bed and clean yourself up! Then come to the library.' Edward Sutton's voice was icy with contempt. '*At once!*'

Guiding his wife to the third door along, he pushed it wide with his foot, supporting her as she slumped against him for fear she would fall in a faint. 'Clemmy, calm yourself . . .'

'Madam!' Feet pounded the landing, the stairs, the passage. 'Oh, *madam* . . .'

The housekeeper and two agitated housemaids came running, and, in the hall below, glimpsed over the banister rail, the butler gazed up, enjoyment evident upon his face.

'Please take care of Mrs Sutton.' Thankfully her husband stood aside. 'She is not well.'

'There, there, madam. Let me send for Monique to help you to bed?' In an agitation of skirts, the wide-eyed housekeeper whisked out of the room. 'And shall I have Doctor James sent for, sir?'

But Edward was gone, slamming down the stairs white-faced, jaws clenched hard on his fury.

What had his son been up to? Set upon by a debt collector's thugs; brawling in some alehouse? He'd taken the motor last night; been absent from dinner without excuse or apology, so where had it happened? Leeds again, or had a vengeful butcher caught up with him – or *any* irate father of a daughter?

Opening the door of the safe, cloister-like room that was his peace and haven, he made for the table where decanters of brandy and sherry stood on a silver tray. Edward Sutton rarely drank before evening, but this morning he downed a measure of brandy with sacrilegious haste, as if it were physic to be gulped of necessity rather than with pleasure.

161

Damn the stupid youth! He hadn't crashed the motor, that was certain, or he'd have made great play of his injuries and not slunk into his room. Oh, no. Retribution had caught up with him at last. His son was in trouble of his own making; trouble with a nasty stink to it.

'Father?' Elliot stood in the doorway, a robe over his nightshirt, his hair uncombed, defiance in his eyes and in the half-smile that tilted his lips.

'I asked you to make yourself respectable! How dare you show yourself in that disgusting state? And do not smoke. I will not have the stink of your cigarettes in my room!'

'*Your* room, father?' He opened the gold case, selecting a cigarette with studied defiance. 'Your *anything* in this house?'

'Damn you!' Edward Sutton covered the space between them, white-hot rage at his heels. Grabbing the silk-quilted lapels, he dragged his son to the chair beside the desk, flinging him into it, sending the cigarette case flying. '*My* room, *my* house, and never from this moment forget it! And I want an explanation of the state you're in or by God I'll beat it out of you!' Knock, pummel, punch him until years of frustration were gone; do what he had longed to do for longer than he could remember – what, as a responsible father, he should have done at the first surfacing of the rottenness in his firstborn. 'And I want the truth. This is not your mother you are dealing with now!'

'Then at least allow me to close the door.' Elliot Sutton brushed an imaginary speck from his robe. 'I do so dislike washing dirty linen in public.'

'You're admitting it then – *dirt*? Because you didn't get that face in church on your knees! Where were you last evening and what were you about?'

'I took the motor, father, and ran out of fuel, and two or maybe three thugs set about me. It was dark – how could I know . . .'

'Liar! Don't insult my intelligence. Those are scratch marks on your face. Which woman did it, and where? Up to your tricks again in Creesby, were you?' Fist clenched, he thumped the desktop. 'Well, you have upset your mother for the last time. From now on you answer to me, and when Doctor James arrives, you'll have him disinfect your face before it goes septic.

'Then you will shave as best you can and remain out of sight until I get to the bottom of this. For the truth I *will* have, Elliot, no matter how unsavoury. And restitution you *will* make, of that be very sure. And now get out of here, for the sight of you sickens me. Indeed, there have been times, lately, when I have looked at you and wondered how I got you.'

'Ha! So that's it! I'm not your saintly Nathan; I'm not Sutton-fair, like Albert! I'm dark, aren't I, a throwback from the Pendennis woman? I could have been Mary Anne's, couldn't I – the son of a herring-wench?'

'That herring-woman you so despise was honest and hard-working. It was she who laid the foundations for what you take for granted, by gutting fish and taking in washing. Would you had *more* of her in you!'

'You say that easily, Father, when your own breeding is flawless; when you were born a Sutton. But none of your friends act as if *I* were. And I *am* a Sutton – every bit as much as Nathan and Albert.'

'You'll be a Sutton when you have earned the right to be one; earned the right to be treated with respect in society. Servants despise you, as do your equals. There are times I think you are not fit to bear the name!'

'Well, I *am* yours – me and Albert both.' The pouting lips made a sneer of contempt. 'Didn't do very well, did you, come to think of it? Two black sheep out of a flock of three?'

'I see no wrong in your brother.' The words came through tightly clenched teeth. 'He married where he thought best.'

'As you did, Father.'

'Albert did what he thought right for himself,' Edward ignored the taunt. 'And has now settled comfortably in Kentucky.'

There had been a letter, not a week ago, from Albert's wife; a charming letter, giving their address, now permanent, expressing the wish to meet her husband's English family, Edward recalled. He had felt great relief, though Clemmy had shrugged it off as social climbing and declared her intention to ignore it.

Well, now she would no longer ignore it. Now she would reply, welcoming her son's wife to the family, thanking her for the offer of hospitality; an offer, did Clementina but know it, they were soon to accept.

'Ha! Breeding horses, aren't they?' Elliot laughed derisively. 'And horses are all he'll ever get, bedding a woman that old, the stupid . . .'

'Stop it! I won't listen to your gutter talk. Your coarseness disgusts me. Get out of my sight! Go to your room and stay there until the doctor has seen to your mother, and that's an order! Show your face outside this house and you'll be sorry, I guarantee it. Get out, before I lose control and finish what was started last night, because I'll tell you this, Elliot; whoever did that to you has my heartfelt gratitude!'

'There now – wasn't the climb worth it? You say Rowan-garth is beautiful – ' Julia's sweeping arm took in fields and trees, cornfields still brightly green, meadows of grazing cows. From Holdenby Pike they saw woodland below them and farmland and red-tiled cottages in early summer gardens, ' – but that is a view to take with you back to London. And over there – in the clearing – that's

Pendenys Place, where the other Suttons live. Isn't it grand?' she laughed.

'Grand? It's like a Scottish castle gone wrong! What a bleak place it looks.'

'Bleak and proud, Andrew, and just a little vulgar, I'm afraid. Pa's brother lives there. I like Uncle Edward, but Aunt Clemmy has moods; tempers, too. I think, sometimes, that she and Elliot deserve each other. And maybe now some good will come out of what happened in Brattocks, because Elliot got a hiding from Dwerryhouse and he'll have his father to face, too.

'And since cousin Elliot will take quite some time to apologize for his behaviour, we won't have to endure his visits to Rowangarth. Sit down, darling.' She sank on to the tough, springy grass, pulling her knees to her chin, clasping them with her arms. 'You know, Andrew, I only hope Aunt Clemmy won't try to stop Nathan visiting when he comes home. Nathan's the middle son – the nice one. Giles and he are good friends, so Giles wouldn't like it either. But at least Hawthorn seems none the worse. You're *sure* she's all right?'

'She'll be fine. I could find nothing seriously wrong with her. She's taken it remarkably well; I can see no reason why she shouldn't walk in the woods as she always did, to meet her Tom. She should be quite safe with the ferocious Morgan to protect her.'

'That spoiled old dog; who'd have thought it? But it would be awful if she couldn't see Tom – even though it's only for a few minutes. Still, there'll be two keepers on the lookout, now; and one of them with a very itchy trigger finger.' Julia laughed her delight, then all at once was serious. 'I mustn't make light of it, though. Just think what might have happened if he'd – well – '

To be raped by Elliot Sutton would be terrible enough; to bear a child of that rape was unthinkable.

'But he didn't, Julia. Don't upset yourself by what might have been. Dear little Hawthorn will soon be over the trauma of it. Everyone has been kind to her, and understanding – and she has her young man to comfort her.'

'Yes, I accept that.' Julia would not be gainsaid. 'But what would have been done about it if he'd got her pregnant?'

'Done? Well – he could have been sent to prison.'

'And what about Hawthorn? And not just Hawthorn; *any* woman attacked like that? Well, I'll tell you. Society would tut-tut, then send the poor soul to the nearest workhouse out of sight, if she didn't have an understanding family to support her. And the child labelled illegitimate, too, yet both of them innocent. No help for a woman, though; no *moral* help to save her having to suffer so. Is that fair, Andrew; is it right?'

'Julia, my love, it is neither fair nor right, but to end a pregnancy for any reason at all is illegal. I don't make the laws, I just obey them; no matter what I might think to the contrary.'

'Then you agree with me? You agree there should be some form of birth control for a woman; some say in what happens to her? Would you believe, Andrew, there is a woman in the village carrying her eighth child, with heaven only knows how many miscarriages in between. The midwife fears for her safety this time, so why can't that poor, worn-out woman call enough and be allowed to limit her pregnancies? Because it *is* possible; you know it is.'

'Possible – *desirable* – but forbidden.'

'I know. Everything is forbidden, isn't it, if it even remotely benefits women! And forbidden by men who make the laws, too!'

'My darling lassie – I agree with all you say. I'm not supposed to, but I do. I think women should have the right to a say in what affects them most. Some uncaring men have been legally killing women for as long as I can remember. And I think women should have the same voting rights as men. And it will come; it *will*.' Gathering her close, he smoothed back a tendril of hair which had blown across her face. 'But please try to take life one hurdle at a time. Don't put down your pretty head and charge in without thinking. Take things quietly and you'll get there quicker, in the end. And will you stop your protesting so I can tell you how much I love you – because I do. Right from the start, I loved you.'

'At first sight, you mean? Don't tell me the dour doctor believes in such romantic nonsense?'

'He didn't, but he does now. You have turned him into a poor creature,' he smiled. 'Do you realize that I knelt beside you that night, picked up your wrist and thought, "This is the woman I will marry." It was a shock; uncanny. I could hardly count your pulse beat. I still can't believe it.' He shook his head, bemused.

'Darling. It was the same for me, too.' Cupping his face in her hands, Julia was instantly serious, her eyes all at once luminous with need. 'And if I promise not to rant and rave, will you kiss me? And tell me you'll always love me? And will you please marry me as soon as we can manage it, because I have such feelings – such wonderful, *wanton* feelings – tearing through me, that I don't know how I'm to put up with the waiting till I'm twenty-one, let alone for a whole year.'

'Sweetheart.' His lips found hers. 'We *will* wait. We must. I can't support you properly yet. Another year will make all the difference.'

'But, Andrew – I've got money of my own, or I will have, when I'm of age. Father left it to me. And there'll be jewellery to come from Grandmother Whitecliffe – on my mother's side. I'm not sure how much, but it could

167

help to buy you a practice – in Harrogate, if you'd like it. Please think about it? Seriously?'

'Your generosity makes me feel very proud – humble, too – but I will support my wife. You call me dour, Julia – well it's the way I am; though if you have money to spare you could settle some of it on our children.'

'Our children,' she murmured, eyes closed. 'How many? Four?'

'Three, I think. First we will have a daughter for you – and she must be beautiful, like her mother – and then you shall give me two sons.'

'Happily,' whispered the sensuous, wanting woman she had become. 'I love you, Doctor MacMalcolm, and it is so *wonderful* being loved.'

'I know.' He took her hand, slowly, gently kissing the tips of the fingers curled possessively around his own. 'My dearest girl, I know it.'

'Then is there an explanation for the way I feel at times?' Frowning, she raised her eyes to his. 'Sometimes I think we are too lucky; that no one has the right to be this happy.'

'I think,' he said softly, 'that we get what we deserve in life.'

'So you don't think the Fates will be jealous?'

'Not a bit of it,' he laughed. 'How can they be when it was Fate, pure and simple, that brought us together in the first place? Stop your foolish blethering, woman,' he said fondly.

Foolish blethering? Of course – that's all it was, she echoed, contentedly snuggling closer. And may it please those Fates, whispered a small voice inside her, to let them keep that love? For ever and ever?

The mistress of Pendenys did not look up from her desk-top when the door opened and closed; nor when footsteps crossed the room and came to a halt behind her chair. Yet she knew that whoever stood there was either her son or her husband – no one else – for no other dare enter her sanctuary except to clean it. The room was hers alone; her one private place in this rambling, echoing, too-large house. Clementina's little room held her precious, private things, and was dear to her. The tantrum room, her servants called it, for in truth that was really what it was; the room the mistress most often retreated into after an upset; when she had flung her final accusation, slammed her last door. It was where she went to pace and fume silently, to simmer down, perhaps even to weep. And the best of British good fortune to it, said the servants, for whilst madam was closeted away, they were safe from the suspicious workings of her mind, the stabs of her tongue.

'Yes, Edward?' Clementina turned to face her husband.

'Please put down your pen, my dear. I wish to talk to you and I shall require your full attention.'

'Very well. You have it.' She knew better than to argue. Her husband was a mild, gentle person; a man who could be expected to have fathered the considerate, contented son who was Nathan; but sometimes there was harshness in his voice and anger in his eyes, and she knew, then, it would be to her cost to challenge the Sutton steel that ran the length of his backbone. 'What can you have to say, I wonder, except to remind me yet again how indulgently I have reared my son?'

'*Our* son, Clemmy. And the word is spoiled – *ruined*. Elliot has gone too far this time. London, Leeds, even Creesby we can hush over, but last night, on his own doorstep – '

'On Rowangarth's hallowed acres, you mean; on Helen's land?'

'Too near to home. Too near for comfort. And not a street woman this time, but a young girl.'

'Last night, Edward, was different. Elliot had been drinking – perhaps a little too much,' she murmured uneasily. 'But how did you find out?'

'Last night, tomorrow night, drunk or sober – where's the difference? Is no woman safe from his brutish ways? And I got the truth of it from Giles. I met him, walking over to see me, and he told me what Helen told you this morning. Why didn't you tell me she had visited?'

'Because I didn't believe what she said – about Elliot, I mean. Everyone is against him – even you, his father. You call him a brute, your own son,' she gasped, rising in agitation to her feet. 'But he's yours! He's a Sutton, remember; as much a Sutton as Nathan and Albert and that precious pair over at Rowangarth. But after this you'll say he isn't one of your breeding, but a throwback from Mary Anne. He isn't fair, like a Sutton should be, but dark like a Cornishman. Well, you married me, Edward. You were eager enough to trade my fortune for your seed!'

'Clementina! That is enough!' God! Must her talk be so direct? 'But if that is what you want, I'll admit it. You married my name and I went along with it. I had little choice. But I will stand by no longer and see Elliot sink to the gutter and take the Sutton name with him. Enough is enough. Either Elliot goes, or I go! Elliot goes to America for *at least* a month, or I shall move out into one of the almshouses!'

'Almshouses? You can't mean it? The talk! The *scandal*.'

'I mean it. There has been a Rowangarth almshouse empty for months, and it would be heaven to move in there, God only knows. And would a little more scandal make all that much difference? Scandal is nothing new to the Place Suttons. Our son has seen to that!'

'You mean it, don't you, Edward? This is your way of getting back at me. Well, Elliot shall *not* go to

Kentucky, no matter what that woman of Albert's says!'

'Albert's *wife* wrote you a perfectly civilized and kindly letter, once they had settled into a place of their own. I believe her when she says that any of Albert's family will be welcome in their home.'

'She's nothing but a social climber! And can you imagine it – Elliot returning home with an ambitious American heiress on his arm!'

'And would that be so bad?'

'You know it would. He doesn't need to marry money. Nathan maybe, but not Elliot. What I want for him is a title.'

'I know, my dear. But marriage to the daughter of a duke, even, could not give him the title he – *you* – so want. Your father tried to buy one for me, and couldn't. Accept it, Clemmy. The Sutton title belongs at Rowangarth, where it will stay. John left two sons, so there is no chance it will sidestep to me. And no accolade from the King will ever make a gentleman of Elliot, so forget your dreams for him. He goes to Kentucky to cool his heels – *or else!*'

'Edward, how *could* you?' Tears filled her eyes, then ran down her cheeks. She could take no more. It was either tears or temper, and in her husband's present mood she knew which would serve her better. 'How can you say such things about our own son? Brutish. Not a gentleman. You'll be saying next that he isn't yours – that some passing tinker . . .'

'Stop it, Clemmy! He's mine, though, I wish he'd been born last rather than first!'

'Aha! There we have it! It's Nathan you favour most; Nathan who looks like a Sutton and acts like a Sutton. Are you sure *I* bore him?'

'My dear – please listen? I am here to talk seriously with you, not flit in and out of the realms of fantasy. So dry your eyes. Tears will get you nowhere and will make you ill again. What Elliot did is completely unacceptable. I have never in my life been so near to giving him the thrashing he deserves. Helen's keeper didn't do half enough, to my way of thinking, and you can thank the good Lord the man had sense enough to hold on to his temper.

'So will you compose yourself? I have made up my mind. Defy me in this and I leave this house. The choice is yours, Clemmy.' He offered his handkerchief, hand on the bell-pull. 'Now I shall ring for tea for you and, no! not another word,' he said softly. 'There is no more to be said. You will drink your tea, calm yourself, then tell Elliot what has been decided. After which you will write a kindly letter to Kentucky, thanking your son's wife for her offer and availing yourself of it. You will grit your teeth and do it – do you fully understand? Ah . . .' He paused as the door opened to admit a butler who had answered the summons with unusual alacrity. 'Mrs Sutton would like tea. Serve it in here, if you please, then ask Mr Elliot to join his mother.

'And now I shall go for a walk; a very long walk,' he murmured when they were alone again. 'I shall walk this terrible anger out of me, and when I return I expect Elliot to be in no doubt as to what is expected of him. A very great deal is expected of you, too, Clemmy, but I know you will do as I wish in this respect. And there is no compromise, remember. It is Elliot, or me!'

'This is very cosy,' Helen Sutton smiled. 'Just the three of us. I do so enjoy luncheon in the conservatory.'

'Where is Giles?' Julia murmured, forking meat on to plates, handing them round. 'Don't tell me he's left his precious books?'

'He has been known to. My son,' she addressed her reply to Andrew, 'has been out all morning. First he went to Pendenys, and now he'll have arrived in York, on estate business. There are repairs to be done before winter to two cottages and one of the almshouses. I so hope the agent won't tell him we can't afford it. But meantime, doctor, I have a great favour to ask of you.'

'Is it Hawthorn, ma'am?'

'No, though I am grateful to you for seeing her and setting my mind at rest. The favour, I'm afraid, is a little embarrassing because it concerns family.'

'But Andrew *is* family,' Julia protested. 'Well, as good as . . .'

'Yes, indeed. And I suppose it is reasonable to expect every family to have a skeleton somewhere about,' Helen sighed. 'It's about Friday night, you see.'

'The dinner party,' Julia offered. 'I think Mama is a little apprehensive, not having entertained for – for – '

'For some time,' her mother supplied quickly. 'But it isn't that. Pendenys won't be coming now, I'm afraid, which will leave me with thirteen at table.'

'And is that serious? Is it really a fact, ma'am, that people never sit thirteen to a meal?' Andrew demanded, eyebrows raised.

'Not *never*, exactly, but not if it can be avoided. And that is why I must ask you – and I'm sorry if you think it an afterthought, but I didn't even know of your existence when the invitations were sent out.' She lifted her eyes to his, looking at him, he thought, as Julia did; without flinching, even though her cheeks were pink with embarrassment.

'Mama! You're asking Andrew to make up numbers,' Julia gasped. 'But how wonderful! You'll say yes, won't you, darling?'

'Accept, even though it would mean staying the night?' Helen murmured. 'We have no motor, you see, to return you to Harrogate, and it seems an imposition to ask

William to take you to the station so late. And we shall finish very late, I'm afraid . . .'

'Lady Sutton – I would have been glad to accept, but sadly I cannot. I have no evening clothes, you see.'

'Oh, dear. You didn't pack them?'

'I have none to bring with me,' he smiled. 'Evening dress is on my list of necessities, but quite some way down. There are other things must come first, you see, though I'll admit I've had to miss many medical gatherings with after-dinner speakers I'd have liked fine to have heard, because of it. I wish I could have helped your numbers. I'm sorry.'

'Oh, *no*.' Julia's face showed disappointment. She would have liked nothing better than to show Andrew off, have him introduced to her mother's friends. It would have set the seal on her family's approval; been as good, almost, as an announcement in *The Times*. 'Are you sure you – '

'Very sure, Julia, though I promise you I shall think more urgently, now, about the matter. And I would have been happy to accept – you know that, Lady Sutton?'

'Then in that case would you – oh, dear, this is going to make things even worse.' Helen's cheeks burned bright red. 'Would you, for my sake and Julia's, perhaps consider borrowing?'

'Of course I would – if you can find someone with a suit to spare – and one that fits. I'm not so foolish, ma'am,' he said softly, 'that I'd let pride stand in the way of such an invitation.'

'Then I thank you, and I'm almost certain we can find something. My husband, you see, would never throw anything away, and the smallest – the *slimmest*,' she corrected with a smile, 'of his evening suits is still hanging there. It is the one he wore when first we were married, but it isn't at all dated. You are his height and build, doctor. Will you – after we have eaten – consider trying that one on? And I'm sure that somewhere there'll be a

174

shirt to fit, and shirt studs, though shoes I'm not too sure about. But would you . . .?'

'I would indeed,' he replied, gravely.

'But, Mama,' Julia gasped. 'You never – I mean – '
Nothing that was her father's had been discarded. Nothing that was his had been moved, even, since the day he died. His pipe still lay on the desk in the library; the loose coins from his pocket on the dressing-table where he had placed them; his cape and driving goggles still hung behind the garage door.

'It's all right,' said Helen gently. 'I have come out of my black and accept that I must face the world again. And I am bound to confess that the doctor is so like your pa once was – even the colour of his eyes – that I shall take no hurt in seeing John's clothes on him,' she whispered. 'Please indulge me, Andrew?' she asked, using his name for the first time. 'I think perhaps that on Friday night I might feel a little unsure and need John with me, but if you are there, and Giles . . .'

'I understand, ma'am. And far from taking exception to your offer, I take it kindly. We must hope,' he smiled, 'that the suit fits me.'

And Julia closed her eyes and fervently hoped so, too, and thought that she had never loved her mother as she loved her now.

'Vegetables?' she smiled, offering a dish, her eyes bright with affection, her heart so full of happiness she felt light-headed. 'And if they don't quite fit, I'm sure Hawthorn could do a quick alteration on them – I'm *sure* of it.'

And dear, sweet Lord, thank you for my lovely family and for this great singing happiness inside me.

And please let me keep it?

Alice held Morgan's lead tightly, reluctant to release him. She wanted with all her heart to see Tom, even if it meant walking alone in Brattocks again, but she had felt relief, almost, when Miss Clitherow had asked her to sponge and press the suit.

'The doctor's evening dress. He'll be coming to the dinner party,' was all that was offered by way of explanation, but Alice at once suggested it be hung out to air, so strong was the camphory smell of mothballs on it. The suit wasn't really the doctor's, Alice knew; rather something long stored away and in need of a good valeting. Yet Doctor Andrew being asked to the Friday night dinner – now that *was* good news, she had thought, as she pegged the hangers firmly to the drying-green line. And then she had felt so guilty about Tom that she had taken Morgan's lead and run to the library, where the impatient creature waited, tail wagging.

And she must face Brattocks Wood again. She had promised Mr Giles, him being away seeing the agent, that she would take Morgan out; had said it would be all right, that the doctor had even suggested that she do it.

'A bit like falling off a horse,' he'd assured her. 'You get straight back in the saddle . . .'

Yet now here she was at the woodland fence – unsure, and wanting to keep Morgan beside her, even though she was certain that Tom would be there and Elliot Sutton would not; even though her hatpin, on good advice, was secure beneath the lapel of her jacket.

'You never know,' Tilda said sagely, recounting one of her love-book heroines who had defended her virtue with the pin from her Sunday hat.

'No,' Alice whispered to the animal who had become used to being released at the fence. 'Stay now, there's a good dog.' Carefully manoeuvring the lead from hand to hand, she climbed the stile, then stood, ears straining for the snapping of a twig that might betray some other presence. But Tom walked without sound as a keeper should, and the silence comforted her. 'Tom?' she called. 'Tom Dwerryhouse?'

At once she heard his answering whistle. It was all right! He was waiting for her! Bending, she released the lead, relief pulsing through her. Nothing could harm her, she should have known it, and taking in a deep, calming gulp of air, tilting her chin high, she began to walk the narrow, moss-edged path.

She needed to see Tom, she urged silently; wanted him to hold her, touch her, because last night she had discovered the depths to which a man could sink and she needed to be sure that men like Elliot Sutton were few and far between. She wanted to close her eyes and lift her mouth to Tom's so she might forget the way another man had kissed her; but most of all she wanted to know she had not changed, that what had happened only a few yards from this spot had not caused her to mistrust all men – even Tom, who loved her.

'Alice, sweetheart . . .'

He was there, Morgan at his heels; the same Tom. So why did some strange voice inside her demand she must be sure that he should know the line that divided love from lust – and never step beyond it?

'Alice?' He walked slowly to where she stood, rooted to the ground, her feet all at once useless.

She ran her tongue round her lips, then moved them consciously into the shape of a smile, thinking for one wild moment to turn and run back to the stile and climb it again; place it like a barrier between them. But she did not, could not.

'You came, then,' she murmured, eyes on her boots.

'You knew I would. I came at teatime, too, though I thought you'd not want to venture here again just yet.'

'I did, though. Well – Morgan is with me,' she defended.

'Aye. He'll not let anyone harm you.' Carefully, as if she were some small, cornered animal, he raised his hand; gently he placed his fingertips to her face.

'Poor little love. Does it hurt bad?'

'Hardly at all. It looks worse than it is.'

'I wanted to kill him, last night,' he muttered, thickly. 'I wish I had.'

'No, Tom. Never wish that – he's not worth it.'

'He harmed you, *dirtied* you. I'll not forgive him for that!'

'It's over,' she urged, her voice no more than a whisper. 'It's behind me.'

'But *is* it behind you? Can you be sure, lass? Can you be certain that what happened hasn't set you against me, against all men?'

'No!' she cried, unnerved that he could look into her eyes and read the thoughts behind them. 'Why should I think that?'

'I don't know, though I wouldn't blame you if you did. But I won't ever harm you, and you must know it, or there's no future for you and me. So tell me why you're holding yourself back from me – because you *are* . . .'

'Tom!' She glanced wildly around her, unwilling to meet his gaze. 'How am I to know? How can I be sure that once we're wed you won't turn into – '

She stopped, tears choking her words, sudden fear making her want to run away from this encounter; run back to the warmth of Rowangarth kitchen; to Mrs Shaw and Mary and Tilda and Bess. And Miss Clitherow, looking down her nose.

'That I won't turn into an animal like the one that attacked you last night? Well, I won't, Alice. I love you. It would be sweet and gentle between us.'

'And you wouldn't change, and look at me wild? And you wouldn't hit me, tear at me? Because, Tom, if that's the way of it, if that's the way it happens . . .'

'It *isn't* the way of it. With love between us it'll be giving, not taking. And I shall make you want me, sweetheart, not make you feared of me. Loving, *real* loving, isn't like it was with him, I promise you it isn't.'

'Then you'll give me time . . .?'

'All the time it takes. All the time in the world.'

'Tom!' She took a step towards him; one small step across the divide, and it was all she needed. 'I'm sorry. It was wrong of me to think as I did. And I'd be obliged if you would kiss me like you always do when we meet, for I've wanted you near me so much, even though I was afraid . . .'

'Alice, my little love.' Gathering her to him, he rocked her in his arms, whispering into her hair, hushing her, waiting until he felt her relax against him. Then he tilted her chin as he had done the first time, and placed his mouth tenderly on her own. 'Will I kiss it better for you?' He murmured, his lips over the bruising on her face, all the time making little comforting sounds, as if she were a frightened bird he had loosed, hurt, from a poacher's trap. 'I love you, Alice Hawthorn; love you – do you hear me?'

'And I love you. And you aren't like him – I think I always knew it. But forgive me for doubting?'

Slowly she raised her arms, clasping them around his neck, lifting her face for his kiss.

'Will I tell you something?' he smiled. 'Reuben told me an' it's on Mr Giles's orders. If that Sutton so much as sets foot on Rowangarth land, he's to be treated like we'd treat a poacher. My, but I wish he'd try it. I'd like nothing better than to kick his backside off the place. Hell! I do so detest that man!'

'Then don't. He isn't worth your hatred. Elliot Sutton will get what he deserves one day, so leave him, Tom; leave him to God. Promise me?'

179

And because he loved her, his lips formed the words she wanted to hear, whilst secretly he swore he'd have justice for her, should chance ever offer the means.

'All right, then,' he said. 'I promise.'

Then damned himself for a liar.

10

Friday came in clear and blue and bright, so that Tilda didn't grumble overmuch at leaving her bed an hour earlier to clear the oven flues of soot, and when Mrs Shaw made her sleepy-eyed appearance, the kitchen range shone with blacklead polish, the fire glowed red, and a kettle puffed lazy steam from its spout.

'Good girl, Tilda,' Cook approved. 'You'd best mash a sup of tea and make us a couple of toasts. And them as lies in their beds till the dot of six are going to miss out on it, aren't they? Think we might open a jar of the strawberry,' she added comfortably, knowing the kitchenmaid's fondness for her ladyship's special conserve, and knowing too that so small a reward would be repaid in extra effort during the day ahead; the hot, hectic, dinner-party day just beginning.

William called, 'Hup!' and the horses broke into a canter. On the carriage floor lay the ice, collected from the fishmonger in Creesby, and, atop it, to keep it cool, a parcel of lobster meat for Mrs Shaw's thick fish soup.

Fuss and bother, that's what dinner parties were, the coachman brooded. All coming and going and do this, William, do that. He brought down the reins with a slap. Best get a move on or Miss Clitherow would glare and he'd be in trouble with Cook an' all. She could be a bit of a battleaxe when the mood was on her, none knew it better than William Stubbs, though she was usually good for a sup of tea and a slice of cake when it wasn't. But all thoughts of fruit cake were quickly dismissed from William's mind when there were matters of greater importance to think on. The carry-on in Brattocks, for one, and the to-do it had caused at Pendenys. He'd got it from the under-gardener there, so it was fact – Elliot Sutton with a badly face; his father going on something awful, and Mrs Clementina throwing a fit of the vapours so that Doctor James had to be brought in the motor.

Mind, you couldn't expect much else from the likes of Elliot Sutton. Not real gentry, the Place Suttons. Not like Rowangarth, so you couldn't entirely blame Pendenys for their lack of refinement, them being half trade, so to speak, and liable because of it to throw a wrong 'un from time to time. But the atmosphere over at the Place was cold as charity if talk was to be believed. Something was going on there, or why had the laundrymaid been ordered to wash all Mr Elliot's linen and boil and starch his shirts – every last one of them? Taking himself off, was he? Away to London again, out of the reach of his mother's tongue? And a fair wind to his backside if it were true, thought William with grimmest pleasure. A good riddance, and no mistake.

There had better, warned Mrs Shaw, getting things straight right from the start, be no idling this morning. Indeed, they should all count themselves lucky there had been time for breakfast, so pushed were they going to be. True, the soup was well in hand, two salmon lay cooling on the cold slab in the meat cellar, and the four ribs of beef – any less would have seemed penny-pinching – had been quickly browned in a hot oven to seal in the juices, and now cooked in slow contentment on the bottom shelf.

The ice-cream and sorbet were Cook's biggest worry, though both were safely packed with fresh ice now, and should turn out right, as they almost always did.

'That's the soup and salmon seen to, the beef doing nicely, and the savoury part-prepared . . .' Cook was in the habit of thinking aloud on such occasions. 'And the meringues for the pudding done yesterday, and please God that dratted ice-cream is going to behave itself. Tilda!'

'Yes'm.' Tilda gazed mesmerized at the pile of vegetables brought in by the under-gardener at seven that morning; a pile so enormous it had set her longing for the day she would rise to the heights of assistant cook – or even under-housemaid would do – and so be able to watch some other unfortunate scrape carrots, peel potatoes, slice cucumbers and pod peas. Yet, she conceded, as the scent of strawberries – the first of the season and straight from the hotbed in the kitchen garden – teased her nostrils, being a kitchenmaid did have its compensations, for no one would miss the plump half dozen that would find their way to her mouth when no one was looking.

'Think we can manage a breather,' Cook murmured, hands to her burning cheeks. 'Might as well have a sup of tea.' Heaven only knew when there'd be time for another. 'Put the kettle on, Tilda, then pop upstairs and fetch Mary and Bess and Ellen . . .'

Mrs Shaw's long, dramatic sigh masked the excitement that churned inside her. Dinner parties at Rowangarth again! Oh, the joy of it, and herself thinking she would never live to see another. Goodness gracious, what a hustle and bustle and delight this day would be.

Ellen had arrived early that morning, leaving her children in the care of her mother-in-law, walking the half-mile to Rowangarth with a lightness of step. In the brown paper parcel she carried were her carefully folded frock – her best one, in navy – and a stiffly-starched cap with ribbon trailers and a bibbed apron, wrapped carefully around a rolled newspaper to prevent creasing. It would be grand to be with them all again, and tomorrow there would be a knock on her front door – her ladyship was always prompt with her thanks – and William would deliver a letter marked *By Hand* in the top, left-hand corner; a letter signed Helen M. Sutton and containing five shillings for her pains.

Five beautiful shillings. Ellen's step had quickened, just to think of it. It would buy material for a Sunday-best dress and tobacco for her man, and a bag of jujubes for the bairns.

Now, in what had been her second-best uniform, and which still fitted her even after two pregnancies, she and Mary and the head gardener, his feet in felt slippers so as not to leave marks on the carpet, were setting a table splendid to see, with sweeps of fern looped around the table edges and, at each corner, a ribboned posy of carnations – carnations being known to keep fresh the longest. And thank goodness for Rowangarth's heated glasshouses: peaches and nectarines, ready long before nature intended, made up part of a magnificent, two-feet-tall centrepiece of fruit, roses, lilies-of-the-valley and maidenhair fern. Already she had checked the fingerbowls, laid ready to be filled with water and sprinkled with rose petals later in the afternoon, and now, menu in hand, she checked the cutlery for correctness, walking round the table unspeaking.

'Will it do?' Nervously, Mary moved glasses a fraction of an inch, wondering if she had folded the table napkins into anything less than perfect waterlilies. 'Have I done anything wrong?'

Ellen continued her progress from chair to chair, then looked up, smiling.

'It is perfect, Mary. I can't fault it. It would seem I taught you well. You can tell Miss Clitherow that only the place-cards need to be seen to now, for where guests will sit is nothing to do with us. Then we shall do as Tilda bids, and be off to the kitchen for a sup.' She took the parlourmaid's arm and tucked it in her own. 'I wouldn't be at all surprised if Mrs Shaw hasn't made cherry scones: she always used to on dinner-party days. I still remember those scones. Oh, but this is going to be a rare day for me, Mary. It's so good to be back at Rowangarth.'

Mrs Shaw sat herself down in the kitchen rocker and, taking a corner of her apron in each hand, billowed it out like a fan to cool her burning cheeks.

'You can pour now, Tilda, and pass round the scones, for I'm fair whacked already . . .'

And loving every minute of, Ellen thought, washing her hands at the sinkstone; loving it as she always had before Sir John was taken and there had been a dinner party at least once a month.

'Come now, Mrs Shaw,' she admonished with a forwardness permitted only because of her marital state and her past years of service at Rowangarth. 'You know you'll be queen of the kitchen tonight, and all of them upstairs exclaiming over your cooking.' And though she knew that a parlourmaid must never repeat table talk, it would be expected of both herself and Mary to pass on overheard compliments. 'I can say for certain that Judge Mounteagle will allow himself to be persuaded to take another of your savouries, and you'll have seen to it there'll be extra, especially for him.'

Glowing, Cook accepted the plate and cup placed at her side, knowing everything Ellen said to be true, for wasn't she indeed queen of her own kitchen, and as such had never seen the need for wedlock when all her heart could ever want was at Rowangarth. Here, she could go to bed master and get up next morning her own mistress, for the title of 'Mrs' was one of kindness, allowed to unmarried cooks and nannies. Truth known she was *Miss* Shaw and for ever would remain so.

'Aah,' she murmured, drinking deeply, smiling secretly. 'Queen of nothing I once was. I remember it like it was yesterday. It was my twelfth birthday and the next day I left school. There were nine of us bairns; all to keep on a sovereign-a-week's wages. I was one of the middle three, the fifth, right in the middle, and middle children had a hard time of it, I can tell you.'

She closed her eyes, calling back the firstborn brothers, well able to stick up for themselves, and the three youngest, petted like the babies they still were.

'Us in the middle were all girls, all mouths to feed and backs to clothe; so Mam had no choice. Taken to Mother Beswick at the Mop Fair all three of us were: in them days, servants was hired at the Mop Fairs. I remember when it was my turn to go, and Mam telling me to work hard and not complain and say my prayers at night. Then she kissed me and gave Mother Beswick a florin and asked her to place me with an upright family if she could manage it. I never saw my mother again . . .'

'And?' prompted Ellen, as the elderly cook lapsed into remembering and Tilda sniffed loudly and dabbed her eyes with her apron.

'And I was the luckiest lass in the North Riding that day,' Cook beamed, 'for didn't Mrs Stormont's housekeeper take me? Lady Helen's mother, Mrs Stormont was, and a real gentlewoman. And I was trained up to under-cook, then came here to Rowangarth with Miss Helen when she married Sir John.'

'Ar,' sighed Tilda, who liked happy endings, 'but what if you'd been placed middle-class? What if some shopkeeper's wife had taken you for a skivvy?'

'What if *nothing*!' Cook selected another cherry scone. 'I ended up here, didn't I, and determined never to wed and have bairns to rear to line Ma Beswick's pocket; a lesson you'd do well to heed, young Tilda.'

'Yes, Mrs Shaw,' agreed the kitchenmaid, though she was only waiting, like the heroines in her love books, to be swept off her feet by the romance of her life. Exactly like Miss Julia had been; snatched from the jaws of death by a young doctor who'd been waiting for a beautiful woman to fall at his feet in a faint. Miss Julia, who was head over heels in love.

Tilda drained her cup, then resumed her peeling and scraping and slicing and podding. Resumed it for the time being, that was. Until *he* came.

On hands and knees in the great hall where tonight milady would be receiving, Bessie rubbed tea-leaves into the rugs. For the past two days, teapots had been drained and the swollen leaves squeezed and set aside for carpet cleaning. There was nothing like them for taking away the dusty, musty smell and freshening jaded colours, Miss Clitherow insisted.

Bessie brushed the tea-leaves out vigorously, mindful that the under-gardener waited outside with a barrow filled with potted plants and ferns from the planthouse, to arrange in the hall so that tonight it would seem as if the garden had crept inside.

Bessie sighed happily. Tonight, in place of Alice whose face was not yet presentable, she would be on duty in the bedroom set aside for lady guests, on hand to receive cloaks and wraps, offer small gold safety-pins if required, and smelling-salts where necessary, and listen, eyes downcast, to the gossip. And, best of all, she would see the beautiful dinner gowns at first hand instead of being stuck below stairs, seeing nothing, hearing nothing.

She didn't mind the extra work at all, because this sad old house had come alive again, and there would be luncheon parties and dinner parties galore from now on. And there would be at least a shilling in tips left for her on the dressing-table, she shouldn't wonder.

'You can come in now,' she told the young man she had kept waiting for the past ten minutes. 'I'll leave the pan and brush so you can sweep up after yourself if you make any mess, for I'm too busy to do it,' she declared, whisking away so that her skirts swung wide, offering a glimpse of ankle that made him flush with pleasure.

He formed his lips into a long, low whistle, a sound that stopped her in her tracks. She turned to face his slow wink of approval. 'Cheeky!' she said airily. 'And you'd best leave the pan and brush at the kitchen door when you're done,' she ordered.

Cheeky he might be, but when he returned the pan and brush, she just *might* return that wink . . .

'Now tell me,' whispered Ellen, as she laid her best dress and apron on Mary's bed, 'if it's true what I hear – that Miss Julia has an admirer?'

'It's true,' came the unhesitating reply, for Ellen was entirely to be trusted. 'Met him in London, in Hyde Park. Ever so romantic. She tripped and fell, see, because of her tight old skirt, and he was there like a shot, holding her hand, seeing to her. It was meant to be, if you ask me. And he's so nice and kindly in his manner. Make a lovely couple . . .'

'Then I'll be back, I shouldn't wonder, to help out at the wedding.' Ellen undressed without embarrassment, she and Mary having shared this very room in the old days.

'Wouldn't be at all surprised. But I'll just fill your basin, then you can get washed and changed. And you can use my scented soap, Ellen, and my talcum powder.'

'Oooh, thanks, love.' Since she had married, such things were a luxury; though she knew that a parlourmaid, when serving at table and reaching and passing, must never, ever give offence. 'I'm grateful.'

And oh, wasn't it going to be just like old times again tonight, and wouldn't it be grand having five shillings of her own to spend exactly as she pleased?

She plunged her hands into the basin of cold rainwater, made a violet-scented lather on top of it, and sighed with pure pleasure.

'Are you decent, or in disarray?' Julia entered Andrew's bedroom without embarrassment. 'I'm here to see if you need any help. Sorry we haven't a valet to help you dress.'

'*Help me dress?* Good grief, woman,' he gasped, 'I've been dressing myself since I was out of napkins, though I'd like fine for you to see to this tie – I've made a bit of a mess of it.'

'Yes, you have, my darling. But don't worry. Mama always tied Pa's for him, and Giles is worse at it than you. You've got the studs in all right, I see.' She glanced with approval at the shirt front, sparkling with diamonds.

'That much I could manage. Don't they look grand. Are they real?'

'They are, so you're very honoured. Mother bought them for Pa as a silver wedding gift and oh, Andrew, you won't do anything careless and get yourself killed like he did when we've only been married twenty-six years, will you?'

'I won't. I promise to grow old with you.' He cupped her upturned face in his hands. 'I couldn't bear to leave you, either. And now will you see to this tie, then help me pin on the rose you sent up for me, though I'd heard that in London fashion it's usually a carnation a man wears.'

'London is London; here, we wear what we like, and your lady chose a white rosebud, so – ' She gave a final pull to the bow tie, then reached on tiptoe to place her lips gently against his own. 'There now, doctor,' she murmured. 'You'll be the handsomest man at table and Mrs Mounteagle will faint at your feet. And you'll remember, when you see her,' she rushed on, 'to thank Hawthorn for sponging and pressing your things so beautifully? She's so pleased you've been asked tonight.'

'I'll make a special point of it. You care for Hawthorn, don't you?' He reached for the smallness of her waist, drawing her closer.

'Yes, I do.' She took a step away from his disturbing nearness. 'She's fun and she understands about you and me because she's in love, too. She's also my friend.'

'Even though she must call you miss, or Miss Julia, and curtsey to you? Even though you call her Hawthorn, and never Alice?' he quizzed, eyebrows raised.

'Even though. It's the way it is and Hawthorn would be embarrassed to have it differently. It doesn't change the way she and I trust each other, and anyway, no one here expects to be curtseyed to. This isn't Pendenys. But let me have another look at you.' She smiled tenderly, eyes large with love.

'Will I do, ma'am, in my fine feathers?'

'You'll do.' Dear sweet heaven, but he was good to look at. 'Tell me, darling,' she murmured, trying to sound flippant and failing dismally. 'Why are you twenty-seven, almost, and still unmarried? Because I don't know how you've managed to stay single for so long. Hasn't there been *anyone* . . .?'

'There has not. I'm a bachelor still, because one thing I'm sure about is that two *can't* live as cheaply as one, and because – ' he placed a kiss on the tip of her nose – 'because you and that hefty constable took so long getting down to fisticuffs in Hyde Park. Heaven help me – there I was, walking in the park day after day. What took you so long?'

'Darling!' She slipped her hands beneath his coat, hugging him to her, closing her eyes tightly as happy little tears misted her eyes. 'I do love you. How will I bear it when you leave me?'

190

'Me, too – about loving you so, I mean, and dreading Sunday coming. And I know we aren't engaged and shouldn't buy presents for each other, but – ' He dipped into his pocket and brought out a small box. 'It's only a bauble, sweetheart, and secondhand into the bargain. But when I saw it, it seemed so right that I had to have it for you.'

'Andrew!' Her cheeks flushed red. 'You shouldn't have, but darling, I'm glad you did.' She opened it to show a small, heart-shaped box that held a dainty, heart-shaped brooch.

'It's gold, Julia, and look.' His finger outlined the two letters entwined within the heart. 'J and A. Julia and Andrew, I thought at once, though maybe it was James who bought it for Anne, or Albert for Joan.'

'Andrew, it's beautiful. Your initial and mine. I shall wear it tonight – wear it always. Oh, I wish you knew how much I love you. It's like a great ache inside me.' She closed her eyes, because she could hardly bear to look at him.

'I know. I have a pain just like it,' he said gravely. 'And I'm glad to say there is no known cure for it. But should you be in a gentleman's room, Miss Sutton, and you not married to him? What if anyone saw us? Your reputation would be in shreds.'

'I know,' she smiled. 'It's quite delightful, isn't it? You'd have to marry me then, wouldn't you? But I won't compromise you, doctor dear. I shall go and see to Giles's tie. I think I shall feel a lot safer in his room than here,' she said softly, pinning the brooch to her dress.

'I understand exactly.' He took her hand in his, lingering his lips in its upturned palm, kissing it sensuously so that exquisite shivers of delight sliced through her; made her wonder how she would endure a year, almost, until they could rightfully close their bedroom door on the world. And she wondered, too, why just to look at the ordinary double bed in which Andrew would sleep tonight, all at once made it loom so large and tantalizing. 'I'll see you in the conservatory,' she murmured. 'In five minutes . . .'

Helen Sutton let go a small sigh of contentment, grateful that her very dear friends – those who had comforted her and been close to her during her years of mourning – were with her tonight. Dear and precious friends, and her family too. There was Judge Mounteagle and his formidable wife; though had Helen been fighting, back to the wall for her very life, it would have been Mrs Mounteagle, truth known, she would have wished at her side. There, too, was Doctor James, and Effie, and the Reverend Luke Parkin, and Jessica, to whom she owed so much; and she was guiltily glad that neither Clementina nor Elliot were coming, though she felt sad that Edward would not be able to enjoy his favourite pudding which Cook had so laboriously prepared for him.

She sat unspeaking, wanting John beside her, yet counting the blessings of this night. The sun, losing its brilliance now, lit the glass room softly, showing off the display of vines that climbed to the roof; exotic shrubs that could never have survived outdoors, and pots of flowers, grown specially for such an occasion in heated glasshouses, and carried inside to give pleasure. Orchids of every colour, save creamy-white; brilliant geraniums, sweet-scented jasmine and campanulas, blazing blue as a summer sky, all weeks before their time.

'I see,' remarked Mrs Mounteagle tartly, 'that Pendenys is late, as usual.'

'Ah – no. My sister-in-law,' said Helen softly, 'is a little unwell and cannot be here.'

'Ha!' the lady shrugged, the look of satisfaction ill-disguised on her face. 'It comes to us all, I suppose – that certain age, I mean.'

She slanted her gaze at Mrs James who, caught off balance by such directness, could only glance appealingly at her husband.

'Mrs Sutton is – er – a little under the weather; a *little*, that is all. Tomorrow, when I call, I fully expect her to be her old self again . . .' the doctor offered reluctantly.

'I see.' Mrs Mounteagle was in no way convinced, and made a mental note to discover exactly what 'a little under the weather' embraced. 'I shall leave my card when passing,' she said without so much as a blush. 'When will that son of hers be finished with Cambridge? Nathan, isn't he called?'

'Soon, now. We hope to have him back in just a few weeks. He's a fine young man,' Helen smiled, eager to be rid of the subject of Pendenys's absence. 'Giles particularly will be pleased.'

'And then what? Find himself a position, will he?'

'I rather think,' Giles offered cautiously, 'he'll take holy orders. He's a good man; he'll make a fine priest.'

Mrs Mounteagle gave in gracefully. She had tried, but failed, to get to the bottom of the rumour currently circulating about Elliot Sutton; that he had been set upon and his injuries so dreadful that his mother had fallen in a faint just to look at him. That Doctor James had been summoned there was no doubt, since he'd been seen by two ladies of her acquaintance in Pendenys's chauffeur-driven car which had, so talk had it, been sent to collect him with all haste.

But the Suttons – and Doctor James, too – had closed ranks, and though it was common knowledge that often the Garth Suttons and the Place Suttons did not see eye to eye, it was taken for granted they stood together at times of stress or scandal. She sighed, then glanced meaningfully at her husband, passing the conversation to him.

Julia Sutton had never, in the whole of her life, loved

193

her mother so much. Screened by the thick, broad leaves of a potted palm, she could gaze unnoticed, almost, across the room and think with wonder: *Once I was her daughter, but only since Andrew is she no longer my beautiful mama. Now, she is my mother, my dearest friend, who loved as I love. She is alone, and only now can I begin to know how great her love was, how awful her loss.*

Helen, Lady Sutton, sat head erect on a high-backed chair, exquisite in blue silk, a creamy-white orchid at the point of her cleavage, another in her upswept golden hair. Always her eyes were the first thing a stranger noticed and most remembered, but tonight those eyes reflected the deep, bright colour of her gown, making them especially brilliant and unbearably distant.

Where are you now, Mother? Julia mused. *Is this the night of your first ball; the night you wore white roses and fell in love for the first and only time? Is Pa at your side, still, and are your eyes loving him as mine love Andrew?*

Her fingers touched the brooch pinned a little to the left of her bodice, where her heart lay. Andrew sat beside Mrs James, who seemed to have forgotten her painful shyness with strangers and was talking to him with obvious pleasure. He listened with rapt attention to her stumbling words, putting her at ease, smiling into her eyes as though he had travelled all this way for just such a meeting. Dear, kind, wise Andrew, who would one day be the finest physician in the country and be given a knighthood by the King.

'And I tell you, ma'am, they are up to no good!'

Julia started, Judge Mounteagle's rasping words penetrating her thoughts. His presence commanded attention; his opinions were pronouncements. He had become that way, she supposed, to get the better of a wife more forceful and commanding even than himself.

'Another battleship launched! Why, I'd like to know! But they'll never change, those Prussians!'

'Oh, but I think we're supposed to call them Germans now,' offered the vicar's wife anxiously.

'Huns? Prussians? Germans? Whatever you call them, ma'am, it don't make any difference to the number of warships they've got!' The judge rode his pet hobby-horse with a patriotic fervour not even his wife's glances could halt. 'Becoming industrialized, like us, and credit where it's due, they aren't half bad at it. But they're after our overseas trade, and they'll be after our Empire next, mark my words! Means nothing but trouble, in my opinion.'

'*Trouble*, Judge?' the vicar murmured.

'And they *are* entitled to a navy,' Mrs Mounteagle boomed.

'Granted, m'dear. But soon they'll have more ships than we do, and what then, eh?'

'Launch a few more of our own,' she snapped.

'What'll we do then, I ask? We'll have to fight them; show them what's what and who's boss!' He was not to be gated. 'But it's a pity, Helen, that the old Queen has gone. One word from her and they'd all have toed the line. Stood to reason, didn't it – her related to every royal house in Europe, so to speak.'

'Fight? You wouldn't go that far? Surely a little trade, sir, a little land,' Giles challenged, 'isn't worth fighting over?'

'There are some,' the judge tapped his nose with a knowing forefinger, 'who would fight at the drop of a hat – or why suddenly all the ships and guns, eh?'

Julia turned to her brother. She knew his horror of killing, his dislike of war; needed to let him know she was on his side, to beg him silently not to rise to an old man's baiting. But Giles Sutton's eyes were on his mother, her face all at once pale with apprehension, yet because the judge was their guest, he could do no more than he had done.

But she, Julia, could and *would*! The man had no right to air his opinions so forcefully, fill women with fear. He was old, so he didn't care. Old men didn't go to war. Old men spawned wars with their senile tongues, then stood aside for the young men to fight them.

'If you will pardon a woman, judge,' Julia looked to Andrew for support, 'for having an opinion of her own, I think that you are – '

She got no further, for Andrew was relaxed and smiling and the eyes that met hers warned her into silence.

'With respect, sir, I think that on this beautiful summer night,' he said slowly and clearly, so that even the judge was forced to stop and pay heed, 'and in such happy company, there is a matter of far greater importance than the latest addition to the Kaiser's fleet – and much more worthy of our interest. Tell me, Lady Sutton – will the King's horse win the Derby next week? Is it to be hats-off for His Majesty?' Andrew laughed.

Relief flowed like a blessing, lips relaxed into answering smiles, the Kaiser's fleet and his country's ambitions dismissed.

'I most certainly hope so,' the vicar beamed. 'I intend to wager a few shillings for the King myself – and put my winnings in the Poor Box,' he added, triumphantly. The vicar of Holdenby parish was a pacifist through and through, and not even for King or Empire could he condone war or even talk of it. Often he had thundered his beliefs from his pulpit, banishing for all time any hopes he might have nurtured of crozier and gaiters.

'Then I shall follow so worthy an example,' Helen said softly, thankfully. 'My sister-in-law in London is a splendid judge of racing form, and vows there isn't a horse to beat it.'

She turned to smile at Andrew, silently thanking him

with eyes all at once free from anxiety, and thought, with sudden contentment, how right her first impressions had been.

'Ah, Miss Clitherow.' She nodded as the housekeeper crossed the room and bent to whisper in her ear. 'Will you all excuse me? The rest of our party is arriving . . .'

'My dears.' She was waiting at the foot of the staircase with pleased anticipation when Mary opened the door, and she held out her hands, her delight genuine.

She had arranged for the Draytons to collect the Lanes and bring them here. Sir Edwin and Lady Tessa Drayton were extremely rich, and kept a horse and carriage in addition to a fine new motor. Martin and Letty Lane were extremely poor, and owned neither. All four were Helen's cherished friends; all had helped sustain her through the bleak years, and she wanted them with her tonight. 'Tessa, Letty – how good it is to see you.'

She kissed them with affection, all at once relieved that Clementina had declined her invitation; now, all who sat at her table would be there because she wanted them to be. Tonight, she admitted with silent relief, could well turn out to be less of an ordeal than she had feared.

'Ladies upstairs in the South bedroom. Bessie is there to look after you,' she said softly. 'Then join us in the conservatory? There are some very fine orchids I want you to see.'

Much, much less of an ordeal . . .

'Wasn't it a wonderful evening?' Julia reached for Andrew's hand.

'Was. Still is.' His fingers tightened around hers.

'Mother was nervous, I could tell. Tonight was the first time she hasn't had Pa with her.' She frowned. 'It was good of you to put the judge in his place.'

'Did I? I hadn't intended – was I *that* obvious?'

'No, darling. But you were firm, and shut him up.

Why must past glories be so important to the old?' she demanded, her cheeks pinkly indignant. 'Have they forgotten how dreadful wars are?'

'Ssssh, darling. Don't you realize we are completely alone? Don't let an old man's grumblings spoil it for us.'

'Sorry.' Alone, indeed. Romantically, blissfully alone, with beauty all around them. A single light shone gently in the conservatory, touching ferns and flowers and trailing plants with lamp glow, inviting moths to throw themselves against the glass with little fluttering taps. 'You are right, of course, but will you tell me what business it is of ours what the Germans do? Why should they need to be taught a lesson?'

'No need at all, so please don't look so angry. Germany is a rising nation; must see to it that factories and shipyards provide employment. They are looking after their own; doing exactly as we are doing, but a little more thoroughly, I suspect. Judge Mounteagle shouldn't have said such things in front of ladies.'

'I know. Mother looked quite upset. So would any woman with sons. I was furious.'

'Yes, you were,' he laughed indulgently. 'I saw it in your eyes. It was why I said what I did.'

'Then I'm grateful. I was about to speak my mind, which would have been unforgivable. But you have more control than I. Will I ever learn to watch my tongue?'

'I hope not. Angry, you are a delight.' He reached to touch her cheeks fondly. 'If you hadn't been angry in Hyde Park, I should never have met you.'

'I suppose not.' Instantly her pique was gone. 'Darling, isn't it good that you are staying here until late tomorrow? I shall think only of that and try to forget that on Sunday you will be in London again.'

'Julia! London isn't the far end of the world when there are express trains and telephones.' He laid his arm around her shoulders, drawing her closer. 'And we shall write every day, even if we are so busy, sometimes, there might only be time to say I love you. We've come a long way, you and I. Who'd have thought I would be made so welcome? And only a week ago you worried in case we wouldn't be able to find a way to meet.'

'I did. But both Giles and Mother like you. I was so proud when she introduced you tonight. 'Doctor MacMalcolm – Julia's friend . . .' and she calls you Andrew now. I love her for calling you Andrew.'

'I love her, too. Will you grow like her, Julia? To please me, will you?'

'I don't know if I can. I don't think I can ever be as gentle as she is. I get angry; shout at life. I want votes for women and birth control and all the things Mother wouldn't even dream of saying out loud. And I shall never be as beautiful. And talking about Mother – she has decided you are to keep Pa's evening suit. It must have taken a lot of courage to see you wearing his things, so you won't go all stiff-necked and proud, will you, and refuse them?'

'I certainly will not. I'm most grateful to her. I could never have afforded such quality.'

'Well, you're to have the shirt, too, and the tie, it seems, though she'd never part with the shirt studs.'

'I wouldn't expect her to. It wouldn't be proper.'

'I agree entirely – so I shall buy you a set of your own. Oh, not diamond ones, be sure of that,' she laughed. 'But we are almost engaged, so it's all right for us to give each other presents. Will you let me do that, for your birthday? And will you tell me which date in August it is?'

'The last day. Another hour, I believe, and I'd have been a September child.'

'Very well. I shall buy a set and post them to you. And when you have gone, I shall sit here, and close my eyes, and will you close to me. And I shall plot and scheme so

I can visit Aunt Sutton very soon. You won't forget me, will you?'

'Not for a minute. I shall think of you, sitting here in the lamplight in your blue gown. Or shall I remember you in that silly skirt, when first we met?'

'Or on top of Holdenby Pike, with the wind blowing my hair all over the place?'

'So many memories already, darling girl. And we'll be married just as soon as I can support you. Does that suit you?'

'No, it does not. I'd marry you tomorrow if I could, and live with you in Little Britain, and wash your shirts and cook your meals – ' She stopped, eyes on her fingers.

'And?' he prompted.

'And sleep in your arms, because since we met I haven't been able to think of much else. Did you realize, love, you've proposed marriage to a shameless hussy?'

'I did. I think I'd been looking for her for a long time,' he whispered, his eyes making love to her, 'and never thought to find her. So will you give me your arm and take a turn around the garden with me, because I have a desperate need to kiss you?'

'Then kiss me!'

'Here? Illuminated in this glasshouse for all the world to see?'

'Andrew – there is no one out there – well, maybe only Hawthorn and Dwerryhouse.'

'Alice and her young man? Why do you say that?'

'Because,' she confided, her expression one of pure innocence, 'when dinner was over, I slipped up to Giles's room and let Morgan out. The poor creature needed a run and I thought that alone, he'd look for Dwerryhouse.'

'I see. And Tom would return him to the back door, and . . .?'

'And with luck,' Julia finished, laughing, 'Hawthorn will have been able to slip out for a few minutes. They've been so busy downstairs that she won't have seen him for ages. So are you going to kiss me, doctor?'

'I think perhaps I better had.' He rose to his feet, drawing her close. 'Do you know how much I love you, Julia Sutton?'

'I think I do,' she whispered, reaching on tiptoe for his lips. 'And, oh darling, hasn't this day been unbelievable? Everything about it has been almost unbearably beautiful – or would be, if only you'd kiss me.'

And never, ever stop, my love? Not ever?

11

Alice blinked open her eyes. There was no need for an alarm clock on mornings such as this; not with every bird in creation singing its heart out. Such a din from those tiny throats; such a singing and cuckooing that she could feel their joy, and share it.

She swung her feet to the floor, reaching for her red felt slippers, peering into the wall mirror. Her face, she decided with a breath of pleased surprise, looked altogether improved this morning. The swelling beneath her eye was gone and the bruising fading and, as for those vicious little scratches, give them a day or two more and they'd hardly be noticeable.

Turning her back on her reflection, she walked carefully to the washstand, with its china bowl and jug and matching soapdish. Here, she must always walk carefully when the sharp slope of the ceiling rendered half her attic room almost useless. But the room was hers alone, precious and private; a privilege, almost, when in some houses servants not only shared a room, but shared a bed, too.

Carefully she filled her washing bowl with water sharply cold, making a lather with the coal-tar soap Miss Clitherow insisted she use to help the healing of her face. Gently she soaped, rinsed, then returned to the mirror to pat dry her face. It would soon be back to normal. By the time her birthday came round, it would be completely healed.

Eighteen! Far more grown up than seventeen. Sweet seventeen, and never been kissed, boys teased. Well, she *had* been kissed, by Tom who loved her; by Thomas Dwerryhouse, who had asked her to marry him!

Her cheeks pinked just to think of him, and her eyes

shone. She smiled at Alice-in-the-mirror, then drew on her stockings and garters, bloomers and chemise. Then she brushed her hair briskly, combed and pinned it into a knot at her neck, and slithered into the long blue cotton dress she wore when working in the kitchen.

Blue did not become her, she decided, fastening the buttons at the neck; not when she had brown hair and brown eyes. Green was her colour, even though she almost always wore grey or black – servants mostly did – and white, starched pinafores like the one she was tying on now. And servants wore soft black boots, buttoned to the ankle; a uniform of servility, she supposed, except that at Rowangarth no one at all was made to feel servile.

Taking her washing bowl, she emptied it into the large slop-bucket that always stood on the landing. Oh, my goodness, it was almost full, which meant she was last up for two days running.

She hurried to the familiar closeness of the kitchen, where Tilda would be seeing to the fire and Bess setting the table for the servants' breakfast. And if she were lucky – and most mornings she was – there would be a pot of tea in the hearth, keeping warm beneath its bright knitted cosy. Come to think of it, she was lucky all round: to be at Rowangarth, to have Tom's love, to be forgetting already what happened three days ago in Brattocks Wood.

'Morning, Mrs Shaw; morning all.' Quietly she closed the kitchen door. 'Might I pour a sup of tea?'

'You might,' Cook nodded, noting that the lass's face seemed much healed and, because of it, deciding against asking her how she felt. The sooner they stopped dwelling on the matter, the sooner it would be over and done with.

Alice spooned sugar into the large breakfast cup, glad that, after today, when the dinner-party commotion had completely died down, she would return to the

203

sewing-room. She liked the light, bright, upstairs room at the back of the house, in which she answered to no one – save to Miss Clitherow, that was – and from which she was better able to slip out each afternoon.

'Can I help, Bess?' Alice rinsed her cup, wiping it dry. Bess almost always cooked servants' breakfast now. It was part of her training up from housemaid to cook. Soon she would take on the cooking of suppers and, in the full course of time, when Tilda had been raised to housemaid and a new kitchenmaid found, Bess would take over most of the cooking for below stairs. It would liberate Mrs Shaw, the housekeeper said, and in any case it was the natural progression of things; the way it was done. 'Shall I make the toast?'

'Would you, Alice, then I can see to the porridge. And there's Miss Clitherow's morning tray to take up, if you'd do that? I'm a bit pushed for time . . .'

Alice would, and did – nothing was too much trouble these days – and by the time she had carried up the tea tray and filled a dish with toasted bread and placed it on the rack above the fire to keep warm, Bess had caught up with herself. Servants' breakfast would be ready on time. It always was.

They stood, heads bowed, whispering *Amen* to Mrs Shaw's prayer. Then chairs scraped, and the first meal of the day began the moment Cook picked up her porridge spoon. No one spoke until Mrs Shaw did, for Cook regulated table talk, as befitted her position.

Tilda sprinkled sugar over her porridge, grateful for the silence. Because of it, she could allow her own private thoughts and not have to keep an ear open for table talk. She was glad the dinner party was over. Now there would be time again for her love books; to escape from mounds of vegetables into her secret world of happy-ever-after. And even though she wished fervently never to set eyes on another unpeeled potato until a week next

Tuesday, she had to admit that her very first dinner party had been better than she thought, if only because of leftovers, and especially because of the ice-cream they'd had to eat there and then. And the secret strawberries still made her close her eyes in ecstasy. Dinner parties, she was prepared to admit, weren't half so bad as she had feared.

'This porridge, Bessie, could do with a pinch more salt – otherwise it's very good,' Cook pronounced.

'Yes, Mrs Shaw. Thank you,' Bess murmured, the silence broken, 'and wait till I tell you about Lady Drayton's dress. Beautiful, wasn't it, Mary? Pale blue satin with a white lace overskirt and white camellias in her hair,' she sighed, though since that lady had left a shilling on the dressing-table – a shilling, mark you – everything about Lady Tessa Drayton appeared beautiful.

'And Mrs Mounteagle would be in her black velvet, with the red satin roses?' Cook remarked.

'She was, Mrs Shaw.'

'As usual,' Mary giggled. 'And Mrs Lane in her pale pink – *as usual*! She wore that old dress last time she came here to dinner, more'n three years ago; just before – well, you know . . . I remember it. You'd think they'd make the effort to wear something a bit different, wouldn't you?'

'That will do, Mary.' Mrs Shaw laid down her spoon, rounding her lips into a button of indignation. 'You did very well last night by all accounts – don't blot your copy-book. Mrs Mounteagle isn't known for being a stylish dresser, and if her ladyship don't mind about Mrs Lane's old dress, then I can't see it being any concern of yours. Mrs Lane is Lady Sutton's friend – her *good* friend – and the poor soul hasn't the means to dress as Lady Drayton does.'

Poor as a church mouse, in fact, but one who had sustained her ladyship and always been there when a

205

sympathetic ear was needed, or a shoulder to cry on. Mrs Shaw knew it to be true, and it excused much.

'People come here because they are her ladyship's friends – well mostly,' she amended, all at once remembering Pendenys. 'And pink suits Mrs Lane,' Cook added for good measure. And just to make sure the parlourmaid didn't get above herself on the strength of one dinner party, she murmured, 'And though you excelled yourself last night, Mary Strong, I'm sure you were glad that Ellen was there, and you had the good sense to learn as much as you could from her.'

'I did, Mrs Shaw, oh, I did. And I'm sorry. I shouldn't have said what I did, should I?'

'No, lass, you shouldn't, but we all make mistakes, which is only human. But best we don't make the same mistakes twice – is that clear?'

'It is, Mrs Shaw.' Suitably chastened, Mary made note never again to criticize her ladyship's true and dear friends within Cook's hearing; Mrs Clementina, maybe; Mrs Lane, *never*.

'And Miss Julia?' Cook picked up her spoon again, the matter closed. 'How did she seem?'

'I'm not quite sure what you mean, Mrs Shaw.' Mary was a quick learner; was not about to repeat her fall from grace.

'*Seem*, girl. Her and the doctor.'

'Miss Julia wore blue – but you'd know that, Mrs Shaw.'

'Hmm. You'd think, with them lovely hazel eyes of hers, she'd go more for brown or maybe green. But how did she *seem* . . .'

'We-e-ll, she didn't eat a lot, but I put that down to the fact that she was busy taking in every move the doctor made, every word he uttered. She's plainly in love.'

'Aah,' Cook sighed, relieved it had nothing to do with the food.

'And Judge Mounteagle – you should have heard him

206

going on about your savouries. Two he had, then he said, "Your cook, Helen, is an angel." '

'Well, now . . .' Mrs Shaw's cheeks flushed pink.

'It's my opinion he'd have taken another,' Mary rushed on, 'if Mrs Mounteagle hadn't glared at him.'

'There now . . .' Cook's delight was complete, Mary's sin atoned for. 'You can collect the plates, Tilda, and pass round the eggs. And since there's cream left over from last night, I think I might just find time to bake a tray of sweet scones for tea. We'll eat 'em with whipped cream and strawberry jam – now what do you all say to that!'

There were worse places to be than Rowangarth, thought Alice, as she sliced the top from her brown boiled egg. Far worse.

'Are we alone?' Andrew whispered hopefully.

'Completely. Mother never breakfasts after a late meal. She's having tea in her room. And Giles bicycled to the station and caught the early train to York. He's got to see the agent about work on the house.'

'Must he ask the agent about everything?'

'It's wise, if it involves money,' Julia frowned. 'And it's going to cost a lot, I believe, once they agree to make a start. Pa decided to have it done, but then it got laid aside, sort of. But it can't wait. Lamps and candles can be dangerous, though we've been lucky over the years and not had a fire. What has really helped him make up his mind, I suppose, is all the extra work it causes staff. And darling, we serve ourselves at breakfast.' She nodded to the side tables where pots of tea and coffee stood, and plates of hot rolls, muffins and toast. And beside them, kedgeree and eggs and bacon, kept warm in chafing dishes. Breakfast was an informal, relaxed meal for the Garth Suttons, taken at a leisurely pace at any time between eight and nine. 'If you need more tea, or anything warmed up, just ring, will you?'

'This is nice,' Andrew smiled. 'Just the two of us. Say you love me, then tell me about the work on the house.'

'I love you,' she whispered across the table, forming her lips into a kiss. 'Very much. And as for the house – well, we're to have electricity put in – didn't I tell you? – and up-to-date plumbing, and baths. There's gas lighting down in Holdenby, but it never got as far as Rowangarth. That's why we seem to have been stuck with candles and lamps. It'll be good, though, just to press a switch, and there'll be a lot of work saved, filling lamps and polishing lamp-glasses, and all that sort of thing. And no paraffiny smell.

'Aunt Sutton changed to electric lighting four years ago, and at Pendenys they've had electricity since the house was built. A bit of a nine-day wonder, Pa said it would be, at the time.'

'So there'll be bathrooms? Bathrooms will save a lot of work, too.'

'We're depending on it,' Julia smiled. 'And won't staff be pleased, not having to heat bath water and carry it upstairs?'

'And carry it downstairs again afterwards,' he reminded her.

'Exactly. It's going to cause a mess, laying pipes and wires under floorboards and all that sort of thing, but it'll be worth it. Giles wants it all finished by the autumn. To have the place in an upset in winter just doesn't bear thinking about.'

'But you'll be able, still, to get a few days in London?' He reached for her hand across the table and held it tightly. 'You won't have to stay here and help?'

'Goodness, no. I'd be more of a hindrance. Maybe, though, if the upset gets too much, I'll be able to get away and persuade Mother to come with me. She hasn't been able to go to the London shops these past three years; I think a trip to Aunt Sutton's would do her the world of good. Come to think of it, darling, I shall write to her suggesting it as soon as you're gone. Oh, dear – just eight more hours, then you'll have to go back to Harrogate.'

'I'm afraid so. Services to London aren't very good on Sundays. I must get the overnight train to get me back in good time. But this holiday has been unbelievable, darling. Now, when you write about this thing or that – when you say in your letters you've been walking on the Pike, or Hawthorn is out with Morgan in Brattocks Wood, I shall know exactly what it is like.'

'And the conservatory? Will you remember it was there you kissed me, lit up for all the world to see?'

'The conservatory, too,' he said softly. 'But will Giles be back before I leave? I'd like to thank him for not throwing me out, that day I called on your mother.'

'He wouldn't have done that; not Giles. He's in rare good humour these days. I think he's the only one of us looking forward to the workmen arriving. He's very clever, really. He knows about plumbing and understands about electricity, too. He should have gone to university when Nathan did, but with Robert in India it just wasn't possible.'

'You care for Nathan, don't you?' Andrew murmured, eyebrow raised. 'I can tell by the way you speak of him.'

'Yes, and so does Giles. Nathan is fair, like we Garth Suttons. Elliot and Albert are dark, like – well, like their great-grandmother Pendennis, I suppose. And Nathan's nature is sunny, whilst Albert and Elliot are inclined to moods.'

'And would you have married Nathan?' he asked her from the side table, concentrating on forking bacon on to his plate. 'If we hadn't met, I mean?'

'I don't know. I think perhaps some might have expected us to – let me help you, darling?' She pushed back her chair and went to his side. 'But marry Nathan – I don't think so. I'd have known long ago, wouldn't I, if he'd been the right one? We grew up together, he and I. We know each other too well ever to be lovers. I could tell him my most secret of secrets, but I didn't once see him as a husband.'

'Good,' he murmured, as she filled up his plate.

'You're jealous, Andrew! Your eyes have gone from grey to green! Darling, I *do* love you, so don't worry about Nathan and me. Can you imagine me as a parson's wife – because that's what he'll be. And I've just had the most wonderful thought! Wouldn't it be splendid, once he's a priest, if Nathan were to marry us? He'd do it so beautifully and with such sincerity. Yes! When he comes home, I shall tell him to hurry into the Church so that he can marry us as soon as maybe!'

'Julia Sutton . . .' He shook his head in bewilderment. 'Do you know that before I met you, my life was uncomplicated and serene? I knew exactly what I was doing, where I intended going. But now I'm in a whirl, and all because of you. I find myself thinking about you when I should be thinking of other things, and when you aren't near me, I have to stop what I'm doing and close my eyes, so I can hear your voice. I think, perhaps, that your cousin *had* better hurry into holy orders . . .'

'So no more dark thoughts about Nathan and me?' Julia regarded him, chin on hand, across the table, her eyes dark with need. 'I care for him dearly, but it's you I love, you I want. And can we hurry outside and find a place where no one will disturb us? I want to spend every minute with you until your train leaves. I want to touch you and kiss you.'

'Mm. Brattocks?'

'Or the far side of Holdenby Pike. Or better still, let's run away like Albert and his rich lady. Did I tell you about cousin Albert who married a lady fifteen years older, and went off to St Petersburg? Now they've settled in America, I believe, but we can't know if it's true or not unless Uncle Edward sneaks over to see us, that is. And I

210

don't think he'll do that just yet.' She wrinkled her nose impishly. 'Not until things calm down a bit at Pendenys. Oh dear – such skeletons in the Sutton cupboard!'

'You are perfect, Julia,' he smiled, 'skeletons and all. And unless Lady Helen has other plans, I think the far side of the Pike sounds the ideal place to be.'

When the spaniel bounded towards him, whimpering with delight, Tom knew that Alice should not be far behind. He had done the woodland rounds that afternoon, yet she had not come, and it made him wonder if she were afraid, still, of venturing too far alone into the whispering deeps of Brattocks Wood. Come to think of it, he'd spent too much time hanging around Brattocks in case she came, and all the fault of Elliot Sutton! Lord alone knew what damage the man might have done, in spite of the front the lass was putting on it. Did she still think that all men turned into beasts when the mood was on them – because they didn't, not by a long chalk. Mind, you couldn't blame any man for trying – Tom was nothing if not fair-minded – it was all part of the game, though it was accepted, right from the start, that it was a lady's privilege to say no – and be respected for it.

Then why did young Sutton take it for granted that along with money and position came the God-given right to do exactly as he pleased, ignore the unwritten rules? A woman who said no to him was a challenge, and he always got her in the end. Or so he'd thought till now; till he had realized Alice was not for any man's fancying. Where Alice was concerned, Elliot Sutton would be in for real trouble if he tried it again!

Tom stopped suddenly, pulling in his breath, listening. Wasn't that a blackbird flying disturbed from the bushes ahead, giving its indignant *clock-clock* of alarm? She was coming.

'Alice?' He whistled softly.

She came to him running, smiling. He held wide his arms and she went into them eagerly, hugging him close, lifting her face for his kiss.

'Where on earth have you been, lass? It's been two days . . .'

His mouth took hers and the eagerness with which she kissed him back told him his fears were without substance. Holding her a little way from him, he smiled into her eyes.

'Let me look at you. Soon be better, that face of yours . . .'

'That's just what Tilda said. And I'm sorry I couldn't slip out when you brought Morgan back last night. I was helping Miss Clitherow wrap up the best silver and lock it away, and I didn't know you'd been till it was too late.

'And this afternoon Miss Julia and the doctor took Morgan with them to the top of the Pike, and I couldn't begrudge them that. It was their last time together for goodness knows how long. He went back on the half-past five train, and she's ever so sad now, poor love.'

'So would I be, if you'd gone off to London. I'd miss you something cruel. I was getting a bit worried when you were late coming – thought you still might be feared on your own. But you needn't be, if what I heard is true.'

They began to walk, arms linked, to where the fallen beech tree lay. Soon it would be cut into logs for the needy in the village, but until then it had become their sitting-place. 'Got a bit of news for you. Only tittle-tattle, mind, from Will Stubbs. He'd gone to the smithy with one of the horses, and the groom from Pendenys happened to be there an' all, getting Mr Edward's hunter shod. It was him told Will.'

'Tom! Surely you know not to take overmuch notice of William? Everyone knows he's a gossip.'

'He's always got a tale to tell, I grant you – but this time I'm inclined to believe what he said.' Tom sat down, taking a red-and-white handkerchief from his pocket, arranging it for her to sit on. 'What he says rings true, somehow. Seems that Elliot Sutton is going to America, to Kentucky, to his brother's place. It came from the Pendenys valet, who'd been told to pack for Mr Elliot – *for a long stay*. An' what's more, the van from the railway has been ordered to collect the trunks.'

'Going away?' Relief wrapped Alice round. 'Soon?'

'Sailing to New York, I believe, on one of the new liners. It's nothing but the best for that one, though with a bit of luck he'll be seasick all the way over.'

'Not him! The wind daren't blow on him; his mother would see to that. I'm glad he's going, though – if it's true, that is.'

'It'll be true. Even William couldn't make up a story like that. It'd suit me if he never came back. I did hear that Mr Edward is going round with a face like thunder, which makes it all add up. Reuben said the Suttons – the *real* Suttons as Mr Edward is – are most times slow to anger, but when they do get annoyed, folk can look out.'

'Mm.' Alice could well believe it, and so, if she rightly recalled, had those London policemen, whose shins another Sutton had kicked. Miss Julia had turned into a little fury that night, with her skirt pulled up to the most unladylike height. 'I feel sorry for Mrs Clementina, though. She does so dote on that eldest of hers. She'll be grieved he's going away.'

'Being *sent*, more like. I'd have shipped him off to the North Pole, if it'd been left to me.'

'I don't care where he goes as long as it's far enough from here.' All at once she shivered and reached for Tom's hand. 'But don't talk about him.'

'Aye. Let's talk about us.' He laid a protective arm around her shoulders, drawing her closer. 'Let's talk about what Reuben told me this morning.

'You'll know he'll be seventy soon – well, that's when

213

he intends retiring. It's official. That's why the end almshouse hasn't been let again. It's on Mr Giles's orders; to be kept for Reuben. Which means that Keeper's Cottage is going to come vacant before so very much longer, and Reuben says it's almost certain it'll be mine – ours.'

'You think so, Tom? Oh, my goodness!'

'That's what Reuben says – so long as I keep out of trouble.'

'And don't go hitting your betters.'

'*Betters*?'

'Happen not. But don't lose your temper again. He isn't worth it,' she urged, eyes anxious.

'I won't – as long as he leaves you alone. But we've got better things to talk about – like me, going to York to be measured for my suit. I'm to go to the man in Stonegate.' To the tailor who always made the suits that were part of Rowangarth keepers' wages: one suit a year in good tweed, and brown boots and leggings for special occasions like shoots and game fairs, when it was politic to do Rowangarth proud.

'Then if you're to have a suit, it means they're satisfied with your work. They must be keeping you on, and we *will* get Reuben's house when he leaves it.'

'Seems we will. I'm to go on Monday morning and, with luck, there'll be time for the shops. What would you say if I looked at wedding rings, love?'

'If it's a ring for me, then I'd say I was glad. But don't buy one yet, Tom?' Buying a ring when they couldn't get married for perhaps three years was tempting Fate.

'I won't, but I want to get an idea of how much I'll have to save, and I want to do a bit of shopping anyway. And will I tell you something else, since good news always comes in threes? That new suit I'm to have is going to do me nicely for my sister's wedding. I had a letter from her yesterday. Reuben's certain I'll be able to have the day off. Next month, it's to be, and I can get there and back in a day. Marrying a farmer's son – done well for herself. They're having the wedding tea at the farmhouse; it'll be a grand affair. My sister Ruth, I'm talking about.'

'Is she pretty, Tom?'

'Reckon she is, since you ask. And then there's Maggie, who's a year younger. She'll be standing bridesmaid for her.'

'Wish I had a family, Tom.' Not that she was complaining. She had Rowangarth and Reuben and now Tom. And one day, Tom would be her real family. 'Close, I mean.'

'Aye, an' talking of close, there's another thing. You know what weddings are like? They're going to be pulling my leg, asking me when it's going to be my turn. So what am I to say, Alice? Will I tell them that you and me are walking out serious? My brother Jack is wed already, so shall I tell them that you and me will soon –'

'Be affianced, Tom,' she confirmed, gravely.

'Affianced – yes.' He liked the word. There was a ring of stability about it. 'And will I ask Mam to write to you, since it's settled? Would you like that, lass – to be family, official like?'

'I'd like it very much. Oh, my dear . . .' Happiness took her, wrapped her round like a soft, warm cloak; tears of pure joy misted her eyes. 'Am I too happy? Is something going to happen to spoil it?'

'Why should it?' He brushed her cheek with gentle lips. 'I won't let it.'

Nor would he. She would be safe with Tom. All her life he would care for her. They had such love between them, it would last for ever. But it was all too much, this sudden, singing delight inside her. She must share it, tell it to the rooks – ask them to keep her love safe.

'I'll have to go soon. Kiss me, will you, then walk me to the stile?'

'If you'll tell me you've forgotten what happened,' he said softly, 'and promise me it won't make any difference to you and me?'

'It won't. It can't. I promise you it's behind me.'

She closed her eyes, lifting her face to his. It was forgotten completely. Wherever he was tonight, whatever he was doing, she could almost find it within her to feel compassion for Elliot Sutton; pity that his sort could never know such joy as she and Tom.

Her pity was wasted, could she have known it. Elliot Sutton lay on his bed, eyes fixed unblinking on the ceiling, his mood black. He was being sent away in disgrace; punished like a child caught with its fingers in the honeypot. Didn't they know that all was fair in love and war? And hadn't the girl asked for it, wandering alone in the woods?

He drew deeply on his cigarette, flicking ash to the floor. Already the servants were sniggering behind his back, and all Holdenby gossiping about it, he shouldn't wonder. And it would be alehouse talk in Creesby before so very much longer. It was degrading and humiliating, and the fault of a servant and an under-keeper who'd forgotten his place. It shouldn't be allowed, he seethed, shifting his gaze to the cases, hatboxes and trunks that crowded his room. But Garth servants thought they were a cut above the rest – always had done; imagined that because they were pandered to by his aunt, any one of them could defy Elliot Sutton.

He pulled in his breath sharply. A pity this wasn't Russia. It could never have happened there. In Russia, the keeper would have been flogged and the girl only too glad to accommodate her betters.

Damn her, with her big brown eyes and provocative nose. It wasn't as if he'd particularly wanted her. That night in Brattocks when he'd been a little the worse for whisky, any female could have satisfied the lust inside him.

He rose to his feet, stretching slowly, walking to the dressing-table. Arms folded, he gazed long and dispassionately into the mirror upon it.

He was handsome – far better to look at than either of his brothers. Even allowing for the mess his eye was in, there was still no denying it. And by the time, he considered, he had crossed the Atlantic and arrived at his brother's estate, his looks would be completely restored.

He smiled, satisfied, at his reflection. Truth known, he didn't mind going to America: it was being ordered there that stuck in his craw. Come to think of it, Kentucky could well be virgin territory, in a manner of speaking. And as for the servant – wouldn't she still be there when he returned?

Oh, she'd fought him off like a wildcat, but her sort were like that, saying no when they meant yes. That she had gone through the motions, scratching and struggling, had only added to his excitement. But come another day, another opportunity, and it might well be different. He always got what he wanted, and he would have her – and her wide-eyed innocence – in the end.

'Hawthorn! Will you *look*!' Julia flung open the sewing-room door, a morning paper in her hand. 'Go on – *read it*!'

Alice felt shame she had been going to say she was about to go down for breakfast; that Mrs Shaw didn't hold with lateness and couldn't it wait? But she had not said it because Julia Sutton's face was drained of colour, and her eyes, dark with pain, had warned her into silence.

'Look at it!' A finger jabbed at the picture of a woman.

The newspaper was dated June 13th, though Alice saw the inch-high headlines first; gazed at them, frowning, for several seconds before they made any kind of sense:

217

SUFFRAGETTE THROWS HERSELF AT KING'S HORSE.

Then her eyes were drawn to the picture of a slim woman with high cheekbones, her hair rolled back from her face; a woman in the cap and gown of an academic.

Emily Wilding Davison, the caption proclaimed, but even before she had read it, Alice already knew.

'The lady selling papers that night! It's her!'

'And she's very seriously hurt,' Julia whispered. 'Even now, she might even be –'

'*Dead?*' Not the suffragette who had stood at the park gates, eyes watchful? 'Oh, I know women should have their say about things, but did she have to risk her life for it?'

'Risk? I think she might already have lost it. That's how much she believed; how important it was to her. She was there that night I got hurt – when I met Andrew. In a round-about way, she was the start of it. It's because of her, you could say, that I'm so happy, yet now –' Tears filled her eyes and she dashed them impatiently away. 'It happened yesterday, Hawthorn, at the races. It was the Derby; she ran across the course and threw herself at the King's horse. Imagine it – so brave . . .'

'She shouldn't have done it.' Alice closed her ears against the fearful sound of charging, thundering hooves. No one should die like that. Not for all the votes in England. 'It wasn't worth it.'

'She thought it was. It was her choice. I don't think I'd have done it, though. Something like that needs a special kind of courage. But I'm on her side, Hawthorn. From now on, I shall speak my mind. Women should have rights and I'm going to say so, every time I get the chance. I feel so angry and – and *proud*, that I'd go and join the suffragettes this minute if I could – and Andrew would agree with me, too!'

218

'Yes, miss.' Happen he would an' all, so it was maybe as well she would have to go to Liverpool to do it, or Glasgow, or London. 'But next time you go to stay with Miss Sutton, you won't – well, you wouldn't do anything without thinking on, would you?'

'I'd talk to Andrew first. And I'd never knowingly cause my mother to worry. But, from today, I won't stand by. Why, will you tell me, can't we be given the chance to prove we aren't stupid? Do you realize that a woman can be a doctor now, can hold the power of life over death by her learning and skill; but still she may not vote!'

'So we'll keep hoping for a miracle.' Alice mourned, because all at once – even though she didn't know what she would do with it if ever she got one – she was in full agreement with every word Miss Julia said. A woman *should* have a vote! 'Well, they do say that hope is akin to prayer.'

'Hope? It's action we need – like yesterday – as well as one of your miracles, though miracles never happen, do they? But we'll pray for Emily Davison, won't we?' She said it, even though she knew inside that already it was too late.

'We will, though I'll not say anything downstairs at breakfast, miss, if it's all right with you. Cook don't hold with suffragettes, so I'd be obliged if you wouldn't let on that I know. And they'll hear it for themselves,' she sighed, 'afore so very much longer.'

'Not if you don't want me to. Cook is entitled to her opinions. But isn't it a sobering thought – you and me so happy and wrapped up in ourselves, I mean. Are we too happy, Hawthorn? Is there a price to pay for everything in this life?'

Alice hoped not. And she would pray for the poor lady, and that what she had done would make folk think on about things.

She closed her eyes tightly, all at once apprehensive. What price happiness then – hers and Tom's?

'I'll remember her tonight,' she said. 'I promise.'

Her birthday! Born one year exactly before the old Queen's Diamond Jubilee on the 20th of June; a very special date on which to be born.

Alice almost sang with happiness as she crossed the drying-green and made for the tree-scattered wild garden that stood between the lawns and Brattocks Wood.

Such a day it had been, with a kindly smile from Miss Clitherow when she had taken up her morning tea tray – and that lady didn't smile very often – and a posy of flowers beside her plate at breakfast time. A card, too, rose-covered and lace-edged, proclaiming *Happy Birthday, Alice*, and signed *Mrs M. Shaw, Mary Strong, Elizabeth Thompson, Matilda Tewk*.

'And these are from us all.' Tilda had blushed pink with pleasure. 'Damask rose and sweet violet – go on, smell them,' she urged, taking the prettily wrapped soap from her apron pocket.

'And for a special treat, I shall bake buns for tea,' Cook beamed. 'Iced, and a cherry on top.'

All at once, Alice felt near to tears, reminding them sniffily that they couldn't call her sweet seventeen any more.

And as if that hadn't been enough, Miss Julia had tapped on the sewing-room door – a thing she rarely did, since most times her entrances were touched with drama.

'Happy birthday, dear girl,' she had smiled, taking a ribbon-tied packet from behind her back. 'This is for you because you've been so good to me and put up with my ways and – oh, open it, do!'

Alice had not expected anything quite so beautiful, so elegant. Pale pink and in silk; three roses, smelling as if, Alice thought, Miss Julia had touched their petals with

220

the real scent of roses from the bottle on her dressing-table.

'For your Sunday hat, Hawthorn, and the little bud is to wear on the lapel of your jacket.'

'They're the most beautiful things I ever did own.' Flowers fit for a wedding hat, that's what, and she must never, ever let it rain on them. 'What can I say, Miss Julia?'

'I don't want you to say anything. I just want you to like them because – well – do you remember when Andrew wrote that he was coming to Harrogate and I was desperate to get away to meet him? And Mother said you couldn't be spared to go with me because of the dinner party. So I told her I didn't want anyone with me, especially you, because I wanted to buy something for your birthday.' She stopped, taking a deep breath, remembering how it had been.

'And I *did* mean to buy your roses, Hawthorn, I really did – though all I could think about was being with Andrew. But it turned out better than I'd ever hoped, and I was so happy when I bought them for you, and you'll always remember that, won't you? Always remember I was so bursting with joy that day, I could have bought the whole shopful for you!'

'Mm.' Her *happy* roses. Alice nodded. 'They'll remind me how everything turned out so well for you and the doctor and they'll remind me of London and the grand time we had: you hurting your head and Doctor Andrew telling people to stand back so he could see to you. And –' She stopped, her eyes suddenly sad. 'Emily Davison won't wear her Sunday-best hat ever again, will she?'

'No, but you and I will always think kindly of her. And one day, when they give us the vote, you must wear your happy hat and think, when you mark your cross, that once we met her.

'And by the way – I've warned Giles,' she had whispered

from the doorway, 'that he's to let you take Morgan out this afternoon and this evening, too – so don't forget . . .'

There would never, Alice had sighed as she sewed a mother-of-pearl button on Giles Sutton's shirt, be such a day as this. She was so fortunate, so loved, she would remember it for the rest of her life. And this afternoon, after servants' tea, she would meet Tom and he'd give her a special birthday kiss. Just to think of it had been almost too much to bear.

'Hullo, lass.' Alice was brought back from her remembering. 'Thought I'd missed you.'

Reuben, waiting at his garden gate, beckoning her with his finger, inviting her into his kitchen. 'I know you're off to meet Tom so I'll not keep you – but I mind what day this is.'

He bent to kiss her cheek and she was reminded of the day he'd visited Aunt Bella's house so long ago. He had kissed her then and his moustache had tickled her cheek. Dear Reuben, who had spoken for her at Rowangarth. That had been the start, though he couldn't have known it then, of such happiness for her.

'Thank you, Reuben, for all you've done for me.' She reached up, locking her arms around his neck, kissing him back, hugging him to her. 'It was a lucky day when you asked Miss Clitherow –' She stopped, remembering the woman who had reared her. 'I shall write to Aunt Bella and tell her I'm doing well – and courting,' she added. 'I sent a letter on my last birthday, but there was no reply. I'll write again, though.' Not with love, or even affection, but from duty and politeness and because, to be fair, Aunt Bella *had* saved her from the workhouse.

'I wouldn't worry. She's not a letter-writer. When I came to collect you that day you came here, she as good as told me that she'd done what conscience required of her and from then on she considered you were off her hands. Gave you over to me, she did. And I was glad of it, an' all,' he hastened to add, so she shouldn't feel unwanted, 'for I had no one close to call my own.

'But that's what I want to talk to you about, lass. You're old enough now.' He opened a drawer, taking out a black tin cashbox. 'There's something I've been keeping for you these last five years. Bella gave it to me. Said you were to have it when you'd got sense enough to take care of it. I think it's time,' he said gently, handing her an envelope 'to give it to you.'

'Reuben?' Cheeks flushed, she looked inside. What she had expected, she didn't rightly know. A letter, perhaps, from her past; a lock of hair, a photograph?

It was a ring in heavy gold, a wedding ring; and she laid it on her palm, eyes questioning.

'Your mam's,' he said softly. 'All else that was left, Bella sold to help feed you. But the ring she kept for you, so she wasn't altogether bad. Look after it, lass, and when the time comes, wear it for your mam, eh?'

She tried hard not to, for didn't folk say, 'Weep on your birthday, weep all year'? But though she blinked hard and squeezed her eyes tight shut, a tear still escaped.

'I'm sorry,' she choked, as he dabbed awkwardly at her cheeks with his handkerchief. 'Only I'm so happy, you see.'

'And so a bonny lass of eighteen should be, so wrap it up and put it safe in your pocket. And happen you'd better write to that Bella woman and let her know you appreciate what she did.' The one good thing she'd done, Reuben amended, silently. 'Likely she'll not write back, but it'll be appreciated, I shouldn't wonder.

'Now there's one thing more I want to ask you. Tonight, if you happen to be this way along, will you bring Tom in? I'd like a word with the both of you – and don't ask me what, for I shan't tell you.' He nodded, mysteriously. 'I'll have the kettle on about eight, so think on.'

'I will, Reuben. We'll come . . .'

She smiled shakily, closing her fingers round the envelope in her pocket, stopping beside the stile to let Morgan run free. Tom had been to the tailor in York yesterday; had met her last night with eyes that teased – as if he knew a secret she did not. Tom, her young man – her fiancé, she should be calling him now. Tom, who loved her and cared for her and had defended her good name.

She smiled tremulously, for only that morning Bess had confirmed what Tom had told her about Elliot Sutton.

'It's fact,' Bess insisted. 'Came from the chauffeur from Pendenys. He's to drive Elliot Sutton to Liverpool in the motor. The ship leaves on the evening tide, so they're having to leave good and early. The *Mauretania*, he said it was.'

So it *was* true, and by now, Alice calculated, he should be well on his way and the other side of the Pennines; almost at the dockside. And by the time he came back, she hoped Mrs Clementina would have made her peace with her ladyship and all the unpleasantness would be forgotten. But wasn't this her birthday, and shouldn't she be thinking of anyone but Elliot Sutton?

'Tom, love!' She looked up from her brooding to see him standing there. Their kiss was special and urgent, and made her ask herself yet again how it was possible for two people to be so in love.

'Happy birthday, sweetheart.' He took her hand, tucking her arm in his. 'Let's sit down at the tree. I've got something in my pocket I hope you're going to like.'

'And I've got something in mine to show you an' all,' she laughed, her cheeks pink with the excitement of it. 'But yours first, Tom.'

'Right, bonny lass.' He held up his first and second fingers, then dipped them into his pocket, slowly, like a conjuror performing a trick. 'Here you are. This is for my birthday girl.' A small, square, red box lay on his upturned hand, 'For her to wear, always, with my love.'

It was a locket and chain; oval, with the front worked with leaves and minute flowers.

'Tom! It's – oh, it's . . .'

'Open it. Push your fingernail into that little groove.' He smiled with pleasure at her delight. 'Your fingers are daintier than mine.'

There was a picture inside the locket of a small boy looking uncertainly into the camera, his forehead wrinkled, one eyebrow raised expectantly.

'Me,' he said. 'When I was ten, on the Sunday School outing. Haven't had one taken since, so it'll have to do for the time being.'

'It's beautiful.' Beautiful and precious, and she would wear it next to her heart always. And when he wasn't with her, she need only touch it to bring him close.

'Shall I fasten it on for you?'

'Please, Tom.'

She turned, lowering her head, holding aside her hair. The nape of her neck was soft and slender. He brushed it possessively with his lips to send so exquisite a feeling flaming through her that she had to snatch in her breath and close her eyes tightly against it.

'What will you put in the other half – a photo of you, will it be? You and me in a locket, together?'

'*Me?* Oh, my goodness.' How could she have lived out eighteen years and never once had her picture taken? 'Tom, I don't have one,' she blushed, embarrassed.

'Then no matter. The day we get wed we'll have ourselves taken in all our finery. And not to worry, love. Between us we'll think of something afore so much longer.'

'I've thought of it already, and it's better than a photo.' She snuggled closer, resting her head on his shoulder. 'Do you remember the time you gave me those flowers?'

225

'Aye – buttercups. You wanted orchids, but –'

'No, Tom. I'd been telling you about her ladyship wearing her own special orchids, but I didn't want one. Flowers like that aren't for sewing-maids. That night, you said I was a buttercup girl; you picked some for me. I pressed some in my Bible, to keep them safe and special. So it's a buttercup I shall wear in my locket, to remind me of the night you said you loved me, and I promised to be your girl . . .'

'My *buttercup* girl,' he whispered, raising her hand, kissing it gently. 'Now, are you going to tell me what's in your pocket?'

'I am, Tom.' She placed the ring on his upturned palm, smiling at his puzzlement.

'Where did you get this, Alice?'

'From Reuben. It was my mother's. Aunt Bella saved it for me – gave it to Reuben to keep for me till I was old enough. Reckon he thinks I am, now . . .'

'Or happen he thinks you might be in need of it one day. Shall you be wed with it?'

'I'd like to be, if you don't mind? Something old, don't they say?'

'Then I think you should keep it somewhere safe till the day comes. It's a far better ring than I could have given you, sweetheart.'

'That's settled, then.' She made to return it to her pocket, but he told her no, that he had a better idea.

'Slip it on your chain; wear it with your locket. It'll be safe there. Here – let me . . .'

He unfastened the chain, slipping the end through the ring.

'There now; all safe and sound. So what else have you to tell me?' he asked, softly.

'That I love you, Tom Dwerryhouse, and that Reuben expects us at Keeper's tonight, at eight.'

'Did he tell you why?' he frowned.

'No. But I said we'd go. He's an old man, Tom, and alone. We can spare him a few minutes.'

'Of course we can, though happen he's forgotten he told me about retiring.'

'Happen. But forgetting is the privilege of the old, now isn't it? And he'll not forget to have the kettle on, so tonight I'll try to slip out a little earlier. Now, what were we talking about?'

'That you love me.' He kissed the tip of her nose. 'And that I love you and we'll be wed as soon as maybe.'

'Just as soon,' she whispered, tilting her chin so their lips were only the distance of a kiss away. 'And sooner than that, if we're lucky.'

'We'll be lucky, I know it. See you at eight, then, at Reuben's gate?'

'At eight. And I'll have to go . . .'

No one below stairs begrudged her these few minutes with Tom; best she shouldn't take advantage of their good nature.

Four hours to go, he thought as she walked away from him. Time to finish the rounds, check the traps, then see to the feed in the rearing field. Then a wash and shave, and into his new tweed suit in honour of her birthday.

His eyes didn't leave her until she was over the stile and out of his sight, Morgan at her heels. He felt less wary, now, knowing Elliot Sutton had gone; that every hour took him further away from them.

Take care, sweetheart . . .

'You'll be wondering why I've asked you both here,' said Reuben as they settled themselves at his fireside.

'I'll admit I'm curious,' Tom acknowledged, 'though if it's about my intentions, then best I should tell you they are –'

'Gentlemanly, I hope – if it's Alice you're talking about,' Reuben admonished.

'They are, and it is. And you might as well know that we plan to wed when the time is right.'

'Then that, in a round-about sort of way, is why I asked you to come,' he nodded. 'And take your eyes off that door, lass. The dog's all right on his own. Knows his place, since Tom took him in hand.'

Tom smiled, accepting the compliment. You couldn't blame an animal for anything, he always maintained. To his way of thinking, there was no such thing as a bad dog – only a bad owner. And since Mr Giles had taken it upon himself to spoil the animal and overfeed him into the bargain, Tom thought it no less than his duty to teach the creature a bit of obedience and a few good manners.

'So why are we here, Reuben?'

'Because there's something I've got to show you.' He rose to his feet, pushing the iron kettle further into the coals, then beckoned them to the staircase.

'There now.' He opened the door at the head of the stairs, nodding to his left. 'What do you think to that?'

It was a tallboy, six drawers high, set against the wall.

'It's beautiful, Reuben. Solid mahogany, too.' You didn't work for the gentry and not know good wood when you saw it, and Alice longed to take a moist leather to it, wipe away the neglect of years, then wax and polish it back to beauty. 'Would you like me to give it a bit of a clean-up for you?'

'Nay, lass, it'll do well enough as it is. Took me and the wife – God rest her – the best part of a morning to get the dratted thing up here, so I'll not be chewed up getting it down again.

'You'll know I'll be away, a year come August. It's all settled now. Well, the bedroom ceiling in that little almshouse is too low by far for that great thing, so I aim to leave it behind me when I go.

'It's yours, Alice. When you're wed and come to live

228

here, it'll take care of your drawer space. A wedding present to you both, it'll be. Just thought I'd tell you.'

'Oh, Reuben . . .' She ran her hand over the silky surfaces. She liked wood. Touching it made her feel she was embracing all nature; hundreds and hundreds of years of growing. She turned, arms outstretched, placing her cheek on his. 'What am I to say? It's so fine. I'm not going to tell you you shouldn't do it, because I'd be out of my senses not to want it. I'll treasure it, always. And I'm glad,' she added shyly, 'that Aunt Bella gave me into your keeping.'

She blinked away a tear. Come to think of it, this day had been punctuated with happy tears, and she would remember it for the rest of her life. Didn't she have a ring to be married with, a house to live in, and a fine tallboy into the bargain? And best of all, in a year come August, they could start making their plans.

'Oh my word,' she sniffed, when they were alone. 'I'm so glad I'm Alice Hawthorn. I wouldn't want to change my life with anyone. There's such joy inside me, I can't begin to tell you how much. Nothing's going to change, is it, Tom?'

'Of course it isn't, lass.' He took her hand in his own, smiling tenderly. 'Just give me one good reason why it should?'

And for the life of her, Alice could not.

12

July came in on a dance of heat, trailing a blaze of colour like an exotic skirt. In fields and lanes grew blue forget-me-nots, their colour stolen from the sky; pink bindweed, bright yellow trefoil and honey-scented meadowsweet. The buttercups had flowered golden and were gone until another year, Alice sighed fondly, but now the hedgerows were a tumble of wild white roses and bryony and honeysuckle and, in Brattocks Wood, tiny spotted orchids grew in the shelter of tall foxgloves. It was beautiful; the whole world was beautiful as she and Tilda carried jugs of water and cold tea and thick beef sandwiches to those who worked in the hayfield in the shimmering heat of a high sun.

They walked down the avenue of linden trees, glad of the cool, shifting shade thrown down by branches thick with blossom.

Tom was working in the hayfield; William too. Anyone who could be spared worked steadily with sickles and scythes, cutting the tall, herby grass. It was important, said the gaffer who came each year to oversee the hay-making, that the fields be cut, turned thrice daily until the grass was dry as old bones, and carted away and stacked before St Swithin's day. He took no chances with the weather. The crop must be gathered, he declared every year alike, before the fifteenth day of the month.

The hay was important to Rowangarth, which had not changed to motors but still kept two carriage horses and a pony to pull the little governess cart. In winter, when the grazing was scant, a barn filled with hay was worth much, William declared.

'There'll be a sup of ale this afternoon,' Alice confided to Tom who worked, stripped to the waist, his back shiny with sweat. She had never seen him this naked, and the sight pleased her. Her man was shapely with muscle; had not a pick of fat on the whole of his body – or not on that much of his body she could see, she amended silently. 'Miss Clitherow ordered it, and me and Tilda are to bring it about two . . .'

'Then see that it's good and cold,' Tom smiled, sinking to the ground, taking sandwiches from the basket lined with paper and topped with a white starched cloth.

'The barrel's in the cellar, so it will be, and Reuben said I was to tell you to go straight back to the bothy when you're finished here. He'll do the rounds, he said, and see to the feeding in the rearing field.'

'Aye – we'll be working while the light lasts, so I'll have a mind for my bed, nothing's so certain.'

'Then I won't expect you tonight, Tom.' That much was understood.

'No, sweetheart. And if you take the dog out, stick to the lane and the cow pasture?' He didn't want her walking alone in Brattocks, even though it was safe now, with *him* gone. 'And I'll see you later on, won't I?'

'When we bring the ale,' she smiled fondly. And the haymaking would soon be finished – Tom's part in it, that was, for once it was cut the worst was done with until stacking time. 'We'll have to go now.' Best not to linger. Cook did not allow servants' dinner to be upset, not even for haymaking.

She formed her lips into the shape of a kiss, then picked up the basket.

'You're going to wed Tom Dwerryhouse, aren't you?' Tilda demanded as they walked back. 'That's what folk are saying, any road.'

'Then for once, folk have got it right,' Alice laughed, 'though when it'll be, I can't tell you.' It was best to say nothing about Keeper's Cottage. 'But when the day comes, I shall want you to come to the wedding, Tilda. Rowangarth is all the family I've got, 'cept Reuben, that is. If we want to get wed before I'm of age, it'll be Reuben I'll have to ask. Tom's going home soon, for his sister's wedding,' she confided, 'and he's to tell his family about us; make it official like.'

'Hmm,' Tilda sighed, wondering whether it might be politic to cast her favours to the winds and see what blew back, or whether to wait for her dream lover; one of those about which she read so avidly. But she wouldn't be sixteen for another month, so there was no call yet to leave the comfort of Rowangarth. Hitherto, her entire experience of wedded bliss amounted to an overcrowded cottage, an overworked mother almost always expecting, and a father she rarely saw save at Sunday dinnertime, so busy was he taking on extra work to help keep his brood, or digging his garden to help feed them. So for the time being, Tilda was content to allow the natural progression of things to take its course. One day she would be raised to housemaid, then taught to cook, and once she was skilled in all aspects of running a home – she being properly taught in a gentleman's house – there would be many a young farmer in need of such a wife. And until then, she was well content with her dreams and fantasies. 'Hurry up, do, Alice. I'm hungry.'

Nathan Sutton came down from college to be met at the station by the Rolls-Royce, it being the largest of the three motors, and better able to carry all the paraphernalia of a three-year stay at Cambridge.

'The master says to tell you they're sorry they aren't here to meet you,' the butler said, immediately upon opening the door. 'Business in London, Mr Nathan, and them not knowing exactly when you'd be arriving. They'll be back at eight tonight, I'm given to understand.'

'That's all right.' He was home now, and when he'd got used to the quietness of everything, and ridden his hunter to the top of Holdenby Pike, or walked the entire boundary of Pendenys land, he could begin to think about his future; maybe even discuss it with his father.

Nathan felt completely at home in the countryside around Pendenys, though never in Pendenys itself; a house that echoed and whispered and watched. The house was a joke, really: a pile of slate and stone trying to be a home and failing dismally. There was a sternness about his own room, even with his own things littered around him. It was too perfect, too precisely planned – too lacking in love, if the truth were known. But such was his nature that he at once dismissed all lack of charity from his mind. Unlike many of his fellow students, he had sat all his examinations and obtained a first-class degree. Now he could become a priest. It was what was almost always expected of a second son, and it was what he most wanted to do. Nathan Sutton liked people: they interested and intrigued him, and people liked Nathan Sutton. He could do good in the Church, he hoped, though Mama would not be content until he became a bishop. Best remember not to mention his feeling for missionary work – not yet . . .

'Shall I order lunch, Mr Nathan? In the library, will you take it?' The library. Always the library for the strange, bookworm son who favoured the Garth Suttons instead of his own.

'No, I think not. Just have my things taken up, will you? I'd like to walk outside first – get some fresh air.'

Walk to Rowangarth to see Aunt Helen and Julia and, best of all, to see Giles, who was more of a brother to him than Albert and Elliot. Aunt Helen would be taking luncheon soon; where better to eat than there? What happier place, with its sloping floors and dark corners and little criss-crossed patterns of sunlight on the floors. And flowers everywhere, and the smell of damp

233

chimneys that didn't quite dry out, even in high summer. Rowangarth. He wished he could have been born there, been a Garth Sutton. He wouldn't have minded being dependent, almost, on the whims of nature giving a good tea crop, nor cared one jot that money, there, did not appear from an inexhaustible fount. Aunt Helen was kind, her mouth always ready to tilt into a smile of welcome, and Giles and he were so close that they might have been twins had they not been born two months apart and to different mothers. As for Julia – bossy, bonny, straight-as-a-die Julia – oh, dammit, it was good to be finished with schooling, if only to see more of her.

'By the way,' he asked, almost as an afterthought, 'is my brother in London, too?'

'*Mr Elliot?*' The pompous eyebrows arched up, the mouth turned down. 'Didn't you know? Mr Elliot has been in America – in Kentucky – for near on three weeks now. I'm surprised that –'

'Sorry!' Nathan interrupted. 'Stupid of me to forget. Exams, I suppose . . .' Kentucky? What on earth could Elliot be doing there? And why, he wondered, had his parents not thought fit to tell him? 'I'll just have a wash, then I'll be off out.'

But Giles would know – or Julia – he thought as he took the stairs two at a time, and Elliot was always doing things on the spur of the moment. But why Kentucky . . .?

Julia saw Nathan from her bedroom window as he made his way through the wild garden and was running across the lawn calling, 'Nathan! You're home!' long before he'd so much as set eyes on her. 'It's so good to see you! And this time it's for keeps!'

She ran into his outstretched arms, hands clasped around his neck as he swung her high.

'Tell me you've missed me?' She placed a smacking kiss on his cheek. 'Because I've missed you – we all have.

234

You'll stay to lunch? Mother is doing calls and Giles is in Creesby talking to the plumber. You know we're to have plumbing and electricity? There's so much to tell you, so much to catch up on.' She tucked an arm into his, pausing to take breath. 'Oh, Nathan my dear, *so* much news. You *will* stay, though when Giles will be back, I can't say. But lunch will stretch to one extra, I know it will – unless I'm being selfish and Aunt Clemmy wants you to herself?'

'My parents are in London, and Elliot, it would seem, has been in America these past weeks – though no one thought fit to tell me.'

'Oh, well – they probably forgot.' Julia's cheeks pinked 'But I've such news for you – apart from the workmen coming, I mean. Giles – I'm going to be married!'

'*Married?*' The word struck him like a blow. 'I – I'm delighted, of course, but when was the announcement made and why wasn't I told? Why does no one tell me *anything*?'

'There's been no announcement yet. We are to wait a year,' she hastened, 'just to make sure, then it'll be official.'

'But, *who*, Julia?'

'Andrew MacMalcolm. *Doctor* MacMalcolm. You haven't met him yet but he's at St Bartholomew's at the moment, though he's got a few patients of his own – most of whom can't pay.

'But, Nathan, I do love him. Right from the moment I opened my eyes and saw him there – at Aunt Sutton's it was – and . . .'

'Opened your eyes? You were ill?' He still needed time to take in the enormity of it.

'No, idiot. Just knocked out. It was my own silly fault, I suppose – with a little help from a twenty-stone London bobby. Well, it *felt* like twenty stones at least! We were in Hyde Park, Hawthorn and me, looked for a suffragette meeting. Remember the lady who was killed – Emily

Davison – well, we met her that night. The police were awful – they knew, of course.'

'Julia, dear girl – *please* . . .'

'Sorry. I do go on, don't I? Look – why don't we go inside and get Cook to make us a pot of something?'

'I think we better had, then you shall begin at the beginning and tell me about your doctor – *all* about him.' Tell him, though he didn't want to know, had not realized until now how much he had taken his cousin for granted. 'Though first can you throw any light on my parents and why they are in London? And why no one told me that Elliot –'

'Nathan – do hurry inside. Come and say hullo to Cook, if you like, and tell her you'll be staying to lunch. As for London,' she shrugged expressively, 'I can't tell you why Aunt and Uncle are there. They don't tell us everything, you know . . .'

Nor would tell them now, she supposed. Not at least until Elliot had promised to behave himself, or Uncle Edward chanced his luck and managed to visit without Aunt Clemmy finding out. Even their scant knowledge about Elliot and Kentucky had come to them by way of stable talk and below-stairs gleanings.

'I suppose not. But I know you're determined to tell me about London and Emily Davison.' And about her Doctor MacMalcolm, too. Because nothing was so certain: Julia was in love. He would have been blind not to notice the softness of her eyes, the catch in her voice when she spoke about him, the colour that pinked her cheeks. The Julia of their youth was gone. Now she was a woman deeply in love, and he had lost her even before he realized he cared – cared for her as a woman, not as a sister. 'Although I wish I knew why you are so determined not to talk about Elliot. What is it?'

'Nathan.' She took a deep breath. 'It really isn't any of our business, but you'll have to know, sooner or later.

And best you hear it from me, I suppose, in case Mother returns early. And when I've told you, try not to mention it in front of her. She'll still shocked and angry about it.'

'About *what*?' About Elliot, he knew it.

'Sssh.' They were walking across the hall now, and not until they were sitting in the conservatory did she continue. 'That I don't know much about Elliot being in America is true. News comes to Rowangarth now in a round-about way, you see. We've heard that Albert has settled down in Kentucky and that that's where Elliot is now . . .'

'You don't know? But surely you'd be the first to be told that Elliot had gone to stay with Albert?'

'Not any longer. And not gone – *sent* – or so talk has it. But we haven't seen your mother in weeks and Uncle Edward, poor love, must needs keep away, too. And that's sad, because he does so love Rowangarth.'

'My dear,' Nathan sighed, 'you still aren't making sense.'

'No, I'm not. All right, then! Elliot misbehaved, and Giles wants an apology. And until he gets it, Mother said Elliot is not to come here; not even to set foot on Rowangarth land, or he'll be marched off it like a common trespasser, or worse! There! Now you know!'

'*But what happened?*'

'Trouble, that's what. Our under-keeper knocked Elliot down and blacked his eye. I tell you, Nathan, relations between Place and Garth are a bit strained, to say the least.'

'Julia, love.' Nathan gathered his cousin's hands in his own. 'What did my brother do that needed an apology? A bit tipsy, was he? Said something out of turn?'

'*Very* tipsy. Drunk, actually. If you want the whole, unvarnished truth, he was in Brattocks and, to put not too fine a point on it, he tried to rape our Hawthorn. And

237

he'd have got away with it, too, if she hadn't had Giles's dog with her. The creature flew at Elliot and Hawthorn was able to run away.

'Then Dwerryhouse arrived on the scene and set about Elliot. Dwerryhouse and Hawthorn are walking out, you see, so you couldn't blame him. And now there's an atmosphere and heaven only knows where it's going to end . . .'

'And Mother took Elliot's part, I suppose?'

'She did. Your father got in a rage, though – or so we heard – and ordered Elliot to Kentucky until it all blows over.'

'Then I'm sorry and deeply ashamed, though I can well believe it,' Nathan said, tight-lipped. 'But how is the girl Hawthorn? Was she badly hurt? He didn't . . .?'

'No, which is something to be thankful for. Her face was scratched, though – she fell into a bramble bush – and he tore her clothes. She was very upset – he hit her, you see, though she's all right now. But her face was bruised for quite some time. We tried to keep it quiet for her sake, mainly, and it was lucky Mother didn't have to send for Doctor James. Andrew was staying here when it happened, so he looked after her. But it's bound to get out sooner or later – that's if it hasn't already. Sorry I had to be the one to tell you, Nathan; like I said, best you should know. And don't look so upset. You aren't your brother's keeper.'

'But I *am*, or I should be. I want to be a priest and I *should* care about him, even though what he did is unforgivable. Yet I'm so angry, so disgusted, I'd set about him myself if he were here. I'm sorry such a thing could happen, and I'm sorry it's caused bad feeling between the families. And as for that poor girl . . .'

'I told you, Hawthorn is fine now,' Julia urged. 'Her face is better, and she's got Dwerryhouse, remember, to watch over her. So tell me about your plans for the

238

Church, Nathan, because there'll be no wedding – and Andrew agrees with me – until you are ordained and can marry us. We want to be your first marrying, my dear.'

'But Julia – ordination takes time: more than a year. And you'd be married here, wouldn't you? How would the vicar feel about it? He'd want to officiate, now wouldn't he, in his own parish?'

'Mm.' Nathan was right of course. He always was; and always willing to see the other's point of view. 'But you could be there, couldn't you? Mr Parkin would understand, it being family. You could assist if nothing else. I've set my heart on it.'

'Then I'll be there. Nothing shall keep me away.'

'Good! That's settled then.' She smiled sunnily. 'Now, are you coming with me to see Mrs Shaw, or shall I just ring for coffee? And don't worry – about Elliot, I mean. These things blow over and it needn't make any difference to you. You won't be like Uncle Edward, will you, and stay away for the sake of peace and quiet? Promise you won't?'

'I shall be very tactful – that I can promise you,' though how he was to help heal what seemed so serious a rift he had no idea. 'And I'm so very sorry and ashamed about what happened – you realize that, don't you?'

'Ssh! Not another word till I've seen to the coffee. Then I shall tell you about Andrew and how we met and oh, everything . . .'

'Good,' he murmured as she whisked off to the kitchen. Everything? Must she? Why had she grown up so suddenly, so beautifully? And why hadn't he realized it until it was too late?

Nathan Sutton thought a lot about it that evening in the echoing gloom of Pendenys. He'd had time, now, to think; more time indeed than he cared to contemplate, since his parents had telephoned to say they would be

239

staying in London for another night, to visit Aunt Sutton and have dinner with her.

Julia must have been staying with Aunt Sutton when she and Andrew MacMalcolm met, he realized. Dear, headstrong Julia, who had only to stamp a bossy little foot and he and Giles would do exactly as she wished – even as children. He smiled fondly. He was touched she should want him to marry her; he would do it, were it possible, with wholehearted affection – yes, and christen her children, too, when the time came.

Yet his ordination into the priesthood was a long way off: much could happen before then, he frowned. In the meantime, he decided, he would not eat alone tonight in this empty house. Giles must surely be home by now, and there was six months apart to be caught up on. Aunt Helen, he knew, would make him welcome despite the coldness between Place and Garth – something he must do his utmost to heal. This longed-for homecoming must not be spoiled by ill-feeling, no matter what Elliot had done; though why his brother had grown up so thoughtless and self-centred was beyond him.

Was it because he had been so spoiled, so indulged, or had there always been a selfish streak in him? Oh, he'd known about his brother's womanizing, and accepted that some men needed to get their wildness out of them before settling down into an arranged marriage they needs must accept – an eldest son especially. But attempted rape was altogether something else, he frowned, and maybe a spell in America in disgrace was nothing less than Elliot deserved.

'Oh, *damn* my brother!' he spat.

After a great deal of wavering, Helen Sutton finally decided to go to London while the electricity and plumbing were installed. Julia let go a breath of relief and assured her she had made entirely the right decision. 'There'll be such a banging and knocking, dearest,' she reminded her mother, never mind the upset of levering up floorboards undisturbed since before the age of the nail. And her mother, Julia knew, would fret and fuss and worry in case they were not replaced exactly as those long-ago carpenters had set them, secure with little wooden pegs. And she would worry, too, about panelling being taken from the walls and ages-old plaster being chipped away to accommodate wires. In fact, she would probably get herself into such a dither that she would cry, 'Stop! No more!' and all hopes of electric lights and hot water in bathtaps would fade for ever. At Aunt Sutton's, her mother would be away from it all, leaving the supervising and worrying to Giles, who cared for Rowangarth every bit as much as any of them, and would make sure it came to no harm.

Yet what had finally made up Helen Sutton's mind was the realization that sight of the London shops was more than three years overdue, and the ordering of new curtains for two of the downstairs rooms and the choosing of shades for the new lights and lamps was now a necessity rather than an indulgence. And it would be good, she conceded, to be with Anne Lavinia; be with someone who understood her need to talk about John, and who would listen with sympathy, since she too missed her brother sadly. Anne Lavinia must be told, too, about Julia's headlong leap into love, and be asked to receive Andrew.

Andrew was so like John; his safeness and stability – the way he looked, held his head even. It was good, Helen thought, to feel so entirely happy that one day he would marry her daughter; confident, too, that her sister-in-law would be in complete agreement with her views on him, once she had met him.

She sighed volubly, wishing Robert and Giles were half so eager to be married as their sister. They should both now be thinking seriously about taking a wife and rearing children – sons, especially – but all Giles could enthuse about presently was the electrifying and plumbing of Rowangarth, and all her elder son seemed interested in was the growing of tea. That it was extremely good tea, she allowed without hesitation; tea which provided the means to maintain the Rowangarth estate in a reasonable manner of comfort. But oh, dear – to be so wrapped up in tea when he ought to be thinking about young ladies . . .

She sighed again. Robert was in India, many miles away from her influence. He was a grown man, though, who would no doubt marry when he pleased. His last letter had been full of approval for the improvements to the house, and indicated nothing less than contentment with his way of life. And who was to say that Giles would not be the first to marry? Who could be sure he wouldn't do exactly as Julia had done and fall immediately and for ever in love in the most unexpected circumstances?

Meantime, London beckoned, and Anne Lavinia's earthy wisdom, and the turning out of drawers and cupboards, the taking up of carpets, the taking down of curtains and the shrouding of furniture could safely be left in Miss Clitherow's more than capable hands. And staff would be busy enough without having family to cook and fetch and carry for, Helen reasoned. A visit to London was the only solution.

Thus finally convinced, she set herself to the once-a-year clearance of unwanted clothes which had become as much a ritual as spring cleaning and the staff Bank Holiday Monday outing. There had not been so many clothes to discard during the mourning years, Helen acknowledged, it making no sense to throw out one dreary black dress in favour of another dreary black dress. But now she must do as Giles and Julia had already done and add her contribution to theirs, for the clearance wasn't only a throwing-out of clothes that were no longer needed: it went a great deal further than that.

The first to benefit from it were staff who, in order of seniority, took their pick of shoes, skirts, blouses, socks, shirts, waistcoats, stockings, chemises and all sorts of ladies' underpinnings. Not that the ladies of Rowangarth need ever expect to see last year's morning dresses in Creesby High Street, or their dinner dresses or ball gowns waltzing in the village hall at Holdenby. Such recognizable (and costly) items were removed by Miss Clitherow from the tea-chests into which they had been placed and set aside for the Leeds Lady, who called upon the houses of the gentry and relieved them of all unwanted garments too good to cast to the winds of charity. The Leeds Lady had a keen eye for a good line, and her establishment in a side street off Briggate offered superior bargains at ordinary prices. Who had worn the dresses and costumes and coats so eagerly snapped up was never disclosed. Discretion had helped build up her business and she was completely trusted by the ladies who sold to her.

Only once had Helen Sutton relaxed her rule and insisted that Ellen, who was leaving to be married, should be given an afternoon dress that had seen little wear, and biscuit-coloured shoes to wear with it and its matching hat. A radiant Ellen had worn the ensemble proudly on her wedding day and only twice since: at the christening of her two children, and at her sister's wedding, when most had said that she was better dressed than the bride.

Thus, when the Leeds Lady had been and gone, leaving payment in a sealed envelope with Miss Clitherow – it was the housekeeper who conducted the selling – staff took their pick of the items, after which Jinny Dobb was invited to make her selection. Jin, who wasn't exactly staff, came to Rowangarth each Monday and Tuesday to wash and iron the household linen and non-personal items, after which she cared for the young men who lived in the bothy – a house in which unmarried outdoor staff lived: the coachman, the stable lad, the under-keeper and two young garden boys. It was Jin Dobb who saw to it their bedding was changed regularly, who swept and dusted after them and, for a shilling each a week, washed their shirts and cooked them a Sunday dinner. She had even been known to rub aching chests with goosegrease when winter coughs struck, though nowadays the fashionable name for that ailment was influenza.

Jin looked forward to rummaging in the tea-chests, from which last year she had selected a pair of slippers of a quality never seen in Creesby market and a long black skirt: washerwoman or not, she was content. There were far worse employers hereabouts than her ladyship – no names, no pack-drill, of course – and with the coming of the workmen to the Garth, extra scrubbing had been promised her when the time came to clear up the mess. Unwed or not, thus far she had managed nicely, thanks be to her ladyship and not forgetting the Almighty. It would be a sad day for Holdenby, she had often thought, if the Garth Suttons ceased to exist. But they would go on for ever. Rowangarth had produced sons since the date was chiselled over the front door all those hundreds of years ago. There was no need to worry.

Then, when the washerwoman had bobbed a curtsey of gratitude to Miss Clitherow, the remaining clothes would be repacked and sent to the vicarage for distribution to needy villagers and inmates of Creesby workhouse by Jessie Parkin. Sorting through drawers and wardrobes was a necessary but thankless task, Helen sighed, when she would far rather be outdoors, taking pleasure from the garden walk or visiting the glasshouses or the planthouse, talking earnestly with the head gardener. But clear out three years of black she must; throw away, she supposed, the most unhappy years of her life.

She reached for the silk dress and jacket she had worn

to her husband's funeral and dropped it, eyes averted, into the tea-chest. There now, she shuddered; the worst was over. Ridding herself of whatever else remained of the bleak years would not be half so bad.

'John, my dearest,' she whispered. '*Why* . . .?'

It was all decided. On Monday morning, Helen and Julia would leave early, take the milk train to York station, and from there the fast train to King's Cross. For this journey, a chaperon would not be necessary, since they had reserved seats in a ladies-only compartment. A luncheon basket, thoughtfully packed by Mrs Shaw with drinking water, a bottle of white wine, an assortment of dainty sandwiches, and fruit cake cut into easy-to-eat fingers, would provide sustenance for the journey, in addition to the carefully wrapped peaches picked that morning at sunrise.

A break from Rowangarth, which had seemed to confine her with her grief for so very long, might be exactly what was needed to make her finally accept that John was gone, Helen was now coming to realize; that the terrible pain and loneliness she had lived through these past three years had not been a nightmare from which she would awake with blessed relief; that she was indeed a widow who could never even contemplate marrying again. Anne Lavinia would listen, unspeaking, to her outpourings, give an opinion when asked to, and send her back to the North Riding with a pocket filled with blessings and the sureness that life was for the living, even without John at her side. She had so much to be thankful for. Even to return to Rowangarth after the hurry and scurry of London would be nothing short of delightful. Indeed, she had never been quite able to understand why London always beckoned so excitingly when she was at home and why the north country always called her thankfully back after very few weeks away. This time, she thought with pleasure even before she had left it, she would return to a house immaculately refurbished, with instant lighting and blissfully hot water in baths, which would then gurgle away with no more effort than the pulling out of a plug. It would be a splendid improvement, and save untold effort for those who worked at Rowangarth. She was fortunate, she pondered, in all her servants, who cared for her and her family with devotion. And, in her turn, she cared for every one of them, and would think of them all every day she was away and hope that the Upheaval, as it had already come to be known, would not cause them too much bother. And at next quarter day, when they were paid, a week's extra wages would be placed in each envelope – it was the very least she could do – and perhaps she would give them an extra half-day off too, as an additional thank you.

She smiled again, then gave herself up completely to the pleasure of visiting London again after so long.

'Hawthorn, what *is* the matter with all the clocks!' Julia flung open the sewing-room door with her usual energy. 'They are standing still, I'd swear they are, and doing it only to annoy!'

Had a day ever crawled by with such irritating slowness? How was each passing hour to be borne, and with what delight would she be awakened on Monday morning – if ever she'd managed to sleep, that was – to the realization that before so many more hours; before all the miles between had hissed and rattled away, she would be with Andrew and holding and touching him. More than five weeks apart, it would be – five lifetimes – and how she could have endured them without his read and read-again letters she did not know. 'And is my blue fit to wear, do you think?'

'Your blue,' smiled Alice who knew how much the doctor liked that particular dress, 'is hanging on the door behind you, waiting to have a button sewn on it and the pleats pressed. As if I could forget your blue!'

'I know you wouldn't. Oh, do you remember the afternoon I wore it? You let us walk out alone and there were scones for tea – and Andrew said that if ever we were able to meet again he hoped I'd be wearing that dress . . .'

'And you did meet him again, in Harrogate, and you *were* wearing it and everything turned out just as if it was meant to be.'

'Yes – and when the time comes, Nathan will marry us if he can, or at least be there to bless us if he can't. Are we too lucky, you and me both? Will Fate suddenly get jealous of our happiness, Hawthorn?' she frowned, her eyes all at once anxious.

'No miss, Fate *won't*.' Alice bit off a thread with practised preciseness. 'I'm of the firm belief that we all get what we deserve in this life, and –'

'And we both deserve our lovely young men,' Julia finished, happy again.

'That's it. So you're to go to London and have a right grand time and tell Doctor Andrew from me that he's to keep a tight hold on you in Hyde Park and steer you away from meetings. And now, if you'll excuse me, miss, it's time for downstairs supper and I saw Mr Nathan not two minutes ago, walking in this direction, so you'd best be off yourself. I'll see to the blue for you and make sure it's all nicely pressed and packed and, Miss Julia, don't take that dratted hobble skirt with you. Get rid of it.'

'I was wearing that dratted skirt when Andrew and I met,' Julia grinned. 'Wear it again I shall not – it's a silly, mincing thing. But get rid of it? That I'll *never* do!'

Giles and Nathan sat in the conservatory, drinking coffee

247

rather than the usual after-dinner port, watching a near-full moon rise slowly over the tip of Holdenby Pike.

'Are the ladies not joining us?' Nathan eyed the box of cheroots with longing.

'I think not. Smoke if you want to. My mother, I'm sure, intends to leave us alone to catch up, and my terrible sister is far too busy with other things. She *says* she wants to see to her clothes for London, but more than likely she'll be writing another letter to Andrew, even though she'll be with him on Monday.'

'She's serious about him, then? It's not just a case of first love?'

'Completely serious. We get Andrew from morning to night. And when she isn't talking about him or scribbling notes to him, she's thinking about him. You can always tell. She goes off into a kind of smirking trance,' Giles laughed, 'and hears not a word anyone says to her. The sooner she's married the better, if you ask me, though she's agreed to wait a year before anything is announced.'

'And he's a decent sort?' Nathan's concern was genuine. 'He'll be good to her?'

'Mother likes him. He's a self-made man and you can't but admire him for the way he must have worked. And there's a steadiness about him as if he'd be slow to anger – yet watch out, if ever he does.

'Now take Mother's dinner party a few weeks back. The judge was on his high horse about the Kaiser getting too big for his boots, and how Germany would have to be stopped, even if it came to war. Mother was very upset by it, and Andrew shut the old boy up with great diplomacy by changing the subject to Derby Day, if you like, as though there were far more important things than the size of the German navy. I was grateful to him.'

'Even though there might be a grain of truth in Judge Mounteagle's prophecies?' Nathan shifted uneasily.

'*War?* Oh, surely not? And you almost a priest!'

'Don't misunderstand me, Giles. I'm as much against wars as you are. But college debates aren't always a lot of hot air. Some students have strong views.'

'About what?'

'Well – Germany is a young and brash nation wanting world markets – '

'*Our* markets,' Giles persisted.

'Certainly. But not by God-given right as we seem to take for granted. Germany and Austria are natural allies, and the Serbian matter could make for trouble. Serbs in Austria want unity with their homeland, and Russia sympathizes with them – openly encouraging them at times.'

'You seem well-informed.' Giles refilled his cup, frowning.

'At college you can't avoid it. Here, you can pretend that the outside world doesn't exist . . .'

'And here in the north we've got our heads in the sand?'

'I'm afraid so. Russia and France have formed an alliance; France is for ever demanding the return of Alsace and Lorraine from Germany; Germany is determined to hold on to them at all costs – and Austria is backing Germany.'

'So these college debates of yours are changing your opinions?' Surprise was evident in Giles's voice.

'No. I'm against war and I always will be. But Cambridge opened my eyes. Europe is seething, Giles; the tensions are below the surface most times, yet still there, especially in the Eastern states.

'But there are other more pressing things to talk about than what might or might not surface in Europe. And we *are* an island, remember. Here, we can cut ourselves off from it all. We have seas all around us and are safe enough, be sure of that.

'So now we are alone, tell me what is going on at the

Place. I can't make head or tail of it. No one seems to have thought to tell me anything . . .'

'About what, Nathan?'

'About what my parents are doing in London that's so secret. And why no one thought to tell me that Albert had settled in Kentucky or that –'

There was a silence, then, each knowing that what the other wished to avoid must soon be brought into the open.

'It's getting dark. Have you a match?' Giles removed the glass shade and carefully held a light to the wick of the oil lamp. 'There now, that's better.'

The flickering flame touched palms and ferns and flowers with a soft golden glow, while outside trees were outlined and silvered with moonshine. It was too beautiful a world, too peaceful, in which to discuss Elliot.

'My brother,' Nathan began. 'We must talk about his behaviour, though I didn't mention it at dinner. Julia warned me it mustn't be discussed in front of Aunt Helen.'

'Julia told you, then?' He might have known it. 'How much?'

'Enough to know that Elliot behaved very badly and got a thrashing.'

'Not a thrashing, exactly, though our keeper hit him good and hard and sent him flying. But it was Morgan we have to thank. The lazy old creature hurled himself at your brother like a wild thing, it seems. Never thought he had it in him.' Giles's pleasure was evident. 'Hawthorn is fond of the animal. Giving him a run means she can meet her young man, you see.'

'The keeper who hit Elliot?'

'That's him – Dwerryhouse. But you'll hear all about it from your father, I shouldn't wonder. I'm sorry if it puts you in an embarrassing position, but your brother must apologize, Nathan, and behave himself where Rowangarth staff are concerned. Mother insists on it, and so do I.'

'I agree with you. Oh, we all know about Elliot's fondness for women, but he's got to learn it can't be allowed on his own doorstep. But had you thought,' Nathan smiled wickedly, 'that some young lady from Kentucky might get him in a hold he can't get out of?'

'It's certainly a thought, but it wouldn't go down at all well with Aunt Clemmy. Oh, my Lord – imagine it!'

All at once they were laughing, for wasn't this a July evening at Rowangarth, a homecoming evening, and for a little while longer couldn't Europe and Elliot be forgotten?

'I've missed you, Nathan,' Giles said soberly. 'I'm glad you're back.'

'Me, too. It's good to come home . . .'

Though to what, exactly, Nathan Sutton could not be entirely sure.

13

Julia was glad to return to London, to the city of their meeting. To her surprise and utter delight, Andrew had been waiting at King's Cross station, and it was all she could do not to run the length of the platform and fling herself into his arms.

'I have a cab waiting,' he'd said after his restrained greeting, mindful that this was a crowded railway terminus where not even husband and wife would dream of exchanging more than the small politenesses allowed in public. 'Let's gather your belongings together, then I can see you safely on your way. Perhaps later tonight I can call – to know you are comfortably settled?'

'But of course! Aunt Sutton always eats early – about half-past seven should see us nicely finished.' Julia turned appealing eyes to her mother. 'I do so want her and Andrew to meet.'

'Then perhaps eight would be a little more appropriate,' Helen smiled, knowing her daughter's capacity for chatter.

'Oh, *yes*!' Her mother *was* on her side, she should have known it. 'And you'll like my aunt, Andrew – it's just that she's a bit awkward about receiving.' Worse than awkward. An invitation from Aunt Sutton was as rare as a summons to Buckingham Palace. Not for her the simpering ways of society; of card-leaving, of calling and being called upon. Either she liked a person or she did not, it was as simple as that; and this philosophy served to keep her intimates to a manageable few. 'Don't for a moment think she doesn't want to meet you or –'

'What Julia is trying to explain, Andrew, is that my

sister-in-law is not a social person. She considers herself entitled to pick and choose her friends and not be bothered by climbing callers, as she calls them,' Helen explained, the corners of her mouth tilting into a smile of affection. 'But if she takes to you, you have a good friend for life.'

'I shall be on my very best behaviour.'

'Just be yourself,' Helen said softly, 'and you won't go far wrong, I'm sure of it.'

'Then I'll call at eight and, meantime, will you check your luggage and make sure it is all there?' Andrew nodded towards the trolley piled high with cases, bags and boxes, then offered his arm to Helen. 'I'll see you on your way then be off. I have a surgery at six.'

'We can't drop you anywhere on the way?' Julia murmured, unwilling for them to part.

'Sadly, no. But I shall look forward to tonight, and hope.'

'She *will* receive you, darling, I know it.' Julia turned anxious eyes to her mother. 'She must. You shall tell her, dearest, that –'

'I shall tell her nothing,' Helen laughed. 'But I will *suggest* the time has come for your aunt and Andrew to meet. More than that I cannot do.'

'Oh, dear.' She had been so sure her aunt would welcome Andrew. She could not envisage that anyone could find even the smallest flaw in his character, conveniently forgetting that her father's sister was abrupt in her manner, plain in her speaking, and difficult to know, too, should she decide a person not deserving of her attention. Time, Aunt Sutton always insisted, was the most precious of all things, and not to be squandered on fools. 'Never mind,' she whispered, as her mother arranged her skirts over the cab seat, 'there's always the park, and, darling –'

Briefly her eyes held his and without sound her lips formed the words, *I love you . . .*

'Tell me then – what did you think of him?' Helen demanded. 'Am I right in allowing Julia to consider herself engaged?'

'Allow? My dear good woman, do you think you have any say in the matter?' demanded Anne Lavinia Sutton. 'It's obvious the girl is head over heels! But she's her father's daughter, and nothing you or I say will make a scrap of difference. The sooner we acknowledge it, the better.'

'John's daughter?'

'You don't remember? Ha! "What am I to do, Sis dear?" He always called me Sis when he was soft-soaping me. "The most beautiful girl – I've got to see her again! You must help me find out *everything* about her!" Besotted, he was, the minute he set eyes on you. Julia is only running true to form.'

For a moment Helen's face was still as she called back that night of their meeting. 'But do you think Doctor MacMalcolm is suitable – first impressions, I mean.'

'My first impressions were that he's equally taken with her – if any impression can be formed from the few minutes he was here.' Before her niece had impatiently guided him to the door, that was. 'But that isn't the point, is it? Can he provide for her, keep a firm hand on her, because she's strong-willed and rushes headlong into any fad that takes her fancy – we all know that!'

'Andrew isn't a fad, and I truly think that given time he'll do well. He qualified the hard way; he makes no bones about it. He's got little money and no expectations but . . .'

Helen sighed, lapsing into silence, leaning back against the bright chintz cushions in the little white-painted sitting-room. She was beginning now to feel the effects of the long, jolting journey; though Julia had barely had time to finish her meal before she was off, on Andrew's arm.

'But do *you* like him?' The older woman's voice broke into her silence.

'Yes, I do. And Julia will have money of her own soon, so she won't have to ask permission for every new dress she orders. But doesn't he remind you of anyone?'

'He does.' She had wondered when the conversation would get around to it. 'It was the first thing I noticed about him. He reminds me of John.'

'Ah,' Helen sighed, delighted. 'I thought it was just me; that deep down inside me I wanted Julia to marry someone like her father. But apart from the colour of his hair, they are so much alike it's uncanny. His build, the way he holds his head, his quiet way of speaking . . .'

Anne Lavinia did not resemble her brother at all. Her face was angular, her eyes shrewd, though her white hair waved softly on her cheeks and softened her finely cut features.

'And his eyes, Helen – the same colour. I noticed them especially because he met my eyes when he spoke to me. I liked that. Can't abide a fellow who don't look you straight in the eye. But here is the coffee.' She smiled at the elderly servant. 'Put it on the table will you, Figgis? We'll help ourselves. Away to bed with you.'

'But what about Miss Julia, ma'am? There'll be no one to open the door.'

'Leave the door on the latch, there's a good woman. She's got sense enough to turn the handle and let herself in. Off you go. She's getting old,' Anne Lavinia confided when they were alone again. 'Poor Figgis gets tired, y'know. Do you realize she was under-housemaid at Rowangarth when John and I were small? She must be well past seventy, though she'll never admit it. Came here to London with me when I left the Garth.'

'Yes – when John and I were married. Strange, but it's

255

as if I've lived there all my life, yet you and Edward and John were all born there.'

'And love it still. No matter where in the world I am, Rowangarth is still home. But the coffee is getting cold. Black, isn't it?' she murmured, rising to her feet just a little stiffly.

'Please. Oh, I'm so glad to be here, Anne. It's been so long. I've missed this dear little house – so pretty and light.'

'It suits me,' Anne Lavinia acknowledged. 'Now, before I settle myself, would you like a sniff of brandy? No?' She sank back into her chair, arranging the cushions, kicking off her shoes without ceremony. 'We were talking about the doctor. You think he'll suit, then?'

'I do. He's so kind. He was waiting at King's Cross when we got there. We didn't expect it, but it's just the sort of thing he'd do. Thoughtful.'

'And now he's walking in the park with Julia. He seems to have a lot of time to himself.'

'Not really. Apart from his hospital work he has patients of his own, but he arranged to change his duties when he knew we were coming. He's doing night work for the next few weeks, which means he can sleep mornings and have afternoons and evenings with Julia.'

'Hm. So when is the announcement to be?'

'Not just yet. They have agreed to wait a year, just to be absolutely sure, but – '

'But we can take it as settled, thank goodness.' Anne Sutton gazed thoughtfully into her glass then said abruptly, 'When are you going to let Julia drive? You know she's keen to. I'm fond of the girl and I'd thought to give her a motor of her own for her twenty-first. But it isn't going to be a lot of use if you won't let her have it at Rowangarth. And there's Giles, too, having to watch his cousin Elliot driving his smart sporty motor and himself riding a cycle like a penniless artist. I respect your feelings, Helen, and

I understand them, but it's three years since it happened, you know.'

'Yes. But I made a vow – no more motors at Rowangarth. Imagine if the same thing happened to Giles or to Julia. I couldn't bear it. I'm sorry, but I – '

'All right. All right, my dear. Don't get upset.' She spoke softly as if to calm an agitated filly. 'Your decision entirely. But I'd half promised Julia she could take a turn in my motor – John taught her to drive and she's got enough confidence. Might I not let her – just to keep her hand in?'

'We-e-ell – if you'd give me your word she wouldn't be allowed to go fast. And you'd sit beside her . . .?'

'I would indeed. I'll take her on the park road, and no one speeds there on account of the horses, you know.'

Horses. John's sister's first love. And most young people could drive a motor these days, Helen pondered. Had she the right to impose her fears on her children?

'Well, Helen?'

'I'll think about it. Perhaps I am being too cautious.'

'Good. Think about it – that's all I ask. Talking about such things, did you know that Clementina has bought a Rolls-Royce? That makes three motors now at Pendenys. That woman spends money like a drunken sailor!'

'Another?' Helen frowned, suddenly apprehensive. 'Who told you?'

'She did. They came here last night, to supper. Telephoned from the Savoy – almost invited herself, if you please. I didn't say no, because it meant I could see Edward, poor man. And Clemmy looked so cockahoop, I knew she'd only come to tell me – get me on her side.'

'Tell you?' Helen murmured. Surely not about Elliot and Hawthorn? 'Not – ' She stopped, her cheeks flushing.

'Not about *what*? Surely you know – about the house they've bought?'

'I don't, I'm afraid.' A *house*? 'Clemmy tells me little . . .'

'Edward, then? Didn't he tell you, though I seemed to

get the impression he wasn't best pleased about it. After all, he's never liked London, except in small doses.'

'Anne, dear – you'd better know. I hear nothing of what is happening over at the Place. There have been words between us, you see.'

'Ha!' Anne Lavinia slapped her knee triumphantly. 'I knew it! Thought there was something up, the way Clemmy changed tack when Rowangarth was even remotely mentioned. Tell me, what's to do between the two of you?'

'I'm afraid it began as a matter of principle. Elliot behaved badly and Giles asked for an apology. But I went further than that. I insisted Elliot mustn't come to Rowangarth until he did.'

'And his doting mama took his part at once, then forbade Edward to interfere?'

'I think she must have, because it is as if we don't exist now. But I won't relent. Elliot may do as he wishes at Pendenys, but in my home he must conduct himself like a gentleman!'

'My word!' The elder woman noted the tight set of her sister-in-law's mouth, the bright splashes of colour high on her cheeks. 'What did he do, then? Made an ass of himself in public? But Elliot was always a loud-mouth – even as a boy.'

'Nothing like that. I really hadn't intended telling you, but it's best you know, I suppose, though you are not to tell Clemmy I've spoken of it to you. You'll give me your word?'

'Word of a Sutton. And you know I'm not a gossip.'

'No – but you are like Julia; you'll have your say no matter what – and when you hear what it's about . . .' She shrugged, twisting the rings on her finger, eyes downcast. 'Elliot attacked our little Hawthorn. In Brattocks. She said she didn't give him any encouragement, and I believe her.'

'Attacked?' She sat suddenly upright, eyes narrowed. 'He tried to interfere with her?'

'He did, though I would call it attempted rape.'

'Good grief!' She stared, shocked, at her brother's widow, never believing she would hear such a word on her lips. 'Any damage? I mean – he didn't . . .?'

'Not *that*. Giles's dog was with her and he went for Elliot. Then Dwerryhouse – he's our new keeper – arrived on the scene and knocked Elliot down; Dwerryhouse and Hawthorn are walking out, so you can't blame him.

'But she has fully recovered and I understand that Elliot has gone to America to visit his brother. Nathan ate with us last night, though he wasn't able to tell us any more than we'd already gleaned.'

'Damned young ram!' The elder Sutton did not mince words. 'But I blame Clementina. She's ruined Elliot. Thinks the sun shines out of his eyes, though if Edward had taken a strap to him long ago he'd maybe have grown up less obnoxious. And Elliot *has* gone to America. Seems Albert and his wife – Amelia, she's called – have settled down at last. Clemmy was singing her praises last night, though rather insincerely, to my way of thinking. But this Amelia seems a sensible sort.' Anyone who bred horses had her full approval. 'And she's well-heeled enough to keep young Albert, so I'm told.'

'Albert can't be blamed,' Helen murmured. 'Younger sons must shift for themselves. Giles will have to do the same and marry a girl with means of her own. I often wonder who he'll end up with – if he ever takes the plunge, that is.'

'Yes. Edward married that harridan Clementina – but what choice did he have, poor man?'

'Not a lot. But you were talking about a house.' Helen was eager to put the Place Suttons out of her mind. 'I can't say I blame Edward – Pendenys isn't at all to my liking.'

'Not Edward. Clemmy bought it. Seems they'll still live in Yorkshire, but this "little place", as she calls it – off the Chelsea Embankment – will be nice for visits, or so she says. Paid the earth for it, the silly woman, *and* bought the leasehold as well. I got the impression she'll do quite a bit of entertaining there – try to get Elliot fixed up, if she can, though heaven help the girl who takes him. Clemmy is looking for a penniless earl with a surfeit of daughters, I shouldn't wonder; determined, still, to have a title in the family. It has almost become an obsession with her.

'And talking about weddings, when is Robert going to stir himself and get some sons? Acting like a contented bachelor. He should be thinking about taking a wife. How old is he?'

'Twenty-seven – there's time enough – but I too wish he'd get married.'

'Then let's hope they'll both surprise us before so very much longer. Wouldn't want the title to go to Pendenys, would we?'

'It won't. They'll both marry, don't worry. There have always been sons at Rowangarth. And at least one of my brood is eager to be down the aisle. It wouldn't surprise me if she isn't plotting this very minute to get Andrew into a practice of his own – in Harrogate, I shouldn't wonder.'

'Could do a lot worse. Polish up his bedside manner. He should be all right there. Plenty of money in that quarter.'

'He doesn't need to polish anything. Andrew is naturally kind and courteous; he even charmed Mrs Mounteagle, *and* very tactfully stopped the judge airing his opinions.'

'What's old Mounteagle been on about now?' Anne Lavinia chuckled.

'He was talking about the Kaiser,' Helen frowned. 'Said his navy and army are getting altogether too ambitious. Said Germany will have to be put in its place, even if it means war. You don't think he could be right, do you?'

'Not really. Mind, Germany is bursting at the seams and eager to expand, but they wouldn't risk war, though the French would soon sort them out if they overstepped the mark.' France had her full approval. She loved it almost as much as she loved her own country. 'Don't concern yourself, my dear. What happens on the Continent needn't worry us. We are no part of them. We are an island, thank God, and can hold ourselves apart from European bickerings. Forget it, Helen!' She waved an airy, dismissive hand. 'Mounteagle doesn't know the first thing about it!'

'You think not?' Relieved by so firm a pronouncement, Helen relaxed into the softness of her chair, wondering why she had let herself become so agitated by an old man's meanderings. 'Do you know, my dear, I think I *would* like a very small brandy,' she smiled.

Then she would take herself thankfully off to bed the minute Julia came in . . .

Julia had no intention of returning to Montpelier Mews a second before she had to.

'I don't believe this – any of it,' she laughed. 'It's been so long . . .'

'Six weeks?' he said, indulgently.

'Six *years*. I don't know how I endured them. Tell me you love me?'

'Again?'

'Yes. And again and again. And do you know where we are?'

'Hyde Park?' he murmured.

'There now! You've forgotten already!'

'No, I haven't, though it's a little further on – nearer to the gates – that we met. I come to our place often, and I think of the night a young lady, such a beautiful young lady, wearing a fashionable but rather silly skirt, took an incredible flying leap through the air and landed at my feet, unconscious. I haven't been able to get her out of

261

my mind since, and when she wears blue, as she is doing tonight, I am simply besotted.'

'Andrew, I do so love you, though if I let myself think how easily we could have missed each other that night, my blood runs cold.'

'We'd have met – somewhere. We were bound to,' he smiled confidently. 'Did I tell you I have a new patient?'

'*Another* who can't pay?'

'Indeed, no! This one settled my account the moment he got it. A wine importer – quite rich, in fact. Came to me in a sorry state and nothing at all the matter with him that losing seventy pounds wouldn't cure. He's more than a stone lighter already and much the better for it.'

'A few more like him and you'll be rich, darling.'

'I think not, but I have no conscience at all about frightening the living daylights out of the man, then charging him for prescribing a simple way of eating and weighing him once a week. It helps make me feel less angry when I see children who are dying because they can't get *enough* to eat. It's a strange world we live in.'

'But you and I together, Andrew – we'll be all right? And we'll be married just as soon as we can?'

'Just as soon as I can support you,' he said gravely, smiling into her upturned face, wanting her with his eyes. 'It shouldn't be too long. But tell me about Alice. Is she fully recovered? Is she happy again?'

'Completely, especially since Elliot has been sent – in disgrace, we think – to America. Tom and she have an understanding, now. He gave her a locket for her birthday and she was given her mother's wedding ring, too.'

'So she's got the man and the ring – no wonder she's happy.'

'Yes, and I'm glad for her. Believe me, if she hadn't been there for me to talk to – about you, I mean – I'd have gone completely mad, or run away to London. Just think of the scandal that would have caused.'

'Just think.' He looked at her. all at once serious, tracing the outline of her face with gentle fingertips. 'I love you,' he whispered, 'and I don't want to leave you, but I must be at the hospital soon.'

'I know – but we'll meet tomorrow?'

'And tomorrow, and tomorrow.'

'We are so lucky,' she smiled. 'Me and Hawthorn, both. You don't think we're too happy, do you?'

'Too happy? I don't know, darling. I see such suffering that perhaps I could be forgiven for thinking we all are.'

'But we won't lose each other? Promise nothing shall part us?'

'I promise. I love you too much.' He tweaked the tip of her nose. 'I'll call for you at three tomorrow. Will that suit?'

'It will suit, doctor,' she replied gravely, lifting her lips to his. 'It will suit very nicely indeed.'

Alice sat back on her heels, polishing cloth in hand, and gazed at the tin trunk at the foot of her bed. It was a fine piece, she considered gravely, the inside painted pale blue; the outside with brass handles at either end and a brass hasp and lock set squarely at the front. She had bought it for a shilling in the second-hand shop in Creesby, though it had cost her another sixpence to have it delivered to the back door at Rowangarth. Yet had it cost her twice as much, she would have loved it, because for all its ordinariness it was the start of their home – hers and Tom's – the chest in which she would store her linen. Household and personal linen, that was. Three of everything, there must be, before it was filled to the top. Three pairs of drawers, three chemises, three petticoats. Stood to reason. One in the wash, one airing and one wearing, or so the saying went; and added to them, all in good time, would go three nightgowns and a bed-shawl; all to be painstakingly hand-sewn – except for long seams when she might possibly cheat and use the machine in the sewing-room

After the personals would go pillow-slips and bolster-cases and sheets of the best quality she could afford, bought from the huckster who travelled the markets, his cart piled high with towels and tablecloths and cotton yardage and linen yardage in widths varying from cot size to double-bed size; cut from the roll with such straightness it was amazing, and ready for her to hem, top and bottom.

It was said, in Creesby, that a body could always tell the lass who was spoken for and the one who wasn't. Those still heart-whole bought knick-knacks and trinkets from the market stalls; those who were walking out steady bought from the huckster and wore small, satisfied smiles as they gave him their order.

Alice had counted the coins in her purse, then selected a towel, white and soft, with which to start her linen collection. The huckster, sensing a new and regular customer, had added a smaller towel, compliments of the management, and said he hoped to see her again in the very near future.

'Thank you kindly,' she returned gravely, 'and I shall see you again as soon as maybe . . .'

Not for three weeks, she sighed, for tomorrow the workmen would be arriving, their carts piled high with all manner of paraphernalia to begin the plumbing and electrification. There would be no more half-days off, then, for any of them until the work was finished.

She had made a start, though. Her towels lay on the bottom of the trunk with her birthday soap to scent them; quite the softest, most beautiful towels she had ever seen, and when next she visited Creesby she would, she considered, buy yardage to sew into pillow-slips and maybe even trim them prettily, though to imagine Tom's head on a lace-trimmed pillow made her wonder if maybe she shouldn't leave them plain. But such decisions could wait. At this moment all she could think about as she looked out into a perfect summer twilight, was how completely happy she was.

Her fingers strayed to the locket at her neck, and the ring hanging with it, and she closed her eyes, thinking of Tom and the tallness of him and the fairness and the way his smile wrought havoc with her insides. There was the letter, too, to set the seal on their understanding; a letter from Tom's mother, welcoming her to the family, inviting her to visit as soon as her son could take her there. And with the letter had been a slice of Tom's sister's wedding cake, wrapped in greaseproof paper for her to close her eyes and wish on before she ate it.

Such had been her joy, though, that she had cut the cake into four pieces and given one each to Tilda and Mary and Bess, to tuck beneath their pillows so they might dream of the man they would marry. Her own piece she had eaten quickly without so much as a half wish, because she had everything in the world she could want – and as for tucking it beneath her pillow – well, didn't she *always* dream of Tom?

The scents of the summer night drifted in at the open window, causing her to hug herself tightly, wanting everyone she knew and cared for to be this happy.

Slowly she undressed, folding her underwear neatly, hanging her dress on the peg behind the door. Then, slipping into her nightdress, she sank to her knees at her bedside. Head bowed, fingers clasped, she whispered her prayers to a God in whom she believed utterly and trusted completely; to a Creator who had made so perfect and happy a world and given more than her fair share of it to Alice Hawthorn.

She whispered, 'Amen', then opened her eyes, kneeling there still, thinking about Miss Julia and the doctor; wondering if they had managed to meet, hoping they had, and that they were in Hyde Park walking hand in hand without a care in the world. Carefully she opened the locket at her neck.

'God bless you, Tom' she whispered to the faded brown photograph with the buttercup beside it. 'Goodnight, my lovely lad.'

14

Lady Helen Sutton and her daughter Julia arrived home a little after nine in the evening, which was, Miss Clitherow said, the most opportune of times, for then the new electric lights could be switched on and seen to their best advantage. They would, she considered, give her ladyship the welcome she deserved; show how much improved was the old house and how fresh and clean again after the Upheaval.

'They're here!' called Tilda, who had not taken her eyes from the window above the sinkstone; a window level with the drive and from which she could see only feet and shins and the bottoms of carriage wheels. 'Hurry an' tell Miss Clitherow, Bess!'

'Oh, my word!' Cook lifted the kettle from hob to hot-plate, knowing a tray of tea would be the first thing milady would call for. 'Up you go, all of you!'

It had been decided by staff and approved of by the housekeeper that they should all be there to welcome the mistress home, if only to see her pleasure and amazement when the switch at the front door was dropped and the two chandeliers, each enhanced by sparkling glass shades sent by post from London, blazed into blinding magnificence.

Tilda dried her hands, fastened on a clean apron, and hurried to take her place at the back of the great hall.

Lady Helen had been missed; she always was when she went away, though goodness only knew, Cook had said, that it was so long since she'd been anywhere that the poor soul would be bothered to death by the noise of London and glad to get back to the peace and quiet of Rowangarth.

Home, Helen thought as William opened the carriage

267

door then walked a step ahead of her to place his forefinger firmly on the bell. And because everyone had been waiting for his ring, the door was opened at once by Mary, whilst Miss Clitherow stood, finger at the ready, beside the switch.

'Goodness!' Helen gasped as the hall, steps – even the coach outside – were all at once illuminated in a dazzle of light. 'How fine it all is and – ' She gazed around her at potted plants in abundance, at old wood polished to a glowing sheen, and at smiling servants, delighted by her amazement. 'And what a joy it is to be home again. Thank you all for working so hard.'

It was indeed a joy, even though she and Andrew were apart again, Julia thought, reaching for the switch, turning off the lights, snapping them on again.

'Stop it!' her mother chided, fighting a smile. 'The electrics are *not* to be played with.'

No indeed, agreed Tilda, who had done much the same thing until Miss Clitherow had been obliged to tell her that constantly switching the lights on and off could play havoc with the bulbs.

'Everything is in order, milady,' Miss Clitherow said when Helen was seated in her favourite chair, a tea tray at her side. 'The workmen were finished two days before expected, which was a great help.'

'And is everything to your liking?'

'It certainly is. No more lamps nor candles,' the house-keeper enthused. 'And the boiler works splendidly; there's hot water and to spare.'

'And an end to all the fetching and carrying . . .'

'Indeed.' Though Agnes Clitherow, having been the first to sample the delights of the new plumbing, had wondered how it would be in winter, with the newly partitioned bathrooms having no fireplaces. Up until now, baths had been troublesome things, but at least they were taken in bedrooms in front of a blazing fire, with towels

268

laid to warm on the fenders. True, the bathrooms were all newly decorated and tiled and splendidly modern, with glazed glass set in the window-panes; but how cold might they be come winter, her practical mind had debated? Yet such was her ladyship's pleasure at being home again, seeing the house so transformed in less than three weeks, that it would be downright unkind to voice such thoughts.

'Hawthorn has all but finished the curtains. They're mostly ready to hang, then you'll see for yourself how the bathrooms look. I've been waiting for you to decide, milady, which colour is to go where.'

'Then I will drink my tea and you shall show me all,' Helen smiled. 'And it *is* good to be back.'

It really was.

Alice sewed the last of the brass rings on to the new curtains and sighed her pleasure at a job well done. So smart and cheerful they would look when hung; when her ladyship had decided where the blue flowered ones would hang, and those with pink flowers, and the chintzy yellow ones, though it was almost certain that those with the autumn leaves would end up in the small, end bathroom Mr Giles had already claimed as his own.

Alice had missed Miss Julia. It was why she was here, now; waiting for the throwing open of the sewing-room door, the dramatic entrance. There was gossip to exchange, too, because since the return from London of the Place Suttons more than two weeks ago, talk and speculation had raged.

Mr Elliot had *not* gone to America, despite the fact he had been deposited on the dockside at Liverpool. Indeed, Mr Elliot had taken up residence in London in a house bought by his mother so near to Buckingham Palace that he would have to behave himself or be in deepest disgrace.

Mr Elliot *had* gone to America, another said, but he had

turned round and come straight home again on the next liner and would shortly be living in a house very near to that of his aunt Sutton in order that the worthy lady might keep an eye on his carryings-on, since his mother had finally given him up as a bad job.

Yet the truth of the matter, as Alice well knew since William had heard Giles and Nathan talking, was that Mrs Clementina had bought a house in Cheyne Walk – at the Chelsea end – at which she would give parties, receive her friends, and escape the unbearable cold of a northern winter.

Miss Julia, though, could choose which version best suited her, Alice decided, because even though there was known to be a grain of truth in all below-stairs gossip, a lot of it could be taken with a pinch of salt.

Julia arrived as expected, though with an unusual quietness about her.

'I'm missing him already, Hawthorn!'

'Never mind, miss. He hasn't gone to Timbuktu, has he?'

'No, thank heaven.' Only eight hours away if the longing got too much for her. 'Aunt Sutton goes to France tomorrow, but when she returns I'm to be allowed to go to London alone to stay with her – provided I'm put on the train at York and met at London, that is,' she smiled. 'And Andrew sent his warmest regards and asked especially if you were fully recovered after – well, you know . . .'

'I am, miss. And talking about *that one* – did you hear about the house in London? Is it true, then?'

'The one in Cheyne Walk – yes, it is. I didn't go to look at it – Mother wouldn't have wanted me to – though I'd have liked a peek at it. But why Aunt Clemmy didn't think to buy something central, I don't know. Aunt Sutton says it's because she's got to the whimsical age, whatever that is, so there's no accounting for what she might do.'

270

'And Mr Elliot Sutton is still in America and not in London, like talk has it?'

'Still away, but let's not talk about him. Can you keep a secret, Hawthorn – *really* keep it – because I've got to tell someone.' Julia's cheeks flushed pink, her eyes shone. 'Andrew says that in a year's time we can set a date for our wedding – sometime in September, he hopes. He says he'll be able to set up in general practice by then, though if he'd let me help him we could be married months sooner. But he's a proud, prickly Scot where wives are concerned. Grandmother Whitecliffe's money, when I get it, must remain my own, he insists, and fourteen months will soon pass, won't they?'

'I won't tell. Not a word,' Alice smiled. 'And me and Tom mightn't be so very far behind you. Reuben's retiring before so very much longer, as likely you'll know, and Tom's hoping he'll be able to move out of the bothy when that happens. I'll have to get Reuben's permission, but it'll be all right. He likes Tom . . .'

'We're lucky, aren't we?' Julia sighed. 'In a little over a year we could both be married.'

'Depending . . .' Alice cautioned, fingers crossed.

'Yes – that Andrew finds a decent practice.'

'And on whether or not Tom gets Reuben's job.'

'He'll get it,' Julia grinned. 'He found favour with Mother when he thumped Elliot. She said, "Good for Dwerryhouse!" But I shall be wishing my life away until next September. I feel so lost without him. I've already sent him a letter. I wrote it on the train and posted it at York. He'll have it second delivery tomorrow. Oh, Hawthorn, let's talk about weddings.'

'And wedding dresses . . .'

'And white satin shoes and silk nightdresses.'

'And next September . . .'

'And honeymoons and never being apart again. How are we to bear it until then, will you tell me?'

'We'll manage. It'll be here before we know it. And Miss Julia – it's grand to have you home.'

Grand, she thought again, as she brushed her hair at the open window of her bedroom, looking out across the sweep of lawn and the kitchen garden to where the bothy lights shone brightly. She knew which window was Tom's, and she sent her love winging out to him.

'Never being apart again, Tom,' she whispered. 'Together for ever – if we're lucky . . .'

Alice, with Morgan in tow, found Tom at the gallows tree on the far edge of Brattocks Wood. It was something Alice didn't like; a dead, leafless tree that looked out of place in summer, and with its branches hung with animals in varying stages of decomposition, just to look at it made her shudder. Yet it was necessary, for a gallows tree was where a keeper hung the pests and vermin he had killed – magpies that took birds' eggs or even their tiny young; stoats, weasels and carrion crows that were known to kill a newly-dropped lamb. And a gallows tree served to show an employer, should he walk that way, that his keeper was doing his job.

'Hullo, bonny lass.' Tom hooked a rat on to a branch. 'What are you doing in these parts – and out so early, an' all?'

'Not so much to do, now that the house is straight again, and all the curtains finished. Cook said no need to be back till teatime. Best part of an hour, we've got . . .' she smiled, lifting her face to be kissed.

'Then put Morgan's lead on him, then walk with me to the game cover. We've got the young birds there now, and they need a bit of feeding.'

Growers, Tom called them. Pheasants and partridge, chicks no longer, newly separated from the hens that fostered them; taken from the coops in the rearing field and put out to fend for themselves. And Tom was taking

272

wheat and barley to them, not only to make sure they fed well enough, but to keep them from straying to find food. Regularly fed birds didn't move far from where corn would appear, twice a day.

'Are the young birds doing well?' It was important to Alice, soon to be a keeper's wife, that they should.

'They are. Any road, Reuben's pleased enough, though Mr Giles don't say a lot.'

'He wouldn't. You should know what he thinks about killing, in any shape or form.'

'He's entitled to his opinion,' Tom answered comfortably, taking her hand. 'Did Miss Julia enjoy London, then?'

'She did, though she's missing the doctor something awful; sent him two letters already and she only said goodbye to him yesterday morning.'

'Reckon she's in love,' Tom smiled, and Alice's heart gave a thud of delight.

'She's in love, all right. In fact she's . . .' She stopped, all at once remembering that no one – not even Tom – could share their secret. '. . . she's as much in love as I am,' she whispered, blushing for shame that she could say such a thing and remembering the need to watch her tongue in future. And that wasn't easy when you wanted to share everything with the man you adored.

'Why the sigh, sweetheart?'

'I – oh, nothing, really, except that I'm happy.'

He squeezed the hand that lay in his, loving her, wanting her; loving her innocence, wanting to take it.

'Wait there. Stand still,' he said sharply. 'And keep a hold of Morgan while I thrown down this corn.'

He made a tock-tocking call and the birds came at once from out of the cover then stood a little way off, still unsure in their strange, open surroundings.

'There now, they'll do . . .' Tom threw wheat, flinging it wide. 'They're coming on a treat – providing that vixen from up the Pike leaves them be.'

'You haven't caught her yet?' She hoped he wouldn't, just yet. Her cubs, though no longer suckling, must still depend on her for food until they learned to catch their own, and in her present state of shining happiness, Alice loved all creatures.

'No, but I'll have her before so very much longer.' Best he should get the vixen. His gun was quicker and kinder than a pack of half-starved hounds. He turned towards Brattocks and the sheltered spot in which he could take her in his arms. 'And by the way, Alice Hawthorn, I'm happy too – being with you, I mean. I want always to be with you – you know that, don't you?'

'I do, Tom, and you shall.' Nothing would part them, ever. The happiness that for the most part lay warm inside her, yet flamed all at once into need when they met and touched and kissed, would suddenly not be denied and, reaching on tiptoe, she placed her mouth on his. 'I've told it all to the rooks, so it'll come right for us.'

'Talking to rooks? Alice, lass, it's a lot of nonsense.'

'It isn't! I always tell special things. Rooks never give away a secret.'

She pointed to the tallest tree in the wood; the elm some said was a hundred years old. One hundred years of secrets, it had heard, and if its rooks should ever leave it; if ever one spring they deserted their nests and went to some other place to build, then disaster would fall on Rowangarth. Or so folk hereabouts said.

'They're good birds, I'll grant you,' Tom acknowledged, reluctantly. Rooks weren't vermin; didn't fill their crops with the seed a farmer planted, like pigeons did. Rooks ate grubs and leatherjackets and didn't rob a bird's nest of its eggs. 'And did you know that a rook stays faithful all its life? You'll mind that most birds mate and couple afresh every spring?'

'Aye. On Valentine's Day, isn't it?'

'So some will have it. But those old rooks keep the same

partner year after year and don't want none other – well, not until one of them dies, that is.'

'Faithful,' Alice murmured, her cheek impervious to the rough tweed of his jacket. 'Like you and me. We'll be together always, won't we?'

'Always. There'll be no one else but you.'

'Mm.' She couldn't imagine loving again. It was Tom she wanted; him and no other. 'Not even if you were to leave me and I knew you were gone for ever would I want to love again. Why have you spoiled me for any other man?'

'I don't know, lass, though I'm glad I have. But why all this daft talk? You won't leave me, Alice Hawthorn, and I shall *not* leave you. We'll be wed, I promise, and live in Keeper's, and be happy. There now – does that please you?'

'It does. I do love you, Tom. I promise there couldn't be another,' she said fiercely, stubbornly.

'I know, bonny lass. I know.' His lips gentled her cheek. 'And I reckon the sooner we're wed, the sooner you'll be rid of your daft fancies. And we shall be, just as soon as maybe; once I know for certain that Keeper's Cottage is mine. So stop your worrying. Nothing and no one shall part us, so you'd best tell that to your rooks, an' all!'

'I'll tell them,' she smiled. 'And I don't usually take on so – it's just that I'm so full of happiness.'

'I know, sweetheart,' he said softly, wondering yet again how he was to bear loving her so much and wanting her so badly for nigh on a whole year. 'And let's get you back, or Cook'll go on something awful if you're late for tea, and Mr Giles'll think you and Morgan have run away with the gypsies!'

She had just opened the library door, given Morgan a quick pat and pushed him inside, when Julia walked along the corridor, envelope in hand.

'Hullo, Hawthorn. I'm just going cycle down to the pillarbox. Anything you want from Holdenby?'

'Oh, miss, not another one?' Alice chided.

'Another. Suddenly it all gets too much and I have to tell him – that I love him, I mean.'

'I know. It's all inside you and if you don't let it out you'll burst of happiness, for sure.'

'Burst,' said Julia, soberly. Then she smiled the lovely smile that could have come from no one else but her ladyship, Alice thought. 'But aren't we lucky, you and I? Was anyone ever as lucky as we are; so happy?'

'Happy,' Alice echoed. Yet surely, she frowned, there was some other word – some special, once-in-a-lifetime word to describe this – this *happiness*? 'Well, best be off for my tea. 'Bye, miss.'

'Goodbye,' Julia smiled, watching as Alice tripped downstairs, feet hardly touching the carpet. 'Happy,' she whispered softly, eyes closed. 'So *very* happy . . .'

15

The pink silk roses on Alice's Sunday hat did not make
her as happy as they usually did; not today, when the
Reverend Parkin had prayed in church not only for
Ireland, but that peace may yet prevail in Europe. His
words had sent sudden fear crawling through her, because
war couldn't happen – not in this lovely world she lived
in; not to her, not to anyone.

'It won't, will it?' she had asked of Tom as together
they walked back to Rowangarth. 'Happen, I mean.
War.'

'Of course it won't. What folk on t'other side of the
Channel get up to is nothing to do with us. Volatile, that
lot over there are.' *Volatile.* He like the word. Reuben
had used it and it explained a lot. 'And even if there is,
it'll all be over and done with by Christmas.' Reuben had
said that, too, though it had to be faced that Mr Giles had
said nothing at all lately about Reuben moving into the
little almshouse come September. It was as if he were
biding his time; waiting as the rest of the world waited,
to see what would come of the assassination. But no man
with a grain of sense in him thought about war with a
bonny lass on his arm. Glancing to right and left, he tilted
her chin for a parting kiss.

'See you tonight, sweetheart?' Tom Dwerryhouse
believed in putting first things first. 'Same time?'

'Mr Giles?' Alice murmured that evening after supper,
still apprehensive. 'Can you explain it to me – the carry-
on in the newspapers that's causing all the talk, I mean.'

'Talk of war?' He turned to look at her with troubled

eyes and her fear returned. 'What's got them into such turmoil?'

'Aye.' She twisted the dog lead in agitated fingers. 'Where did it all start and *why,* all of a sudden?'

'Start? Sarajevo, I suppose.' With the killing of Archduke Franz Ferdinand and his wife. 'But *why,* God only knows.'

'Then hadn't He best be sharp about it and sort it all out?'

'It isn't as simple as that. Sarajevo was the excuse, not the cause, Hawthorn. The Austrians have captured the assassin – a Serb – but there would be an outcry were they to shoot him: he's little more than a schoolboy. So they are demanding impossible reparations of the Serbs – sabre-rattling at the Russians who are on the side of Serbia, I suppose it amounts to. Both Germany and Austria mistrust the Czar, you see, and the killing in Sarajevo could provide them with what they want – a match to light the fuse with.'

'It seems, then, as if the Kaiser wants a war.' Alice swallowed noisily. 'And the Austrians, too.'

'I'm afraid so. It's mostly Germany's dislike of France and fear of Russia that's behind it all. Seems the German High Command have wanted a confrontation for years now, even though the Kaiser and the Czar are first cousins.'

'That lot in Europe are all cousins, but it isn't making much of a difference.' And Alice had to admit she was sorry for the Archduke and his wife; even sorrier for their two children made orphans – she knew all about being an orphan. But was it reason for war? 'Ah, well – there's nothing you and me can do about it, Mr Giles, so I'll give Morgan his run, like always, and maybe – '

'Giles!' Julia burst into the room. Julia, thought Alice, startled, almost always burst into rooms. 'I've just been on the telephone to London and Aunt Sutton is hopping mad. D'you know what is in the London evening papers?

That Germany is demanding – *demanding,* mark you – that Russia stops calling up its reservists immediately and that France announces her neutrality at once! And, would you believe, it seems they want France to surrender a couple of frontier towns – Toul and Verdun, I think she said – as a guarantee of goodwill!

'Aunt Sutton said the hell the French will and she says the Kaiser knows the French will refuse. Germany *wants* a war!'

'So what will France do, did she say?'

'Aunt Sutton says they should cock a snook at the Germans – call their bluff – and order general mobilization at once!'

'But would that be wise?' Giles frowned. 'Wouldn't the Kaiser immediately do the same?'

'Heaven only knows. Oh, Hawthorn – I didn't realize – I know I shouldn't go on so.' A glance at the stricken face warned Julia it was time to draw breath and calm down. 'I'm sorry if I upset you – we're *all* upset . . .'

'Yes, miss, I know. But the poor old dog don't understand a thing about it, so best I take him out,' Alice whispered, cold with fear.

'Lucky old dog,' Julia shrugged when they were alone. 'So what do you think the King will do, Giles?'

'I don't know. Would to God I did. But, Sis – don't go on about it in front of Mother? You know how upset all this war talk makes her?'

'I won't. But what will we do? Surely we can keep out of it?'

'I doubt it. We have guaranteed Belgian neutrality, remember. If the Germans or Austrians invade Belgium, we'll have to stand by our word.'

'But why should they invade? What have they got against Belgium, will you tell me?'

'Nothing at all, I'd say. But they would have to cross Belgium to get at France. And both fear France . . .'

'Oh, God!' Julia covered her face with her hands. 'Seems they're determined . . .'

'Seems so, old girl. Everybody seems linked by treaty or pledge to everybody else. But don't worry. If it comes to a fight, we'll be all right. We have the finest navy in the world and plenty of reservists to back up the army. And there's the Channel, remember, so don't worry your head about it. Even if the worst happened, it would be over by Christmas. They just want to let off steam, I'm sure of it.'

'Bless you, love.' Julia laid her cheek to her brother's. 'I'm so afraid, though. It's as if my lovely world is crumbling all around me. Why didn't we see this coming? Were we too busy being happy? Is being happy such a sin?'

Being happy; *too* happy. Her world had been one of gentleness and beauty; and from the very moment of her meeting with Andrew, everything she looked at seemed touched with gold. They had all been living in Arcadia: were the golden days gone for ever?

'Go to Mother, Julia. She must be feeling every bit as anxious as we are. Try to cheer her up, there's a good girl.'

'Yes. But come with me, will you? I'm always going off like a firecracker, but you'll be able to reassure her.'

'Very well.' He placed a marker in his book and closed it gently. 'Since Hawthorn has taken the dog for his run, I have no excuse, I suppose.'

'Poor Hawthorn. I upset her and she must be every bit as worried as I am. I'm a selfish brat, aren't I?'

'Not always, but tonight you shall make atonement by comforting Mother.' He held out his hand and she grasped it gratefully. 'And, awful as you are, I wouldn't change you,' he smiled.

Helen sat in the darkening conservatory, watching as the sun dropped behind the far elms, wondering if she were living through one of the last days of peace.

It had come so suddenly this war, for war there must

surely be unless God send down floods and bolts of fire on the turbulent Eastern Europeans. And miracles, she sighed, were few and far between.

Not that she cared for herself. She had known complete happiness; known more in the twenty-five years she'd had with John than five women in five lifetimes. It was her sons she worried for; for Robert – and please God he would stay safely in India – and for dear, gentle Giles. If war came, could our army take on Germany, or would young men be expected to enlist? Would they take her sons, part Julia and Andrew?

She looked up as the door opened, then smiled at her son and daughter, holding out her arms to them.

'My dears – come and join me.'

'What were you brooding about?' Giles took his mother's hand.

'Brooding? Oh, no. I was watching the beautiful sunset and thinking that perhaps I might ring for a tray of tea. Sit down and join me, won't you? How lovely it is. A sunset like that is always a sign of a good day tomorrow.' She smiled her beautiful smile as if all was well with her world and her heart not near to breaking. 'Come and sit by me, both of you. Let's hold hands and think how lucky we are . . .'

Oh dear, sweet Lord, Julia closed her eyes, all at once ashamed of her selfishness, *why didn't you make me more like my mother? And will you remind me when I get upset and worried about what is happening to me, that she is alone now? And please, if I swear to try to be a better person, will you let me keep Andrew, because he is so precious to me . . .*

'Darling.' She lifted her mother's hand to her cheek. 'I love you very much. I know I don't often tell you so, but when I'm being horrid, will you try to remember that I do? And shall I go downstairs for a tea tray whilst you and Giles wallow in your sunset?'

Because if I don't, Mama, I shall weep, and that would never do, now would it . . .?

August, like a woman in her prime, came in on a dance of sunlight, smiling benignly on fields of near-ripe corn, whispering to fat grouse on the heather-covered tops to beware, and count their days.

'It's a pity,' Tom said to Reuben, 'that Mr Giles don't care overmuch for shooting. We've some fine birds on the tops, yet no one bothers about them, 'cept poachers.'

'Aye.' Thoughtfully Reuben lifted his gun to the light, gazing, one eye closed, down the barrel he was cleaning. Like glass, his gun barrels must shine before he was satisfied and stopped his pulling through of the piece of soft, red flannel. 'A scholar, Mr Giles is. He was never cut out to be a country gentleman. It's his brother should be here, now that the shooting's starting. By the heck, it must be a right bonny lass that's making him turn his back on his birthright.'

'There's a woman at the bottom of it, you reckon?'

'*Cherchez la femme,*' Reuben shrugged. They were some of the few words of the French language Reuben knew but, give him his due, he pronounced them well.

'Then why don't he bring her here and settle down to some shooting and get on with rearing a few bairns for her ladyship?' It worried Tom that the estate employed two keepers yet few shoots took place. 'And has Mr Giles mentioned when you'll be moving? Not that I'm pushing,' he added hastily.

'He's said nowt, though I thought the matter was settled. Me to move out before pheasant shooting started, I always understood. And I want to, lad. There's times I'd like nothing better than to put my feet up and take things a bit easier. Happen it's this war talk that's made him forget.'

'You think it'll come to war, then?'

'If I could tell you that, Tom, I'd be working for the Government and not earning a living rearing game-birds for the gentry. Any road, I don't hold with wars.'

Wars, reasoned Reuben's philosophy, were downright immoral, though he admitted that from time to time some king or grand-duke or czar must feel the need to flex his muscles and put on a show of strength. But wars were wasteful and cost lives, when differences could have been resolved in a more gentlemanly manner by the simple expedient of two teams of guns. Let them shoot it out, he'd always maintained; not shoot at each other but at clays, rather, or at verminous pigeons and carrions and magpies.

'Whether you do or not, Reuben, I fear there's one coming and there's little the likes of us can do about it. Blasted Serbs . . .' Tom hadn't even heard of Sarajevo till a few weeks ago, yet now folk talked of little else. 'And Alice has got herself worried sick about it. Wish they'd get it over with, so things can get back to normal.' A good sea-battle, happen, to settle things once and for all. 'Well,' he reasoned on seeing Reuben's stony stare, 'folk are getting sick and tired of all the shilly-shallying. That Kaiser wants teaching a lesson.'

'Then I hope there'll be no order from London calling for our territorials to mobilize; and I hope that daft lot in Europe see sense afore it's too late, because once it starts, *if* it starts, they'll be at it like two hungry dogs over a bone. They'll neither of them let go . . .'

'Happen you're right.' Tom glanced at the mantel-clock. It was time for Alice to come – if Mr Giles didn't decide to walk the dog himself, that was. 'Reckon I'd best be off – see if Alice is about. And don't worry yourself, Reuben. I'll not upset her with war talk.'

'I should think not,' Reuben chuckled. War talk, with a bonny little lass like Alice there for the kissing? 'Get yourself off, and best we don't worry because it's like folk al'us says; it'll all be the same a hundred years from now.'

He placed his gun on the pegs on the chimney breast, then set the kettle to boil.

War? he frowned, gazing into the bright red coals. By the heck, but he hoped not!

The Kaiser's army marched into Luxembourg. It was a probing occupation; one to test the mettle of other governments and heads of state, and reaction was swift. France and Great Britain ordered general mobilization. In every newspaper, notices appeared calling reservists to the colours; hastily printed proclamations were displayed outside town halls, police stations, and even nailed to trees and barn doors in villages and hamlets.

Soldiers and sailors jammed the railway stations, making for ports and barracks. Overnight, women found themselves alone, mother and father, now, to their children; and provider, too, for a fighting man's pay was meanly given.

'I must go to the village,' Helen whispered. 'See what I can do . . .'

There would be many in need of comfort, even in Holdenby, and the reassurance that they were not completely alone might be some small help, she reasoned.

Already she had come to dread the delivery of morning and evening newspapers, and the ringing of the telephone sent apprehension slicing through her. Had she followed her instincts, she would have found a small, safe corner in which to hide; yet every house in the village belonged to Rowangarth, and those who lived in them were connected in some way or another to the Suttons, so hide she could not.

Instead she must hold her head high, smile often and resolutely, stand shoulder to shoulder with bewildered women, their faces taut with shock; must offer a comforting hand to those who bravely held back tears to wave their men goodbye.

Best she should go to the vicarage, to Jessica and Luke; it would be to that house the constable would first take any news or orders from high places. But first she would slip quietly into church, make one last desperate appeal that this should not be the final day of peace, the last day of her world as she knew it. For if the worst happened; if men were to forsake sanity, then nothing could ever be the same again.

'They'll requisition all the horses, see if they don't,' Cook mourned. 'Will Stubbs told me that the young veterinary is a reservist, and he'll be one of the first to go.' Stood to sense, didn't it, when horses still outstripped motors in the British army? 'There'll not be a thing left by the time the Government's finished.' Had had its thieving way; taken all it could lay its hands on in the name of national emergency. Already young men were flocking to enlist on a great wave of patriotism. Here was adventure, not to be missed; one sweet, fierce moment of glory, then back home for Christmas.

Motor buses from Creesby had already been commandeered to carry reservists to the mainline railway stations since both trains out had been packed to capacity. And this had not been without its inconvenience, since most ordinary folk had been left with little choice but to cycle or walk to their places of work.

Worse than that, some even suggested that the gentlemen from the Government might even go so far as to take Rowangarth to use as a billet for soldiers, or turn it into a hospital for the wounded.

'Take Rowangarth?' Mrs Shaw had snapped, gravy ladle poised belligerently. 'And why, will you tell me, that out of all the gentlemen's houses the length and breadth of this land should they pick on us?' And any road, Pendenys would be nearer the mark, would make a far better hospital than higgledy-piggledy Rowangarth;

could accommodate four times as many soldiers. Cook smiled secretly to think of a protesting Mrs Clementina being moved out and the army tramping in.

'They'll probably come,' Tilda said darkly, 'and take all our food.'

If they were to billet soldiers at Rowangarth or Pendenys, then they'd all have to be fed, now wouldn't they?

'Food!' Cook snorted, remembering with gratitude the extra fifty-six pounds of sugar she had bought in only last week. 'Our lot don't go taking food!' The Germans, maybe; those swaggering Prussians would stop at nothing. But it could not happen in England; in this bastion of all that was good and sound and safe. 'And talking about food, will you all put those dratted newspapers down this instant and be about your business! We ain't at war yet, and if you take my advice, all of you, you won't believe the half of what you've read!'

Scaremongering, that's what the newspapers were doing. Upsetting everybody with their wild stories and suppositions. Newspapers ought to be banned at times such as this, and though she had devoured every printed word she could lay hands on these past few weeks, Mrs Shaw was still inclined to believe only what she wanted to. This morning, all she had chosen to believe was the date printed boldly on the front page, though she had checked even that with the calendar!

War, war, *war*! She was sick and tired of it already and it hadn't even started. And oh, please God it wouldn't.

The telephone in the great hall began its ringing as Julia was passing. Without thinking, she picked it up, unhooked the receiver, placed it to her ear, then gave out a cry of delight.

'Andrew! *Darling!* Why are you ringing? Is everything all right?'

'I'm at your aunt's house, and everything is fine, though London is in a ferment. Families crowding the railways to get home and Territorials packing the trains to get to their regiments and rumours everywhere . . .'

'But you're all right, Andrew? Why are you at Aunt Sutton's?'

'I'm all right and I'm here because your aunt called me to Miss Figgis. She has a stomach upset but is over the worst, I'm glad to say. She'll be taking nourishment tomorrow, I'm sure of it. Miss Sutton suggested I give you a call to let you know she is well – though a little disgruntled that the worst might happen and prevent her visiting France.'

'Then give them both our love, though I was hoping you'd tell me that you've heard some wonderful news – that they have all seen sense.'

'I'm afraid not, but at least I can tell you I love you.'

'And I love *you*. Andrew – let's be married? Let's not wait another week?'

'If I have to go, then I promise you we'll bring the wedding forward.'

'What do you mean – *if* . . .' Panic screamed through her.

'I mean if my conscience won't let me stay out of it – if it happens, that is. Julia, dearest, if there are to be wounded men, then I must be with them.'

'But not just yet, darling?' Of course he would go, but please not before they'd been married! 'You wouldn't do anything without telling me?'

'Of course I wouldn't. I love you too much. But I must go, now. Your aunt is well and Miss Figgis on the mend. We are all fine, down here – just a little on edge.'

'Goodbye, Andrew. I love you. And if you can't find time for letters I shall understand. But please just write that you love me?'

She closed her eyes tightly against the hopelessness of

it all; because there was nothing she could do but wait and hope and pray.

Taking a pencil, she wrote on the pad, *London phoned. All well.*

Her mother would see it when she returned from the village. These days, especially, her mother glanced at the telephone pad before she had even removed the pin from her hat.

Yet all wasn't well. Tomorrow or the next day could see them at war, and even if it only lasted the few months everyone predicted, Andrew *might* join the Medical Corps and he *could* get hurt, even though common sense told her that hospitals would be sited well away from risk.

She closed her eyes again and sent her thoughts high and wide.

If you go to war, Andrew, I swear I'll follow you. Somehow, I will find a way!

At first light on the fourth day of August, the Kaiser's soldiers crossed the frontier into Belgium. At half-past ten that morning, the King held a privy council meeting at Buckingham Palace to discuss the gravity of the situation and to advise Mr Asquith at Downing Street that a proclamation of war with Germany was being prepared. An hour before midnight, Great Britain, with her Empire and Dominions, was at war with Germany. King against Kaiser; blood ties forgotten.

At once, all military areas were closed to aliens, trade with the enemy forbidden and merchant ships requisitioned for use as troop transports.

It was a sad state of affairs, most thought, that it should come to this. Up until that day, no restrictions had been placed upon the British people, who could leave the country and re-enter it at will; there had been no restrictions, either, upon foreign nationals who wished to live in the United Kingdom. Yet now, some said, the need to carry a passport would be imposed; there might even be compulsory military service.

Already, in the space of a day, things were changing. Those who could afford it bought in flour and sugar, butter and bacon; those who could not had to accept that beer, their only luxury, was to be watered down by Government order and the licensing hours of alehouses severely curtailed.

At a little before midnight, Miss Clitherow walked slowly down the back stairs and opened the kitchen door to find everyone sitting round a dying fire, reluctant to go to their beds until they knew. Five pairs of anxious eyes met hers.

'I'm sorry,' she whispered. 'Miss Sutton has not long telephoned from London. I'm afraid – '

'War?' Cook whispered.

'Yes. An hour ago. We and the French . . .'

There was a stupefied silence as if no one else could speak; a silence so complete that it almost screamed *No*! 'A police constable from Creesby called earlier, warning her ladyship to be prepared – but you'd all know that?'

They knew. Mary had realized from the set of his face as she opened the door to him that he had not brought good news.

'He said it is best – and her ladyship agrees with him – that we show as little light as possible. Close the curtains before you switch on a light at night. And from now, I understand, the gas lamps in Creesby streets will not be lit – just as a precaution. But we are not to worry unduly, the constable said. We are all safe, her ladyship said I'm to tell you . . .'

Her words trailed into nothing and were lost in the silence.

'Safe from what, Miss Clitherow?' Tilda was the first to find her voice. 'From them Russians that are here?'

'Those Russians do not exist, Tilda.'

'But they've been seen, miss; thousands and thousands of them, going through York station by the trainload! What are they up to?'

'Yes, and those same mysterious Russians have also been seen in Manchester and in the Midlands and heaven only knows where else. Those are silly rumours, and we must not listen to rumours, Tilda. Even if any of it were true, there would not be cause for alarm. Russia is on our side. Czar Nicholas is our King's cousin.'

'Aye, and so is the Kaiser!' burst out Cook indignantly, 'And it didn't stop *him*!' But Kaiser Wilhelm would bitterly regret what he had started, Mrs Shaw brooded silently; would wish he'd never taken on the might of the British Empire.

Kaiser Willy: 'Silly Willy', folk were already calling him; Willy with the withered left arm. And *that* could only have been caused by cousin marrying cousin!

'Well, if we don't have to bother about the Russians,' Tilda persisted, 'then what are we supposed to be safe *from*? Zeppelin attacks, is it?'

'*Not* zeppelins, Tilda. Why would a zeppelin come here? What is there to drop bombs on? London, maybe, but not here. By *safe*, I think her ladyship meant in general terms. She meant to convey, I think, that she and Mr Giles will take care of us. And she would want you to worry as little as possible and, now that the stress of the last few weeks is over and we know where we stand, I think she would want us all to try to look on the bright side and to count our blessings too.'

Blessings? Alice thought, as cold, cruel hands clutched at her insides. What blessings, when Tom might have to go and Mr Giles and Doctor MacMalcolm? Where was the sense in war? Why couldn't folk live and let live? And just six weeks ago, not one of them had even so much as heard of a place called Sarajevo!

'I think,' said Cook, after Miss Clitherow had begged

them to say their prayers most earnestly tonight before making a tearful departure, 'that we should all have a cup of tea with a sniff of brandy in it. For our nerves.'

'Brandy?' Bess breathed.

'Aye. Only the cooking stuff, mind, but I reckon we all needs and *deserves* a drop tonight.' Her lips trembled and she dashed away the tear that trickled down her cheek. 'Well come on then, Tilda girl! Get some kindling on that fire and set the kettle to boil! Just because we're fighting a war don't allow for slacking – oh my word, no!'

Helen glanced at the mantel-clock. Just five more minutes of this awful day to run, yet still she could not bring herself to go to bed.

'We must remember, Giles, to remove the bulbs from the conservatory lights as the constable suggested.' She stirred restlessly. 'Oh, I can't believe it. It came on us so suddenly – and all because of what happened at Sarajevo.'

'No, dearest.' Giles reached for his mother's hand and the coldness of it shocked him. 'It is because we have ignored the Germans far too long. Judge Mounteagle was right. The Kaiser's advisers have been planning for war. The assassination was the excuse they needed, that's all.'

'What was it the Foreign Minister said about the lamps going out all over Europe? Giles, you won't enlist? Not just yet? I ought to be patriotic, send you to war with my head held high, but I don't want to!'

'And I don't want to go. You know I am against all killing. I can't take life, not even for my country. I shall not rush to enlist, and there'll be no need to, anyway. Your lamps will be shining again, I promise you, by Christmas.'

'Bless you, Giles. These past few weeks have been a trial, and not for anything would I want to live them again. And perhaps things will be more bearable now that we know the worst and when we've had a chance to get used to it.'

'Of course. Nothing much here will change. Little Hawthorn will still tiptoe off with Morgan, and Julia will write every bit as furiously to her Andrew. Germany and Austria will come to see the futility of it all before so very much longer, just see if they don't. Wars cost lives and they also cost money, and they'll all of them – yes, and our own country too – soon be looking for ways to end it all without anyone losing too much face.'

'Then I shall pray you are right.' Pray, too, that in the morning she might awaken to find the past weeks had all been a long, terrible nightmare. 'And Giles, if Julia and Andrew want to marry sooner than they'd planned – have just a quiet affair – say you won't forbid it?'

'Julia is twenty-one, now. I wouldn't even try.'

'Good. And you, Giles – are you sure there isn't someone? I wouldn't want you to sacrifice your own interests to Rowangarth. You know I want dearly to see you married too.'

'There is no one, Mother. Even if there were, I'd think twice now about marriage. If the unthinkable happens and the war drags on, I feel it would be wrong for me to marry then go to France, perhaps leaving a wife with a child to bring up alone.'

'But *your* child, Giles . . .'

'A son for Rowangarth, you mean?' He said it tongue-in-cheek, his eyes teasing.

'Giles, I *want* you to marry and have children – for you, for me and yes, for Rowangarth too. I *deserve* grandchildren,' she added defensively.

'Then write to my brother and tell him that,' he laughed.

'Robert,' she murmured, frowning. The son in far-away India she hadn't seen for almost three years.

Stay where you are, Robert. Don't come home, to this.

She felt no shame for her lack of patriotism, for wasn't she first a mother? Which mother wanted a dead hero for a son?

'Don't frown, dearest. I was only teasing.' Giles cupped his mother's face in gentle hands. 'All of this will come right for us. One day soon, we shall all look back and wonder why we worried so.'

'You think so?' Eagerly, she snatched at the crumb of comfort.

'My dear, lovely mama, I am *sure*. Now shall I bring you hot milk and shall you stop your worrying and go to your bed like a good, sensible lady?'

'No milk, I thank you. I think a glass of sherry will help me to sleep, though, but only if you join me.'

'Gladly. And we'll raise our glasses to the quick return of sanity and goodwill.'

Helen smiled as her son patted her hand, then went in search of decanter and glasses. And he was right, she sighed. War was futile and wasteful, and soon all nations would come to accept it. It *would* be over by Christmas; everyone said so, she reasoned, tilting her chin higher.

Then if that were so, she silently demanded, why was she so very afraid?

16

Charming though his new sister-in-law had proved to be, Elliot Sutton, having tired of Kentucky hospitality, took himself off to New York on the very day of the assassination in Sarajevo. It surprised him that the newspapers there should give such prominence to an event he dismissed as typical of Eastern European peasants, and he began a round of eating, drinking and theatre-going with dedicated indulgence. Yet, by the time he returned to his brother's home, the European situation, as it had come to be known, was being treated with concern, for what affected Europe in general, and France and Britain in particular, could well affect the United States of America.

'Will there be war?' Amelia demanded, 'and shall you enlist, Elliot, if there is?'

'War? I doubt it, my dear, though if the balloon bursts, naturally I would take a commission in the army at once.' But the balloon wouldn't go up, let alone burst, though he was flattered by the admiration in her violet-eyed gaze. 'Mind, I don't advise it for you, Albert,' he hastened, meeting his brother's narrowed eyes with equanimity. 'You have your responsibilities now, and your first duty is to your wife and home.'

Albert nodded, mollified, even though he had not so much as considered returning to the country of his birth, should the need arise. He was in the process of applying for American citizenship – Amelia had insisted upon it – and had no intention of exchanging a life of ease for that of an army subaltern.

'You must be worried,' Amelia laid a hand on Elliot's

arm, 'about your folks back home. They do say Germany has zeppelins capable of dropping bombs on London.'

'The Germans have made advances, especially in the field of mass production,' Elliot acknowledged, 'and though their army is efficient enough, our navy is second to none. Should Austria and Germany be so foolish as to challenge the British Empire, I think you will find that one all-out confrontation will put paid to their aspirations once and for all.'

'Is that so?' Amelia's lips pursed with sudden annoyance, though she was too genteelly reared to remark that the United States had a navy, too, and as for the British Empire – which in America amounted to nothing less than an arrogant grabbing of half the world – well, words failed her! She breathed deeply, grateful that her dear Albert showed no signs of his brother's conceit and condescension. Had it not been for the fact that her brother-in-law just might, one day, inherit a title, she could, on many occasions, have been driven to remark that his manners left much to be desired. 'I shall leave you to your port, gentlemen.' She pushed back her chair, outwardly serene. 'Join me for coffee in the boudoir – ' she looked directly at her husband – 'in ten minutes.'

Albert and Elliot rose automatically to their feet as she prepared to leave them.

'Please don't get up,' she smiled. My, whatever else, didn't you just have to admire that English old-world courtesy? You could, she admitted, almost forgive them their brass-necked pride. 'Ten minutes, remember . . .'

'I think,' Elliot murmured, reaching for the decanter as the door closed, 'that should the situation in Europe get worse, I must consider returning home. Mama will be worried; someone must be there to comfort her.'

'She's got Pa, hasn't she,' Albert scowled, 'and Nathan?'

'Yes, indeed. But as you know, Bertie, Pa never seems

to be there when he's needed, and Nathan is awaiting ordination and has thoughts for nothing but the Church.'

'When do you intend leaving?' It surprised Albert he could have forgotten how he had so disliked his eldest brother. 'If it comes to a showdown, a passage home might not be easy to get hold of, if you delay. Could be a dangerous crossing, too,' he added with relish. 'Submarines, I mean . . .'

'You could well be right. Might be wise to get in touch with Cunard right away.' Elliot had had his fill, anyway, of Kentucky. American tarts had proved expensive; American young ladies were more carefully chaperoned than in England – and surely the sewing-maid incident should have long ago blown over? 'Wouldn't do to have people thinking I'd sat out the war in safety – if it comes to a scrap, that is.' The angry flush on Albert's cheeks prompted him to drain his glass quickly and rise to his feet. Pointedly, he glanced at his watch. 'Shall we join your wife?' he smiled.

Alice was determined to put the war behind her and not to trouble it until it troubled her. She had volunteered at once to knit khaki gloves for the troops; to cut three-inch strips from lengths of cotton, then assist in rolling them into bandages with her ladyship's 'Comforts for the Troops' circle. This afternoon she had also given up her half-day off to shake a tin in Creesby market, collecting pennies and halfpennies for the Red Cross. Now, with just a few minutes to spare before the bus left, she paid a visit to the huckter's stall, there to buy trimmings for the pillow-cases she had sewn for her linen chest, for not even the Kaiser was allowed to upset that. The war would not last long: Tom said it wouldn't, and he hadn't joined that first fervent rush to enlist, declaring it would be a waste of his time and the Government's money in training him up as a soldier for so short a duration. This greatly reassured Alice, and she had settled down, albeit with eyes still devouring the morning papers, to as near normal a life as possible.

Mind, Cook had been put out by the temporary shortages in the food shops, caused by people who had panicked because the Germans, it was said, would at once blockade every yard of the coastline and prevent food coming in and fishing smacks going out. Yet, this far, it had not happened. The food shops had replenished their stocks, though now they refused to sell what they considered to be more than their fair share of sugar, butter, bacon and flour to their customers. It pleased Cook that not so very long ago she had laid in extra sugar, a wise move, since sugar would be one of the first casualties of the war, she calculated, no one having noticed until now that Germany was the principal refiner of sugar in Europe. She was sure the British would be forced to curtail their liking for sweetness in the not-so-distant future.

Alice placed the broderie anglaise edging in her basket, together with the collecting tin, a twist of tobacco for Reuben and a bag of mints for Tom, smiled a promise to the huckster to see him next week, then made for the omnibus stop to wait. Things were returning to some kind of order at Rowangarth – or as near as made no matter now that the awful waiting was over and the first breathless panic had subsided into an acceptance of what might come. Times spent with Tom were now more precious, and each meeting seemed more special than ever before.

But governments would see sense; they would have to before so very much longer, Alice brooded. Will Stubbs was of the considered opinion that the Kaiser had bitten off more than he could chew; had thought the British would turn a blind eye to his invasion of Belgium and, now that Britain had declared war on him, was worried sick about it and looking for ways to get his troops back home, double-quick. Mind, there was also the school of thought that the King had sent his German cousin a sharply worded telegram, telling him to mind his p's and q's, which might have accounted for the Kaiser's change of heart. And there was still the mystery of the missing hundred thousand Russians, shunting hither and thither on the London and North-Eastern Railway. Very peculiar indeed, Alice reckoned, since there never yet had been smoke without fire, though what they were doing so far from St Petersburg, no one had yet caught up with them to ask.

She was relieved to see the bus turning the corner. At least the motor buses were back to normal running after their frantic shuttling to York with Territorials and reservists. Maybe soon, the rest of Europe would get itself into some kind of order again.

And tonight, no matter what, she smiled, she would be seeing Tom.

'Oh, my lordy!'

Cook unhooked her spectacles, then, letting the morning paper slide from her shaking fingers, buried her face in the folds of her apron and sobbed bitterly.

'Poor lads. Ah, them poor young lads . . .'

'Mrs Shaw – what is it?' Bess dropped to her knees beside the furiously rocking chair. 'Whatever has happened?'

Cook always had first use of the servants' morning paper, reading out snippets, snorting comments as befitted her interpretation of the war news, but never, in the two-and-a-bit weeks since it started, had she been so distraught, so overcome.

'A battle.' She lowered her apron to gaze tearfully around her. 'In Belgium, at a place called Mons. Our lads got the worst of it – had to retreat when it got to night-time. And the Germans set out after them to cut them down. And then – oh, dear – ' The tears flooded afresh, and she retreated once more into her pinafore.

Speedily, Bess scanned the headlines. 'There *was* a battle – a big one. And our troops did retreat but then – oh, my goodness, listen to this! An eye-witness account from the Front is prepared to swear that, as our army was forced to withdraw, a mighty vision of brightness appeared above our ranks and between them and the advancing Germans, and as they gazed, the brightness could only be described as a host of angels, hovering protectively around our men,' she gasped. 'And what was more, those Germans must have seen them, an' all, because they turned tail and ran and our troops were left unharmed to march back to safety. Oh, isn't that wonderful?'

'Yes, an' it's in the paper, in black-and-white for all to see,' Cook added, forgetting her mistrust of the printed word. 'A miracle, that's what.'

The tears started afresh, and the to-and-fro rocking, and Tilda, who quickly ascertained that if it went on for much longer there'd be no breakfast for anybody, laid down her dishcloth and declared with splendid aplomb, 'Then what are you all bothering about? If we've got the angels on our side, it's bound to be over by Christmas, now isn't it?'

But Cook and Bess were so overcome at the miracle of the Angels of Mons – ghosts returned from Agincourt, they had to be – that Tilda set the iron frying-pan on the hob to heat and brought the plate of newly rinded bacon from the pantry.

'First, it's the disappearing Russians,' she muttered, 'and now angels!'

Whatever next?

Elliot Sutton had arrived at Pendenys on the day the German hordes swept into Belgium, and such was his mother's delight at seeing her firstborn back home that she ran down the steps crying, 'Elliot! Oh, my dear, *dear* boy, you are safe!' as if he were returning battle-stained from the war. 'Why didn't you let us know? Just a cable and we could have met you at Liverpool.'

'I decided against it – didn't want you to worry about the crossing,' he smiled, gathering her to him, kissing her with studied tenderness.

A bare-faced lie, nonetheless. He had kept secret his return the more to enhance the surprise of his arrival. And it had worked. Even his father held out a hand of welcome and his brother, smiling, said, 'Elliot! Good to see you safely back. Now Mother can sleep nights again.'

'We are almost ready for dinner; I'll ring and delay it until you're bathed and changed, my dear.' Clementina pulled hard on the nearest bell-rope, not knowing whether first to summon a valet or send a message to the kitchens.

Clemmy was like a dog with two tails, Edward thought sourly; not knowing which of them to wag the more furiously. Then he chided himself for his lack of charity. Elliot was his son, and the centre of his mother's existence: naturally she was pleased he was back. Who knew but that a spell in disgrace had been just the shock he'd needed.

'If dinner is to be late, I'll take a turn around the grounds,' Edward said to a wife still delirious with delight. 'Have me called, will you?'

Outside, he kicked moodily at a fallen fir-cone. Damn and blast it - how was it possible to dislike his own flesh and blood so?

After he had extolled the delights ot Kentucky, and passed photograph's of Albert's wife, Albert's house and Albert's splendid bloodstock around the dinner-table, Elliot went on to stun his family with the amazement that was New York.

'Those great, tall buildings – skyscrapers, they call them – are springing up everywhere. And life is lived at such a pace that it makes London seem a sleepy backwater by comparison,' he enthused, determined to prove that his banishment had turned out nothing less than a delight; that had it not been for the seriousness of the situation in Europe, he wouldn't have so much as dreamed of returning for many months.

'And the working man's standard of living is such that many of them own motors. *Own* them! Mind, it's all due to Mr Ford. He's got it to a fine art; almost as bad as the Huns, those Detroit manufacturers with their factories and production lines.

'The first of those little motors came on to the market last year, though they're what you'd call a working-class job, and not to be compared with British and French engineering. Only one fault, for all that. Each and every one of them is black, but with decent brass trims to all the lamps, and – '

'You seem much taken with the New World,' Nathan smiled.

'Taken? America is a splendid country, full of opportunities. You should go there, brother; make your way in the world.'

'Nathan has given his allegiance to the *English* Church,' Edward remarked, pointedly. 'His future lies in his own country.'

'Sorry. I'd forgotten. And losing Albert to America is sufficient, I suppose. He'll be staying there. Well, he *is* a married man, with all the responsibilities that entails, whereas I – ' he paused to smile in turn at each one sitting at the table – 'whereas I came home specifically to enlist.'

'Elliot! *No!*' Clementina's face blanched, her spoon fell with a clatter from suddenly useless fingers. 'Elliot, you *can't!*'

'Can, Mother, and will!' He would look more handsome still in uniform – after giving consideration before enlisting, of course, to the one most becoming to his colouring and

301

height. 'It is my duty. What about you, Nathan? You'll go, too?'

'My ordination is in two weeks' time. When I am finally a priest – the humblest of curates – then I, too, shall volunteer. The army will need chaplains.'

'No! Please, *no!*' Clementina reached for her water glass, taking great, choking gulps from it. 'Oh, this is altogether too much! You should have stayed there, Elliot, away from it all. Who's to say this idiot Government won't bring in conscription? There won't be an able-bodied young man left then.'

'Some young men would stay. They'd defy call-up,' Nathan spoke quietly, remembering his own dislike of killing and that of his cousin, Giles.

'Not go? But that is monstrous!' Elliot spat contemptuously. 'Cowards like that deserve the white feather!'

The white feather. The badge of cowardice.

'I would not kill.' Nathan spoke quietly, his eyes steadily holding those of his brother.

'Well of course *you* wouldn't – you're damn nearly a priest. But you've been talking to Rowangarth, haven't you? A sissy, that's what cousin Giles is. And will Robert come home? You bet he won't! Robert Sutton will sit out this war skulking behind his tea bushes, mark my words if he don't!'

'Elliot! You disgust me!' Nathan brought down his fist on the table-top, turning to his father. 'Excuse me, sir, and you, Mama? Suddenly I'm not hungry!'

'Come back! At once, I say!' Clementina cried as the butler began to shepherd out footmen and parlourmaids who had already, in his opinion, heard too much.

'Stop!' Edward motioned with his finger. 'No one else is leaving and I for one wish to be served!'

'But I *don't!*' Elliot jumped to his feet. 'A fine homecoming this has turned out to be! I should have stayed, dammit; stayed where I was welcome!'

'And I,' Clementina sobbed, making for the door, 'could not eat another bite at this table – at *my own* table. I must lie down! It is all too much!'

'As you please, my dear.' Edward Sutton dabbed his mouth with his napkin then nodded to his butler. 'The soup was excellent; now I will take a cut of beef, if you please. Sit down, Elliot, if you intend to stay; though why you had to upset your mother and brother is beyond me. Do you take a delight in being so perverse?'

'Father! Opinion has it in the United States that the war will not be over by Christmas. There, they think it will go on for years. You cannot, therefore, blame me for wanting to make sure I don't wait and end up foot-slogging in the infantry!'

'You seem to set great store by America and American opinion,' Edward remarked, blandly. 'Tell me, when will they join our cause?'

'Never, like as not. It isn't their war. They can stay out of it – and wouldn't you, with the Atlantic between you and the fighting?'

'That, I imagine, is a matter for American consciences. Now sit down, boy, and finish your meal.'

'Sorry! Not where I'm not wanted!' Elliot glared the length of the room at his father, then slammed the door behind him.

Edward gazed round the empty table and at servants who stood embarrassed, eyes on shoe toes. At least, he sighed, he could now eat in peace.

'Finish serving me,' he said quietly, 'then put a little cheese on the side table and I will see to myself. After that, you may all leave.'

Elliot cannot be my son, he thought, cutting viciously at the meat on his plate. He simply *cannot*!

Later that evening, Edward tapped on the door of his wife's bedroom, then closed it quietly behind him. She was not sleeping, so he whispered, 'Are you feeling better now, Clemmy? Have you composed yourself?'

'Composed? Better? I shall never be well again! And all because I am a mother; because the prospect of losing my sons to this wicked war dismays me! What am I to do then – laugh my head off?'

'You might try accepting the situation – as all mothers in all stations in life have tried to do – with a little more dignity.'

'*Dignity!*' She sat bolt upright, eyes bright with anger. 'Like your precious Helen across the fields, I suppose? But she's all right, isn't she? One son in India and the other an effeminate bookworm. I notice neither of those two have rushed to the colours!'

'That's enough, Clementina! Giles is no more effeminate than Nathan, and there's nothing pansy about *him*! Just because neither of them goes rampaging round whorehouses as Elliot does, casts no aspersion on their manhood!'

'So! Now we're back to *that* again! Can't you forget what happened in Brattocks?'

'I have tried, so help me, I have tried.' Indeed, he'd almost succeeded, until his elder son had appeared, unheralded, like the prodigal son, all sins forgiven. 'I only hope the poor girl he assaulted has also forgotten!'

'I told you before – she asked for it. And was aided and abetted by Giles who has had the little slut himself, I shouldn't wonder!'

'Clementina – will I tell you something?' Edward asked much, much too quietly. 'There have been many times I had cause to wonder if Elliot was ours, but now I know that at least he is *yours*!'

'How *dare* you!' Her voice rose to a scream, then she pummelled the pillow with vicious fists before flinging it in his face. 'Oh! Oh – aaaagh . . .'

All at once speechless, shaking with breathless fury, she

flung herself on to her stomach, covering her head with the quilt.

'Get out!' she sobbed. '*Go!*'

Alice stood by the stile where wood and wild garden met, reluctant to venture too far in or too far from sight and sound of Reuben's cottage. She bent to release the spaniel, whispering to him to go. Morgan would find Tom, let him know she was here. And wasn't it downright foolish to be like this when she knew lightning never struck twice – not in the same place, anyway.

She heard a short, delighted yap and Tom's answering whistle, and ran towards the sound, calling his name, throwing herself into his arms.

'Tom! He's back! Last night, unexpected!'

'Hey! Hold hard, lass.' He tilted her chin, placing his lips to hers. 'There now, that's better.'

'Tom! I'm trying to tell you he's – '

'Young Sutton – back from America, you mean? I know. Their keeper told me this morning.'

'You went to Pendenys?'

'I did. One of their keepers knows I'm in the market for a dog of my own; sent a message for me to go over – look at some pups . . .'

'It's got me worried – well, just a bit. But he won't come here again, will he?'

'Reuben's dogs are getting on, now, and a bit slow for the guns – reckon he'll take them with him when he goes. A bit of companionship, sort of,' Tom went on, putting first things first. 'Couldn't have a dog of my own in the bothy – Jin Dobb would have seen to that – but I'll need one once I move into Keeper's. There's a fine bitch at Pendenys; I've always had a fancy for one of her pups.'

'Will you listen! I'm trying to tell you that Elliot Sutton is back and you seem not one bit bothered!'

'I'm not, and neither should you be, Alice Hawthorn. He'll not set foot on Rowangarth land nor anywhere near you, be sure of that; knows what he'll get if he does. Forget him. There's more important things to talk about than that young buck – my own dog, for instance, and what I shall call him.'

'But you aren't in Keeper's Cottage yet. Aren't you worried about Mr Giles not saying anything about Reuben moving out?'

'Course I'm not. Reuben wants to go and Mr Giles'll get round to it in time. Slipped his mind, I shouldn't wonder, with all that's been happening.'

'But, Tom – a pup takes a long time to train for the gun. Are you sure it'll be all right?'

'That I shouldn't be taking on a dog when I might have to go for a soldier, don't you mean?'

'Only *if* . . .' She shouldn't have said that. Tom wouldn't have to go.

'Heaven help me, lass, but it's a real worrier I've found for myself! I won't be enlisting, Alice. We've got an army and enough reservists and a man doesn't have to go if his conscience tells him otherwise. This war isn't going to last, everybody says so; so where's the need to go rushing off without so much as a thought? When they bring in conscription – *if* they do – when a man has no choice but to go, then I'll step forward, sweetheart. When the time is right, I'll enlist.'

'So you don't think it's over-serious?'

'I don't, but what I *do* think is that you've worried yourself into a tizzy over what the papers say. You can't believe all you read.'

'That's what Mrs Shaw says,' she admitted, dubiously.

'Well then, there you are!'

'But it still don't stop her reading them. There's been a terrible battle, Tom.'

'There's bound to be battles – stands to sense. But the

306

Kaiser's a fool and Franz Joseph of Austria's an old ditherer. There's nowt for us to worry overmuch about, to my way of thinking.'

'But don't you love your country?' Alice persisted.

'Suppose I do. Haven't given it a lot of thought. But when the time comes I'll fight for it, and for you too, though the time isn't now.' He took her in his arms, kissing her gently. 'I can see I'll have to wed you pretty quick once I've got moved into Keeper's, then I can put you over my knee and spank you when you nag me!'

'Married, Tom? So soon, then?' Her cheeks pinked with delight.

'Don't see why not. You'll be under-age, but I reckon Reuben won't have any objections. So don't let's spoil things by talking about war, or Elliot Sutton. Let's talk about you and me, and how much I want you. Or better still, let's not talk at all.'

She was, Alice admitted as she nestled closer, just about the luckiest girl ever born. And Tom said she wasn't to worry, so she wouldn't.

She lifted her mouth to his and he kissed her so thoroughly, so beautifully, that the war and all her worries about it faded. Come to think of it, she didn't know why she'd got herself into such a state over Elliot Sutton either, when Tom was there – yes, and Morgan too – to see she came to no harm.

'Kiss me again,' she murmured.

With Tom's safe young arms around her, it was easy to be brave.

Julia sat in the corner of the ladies-only compartment, counting telegraph poles as they slipped past the window, thinking it had been easier than she could ever have hoped, getting permission to travel alone to Aunt Sutton's.

'Mother, please – *please* – let me go to London? I promise to behave and do nothing to upset Aunt; I'll even stay only the one night if you say I must, but I ache to see Andrew, talk to him. He'll enlist, if I don't. Oh, I know that if the war doesn't end soon he might *have* to go, but I do so long to see him. Please say yes?'

'But the trains will still be packed with troops and London *could* be raided by zeppelins – had you thought of that?'

'But that's just rumour. It wouldn't surprise me one bit if the Kaiser didn't have spies here, especially to spread fear and despondency. Goodness, we have fighter planes that would only have to fire one shell into those great, slow-moving things and they'd catch fire. Can't you understand? There might be so little time left for Andrew and me.'

'I understand, Julia.' How well she understood. If John were in London, now, she would walk there barefoot – no! crawl there on hands and knees – just to see his face; to lay her lips on his and whisper the goodbye they never said. 'I understand only too well. But I know that at times like these, feelings – *needs* – could take over our senses and cause us to act wrongly.'

'I promise not, Mother. Oh, *I* would! Sometimes I want Andrew so much I'm ashamed. But he is better able than I to keep his emotions in check. Your daughter might forget herself,' she smiled wanly, 'but not Andrew.'

'But the journey, Julia – travelling alone . . .'

'Dearest! We are at war! There are far greater dangers than travelling in a ladies-only compartment to London. Don't you see? Women are volunteering to work in factories, nurses are already on their way to France to care for the wounded! I *will* be all right!'

'Yes, I suppose you will.' Gently Helen touched her daughter's cheek. She was a child no longer, but a woman in love. She, Helen, had known the same desperate longing; would have run away with John at the crooking of his finger and lived with him unwed, in a garret. 'Just give me time to arrange a seat for you and to ring up Anne Lavinia, then William shall take you to York and see you safely on the train,' she had smiled.

Darling, darling, Mother. She understood. Wasn't it something special to be the child of love and not one of a coupling of convenience? And all her children – hers and Andrew's – would be children of love, she thought, and *why* did this train travel so slowly, and would they *never* reach London?

Andrew was there to meet her at the station. She flung herself into his arms, not caring who might see them, for this was a country at war and a kiss in public mattered little now.

'Darling, I've missed you so. Are you on duty or can you come with me to Aunt Sutton's? How much time do we have?'

'Very little, I'm afraid. We are so busy at the hospital. The wounded, you see, from Mons. It must have been a terrible battle.'

Wounded! How could she have been so completely selfish, not to have noticed the pallor of his face, his dull, tired eyes?

'They've come to you?'

'To any hospital with beds to spare. They couldn't cope with them in Belgium – nor France, either. Just had their wounds dressed as best they might, then sent on to England. The journey back here must have been hell.'

'I'm sorry. I didn't think . . .'

'How could you be expected to? It was a shock to me too. Wounded are arriving by the trainload – their injuries are unbelievable. If the war goes on, field hospitals will have to be set up over there. The wounded must be treated sooner. One died from loss of blood on the journey over; many were delirious when they got to us from untreated wounds which had turned septic.'

309

'I shouldn't have come,' she choked, 'but I did so want to see you, darling.'

'And I you, Julia. Just to stand quietly in the middle of that nightmare and think of you helps keep me going. And I'm due time off. I've been on duty for two days and nights, and even a doctor must sleep. I'll come to Montpelier Mews just as soon as I can.' He tilted her chin. 'I want to kiss you.'

'Then kiss me! Who cares?'

'I'll come to you the minute I can.' He touched her lips gently with his own. 'And I love you . . .'

He came when she had given up hope; when she had almost decided to ask Figgis to unlace her corsets so that she might undress for bed.

'It's all right! I'll go!' she called as the doorbell rang. 'Darling! I thought you'd never come!'

He closed the door before wrapping her in his arms; not kissing her but holding her close, resting his cheek on her hair.

'We must talk, Julia.'

'I know,' she whispered, sensing what was to come. 'But come and sit by the fire and pretend we're an old married couple. Aunt Sutton has gone to bed, but Figgis is still up. Shall I ask her to bring tea – or coffee?'

'Thanks, darling, but I'm awash with coffee – keeps me awake, y'know. I wouldn't say no to a dram, though.'

'Give me your hat and take off your jacket, then I'll pour you one. Then we'll have that talk, because I have something to say too.' And say it she would. Now. Before her courage failed her. 'I want us to get married. Never mind waiting for your own practice so you can provide for me. I want you – I need you – *now*.'

'I know.' He sank back into the cushions, closing his eyes. He needed sleep desperately, but there were things to be said. 'The war isn't going to be over by Christmas – you realize that?'

'I didn't – but we can still hope . . .'

'Hope!' She hadn't seen the mutilated bodies, or walked through wards packed with dying men. They, too, had hoped.

'All right, then – it could last a year. But will you have to go?'

'I'm a doctor and doctors are needed out there. Nurses, too. Some have already gone in a civilian capacity, and the day will come when I can no longer put it off. It's likely, Julia, that I shall offer myself to the Medical Corps when my contract with the hospital runs out in October.'

'I see.' Fear touched her with an icy hand, and she shivered. 'So you won't want the encumbrance of a wife?' She looked down at nervously entwined fingers. 'I'm sorry I was so forward, but I love you very much. And I do accept you might have to go, but a little time together was all I asked . . .'

'Yes, you *are* forward; you are direct and honest and there isn't one conceited bone in your body. Look at me.' Gently he traced the outline of her face, forcing her to meet his gaze. 'And I'd be the biggest fool alive if I went to war and left you behind, unwed. So when shall it be, my darling, and where?'

'You *will*?' She took the glass from his hand, throwing herself into his arms. 'Dearest Andrew, I thought your dour, Scottish common sense would make you say no; that only a fool married in wartime.'

'My good Scottish sense left me the night I met you. And I, too, want all the time together we can have. I don't know when I'll be able to come to Rowangarth – make it all right with your family . . .'

'Write to them. They'll understand.'

'I'll buy you a ring – that much I can do. Shall we choose one tomorrow?'

311

'No, darling. Oh, I want to let everyone know, but rings cost money, and I know you need all you've got. And it would be plain silly to go to such expense when I inherited Grandmother Whitecliffe's jewellery last year. It's all in the bank, but when you next come to Rowangarth we'll get it out and you must decide which of the rings you like best, then put it on my finger for me. How does that suit you?'

'And it's supposed to be we Scots who are canny!'

'Just good northern common sense. I've been known to have the occasional bout,' she laughed, all at once light-headed with happiness.

'I don't believe any of this.' He shook his head, bemused.

'I do,' she sighed. 'But then, I've always had a head-start on you. The moment I laid eyes on you, doctor dear, your days were numbered. You had no chance at all, had you known it. So tell me you love me and kiss me goodnight. You look as if you could sleep the clock round.'

Yet she, Julia, would not sleep. She would lie in the little white bed in the little white room and think about their wedding and being able, after so much wanting, to sleep in Andrew's arms.

And I am old enough, now, to marry without your permission; but please, Mother, and you too, Giles, give us your blessing and your love?

'Goodnight, my love,' she whispered, as he left her. 'You won't change your mind?'

'Never,' he said hungrily, kissing her gently. 'Never as long as I live . . .'

17

Julia remained only a week in London. Already, St Bartholomew's Hospital had taken all it could of the casualties from Mons; now it remained for the doctors and nurses there to work the clock round to drag the injured back to some semblance of health. Because of it, meetings had been few and brief, and it pained her to see the fatigue etched deeply into Andrew's face.

'I must go home,' she had whispered at their last meeting. Time snatched with her he could better spend sleeping and, besides, there was a wedding to arrange. 'When things calm down a little, try to get to Rowangarth? You need a break.'

What had the army been about, she had demanded over and over again, sending men to war without making proper provision for the wounded? This was not a bows-and-arrows war, but a fight to the death. Germany had been preparing for it for years, it would seem, yet the British had been caught on the hop. Men, munitions, horses and motors Britain had in plenty; common sense we had not, and if fighting did not end soon, Julia thought despairingly, it would become a stalemate and go on and on and on, devouring young lives.

'We must talk,' she said without preamble, the moment she was home.

'I'd thought we might.' Giles was not one jot surprised by her sudden return.

'About what?' Helen stirred her coffee, knowing what was to come.

'About Andrew and me. He'll be writing, very soon. I told you about all the wounded, didn't I?'

'You did, and it horrified me. Andrew must be worked to a standstill.' Giles's face was grave with concern.

'He was – still is – and though he didn't say it in so many words, he thinks the war won't be over as quickly as we'd thought.'

'Yes – we're all coming to accept it; yet please God there'll be a miracle, even now.' Helen paused, drawing in her breath. 'So you wish now to be married? Is that what Andrew will be writing to us about?'

'It is. He'd come and ask permission properly, but to get time off just isn't possible, and we want to start making plans, you see.'

'And these hasty war weddings – you know what people are calling them, Julia?'

'I do. "Foolish marriages", they're saying, but it isn't *people*'s business, is it? And anyway, there won't be anything hasty about our wedding,' she added, chin tilted. 'I've been thinking about little else since the day we met, if I'm to be honest.'

'You're nothing if not that,' Giles smiled. 'And I'm grateful to Andrew for wanting to observe the courtesies, but we're well aware you are of age now.'

'Then you'll both of you give us your blessing?'

'You have it, my darling. But nothing too hasty?' Helen smiled gently. 'Andrew doesn't intend giving up his post at the hospital, surely?'

'Not yet. His contract runs out at the end of October, and that's when he'll have to take stock. But he says there's a crying need for hospitals in France and, just in case he volunteers, I'd like everything cut and dried. If you'd agree to have the banns called, it would be a start.'

'That should be no problem. Luke and Jessica are coming to dinner tomorrow evening – talk to him about it then. But there'll be so much to do, Julia – your dress

314

to be made and your trousseau and invitations . . . And there'll be food, too. Some things are already hard to get. A big reception might just not be possible.'

'I don't want a big affair.' Julia shook her head vehemently. 'All I want is to marry Andrew – for us to have as much time together as the Fates allow. No satin and lace, Mother, and *not* half the Riding there. It's between Andrew and me. Just a quiet wedding for family and closest friends. Besides, Andrew has no family left that he knows of, so it's better we do it my way. You won't mind too much, will you?'

'Not if you promise to be happy together.'

'And give Mother some grandchildren to fuss over,' Giles grinned.

'Both I can guarantee,' Julia whispered, the tension all at once gone.

'Then do just one thing for me, when the time comes – for me and your pa,' Helen said softly. 'However quiet a wedding, will you carry Pa's orchids to church with you?'

'*Your* special orchids? But darling, they are your very own flowers. No one else has ever worn them. Pa always insisted they were yours . . .'

'Maybe so. But he never once said that our daughter shouldn't carry them. So will you, Julia? It will make your father seem nearer to me, if you do.'

'Then I will.' Her lower lip trembled, and she bit on it, hard. 'And thank you,' she whispered. 'I love you both very much, and I'm sorry if I don't tell you more often. You'll give me away, Giles?'

'Happily. Glad to be rid of you!'

'Then I'll write Andrew at once – and ring up Aunt Sutton, too. And will you excuse me, please?'

Because all at once I'm so happy that if I don't go to the top of the pike and shout it out to the four winds, I shall die of happiness – I just will!

Or would it, perhaps, be better told to the rooks?

The letter from India arrived next morning. It bore a postmark dated August and Helen's fingers were suddenly clumsy as she tore open the envelope.

Dearest Mama and Giles,
   The news has shocked me and I want you to know that plans are already in hand to leave matters in good order here, so I might return to England at once. Thus far, I have not been able to get a passage; it seems that everyone who can is coming home. But with luck and fair seas, I should be with you early in November.
   I will write again, or cable, once I have more to tell you. Meantime, take care, and God keep you all safely.
   Your devoted, Robert.

'So he's on his way . . .' Not knowing whether to be sad or glad, Helen handed the letter to her son. 'Heaven only knows I have longed to have him back, but inside me I was willing him to stay in India. He's coming home to enlist, you realize that?'

'I do. It's his decision and I respect him for it. But you know the way I feel, dearest? I'll do anything they ask of me but fight. You won't be too ashamed of me?' Giles said softly, his eyes dark with sadness.

'I won't.' She reached across the table for her younger son's hand, squeezing it tightly. 'In fact, it's going to take a very special courage to stand up for what you believe in so passionately – you know that, don't you? When Robert and Andrew and your cousins have all gone, people will wonder, and talk.'

'I accept that, Mother, but I won't take life.'

'Then I shall stand by you, be sure of that. And had you thought – ' deliberately she turned the conversation, forcing a laugh to her lips, a smile to her eyes – 'your brother's letter has relieved you of the necessity of walking

316

down the aisle with your dreadful little sister. Now, do you suppose we can persuade the impetuous young miss to wait until November, till Robert gets here? And where *is* she? It's long past getting-up time!'

'She probably sat up half the night writing to her dearly beloved.' Giles quirked a knowing eyebrow. 'Fast asleep, now, I shouldn't wonder, dreaming of weddings . . .'

'Perhaps you are right.'

Helen set down her knife and fork, laying her hands to her blazing cheeks.

Robert – *home*. In the time it took to sail from Bombay, he would be here. There would be the joy of reunion and of Julia's wedding – and then what?

'Hawthorn! Such news! Andrew and I are to be married and Robert is coming home. November, he thinks, so that will be in nice time for him to give me away! Now, what do you think to that?'

'Married, miss – and Sir Robert back?' Alice pressed her foot down hard on the treadle, jerking the sewing-machine to a stop. Flipping heck. Miss Julia wasn't half a one for dropping bombshells. '*Married*, all of a sudden?'

'What do you mean, *all of a sudden*? It's taken me two years – yes, and a war, too – to get that man down the aisle! But say you're happy for me, Hawthorn? Please be glad?'

'Glad? I could fair weep for happiness. And if I was looking just a little – well, dubious, sort of – will you tell me how I'm to cope with your trousseau, let alone make a wedding dress by November? Because it might sound uppity of me, but I've dreamed of making your wedding dress, all full and flouncy and sewn with pearls . . .'

'Then I thank you, Hawthorn, and I know you'd have sewn love into every stitch of it. But I don't intend having a big wedding. Just family and dear friends – and Pendenys. And *no* bridal gown. I intend wearing my blue.'

'Your *blue*?' Not her sneaking-off-into-Hyde-Park blue? 'Oh, *no* . . .' Not when she had set her heart on the loveliest, the most romantic of dresses, and yards and yards of lovers'-knotted veil, and a blue garter to wear above her knee! 'It ought to be something special!'

'And what more special than the blue dress Andrew likes so much? I shall wear the special orchids, though, in my hair. Might look more bridal than a hat . . .'

'Then if you're set on the blue, miss, let me at least make your bridal nightdress?' Silk, it would be; hand-stitched and lace-trimmed and threaded through with baby-blue ribbons.

'Yes! It shall be your wedding present to me. And Hawthorn – you'll always be my friend, won't you? Say you will?'

All at once, her eyes filled with tears, and apprehension tingled through her. Because she was too contented; she knew it. In a world where already lives had been shattered and hearts broken, how could one person presume to be so shiningly, gloriously happy?

'Course I will, Miss Julia – you know I will. For always.'

And always was a long, long time.

So much had happened since the ghosts of Agincourt's dead rose up at Mons. The German armies had swept unhindered through Belgium and into France and, proud on horseback, with lances high, the Kaiser's dreaded uhlans, the worse for looted wine, followed closely to plunder and maim.

Belgians, fleeing the fighting, were joined by French women and their weeping, clinging children, mixing with the pathetic straggle of carts and farm waggons, all hastily commandeered to carry back the wounded.

Those who had means of escape did so; those who had not secured shutters, locked and bolted doors, and took trembling refuge in cellars until the tide of war reached them and raged past.

They must, Helen thought despairingly, be living through a nightmare from which there was no awakening. She sent up a prayer of gratitude for the blessing of the strip of water that served to keep her own country safe and apart.

The first patriotic rush to the colours had ended. Now, Lord Kitchener's eyes challenged those of young men who had stayed behind; his jabbing, accusing finger reminding them of their country's need. In towns and cities, gas lamps that had shone on the streets so brightly had been lowered to no more than a glimmer. London awaited the dreaded zeppelins.

Yet still there were those who tried hard to ignore the European skirmishings, refused to give them credence by calling it war; and there were others – many others – who clung stubbornly to the belief that it would all be over in time for Christmas.

Yet it was there, still, like a thundercloud ready to burst; to release bolts of fire, the effects of which Europe could scarcely begin to imagine. It hung, menacing, a constant reminder of what might be if nations were not soon to find their senses.

Already in Holdenby, the dreaded small envelope had been delivered; twice in as many days, and to the same house – the telegram of death.

'Sam Dobb's boys; both of them,' Agnes Clitherow told Helen. 'Joined the same regiment, you see. One killed, the other died of his wounds. At Mons, milady . . .'

'Jinny Dobb's nephews? *Our* Jin's?'

'Yes. You'll go?'

Helen Sutton would go at once. She would wear the hated black again, pin on her black hat, pull on her black gloves; would hold the hand of a weeping woman as her station in life demanded, and all the time begging the Almighty it should not happen to her.

It did not seem right, Julia thought soberly, that she should be so happily planning her wedding; that she had sat in church, blushing pink, through the first reading of the banns last Sunday, when already so small a village had been singled out for tragedy. Yet tomorrow was Andrew's birthday, and she closed her eyes to picture him opening the small package she had left behind her with instructions that it was not to be opened until the last day of August.

A set of studs for his dress shirt – she had not intended they should be replicas of those Mama had bought for Pa, yet she had dipped deeply into her inheritance and bought them without a qualm.

To my darling, because I love you, read the inscription on the tiny, gold-edged card inside the box. Her country was at war; soon the man she loved might be forced by conscience to enlist. Such a gesture was justified.

She had not long welcomed back her pale-faced mother, entreated her to take off her black and place it at the back of her wardrobe, when the doorbell rang with an urgent clamour.

'Miss – it's the Pendenys coachman,' Mary whispered, handing the card to Julia. 'He says Mrs Clementina's waiting in the carriage outside . . .'

'Then bid him ask her in,' Julia replied calmly. Her aunt might be bringing trouble, but at least it was she who had given in; she who had come to call a truce.

'Good morning, Aunt.' Quietly Julia greeted the woman whose pride must be making her feet ache something terrible, Mary thought, as she hurried away to report to the kitchen staff. 'Mother has only just returned from Holdenby – two of the Dobb boys were killed at Mons. I know she'll be glad you've come, but can you give her a minute? Perhaps you and I could sit in the conservatory?'

'I hear,' said Clementina when she had composed herself sufficiently to attempt conversation, 'that your banns were read out at Eucharist, last Sunday. May I offer my dearest wishes for your happiness?'

'Thank you, Aunt Clemmy.'

'And when is it to be? So sudden. It took us all by surprise.'

'I'm not yet sure. Soon, I hope. The banns are really a precaution against Andrew leaving for France. Perhaps on my birthday might be as good a day as any. And it *will* be quiet,' she warned. 'The war . . .'

She was relieved that, at that point, before her aunt could hint at an invitation, the opening of the doors caused Clementina Sutton to turn anxiously. And, Julia frowned, if Nathan were to be at the wedding as she so fervently wished, she had best get used to the idea that Pendenys – all of them – would have to be asked.

'Clemmy!' Smiling, Helen held out her arms and, almost tearful with relief, her sister-in-law went into them.

'Helen – it's been so long . . .' She glanced up to see the undisguised satisfaction on the face of her niece, then lapsed into embarrassed silence.

'Julia, be so kind, ask Mary to bring us tea. For *two*.' Helen murmured, emphasizing that what might be said thereafter was not for her daughter's eager ears. 'There, now – this is so nice, Clemmy. We seem to have so much chatter to catch up on. Tell me, how are you and how are my nephews?'

'Albert seems nicely settled; Nathan is to be ordained next week and – and Elliot is home . . .'

Then, all at once, it was much, much too much. At the mention of her eldest son – he who had been the sole cause of the coldness between Pendenys and Rowangarth – Clementina broke into wails of distress, fumbling for her handkerchief, desperately dabbing the tears that ran down brightly flushed cheeks.

'Oh, Helen, it has all been so *awful* and now this dreadful war. It's more than a body can bear. I simply had to come.'

'And I am glad you did. We mothers must comfort each other.'

'Ah, yes. Elliot is set on enlisting.' More tears, more hasty dabbing. 'Things have happened in the past – how am I to say this? – things we must both be regretting.'

She opened her handbag, taking out another handkerchief, holding it to her face. This interview was not going as she intended, though she had brought it upon herself. Not for a moment had she meant to allow the indignity of tears, but Helen had been so welcoming, so damned ladylike, that all the carefully rehearsed words were rendered useless. It was Helen's way, though, always to be gracious and kind; was the way of her breeding never to raise her voice, to be impossibly polite in all circumstances. She, Clementina, had intended an honourable truce, yet here she was, weeping like a servant. And all she had come for was to ensure that, at Nathan's induction, all the Suttons should be there. She would die of shame if they were not. Everyone who was anyone would be there – folk always turned out when the Archbishop graced the occasion – and if the Suttons were not seen to be standing together, it would provide tittle-tattle at every gathering of society.

'Regretting?' Helen said softly when Mary had set down the tray of tea and closed the door behind her. '*Both* of us?'

'The girl.' Clementina shifted uncomfortably, eyes fixed on a flowering plant. 'The incident in Brattocks. Elliot was naughty and Giles overreacted. Isn't it best forgotten?'

'Aah.' Carefully Helen poured tea. 'Forgotten? Oh, dear – but I'm afraid it isn't possible to forget Hawthorn's distress and – '

322

'Hawthorn? You're taking the part of a – a *servant* against your own flesh and blood?'

'My *sewing-maid*,' deliberately, softly, Helen stressed the words, 'was hurt and humiliated.'

'And what about my Elliot? What about your keeper who attacked him!'

'One punch, Clemmy. And he deserved it!'

'You encourage your servants to strike their betters?' Her voice rose stridently. 'Does family mean nothing to you, then?'

'Clemmy.' Helen rose to her feet, cup in hand. 'I advise you to take a deep breath and drink your tea. Then, when you are a little more calm, we can talk about Elliot and the apology he will make to Giles. And – ' she held up her hand as the red-faced woman opened her mouth to protest – 'when that has happened, I shall visit Pendenys and you and I can talk about Julia's wedding and Robert who is on his way home and, most importantly of all, about Nathan and that wonderful evening in the Minster I should so much like to share with you. It will be a splendid and moving ceremony – the Archbishop always adds to the sense of occasion, don't you think? I would feel hurt and deprived were I to have to miss it all.' Her eyes sought and held Clementina's. They did not waver; their message was plain to see. *Either Elliot apologizes or we shall boycott Nathan's induction and none of you will be invited to Julia's wedding.* 'Do I make myself clear?'

'You mean it? You'd do that, just to get at my Elliot?'

'That, and more. And *get at*, Clemmy? I don't seek to humiliate your son – I fear he does that for himself with every new indiscretion. Elliot *will* apologize,' she said, her voice steely soft, 'and you, his mother, will insist that he does.'

The silence was broken only by the tinkle of a teaspoon, the clink of cup against saucer, the indrawing of Clementina Sutton's breath as quickly she weighed up the situation. She knew she was no match for the gently smiling woman who sat opposite.

'Elliot will telephone Giles for an appointment. I trust that when he calls he'll be admitted?' she hissed through lips stiff with defeat. 'And I would like another cup, Helen, if you please. Good and strong.'

'Splendid. But first I shall ring for Miss Clitherow to make you up a parcel of tea to take home with you. The consignment we have just received from India is particularly fine; conditions, I understand, were perfect. Robert said in his letter that the entire crop was bought, even before it had been picked. Such a relief . . .'

'That is most kind.' Clementina spooned sugar into her cup, stirring it furiously, almost choking on her anger. *Why* did Helen always better her and why, fool that she was, could she not take a leaf from her sister-in-law's book and learn to think before she spoke?

Oh, but Elliot would apologize; she'd see to that! Elliot would ask forgiveness if only for the humiliation she, his mother, was enduring because of him! He would pay for this little carry-on. Only let him wait until next time he was in trouble!

Her eyes narrowed with anticipation, then she lifted her head and smiled into Helen's eyes. 'Sutton Premier is always such quality tea. Be sure we shall enjoy it.' *Only let him wait!*

The armies of the Kaiser were eager for spoils. Already they had marched through Brussels and now they scented Paris; now, the subjugation of the detested French was almost within their grasp, and all that stood between them and the Eiffel Tower were British soldiers; well-trained regulars who gave the unblooded German reservists a lesson in warfare and an unexpected shock. And, further along the line of battle, their comrades had received a similar mauling at the hands of French marksmen, convincing them, finally, that their unhindered advance was soon to end.

Just thirty miles from Paris they were finally halted. The capital city waited, tense behind ancient fortifications, for the field-grey flood that, though heard, was not to be seen. By the middle days of September, when purple daisies flowered in Rowangarth's gardens and chestnuts gleamed brown beneath yellowing leaves, the German armies began to dig themselves into positions of defence.

They needed to tend their wounded, bury their dead, regroup to count the cost. And, exhausted but defiant, the French and British did the same, digging deep bunkers the length of their lines, implanting machine-guns. Between the emplacements, they frantically dug connecting passages, many feet deep.

Autumn came and the defences were fortified with tangles of barbed wire and hastily buried mines. Between those lines, from which each side thought to break out to annihilate the other, lay a tract of land where no man ventured; land, had either side but known it, that would be fought over again and again. But the break-out was slow to start, and the tract between remained still and empty. Dugouts were made yet stronger, and the communication passages, now reinforced with timber, became muddy and began to stink.

The old order of fighting pitched battles gave way to a new order of stalemate and checkmate they came to call trench warfare. Army faced army across No Man's Land. By day, sharp-shooters waited in church towers and on the roofs of shell-torn houses, rifles at the ready for the careless head that showed an inch above the dugout top. By night, raiding parties braved the wastes of No Man's Land to reconnoitre, bring back prisoners for interrogation and, with luck, to kill.

At home and at the Front, people spoke about poison gas and prayed that neither side would be the first to use it. Trenches became deeper, safer.

The war was not to be over by Christmas.

Robert Sutton settled himself in the corner seat of the compartment. Almost there. Fifteen minutes to Holdenby, then a short carriage drive to his home.

He had been glad to tie up at Tilbury after so long at sea; to disembark and check his trunks and boxes on the quayside. The SS *Pindah*, out of Bombay, had missed the morning tide and been late docking; thus was he faced with a choice. Either to take the overnight express to York, or to beg a bed from Aunt Sutton and make an early start in the morning. And, since his aunt was extremely dear to him, there had been little hesitation. Besides, he needed to talk to her, sort things out in his mind before he went home to Rowangarth.

'I've come back to enlist, Aunt, but I suppose you'll know that?' he'd murmured, eyes on his glass as they sat companionably after dinner. 'The Green Howards, I suppose, or one of the local regiments . . .'

'And how will your mother take it, do you suppose?' she had demanded abruptly. 'Seeing you after so long away will be drama enough; to greet her with news such as that will bowl her over. You'll have to handle it gently.'

It was then she had thrown him completely off balance. 'Tell me, Robert, why you went back to India after your father died,' she flung without warning, 'when you'd have been better to have stayed to look after your inheritance? And why, having chosen India, have you returned to enlist? Has she been worth all the upset?'

It was a shot in the dark, but it found its mark. Robert had accepted that now it would have to be brought into the open.

'I'm sorry to have been so underhanded, but you are right in what you suppose, Aunt. I must tell Mother first,' he said softly, 'but you *shall* know . . .'

'It'll wait. You'll tell me when you're good and ready, I suppose. And I wasn't prying. Curious, maybe and – '

'And direct, as always,' he smiled. 'Julia is like you. Blunt, I think best describes her. But to tell Mama first is only right. After that – '

He shrugged, realizing he was not looking forward to the telling of what they must all have been bursting to discover for the past four years.

'You look as if you could do with a good night's sleep.' She had touched his hand, briefly. 'And I don't aim to interfere, you know that?'

'I do, Aunt. And after Mama, you'll be the first to be told.'

The sudden jolting as they swayed over the level-crossing cleared his mind of all thoughts. The engine driver tugged on the steam release to let go a shrill, warning whistle, and the train began to slow as it took the incline that ran alongside Brattocks Wood. Robert Sutton rose to his feet, taking his hat and coat from the rack, wondering if anyone would be waiting to greet him.

Julia jumped eagerly to her feet at the far-away whistle and walked to the centre of the platform. The train must just be passing Brattocks; any second now it would appear round the wide bend, half a mile down the track.

In the station yard, Will Stubbs waited beside the small, open carriage, checking the clock for the second time in as many minutes, relieved the train was arriving.

Her ladyship had decided against meeting her son, yet Miss Julia, doubtless eager to see a brother whose face the coachman could hardly remember, now stood at the platform edge, peering down the track with impatience written all over her face.

'Stand well clear if you please, Miss Sutton! Holdenby Halt!' the stationmaster called importantly as the train squealed and shuddered to a stop.

'Robert!' Julia ran to greet her brother, arms wide. 'It's so good to see you!'

She hugged him tightly and he fastened his arms around her middle, swinging her round in the giddy whirl she had always demanded as a little girl.

'Sorry, Sis,' he laughed, realizing that in four years she had left behind her gawkiness and grown into an attractive young woman. 'My word, but you've changed.'

'You, too.' He was handsomer than ever, truth known. His apricot skin against the sun-lightened fairness of his hair was enough to make any woman take notice. He was thinner, though – really grown up. How old was he, now? Twenty-eight, wasn't it, and still not married!

'Afternoon, Sir Robert.' The coachman touched the brim of his hat with a respectful forefinger, then shouldered the first of the trunks with ease. 'Just leave everything there; I'll see to it.'

'Remember William?' Julia whispered. 'He was stable lad when Pa died. He's made a good coachman but – ' she raised a warning eyebrow – 'he just doesn't like to miss anything.'

'Nothing changes, I'm glad to hear,' Robert said softly. This was what he'd been looking forward to. The little railway station; the drive through the village in which almost every house belonged to him, the flower-filled lanes and then, suddenly, the gate lodges and the tall iron gates. When he was in India, he had longed for it; now that he was home, India already called him back.

'I'm getting married,' Julia said when they were driving along at a pace. 'I'd have told you, but you were already on your way.'

'I know. Aunt Sutton told me. I'm happy for you, Sis.'

'You've seen her?'

'I stayed there last night. I thought you knew. We were late docking, so it seemed the sensible thing to do. When is the wedding to be?'

The abruptness with which he dismissed his stay in London made her uneasy, but with William up front, she decided it was best left until later.

'When? Nothing is settled yet, but the banns have been called and now you are home to give me away, I'd say it'll be in about a fortnight. Very quiet, mind. It's the way we both want it.'

'Because of the war?'

'I suppose so,' Julia frowned. 'Andrew hasn't enlisted yet, but his contract with the hospital he works at runs out soon. I'm trying not to think what will happen after that.' Then she smiled. 'Except the wedding, of course.'

'Aunt Sutton likes your doctor.'

'Everyone likes him,' she retorted sunnily. 'Me most of all.'

They lapsed into a contented silence, because just around the bend in the narrow little road lay Rowangarth gates, and this was not the time to demand of her brother when *he* was going to be married.

'Home,' she said softly as William pulled on the reins, guiding the coach into the drive. 'What's the betting that Mother is waiting at the top of the steps?'

Home, he echoed silently – but to what?

Because his brother was expected to arrive within the next half-hour, and because he thought it best that Elliot Sutton be kept as far away from Rowangarth as possible – at least for the immediate future – Giles had said, 'Can't it wait a couple of days?' He had known exactly why his cousin was telephoning, yet wondered why on earth it had to be today – *now*. 'Perhaps you could ring again later, Elliot?'

'That won't be possible,' came the peevish retort. 'I mean, either you want me to grovel, or you don't. I've offered to come over and see you, but if you think it unimportant, then that is your decision entirely. Tomorrow I'm going to London.' Which was another way of saying that Giles had little option.

'No one has asked that you grovel, Elliot. All I want is an assurance there will be no repetition of the incident in Brattocks, that's all – and that you regret what you did, of course.'

'Now see here, old man – why blow it up out of all proportion? It was anything or nothing. Some girls will, some won't. I got it wrong, that was all.'

'And you regret the upset you caused, Elliot?'

'If that's what I'm required to say – yes . . .'

'Then I shall tell Mother you will behave yourself in future and that such behaviour will not happen again. Do I give her your apologies, too?'

'Of course.'

His tone was flippant and Giles was given the impression of a completely bored young man who really did not know what all the fuss was about.

'And I'm to tell Miss Hawthorn that you deeply regret the anguish and injury you caused her; that you apologize to her too?'

'Now see here, Giles – isn't that a bit much? You said you didn't require me to grovel.'

'Very well. You will *not* apologize to Miss Hawthorn. There is no more to be said, then, save to remind you that if you set foot on Rowangarth land you'll be ordered off it. And I take it you have no wish for us to be at the Minster for Nathan's induction and that Aunt Clemmy has no interest at all in being invited to Julia's wedding?'

Giles caught sight of his reflection in the wall mirror and was not one bit surprised to see that he appeared to be enjoying the conversation. '*Well*, Elliot . . .?'

'Oh, dammit – all right then. I apologize to your servant.'

'Which servant would that be, Elliot? Miss Hawthorn, perhaps?'

'I apologize, then. Please tell Miss Hawthorn it will not happen again. Is that what you want?'

'It will do,' Giles said softly. 'And, Elliot – keep well clear of Brattocks. For one thing, Hawthorn often walks my dog there, and I won't have her upset again; for another, Dwerryhouse is still very angry about what you did, so you'd best give it a wide berth.'

There was a cold, disbelieving silence, then the receiver at the other end of the line was replaced with a sharp click.

'Oh, my word!' Giles quirked an eyebrow at his reflection. 'Cousin Elliot seems a little put out. Now what, do you imagine, could I have said to upset him so?'

But he had meant every word of it. Elliot was a fool, and one of these days his nasty little habits were going to land him in very grave trouble. He turned as his mother came down the stairs.

'Who was telephoning, Giles?'

'No one, dear. No one of importance. I'll tell you about it later.'

'Then come with me at once, and wait for Robert,' Helen laughed, holding out her hand. 'I've just seen the carriage from the bedroom window, turning into the drive. Do hurry, Giles . . .'

18

After dinner, as if by unspoken consent, Giles said, 'Mind if I don't join you?' and Julia said she must write to Andrew – it would be all right, wouldn't it, if she went to her room?

'That leaves just the two of us, Robert,' Helen smiled, 'though I rather think they did it on purpose. Shall we sit in the small parlour?'

'Suits me very nicely.' The room was cosy and warm; he hadn't yet become accustomed to the cold and damp of an English autumn. 'There are things to be said – you know that, don't you?' he said softly, taking her hand, tucking it beneath his arm.

'Things to be said?' Helen prompted when she had poured coffee and they were settled easily. 'About you, perhaps; that you've come home to enlist – and when you didn't have to.' Her words were almost a reproach.

'But I *do* have to, Mother, if I'm to be worth my name. And there's another reason, too. When I was little, I used to play a game – tempting Fate, I suppose – and I'd tell myself that if I could hop the length of the path without touching a crack, there'd be jam sponge for pudding. And once I remember telling myself that if the next bird I saw was a swallow, then Pa would buy me the bicycle I so wanted. I still do it . . .'

'And?'

'And a few weeks ago, I told myself that if I did the right thing; if I enlisted and came through the war safely, then everything would turn out all right, for Cecilia and me.'

'Cecilia?' Helen breathed the name as if afraid, almost,

to say it out loud; as if, now that she was soon to know the cause of her son's secrecy, she wanted to put off the telling.

'Cecilia Jamilla Kahn.' He said the name gently. 'The lady I've loved for a very long time.'

'Aaaah. I'd thought – hoped . . . Robert, she isn't married?'

'She isn't married. She teaches in the English school in Shillong, up in the hills. I met her in Calcutta, at the railway station. She was so beautiful I couldn't help but notice her, and when I realized we were to take the same train, it seemed my luck was in.

'Before we reached Shillong we'd spoken, and I'd given her my card. Not the most auspicious of beginnings, but she was travelling alone and I had to be careful. It was obvious she was most properly reared, you see.' He paused, smiling, as though some of the tension so evident since his return had left him merely to say her name.

'Cecilia Jamilla,' Helen frowned. 'The one name is European, the other is Muslim, surely?'

'She is named for her saint. She is a devout Christian. She was born on St Cecilia's Day – the twenty-second of November. Jamilla is her grandmother's name.'

'I see.' Helen did *not* see; could not understand why a love so obviously deep had been kept a secret – and when Robert knew she wanted him to marry. Why had there been no mention of her – not so much as a word?

'No, Mother, you don't see, but this will help you.' He slipped his fingers into the inside pocket of his jacket and drew out a photograph. Then he handed it to her, his eyes asking that she should love her too. 'This is Cecilia,' he said.

The photograph was a formal one but, even so, it did nothing to hide such beauty: the smile that showed small, even teeth, the dark, limpid eyes, the facial bones so

333

perfect they might have been the work of a brilliant sculptor.

'Robert! She is exquisite!'

'Yes, but you miss the point. Surely you can see that Cecilia is what people hereabouts would call "*coloured*" Do you realize,' he rushed on, 'that I have committed the unforgivable? I've *gone native*, as people out there would say. I am white and I want to marry an Indian lady. Here in England it is unacceptable; in India, too, it is frowned upon.'

'But my dear – you love each other. Where is the wrong in it?'

'Mother!' Agitated, he jumped to his feet. 'Don't you see? Cecilia would never be accepted here just as I am not acceptable to *her* parents. Christians they may be, and forward-thinking, well-educated people; yet they still have no wish to see their daughter marry outside her own race.

'What are we to do? Cecilia is a devoted daughter, an only child; she doesn't want to upset her parents. If she defied them and married me without their blessing, I would have to bring her to England to live. And then we would be frowned on by *my* race! It would be a mixed marriage and totally unacceptable to both sides. Why must people be so blinkered? Even you were a little shocked to see her picture; it showed on your face!'

'Not shocked, Robert. What you saw was profound sadness, because I am bound to agree with everything you say. It is wrong, but it – '

'It exists,' he finished savagely. 'Prejudice!'

'Then what will you do, my dear? Do you go on tearing each other apart, for it seems that is what you are doing now. Is that why you have come home – to separate yourselves from each other and see if it will survive?'

'Something like that, I suppose. It was hell, leaving her there, not knowing if I'd ever see her again. She cried when we parted and I hated myself for bringing such misery on her. She's given me five years of her life; five years of refusing every man who wanted to marry her. It hasn't been easy for her.'

'Nor for you, Robert.'

'Nor me. But I was better able to take the digs and sneers about my *native woman*. And the sneers were mostly from white women, would you believe? Men seemed more tolerant. But tell me what *you* think, Mother? Tell me truthfully. I'd be more inclined to accept it from you, because you've always been the fairest person I know.'

'Shall you give her up, do you mean; go to war and, when it is all over, stay here – leave the plantation to someone else to manage? Or will you tilt at windmills? Will you marry her and risk being cast out by both sides? I'm sorry, but that decision is for you and your Cecilia to make. Yet there is something I must say that I hope will help.

'What other people think doesn't matter; not what we here might think, nor her parents in India. You see, it is all so blazingly clear to me, though if you can't see it then I certainly shan't tell you. Will you just remember, though, that I do know what it is like to love deeply, and for ever. I would have followed your pa through fire and water – given him my life, even, had he asked it of me.

'Oh, he had all the right qualifications, so there was no problem, but I fell in love with him the first time I set eyes on him, and it wouldn't have mattered to me who objected to our loving. He was the man I wanted.'

'You mean – ' He turned, then dropped to his knees beside her chair, taking her hands in his, gazing into her eyes. 'You are trying to say that I should – '

'All right, then!' she said fiercely. 'I'm saying you should get this dreadful war over and done with, then go back to India and marry your Cecilia and to the devil with the lot of them! Come home safely and you shall have my blessing. Only come back to us, and nothing else in the whole of this world will matter, I promise you.'

'Dear, lovely Mother, what am I to say?' he demanded huskily. 'I didn't expect – '

'Didn't expect me to want you to be as happy as I was? How little you know me! Now off with you and ask Miss Clitherow to chill a bottle of the good champagne. Then call in Giles and Julia and we shall raise our glasses to your happiness – yours and Cecilia's!'

Taking his face in her hands she felt great happiness that he was home – for however short a time – and in love.

'Robert Sutton, I have only just realized,' she said softly, 'how very much I have missed you.'

It had been, thought Helen, as she climbed the creaking, uneven stairs, the most satisfactory evening. She gazed, as she almost always did when going to bed, at the gilt-framed portraits of long-gone Suttons, hanging silent on the wall. At Dickon Sutton, who sailed with Frobisher against the Armada; James, who'd hidden the Sutton silver then galloped off to fight the Roundheads. And beside him Gilbert, who had fathered six sons then covered himself with glory at Waterloo; and another Gilbert, who had fought in the Crimea then returned to Rowangarth to marry Mary Whitecliffe and beget John and Anne Lavinia and Edward. All had gone to war; all had survived to die peacefully at Rowangarth.

So why should history not repeat itself and Robert come home safely, too? And any other Sutton who went to war?

She snapped on her bedroom light, then rang for the housekeeper to unhook her gown and unlace her corsets so she might undress for bed.

'Might I say, milady,' said Agnes Clitherow as she struggled with the knot she had tied too enthusiastically only a few hours earlier, 'how good it is to have Sir Robert home – there now, I'll ease off the lacing if you'll just unhook the front . . .'

'Good, yes. He looks so well, doesn't he?' Helen unfastened the metal clasps, sighing with relief. 'Sad that soon he'll be going to fight. I was looking at the paintings as I came upstairs, and it occurred to me that many Sutton men have gone to war over the centuries, and all of them returned safely.'

'Indeed, milady. And Sir Robert will come home safely too. We shall remember him every day in our prayers.' Agnes Clitherow was a great believer in the power of prayer; had tangible proof of its efficacy. 'Now, shall you slip into bed whilst I make you a drink? You've had an exciting day, if you'll pardon me, and a glass of hot milk and honey is a great aid to sleep.'

She had been right, Helen thought, as she switched off her bedside light. It *had* been an exciting day, in all ways.

The last flickerings of the dying fire touched the silver-framed photograph of her husband on the table beside her, and picking it up she smiled and whispered, 'That's two of them, John, my darling; Robert and Julia both very much in love. It won't be easy for our son, but it will work out, I know it.

'But will you tell me what I'm to do about Giles,' she frowned, 'for I think he's determined to remain a bachelor – I really do . . .'

November, declared Rowangarth's head gardener, was just about the most awkward time in the whole of the year to have a wedding, and Miss Julia the most awkward of lasses to decide to have hers when there was next to nothing by way of vegetables and less than nothing, except chrysanths, when it came to flowers. And as for her ladyship asking that the special orchids be brought on – well, wasn't it just like a woman to imagine that any bloom, much less an orchid, could be coaxed into flowering at the dropping of a hat? He had mumbled and grumbled and sucked noisily on his empty pipe as he always did when put out, then stumped off to the forcing house to take stock.

There were more, now, of the special orchids, he admitted, as he settled himself on a box to contemplate ways and means. Now there were six plants of milady's orchid, as it had come to be known. From the one brought to Rowangarth at the time of her wedding had come abundance, and all from that long-ago parent.

Yet the forcing of orchids into unseasonal flowering upset them something cruel, to his way of thinking, so they were forced to go into a decline after such treatment, and often showed their displeasure by refusing to flower the following year.

He reached for the humidifier and began to fill the air with thousands of glittering droplets of water. Orchids liked dampness; orchids were beautiful creations and temperamental because of it. Place a potted orchid in a bathroom and you had growing conditions just about right, though what that housekeeper woman would have to say about pots of orchids in the precious new bathrooms didn't bear thinking about!

He began to feel more calm. He liked it here in the forcing house, especially in November when all outside was raw with cold; liked the moist air which was good for his bronchitis, and the warmth that sank into his bones to soothe and please him. And, all things being equal, he just might manage to produce a few sprays of the special orchid in time for the wedding.

And that wasn't right, either. Rowangarth weddings were expected to be fine affairs, with half the gentry in the Riding there. Marquees on the lawns, there should be, and the gardens full of colour and perfume and a pleasure for guests to behold. But the gardens were sad things in November, so happen it was as well it was a quiet do, and as long as he provided corsages for the ladies and buttonholes for the men and saw to it that the dratted orchid flowered in time, there was little more he could do.

Yet winter weddings he did *not* hold with, and Miss Julia's was the fault of the war. Foolish weddings, they were coming to be called: in his opinion, those who couldn't wait until June – the right and proper month for weddings, when every flower was blooming and roses grew in abundance – were indeed foolish! Or three months gone with child.

'Are you there, Mr Catchpole?' Tilda, shawl-wrapped, hurried gratefully into the warmth. 'Sorry to barge in on you, but could you let Cook have a few sprouts? She knows you like to keep them back till they've had a frost on them, but Sir Robert fair loves them and he doesn't get them in India. So Cook says will you be kind enough to send at least a pound?'

'Ha! It's all on account of that wedding,' he snarled, settling down for another grumble.

'I know. Isn't it lovely? Wouldn't it make your heart glad to see her ladyship so pleased with herself, even with all the bother it's causing?'

'Not in November it isn't lovely,' said Catchpole sourly. 'And I'll see Mrs Shaw gets her sprouts, though if they go on like this, there won't be a single one left for Christmas.'

'Won't there?' Tilda didn't care at all about Christmas, all of six weeks away, when the wedding was next week and ever so much more romantic. 'Well, I'd best be off. Up to the eyes in it we are, and Cook wanting to get the almond paste on the wedding cake today an' all . . .'

She left, singing, leaving the glasshouse door wide open and causing the gardener to jump up and close it at once before damage was inflicted that could prove costly.

Weddings in November! Pah!

'Could you let me have the use of the table, Mrs Shaw?' asked Alice. 'Just for ten minutes.'

Over her arm lay a froth of silk and lace, finished with a day to spare.

'It's done, then?' Cook held out her arm and Alice draped the nightdress over it. 'Oh, my word . . .'

'It's *beautiful*,' breathed Tilda, who had already laid the ironing blanket on the table-top and was covering it with a sheet. 'The fire's just nice. I'll put on the irons.'

'If she'd given me a bit more notice,' Alice shook out the flimsy garment, inspecting it critically, 'I'd have made a better job of it,' she frowned.

'You couldn't have, girl.' Hawthorn had done Miss Julia proud. A voluminous skirt hung from a tiny, pin-tucked yoke supported on lace-trimmed straps. At the front was a lover's knot in palest blue to match the lace, entwined with the initial 'J'. Every seam and tuck was hand-sewn like all the best bridal wear you bought in Paris and London. Cook knew about such things. 'No one could have done better. You could make a living at it – sewing trousseaus for the gentry.'

'Happen I could,' Alice blushed with pleasure, 'if I fell on hard times. But I'm suited where I am, Mrs Shaw. All the little fiddling tucks take a lot of time, by hand. Only did it as a favour for Miss Julia.'

'Pity we'll never see her in it,' Bess sighed.

'Does anyone know where they're going for their honeymoon?' Blissfully, Tilda closed her eyes. This, the real-life thing, was better by far than anything in her love books.

'I'd heard,' Mary offered, 'they'll be spending their

wedding night at York, in the hotel by the station; but after that I suppose they'll go to Scotland.' Stood to sense, didn't it, the doctor being Scottish?

'Well, they can't go to Paris or Venice or anywhere like that now.' In a sentence, Cook dismissed abroad. And they wouldn't go to Bournemouth or anywhere on the south coast – too near to the war. 'Happen you're right, Mary. It'll be Edinburgh.'

'It'll be London. That's where they met, isn't it?' said Tilda with certainty, holding the flat-iron to her face. 'Coolish, isn't it, for silk?' Vigorously she rubbed it in a tray of powdered bathbrick to clean and polish it before setting it carefully on the trivet.

'Thanks.' Alice tested the iron on a scrap of silk. 'Just right, Tilda. Keep an eye on the other one, will you? Don't let it get too hot?'

A dream nightgown, that's what. She would make one exactly like it for herself, Alice vowed silently. Not in silk, mind. They'd sent specially to a warehouse in Leeds for the silk and for the special thread, too, and the baby-blue lace and ribbons. Cost the earth, it must have. She'd been worried, at first, making the first cut into the pattern-pinned material. Yet maybe she'd make one in finest lawn for herself, with a yoke embroidered with little pink rosebuds and –

'What are you thinking about that's making you smile so?' Bess demanded. 'Or can't you say in front of young Tilda?'

'If you must know, I was thinking I might make one for myself – only a cheaper version,' Alice laughed.

Then she frowned, wondering when, for still nothing had been said about Reuben moving out and Tom taking over at Keeper's Cottage. But it was the war, and everybody was waiting to see what would happen, telling themselves it would soon be over and done with and they could get back to normal again.

341

Only it *wasn't* going to be over by Christmas. Mr Giles had said so, and that was why Miss Julia was having such a quiet wedding; because any day now the doctor might be going to a field hospital at the Front. And not just the doctor. Sir Robert had come home to enlist – everyone knew it – and now that Mr Nathan was properly a priest, talk had it that after the wedding he'd be off to Strensall Barracks to be chaplain to one of the regiments there.

There had even been talk that Elliot Sutton was going an' all. Will Stubbs had had it on good authority that Mrs Clementina had made sure he'd got a commission in the regiment of his own choosing – likely one that wouldn't be going to the Front, just yet. Someone in high places, William said, had owed that lady a favour, and she'd called it in without so much as a quiver of conscience. Mrs Clementina did things like that.

Alice frowned. They would all be in khaki before long if someone didn't put a stop to the war. It didn't bear thinking about – she *wouldn't* think about it; not when there was so much to be happy about. She would think instead about the wedding; that they had all been invited – to the service, that was. All the house staff – Miss Clitherow included – were going to be driven to church by William in the carriage and two. Sad that Miss Clitherow wouldn't be taking her rightful place; because if Miss Julia had been wearing white and a long veil like she should have, Miss Clitherow would have driven with her in the bridal carriage to arrange her skirts and petticoats so they shouldn't crease, then would have helped her out at the church, making sure her veil didn't catch and her lovely long gown was hanging exactly right before she began her walk down the aisle.

Only Miss Julia wasn't wearing yards and yards of satin and lace, nor a floaty veil, either. She was wearing the blue dress the doctor liked so much. She, Alice, had picked off the white lace collar, carefully washing and pressing it, then sewing it back on again. Then she had sponged the dress and pressed the pleats and the hem, all the while sad that it couldn't have been a white wedding; a peacetime wedding.

Not that Miss Julia minded. 'We're getting married and that's all that matters,' she had said, and if she was happy about it, then who was Alice Hawthorn to want different?

'I suppose you all realize that we'll have to be back here pretty sharpish after the wedding?' Tilda demanded, briskly polishing the second iron. 'As soon as they go into the vestry, we're to be brought back here in one of Pendenys's motors so we can change into our uniforms and be ready to wait on. Miss Clitherow said it was a good idea, since the bride and groom will want the carriage, and kind of Pendenys to let us have the use of a motor *and* a chauffeur.'

'Kind,' sniffed Cook, who thought it poor exchange for all the trouble there'd been from that quarter.

'And did you know that Jinny Dobb is coming to keep an eye on things here whilst we're all at church? Miss Clitherow said it was a kindness to the poor soul, her having lost two nephews already . . .'

'Who told you all this?' Alice murmured, smoothing the silk as she pressed.

'I heard it. Her ladyship and Miss Clitherow were talking. The door was open, so I listened.'

'You're getting as bad as William. What else did you hear?'

'That we're to have all the food that's left over from the wedding breakfast at our party – and more besides. Her ladyship said there hadn't been a wedding at Rowangarth for longer than anyone could remember and, war or no war, we were all to enjoy it.'

'And we will.' Alice was looking forward to the servants' dance, after the bride and groom had left. Tom

343

would be there and Reuben – even Catchpole and the under-gardeners: everyone from the estate. There was to be ale for the men, so talk had it, and sherry for the ladies to drink Miss Julia's health. It would be a beautiful day, November drear or not; a day to remember with the war forgotten for just a little while.

'There now, that's it finished with.' Alice held up the nightdress, giving it a shake. 'I'll smuggle it up the back stairs and lay it on her bed to surprise her. She doesn't know yet that it's finished.'

Yes, Alice *would* forget about the war; not so much as think once about it until the party was over. Only then would she allow it back into her life – hers and Tom's. Come to think of it, she would have to, because it wasn't going to go away. The awfulness of it would always be there like a little ache inside her, along with the silent fear that chilled her through each time she looked at Tom.

Oh please, not yet. Don't leave me just yet, Tom.

Julia Sutton sat at her dressing-table, gazing into the mirror, wishing away the minutes until it was time to leave. Her hands were alternately hot and cold, her cheeks flushed too red and in need of cream and powder to tone them down.

She wished she were beautiful. Why wasn't she beautiful like her mother? And why was her heart making such a noise? They'd all hear it in the church.

'There now, Miss Julia; almost done.' Agnes Clitherow smiled indulgently. 'I'll just pop in a couple more hairpins – make sure your chignon is secure, then if you'd slip into your dress I can pin on the orchids.'

No wedding veil, the housekeeper sighed inside her; just a circlet of white orchids on her upswept hair. The special orchids. The first time anyone save her ladyship had worn them.

'My stays,' Julia grumbled, 'are far too tight. When I

344

kneel down there'll be the most unholy noise and it'll be me, bursting at the seams!'

'They are *not* too tight. I made sure they weren't. Now hold up your arms and I'll slip on your dress. I must say your hair suits you, swept up.'

Miss Julia had beautiful bones, did she but know it; not so fine as her ladyship's, but good for all that, and enhanced by the upcombing of her hair. 'And with the orchids just like a ballerina wears them – oh, most bridal . . .'

'Julia, my dear!' Helen stood in the doorway. She too wore blue; a colour, Julia thought, that might have been especially invented for one with such startlingly blue eyes, so fair a complexion. How dare any woman be so beautiful? How, at touching fifty, *could* she?

'Come in, Mother, do. I need someone to hold my hand. 'I'm shaking like a leaf. I wish it were all over!'

'You do *not* wish that! The next hour will be the most wonderful you will ever spend, and you will enjoy it – every minute of it! I insist that you do!' She touched her daughter's face with gentle fingertips. 'And has anyone told you yet how lovely you look? She has that bridal look hasn't she, Miss Clitherow – that glow from inside that makes all brides especially beautiful?'

'Radiant is the word, milady. And might I be excused now? I think the carriage is waiting. God bless you, Miss Julia,' she whispered, her eyes misting over.

'Radiant? Am I, Mother?' Julia whispered when they were alone. 'But, more to the point, is Robert ready yet? I haven't had sight nor sound of him all morning.'

'Your brother is ready and waiting downstairs.'

'All right – but what if Andrew is late at the church? Suppose he doesn't turn up?'

'He'll be there. Giles is with him. He'll be on time.' The best man and groom, as custom demanded, had stayed the night with Edwin and Tessa Drayton. 'Tessa

345

will have everything organized. Now just give me a hug and a kiss, darling, and promise you'll walk slowly down the aisle – head high?'

'I will. I'll do it for Pa – that's what you want, isn't it?'

'That's what I want. And you'll be wearing his orchids and carrying them, too.' She lifted the tiny bouquet from the box in which it lay; a spray of ten orchids and a sprig of white heather, looped underneath to fit snugly on her daughter's middle finger. 'Catchpole has done well. You'll remember to thank him?'

'I'll remember. And, Mother, thank *you* from me and Andrew – for everything.'

'Thank me by being happy.' Her smile was gentle, her eyes gazed across the years to another bride who had carried white orchids. 'See you at the church – and only one minute late is allowed, don't forget.'

'One minute.' All at once her heart stopped its frantic thudding and she was calm and very sure that what she was about to do was right and good and that she and Andrew would be happy together. For ever. 'And I love you very much – you know that, don't you?'

'I know it,' her mother smiled, closing the door gently behind her, pausing to mop the tear that slid down her cheek. *And I love you, my darling girl; be happy with your Andrew.*

19

Agnes Clitherow wriggled her toes inside her felt slippers, relieved it was all over, pleased the day had gone so well. Now, in the quiet of her little sitting-room, she could relax and think back on it with pleasure, for nothing had gone wrong; not one hitch.

The day had been crisply cold but sunny; Catchpole had produced the orchids on time, and Mrs Shaw had excelled herself with a cold collation for the guests that was nothing short of amazing considering the shortages already being felt. Wartime wedding or no, it had been a joy from first to last, she sighed, especially for the servants. The drive to church in the carriage; the drive back in one of Pendenys's motors and Mr Elliot in the fine dress uniform of a Hussar, driving them back, if you please!

Mind, she was not at all sure Elliot Sutton should have been wearing that uniform, since no one could be absolutely sure his commission had yet been granted, though she was relieved that Pendenys and Rowangarth were on speaking terms again, with Mrs Clementina being the one to climb down. Had she not done so, there would have been none from Rowangarth at Mr Nathan's induction, and no one from Pendenys invited to the wedding. Foolish as she was, Mrs Clementina had found the sense to bow to the inevitable and choke on her pride in doing so.

She reached for a log, laying it on the fire, setting her chair rocking gently, thinking back. The doctor had not seemed one bit nervous sitting waiting in the church, though Mr Giles had checked his pocket-watch more than once as a best man usually did, and turned often to watch the door for signs of his sister's arrival.

Such a shame it had been so quiet. Could things have been different, there would have been bridesmaids and scores of guests in amazing hats, but everything had been so suddenly changed by the war. Because of it, couples got married as and when they could, and forgot all the fuss and bother of fancy weddings. Yet, in spite of everything, it had been a splendid day, with everyone happy and not so much as a mention of the fighting in France, nor of the Government doubling income tax at a stroke to pay for it.

Today, Miss Julia had married her doctor and been so radiant she had put the winter sun to shame. It must have been a comfort to her ladyship that the bride should have thought to pause at her father's grave as she left the church and lay her orchids there, then turn to her mother, smiling gently. But that was how the gentry – the *real* gentry – did it; always correctly, without even having so much as to think about it. Not like one she could think of who'd never be a lady if she lived to be a hundred. That one would be an ironmaster's daughter till the end of her days. Agnes Clitherow could recognize breeding; had lived with it since the day she left school, a twelve-year-old child; served the gentry for the better part of her life and learned from it, she hoped, to conduct herself in a proper manner. And though she had started life as a kitchenmaid and risen by sheer determination to the position of housekeeper, she had been astute enough to keep her place at all times.

Mrs Clementina had not. Two generations ago, her folk had been working-class and the old saying was right: you could never make a silk purse from a sow's ear, and those who thought differently and married above themselves must surely live to regret it. The working classes, however they may prosper, should never presume to step out of their station; not if they knew what was good for them: of that the housekeeper was certain, and the knowledge had served her well.

Her head dropped sleepily and she at once straightened her back, blinking her eyes rapidly. It had been a long day and she was tired. Events such as this, however joyous, made her years weigh heavily. Best she should look in on the party to make sure it wasn't getting out of hand. She had remained there long enough only to drink the health of the bride and groom and eat a finger of wedding cake. Then she had left, not wanting her presence to dampen the evening. Yet she didn't want it to to develop into a romp; her ladyship would be too kind to complain if it did. Food in plenty there was, and the tea-urn full, yet there was not so much ale and sherry to cause anything untoward to happen. But she would make sure that the party would not go on too long, it being the Sabbath tomorrow; and then she would undress, say her prayers, and creep thankfully into her bed, not allowing so much as one unhappy thought to cloud the joy of this day.

In the morning she would awaken once more to the awful reality of war, but for the remainder of this day she would forget the worry and futility of it, because tomorrow would come soon enough.

She buttoned her shoes, opened her door quietly, then tiptoed down the long corridor and past her ladyship's bedroom door. She would be long asleep; best not awaken her.

Helen Sutton was not asleep. For a long time she had lain awake, recalling every word and smile, every smallest detail of her daughter's wedding day.

Everyone, she was forced to admit, should have small, happy weddings with only those there who ought to be: family, close friends and godparents. Banished should be

349

the big affairs with the world and his wife present and half the guests not knowing the other half.

Julia's wedding, Helen smiled, had been small and intimate. Even Clemmy had acted as if she were enjoying herself, and Elliot for once had been charming and attentive in his fine new uniform.

Yet she had felt just one sadness, Helen admitted, staring at the dimly outlined mouldings on the ceiling, as Robert had stood there with Julia on his arm. The pain which sliced through her had left behind it a dull ache, exactly where her heart was. She had closed her eyes in an effort to compose herself, then mercifully opened them to see Andrew looking at her and smiling, as if he understood exactly how she felt; how much she needed John beside her.

Andrew had great strength. He was so right for Julia, who was either up on a cloud or down in angry deeps. Andrew would care for her always, she was very sure of that, though now it was Robert she wished to see happily married. How sad he must have felt in church, giving his sister to the man she adored, with his own love half a world away.

Irritated, she threw off the bedclothes and drew back the window curtains, as though a solution would be there, written plainly in the frosty-bright stars.

She stood, listening to the music and laughter heard faintly from across the stableyard where the hayloft had been cleared and cleaned and now shook with the sounds of partying. Surely everyone was happy tonight, except Robert. What could she do, Helen frowned, to give him comfort and hope? Was there any way, even at this late hour, for him to marry his Cecilia?

She looked to her right and was not surprised to see the light in his room shining brightly. At once she took her wrap, then hurried along the passage to his door.

'May I come in?' she called, tapping softly.

'Mother!' At once the door was opened to her. 'Is anything wrong, or are you like me?'

'Can't sleep? Something like that. Thinking about – oh, *everything*. Thinking about Julia and what she is doing and – oh, *dear*!' She placed her hand to her mouth.

'Lady Sutton!' Robert scolded, lips pursed, eyes laughing.

'I know. Sorry,' she murmured, cheeks pinking, eyes on the toes of her slippers. Then, suddenly defiant, she tilted her chin. 'No, I am *not* sorry! I hope with all my heart they aren't wasting a minute of their first night together. Robert,' she murmured, changing tack with alacrity, 'do you think it wise to show so much light? We have been asked to draw curtains across windows if it's at all possible.'

'Of course. Foolish of me.' He closed the curtains at once. 'Though I think that particular directive applies more to London and the big cities. They could be bombarded from the sea, I suppose, or bombed from the air – though I very much doubt it.'

'But the zeppelins? Everyone says they will come.'

'Not to Holdenby, dearest, so stop your fretting. It's such a little place, I doubt they could find it, let alone drop bombs on it. I got a letter from Shillong – did you know?'

'I did. I saw the stamp. From Cecilia?'

'She misses me already,' he nodded. 'She wrote the letter immediately I left. I wrote one before I sailed and left it behind to be posted – for her birthday, I mean.'

'Ah, yes – just one day after your sister's. Is Cecilia well?'

'She's well – and asks if she can write to you. Shall I tell her yes?'

'Of course she must write!' Why hadn't she thought of it herself? 'Better still, I shall write to *her*. I shall wish her a belated happy birthday then tell her all about the wedding and how I wish that you and she could be married too. Is there no way,' she frowned, 'that she can come to you? I know you intend to enlist, but even if they send you to France, surely you'll get leave. Cecilia could be married from Rowangarth and Giles or Edward would give her away. If she sailed at once, we could have everything arranged for your first home leave. A summer wedding would be so beautiful,' she finished, breathlessly.

'Dearest Mother, how good it is to hear you say that.' He took her in his arms, laying a cheek on her hair. 'And I would give anything for it to happen. But when I came home I tried to get a passage for Cecilia too, but I couldn't.'

'Then she must try again. There must be dozens of ships bound for home. Why didn't I think of it before – and there must be *some* lady on board willing to chaperon her.'

'No. There'll be no lady to do that.' He shook his head, his eyes sad. 'Women aren't allowed to sail, you see. The shipping lines won't accept responsibility for women and children. I suppose they haven't yet forgotten the *Titanic*, only now the danger is submarines. Already ships have been sunk, though the Government seems not to admit it. I'm sorry, but even a woman sailing with her husband is refused a berth. It seems that women and children must stay behind in India until the war is over.'

'And I am sorry, too. It seemed such a good idea.'

'That's what Cecilia and I thought. Never mind,' he smiled. 'We've accepted it, now . . .'

'But you mustn't give up! Had you thought the army might well post you back there? We can't leave India undefended and you do speak the language.'

'*One* of the languages, Mother.' He touched her cheek gently, fondly. 'And you are the eternal optimist to think that something so utterly improbable could happen.'

352

'Maybe, but we can hope. Why don't we wish Cecilia happy birthday *now*?'

'Of course! And we'll send her our love too.' He held out his hand. 'Let's go downstairs and pour ourselves a whisky.'

'Sherry for me, I think,' Helen laughed, as they walked softly along the gallery to the stairhead. 'It helps me sleep. Ssssh! We mustn't waken Giles and oh, dear – I think we've been caught.'

At the foot of the stairs the housekeeper waited, nodding briefly.

'Goodnight, milady, Sir Robert. The party will soon be over. When Mary returns she will see that the house is secure. I am going to my bed now, if there's nothing you want.'

'Nothing, Miss Clitherow. Off you go. And thank you,' Helen smiled, 'for all your help.'

'But I enjoyed it. Every minute of it, milady.' Helen was rewarded with one of the housekeeper's rare smiles. 'It was the nicest wedding ever.'

'Yes – and yours is to be the next,' Helen said firmly as she closed the dining-room door behind her. 'I have set my heart on it. Somehow there must be a way to get Cecilia to England and she shall be married from this house.' She raised her glass, smiling over the brim. 'To Cecilia – a happy birthday. And may you soon be together again.'

'Bless you.' He touched her glass with his own. 'Hell, but if you knew how I miss her, want her. I shouldn't have messed about so. It's taken a war to make me see sense, and now it's too late.'

'It is *not* too late – and Robert, I do know how you miss her; I truly do. But you *will* be married. You *will* come through this war, and all will be well for you both – I know it.' All at once she was very sure. One day there would be another wedding at Rowangarth. One day this awful, unnecessary war would end. 'God will keep you safe and you will come home. I know it in my heart.

'To happy birthdays and lovers' meetings,' she smiled. 'And it is so good to have you back again. I am the *luckiest* of women.'

Forty-eight, forty-nine, fifty. Alice laid down her hairbrush and gazed, chin on hand, into the mirror. She wished she were beautiful like Miss Julia had been today, her eyes so full of love, her hair done up real bonny with the circlet of orchids tilted on to her forehead, like the ballet dancers they had seen on the paintings in the London gallery. And it had been so like her to stop beside her father's grave as she left the church, and lay her orchids there. Not that she'd seen her do it; by then they had all left in Pendenys's motor. But Miss Clitherow had been there to watch it.

Pendenys's motor; that grand carriage with soft leather seats and carpet on the floor, shiny brass lamps and shiny door handles. Alice's first ride in a motor; sad that Elliot Sutton should be driving it. But there was, as Mary said afterwards, no show without Punch. Elliot Sutton, Mary said, had looked like something out of Floradora in that get-up of his, and him all the time knowing how handsome he looked.

Mr Nathan, now, had been altogether different. It was as if, Alice considered, the gypsies had taken away the real Elliot Sutton; stolen him from his perambulator and left a black-haired, black-hearted bairn in his place. Elliot wasn't one bit like his brothers and cousins. A changeling, that's what he was, with gypsy blood and gypsy passions and she, Alice Hawthorn, should know it.

She set her mouth button-like, as Cook did when she wasn't best pleased, whilst common sense told her that Elliot Sutton wasn't worth the time of day and not a patch on Nathan. Should Mr Nathan be called

354

the Reverend now, she wondered, or Father Sutton, or Padre, maybe, since he was almost in the army? Nathan had been there, helping at the marrying. At the end, when they'd been pronounced man and wife and for no man to put them asunder, the Reverend Parkin had stood aside and Nathan, his eyes full of love and his voice gentle, blessed them as they knelt there, laying his hands on each of them. His voice had been beautiful and sincere, Alice smiled, and if two people were ever sure of happiness and long years together, it was Miss Julia and the doctor. Doctor and Mrs Andrew MacMalcolm . . .

It would be her own turn, soon, Alice considered gravely, because tonight, as Tom kissed her goodnight after the party, he'd said it in no uncertain terms.

'I was wishing it could have been you and me today, sweetheart. We've been courting every bit as long as Miss Julia and the doctor; by rights it's our turn next.'

And what was more, he'd said, he was sick of waiting, and intended getting things straightened out, once and for all, about Keeper's Cottage.

'I'll see Reuben,' he said, 'tomorrow.' He would ask him to have a word with Mr Giles about Keeper's and when they could expect to move in there. 'A man has the right to know where he stands, especially when he's been as good as promised it.'

Mind, Tom had had a pint or two at the party, but it hadn't been ale-talk. He'd held her close to him as they waltzed and she had closed her eyes and clung to him, unsteady on her feet on account of never having waltzed before, and whispered that, if they didn't get wed soon, she didn't know what she would do for loving him.

She glanced fondly at the tin trunk, full to the brim now with her linen, and thought of the magnificent chest-of-drawers in Reuben's front bedroom, and it made her want Tom so much it was like an ache inside her.

Be happy, Miss Julia, and I bet you look real beautiful in that nightdress . . .

'It was amazing,' said Miss Clitherow to Mrs Shaw next morning, 'how suddenly she was the living image of her ladyship. I'd always thought that Miss Julia wasn't exactly a Sutton; more like her aunt Anne Lavinia, who favours the Whitecliffes,' she confided. 'But when she walked down the aisle – and how blue suits her – with her eyes on the doctor, she seemed somehow to change. Completely beautiful. Another cup, Mrs Shaw?'

Cook nodded, enjoying the rare intimacy of an invitation to the housekeeper's sitting-room; being honoured by the silver teapot and the seldom-used china cups, a gift from a past employer.

'And I'm bound to say, Cook, that in these terrible times, I was pleased to see the rift had been healed between Pendenys and Rowangarth. Nice to see the Suttons together again, even though it took a wedding to do it.'

'Hmm!' Cook grunted, stirring her tea. 'Talk did have it that Mrs Clementina was forced to make the first move. Never thought, she hadn't, that her ladyship would have so much steel in her backbone. Thought Lady Helen would give in, but it was Pendenys as had to come calling first. Just after young Sutton came back from Kentucky, I heard it was.' She raised an eyebrow, waiting in vain for confirmation. 'Mrs Clementina would have died of shame if Rowangarth hadn't been at the Minster for Mr Nathan. And think of the talk if Pendenys hadn't been asked to the wedding.'

'The Reverend Nathan would have been asked, choose what,' Agnes Clitherow offered cagily, 'with Miss Julia so set on him marrying her. Not that he could, of course, but it was a lovely blessing he gave them,' she smiled dreamily. 'Strange,' she murmured, 'but I always had it in mind that he and Miss Julia might one day have announced their engagement, but it wasn't to be . . .'

'Aye. And happen the lass knew all along what an unholy terror Mrs Clementina would have been – as a mother-in-law, I mean. Nobody, not even a Rowangarth Sutton, would have been good enough for that one's sons. And she can see no wrong in Elliot – not even after what happened in Brattocks. But thanks be we'll soon have rid of him and his fancy uniform. A spell in the army might do him a power of good.'

'I doubt it – and he won't go anywhere near the fighting, his mother will see to that,' murmured the housekeeper archly. 'My word, Mrs Shaw, if you'd seen the distress of poor Hawthorn that night Reuben Pickering called me to her, you'd have had Elliot Sutton horsewhipped; and horsewhipped he'd have been had Sir John been alive or Sir Robert at home. And talking about Sir Robert – did you know we've all been worrying over nothing – about his staying unmarried for so long, I mean.

'Her ladyship told me,' she dropped her voice to a whisper. 'And this is in the strictest confidence – not one word to anyone else – that he has a young lady he hopes to marry when things get back to normal.'

'Well, now. It all goes to show!' said Cook comfortably.

She hoped her face registered the correct degree of surprise, for Agnes Clitherow rarely unburdened herself to the lower orders; not even to herself, who'd been cook to the gentry for more years than she cared to tell. Because, Mrs Shaw thought gleefully, she had known all along about Sir Robert's young lady; had got it from Bess, who'd been dusting his bedroom and been caught with the photograph in her hand.

'And is she to your liking?' Sir Robert had asked, all at once appearing, to which Bess, all flustered, had said she was just about the most beautiful young lady she'd ever clapped eyes on. And Sir Robert had smiled very

357

mysteriously and said, 'That is Miss Cecilia Kahn and yes, I think she is most beautiful too . . .'

And when no one was about, they had all crept up the back stairs and had a look at the photograph at his bedside, and been ever so glad she was a Miss.

'It all goes to show,' Agnes Clitherow agreed. 'And I think, Mrs Shaw, that since there was a half-empty bottle left at the party – which I brought up here, not wishing good sherry to be wasted – we should raise a glass to the future happiness of Doctor and Mrs MacMalcolm.' And then perhaps raise them again to Sir Robert and the most beautiful Miss Kahn. And even though she knew she would pay with a headache for such indulgence, the housekeeper, for once in her blameless, straight-laced life, did not care.

'To Miss Julia and her husband,' she murmured, raising her glass. 'And may they have a lovely honeymoon – wherever they are spending it!'

Julia lay in her husband's arms, her body warm from loving, exulting in their nearness, unbelieving, still, of the wonder of their coupling; that mixing of loving and lusting and naked bodies close. Never, not even in the early days of knowing him, wanting him, wondering how it would be, could she ever have imagined the joy of giving and taking.

On their wedding night, in that splendid room in the York hotel, she had been apprehensive; had sat at the dressing-table brushing her hair, wanting him to take her; wanting him not to take her – to leave her dreamings unspoiled. But he had walked in from the bathroom, towel-wrapped, hair wet and tousled and said, 'Julia, darling . . .'

She went to him then, in a float of silk and baby-blue lace and knew, all doubts gone, it would be all right.

'I love you, I want you,' she had whispered as he'd

slipped the straps of her nightdress from her shoulders so it fell to her feet in a gossamer drift.

'And I love you, wife,' he'd said as he had lifted her in his arms and carried her to the bed.

Nothing, she had thought, could ever be as wonderful as that first loving in a bridal suite, flower-filled and opulent. Yet here, in Andrew's lodgings in Little Britain, it had been better, fiercer, more passionate. Here, in Andrew's bed, she felt she truly belonged.

'Are you asleep?' she whispered, her lips across his cheek.

'No.' He kissed her softly. 'Close your eyes . . .'

'I don't want to. Don't want to waste any of tonight.'

'Go to sleep, woman.' His voice was low, indulgent. 'There are four nights more – '

He stopped, knowing it was too late; knowing it by the sudden stiffening of her body.

'Four nights? Why four nights? What are you keeping from me?' Her voice was sharp and high with sudden fear, and she groped in the darkness for the matchbox, lighting the bedside candle with hands that shook. 'Tell me, Andrew!'

'I'm sorry, sweetheart. I was half asleep – just wasn't thinking . . .'

'Where? *When?*'

'On Friday – I report to Aldershot. I'd have told you – maybe tomorrow. I should have gone last week, but I telegraphed them that I was to be married. They gave me seven days' grace.'

'The army!' Fear screamed through her; cruel hands twisted her insides. 'You knew! All the time you knew and you said nothing!' She pulled the sheet around her nakedness, facing him accusingly. 'Four days – all we've got.'

'And four nights, Julia.' His eyes asked forgiveness. 'I didn't want to spoil our wedding, but I'm glad you know.'

'I'm sorry. It isn't your fault. It's this damned war – and

your conscience,' she whispered. 'Will they send you to the Front?' She reached for him, seeking comfort in his nearness. The shock had receded, but the pain remained.

'I won't know until I get to the barracks. Maybe I'll stay in England for a while. But even if – well, it won't be in the front line, exactly. Dressing-stations are behind the lines and hospitals well out of reach of the fighting.'

'They're taking you from me,' she whispered.

Her face crumpled, her mouth trembled on the edge of a sob, and he held her tightly, hushing her softly.

'It was selfish of me to marry you, knowing I already intended to enlist. But I wanted you so desperately, darling. Forgive me?'

'You know I forgive you and I'll be all right once I'm used to it. And I suppose I'd have been more upset if you *hadn't* married me. And four days is quite a long time.'

'They'll be heaven, Julia. We'll make them so. We'll visit Aunt Sutton and walk in Hyde Park – go to our place. And there is so much to see in London, even in November. The war hasn't closed the theatres and music halls.'

'Go out nights, with the fog coming down and the street lights dimmed? Best we stay here, snug and warm, and make love.'

'Julia MacMalcolm, you are shameless!'

'I know. But having you is so wonderful. Do you suppose we've made a child?'

'No!' His tone was sharp. 'Darling girl, I'm going to war. When we have a child I shall want to be with you, to take care of you. To leave you behind, pregnant, would be selfish.'

'Even though I want your baby – desperately want it?'

'Even though. When the world comes to its senses again, we'll have all the children we can afford, I promise you.'

'I suppose you know best; you usually do,' she sighed, calmer. 'But, oh Andrew – only four days. I knew you would go, but I thought – hoped – not yet . . .'

'I'd thought so, too, but if you'd seen what I have seen these last weeks – the troops need on-the-spot attention. The army is asking for doctors and nurses. It's urgent. There have been terrible casualties at Ypres. I *must* go.'

'I know. Afterwards – how long shall I stay on here?'

'*Until* . . .'

'Until I know there's no chance you might be able to get back to see me? Until I know you've gone?'

'Stay here as long as you want – there's another year of the lease to run. But I'd rather you went back to Rowangarth. You'd be less lonely there, and safer.'

'But I'll be all right here. And Aunt Sutton is near. Why such concern for my safety?'

'Because London could be dangerous to live in. The Germans haven't built all those zeppelins for nothing. London – Britain – *will* be bombed. Already the sea blockade is being felt. Food could become scarce and you'd feel the pinch less in the country. Please, Julia? It's going to be bad enough being parted from you: at least let me know you'll be safe?'

'Very well, if that's what you want. And I'm sorry I was so awful about it when I should be so proud of you.' She wound her arms around him, straining closer. 'And darling, is it very unladylike of me to ask you – *beg* you – to make love to me again? *Now*?'

'I don't know. I've never before been faced with such a delightful dilemma.'

'Then will you give it your most urgent consideration?' Her eyes begged him; every pulse in her body beat out her need of him. 'Please?'

'I will,' he murmured throatily, pulling closer, searching with his lips for hers. 'Oh, I will indeed . . .'

They ate bread and jam for breakfast and boiled the tea-kettle on the single gas ring in the kitchen.

'I'm sorry,' Julia whispered, dismayed, 'but I don't

know how we are to eat tonight. I can't cook. I can't even light the range . . .'

'It doesn't matter. This morning I will forgive you anything. Mrs Sparrow will be in at ten. She'll soon make short work of raking out the fire and cleaning the flues. She has a way with that kitchen range.'

'Sparrow. What a lovely name.'

'Not really. She's really Emily Smith but she's so cheerful and chirpy – a real Cockney sparrow . . .'

'Do you know, Andrew – that day I came here to find you I expected your housekeeper to open the door to me.'

'Nothing so grand! Mrs Sparrow is a daily. But if she had answered the door, I promise she'd have asked you in, made you a cup of strong, sweet tea, and had all your history – and your family's – out of you in ten minutes flat. She loves people. I want you to like her, too, so that if – after Friday, I mean – if you should want to come here, or if you want mail sending on to you, she'll be on hand to see to things. She's got her own key, so she'll keep the place aired – until the coal heap runs out, that is.'

'And you trust her?'

'Implicitly. She is also my friend. And when you meet her, be sure to ask about her rheumatism. She's a martyr to it,' he grinned.

'I'll remember. Now do we leave the bed-making and dish-washing to your Sparrow, or shall I do it before we go to Aunt Sutton's?'

'Leave it to Sparrow. And don't worry. When we set up house together – when I'm in general practice – I think we'll be able to afford a cook and a housemaid. So let's be away to your aunt's. And when we've lunched, we'll walk in the park and be thoroughly sentimental. How does that suit you, wife?'

Figgis answered their ring, bobbed a curtsey, then called, 'They're here! Go on in, ma'am, whilst I see to the coffee.'

362

'My dear!' Anne Lavinia Sutton caught her niece in a hug, then pumped Andrew's hand enthusiastically. 'Bless you both. Be happy, won't you, and forgive me for not coming to the wedding? Can't abide 'em. Vowed years ago that I'd never go to one – starting with my own! Now come in and make yourselves comfortable. We'll have to see about your wedding present. Thought I'd forgotten, didn't you?'

'Of course not. And if you had, it wouldn't have mattered. Where are we to sit?'

'On the sofa, the pair of you. Tell me, what do you think to this?'

It was there beside her chair, as if she had known they would come; a painting in oils in a heavy gilt frame and instantly recognizable.

'It's Rowangarth,' Andrew smiled.

'Yes, and painted in 1750 – look, you can just see the date. I've arranged to have it cleaned then packed and sent up to Rowangarth. Will that suit you, eh?'

'It most certainly will. But are you sure, ma'am?' Andrew frowned. 'It must be very valuable.'

'Only, I think, if you're a Sutton. And it don't hang well on these plain white walls of mine. That sort of painting needs an older house to set if off. There's very little changed, you'll notice, in a century and a half. Your pa gave it to me, Julia, when I left home to live in London, and now I'm giving it back.'

'I'll treasure it, Aunt, and thank you – from both of us.'

'No thanks needed, girl. Just be happy, that's all. You *are* happy, aren't you?' she demanded bluntly.

'Exquisitely so,' Julia laughed, cheeks pinking.

'Good. Then mind you keep a tight rein on her, young man,' she glowered at Andrew. 'The Sutton women are all high-mettled. If you let her get out of hand, she'll turn out like me, and then where will you be?'

Fortune, Andrew was to think, sometimes favours the timid too, for at that moment exactly, the entry of Figgis bearing coffee relieved him of the need to reply.

'I'll pour.' Julia jumped to her feet. 'And did you know, Aunt, that Andrew joins a regiment on Friday?'

'So you've volunteered? Good man. You'll be off to France, I suppose? I'd join you like a shot if they'd have me. It irks me, you know, not being able to go there any more. I swear that when this war is over I'll up sticks and spend the rest of my years there. Mind, I've got irons in the fire, but it's early days yet . . .'

She settled herself comfortably, took a sip of coffee, then, setting it aside, she said abruptly, 'It wasn't that I didn't think about you on your wedding day; I wasn't being an awkward old cuss not being there. Weddings and funerals – I dislike them both. But I did have you in mind – most of that afternoon, in fact. I spent it with my solicitor, you see, changing my Will. I'm not without a sovereign or two, and I've decided that, when I'm gone, you shall inherit.'

'Aunt! But why? Oh, it's good of you – but why *me*?'

'Why not you, Julia? You are like me in so many ways. You look like me and, like me, you won't be gainsaid. There's a lot of Whitecliffe in you too. I gave it a lot of thought. Robert, I decided, doesn't need it; he'll get Rowangarth and the tea garden and that's enough for anyone.

'Giles, if I left it to him, would either spend it on old, expensive books or put it in the bank and forget it. Of my Pendenys nephews, I think that anything Nathan inherited he'd give to the Church; young Albert doesn't need it, if what I'm told is to be believed – and as for Elliot! Tcha!

'So that leaves you, Julia. There's this house and my motor and what's in the bank. It'll come to you when I'm gone. Don't agree with marriage, myself, but you've found yourself a good man, so that at least I'll not hold against you. Now this little house isn't big enough for you to set up in, young sir, but it's a good address and, should you decide to put up your plate in London, it'll be a starting point for you. Now, what do you both think? Did I do right?'

'Aunt! I don't know what to say. The painting – that would have been more than generous; but to leave all this to me – ' Julia waved an expansive hand. ' "Thank you" sounds so – so *feeble* . . .'

'Left it to you both. I'd like it if you kept the house, but it's entirely up to the pair of you. No strings attached. Now tell me, young man, about what'll be happening to you. God knows, there seems to be a crying need of doctors out there . . .'

'If you'll pardon me, Sir Robert, it's good to have you home.' Reuben, in his best keeping-suit, brown boots and leggings gleaming, walked at Robert Sutton's side feeling that, for a little while at least, things would be done right at Rowangarth. 'And shall you be thinking about a shoot? There's some fine young birds this year. It's almost as if we knew you'd be back.'

'It's good to be back, Reuben; good to walk the covers again. I didn't expect you to be still in charge. Thought you'd have retired by now.'

'And me an' all. I'd had it in mind to retire last back end, but nowt came of it. Expect that Mr Giles is leaving that sort of decision to you now. I'd thought to have the end almshouse – the one with the bit of garden to it, but – '

'But you're still here.' They climbed the stile into the wood, Reuben's two retrievers wriggling under it, then taking their place at his heels again. 'The new man – what's he shaping up like?'

'Tom Dwerryhouse? He'll make a good keeper; I've no

doubts in that direction. But it's this war, Sir Robert. The young ones are all unsettled. Dwerryhouse thinks it isn't worth enlisting. Says it'll all be over afore he's had time to fire a shot in anger. But talk seems to have it different now. Got themselves dug in – both sides. Can wait it out for months – *years* – folk are saying. I'm wondering if Tom will go.'

'I understand your doubts, and I'm glad you're still here. I'm inclined to agree with you. And before so very much longer we'll have conscription forced on us, and then all the young men will have to go. It wouldn't do for you to retire, Reuben, then find the new keeper had been called to the colours. Could you stick it out for a little while longer, do you think?'

'You mean for me to stay on at Keeper's?'

'Would you? Just until we see how things go. I'm hoping to meet Dwerryhouse before so very much longer – he'll doubtless let me know how he feels about things. And can you set up a shoot for me, Reuben? I'll be off to join the army in the New Year – a Boxing Day shoot would suit me nicely; might be the last one we'll be able to manage until the war is over.'

Could he set up a shoot? Reuben silently exulted. Hadn't he been waiting – *wanting* – to set one up for years now? There'd even been times when he had wondered at the need for one keeper, let alone two.

'Leave it all to me and Dwerryhouse, sir,' he said, almost with glee. 'And how many guns will there be?'

'About half a dozen, I'd say. Must speak to Lady Helen about it first, though – see how she feels about house guests over Christmas. But I think it'll be all right. I'd thought on a couple of friends and Uncle Edward and the two Pendenys cousins, if they're at home, that is.'

'I'll see to it – get the beaters fixed up an' all,' Reuben said eagerly. 'My, but it'll be right grand to have a bit of a do at Rowangarth again. We seem to have been rearing birds for nowt since Sir John was taken.'

'Then can we take it you'll stay on at Keeper's Cottage – see how things work out? And as for rearing, I think we can dispense with that until things get back to normal. Just leave it to natural breeding, will you? This war could last a couple of years more, and the German navy is determined to blockade us and starve us out. If things get bad – the food situation, I mean – you'll see to it that none of the estate workers goes short of a rabbit or a hare and anything else that might help?

'Things are going to get worse before they're better, Reuben. We'll just have one last shoot here, then we'll let things slow down a bit – does that suit you?'

'To stay on, you mean? If that's what you think best, Sir Robert, I'm willing. Dwerryhouse will be disappointed. He's courting and would like to have Keeper's, but I reckon he'll accept that this war has knocked everybody's plans on the head. By the heck; we could have done well without this dratted old war.'

'We could, but we're stuck with it, so there's precious little we can do about it. Now, let's have a look at the far covers – see what you've been up to whilst I've been away, and what kind of sport we can expect on Boxing Day. And before you ask it, I haven't included my brother in the numbers. You know his views and, besides, he's a rotten shot,' he grinned, drawing deep on the air, pulling it into his lungs. 'You know, I hadn't realized how I've missed these late autumn mornings. There's a smell to them; a scent you'll find nowhere else in the whole world. I've missed England, truth known. It's good to be back, even though it took a war to get me home.'

'And happen when it's over and done with, you'll be staying on here, at the Garth?' Reuben asked with the assurance of one who had known his employer since boyhood. 'Us'd like it if you did.'

'And I'd like it too,' Robert laughed, 'and happen I might stay on and settle down. Happen I just might.'

'Here you are, darling. In line with the gate about ten yards from the seat . . .'

'You've remembered. Imagine, Andrew, we might never have met. If someone hadn't thrown a cricket ball –'

'And your Whitecliffe temper hadn't surfaced?'

'Just think, though. You could well have been on duty that night. What would have happened to me then?'

'Either the constable would have marched you to the bridewell to cool your heels, or Hawthorn would have hustled you off home and telephoned Aunt Sutton's doctor.'

'I know. It's too awful even to think about. But when we are apart, when I'm so lonely for you that I can't bear it, I shall come to this very spot, and you'll be near me again.'

'Will you, Julia? If I were not to come back from the war, is that what you would do – seek me here?'

'Yes, I would. I'd stand here, very still, and talk to you with my heart. And you would answer me, I know it. But supposing it were me who died – where would you go to find me?'

'Oh, there's no doubt! I'd go to Holdenby Pike – right to the very top. You took me there when first I visited Rowangarth, do you remember? It was then that I knew there could only be you for me – for the rest of my life. You were like a free spirit, your hair blowing wild, and I know that if I went there and called your name, you would answer me on the wind.'

She reached for his hand, entwining her fingers in his, lifting his hand to her lips, placing a kiss there.

'We're foolish, aren't we, darling? You *will* come home safely. There won't be a moment I'm not thinking of you or dreaming about you. I shall send my love in great warm gusts, and it'll wrap you round and keep you from harm. And, darling, you'll get leave, won't you? We'll come here again on another sentimental pilgrimage, won't we?'

'We'll come here again and again. We'll come until we are so old we've completely forgotten why we are here and what we are looking for,' he laughed. 'I promise you, my lovely love, that we'll grow old together.'

Of course they would, she thought contentedly. What could part them? What dare try?

20

Waterloo station was crowded yet strangely subdued, with the sad, waiting silence that heralds partings to come and farewells no one wants to say.

The platform was crowded with khaki. Privates, sergeants with chalk-white stripes, officers. Most carried full kit; infantrymen with marching-packs, rifles and ammunition pouches; officers wearing dress of finer cloth and soft, brown boots. There were sad faces; going-back faces, taut with apprehension; bright, fresh faces, too young to be gazing soon upon war.

'Darling,' Julia whispered to the stranger who stood beside her. 'How soon will I know?'

'When, you mean? I'll write tonight – let you know I've arrived.' Too late, now, to regret the absence of a telephone in the lodgings in Little Britain. 'I should know fairly quickly what will be happening. Don't stay here for more than a week, will you?'

'I'm staying here till I know you've gone,' she said stubbornly. 'I won't be alone. There's Aunt Sutton not so very far away, and Mrs Sparrow will be coming in every day.' And why were they talking like this when they should be holding each other close, whispering their love, their need. Yet instead she was forcing her lips into the shape of a smile, pretending to be brave when she wanted to cry out her desolation and not care if the whole of London heard.

'I don't want you alone nights, Julia. Go back to Rowangarth, or at least to Aunt Sutton.'

'I shall stay at the lodgings,' she insisted, 'until I know there is no chance at all that you'll get a pass.'

'Then be careful. Don't go out in the dark unless you must.'

The street called Little Britain was mostly shops and workshops; there were few houses, few lights, many shadowy corners.

'I'll take care.' Once more the smile that hurt her so.

'I heard I'll be joining up with twelve Scottish doctors – *women* doctors. Does that please your suffragette soul?'

'It should, but it doesn't. It just makes me angry I must stay behind, useless.'

She *was* useless. She could do nothing; not even light a fire. Like most of her kind, she had been reared for marriage and motherhood.

'You are *not* to change,' he whispered, taking her hand. 'I love you so much . . .'

They stood beside the open door of the compartment, where already his greatcoat lay folded on the seat, his kit stowed on the rack. She wanted to slam shut that door and cry, 'I won't let you go! They shan't have you!' but she stood there, mute, and the smile stayed set on her lips.

'I'd better get in.' He glanced up at the station clock. 'It's almost time . . .'

'No!' Just a few more seconds? 'Andrew, I love you so. I can't believe they're parting us. Why did we let it happen?'

As if to mock her, there was a blowing of whistles at either end of the train; a guard waved a green flag, calling that the train was about to leave, that they must take their seats – *please*!

'This is it, then.' He cupped her face in his hands; such a lost, fear-filled face. 'I love you, Julia MacMalcolm.'

His kiss was hard with despair, and she clasped her arms around his neck, pulling him closer.

'And I love you. Take care. Come home safely?'

The train began its reluctant filling. Last kisses, the sweeter for being snatched; hugs, handshakes and smiles; false, brave smiles. Heads were held high, mouths set tightly against tears. Bereft, they stood there; wives, sisters, sweethearts, mothers; stood numbed, long after the red rear lights of the train became smaller then disappeared into the gathering dark of the late afternoon. Faces crumpled then. Gone were the smiles. Now they could weep.

Julia did not, would not weep. Head down she turned and ran to the cab rank, calling the address to the driver as she slammed the door, shut out the uncaring world. She sat, shoulders back, head defiantly high, listening to the round grinding of wheels, the measured clopping of hoofs.

'Here y'are, lady – Little Britain. What number?' the cabby called.

'Number 53A. Just past the church gates.' She pushed a florin into his hand, waving away the change, fumbling her key into the lock.

The gaslight flickered and popped in the inrush of cold air; to her left, the closed door of the surgery sent a chill of finality through her that the glow of firelight from the kitchen did nothing to dispel.

'You're back then, mum?' The little cleaning woman came slowly down the stairs, her eyes bright with concern.

'Mrs Sparrow! Oh, I'm so glad you're here!'

Julia went into the open arms, laid her head on the thin shoulder and sobbed.

'He asked me to. "Be there for her," he said. "She'll need someone . . ."'

'I'm sorry.' She blew her nose noisily, dabbing her eyes, taking deep, shuddering breaths. 'I shouldn't have made such a fuss – couldn't help it, though.'

'Not weep, when your man's gone? Whatever next? And I know how you feel. My son went last month.

372

Sparrow understands. Now off you go upstairs to the parlour and warm yourself. The kettle's on the boil. I'll bring you some tea.'

'Would you? And will you have a cup with me? Stay a little while? I'm so miserable I don't know what to do. I couldn't cry at the station. I wanted to, but I didn't. I stood there, smiling, and all the time I wanted to weep and rage and beg him not to go. I stood there and smiled, would you believe?'

'That's my brave girl. That's what he would want. Upstairs with you now. I'll stay till you feel a bit better – see you into bed. And I brought along a little tipple. Nothing like a spot of hot gin and sugar to help you sleep.'

'I feel like getting blind drunk!'

'No you don't, mum, and besides, there ain't enough to get drunk on. Off you go, this minute!'

'You're very kind, Mrs Sparrow. Thank you for being here.'

'No thanks needed. Doing it for the doctor. He's a good man; been kindness itself to me. My rheumatics are going to miss him something terrible. Treated me for nothing, he did,' she sighed. 'It's a sad, wicked world, Mrs Mac, but the doctor's going to be all right. Sparrow's got a feeling for such things and she knows it. He'll come back to us safe and sound, just see if he don't.'

Julia took off her hat and coat and held her hands to the fire, closing her eyes tightly.

Andrew, my darling, wherever you are tonight, think of me? I love you so, miss you, need you. Come back to me? I can't go on living if you don't . . .

She stayed at the lodgings, waiting; watching for the postman, listening for the slamming of a cab door, the sound of her husband's key in the lock. She hardly dared go out and, if she did, so he might not think she had returned to Rowangarth, she pinned a note each time to the surgery door.

Darling. Back soon. I love you, love you.

On the third morning, his letter came. It was no more than a single sheet of paper and bore no address.

Dearest love,
By the time you get this, I shall be on my way . . .

Carefully she read it, folded it, returned it to the envelope. She should have known. No lovers' meetings for them; not for a long time.

Opening her dressing-case she laid it with the other letter; the one she had found on her pillow the night he left.

My darling girl,
This last week was the most marvellous I shall ever know. Thank you for loving me, for marrying me. I promise I shall love you always. You, and only you. There are no words to tell you how much I care. You will never be far from my side. Just call for me with your heart, and I shall be there.
God keep you, my lovely love,
Your Andrew.

Her Andrew. Hers, body and soul, for all time. There never could, never would be another. Not if their brief loving was all she would have for the rest of her days. And now he had gone. *By the time you get this . . .*

Now she too must go; home to Rowangarth, to where his next letter would be addressed. Back to her mother; to Giles and Robert and the warm safeness of the old house wrapping its love around her. Andrew wanted her there, and she would obey him as she had promised in church, just a week ago. Go back to the garden they had walked in, to the church they'd been married in, there to kneel and ask – *beg* – God to keep her man safely.

She would *not* go to Holdenby Pike; not without him. To go there alone would be to cry her grief to the four winds; call him back from whatever is death.

She clamped her teeth tightly, shaking away such thoughts. Mrs Sparrow would soon be here. Taking paper and pen she left a note that she had gone to Montpelier Mews and would be back by ten o'clock.

'So you're off, Mrs MacMalcolm?' she demanded, when Julia returned.

'There was a letter this morning. By now, he'll be on his way to France, I suppose. He wants me back with my family.'

'And are you all ready?'

'Yes.' For the first time in her life she had packed her own cases. 'I'm getting the midday train.'

'I'll come in regular then, mum; keep the place aired, and the bed. You'll write me out your address, so I can send me any letters?'

'I've already done it. Give me yours, will you, then I can send your wages, and let you know how the doctor is? I don't know how much – will a pound a month be enough?'

'That's what the doctor paid me – on the first Friday of every month. Mind, it was more than enough. I'd have cleaned for him for nothing for what he did for my rheumatics.'

'Oh, dear – and how are they today?'

'Something awful, and that's God's truth. But it's a cross I has to bear and there's many a one in that graveyard up the street would be glad to have my pain, I'll be bound.'

'I'll send you money for coal too, Mrs Sparrow. Let me know when it runs out. I'll send you a pound note – that'll be all right, won't it?'

'It'll do, mum.' Not that she entirely trusted the new notes. Scraps of paper, pretending to be sovereigns, to her way of thinking; not solid money, *gold* money. But more and more shopkeepers were taking them now, and it made sense, she supposed, to call in all our *real* money. Gold, people said, was important to the winning of the war, and perhaps it was as well that English gold was safely locked away. 'Not that I agree with paper money. I don't know who thought it up, but they'll have to do away with it once this war is over.' Whoever heard of a paper pound? 'But leave it all to Sparrow. I'll look after the place. And don't fret yourself. He'll be all right. T'ain't as if he'll be up to the kneecaps in mud in the trenches. Hospitals have got to be behind the lines. Even this barmy Government has sense enough to see that.'

'Of course he'll be all right. He *will*. I've already written him two letters, though I can't post them. But I'll write every day, then send them all when I get an address.'

'Then be sure to send him Sparrow's best wishes.'

'I will,' Julia whispered, hugging the little woman to her. 'Be sure I will, Mrs Sparrow.'

Though this was her afternoon off, she might just as well be in the sewing-room turning sheets sides to middles, Alice sighed. Tom was as busy as might be, with Sir Robert's Christmas shoot and him so looking forward to it that it hadn't occurred to him to take even half a day off. But the winter shoots, Tom said, was what keeping was all about, and since Mr Giles didn't agree with rearing and fattening birds only to blast them out of the sky, things had been far too quiet at Rowangarth since Sir John was taken. Now, until his son went into the army, there would be some semblance of normality, Tom enthused, and as fine a crop of pheasants and partridge as any landowner could wish for.

'Off you go, boy,' she commanded, unleashing the dog. 'Find Tom . . .'

Not that she had needed to bring Morgan with her this afternoon, but the soft old thing had got used to his outings and, if she hadn't offered, Mr Giles would have forgotten it was her afternoon off, like as not, him with his nose always in a book. And for all it was a long time since the happening, she still felt safer in Brattocks with Morgan at her side.

Brattocks was drab now. Fallen leaves covered brown, withering grass; no flowers bloomed. Only the trees were beautiful still, their outlines starkly magnificent against the sinking red suns of late November, or a grey sky full of snow.

She hurried into the depths of the wood. Tom, she calculated, would have checked the covers, the vermin traps and the rabbit snares, and should, about this time, be walking Brattocks Wood – if not to catch poachers, then to warn off any who might have designs on a brace of game-birds. She called his name and her heart gave a happy little skip, just as it always did, at his answering whistle.

'I'm here,' she called, running to meet him.

'Hullo, bonny lass.' He wrapped an arm around her, lifting her high, kissing her as she clung to him. 'Don't have a lot of time,' he smiled, setting her down. 'I'm to be at Reuben's place in five minutes; Sir Robert'll be there to talk about the shoot. Shall we go to Creesby to the picture house tonight, or shall we find somewhere warm, and talk?'

'Talk,' she said without hesitation. Much as she liked sitting hands clasped in the flickering, intimate darkness of the cinema, somewhere warm and private was much better. They had found a spot behind the kitchen-garden wall: a corner warmed by the hothouse boiler on the other side of it, and sheltered from the east wind by bushes; and had long ago marked it down as a place to come to when the cold nights came.

Alice needed to talk. Since the wedding there had been such a longing inside her; so great a need to belong. It was the war, mind, putting such thoughts into her head; that war they had said would be over by Christmas. Now, some prophesied it could last as long as two years. Before so very much longer she would be nineteen. Not old enough to marry, she frowned, yet old enough, had she been born a boy, to fight in the trenches. Why then was she considered too young to know her own mind – and when, come to think of it, was Tom to be told to move into Keeper's Cottage?

'You've heard nothing?' she asked him.

'Nothing that won't keep until tonight. What news of Miss Julia? I heard tell the doctor's gone to the war.'

'My word, but bad news travels fast,' Alice sighed. 'All I know is that she rang up this morning from her aunt Sutton's house. She's coming home. The doctor has been sent to France, she thinks. Knew all along he was going, it seems, but he didn't say anything so's not to spoil the wedding. A week a bride, then she's alone again. Poor Miss Julia.'

'Was it worth it, do you think?' Tom murmured. 'Getting a taste of being wed – getting to like it, happen – then it all having to end? Wouldn't do for me.'

'Why ever not, ' Alice countered hotly. 'If a week was all you knew you might ever have, wouldn't you take it, Tom Dwerryhouse, and be thankful?'

''Twould all depend.'

'On what?' To Alice, there was no argument.

'On a lot of things. On if it's fair to marry a lass, then leave her, maybe for a widow, a week later.'

'But wouldn't it depend on the lass? Wouldn't she get a say in it then?'

'Oh, hush your noise.' He silenced her with a kiss. 'A right little vixen you're turning out to be. You'll be joining that suffragette lot next.'

'And so I would if I could. It's about time women had a say in the running of things!'

'Alice, love.' Tom laid down his gun, gathering her close. 'I love you. Even when you get on your high horse and talk nonsense, I love you. But I'll have to go. Can't keep Sir Robert waiting.'

He kissed her long and hard and she murmured, 'See you tonight then? Six o'clock, and mind you're not late, Tom Dwerryhouse!'

'I won't be,' he said softly. Being late was the least of his worries, did she but know it.

She turned at the stile, waved, then called for Morgan. The silly creature had probably picked up Tom's scent and was running round in circles still looking for him. And why should she not be a suffragette? Why shouldn't women have a say in the running of things? Couldn't make a bigger mess of it than the men had done. Had there been women in Parliament, this war would never have been allowed to happen. Women had sons; bore them and reared them to grow into men, not soldiers. 'Don't you dare have any wars!' women would say if they only had a voice. And weren't women begotten and born in just the same way as men? Alice considered, warming to her subject. Weren't women every bit as good as men, even though some would have it they were the weaker of the two and their brains smaller? Yet women were already at the Front. Hadn't lady doctors and nurses gone there already?

'Morgan!' she called again irritably. 'Come here *at once*!'

With relief, Julia saw a light still burned in Alice's bedroom. She wanted so much to talk to her. Unburdening herself

379

to her mother was all very well, but there was a limit to what she could say without upsetting her. Hawthorn would listen; would understand how desolate and alone she felt.

'Can I come in?'

'Oh, it's you, miss.' Alice dabbed hastily at her eyes.

'Hawthorn, you've been crying. You haven't had a quarrel with Tom? I came here for sympathy but it seems you need some yourself. What is wrong?'

'Wrong, miss? Oh, just about *everything*.'

'Then you must tell me. Let's go down to the sewing-room. We won't need to whisper, there. And please don't cry.'

'It's Tom,' Alice sniffed when they were settled in the little workroom. 'Sprang it on me without warning, though I suppose he can't be blamed for it – not entirely.

'He's not to have Keeper's Cottage, you see. And I know it isn't my place to be outspoken, and I'm not intending criticism of Sir Robert, but Reuben told Tom he isn't retiring to the almshouse like he'd hoped. Sir Robert says there's to be no more rearing of game-birds; practically said there won't be any need for two keepers – well, not until the war is over.'

'And?' Julia prompted, taking Alice's hand in hers. 'Please tell me. You and I are friends and I do understand.'

'Oh, I can see the sense in it, miss, but it hurts something cruel for all that. Sir Robert thinks – aye, and Reuben and Tom agree with him – that before so very much longer this Government is going to bring in conscription. Not so long ago, Tom was saying the war would soon be over, but now he seems to be changing his mind.'

'So if conscription came, Tom might be one of the first to be called?'

'That's just about it.'

'And what does Tom think about it?'

'He agrees. Said tonight that there wasn't a lot of sense him moving from the bothy into Keeper's when before so very much longer he'll have to go for a soldier. Said Reuben might just as well stay where he is. The biggest part of the work is the rearing, and if there are no more shoots, they'll not need birds, will they?

'And do you know what else Tom says? He reckons that if men are going to be conscripted, they'll have to go where they're told. But if they volunteered, like now, they could take their pick. Imagine getting called as a conscript, Tom said, and being told what to do and where to go. "I'm a fine shot," he said. "I'd make a good marksman for the army but, if I wait, where are they going to send me? To the cookhouse, like as not!" But I'm being selfish, aren't I? I ought to be saying how sorry I am that the doctor's gone. And I *am* sorry. It must have been a terrible shock for you – him knowing, I mean, and not telling you.'

'It was worse for him, I think, trying to keep it from me.'

'He did what he thought best, I shouldn't wonder. And he'll get leave, miss. There'll be leave to look forward to.'

'I doubt it. I'm not setting my hopes too high. It's the men with children who'll get the leave – *when* they're giving it out, that is. Someone like Andrew won't stand much of a chance. But I shall hope and wish and pray that sometime, somewhere, we'll be able to meet. I don't think I could bear it if there wasn't hope.'

'Then we'll both hope and wish and pray, shall us? Hope that the doctor gets some leave and that that stubborn Tom Dwerryhouse comes to his senses and don't go volunteering before he has to.'

'But if he does you'll be getting married, Hawthorn, and when you do, you must borrow my beautiful night-dress to wear on your wedding night. There now, what do you say to that?'

381

'I'm saying – oh, miss . . .' Alice covered her face with her hands and the tears came afresh. 'Oh, I don't know what's come over me. Can't seem to stop this weeping.'

'What did I say? Tell me?' Julia offered a handkerchief, begging her to dry her eyes. 'Something is wrong and I want to know. You aren't having a baby, are you?'

'No I'm not, but I wish I were. He'd have to marry me then! If you must know, miss, it's something else he said tonight. Said that if he went into the army it wouldn't be right nor proper to marry me, then leave me behind. So I asked him wasn't it up to me to decide and he said no, it wasn't.

'He'd talked to Reuben about it, you see, and Reuben said there was no hope of him giving consent to me being wed. Too young, he says I am. So even if Tom wanted to, Cousin Reuben would put the stoppers on it. I tell you, miss, I'm fair upset.'

'We're a pair of miseries, aren't we?' Julia laughed shakily. 'You with your hopes dashed, and me being a grass widow and wanting Andrew so much. We ought to be making a fuss about this war – or maybe we should make a fuss about not being able to join it.'

'But they'd never let women in the army or the navy,' Alice gasped. 'Not even if we cut our hair off and bound up our busts so we looked like men.'

'I know. I'm talking like an idiot. And let's face it, they mightn't bring in conscription, and Andrew might not be on his way to the Front, even though I'm sure he's in France already. And common sense tells me they'll vote in conscription, too, before so very much longer.

'So let's try not to be too sad, Hawthorn? Tom is still with you and Andrew and I did have a week together. But I love him so much. It was awful, having to stand there and watch him leave me. I want him so desperately that I don't know how I'm to bear it, staying here, doing nothing. I want to help but what is there for me to do? I was brought up to marry and have children. I'm useless. I couldn't even light Andrew's kitchen fire.'

'Kitchen ranges can be very tricky, miss, especially when the wind is in the wrong direction. I can light a fire, all right – I was brought up to clean and scrub and sew – but we are women, so what can we do?'

'I don't know. Good works, I suppose. Mind, there are women doctors in France and nuns from nursing orders, but that's about all. I wish I could go there. What are we to do about it, Hawthorn?'

'We could count our blessings, happen?'

'I suppose so. It's pretty cold comfort though.'

Her face crumpled and she closed her eyes and tried not to think of Andrew and their wonderful, warm nearness; tried not to want him and the exquisite joy of giving and taking and loving and being loved.

'Don't be upset,' Alice whispered. 'I know what it's like – well, I would if Tom and me were married. But I do know how it is to want someone so much that it wouldn't matter one bit if I fell for a baby. It's awful having to count to ten.'

'I know. I did a lot of counting before we got married. But it's nearly midnight. We should be getting ourselves to bed, though I won't sleep.'

She would lie there, fretting for Andrew; wanting his arms around her, his mouth on hers; wanting to climb the dizzy heights of their loving.

'Me neither,' Alice shrugged. 'Cook'll have gone to bed, but I could bring you a glass of milk and untie your stays . . .'

'Thanks, but I can manage.' A small, sad smile tilted Julia's lips. 'As a matter of fact, Andrew threw my corsets out. I'm not to wear them again, he said.' She covered her face with her hands, squeezing her eyes tightly against tears. 'Oh, damn this war! And damn conscription and that lot in London who don't care one bit about wives and sweethearts!' She took a deep, shuddering breath, fighting her despair and the longing to weep until she made herself sick. 'I'm so afraid, Hawthorn. It's as if our lovely world is coming to an end – just crumbling into nothing while we stand by, helpless, and watch it. We were too happy, weren't we? We thought our gentle, ordered existence would last for ever, and now we know it isn't going to and that things will never be the same again.'

'I know. I should've known I was too happy,' Alice smiled sadly. 'Coming here to Rowangarth was like another world. I'd been an orphan, see; a nuisance – unwanted. Then Reuben spoke for me and I didn't think I could be happier. But you are right; it's all changing.'

'Then what are we to do? We can't just sit here! There must be *something*.'

'And there will be if we put our minds to it. But we'll think about it tomorrow. Tomorrow's always the best time. And we'll go and have a word with the rooks. They listen to bad things, as well as good. So get yourself off to bed, miss – you've had a long day. And I shall bring you some hot milk.'

'Bless you. You're such a dear person. Say you'll always be my friend, Hawthorn? Promise you will?'

'Always,' Alice said gravely. 'I promise.'

21

1915

Helen smiled, her eyes following the darting, diving bird that circled the stable block: a swallow – the first of summer. She was always glad when the little birds arrived to build beneath the stables eaves: swallows brought luck with them, Jinny Dobb said. The year the swallows *didn't* nest at Rowangarth would not be a good one, she said, for the Suttons. And the same with the rooks – if ever they deserted the rookery, took off to build elsewhere, then ill would befall Rowangarth.

There were many, of course, who thought Jin a little peculiar. She had 'feelings'; read tea-leaves with uncanny accuracy. But then her mother had been the same; a witch, some had gone so far as to say.

'Tommy-rot,' she chided herself, lifting her face to the June sun, closing her eyes for that first-swallow wish, not to be wasted. She was always careful with wishes; never asked for something so highly improbable that it could never be; would never be so foolish as to wish that on the first of July there would be a great, blazing miracle and the war would end. Better to wish that all those she loved would come safely home from the war. She would settle for that: for Robert, in France now; for Andrew, at a base hospital, Julia thought – and please God he was; and for Nathan, so very like Giles.

Poor Giles, Helen frowned, who had learned to live with pointed enquiries about when he would enlist, and the raised eyebrows that one so young was still a civilian.

'No!' She shook such thoughts from her head and surrendered to the peace of the garden and the birdsong that never failed to soothe her. She was glad it was summer. Bad news seemed never quite so bad when the sun shone; it was less awful on a day such as this to think back on what had happened these last six months.

The winter had not been a good one, there was no denying it. Last Christmas, when everyone hoped to be celebrating peace, they'd all been caught unawares. No one had dreamed the war could strike so close to home; at nearby Whitby and Scarborough. London, maybe, or even the south coast towns – but not two northern fishing ports. Their bombardment from the sea had been vicious; had lasted for more than half an hour before the enemy ships disappeared, without challenge, into the winter mists of the North Sea.

And after that, the zeppelins. They came, as everyone had feared, silently out of the night, leaving death and destruction behind them, and ghosting away, sinister in the moonlight. It was as if, Judge Mounteagle said, the Kaiser had issued a warning.

Don't sit there so smugly, you Britishers, with your seas all around you. You are not inviolate. We can reach you any time we want, by sea and air. And they could, she shivered, despite guns and searchlights around all the cities.

There were good things, though, she smiled, remembering the march on Parliament. Fifteen thousand women asking – nay, *demanding* – the right to work in factories, on farms, or anywhere they were needed. It had pleased Anne Lavinia who, immediately after Christmas, joined the First Aid Nursing Yeomanry, swearing hand on heart she was fifty next birthday, and most put out to find even then she was too old to go to France to drive a motor. Now she had settled for teaching young women to drive, declaring that some were so empty-headed they hadn't the brains to be in charge of a wheelbarrow, let alone an ambulance. Most of them she had sent packing, telling them to come back when they were serious about the war and not merely taken with getting into uniform.

Yet how senseless and futile this war had become, Helen sighed, especially on so beautiful a June day, which had started so well with letters from France and India arriving by the same post. One from Cecilia, one from Robert – a good omen indeed.

Yet there had been the poison gas. How bestial. Men poisoning men; sending over waves of the noxious substance so that British troops had collapsed, half blinded, fighting to breathe. The rats had known, though; had been seen leaving the German trenches in their hundreds. They'd smelled it, and been warned. Such clever rats, to save themselves . . .

Then the sinking of the *Lusitania* within sight of land. That great ship had gone down in minutes. *Stay where you are, Cecilia. Even if you have to wait out the war – stay. What is a year – two years even – if at the end of it you are together again?*

Yet why, she frowned – determined to put the world, if not to rights, then into some semblance of order in her mind – were men plotting in Russia? Those who called themselves Bolsheviks, arrested in Odessa for treason. It had worried her greatly, she remembered, until Anne Lavinia snorted, 'Nonsense! Don't worry your head about Russia. Nothing like that could happen here, thank God.' Or it wouldn't, she'd sniffed, once they had the sense to give women the vote. But even so, Helen pondered, there was something in the wind, or why had Gallipoli happened? It should have been a short, sharp bombardment from naval guns, quickly over and placing the Dardanelles under British control; yet it had turned into a tragic failure. Each day now, more and more lives were lost: she dreaded opening the newspaper.

The action at Gallipoli was intended to open up a shorter seaway to Russia, the Judge supposed – but why to Russia? And were those men in Odessa really so important? Weren't we taking them a little too seriously? Were they our problem?

Yet in spite of it all, today the world had not gone quite to the brink of madness. Today, the swallows had returned bringing wishes with them, so that she *knew* everything would be all right. One day, the war would end and those she loved would come safely home and –

'Mother! You must come – *at once*!' Julia called, running across the grass. 'Will Stubbs is beside himself and wants me to find Giles.'

'Giles is at York – had you forgotten? But why is William upset?'

'You may well ask! Just come, will you, and tell those men to be off!' Impatiently she took her mother's hand. 'Cheeky as you please and without so much as a by-your-leave! Two horses they want, and won't take no for an answer. Tell them they can't do it!'

They found Will Stubbs protesting loudly; telling the men to be on their way before he called the constable.

'What is going on?' Helen demanded. 'Why the commotion, William?' Three men in khaki spun round to face her. Two wore the stripes of a sergeant, the third was an officer. 'My daughter says you intend taking two of my horses. Perhaps you will tell me on whose authority?'

'Ma'am. I am veterinary officer to the Third Battalion, Royal Artillery, quartered at Creesby. This,' he stressed, offering a document to her, 'is my authority. The army needs horses urgently and I am empowered to take them. You'll be paid a fair price.'

'Even when I have no wish to sell?'

'Even so. Your coachman tells me you have four horses.'

'That is so.' Helen lifted her chin. 'Two geldings, a mare in foal, and a pony – all of which we need.'

'Then I am sorry, ma'am. I require the geldings. A rider

388

will come tomorrow to take them away. I'll be obliged if you will make sure they have first been fed and watered. I must remind you we are at war and – '

'Oh, be *quiet*!' Julia's anger seethed over. 'We know all about the war without reminders from you! My husband is at the Front, and my brother. What more do you want?'

'Tomorrow morning, ma'am. Please have the animals ready,' said the young man quietly. 'You will be given a receipt for them and will hear from the Paymaster's office in due course.'

Helen opened her mouth to protest, then closed it, traplike. 'Come, Julia,' was all she said, before turning abruptly and walking away.

'They can't do this!' Julia raged when they were out of earshot. 'How are we to manage?'

'As best we can, I fear. Buy more carriage horses if we can get them,' Helen said flatly, 'and use the pony and the governess cart, meantime.'

'*If* we can get horses! I'd heard those men were around. They're even taking farm horses. It's monstrous. You must complain, Mother!'

'Not I. They are within their rights. They hide behind the Defence of the Realm Act and do exactly as they please. And if the surrender of two horses will shorten this war by even one day, then they are welcome to them!' Helen swept up the steps and into the house. 'And tomorrow, Julia – when the men come again – leave it to Giles and William. Don't interfere.'

'Very well, but I don't know how you can accept it all so calmly. What next will they take from us? The house?'

'If they want to, they can even do that, though I hope they will not.'

Take Rowangarth? Take her lovely old house, John's house? That would be most cruel of all. Please – they would not take her home, would they?

389

'Are you all right?' Julia guided her mother to a chair, settling a cushion at her head. 'Shall I ring for tea?'

'Thank you. I would like that. And don't worry – I'm all right . . .'

But, oh, sometimes – just sometimes – she was so very afraid.

Andrew read the letter through twice, folded it carefully, then placed it in his pocket.

Julia was well, he smiled fondly, though her letters were alternately sad or glad, according to her mood. She missed him, wanted him, as he missed and wanted her.

Was there any news yet about leave? And if so, when would he get it? Where, when he did, she demanded, would they spend it? Longings poured out on paper; yearnings between every line. His Julia was exquisite. She walked the wards beside him, stood at his side, and brought sanity to a world gone mad. She was his reason for staying alive; for breathing out and breathing in, even.

Today he had needed her letter. Today he had looked upon savagely broken bodies; seen more young lives viciously ended. Many had died without protest, like the gentle snuffing out of a candle flame; others had fought death, crying out their right to live.

It was obscene they should die in such filth; in lice-infested uniforms caked with stinking mud. Many had no chance. There were not enough doctors or nurses; though to expect a woman to brave the dangers of the clearing-stations so near the front line couldn't even be thought about. There, medical orderlies and stretcher-bearers patched up the wounded before sending them to the hospital behind the lines or despatching them to Blighty.

A hospital in Blighty. Home, though wounded, to a clean bed in a clean ward and soft-voiced nurses to tell them it was all right; that they were out of the fighting for as long as it took their wounds to heal. Well worth, some said, all the pain and horror they had endured.

Yesterday, north of Hooge, a battle had raged. Infantrymen had gone over the top of the trenches to crawl stealthily – the better or the worse for a mug of rum – through barbed-wire entanglements and into No Man's Land, to surprise the enemy in the trenches opposite; to throw in grenades, spatter the communication walks with gunfire, take prisoners. If they were lucky, that was. If the enemy had not seen their coming: though God help them if they had.

That was why, in the small hours of a silent morning, the stretcher-bearers crawled the cold wastes of No Man's Land to bring back wounded under cover of darkness. Brave men all, taking with them a priest to comfort the dying, give absolution to the dead.

And afterwards, the counting of discs. He disliked even touching them. Corpse tickets, the men derisively called them; the red identity disc taken from the body of a soldier so his death might be recorded officially; the green disc that was buried with him.

When morning came, he held eighteen lives in his right hand; eighteen red discs to slip into his pocket and give to the adjutant when he returned to the field hospital. Eighteen telegrams; eighteen grieving homes. How long could he stand it; how long before he stepped over the thin line that divided compassion and cynicism and learned to accept what he could not change?

He closed his eyes, hearing Julia's voice, feeling the small breath of her whispering close to his ear. He wanted her now; needed the softness and comfort of her. How could he have come here; how could he not have come here? And why did the six months of their parting seem like six lifetimes, six glimpses into eternity?

'Julia.' Her name was like a blessing. He must close

391

his mind to this day. Soon he would be back at the field hospital, would open the door of the small room that was his own; where Julia's photograph stood beside his bed and there was no stench of death. For two days he would be on stand-down: time to sleep, to eat, to clean himself before going back to the forward dressing-station. That was the pattern of his life now. Two days on duty without sleep or food; two days away from it.

Now he knew what hell was made of.

That morning, the army had taken the horses and doubtless it was the last anyone at Rowangarth would see of them. Horses were essential to the war – more so than motors. They heaved loads, pulled guns, munitions carts, even ambulances. Before very much longer, the Government would realize the need to build more and more motors but, until that happened, no horse hereabouts was safe from the covetous eye of the veterinary officer. It all went to show, William said, that horses were of far more use. Stinking, spewing motors needed fuel poured into them; a horse, at a pinch, could find its food at roadsides and in hedgerows. Horses didn't break down; were living creatures, warm and faithful to man, Will declared not three hours ago as the army rider had cantered off with never so much as a word of remorse. All it had taken was a signature on a receipt, Alice told Tom as they stood now in the thickening of Brattocks Wood, arms entwined.

She seemed to exist, now, for their next meeting. A lot of what was of consequence in her life seemed to have happened in Brattocks, this last year. She wondered if it was here that one day Tom would tell her the time was right for him to go.

'Will Stubbs isn't best pleased,' Alice murmured. 'Says what's the use of a coachman without horses? There'll be nothing to keep him here once the mare has foaled.

Be gone to the army, he reckons, before the back end. He'll have to, if he wants to get with horses. Wouldn't be any use him going for a marksman; couldn't hit a pig in a passage, not Will . . .'

'To every man his own,' Tom said comfortably. 'I could take a snipe on the wing, but I'd not be a lot of use with a carriage and pair. 'Sides, I'd look right daft in one of those top hats.'

'Be serious, Tom.' He always made light of it; never gave a yes or a no to anything she mentioned about the army. 'Don't know what's got into you these days.'

'That's because you think I've forgotten your birthday!'

'Tom, love . . .' He'd remembered. She smiled, lifting her lips to his. Nineteen in two days' time, yet still two years to go before they could wed – if Reuben persisted with his stubbornness and Tom insisted, still, that it wasn't right to marry, then to go to war. 'Tell me how we're going to wait – if you still want to marry me, that is?'

'You know I want to,' he said fiercely, his arms tightening around her. 'But we have no house, even if Reuben was to say yes tomorrow.'

'We'd find somewhere . . .'

'Then have me leave you – is that it? You fancy being a widow, maybe with a bairn? Where'd you go then? Who'd take you in but the workhouse?'

'So you're still set on going?' He didn't want her, that was the truth of it. 'You'll go for a soldier, and forget me?'

'Aye. Likely I will. It's got to be faced, sooner or later. The war could go on for years yet. But as for forgetting you, Alice . . .'

'You will! An' all because of this war!' She pushed away from him. Everything had been all right till war came. 'What's happening to us, Tom?'

'Nothing's happening, you silly lass,' he said softly, eyes tender. 'And just to prove it, you shall have your birthday present now. Close your eyes and hold out your hand.'

It was a small, square box, satin-covered. She looked at it, bewildered, then murmured, 'Must I wait, or can I look at it now?'

'Open it, bonny lass – see if you like what's inside.'

It was a ring; a flowerlike cluster of tiny pearls, glowing dully against a velvet bed. She looked at it for a long time, unbelieving, then whispered, 'For me? Does it mean we're engaged, official . . .?' Her cheeks burned, her eyes filled with lovely tears.

'Engaged, official,' he said, tilting her chin. 'Is my buttercup girl happy? Will it fit, do you think?'

'You'd best try. Left hand, is it?'

'Left hand. We'd best do it proper.'

He slipped the little circlet on to her third finger and she gasped with delight that it fitted so perfectly, holding up her hand, loving him so much it was impossible to describe.

'There now, Alice Hawthorn; that ring says I *won't* forget you. Not ever.'

'Can I tell them, Tom – say you're my fiancé?'

'Aye. Tell them. And when they ask when we'll be wed, tell them as soon as maybe; just as soon as this war will allow – that Tom Dwerryhouse wishes it could be tomorrow. I'd have liked it to be diamonds, Alice: maybe one day, perhaps . . .'

'Don't you dare. Buttercup girls don't wear diamonds.'

'Nor yearn for orchids, Alice?'

'Never orchids.' She smiled tremulously into his eyes, so suddenly happy it was like a burst of sunlight inside her. 'Kiss me, Tom – please?'

The meeting of their lips was warm and gentle; a wondering kiss; a kiss of commitment.

'I love you,' he said, his voice rough with wanting. 'I love you so much it's near unbearable . . .'

'I know.' Her voice was little more than a whisper as she sank down on the soft summer grass, holding up a hand to him, begging him silently with her eyes.

'You're sure?' he said, dropping to his knees beside her.

'Very sure, only I don't know how. Show me, Tom?'

'You know I'll be careful.'

'Yes, my darling; I know . . .'

Alice knew from the urgency of the footsteps, the slamming of heels along the passage, that Julia would any moment fling open the sewing-room door.

'Hawthorn!' Her cheeks were bright pink, her eyes shone. 'I've told Mother and now I must tell you! It's all so wonderful! No leave, he said. Don't ever begin to hope – yet listen to this!' She unfolded the letter, reading breathlessly.

> I think perhaps I might tell you, even though nothing is certain, that somewhere before the end of the year there may be good news. Married men can now be considered for ten days' leave. Names go to Brigade HQ – if taken alphabetically, I'm just about half-way.
>
> Please, my love, don't build your hopes too high – nothing in this war is certain – but even I am beginning to hope we might spend our first anniversary together . . .

'Hawthorn! Just imagine! To see him, touch him . . .' Her voice whispered into a sob. 'Dare I hope? He wouldn't say it if there wasn't a chance, would he?'

'He wouldn't, miss. The doctor's a cautious one. It's my belief there's something in the wind or he'd never have written that. And I'm right pleased for you. Funny, isn't it, but luck breeds luck, they say.' Smiling, Alice held up her left hand. 'Go on, Miss Julia – have a wish on it. Everyone else has.' Carefully she pulled off the ring, dropping it in the outstretched palm. 'Slip it on your finger, then close your eyes and wish.'

'Engaged! You never breathed a word!' Impulsively, she kissed Alice's cheek. 'When will you be married? Has Reuben said yes at last? Oh, my word! Tom hasn't enlisted, has he?'

'I didn't say anything because I didn't know. Took the ring out of his pocket all of a sudden. And no, he hasn't volunteered, thank God, yet he will, I know it. There won't be a wedding, though,' she sighed. 'I'm only nineteen, or will be – '

'On Sunday,' Julia finished. 'I haven't forgotten. But tell me about the ring?'

'We-e-e-ll, I was going on at Tom, I suppose, worrying about him going to the war – so I think he sprang it on me before he'd intended.'

'Well, you're half-way there now. Does it feel strange, wearing a ring? I was very conscious of mine. I went left-handed, sort of, till I got used to it . . .'

'Don't think I'll ever get used to it, miss,' Alice smiled shyly. 'I'm sort of – *floating* . . .'

'I know the feeling. Scattering rose petals from a lovely pink cloud. Aren't we lucky? Must fly, though. Got to write to Andrew at once! I'll tell him about you and Dwerryhouse and I'm so happy for you, I truly am. I'll wish and wish you'll soon be married, because being married – you know what I mean – is the most wonderful, *wonderful* thing . . .'

'Yes,' Alice whispered as the door banged and footsteps danced down the stairs. 'I know exactly what you mean, miss.'

She had hardly slept last night for thinking about it; had stared at herself in the mirror, wondering if it showed, if in some way she had changed because of it. But Alice in the mirror had stared back, unchanged except for eyes that held a secret.

Last night had been so good. A gentle giving and taking, too soon over; as if after that first careless soaring they had realized the enormity of it. She had wanted to stay in his arms; to cling to him to prolong the moment, but he had left her, abruptly.

Yet it had been so wonderful, their first fleeting loving. It bound him to her and her to him. Neither of them spoke on the walk home, thighs touching, hands too tightly clasped as though now they must always be close. Bemused, almost, they walked to the edge of the wood.

'Sweetheart . . .' As if, suddenly, she were fragile china, he helped her over the stile. 'What came over us?'

'Nothing that wasn't right and proper. Nothing save love, Tom . . .'

'And was it . . .?'

'It was good, if that's what you're asking, and it'll get better with every time.'

'No!' She felt the tightening of his hand on hers. 'There won't be another time. Tonight we were lucky and I managed – well, I left you before any harm was done. But no more till we're married, Alice. Another time I could lose control and you'd fall for a baby.'

'And would that be so bad?' She had wanted him, then, to take her again, but he'd touched her cheek gently and told her to be away.

'I'll stay here – watch you to the door. And Alice, love . . .' He kissed her again. 'I do love you.'

He'd said it sadly, she thought; said it sort of yearning, as if he really meant it wouldn't happen again – or as if he regretted, already, what had been between them.

But there *would* be another time, she argued fiercely, and if making a child together was a means to an end, then so be it. It would be a love child to bind them ever closer. And if that happened, she thought, laying her lips to the cluster of pearls on her finger, then Reuben would *have* to say yes!

22

Cook was not best pleased. Neither wedded nor bedded, much less a mother, she'd been near overcome to learn that the three nephews she looked upon as sons and to whom would go her worldly goods when her time ran out, had been sent to the Front. All in the same regiment, too, which was downright foolish of the army when she brought to mind what had happened to Jinny Dobb's nephews. Killed, both of them, by the same shellburst, and Jin still a mite peculiar because of it.

'Pah!' She vented her dismay on the bread dough she was kneading: lifting, punching it, slapping, banging it, because that wasn't all by any manner of means. She'd been upset by what she had read in the paper this morning: that nice young Mr Churchill banished to be Chancellor of the Duchy of Lancaster; no sort of a position for a man who'd been First Lord of the Admiralty.

But someone had to be blamed for Gallipoli, she sighed, for they'd never get over the shame of it. She closed her eyes tightly because it hurt to think of the young men who'd come all the way from Australia and New Zealand to die for a far-away King: she'd wager a week's wages that if their womenfolk had known they were going to breathe their last on the soil of a heathen country like Turkey, they'd never have let them come!

'That's going to be a grand baking of bread, Mrs Shaw, the way you're knocking it about,' Tilda observed.

'Is it now?' Cook puffed. 'And less of your sarcasm, miss, or I'll knock you about an' all!'

Tilda smiled, not the least put out. Nothing could upset her now she was in love, deeply, for all time in love; and with the most handsome, eligible bachelor in the world. He was brave, an' all, in France with the Grenadier Guards and even though she knew he wouldn't be allowed within miles of the fighting, to her he was a hero.

She smiled dreamily at the mantelshelf from which His Royal Highness, David, Prince of Wales smiled down from a silver-plated frame, and reaffirmed her devotion with a sensual pouting of her lips.

'And another thing,' Cook flung to no one in particular, 'what's to be done about the dinner party – food being what it is?'

'You'll manage,' Mary soothed. 'You always do. We're well into the shooting season, so the meat shortage won't bother us. It's only to be a small party; it'll run to a partridge apiece – and there's no one like you when it comes to cooking game-birds.'

'We-e-ll . . .' Only ten at table; family and close friends to mark Miss Julia's first anniversary; the date not certain, mind, on account of them not knowing exactly when the doctor would be arriving – if Miss Julia and the doctor decided to spend his leave at Rowangarth, that was.

Just a main course and pudding, her ladyship had said it was to be, on account of them having to follow the King's example and eat frugally. Eat a third less, the Government was asking everyone: two potatoes instead of three, and smaller helpings of meat. Her ladyship was being frugal, all right. Only bacon and eggs, now, at breakfast; sometimes not even bacon – and less toast in the rack, for bread could no longer be wasted. Cook thought sadly about her precious, squirrelled-away sugar. Half a hundredweight she'd laid in just before it all started, yet most of it was gone now. Food was getting more and more expensive, which wasn't right nor decent when the wife of a soldier was hard put to manage on what the army paid her man.

Mind, the grocer in Holdenby was fair. Rowangarth

still gave him their weekly order and hadn't changed to the big shop in Creesby like some had done in the hope of getting a bit more of things in short supply.

'Maister says he's sorry,' said the lad who delivered their order only that morning. 'He's sent what he could of what you asked for – 'cept the sugar. Getting real short of sugar, and no chance of getting any more till next month.'

Two pounds! Two pounds of sugar for a household of nine, and what about the margarine? Who'd have thought to see margarine in Rowangarth's groceries! But use it she must, because butter was so scarce it would be going the way of sugar before long; ceasing to exist, almost.

Sighing, she returned her thoughts to the cooking of the partridge. She couldn't roast them in butter, nothing was more certain. Folk kept what little they could get to be eaten on Sundays.

'Red wine,' she murmured. Yet however the dratted birds turned out, they'd be a lot more palatable than the food the poor lads at the Front were getting. Iron rations, when they were in the trenches, she'd heard. Cold tinned stew and biscuits hard enough to crack your teeth, though they ate better by all accounts when they went behind the lines for a break from being shot at.

The trenches would be getting muddy, now that winter was almost here, and there would be no warm beds in the dugouts. Tommies slept on their feet, though if they had any sense they didn't sleep at all, folk said.

She looked round her clean, well-ordered kitchen and counted her blessings. Then she shaped the bread dough into tins for its first rising, all the time trying to think up a pudding that was careful on sugar. It was her duty, after all, to do her best and not grumble, for the sake of the lads at the Front and particularly for her nephews now in mortal danger. And for Sir Robert, too, and Doctor Andrew and the Reverend Nathan. She almost added

400

Mr Elliot, then decided against it on account of what happened in Brattocks for which she would never forgive him and him not being at the Front, neither. Can-lad to some high-ranking army man at the War Office, so talk had it, and like as not spending every night at his mam's new house in Chelsea in a comfortable bed.

'Miss Julia had a letter this morning. You should have seen her face,' Bess announced, back from checking the upstairs fires. 'From the doctor, I think it was.'

Bess had taken great care over the building-up of the breakfast-room fire: raking it, laying on just enough coal, then painstakingly brushing the hearth; but she still heard nothing worth carrying below stairs.

'She's hoping, now that the doctor's been given official leave, that he'll get it for their anniversary,' Alice said, wishing she and Tom were married and living in Keeper's Cottage as if the war had never been. 'She asked me,' she confided, 'to get her blue out and give it a sponge and press.'

'The one she was wed in,' Bess smiled.

'Yes – it was the one she was wearing when he proposed,' Alice added for good measure, not wanting them to think her uppity because she'd once gone to London with Miss Julia. 'When they used to meet in secret in Hyde Park – with me walking behind, of course,' she added.

'Wonder where they'll spend their honeymoon?' Tilda slid her eyes to the mantel. 'Because it'll be like another honeymoon, won't it, them being apart for so long.'

'In London, would you think, or here at Rowangarth?' Mary ventured.

'I think she'll go to London to meet him,' Alice nodded, 'so they'll have to spend one night there at least – probably at the doctor's place.' Miss Sutton's house was small; no room for them at Montpelier Mews. 'Reckon they'll come home to Rowangarth once the doctor's seen to it that everything's all right at Little Britain. Ooh, but it's exciting for Miss Julia, isn't it?'

'Her'll be dreaming about it all the time,' Tilda sighed.

'Well, I hope that nothing goes wrong. Those high-ups out there can do peculiar things at times,' Mary warned primly.

'Ha! Those high-up officers don't know the first thing about it,' Cook grunted, 'on account of them all being in London, sending their orders willy-nilly to them that's doing the fighting.'

'Not *all* of them,' Tilda sniffed. Oh my word, no. Wasn't her lovely David there – it was Matilda-dear and David, in her imaginings – and didn't he know all about it? Probably on the waiting-list for leave himself, and right at the bottom on account of him having a German name no one could pronounce.

'Well, *all* of you are on war work one way or another, so you'd best be about your business,' Cook pronounced. 'The likes of us also serve, don't forget.' *They also serve.* She liked the phrase, even if she could never quite get it right; because not everybody could march off to war, thanks be. 'Now then, young Alice, are you sewing or working this morning?'

'Miss Clitherow says I'm to help down here, if I'm needed. There's nothing in the sewing-room that won't wait.'

Which made her very glad, because if Tom should call at the kitchen door with the hare Cook had asked for she would see him and that, to her love-starved heart, meant a whole lot more than the peace and quiet of the sewing-room.

Oh, Lordy, she sighed inside her, but how she wished they could be wed.

There were two letters of importance next morning, and both from the Western Front. Julia's was brief. Andrew

402

was counting the days to his leave, which could well be at exactly the right time for their anniversary; she was to take good care of herself and he loved her. But more important even than that was the date at the top of the sheet. *Saturday 13 November 1915*. The letter had taken only four days to get to her, which meant that as little as four days ago he was alive and well and loving her and today he was alive and well and loving her! He *must* be! And when this war was over, she would never let him out of her sight again. *When* it was over; when the killing had stopped and no one need live in dread of the knock on the door and the small envelope the telegraph boy held in his hand.

'He's well; he loves me,' she smiled through her tears. 'What news from Robert?'

'Sssh!' Helen held up a finger for silence, her eyes not leaving the page, her cheeks flushed.

'Mother – what is it? Robert isn't getting leave, too?'

'Listen to this, both of you – just *listen*.' Briefly dabbing her eyes, taking a deep, shuddering breath, she gasped, 'Oh, no, I can't! My eyes – so silly of me. I keep wanting to weep. You read it, Julia; read it out aloud then I'll know I'm not dreaming.' She thrust the letter into her daughter's hands. 'Go on! Hurry! The bit that starts *Do you remember . . .*'

'Do you remember the night of Julia's wedding – oh, *yes*, Mother, I do *so* remember it . . .'

'Go *on*!'

' . . . *of Julia's wedding when you and I wished Cecilia a happy birthday, then spoke of where you hoped the army would send me? I can't actually write it in a letter for reasons of security, but your totally impossible wish is about to come true! I simply don't believe it! Dearest Mother, you are a witch . . .* A witch?' Julia frowned. 'How come?'

'It was after the wedding and neither Robert nor I could sleep. So we went downstairs for a drink, to wish

403

you both luck,' Helen beamed. 'And I – well, I said I hoped that he and Cecilia could be as happy and that I'd wish and pray that the army would post him to India instead of France: he was waiting his call-up at that time, if you remember.

'And my impossible wish is about to come true, he says. He can only be referring to India. They're probably sending him to the Afghan border, I shouldn't wonder. The army does have a garrison there. But if it's true - don't you see? They'll be able to be married!'

'I don't believe it!' Julia cried. 'How lucky can a family get? First Andrew's leave, and now this!'

'Someone must have the luck,' Giles said softly. 'Why shouldn't Rowangarth have its share? But this is what you wanted, isn't it, Mother – all your children married? So are you going to witch a wife on me too?'

'I shall if you don't hurry and find one for yourself.' She held her hands to her burning cheeks. 'And they say miracles don't happen!'

'Might I look?' Giles held out his hand for the letter, carrying it to the window, squinting at the postmark. 'This was posted a week ago. For all we know Robert could be on his way home now.'

'But will he get leave?' Helen murmured. 'They might tell the battalion to pack up and send them lock, stock and barrel to India on the next ship available.'

She wouldn't mind were it to happen that way. She wanted to see him, for however short a time, but the fact that he was being sent away from the fighting in France and back to the woman he loved was all she could ask.

'I rather think he'll be home,' Giles smiled. 'They'll need special kit – shorts, and all that sort of thing. It's hot in India, remember.'

'You could be right, Giles. He might come to Aldershot.'

'Or even York,' Giles teased. 'That's where he reported

when he enlisted. Would York suit you? And had you thought that he just *might* arrive on the same day as Andrew?'

'Don't!' Helen closed her eyes and held up a hand. 'It's all too much!' She mustn't be greedy: Robert was being posted to India and the woman he'd thought never to see again and – 'Oh, my goodness! I must write and let Cecilia know – carefully, of course – just hint, sort of, so she can share the excitement . . .'

'Mother! Robert will have written to her. By the time your letter reaches her, he might already be there.'

'I know, Julia. I'm being foolish, aren't I? All this is just a little too much to take in. I think I'll wrap up warm and take a turn round the garden . . .'

'I'll come with you.' Giles rose to his feet.

'No,' Julia mouthed, reaching for his arm. 'Idiot!' she grinned when the door had closed and they were alone. 'Oh, it's easy to see why you aren't married. You've got so much to learn about women.'

'*Learn?*'

'Yes, you soft old thing. She's going out for a little cry. Leave her be . . .'

'Cry? But I haven't seen her so happy for a long time.'

'Of course. That's why she needs to weep – can't you understand?'

'No. No, I can't at all . . .'

'Oh, Giles Sutton – how I pity the girl you'll marry! And,' she whispered, cupping his face in her hands, 'how very lucky she'll be . . .'

'I don't know what's going on upstairs,' remarked Alice to Tom as they walked carefully in the darkness to the place they called their courting corner, 'but this afternoon, when we were having our sewing circle – for comforts for the Front, I mean – you could fairly feel the excitement.'

'That'll be Miss Julia, I suppose.' Tom unbuttoned his overcoat, wrapping Alice into it as she snuggled against him. 'With the doctor coming on leave, I reckon.'

'No. It was her ladyship an' all. All sort of happy, she was, and smiling and – oh, I just couldn't put a finger on it. But milady's got a secret, if you ask me.'

'She's got a gentleman?' Tom frowned.

'No, she has *not*, and don't you go putting it around that she has. But there's something in the wind, mark my words if there isn't. Could hardly thread her needle, her hands were shaking so much. "Be a dear," she said to Bess, "and do it for me. My eyes are getting old." *Old?* Not her!'

'Then what?' He kissed the tip of her nose; such a pretty nose. Tip-tilted and cheeky, sort of. A kissable nose.

'Couldn't say. But what I do know is that Bess is likely giving notice.'

'An' why is the silly lass doing that? Her and Davie are courting strong, if what I hear is to be believed.'

'Aye, but Davie is out of his time, now, and Mr Catchpole says he's welcome to stay in the bothy, but if he wants promotion he'll have to look elsewhere. Rowangarth don't want no more time-served gardeners – leastways not till things get back to normal. So Davie said, "Right. I'll go for a soldier afore they conscript me." And he means it. Told Bess, and now she's vowing that if he goes she's going, too.'

'I can understand it. Sooner or later they'll bring in conscription and that'll be that. No choosing where we'll go.'

'*We?*' A shiver that was nothing to do with the November cold sliced through Alice.

'We. Davie, Will Stubbs – and me. Will's going an' all. Says he'll see to it they don't put him in the infantry. Wants to be with horses when he goes. And me – '

'You want to be a marksman because you're a good shot,' Alice whispered, stiff-lipped. 'So the three of you'll volunteer.' Alice pulled away from the circle of his arms. 'You've been talking – all of you. You're all of you going before they make conscription into law . . .'

'No, lovey. Not *going*. Just talking it over between us.'

'I see.' There was a terrible shaking inside her; a feeling that if she let herself, she could be sick. 'You're like Bess, aren't you? Can't wait to be off . . .'

'No, Alice. We've been talking, I'll admit it. Can't blame us for that – not for talking; a bloke has to think things out. But we aren't going to rush off and grab the King's shilling if that's what you're bothered about. I'll tell you, I promise I will, before I make up my mind about anything. I give you my word, bonny lass. So give us a kiss and tell us what Bess aims to do. Going to set the world alight, is she?'

'Bess only said *if*. If Davie goes. They're building a munitions factory at Leeds. It'll be making shells – the army's terrible short of shells, it seems. And it's respectable now for women to work in factories – married women, an' all. There's good money in munitions; better than in service.'

'Maybe so. But I hope you won't do anything like that if I should decide the time is right for me to go, Alice.'

'Are you asking, Tom?'

'I'd like to think,' he said, choosing his words carefully, 'that if I went for a soldier I could think of you here, with her ladyship, and Reuben on hand to look after you. I wouldn't want you to go into a munitions factory, lass. Those shells can blow up. There's been some nasty accidents, you know that as well as I do: women blinded, or their hands blown off – or worse.

'And they go yellow, those women who make shells – can't blame folk for calling them canaries. Something in

407

the powder, it is. No amount of money is worth going *yellow* for.'

'Happen not. But they'd give Bess a badge to wear. She'd be in a starred occupation. She says she'd rather have a star to wear than be sent white feathers.'

'Folk don't send white feathers to women, daftie.'

'No, but there'll be some busybody sending 'em soon to Mr Giles.'

'And to me too, Alice.'

'No, Tom. *No!* You aren't a conchie. You'll go when the time is right – you've always said so. But Mr Giles says he won't go; not to kill, any road. And he don't care, he told me, if folk do call him a conchie. And it's a free country, I suppose . . .'

'No love, it *isn't*. Not any more,' Tom murmured, pulling her closer. 'Soon there'll be a choice; fight or go to prison, because that's what'll happen to objectors before so very much longer.'

'Poor Mr Giles,' Alice whispered. 'He's a good man, Tom.'

'He is. You know it and I know it – but tell that to the recruiting sergeant next time he's around, and see what *he* says. But we're wasting good courting time. Here we are, putting the world to rights, and not a kiss between us. Tell me you love me,' he demanded.

'I love you, Tom Dwerryhouse, and I want us to be wed. I want you and me to be married so much that I don't care if I've fallen for a baby . . .'

'You haven't – and Alice, there's got to be no more of *that* between us. We've got to wait. I don't want to walk down the aisle with a shotgun at my back. I want us married decent.'

'Well, I just want us to be married,' she murmured mutinously, 'and I'm giving you fair warning, Tom. I don't care how I get you!'

'We'll be wed when there's a house for us to live in,'

he muttered, stubborn to the end, 'and I don't have a war hanging over me. I'll not marry you, then leave you for a widow.'

'The doctor wed Miss Julia. Are you saying he shouldn't have?'

'I'm saying it's his business – his and hers. And anyway, they're both of them better heeled than you or me. You haven't any kin of your own to go to if you were left with a bairn, Alice. Miss Julia has her family around her – aye, and money of her own too.'

'And she's counting the days to them being together again,' Alice whispered, lips close. 'She's so happy, you wouldn't believe it.'

'And you've got me here every day, so why aren't you happy too, Alice Hawthorn?'

'I am happy, only I want us to be wed, Tom; I want to belong.'

'And I say we'll be wed when the time is right and now isn't the time! So let's not fratch and fight over it. I love you. I've bought you a ring for all to see my intentions, but we won't be wed – happen because I love you too much.'

'All right,' she murmured. 'I'm only saying I love you and want you – you can't blame me for that, can you?' She inched closer, whispering her lips across his cheek, teasing him with soft little kisses until she felt the hardening of his body against hers.

'Kiss me,' she murmured, huskily. 'Kiss me and touch me and hold me . . .'

She lifted his hand to the rounding of her breast, searching with her mouth for his.

Eve had done it with an apple, the Bible said. It had been the same between men and women since ever the world began, so where was the harm in it? She closed her eyes, knowing it was wrong even to think such things. And hadn't Adam and Eve lost Eden because of it?

'Sorry, sweetheart,' she whispered. 'Forgive me?'

23

Julia unfastened the button at her waist, letting her petticoat slide to her feet. Since Andrew demanded she should throw away her corsets, life had become unbelievably comfortable. Now her breasts were where nature intended them to be, and not pushed in and up by harsh, uncomfortable bones.

Unfastening her supporters, she gazed dispassionately at her body in the mirror. For the young and daring, tight bust bodices were out of fashion. Now 'supporters' were all the rage – a brassière, the French called the new undergarment; but by whatever name, it gave such freedom she wondered why something so clever and chic hadn't been thought of long ago.

The light from the peach-shaded lamps touched her naked image. Strange, she thought, that the exchanging of wedding vows should make the hitherto unacceptable into something completely respectable, and the unthinkable into an act of wifely duty, with the generous blessing and complete approval of the Church and society. In short, wasn't sleeping with Andrew an utter delight?

And soon, now, she would hear from him. By letter, would it be, saying he was on his way, or a telegram asking her to meet him at the lodgings in Little Britain? Or would it be a telephone call? Would the phone ring and would she pick it up to hear, 'Darling, I'm at Holdenby . . .'

Yet if she could choose, it would be to meet him in London at the station: to savour the excitement, the anticipation; to watch his train arriving, wonder which compartment door would open and . . .

She laughed with delight as she pulled her nightgown

over her head – her sensible, winter-warm, sleeping-alone nightgown – then placed the guard over the fire. She hurried into bed, impatient to close her eyes and be near to him, for this was a time for counting days and dreaming dreams; to wonder where they would meet, what they would say.

Would it be with a chaste kiss of greeting; a sharing of glances that said, *I want you?* Would she run the length of the platform to him, throwing herself into his arms? People kissed in public now. Lovers apart for a whole year cared not a jot for convention. Even skirts were shorter. Now the human race had discovered ankles, she giggled, hugging the hot bottle to her.

Skirts. When she met Andrew, should she wear the hobble skirt – that *daft* skirt, he'd called it. If she did, though, Hawthorn would have to take it up at least three inches, for it wasn't just ankles that were in fashion. In Leeds, a week ago, Miss Clitherow had seen a lady police constable wearing a skirt no more than four inches below her knee: showing her calves, would you believe?

She switched off her bedside light, then burrowed into the feathers of the mattress to dream again of loving and being loved; of sleeping in her husband's arms and the joy of awakening to find him beside her still.

'I love you, Andrew MacMalcolm.' She ached all over, just wanting him; longed for his caress and the wonder of their coupling. She hoped that this time they might make a child, but at this moment of her terrible need of him, she would settle just for being loved.

God. She closed her eyes. *Thank you for Andrew. Keep him safe for me? Don't let anything awful happen to him.*

Yet awful things did happen, every minute of every day and night. It wasn't fair, really, to ask God to choose, because German women were praying now, exactly as she was and for much the same thing.

411

Best she should send her love to her man instead, send it in great, warm waves; a love so strong that nothing could harm him because of it.

'I want you so much, my darling,' she murmured, as sleep took her.

She awoke to a crisp, cold morning and the first frost of the year. It sparkled the lawn below her window and touched the bare branches of the trees in Brattocks Wood. Mornings such as this gave way to wintry sunshine, she smiled, flicking over the date on her writing-desk calendar. One day nearer.

She took her sponge-bag and hurried to the bathroom, eager to start the day. Perhaps today she would know when he would come and how it would be. Soon they would be together again. She was so happy. Not *too* happy; she dare not be that. Too-happy people made the gods jealous. And today she *must* remember to write to Sparrow; ask her to light fires at the lodging, make sure the bed was well aired. *Why* couldn't she get beds out of her mind!

She slid home the bolt then turned on the taps. Quickly now. She must not be in the bath when the telephone rang! Dear, sweet heaven, how happy she was. Crazily, stupidly happy – and be damned to jealous gods!

Alice could not get Giles Sutton out of her mind. Since it happened she had been upset – aye, and angry, too. This morning it had been – and all because of that Morgan sidling down to the kitchen; gazing at Cook with big, begging eyes, and generally being a nuisance underfoot.

'Take that animal back to where it belongs,' Mrs Shaw ordered. 'Animals in kitchens isn't sanitary!' How Alice wished she'd told Tilda to take him away instead.

'In you go, you bad dog. Sit on your blanket and wait.'

She had found the library door open, the room empty,

and had crossed to the hearth to make sure there was water in the drinking bowl. That was when she saw it: no one could miss it, no one was intended to miss it. A garish poster, spread out on the desk, exactly like the one she had seen in Creesby.

THERE ARE THREE TYPES OF MEN.
THOSE WHO HEAR THE CALL, AND OBEY
THOSE WHO DELAY
AND THE OTHERS . . .
TO WHICH DO YOU BELONG?

She could still remember her shudder of revulsion; how she had wanted to tear down that poster because it was aimed at Tom and Davie and Will. Now someone had sent one to Mr Giles!

'Hawthorn!' He was standing in the doorway. 'What are you doing?'

'I came to bring Morgan back. You let him get out, Mr Giles.'

'I'm sorry. Thank you.' His face was ashen, his knuckles stood out white in clenched fists.

'That's all right.' She stood there waiting, stubbornly, angrily, standing her ground. 'And, sir – you'd better tell me who sent that. Or didn't they put a name to it?'

'No name. There never is.'

'What do you mean, *never is*? You've had one before? Why you? Nobody's sent anything like that to Tom!'

'Nor will they. That poster is aimed at shaming men to enlist. Dwerryhouse will go before so very much longer, but they know I won't: God knows I've said so often enough. I asked for it, I suppose . . .'

'It isn't right. It's not fair!' She snatched up the poster, twisting it into a ball, flinging it on the fire. 'There now – the best place for it! This is a free country and don't let them make you do anything your conscience

413

don't approve of. I know Tom will go, but I'd give anything for him not to – I'll tell you that for nothing!'

'Bless you, Hawthorn. But you won't breathe a word about this, will you? Julia is so happy, my mother too. I don't want anything to spoil it for them. Not a word to a soul?'

'Not one word, sir. I promise.'

'Good. Then while you're about it, you'd better do the same with these.' Cheeks blazing an unnatural red now, he opened a drawer and took out an envelope, shaking it so the contents floated to the desk-top. 'Burn these too . . .'

'Mister Giles – *no*!' Horrified, Alice gathered up the feathers: three white feathers. 'When did these come?'

'Two days ago.'

'Then you should have told me! You can't keep a thing like that to yourself: not white feathers!'

There'd been a man at Creesby who'd hanged himself from a tree; they'd found three white feathers in his hand when they cut him down. Sad that whoever sent them hadn't bothered to find out he was dying of consumption! Some cat of a woman, she supposed. White feathers weren't a man's way of doing things.

'There now – that's them over and done with!' The acrid stink of their burning filled the room, and she opened the window the sooner to be rid of it. 'I'll come for Morgan this afternoon before it starts getting dark, and don't you fret none till then. No one knows but you and me – and her who sent them,' she added darkly.

She worried about it all morning. Who would do such a thing? Who hated Rowangarth so much?

Mrs Clementina? she'd asked herself, then immediately dismissed the thought. Mrs Sutton had sons in uniform, one of them at the Front. She couldn't have sent that vicious poster, nor any of her ladyship's friends, either. But a young man like Mr Giles who stood by what he

414

believed was fair game to the stupid lot who hung on to every word that Baroness Orczy woman said; she who preached that it was glorious a man should die for his country; who openly encouraged women to do their duty and persuade every man they knew to enlist, or award them the Order of the White Feather, present them with the badge of cowardice.

Women of England, she cried at recruiting meetings. *Do your duty! Send your men today to join our glorious army!*

Glorious, Alice fumed. What had been glorious about Artois and Loos and the slaughter at Gallipoli? And Mr Giles wasn't a coward; he didn't deserve three white feathers! Giles Sutton knew what being a conscientious objector was all about. It took a special courage to stand up and be counted.

All at once, her anger spent, Alice felt helpless and bewildered. What was the use of this war, she demanded, and how was she to bear it when Tom went?

Because the afternoon was so sunny and the sky still amazingly light for November, Helen decided that tea would be taken in the conservatory, probably for the last time this year, she thought, relaxing in the unaccustomed warmth, thinking that this could be mistaken for a day in spring. She looked up, smiling, as Mary brought in the afternoon post.

Helen's heart thumped with excitement now, each time the postman pedalled down the drive, anticipation adding to the joy of opening a letter, maybe to discover at last whether it would be Robert or Andrew who would arrive first.

All her children would be at Rowangarth again, even if only for a short time, she thought. She was the luckiest of women. Soon Andrew and Julia would be together and Robert on his way back to Cecilia. And who but knew,

Helen thought: this time next year they might not only be married but Cecilia might well be pregnant.

She cleared her head of such thoughts. She must not wish for such things when already she'd had more than her fair share of good luck. Grandchildren – grandsons – would come in their own good time.

'Well now, what have we here?' She thumbed through the letters, not noticing the look of apprehension on her son's face. 'Two for me, one for Julia and one for you, Giles, from York,' she smiled, recognizing the agent's flowing script.

'I'll read it later.' He set it aside, relieved that no one had sent another poster – or three white feathers.

'Julia's is from Andrew.' Helen held out the letter as the door burst open.

'Mary says there's one for me from France,' Julia cried. 'Probably Andrew knows when he'll be arriving by now.'

Her cheeks were flushed, her eyes shone. She had never, Helen thought, seen her daughter so beautiful. Such happiness was good to see, but then, she'd always known that Andrew was right for her daughter from the moment he'd looked at her with John's eyes. It had been as if –

'No! Oh, *no*! I don't believe it! They *can't* do this!' Julia's voice rose shrilly, trembling on the edge of tears. 'Read it! Go on, read that,' she cried, thrusting the letter into her mother's hand. 'He isn't coming! They've stopped his leave . . .'

She wrenched open the door, running out and down the stone steps, head down across the grass, making for Brattocks Wood.

'Sis! Wait!' At once, Giles made to follow. 'I'll go to her.'

'No.' Helen laid a hand on his arm. 'Leave her. There's nothing you can do; nothing anyone can do,' she whispered bitterly, opening the letter.

416

The writing on the single sheet was small and crabbed as if each word had been distasteful to write. It was dated the fifteenth day of November.

My dearest,
    I am writing this because to send a telegram and throw such news at you suddenly and starkly would be unforgivable.
    I was told this morning that my leave pass is withdrawn for the time being. No explanation was given though none was needed. We are worked to a standstill, almost, and still the wounded flood in. I think the powers that be have only now realized that neither I – nor any doctor or nurse – can be spared . . .

'The poor child,' Helen whispered. 'How could they be so cruel? She was so happy, so looking forward to it.' She folded the sheet into four, unwilling to read on. 'I find it very easy to dislike those lunatics at Sarajevo who caused all this.'

'It wasn't them especially.' Giles took her hand, holding it tightly. 'Europe was ready for war long before then. It was like a time bomb ticking away, and we thought to ignore it. The assassination was the excuse they'd been waiting for. Try not to be bitter. It won't help Julia.'

'No. Nothing will help her. Though when Robert comes home, she's going to feel it even more, knowing he'll soon be with Cecilia.'

'I realize that, but we must let her come to terms with it in her own way and in her own time. We can't intrude, Mother. We must just be there when she asks for our help.'

'Nevertheless, it is my instinct to shield her, comfort her.' Helen glanced apprehensively across the lawn and to the cloud that all at once blocked out the sun, making it November again. 'It'll be dark soon. Perhaps you should go and find her. I don't like her being in the wood in the half light – so many poachers about now. I don't want her mistaken for a trespasser.'

'Don't worry. The keepers know the law. They would call a warning first. But I'll find her. I think I know where she'll be.'

He found her beneath the tallest tree in the wood, leaning against it, hugging herself tightly, her eyes closed and dry of tears. Above her, rooks cawed and flapped as they settled to roost for the night.

'Sis? Come inside,' he said gently. 'It's getting dark . . .'

'You should always let them know,' she said, dully. 'Always tell the rooks – good things and bad – did you know that, Giles?'

Her eyes remained tightly closed as if she were unwilling to open them on so cruel a world. 'I was counting the days, the hours.' Her voice was harsh with pain. 'I want him so much it's like a terrible ache inside me. What am I to do?'

'Dearest girl.' He held wide his arms and she went to him, her face a mask of torment, giving way to her grief; weeping with great, tearing sobs.

He held her gently, making small, soothing sounds, stroking her hair, not speaking. It was a long time before her tears were spent and she let go a shuddering sigh of surrender.

'I'm cold,' she whispered. 'Let's go home, Giles.'

Alice knew Julia would come. News of any kind found its way to the sewing-room sooner or later. It was why she waited now, putting the finishing stitches to the tiny nightgown some soldier's wife would be glad of. And though she wanted to marry Tom so much that she could weep for need of him, she knew he had been right. It would be downright foolish of them to marry. Miss Julia knew it now, only too well. Crying her eyes out, like as not, and only this morning her so excited: jumping every time the telephone rang, waiting for the postman, and all the time a far-away dreaming in her eyes.

Alice switched off her thoughts with a snap. Not for the sewing-maid to put dreamings of a honeymoon nightdress and big, sinful double beds into Miss Julia's mind, though if she wasn't thinking exactly that, then there was something very wrong with her, Alice sighed.

This morning her courses had come, right on time as they always did, and she'd been relieved, she had to admit, that their one snatched loving hadn't got the child she'd thought would bind Tom to her. Their bairns, when they had them, she sighed, would be properly got; made in wedlock in Keeper's Cottage and born into a world at peace, she conceded soberly. Tom was always right.

She broke off the thread, laying the baby gown in the sewing-circle hamper, wondering if she should knock on Miss Julia's door and see if she wanted anything. A bit of sympathy never hurt anybody, and a glass of warm milk might help.

'Hawthorn?' The door opened quietly. 'I saw the light.'

'Come in do, miss, and sit you down. I thought you'd come . . .'

'I'm glad you're here. I don't want to talk about it, though. I shall start weeping again if we do.'

Her voice was flat, her face slablike. But the gentry didn't parade their grief, Alice knew, glad she'd had the sense to take the blue dress from behind the door and hang it out of sight in the wardrobe.

'I went to Brattocks, though.' Julia leaned back in the chair, eyes closed. 'I told the rooks that – '

'Hush, now. No use going on about it,' Alice interrupted in a most unservantlike way. 'You did right, just the same, telling those birds.'

'Superstition, Hawthorn, for all that. What Luke Parkin would say if he found out, I don't know.'

'Well, the reverend isn't going to find out, is he? I shan't tell, nor them birds, neither. Know how to keep a secret, they rooks, and now that you've told them – trusted them, like – they'll make it come right for you,' Alice rushed on, eager to stall fresh tears. 'Your bad news came by letter, so it's the postman you'll have to be watching out for now.'

'You think so?' Julia's eyes opened wide, her shoulders straightened. 'There might be some good news in a letter, you mean?'

'Jin Dobb reckons that's the way it usually goes, and I'm not inclined to argue with her. Mind, my aunt Bella swore by the bees,' Alice added, steering the conversation into safer channels. 'Daft as a brush, her; stood by that hive and the bees all busy and taking not one blind bit of notice of her. Have served her right if she'd got herself stung,' she added with relish, for she had never liked Aunt Bella. 'But you and me'll stick with the rooks, miss, and if you'll pardon me, I'd try to get some sleep now if I were you. And no more weeping? Think I'd best see you into bed with some hot milk, then find some witch hazel for them eyes . . .'

'You're right.' Julia rose to her feet, glad for someone else to make the decisions, tell her what to do. Dear, kind Hawthorn, who had shared her dreams and hopes right from the start; who'd sent the policeman flying that night in Hyde Park. 'Do you know something, Hawthorn? If I'd had a sister, she'd have been just like you.'

'Oh, *miss*!' Sister, indeed! To the gentry?

'She would. One I could share secrets with and who'd always be there, as you are, when I needed her. If we asked the rooks, do you think they could do something about it?'

'Away with your bother, Miss Julia! There's no way at all I could be sister to you. So get yourself undressed and I'll see to that drink.' Yes, and one of Miss Clitherow's

420

herbals an' all, to help the lass sleep. 'And then we'll see to them puffy eyes.

'And not one tear while my back's turned – not *one*,' she added sternly, 'or the sight of you will frighten the horses. The rooks'll put it right,' she crossed her fingers behind her back. 'I promise they will.'

Agnes Clitherow's herbal tablet did its work. Julia slept late and Helen gave orders that her daughter should not be disturbed with the usual early-morning tray of tea.

'I think I won't have breakfast – just coffee here in my room. Mr Giles will make do with tea and toast in the library,' Helen murmured, arranging her pillows, drawing her shawl around her shoulders. 'And will you tell Mary I won't be receiving this morning. No explanations, tell her. She's just to take cards, Bess . . .'

Helen did not feel like callers today; didn't want to have to admit, when asked for news of Andrew's impending arrival, that he wouldn't be coming on leave after all.

'Not at home to *anyone*, milady?' Bess murmured.

'Well, to Lady Tessa and Mrs Lane, of course. Mary will know who.' And to Pendenys, she supposed. 'Mrs MacMalcolm is still upset, Bess. Best she shouldn't have to face callers – not for a couple of days.'

Bess understood; wasn't best pleased herself with the war and Davie getting himself all in a bother about being conscripted if he wasn't sharpish about enlisting.

'I'll tell Mary, milady,' she murmured. 'Not unless it's urgent, you mean?'

'Urgent?' Helen gasped.

'Why yes, milady. Like a telegram message from Sir Robert, saying he's on his way,' she smiled impishly.

Robert. But of course. 'Only if it's that kind of urgent.' Helen returned the smile and Bess bobbed a curtsey, as she always did first thing in the morning and last thing at night, then closed the door behind her.

Robert. The army was giving him a second chance: if the foolish boy didn't carry off his Cecilia and marry her as soon as maybe, then he wasn't his father's son! Robert happy at last, she sighed contentedly, and Andrew's leave was only postponed. Who knew but that he wouldn't make it home for Christmas, she thought, putting her world to rights. What better time to have his leave? They'd all be glad, then, for this setback. And thinking about Christmas, why shouldn't Julia go to London and do some shopping? Not that there would be a lot to offer, so bad were the shortages becoming, but it would take her daughter's mind off things, and there was little risk of air-raids now that winter was setting in. The judge said only recently that a zeppelin had no chance of finding London in winter, what with the chimney smoke that rose in a great thick blanket over it, and the terrible fogs, too. London in November was the safest place imaginable, and Anne Lavinia's booming common sense would soon put paid to Julia's unhappiness. It was a splendid idea. Soon, when her daughter was a little less upset, she would put it to her.

Smiling, she took the carefully folded morning paper and dropped it to the floor beside her bed. She would read it, of course – it was her bounden duty to do so. But later. The newspapers made such depressing reading that, just for once, she might be forgiven for putting off the evil hour. Later she would read the sad list of deaths; of young men killed in action or died of wounds or missing at sea; read it as she always did whilst offering a prayer for wasted young lives and for those left behind to mourn. But not just yet. Later, perhaps . . .

It was ten o'clock exactly, the housekeeper was to remember, when Bess burst into her sitting-room, because she had only then checked her fob-watch with the ponderous booming of the grandfather clock in the great hall.

'Bess! That is *not* the way to enter a room,' she

422

remonstrated, rising from her desk, tilting her chin to its usual angle. 'How many times have I –'

'Ma'am! Oh, come *please*! Mary don't know what to do with it. Standing there, she is, and refusing to take it in to her ladyship. The telegram, I mean,' the housemaid supplied in answer to the unspoken questioning of the housekeeper's eyebrows. "I'm not taking this to her ladyship," she said to me. "I *won't*, not for anything!"'

'And why ever not?' Agnes Clitherow smoothed her skirts, making for the door. 'Milady's been expecting one hourly, almost, from Sir Robert – what on earth has come over the girl?'

'The sixpence, that's what . . .'

'The *sixpence*?' The housekeeper's annoyance was real. Never would Bess Thompson train up into a parlourmaid, she clucked inside her. Indeed, what could be the matter with Mary, who knew how to conduct herself, that she seemed to be so mesmerized by the arrival of a telegram?

'Mary offered it, and he wouldn't take it!'

It was then the housekeeper remembered. A sixpenny piece. Kept in readiness in a small china pot on the hall table, to be given as a tip to any telegraph boy who came on his red Post Office cycle from Creesby. Usually, Rowangarth telegrams or registered deliveries were snatched up at once, for the sixpenny tip represented half a day's wages, almost, and was spat upon for luck before being pocketed. Most folk tipped only a penny – if at all. And the stupid lad had refused it?

'You're sure?'

'Sure. He said nothing. Just clapped the thing into her hand, and when Mary told him to wait he turned tail and was down the steps afore she could hand him his tip. And he didn't even ask if there was a reply. They always ask if there's a reply . . .'

Agnes Clitherow bumped into a wide-eyed Mary at the turn in the passageway.

'Ma'am – take it in, will you?'

'This is no way to act, Mary!' She gazed archly at the small envelope deposited in her hand without so much as a by-your-leave. 'What has got into you? Did the boy say anything?'

'No, and he didn't need to. Didn't wait for his tip. Didn't you know they never take a tip when – ' She stood there, shaking.

'When *what*, girl?'

'You know what I mean, ma'am.'

Death telegrams, those boys called them. Unlucky to take a tip for one of those. Like robbing the dead, they said.

'Good gracious!' There was nothing else for it. She must take it in herself, then give Mary and Bess the talking-to of their lives for acting no better than foolish peasants in a gentleman's household. 'Such nonsense! I shall speak to the pair of you later!' was her parting broadside as she sailed to the winter-parlour door.

Hesitating for only a second before opening it, taking a quick calming breath before walking up to the desk at which Helen Sutton sat, she offered the envelope without so much as a word.

'Thank you,' Helen smiled. 'This is probably from Sir Robert, asking to be met at Holdenby. Oh, dear – and we are still without carriage horses . . .'

She took the pearl-handled slitter, opening the wretched thing so very daintily, the housekeeper thought, smiling as she did it.

The slitter fell to the floor; the small piece of paper fluttered to join it. Helen Sutton's head fell on her hands on the desk-top with a moan so soft it was little more than the letting go of her indrawn breath.

Her face was chalk-white, her head, when the house-keeper took it in her hands, lolled heavily, then fell again with a soft thud.

'Milady!' In two steps she had crossed the room and was pulling furiously on the bell. Then she returned to the desk, calling, 'Help me!' to Bess and Mary, who had been hovering outside the door because they'd known, hadn't they?

'Water and smelling salts,' she hissed. 'Then fetch Miss Julia and Mr Giles! Oh, milady, open your eyes, do,' she pleaded, supporting her as best she was able, rubbing the cold hands furiously.

It was Mary who, having recovered her wits, helped the housekeeper to carry her to the sofa, pushing her head between her knees and all the time begging her to open her eyes.

'I told you, didn't I?' Bess muttered, thrusting the bottle into Agnes Clitherow's hands.

'Be quiet!' she snapped, waving the bottle to and fro, sighing with relief as Helen Sutton's eyes fluttered open.

'Another sniff, milady? Just one more, then a sip of water? And do as I bid you,' she flung at Bess, who disappeared in a flurry of skirts, running as if her life depended on it.

'Mother! Darling – what is it?' Helen was still bemused when Julia arrived. 'Bess said you fainted.'

'A telegram . . .' Helen murmured, eyes closed.

'Here, miss.' Mary had retrieved it from the floor. 'I'm sorry, but I think – '

The message was addressed merely to Sutton, Rowangarth, Holdenby. Its message was terse to the point of cruelty.

Regret to inform you that Lieutenant Sir Robt. Sutton reported missing believed killed at sea on 17 Nov. 1915. Letter follows.

The words swam before Julia's eyes. She had to read them again before the jumble of words formed themselves into any sort of meaning.

'Read this!' She thrust the telegram into her brother's hand as he entered the room, then wrapped her mother in her arms, rocking her, kissing her, trying to say the words her lips could not form.

'That troopship,' Giles whispered. 'In the paper, this morning – men coming home. Torpedoed . . .'

'Damn them! *Damn them!*' Julia's voice, when at last she found it, was harsh with pain. 'Oh Mother, not Robert?' Please, not her brother?

Helen rose slowly to her feet, swaying. Giles gathered her to him, holding her tightly.

'Water, Miss Clitherow,' she murmured. 'If you please . . .'

'Will you telephone for Doctor James please, Mary?' Julia's voice sounded strange and strained. 'Tell him it's urgent. Then ring the vicar. You know the numbers?'

'Yes, miss. What about Mrs Lane and Lady Tessa? Will I tell them an' all?' Friends. A woman needed her friends about her when her son's been taken.

'Just the doctor and the vicar, Mary. The others later, if her ladyship wants them . . .'

'I would like,' Helen whispered, 'to go to my room. Will you help me, please?'

'Put an arm around my neck.' Giles scooped her up as if she were no weight at all. 'Julia and I will stay with you . . .'

'Missing, didn't that telegram say?' Tilda murmured. They were sitting around the kitchen table, stunned by the news. 'Missing means there's a chance, doesn't it? Happen Sir Robert could have been picked up.'

'And happen he hasn't,' Cook wailed, bursting into fresh tears. 'Didn't you read what the paper said this morning?'

No survivors, that's what. Hit twice. *Two* torpedoes. Men coming home on leave. It had happened three days

426

ago, but the Government had held back the news till all the telegrams had been sent. If there had been survivors, they'd have known . . .

'What is her ladyship to do?' Agnes Clitherow whispered. 'She was lying there when I went in, her face like chalk and holding on to Miss Julia's hand as if she was afraid to let it go. Staring at the ceiling, her lips moving yet not saying a word. Like she were praying . . .

'First her husband and now her son. And him going back to India to his young fiancée and her ladyship so pleased about it. There's no justice in this world . . .'

The doorbell rang. It clanged and echoed through the house, sending Mary jumping to her feet.

'I'll come, too,' the housekeeper said. Milady was in no fit state to receive – only those who were close. Agnes Clitherow knew how to deal with unwelcome callers.

Edward and Clementina Sutton stood on the doorstep, he white-faced, she lips pursed.

'We telephoned, Clitherow,' Clementina accused. 'The exchange said there was no answer.'

'Mrs MacMalcolm instructed me to remove the receiver.' It pleased the housekeeper to supply the information.

'How is she?' Edward asked, softly. 'Just a minute – if she's up to seeing us? Just to let her know we've been . . .'

'Will you be kind enough to take a seat, sir, madam? Mrs MacMalcolm is with her ladyship. I'll tell her you are here. Perhaps she'll be asleep. Doctor James has only just left. He gave her a draught . . .'

'If she's asleep, we'll call later,' Edward said gently.

'Yes, sir. Thank you, sir.'

Agnes Clitherow walked stiff-backed up the stairs, swallowing hard. Less than an hour since that telegram arrived, yet that woman from Pendenys Place already in black from head to foot.

Like a carrion crow . . .

24

'I'm sure they will understand, Miss Clitherow. No one at all.' Helen Sutton sat straight-backed at her desk, her face white, eyes red-rimmed from weeping. 'No Pendenys; not Letty or Tessa, even. Ask Mary to take cards – tell them tomorrow, perhaps.'

'Doctor James said you were to stay in bed.' The housekeeper offered the small glass. 'You ought to be resting. Why don't you take the sleeping-draught he left you?'

'Because there is something I must do. And I thank you for your kindness, Miss Clitherow. Everyone is so good, but just for today, I don't want anyone . . .'

So short a time ago she had felt such happiness that Robert would soon be with the woman he loved; now she knew they would never meet again and that it was she who must write the letter to break Cecilia's heart.

'I'll see you aren't disturbed, milady, and if there's anything I can't deal with, I'll ask Mrs MacMalcolm to see to it. I'll go now; tell Mr Edward . . .'

'Thank you.' Helen gazed at the photographs on her desk: the one of her son, the other of the woman he would have married. How was she to find the words? How did she tell someone that the man she loved was dead? How had it been, five years ago, when John was killed? She couldn't remember; hadn't wanted to. She'd shut out the world that day.

'Oh, Cecilia Jamilla Kahn.' She took the photograph in gentle hands. 'I understand, my dear. I do so understand.'

'Her ladyship is not to be disturbed today.' Agnes Clitherow gazed at each in turn. 'Not for *anyone*,' she stressed.

'The poor soul.' Mrs Shaw's eyes were red and puffy. 'I'd shut myself away for ever if it had happened to me. Isn't there any hope? Missing, didn't the telegram say?'

'Missing, believed killed. The survivors have been listed in the morning papers – less than twenty. Sir Robert's name isn't one of them. That is why no one must disturb Lady Helen. She is writing to Miss Kahn – a terrible thing to have to do . . .'

'But won't the army have told her?' Tilda frowned. 'She was his young lady.'

'A fiancée doesn't count. Only the next of kin is told.'

'Her ladyship set great store by that wedding,' Cook sniffed. 'Wanted nothing more than to see them married.'

'And grandchildren. She wanted children to follow on,' Mary added. 'It's going to be up to Mister Giles, now, and him not in the least interested.'

'I hope you aren't inferring . . .' The housekeeper left her remark hanging in mid-air.

'Course I'm not! It's just that he's – well – *bookish*. But he'll have to look sharp and get himself wed, now.'

'No one *has* to do anything, Mary, though we shall all be pleased when he finds a nice young bride.'

'But if he doesn't, then what's going to happen to the title?' Tilda demanded. 'There's been a Sir at Rowangarth for hundreds of years.'

'And please God there always will be.' Tilda, thought Agnes Clitherow testily, had an uncanny way of putting her finger on things; of demanding, in all innocence, an answer to the question they had all been longing to ask. 'And I suppose – officially – that Mr Giles is already *Sir* Giles. But for delicacy's sake – her ladyship being in such terrible shock, I mean – we'd all best leave it for the time being.'

'But what,' Tilda persisted, 'if he doesn't have bairns?'

'Then the title sidesteps,' Cook clucked distastefully, 'to Pendenys. And if you don't mind, I want no talk in my kitchen about Sir Robert's title ending up at the Place!'

'Amen to that,' whispered the housekeeper as she climbed the twisting staircase that led to the great hall, though for Mr Edward to have it would be right and proper, him being born a Sutton, and the late Sir John's brother. But *Lady* Clementina – the Ironmaster's daughter? Oh, my word, no. And worse than that, even, was where the baronetcy would end up. Imagine it? Sir Elliot Sutton – and his doting mama just squirming with delight, should she live to see it.

Well, there'd be no shortage of Sutton heirs in *that* direction, she thought, lips pursed. It wouldn't surprise her if there weren't a few already – hedge children and by-blows, of course. Elliot Sutton had been bailed out of fatherhood more than once by his mother's money! It was the best-known secret in the Riding.

The housekeeper's cheeks pinked at such unladylike thoughts – and at a time when the house was in mourning! *Again.* Her ladyship in black once more; for a year, this time, and Mrs MacMalcolm and Mr Giles for six months and, oh! she was in such a state that she'd forgotten to tell them downstairs to dress soberly and wear black armbands until such time as advised differently. And to remind them there was to be no gossiping in the village; that, if asked, they should say her ladyship was bearing up as well as could be expected.

She sighed deeply, retracing her steps. Best she should tell them and, anyway, Cook would have the kettle on the boil soon. It might be a comfort to take a cup of tea in the kitchen. There might even be cherry scones, she thought sadly. Somehow, Cook always seemed to know when to bake cherry scones . . .

Helen gazed at the envelope. She had written and rewritten the letter inside it, but had found no way to blunt Cecilia's pain. She had hoped never to use those envelopes again, nor the black-edged matching notepaper, left over from the time of John's death. Now John's son was dead, too.

'Is there anything special you want from Creesby?' The door opened quietly and Giles stood there, uncertainly. 'Shall I – post the letter?'

'If you will. And I think I shall go upstairs now, and lie on my bed. I didn't sleep last night.'

'Will you be all right alone? Julia has gone out. Walking, she said . . .'

'To the top of the Pike, I suppose.' Julia always went there when she was very happy – or very sad. 'I'll be all right. I'd rather be alone, truth known.'

She offered her cheek for her son's kiss, then turned, unspeaking, to walk unsteadily up the stairs; past the Sutton men of long ago – those who had fought against the Armada, the Roundheads. She stopped to gaze at the one so like Robert; at Gilbert Sutton who had fought at Balaclava. And all of them had come home to Rowangarth, save her son.

She closed her eyes, gripping the banister rail, walking like a woman suddenly old. At the half-landing she turned and looked down to see Giles watching her, his eyes wide with concern.

'Off you go. I'm all right – just in need of sleep, that's all. We'll have tea in the conservatory when you get back.'

Dear Giles, whose conscience must be heavier, even, than his heart. Brave Giles, because it took a man of courage to refuse to fight.

She smiled down to reassure him. Only Giles left now. Giles, who must give a son to Rowangarth . . .

Elliot Sutton replaced the earpiece of the telephone on his desk and smiled. Not a smile of pleasure, for even he found no joy in the death of any soldier, much less his cousin. He disliked the war intensely, baulked at taking orders and observing rules and regulations; liked still less the ever-present threat of the front line because, sooner or later, he would have to go there.

His smile was more one of mockery, of derision even, that Robert Sutton should have come home to England to get himself killed when he could have stayed safely in India. Little brother Albert had had more sense. Not for anything would he come home to enlist for, like himself, Albert thought nothing of the glory of dying in a stinking trench or choking slowly on mustard gas. Just to think of it made him shudder.

But that was life. Sorry you copped it up on the way home, Robert, old man. Elliot sent his thoughts winging. Not even killed in action, he thought. What a way to go, dammit. A soldier drowned at sea.

They wouldn't get Elliot Sutton so easily, though. He would stay at the War Office as long as he could, and be damned to France and Belgium – foreign countries, both. Mind, he didn't like kowtowing to a penniless aristocrat with one pip more on his shoulders. He didn't mind people at home knowing that all of the fighting he'd seen was from a window in Whitehall. What he *did* mind about was going home to Pendenys in a coffin. No death or glory for Elliot Sutton.

For the first time in his life he was glad he had more than his fair share of Mary Anne Pendennis's blood in his veins. Mary Anne had been a survivor, and so would he be. Sorry, cousin Robert. Bad luck, and all that . . .

Sighing, he took pen and paper and prepared to write, as his mother had just ordered him to, to his aunt Helen; to tell her how shocked and heartbroken he was. Best do it now. He aimed to be at the theatre in less than an hour. Better get it over with.

Tongue-in-cheek, he began to write.

'I'd never have thought – not even with a war on – that I'd be wearing black again,' Julia whispered. 'Somehow,

432

it was going to happen to other people, not to me, Hawthorn. Do you suppose you can find a button for this dress?'

'How's her ladyship today?' Alice murmured, emptying the contents of the button-box on to the table-top, searching carefully through all the black ones.

'Not so good. She's just written to Cecilia; not a very nice thing to have to do.'

'I'm sorry, miss.' There didn't seem anything else to say.

'Sorry? I still can't believe it. Robert was – well – always *away*, somehow. Away at school, or in India. He was like a shadowy person: not as real to me as Giles. Then he came home to enlist when he could have stayed with Cecilia and I saw him differently. He loved her very much, and all at once we understood each other.'

'Life's awful, isn't it, miss? It's wrong for two people in love never to see each other again . . .' Tears filled her eyes then trickled down her cheeks.

'Don't cry, Hawthorn. Please don't cry.'

'I can't help it. It isn't just Sir Robert and his young lady I'm upset about – it's me and Tom and you and the doctor. It isn't fair. I hate this war. It's going to take Tom from me and I'll have to stand by and see it happen.'

'I know. When Andrew walked away from me, slammed the compartment door, I wanted to scream, "*No!*", but I stood there and smiled. I stood there and watched him go when I ought to have lain down in front of that engine to stop it leaving.'

'They'd have carted you away to the lock-up.'

'Maybe so, but I'd have made my protest, wouldn't I? Now I feel it's partly my fault that I'm looking for a black button that's missing from a black frock; because no one has tried to stop this war! And there's my mother, trying to be brave when they've killed her son! She doesn't want

433

Giles to go, you know. She'd support him, stand by him, if he refused to enlist.'

'But he *will* go. They all will. It's getting so they're afraid not to.'

'Not Giles. I think he'd go to prison first. They can call him coward and conchie, but he won't kill – not my brother.'

'Then I pity him with all my heart, miss.' Alice did; especially since the white feathers. 'And you'd best leave the frock. I'll see to it.'

'Black! How I dislike it!' Julia laid the full-skirted dress over the chair arm. 'And it's miles too long! I wish I didn't feel so guilty, Hawthorn. I'm glad, would you believe, that I'm wearing black for Robert and not for Andrew. I'm trying to feel sorry for my mother and Cecilia – and I *am* sorry – yet all the while I'm grateful it wasn't Andrew's name on that telegram. I thought my world had ended when his leave was cancelled, thought nothing worse could happen. Yet now I keep saying thank you to God for letting Andrew live. What is this war doing to us?'

'I don't know. I'd give ten years of my life, though, for it to end, *soon*, before Tom has to go. And I'm really sorry for her ladyship and for that poor lady in India. How long before she gets the letter – telling her, I mean?'

'About a month. Mother's hoping it won't arrive until after Christmas, but it will. Bad news always travels fast, don't they say? Oh, look! There's Giles and your Tom.' Julia drew aside the lace curtain. 'Wonder where they're going?'

'They're making for Brattocks. Happen to see Reuben; happen to talk keeping business.'

Alice stood there, her eyes on Tom's back, loving him with her eyes, willing him to turn and see her. But he did not. Whatever it was they were talking about didn't allow for waving to a young lady in a sewing-room window. Poachers they'd be on about. Poachers, without a doubt.

'So you're all set on it, Dwerryhouse?' Giles dug his hands deep into his pockets, hunching his shoulders against the cold. 'Davie, William and yourself?'

'Well, sir. Davie's out of his time, so it seems sensible he should go, and now that the mare has foaled – and her ladyship not being able to replace the geldings the army took away – '

'There's a terrible shortage of good carriage horses,' Giles frowned. 'We've been trying to match a pair – you'll tell William that, won't you?'

'Will appreciates the position, sir.' Was he to call him Sir Giles, Tom pondered, or maybe, with Sir Robert only being *believed* killed . . .? 'But he says a coachman without horses to see to – well, he reckons he might as well enlist.'

'And you, Dwerryhouse?'

'Same for me. I'm a good shot – that's what I'd be best at. If I wait till conscription comes I'll have no say in the matter.'

'You're off to Creesby then, to join up?'

'If it's all right with you, sir. We're asking for a couple of hours off. Now seems as good a time as any – and after what happened to Sir Robert . . .'

'So when will you be going?'

'Tomorrow. If we walk to the station we can get the nine o'clock train. We'll be there and back by noon, I shouldn't wonder. And, sir – if happen you could keep it quiet?'

'The young ladies?' Giles smiled.

'Aye. They'll not be best pleased.'

Giles Sutton watched the keeper walk away, gun over his arm. Then he turned abruptly, whistling to the spaniel.

'Come on, Morgan.' He bent to fondle the silky head. 'It's getting dark. Let's go home . . .'

'What on earth is going on all of a sudden?' Mrs Shaw demanded of Alice when she came in by the back door. 'Is everybody going mad around here? Bess says Davie's been to volunteer, so she's giving notice. Away to Leeds to make shells, and Mary offering to go with her.'

'Why Mary?' Alice asked dully, holding her hands to the fire.

'Gone all patriotic. She's got a brother in the navy, remember; him that's minesweeping in the Channel. And what's to do with you, lass? You and Tom been having words?' She gazed pointedly at Alice's pale, tear-stained face. 'Been having a weep, have you?'

'Weeping, yes; words, no. Tom's volunteered, an' all.'

'So you'll be going next?' Cook frowned.

'That I won't,' Alice flung. 'What has this war done for me, 'cept take my man? And you're right. Everybody *is* going mad, but me. Because Alice Hawthorn isn't going to work in no factory. There'll have to be someone here to help take care of Rowangarth. They've got Tom now; they shan't have me!'

She hugged her arms around her chest. She felt so cold, even here in the warmth of the kitchen. She ached all over too, and there was a pain exactly where her heart should have been. The way ahead looked bleak and threatening as a winter that never ends.

'You're feeling sorry for yourself, that's what,' Cook pronounced comfortably, arranging the hot coals with the poker, making a bed for the kettle. 'What about poor Miss Julia? Her's all alone in her room and today's her wedding anniversary. And no one but me seems to have remembered.'

'And I'd forgotten, too. Taken up with my own miseries, I suppose. Poor Miss Julia – and her wanting him with her like he should have been, if his leave hadn't been denied him.'

'Then how about if I set a tray and you take it to her, Alice? She'll not be asleep, be sure of that. Just a pot of tea and happen a piece of sponge cake – and you giving her a bit of sympathy, like. Might help the lass to feel a bit better.'

'I'll do that.' Alice took off her coat and hat, patting her hair into order. 'And you're a good soul to remember her. My, but it seems half a lifetime ago, that wedding; and last year Sir Robert newly home and all of us so happy.'

'That's the way it is, lass.' Cook placed a bright red cosy over the little teapot. 'But remember that it'll all pass, given time. Nothing lasts – neither good times nor bad. So off you go. You and her are close. Stay with her for a while; she'll be glad of a bit of company.'

Alice tapped on the bedroom door, softly, in case Miss Julia was asleep, but it was opened at once.

'Hawthorn! I've been hoping you'd come.'

'Do you want a bit of company while you drink it?' Alice set the tray on the dressing-table. 'Cook sent it on account of it – ' She stopped, not knowing what to say.

'Of it being our first anniversary and I'd hoped we'd spend it together?' Her cheeks were flushed, her eyes bright, though dry of tears.

'Something like that.' Alice closed the door. 'And will I make up your fire? – it's all but out.'

'No thanks. We've got to save coal, you know. Tell me why you've been crying, Hawthorn?'

'On account of Tom.' No use denying it.

'Enlisting, you mean? I'd heard. There'll be no one left at Rowangarth, before so very much longer. Only Reuben and Catchpole.'

437

'There'll be Sir Giles.' It was *Sir* Giles now. Lady Helen had as good as said so. 'Ask Sir Giles if he can spare me a minute, will you, Mary?' she'd said. 'He'll see to things.'

'No. He'll be gone, too. He volunteered today, along with Tom and Davie and Will Stubbs. Only he went to York to do it.'

'But he said he'd never take life! Did he say why he did it?' Those white feathers! Damn the stupid woman who sent them!

'No reason given. All he said was that he could enlist without blotting his copybook. They're in great need of doctors and nurses, he said – anyone to help care for the wounded.'

'So he's going to be an orderly?' Medical orderlies didn't fire guns. It was a fair solution, Alice thought.

'No – he's volunteered before conscription comes, he said, so he can have some say in where he goes and what he does. Today, he volunteered for a stretcher-bearer.'

'But, *miss*! Doesn't he know that's just about the daftest, most dangerous thing he could go and do? They send stretcher-bearers into No Man's Land to bring back the wounded and dying as can't help themselves. There'll be barbed wire and minefields to contend with and the German machine-gunners sat there waiting . . .'

Her cheeks flushed pink at her eloquence – and her stupidity, she thought bitterly – at saying such things which could only worry his poor sister. She had spoken out of turn, an' all, but it had to be said. '*Why* didn't he settle for being an orderly? What's he trying to do – get himself killed? Hasn't her ladyship suffered enough already?'

'That's what I said, more or less, but it's done now. And he admitted it wasn't the best of times to have sprung it on Mother. But what choice does a man have when his brother has been killed – and someone has sent him three white feathers?'

438

'He told you, then? He told me an' all, a while back,' Alice choked. 'There's some folk making it impossible to draw breath even, if you aren't in khaki! When does he think they'll send for him?'

'He explained about Robert, so they agreed to defer call-up until the New Year. That should give him time to do what's got to be done here. Did Tom say when he'd be going?'

'No, but he thinks pretty soon. I reckon he'll be gone before Christmas. It's an awful world, isn't it, to be young in?'

'Terrible, Hawthorn. Yet tonight, when I should be miserable, I'm not. And if I tell you something, you won't breathe it to a soul? I wouldn't want it to get back to Mother, you see.' She opened her jewel case and drew out a letter. 'Read this, will you?'

'You're sure?'

'Quite sure. And anyway, you are entitled to see it. You said it was the postman I must watch out for,' she urged. 'You said it would come by letter, and it did. Look – written on the back of the envelope. *Do not open until 20 November*. It came yesterday . . .'

Alice unfolded the single sheet of paper. The handwriting on it was firm and dependable, somehow; just like the doctor.

My dearest love . . .

'You know, miss, I've never had a letter from Tom.'

'You will have, before so very much longer. Your life will come to revolve around letters,' Julia whispered. 'But go on . . .'

My dearest love,

 I write this in the hope that you'll be able to read it on our first anniversary. It makes me sad you'll be alone when you do, and when we shall meet again, it is hard to say. The situation here is near chaos and all leave but the most urgent or compassionate is suspended. This I accept, and although I have not heard from you

439

since, I know your disappointment is every bit as great as my own.

Yet there is a silver lining to our cloud. I was to have left here early on 17th November to arrive at Le Havre for the overnight crossing by troop transport to Southampton. I know now, that if my leave had not been cancelled, I would have been aboard a trooper which was torpedoed mid-Channel with a terrible loss of life.

Now I am certain I shall survive this war and come safely home to you, one day. With such prodigious good luck, my darling, nothing can harm me. Your love has kept me safe. What happened was meant to be.

I love you with all my heart.

Andrew.

'Oh . . .' It was all Alice could say.

'Oh, indeed. Andrew will only now have heard about Robert. When he wrote that letter he had no way of knowing my brother was aboard that troopship. Imagine – *two* of them killed at sea? That's why Mother musn't be told yet about Andrew. And that is why I can't be sad Andrew isn't with me today. If his leave had gone ahead, I'd be a widow now.'

'It's a funny thing, isn't it – Fate, I mean.' Alice ran her tongue around suddenly dry lips.

'Funny, capricious, a chance in a million; whatever you call it, Andrew wasn't meant to come home. I'm so lucky, Hawthorn.'

'But Sir Robert and his young lady – they aren't lucky.'

'No, poor loves – not in this life, anyway. But I *know* Andrew will come home to me now.'

'And you'll wait, miss, and be content?'

'Wait? That I won't! Oh, no! I've decided. *I* am going to *him!*'

'But how?' Alice wanted to smile. It sounded just like Polly Oliver in the song they'd sung at school; Polly, who'd dressed as a soldier to follow her love.

'Simple! There are too many wounded and too few

440

to care for them. I shall drive an ambulance. Aunt Sutton will help me. She's in the First Aid Nursing Yeomanry – she'll put in a good word for me. I don't know why I didn't think of it before.'

'And you'd do that, just to be near the doctor?'

'No – I'd be doing it to help my country and those poor wounded troops, out there and – '

'Truth or dare, Miss Julia,' Alice said, looking her straight in the eyes.

'Oh, all right! I want to be near Andrew, truth known, but if I can do something useful at the same time, then so much the better. I'd at least be on the same continent, if not in the same country. Just think – one day I might look up and see him standing there.'

'And you might spend the whole war just missing each other by hours. Or you might even be sent to the Eastern front, where the Russians are fighting. You'd have to go where they sent you, remember.'

'That's a risk I shall have to take.'

'And her ladyship? She'll be alone. Had you thought of that?'

'Yes, I had.' Julia's face was all at once grave. 'But I know that when I tell her she'll give me her blessing, for all that. She and Pa were very much in love. She'll understand.'

'Then I'll come with you! If Bess and Mary can make shells, then I can go to France!'

'You will? You'll come, Hawthorn? You'd have to learn to drive first, but Aunt Sutton will help, I'm sure she will.'

'Drive, miss – oh, no; not me!' Alice held her hands to her blazing cheeks. 'I couldn't control one of them contraptions, but I could be a nurse, now couldn't I? I'm young and strong and I'm not afraid of hard work.'

'There'd be some terrible sights,' Julia warned.

'Happen. But if you can stick it, Miss Julia, then so

can I. Though if I gave in my notice I don't know where I could call home – with me not having any parents. I suppose I could stay with Reuben if ever I got leave . . .'

'You could. Or you could keep your room at Rowangarth. Well, you did once say that Rowangarth was the only real home you'd ever had. But we'll worry about that later. What is important – and I'll bet you haven't so much as thought about it – is that you aren't twenty-one yet. Men have to be nineteen before they can be sent to the Front and women twenty-one. And you won't be *twenty* till June.'

'*Damn!*' All her life, it seemed to Alice, her age had been against her. 'Well, I'll just have to add a bit on, won't I? I don't suppose they'll ask for my birth certificate.'

'I don't suppose they will.' Julia held out her hand. 'So is it a bargain, then? Shall we shake on it? After Christmas, we're going to France?'

'But we can't just pack up and go, miss. It might take time.'

'I'd thought of that. I shall go to London and see Aunt Sutton. She'll help us, I know she will. In the New Year it shall be, Hawthorn; when Mother has had a little more time to adjust to Robert's death.'

'Seems as good a time as any.' Tom would have gone by then.

'And meantime, we mustn't say a word to anyone about it or Reuben will stop you going and Andrew will think up a dozen different ways to keep me at home. The New Year? 1916?'

'The New Year!' Alice grasped Julia's hand and held it firmly. 'It won't be a bed of roses, but we'll manage somehow.'

She didn't want Tom to go to war, but all at once his going didn't seem quite so awful. And, like Miss Julia said, who was to know that, somewhere in France, just around the next corner, they might not meet? She was still a little uncertain, and afraid, too, if she let herself think too much about it, but being afraid and doing something about it was better than staying at home worrying – if someone didn't discover how old she really was . . .

She glanced in the dressing-table mirror. It was her nose, truth known. It made her look even younger.

'You think we'll get there, miss?'

'We can try our damnedest. Maybe I can't be with Andrew, but at least I can be nearer, without the Channel between us. And just think, we might even be able to be together just for a few hours.

'There's nothing to keep me here, and Mother herself said my first duty is to my husband, though duty doesn't come into it, really. I want him, Hawthorn. I've *got* at least to try . . .'

'Then I'm coming with you.' Alice tilted her chin, breathing slowly, deeply, though it did nothing to stop the shaking inside her.

Alice Hawthorn – going to France? Oh, my word . . .

25

The seventh of December, the Tuesday on which Tom was to report to the army at Richmond, was a date and day written deep on Alice's heart. Tomorrow, when they met, would be their last goodnight, their last kiss. Already William and Davie had gone, and Bess and Mary had left Rowangarth for shared lodgings in Leeds and the hard work – and good wages – of the munitions factory.

Her sweet, safe world was falling apart, Alice mourned. All she held dear, had believed would outlast time itself, was slipping away from her. And how soon would it be, she fretted, before she and Miss Julia were gone too – if their schemes came to anything, that was; if Reuben didn't find out and forbid her to go.

But she would worry about that when Tuesday had been and gone. Tonight, being with Tom was all that mattered, when soon she would be living in a world so bleak, so loveless and empty, that she would die of heartache unless she was able to go nursing with Miss Julia. And if cousin Reuben put paid to it she would never speak to him again. Not as long as she lived!

She switched off the light and drew back the curtains. There was no moon tonight, no stars. She could hardly pick out the bulk of the bothy, shadowy against the skyline. Not a glimmer of light showed from Tom's window, as if he were gone already.

She swished the curtains together again, wondering if Sir Giles had told her ladyship about the letter. It had come on the same day as Tom's calling-up notice, and he'd told her about it, Alice frowned, just as he'd told her about the white feathers.

'I'm to report to Kingsford Camp on the fourteenth of January, Hawthorn – near Salisbury . . .'

'Then best you tell her ladyship as soon as maybe, sir,' she had warned. 'At least give her time to get used to it.'

But as yet he'd said nothing. Giles Sutton was too kindly for his own good; too mindful of the feelings of others. She hoped the war would deal gently with him, but she doubted it, for war took account of no man's feelings. She raised her eyes to the ceiling.

'What were you about, God, to let it happen? Just what, will you tell me?'

Julia met her brother's gaze, held it, then nodded her head in a movement which meant, *Now!* Then her eyes narrowed with a challenge that said, *If you don't, then I will!*

'Mother,' Giles cleared his throat noisily.

'What is it?' Helen smiled, laying aside the sock she was knitting, offering her full attention. 'Tell me?'

'I'm sorry, dearest, truly I am,' he said softly. 'I was trying to keep it until after Christmas, but it's best you should know. I volunteered, you see. Did it on the same day as Dwerryhouse and the others. They said, though, that I could have deferment, because of Robert . . .'

'But he's to go in January,' Julia supplied. 'On the fourteenth.'

For a moment there was a silence so complete it seemed to stretch out, crystal clear and cold, into forever.

'I knew something was upsetting you.' Gently Helen spoke. 'I wish you'd told me at the time, though. It might have helped to share the worry.'

'Say you understand?' Julia begged. 'I know you don't want him to go – who in her right mind would? – but it had to come . . .'

'Yes, and I accept it, even though I shall never know how we came to let this war happen,' Helen sighed

445

bitterly. 'And I admire your courage, Giles. I realize how painful it must have been for you.'

'Not so bad, really, once my mind was made up. The worst bit was getting the feathers. That's why I volunteered. Someone sent me three white feathers, you see.'

There! It had been said. Now she knew she had a coward for a son.

'Oh, my dear!' Helen held wide her arms and he went to her, kneeling at her feet, laying his head on her lap as he had done when a small boy. And she bent to kiss him as she had kissed him when he'd awakened from a bad dream and called out for her in the night.

'You aren't both ashamed of me?'

'Of course not,' Helen whispered.

'No, we aren't! And, darling – can you bear any more? There's worse to come.' Julia's eyes, dark with pleading, gazed into her mother's.

'More, child? Oh, well . . .'

'Mother, I am *not* a child. I'm a married woman,' Julia said, her voice indulgent. 'And that, really, is what it's all about. I want to go too. I know I'm being selfish,' she rushed on, 'and that my duty is here with you, especially after –'

She stopped, wishing she had drawn breath, thought more carefully, not about what she wanted to say, but the way she should have said it.

'It's all right,' Helen prompted. 'And before you say any more, you know I have always insisted that your duty – if duty we must talk about – is to Andrew and not to me.'

'Thank you for understanding – especially now,' Julia smiled sadly. 'But I want desperately to go to France. I want to be nearer to Andrew. If he were given a few days away from duty, then I'd be able to go to him. I'd do anything just to see him. I love him so much, you see, that I have no pride left.'

'Pride, Julia MacMalcolm? What has pride to do with

loving?' Helen's voice was gentle with remembering. 'And I do understand. I loved your pa in just such a way.'

'Then it's all right? You don't mind?'

'No, it *isn't* all right and I *do* mind. No mother wants to see her children walk headlong into danger, but I accept that you are both adults and I respect your wishes. I shall be grey-haired with worry by the time it's over and you are both – Andrew, too – back safely at home. But you shall go with my blessing – and my love.'

And if she could, she would make a bargain here and now with the Almighty; pledging what remained of her life for the safety of theirs. She would do it gladly, if only to be with John again.

'Dearest milady – will I give you an answer to something you have asked me more times than I can remember?' Giles rose to his feet, looking down at her with love. 'Why I haven't married, that is. Well, I'll tell you now. It is because Pa found you first, and if I look for ever, I shall never find another woman who could hold half a candle to you.'

'Stuff and nonsense, flatterer!' Helen jumped to her feet. 'Oh, let's try not to be sad! Let's try to pretend there is no war out there.' For wasn't this Rowangarth, and didn't her beloved house have walls so thick and comforting that nothing could penetrate them unless she chose to let it? And when her children were gone – dear heaven, how would she bear it? – John's house would share her loneliness and comfort her with its warmth. 'And I think we'll ring for a tray of tea.'

Such a comforter. Sutton Premier Tea, picked less than a year ago. The last Robert would ever grow.

'Run down and ask Cook – there's a dear girl.'

It had come, the night she had dreaded since they realized the war was not to be a six-month skirmish. Alice stood quite still, accustoming her eyes to the darkness, then walked carefully across the lawn to the wild garden and the stile.

'Tom?' She stood, head tilted, listening for his answering whistle.

He was out there, waiting – for the last time until it was all over. She wanted this night to be special, to remember every word, every laugh, every kiss; but she would not, because already she was shaking and cold inside and there was a tightness in her throat that was really a hard ball of tears, waiting to be shed.

She called his name again, then saw his outline with its wide-open arms; its safe, protecting arms.

'Bonny lass!' He was gathering her close, whispering his lips across her cheek to her waiting, wanting mouth.

'Hold me,' she whispered. 'I'm cold. Let's go to the corner.' To the warm place, sheltered from the wind that blew from the east; warmed by the boiler fire on the other side of the wall. And private, because no one had bothered, lately, to cut back the bushes that grew beside it.

'We aren't going to talk about the war tonight,' Tom said firmly, 'nor about me going in the morning. I'll be away long before anyone's awake, and I don't want any goodbyes – nothing like that. You understand, Alice Hawthorn?'

They had agreed more than a week ago that that was how it would be. No talk of undying love, of being faithful, of the pain of wanting. Those things they took for granted; no sense wasting good breath saying over again something they had known since the day they first met.

Does this creature belong to you?

No, but he's with me. He belongs to Mr Giles . . .

No one had even heard of Sarajevo that day.

'It was not so far from here that we met – remember? You called Morgan a daft dog.'

448

'And so he was, the spoiled creature. You'll have to look after him when Sir Giles goes – see he gets his walks. Not in the wood, though.'

There would be more poachers in Brattocks than ever, once they knew there was only one elderly keeper to keep an eye on their goings-on. And not only poachers. Elliot Sutton might think to use the woodland path again when next he visited Rowangarth.

'Penny for them, or are they worth more?' Alice smiled.

'Much more. Far more than you can afford to pay,' he lied. 'I wouldn't take a hundred sovereigns for them.'

'And I haven't got that much to offer.'

'Then I might just 'change them for a kiss.'

'About me, were they?' she laughed, teasing him with her lips.

'About a bonny lass with big brown eyes and the sweetest nose ever; about the lass I'm going to marry . . .'

'When, Tom? Soon, will it be?' Their teasing was over, and wanting took her, twisting her insides, setting every small pulse throbbing out her need of him.

'As soon as we can, Alice; just as soon. Happen, if ever they gave me leave, we might persuade Reuben to change his mind. I did read, somewhere, that if all else failed you could ask the Courts for permission.'

'I could never do that. Courts cost money and, anyway, eighteen months will soon pass. They say there's a time and a place for everything and our time will come, Tom. I've accepted it, now. And no matter what happens meantime, you and me will have our day.'

'You think so.' He closed his eyes, wanting her.

'Course I do. I told the rooks about us. They'll see to it that we'll be wed. And tomorrow, when you're –' She stopped, confused. 'Tomorrow, when me and Morgan are passing by, I shall tell them you're up Richmond way, and that they're to take care of you.' She snuggled closer, thrusting her hands into his jacket pockets. 'And they'll – ooooh! What have you got in there?' She pulled out her hand as if it had been bitten. 'A mouse?'

'That'll teach you not to go in your man's pockets – especially if he's a gamekeeper,' Tom grinned. 'Now hold out your hand, because I want you to wish on it.'

'N-no,' she said, dubiously. It was dark and she couldn't properly see. She held out a probing finger and touched the soft fur that lay on his palm.

'It's all right. Only a rabbit's foot. They're lucky, if someone gives one to you. Reuben said I'd better take one along with me. He gave one to Will and Davie, an' all; said we'll be all right with one of these in our pocket. Now take it in your hand and wish, like I told you.'

She took it, stroking it with her forefinger, wishing with all her might for him to come home safely. Then she laid it gently back in his hand, wrapping his fingers over it.

'There now,' she sighed, 'between the rabbits and the rooks, you'll do all right. One day, we'll be together again.'

'You seem so sure, sweetheart.' His voice was touched with sadness, for she didn't know the half of what would face him after this night.

'I'm sure, Tom. Very sure. Our turn will come. But oh, I don't want you to leave me. I want us to stay here, all night.'

Stay for ever, arms entwined, bodies close; stay until they petrified into stone, like the figures in the garden at Rowangarth. And a hundred years on, people would stop a while and gaze at them and wonder who they were. Then those people would pass on, because in a hundred years from now it wouldn't matter anyway.

'Say you'll never love anyone else, Tom?'

'I love you, bonny lass. There couldn't be anyone else for me. And when I'm away and missing you and wanting you near me, I shall picture you beside the stile at the edge of Brattocks. And it'll be a summer's day, in my

450

dreamings. There'll be sunshine and new, gentle leaves, and you'll have buttercups in your hair . . .'

She sat alone in her room that night, dry-eyed and numb, thinking back to their parting and how she had wanted to weep and cling to him and beg him, on her knees if she had to, not to go. Yet she had sent him to war with her head held high and, though he couldn't see it in the darkness, with a smile on her lips.

Now she wanted to throw herself on her bed, to weep into her pillow, beat it with angry fists, but that wouldn't do. She must stay awake until she saw a light in his window. At five, Tom would be leaving to walk across the fields to the station and the milk train that left a little before six. And she would be there at the bothy gate to surprise him; to walk with him, her hand in his, saying all the things they should have said and hadn't, and all the time watching the sky lighten to the east over the Pike.

The room was cold and she wrapped her shawl around her, pacing the room slowly, softly, that she might keep awake. Her eyelids felt heavy; her eyes pricked as if they were full of dust. She clucked impatiently. The room was too bright. Reaching for the matches, she lit the candle that stood beside her bed then, snapping off the light, she pulled her chair to the window to wait.

She had not meant to fall asleep and when, next morning, Tom looked up at her window as he closed the bothy gate, there was only a flickering of candlelight to bless him on his way.

'So long, my lovely lass,' he whispered. 'Take care of yourself.'

For the first time since his childhood his eyes filled with tears. He was glad she was not there to see them.

Christmas was a quiet one that year. Rowangarth was in mourning again, so it had to be. No one said, 'Happy

Christmas.' Even those in Holdenby village lucky enough to have sons and husbands at home didn't go about with smiling faces, for there was little to be glad about.

On the Western Front, the intense cold had done nothing to slow down the fighting; casualty lists in the morning papers were so upsetting, Cook declared, that if things got any worse she would refuse to open another newspaper till peace came.

Food was becoming harder to get. Sugar and margarine had to be queued for now, and the shopkeepers had had neither sight nor smell of a keg of butter since the summer. Food, Cook said, ought to be on official ration, then everyone would get fair shares and a soldier's wife have her entitlement at a price she could afford to pay.

Now, like Julia's, Alice's days were regulated by the thrice daily knock of the postman. Every day she wrote to Tom; most days there was a letter from him. Yesterday's letter had made her laugh.

Imagine, he wrote, *today I learned how to load a rifle and clean it*.

Ha! Trying to tell Tom about guns. As daft, almost, as trying to teach Mrs Shaw to boil an egg.

Yet when they had made a soldier of him, what then? France, would it be, and the trenches? Tom had no say in his destiny now. For as long as the war lasted, he was a name and number: he had ceased to be a person – a real person – the day he signed his name at the recruiting office in Creesby.

Alice gave her full attention to the letter she was writing, the special Christmas Day letter, telling him how much she loved him, how much she longed to see him. And she told him how things were changing now, with all Rowangarth's young men gone and Bess and Mary doing war work in a factory in Leeds.

They had visited, not long ago; each of them wearing the new, shorter coats and smart hats and gloves of softest leather. Very prosperous, they'd looked, except that their fingernails were beginning to turn yellow and the whites of their eyes the colour of saffron, Cook said. And who, Tilda demanded when they had left to catch the motor bus back to Leeds, was going to fall in love with a girl who'd gone a peculiar shade of yellow and looked like her cousin Maud who'd once been so badly with jaundice she'd all but died of it?

'That'll be all from you, miss,' Cook retorted sharply. Tilda Tewk was getting a mite above herself now she'd been promoted to housemaid and Jinny Dobb brought in to do the kitchen work. Though Jin was glad of it, since there was no one in the bothy now for her to look after.

But Cook was fast losing patience with the war. She'd be dead and in her grave, she lamented, before both sides tired of it and filled in their trenches and took themselves back to homes they ought never to have left in the first place! She had brooded deeply and long in church that morning, the beauty of the Christmas gospel and the joy of carols lost to her. Mrs Shaw was becoming increasingly annoyed with a God who could, in her opinion, have stopped the fighting with the lifting of a finger.

Peace on earth, goodwill to men – whatever had happened to it?

Alice was glad that Christmas Day was almost over. It hadn't seemed right, sitting well-fed on roast pheasant when Tom and Davie and Will had dined off bully-beef and biscuits, like as not. The lads in the trenches fared even worse, she brooded, taking the long, heavy pins from her hair and letting it fall over her shoulders.

Yesterday, a letter had arrived from Tom and she had resisted the temptation to tear open the envelope, slipping it beneath her pillow to be saved for Christmas morning. And on this Christmas morning he missed her, loved her, wanted her. She closed her eyes and it was as if

453

he were saying the words. It had helped make the day bearable.

Now she would clean her teeth and brush her hair as if this had been an ordinary day. Then she would get into bed, relieved it was over, because there was no Christmas Day at the Front: men still fought and were killed. Wars didn't seem to stop just because a baby had been born and laid in a manger.

She drew back the curtains, gazing into a star-bright night, looking for the Christmas star – the one the Kings had followed to the stable.

It was there now, brighter than the rest, throbbing with light. Smiling, she reached for her Bible and opened it at the special place. St Luke, Chapter Two. It was still her favourite story and the buttercups were still there – all but the one she kept in her locket. They were no longer golden, but a reminder, still, of the first days of their loving.

Please take care of Tom? Alice raised her eyes to the star. *Don't let him be killed? Let him come home safely? Please? And let me see him – soon?*

Warmly wrapped, Alice watched the spaniel lumber off, nose down, yelping and snuffling in search of some new, adventurous scent. She lifted her face to the pale, winter sun. This was a clear day, a rare day; a day too good to be wasted thinking about war.

The morning had been sharply cold, the grass sparkling with silver hoar. Beyond the trees, the distant hilltops were white with snow that had fallen over a week ago and would lie unmelted until a spring wind blew from the south. Now it glistened under a cold sun, softening the craggy pike into beauty.

Alice walked carefully. The woodland paths were slippery from melted frost, though the sky was still brightly blue; a dazzling backcloth for the dark, winter-bare trees.

Trees were miracles, Tom said. You had to believe in God, he insisted, when you looked at a tree.

Tom. He sprang so easily to her thoughts. Always on her mind, in her heart. Loving him, missing him, wanting him always. She was incomplete without him. Even Brattocks Wood was different, now the chance delight of meeting him was gone.

Where are you, Tom? Are you wishing, like me, that the year to come will see an end to the war?

She pulled her muffler around her ears and over her mouth and nose. It was colder in Brattocks with the small warmth of the sun screened out by the undergrowth. And darker, too.

She called for Morgan and he came at once, skidding to a clumsy halt in the mud; yelping, whining, looking up with pleading eyes.

What had he found? Some creature, hurt and afraid, perhaps, cowering beneath a bush? She stood still, breath indrawn, eyes sliding from left to right. A poacher, maybe? Some man with a family to feed, seeking a game-bird for the pot?

The spaniel yelped again, running forwards, stopping, looking back.

Was he asking her to follow him? Did he want her to forsake the depths of the wood for Reuben's cottage, for that was where he was heading. And why was he standing on the doorstep, tail wagging, barking to be let in?

Alice began to run. Was Reuben ill, had a fall maybe? Oh, good dog, Morgan, to know it!

She knocked on the door, lifting the latch, calling his name.

'It's Alice. Are you all right? Where are you, Reuben?'

The dog pushed past her impatiently, throwing himself at the kitchen door, bounding inside. Then he set up such a barking that she was afraid, almost, to step inside.

'Well now – look who's here . . .'

Reuben was standing, back to the fire, puffing on his pipe. At his feet was a litter of - goodness gracious! A kitbag, a steel helmet, a knapsack! And, leaning in the corner, a rifle and –

'Hullo, bonny lass.'

Not Tom – it couldn't be! That stranger in khaki, holding wide his arms, it couldn't be him!

'Sweetheart!' He gathered her to him, and she wrapped her arms around his neck, laughing, crying, searching – eyes closed – for his lips. He smelled of new cloth; cloth rough beneath her fingertips.

'Say it's you?' She mustn't open her eyes for fear he would vanish. 'What are you doing here?'

'Come to see my girl. I was leaving all this kit with Reuben before I came looking for you. And before you ask it, they haven't given me leave. This is by way of being a two-hour detour.'

Two hours? Half a lifetime! She laughed out loud because she didn't believe any of it. These weren't Tom's arms around her nor Tom's lips on hers. It was all a dream. She had wanted him so much that he'd appeared out of the air and could just as easily vanish again.

'It *is* you?'

'It's me. I have to be in York at five, so let's hope the three-thirty from Holdenby is still running, or I'll be in trouble.'

'But how did you manage it?' She still had difficulty breathing; was still fearful her dream would end.

'My platoon sergeant – not a bad sort, really. I told him, when we could see Pendenys's tower, that my girl wasn't far away from there. Asked him if there was any chance of a stop-off. Didn't think he'd let me . . .'

'That was good of him, Tom.'

'Aye. Takes all sorts to make an army, I suppose. Anyway, he called to the driver to stop and told me that if I wasn't on that platform at York at five o'clock, he'd come looking for me himself and the angels would weep for me when he found me – or words to the same meaning,' Tom grinned.

'But how did you get here?'

'Made a beeline across the fields from the Great North Road – no trouble at all. Didn't expect you to walk in on me, though I'm glad you did. Saved a lot of time finding you. I'll have to be on my way in half an hour.'

'Walking to the station, are you?'

'Can't think of any other way to get there.' His cheeks were flushed from the warmth of the fire, his eyes bright with teasing.

'Then I'm coming with you. She'll let me, won't she, Reuben?' Miss Clitherow couldn't say no, could she? 'I'll run and ask her . . .'

'Don't you be running anywhere. I'll make it all right with that housekeeper woman – and Cook an' all. You stop yourself here, lass, and make Tom a slice of toast and dripping and a sup of tea, and I'll take that daft dog back for you – tell Sir Giles. Though that creature isn't so daft, come to think of it. He knew Tom was here . . .'

'He did – and you're a love, Reuben!' Alice kissed his cheek warmly. 'But what if she says it isn't all right?'

'I shouldn't worry overmuch about that,' he nodded. 'By that time you'll be well on your way to Holdenby. And if she gives you a telling-off when you get back – well, it'll have been worth it, to my way of thinking. So how about you seeing to that tea, and let's all drink it in front of the fire. It'll be a cold old walk to the station, in spite of the sun.'

'And a cold walk back for Alice. It'll be getting dark an' all,' Tom frowned. 'Can't say I like the idea of her coming back alone. Happen you'd best not come, sweetheart. Don't want anything happening to you.'

'I'll run like mad, Tom. I'll soon be back.'

'And just gone three, I'll set out to meet her; she'll be all right,' Reuben offered, comfortably. 'She'll not come to any harm.'

'That's settled, then!' Laughing, Alice set the teapot to warm. 'Oh, I don't believe any of this – I *don't*!'

Alice eyed Tom dubiously. He looked, she thought, like a packhorse, a beast of burden, weighed down with knapsack, kitbag, mess tins, groundsheet and ammunition pouches. But the one piece of his infantryman's equipment that worried her was the bag which contained his gas helmet. She'd seen pictures of those sinister-looking things that turned soldiers into monsters.

'Those gas helmets, Tom.' She looked with distaste at the bag, swinging as he walked. 'If they're really any good, why do men get gassed?'

'Because they don't get them on quick enough! Four seconds, it should take. They show us how. I can do it in three, so stop your worrying!'

'I love you, Tom.' There didn't seem anything else to say. 'I love you for tramping all that way just to be with me for a couple of hours.'

'I'd have come a lot further for a couple of *minutes*. You're my girl, aren't you?'

'I'm your girl, Tom. There'll never be anyone but you. We belong, remember.'

'So you'll think on about that when the train goes? You won't spoil that pretty face crying? I couldn't bear it if your cried . . .'

'I won't weep.' She wouldn't. Tom was going to be all right.

'Not if I tell you that I think we'll soon be in France?'

'Not even if –' She stopped, smiling. 'Kiss me, and I'll tell you something.'

She closed her eyes and lifted her mouth to his. And as their lips met such love of her raged through him that he wanted to take her in his arms and never, ever let them part him from her.

'So tell me, lass?' he said, linking her arm in his; walking on again.

'Well, there are two things, really. They happened to me and Miss Julia both. She hasn't told her ladyship and I oughtn't to be telling you. But remember that the doctor was to come on leave and didn't? Well, she got a letter about a week after. He said if his leave hadn't been cancelled he'd have been on that troopship that was sunk in the Channel.'

'The one Sir Robert was on?' Tom let out his breath in a whistle.

'The one. There'd have been two of them. It'd have been past bearing. Miss Julia said she would never complain again. Said it had been down to Fate, his leave being stopped; a sure sign he'd see the war out. She told me that now, when she wants him something unbearable, she reads that letter and is thankful . . .'

'And you, Alice?'

'It happened almost the same. I wished on the Christmas star; I always have, since I can remember. I know you aren't supposed to tell wishes, but it doesn't matter, now, because mine came true. I wished you'd come back to me – for me to see you, soon.'

And she told him everything, exactly as it had been, from her cheek in wanting to see him, right to the minute she had pushed open Reuben's front door.

'So you see, Tom,' she finished breathlessly, 'you being there was better than a sign – more like a miracle.'

'I reckon it was,' Tom conceded gravely, 'when you consider that the regiment is being moved by train from Richmond to Aldershot in two days' time. I was picked for the advance party – just a few of us sent by motor to York station, then to travel overnight to get the billets ready and the cookhouse set up. Suppose if it doesn't

459

qualify for a miracle, then it's a real bit of luck the driver took the route he did.'

'And don't forget that the sergeant let you off for a couple of hours. It was meant to be, Tom. You and the doctor; you'll both be all right. I know it.'

'Bonny, *bonny* lass. Do you know what a joy you are to me?'

'I do,' she smiled. 'And you won't worry overmuch, will you? What with those old rooks in Brattocks and that Christmas star, we shall end up together in Keeper's, just see if we don't. And you've still got that rabbit's foot, haven't you?'

'Still got it. Safe in my pocket.'

'Well, then . . .' Now, she thought, was the time to tell him. This winter-bright day when they were so happy was when she should share her secret. But would he want her to go to France, lie about her age? Would he want his girl in a ward full of soldiers?

'A penny for them, lass?'

'They're worth more'n a penny.' She swallowed hard. Now was *exactly* the time to tell him, and she couldn't! 'I – I'll take a kiss for them instead.' She reached up on tiptoe, closing her eyes as she always did when they kissed, then sighed, 'If you must know I – I was wondering what it would be like, you and me wed . . .'

For shame, Alice Hawthorn! You never meant to tell him! Not for a moment did you, for fear he'd forbid you to go; demand your word on it that you wouldn't!

'Were you, now?' He smiled, and her heart did a somersault. 'Take my word for it, it'll be wonderful – I promise it will – and well worth all the waiting. Now let's get a move on or I'll miss that train!'

'I love you, Tom,' she whispered, hurrying after him. *And I promise*, she vowed silently, *that for the rest of my life I'll never lie to you or deceive you again. But I need to do something to help win the war, and what you don't know about you can't worry over* . . . And weren't some lies – the white ones, and some deceits – the allowable ones, justified? She and Miss Julia were going to France, and nothing must stand in their way. Not even a promise to Tom.

The sun was still shining; the sky still baby blue when the signal at the end of the platform fell with a thud and a rattle.

'Train's coming,' Alice whispered.

'Aye – and no tears, mind?'

'No tears.' Rooks and rabbits and Christmas stars would keep him safe.

'Kiss me, then, and say so-long.' He gathered her to him and his lips were hard on hers. 'I love you. Wait for me?'

'For as long as it takes . . .'

Her lips found his again. She wanted to cling to him and never let him go, but the stationmaster was calling to them to stand back.

'York!' he shouted. 'Next stop, York!'

Tom picked up his kit, throwing it piece by piece into the compartment. Then he pulled the door shut with a terrible finality, leaning through the open window for a last, brief kiss.

'I love you,' he whispered. 'Take care on the way home.'

'I will, and I love you. Look after yourself. I love you, love you . . .'

She stood there, waving, until the train had rounded the bend. She was still standing there when it was gone from her sight and all she could hear of it was a far-away hoot as it entered the long tunnel, half a mile down the track.

When shall I see you again, Tom? How long . . .?

But he would come back to her. He was coming home safe and sound and however long it took didn't matter!

Head down, she began to run. Reuben would have set out already to meet her and she musn't be late. And goodness only knew what Miss Clitherow would say when she got back; taking the best part of an afternoon off without so much as a by-your-leave!

But Tom *would* be all right. Her love would keep him safe – and the Christmas wish and the rabbit's foot and the rooks.

So why was she weeping? Why the great, choking sobs and tears that tasted salt on her lips? *Why?*

26

1916

Helen could no longer bring herself to read what she had come to look upon as the death column, for now it was no longer a column but a page – *pages* – of wasted lives. Young men killed in action; husbands, brothers, fathers, sons. When Robert died, she had determined never to read it again, though she would still pray each night for all the lost souls, and that their women might find the courage to accept what they were powerless to change. But read it in the papers she would not. Soon, when the Military Service bill became law, there would be even more men called to the colours and even more killing and maiming and blinding.

Yesterday saw the bill passed in Parliament. Mr Asquith had had his way, and now every unmarried man between nineteen and thirty would be called to fight. After all the conjecture, conscription was a fact and, in years to come, when the war was nothing but a bitter memory, it would be considered unthinkable – something to be ashamed of, in fact – never to have fought.

Now, in just one week, her second son was going to war, and after him, her daughter: Rowangarth would be a sad, lonely place. If she let it; if she gave in to self-pity and shut herself off from everything; if she wept and bemoaned her loss and wore her black until the autumn . . .

It was the fault, she thought almost angrily, of the old Queen. Victoria had made mourning fashionable, a religion almost. She it was who refused consolation after the death of her Consort; had taken to widow's weeds with maudlin pleasure. And thereafter, her subjects had done the same. Public mourning became a way of life.

But Queen Victoria was long gone, and her son too, Helen thought with sudden defiance. Now her grandson was King, and the Empire the old woman had once ruled over like a distant, doting mother had taken on a fight to the death. The Empire, Britain – Holdenby and Rowangarth too – were at war, and there could be no time for public mourning. Grief must become a private thing, not something to be paraded and wallowed in! Helen's elder son had given his life – had been killed – for his country, and enough was enough! There was work, *war* work, to be done, wood to be brought in to eke out the coal; the green and perfect lawns around Rowangarth to be ploughed up and planted with potatoes. And there were people to be comforted and the elderly who couldn't queue for food to be fed.

'Julia!' she said so loudly, so decisively, that her daughter jumped visibly. 'I am going to find war work!'

'But, dearest, you already do your bit.' Julia laid down her pen. 'Perhaps when you come out of mourning –'

'I am out of mourning – public mourning, that is!' She felt quite light-headed, but it had to be said. 'Don't you realize that bereaved women are making munitions, heaving coal, working as railway porters? They have to, because the widow's pension that the army pays won't feed and clothe their children! They can't wear black and retire from living, so how dare I?

'Oh, I shall never forgive this war for taking Robert.' She paused, taking a long, trembling breath. 'But that is between me and my son. It is private. Wearing mourning, cutting myself off, won't lessen my despair, nor bring him back. So I shall visit Pendenys. I shall put on some stout shoes and walk there, across the fields.'

'But why must you?'

'Because we have no coachman and no horses. The

exercise will do me good and it isn't far. And there is something I must learn to do for the war effort – you must teach me to harness the pony into the cart. I must be able to drive myself about.'

'But I can drive you to Uncle Edward's. You only need ask.'

'And when you are gone, Julia? Do I stay within these four walls? Or maybe I should learn to ride a bicycle?'

'Mother! You simply can't do that!'

'*Can't?* I see. It is too undignified for a middle-aged lady to be seen pedalling along the roads?'

'It would be a great deal more undignified were you to fall off,' Julia chuckled. 'I don't suppose it's any use suggesting you buy a motor?' It made sense. Alone at Rowangarth, her mother would be virtually isolated. 'Aunt Sutton wouldn't be without hers.'

'No motors here,' Helen said flatly.

'Very well. I'll see to the pony and drive you to Pendenys.'

'No! I shall drive myself there. I'll take the back lane – it's very quiet. I'm not entirely helpless!'

'Just so long as you'll be all right. You're sure, now?'

'I am *not* sure.' Briefly, Helen's defiance flagged. 'But we are at war and it is time I too joined in – *really* joined in. It is everyone's fight, and the sooner I learn to manage the pony and cart, the better!'

'But you've never driven yourself. Are you sure you can cope?'

'I'm sure. Or I will be, by the time I get back. Now be off with you, *please* . . .'

'Milady!' gasped Pendenys's butler, eyes wide.

'Good morning,' Helen smiled brightly. 'Be so kind as to have someone see to my pony.'

'Of course. At once.' He held wide the door. 'I will inform Mrs Sutton you are here.'

'Please don't bother.' Helen hurried past him. Clemmy was always in the morning-room between ten and eleven – her at-home time – and if it was unforgivable to walk in on her unannounced, then so be it. There was so much to be done that Helen no longer had any time for niceties. Tomorrow, heaven only knew how she would feel; in a week's time, when Giles left for Salisbury, she might even feel suicidal; but today she was angry with the war and intended to do something about it.

'Clemmy!' Hands outstretched, she greeted her brother-in-law's wife. 'Forgive me for arriving unannounced, but I need your help.'

'My dear!' Clementina's mouth sagged open. The very last person she had expected was Helen, a stickler for etiquette, and her in mourning until November! 'My help?'

'Yes, indeed. There comes a time, I told myself not an hour ago, when enough is enough!'

'But you should have telephoned. I'd have come at once, if you needed me.'

'I thank you, Clemmy, but all at once I am weary of wearing mourning and have become very angry with the war. I intend to find more to occupy me. I shall do war work.'

'*War* work?' Agitated, Clementina settled her caller in a chair. 'But you are in mourning.'

'I am.' Helen's voice faltered only slightly. 'But that is between Robert and myself and will not end when I come out of my black in the autumn. I believe there is a hospital you work for. I, too, would like to offer my help.'

'But, Helen, it is not the place for a lady.' Denniston House, did she mean? 'And I don't exactly work there. I organize events and gatherings and raise money for comforts for the wounded there. But I couldn't *work* at Denniston House.'

'Why not, pray?' Helen nodded her thanks for the cup of tea Clementina had shakily poured. 'Is it a fever hospital – an isolation hospital?'

'No, but it is full of wounded – in all kinds of distress. Some of them quite awful to look at, I believe. Burns, you know. And some of them with no arms, no legs. Many have lost their sight . . .'

'Then that makes me all the more determined! I can read to the blind soldiers or write their letters. Perhaps those who can't see will be glad of a chat. So will you telephone the matron, Clementina? You know her. Will you ask her if I can be a hospital visitor?'

'Very well – since you seem set on it. But I hope you know what you are doing,' Clementina sighed, wondering what had come over Helen that she must visit wards which were quite awful. And she'd heard that the smell could be quite terrible at times. 'Have you given any consideration to what people will think, what they might say?'

'If helping the wounded causes comment, then I'd be most surprised. But I care little what anyone thinks or says, Clemmy. Suddenly, I decided to do something about the state I was in, and I know that Robert would approve. That is good enough for me. Giles will soon be leaving, and Julia intends to take up driving. I shall be alone with my thoughts then, you see, and it simply wouldn't do. You *will* help me?'

'Completely out of character,' Clementina said to her husband when Helen had left. 'Visiting at Denniston House, I mean. It isn't even a proper hospital – just a house the army took over.'

'It's Blighty to a lot of wounded men, Clemmy. And I think it admirable that Helen wants to help.'

'Well, I *don't*,' she sniffed. 'In fact, I think it a little – *eccentric* to want to expose herself to such terrible sights.'

'Those terrible sights were whole men before they went to war, my dear.'

'Take her side – you usually do!' No use complaining to Edward about Helen-who-could-do-no-wrong! Yet to Clementina's way of thinking, her sister-in-law was acting most peculiarly; a woman who, because of her birth, could get away with anything. Let the daughter of an Ironmaster do the same, and she was reverting to type! Clogs to clogs in three generations, people would say!

Life was very unfair!

'Don't see me off – please?' Giles Sutton had asked his mother. 'Just give me a hug and a kiss and wave to me from the door, just as you did when Robert and I were going back to school.'

'Very well, if that's the way you want it.'

He was right, of course. Partings had never been her strongest suit, though it wouldn't be a parting – not quite yet. Giles would be given leave when his training was over. He wouldn't – couldn't – be sent to France until the summer at least. And by summer the war might well be over, because in spite of all the money being wasted on developing tanks, she had great faith that once the inventors and engineers could make them work properly, those lumbering monsters could prove to be the turning point of the war – and Mr Churchill thought so too!

Now that time had come. Giles's case stood on the top step, and Julia was leading the pony and trap through the stableyard archway. Helen distanced herself from it; stood apart and watched as she would watch actors on a stage. And she would stand there, smiling and waving until they were out of sight, exactly as she had done when the boys were little and John had driven them to the railway station in his latest, newest motor, their school trunks strapped on the back. Nothing to get upset about, she insisted; she had done this before many times: only then she had known they would always come home to her.

'Giles was in splendid spirits when I saw him off,' Julia smiled as they sat that evening in the winter-parlour. 'He seemed very confident, as if he knew he'd do all right. He's sure he'll get leave before they send him to France – if they send him, that is.'

'But I thought . . .' Helen frowned. Of course Giles would go to France. 'Where else are stretcher-bearers needed?'

'In every army hospital in these islands and at railway stations meeting hospital trains and on hospital ships,' Julia supplied, recognizing her mother's need for comfort. 'Nurses don't carry big heavy men around, you know.'

'Perhaps not . . .' Helen lapsed into silence, remembering their last minutes together.

'You are not to worry, dearest . . .' He'd always called her dearest, even as a small boy. 'I know I shall be all right. I'm not worried – truly.' He had cupped her face in his hands and gently kissed her closed eyelids. 'I'm more worried about Morgan. You'll see he's looked after, won't you?'

'Morgan!' Helen gasped now. 'Oh dear – I'd quite forgotten the poor animal. He'll be all alone in the library. Has he been fed, do you think?'

'He's fed at midday – Giles will have seen to it before he went. And he has biscuits morning and night.' Julia jumped to her feet. 'I'd better ask Hawthorn. She usually takes him out. Giles probably arranged it all with her.'

'Hawthorn mustn't take him out at night – not in the dark, alone,' Helen warned.

'All right. If that's what you want. But Morgan is devoted to her. She'll be safe enough with him. Look at the way he went for Elliot: I do so wish I'd seen it!'

469

'Julia! For shame! It was a dreadful experience for the poor girl!'

'I know. But I still wish I'd seen Elliot getting his comeuppance, especially when Dwerryhouse blacked his eye!'

'It all seems a long time ago,' Helen sighed. Robert was safe in India then, and Giles seeing to the books in the library. And Julia, of course, newly, blissfully in love.

'Those days will come back again – well, almost,' Julia said softly. 'Now you're not to get upset. Giles said you weren't to.'

'I won't.' Tonight, she would include Giles especially in her prayers, then leave it all to God. 'Off you go and see if the animal is all right. Maybe someone should let him out for a few minutes . . .'

'Hawthorn and I will take him out. And afterwards, maybe, I'll bring him back here. He'll like it, sprawled in front of the fire, and he's quite well-behaved these days.'

'It's all right, miss,' Alice said. They stood in the shelter of the stableyard gates as the spaniel sniffed and snuffled into every corner, searching for his master. 'Cook will save him kitchen scraps like always and a drop of gravy, and I'll see to his biscuits and his airings. I promised Mr Giles he'd be all right. And I told him I wouldn't stray out of sound of the house at night, so tell her ladyship there isn't any need for her to worry about me – you neither, Miss Julia.'

'I'm not. I'm here because I particularly want to see you and there hasn't been a minute, today, with Giles going off. Have you heard from Tom yet?'

'Not a word.' Not for nearly a week, which could only mean he was on his way to France.

'I'm sorry, Hawthorn. Keep writing to him, though. Your letters will catch up with him eventually. Letters are important to a soldier – especially when he's –'

'At the Front,' Alice finished.

'Well . . . yes. Look, have you thought any more about taking up nursing?'

'Times like this, miss, when there's no word from Tom, I think of little else.'

'Then did you know that women are allowed to drive ambulances in France, now? It was in the paper. Just a small piece and mother didn't see it, thank goodness.' Her mother hardly ever picked up a newspaper, these days. 'It's the First Aid Nursing Yeomanry – that's what Aunt Sutton is in. She'd help me, I know she would. I realize it isn't possible to rush off and leave mother just yet, but I want to go to London as soon as I can; ask Aunt Sutton to put feelers out for me – to go to France, that is.' Nowhere but France. 'Are you still game to come along?'

'Be a nurse? That I am! If they don't go poking and prying too much . . .'

'Then leave it all to me. *Morgan!*' She placed her fingers in her mouth and sent out a piercing whistle. 'Come here, you silly dog! Come here *at once!*'

'Go to London? Why not? I thought you might have gone there before Christmas . . .'

'I thought about it, Mother, but I –'

'But you didn't, because of Robert?'

'Something like that. I'd like to go, though – fairly soon if that's all right with you?'

'Of course it is. I intend to be very busily occupied. There is the sewing-circle and the sock-knitting, and the elderly to call on. And I start my visiting at Denniston House on Monday.'

Julia closed her eyes, lulled by the insistent clacking of train wheels, thinking how easy it had been to get away. Once, she could hardly have left the house without a chaperon or a maid to walk with her. Now, chaperons were a thing of those past gentler days and there were fewer maids to accompany young women like her; there'd be fewer still at Rowangarth if Hawthorn managed to get away.

She looked at the watch on her lapel. The train would be late arriving at King's Cross: held up by a troop train and a hospital train, both of which were given priority. She hoped to be able to get a taxi. London was a city of dimmed lights and unlit shop windows now, and to leave her cases at the station and walk to Montpelier Mews didn't bear thinking about. Because of the war, motor buses were few and far between at night, and the army's need of horses had severely cut back the trams. Nor could Aunt Sutton be expected to meet her with the motor. Petrol was hard to come by for civilians, and what could be had cost ten shillings a gallon.

But she would manage. She would have to. Crossing London unaided was nothing compared to going alone to France. A long time ago she had accepted that the life she had known – the safeness and gentleness of it – was gone for ever. Best she should accept it.

Five o'clock, she sighed. She wouldn't be in London until seven at the very earliest. Three hours late . . .

'That was the best cup of tea I've had in ages, Figgis,' Julia smiled at the elderly servant. 'Now I feel human again.'

'You're sure you don't want a meal?' Anne Lavinia Sutton offered. 'There's soup, if you do, and cold meat.'

'Thanks, Aunt, but Cook packed me sandwiches and apples for the train. It was a hot drink I was in need of. Such a journey!'

'Thought you'd changed your mind; decided not to come. But I might have known you would. It's really all about getting to France, isn't it? Is it the wounded you are thinking about, or is it yourself?' she demanded. 'Are you sure you're not rushing willy-nilly to get to your husband by any means at all; acting like a lovesick milkmaid, are you?'

'No, I'm not! How could you think such a thing?' Her aunt didn't change. Blunt to the point of rudeness still. 'I'm not being selfish. I'm just sick of waiting about, wishing the war over. I want to roll up my sleeves and help. Everyone is helping now, though –' she looked directly into her aunt's eyes – 'if I were to meet up with Andrew, it would be a wonderful bonus. And you can't blame me for wanting that?'

'Good! A bit of sense at last! And you want me to help you?'

'Please, Aunt? Mother knows about it, so you needn't worry. I don't think she wants me to go, but she understands that I need to. And I'd thought that since women can drive ambulances now, in France, maybe you could use your influence to get me in?'

'Be a Fanny, you mean?'

'If that's what they're called – yes. I saw in the newspaper that women of the First Aid Nursing Yeomanry have been driving in France since the New Year. I would like to go too.'

'Just like that, eh? Your Aunt Sutton snaps her fingers and makes it all right? Put another piece of coal on the fire – *one* piece, child. Coal's worse to come by in London than petrol! And what do you say to a sniff of brandy? Getting a bit short on supplies now. Should have stocked up more, but who'd ever have thought it would come to this?' she said sadly. 'I ache for France, you know. Wish I were young and strong like you. Nothing would have stopped me going.'

'And I want to go too, but for different reasons,' Julia murmured, selecting a piece of coal, positioning it carefully. 'You know I can drive quite well. With a few more lessons I'd be good at it. And you said you teach women to drive – why can't I be one of them?'

'You could, like a shot, if I thought it'd do any good. But there are more drivers than ambulances, and that's a sad fact. Motor ambulances are in short supply as yet. Thank the good Lord for horses. At least there's no shortage of them. But women don't drive horse-drawn ambulances; they just don't. You'll have to take your turn. There's a long queue of young women waiting for an ambulance. If you want to get out there, you'd do better to be a nurse. Far better you go for the Voluntary Aid Detachment. The VAD is crying out for nurses – or couldn't you stand the sight of blood?'

'Seems I don't have a lot of choice, and I'm not put off by blood,' she shrugged. 'I just want to help. Hawthorn wants to be a nurse; we could go together. I thought being a driver would get me there more quickly, that's all.'

'Oh, dearie me – if it's getting there quickly you're after, then I'm afraid . . .' The elderly woman offered a brandy glass. 'Sip it slowly. Lord knows when there'll be any more of the good stuff. World gone mad,' she murmured, nose in glass.

'What do you mean, afraid?' Agitated, Julia jumped to her feet. 'Red tape, do you mean?'

'I mean that Julia Sutton can't clap her pretty hands and demand to be in France the moment she thinks fit. You'll first have to do probation in a hospital here at home, and there'll be nursing and first-aid exams to be taken *and passed* before you can even begin to think of an overseas posting.'

'I see, Aunt,' she murmured, her eyes all at once grave. 'Forgive me, but Julia *Sutton* is no more, nor is the world she lived in and thought would last for ever. But Julia MacMalcolm is altogether a different person. And it's sad that we can't go at once, but we'll have to accept it. The sooner we get started, the sooner we'll be there,

I suppose. So when can we begin, and where? Oh, and there's a complication: Hawthorn isn't twenty-one.'

'How old? Twenty?'

'She will be, in June. But it would only be a small deceit – a white lie. And perhaps they won't even bother to ask . . .?'

'They'll *ask* all right, but if she tells them she's old enough – adds a year on – I very much doubt they'll check up on her, especially if she's given good references. You'll both of you need a character reference, you realize that? I could give one to Hawthorn – say that in my opinion she would make a splendid VAD nurse. Or your mama could do it . . .'

'No! I'm sure Hawthorn would be pleased to have you, Aunt, though I suppose family wouldn't count in my case. I'd have to ask Judge Mounteagle, I suppose.' She gave a little laugh. 'Imagine having to ask someone to vouch for me – a Sutton!'

'Your cousin Elliot is a Sutton.' Anne Lavinia pulled down the corners of her mouth, 'and I wouldn't give him a good name for all the horses in the Camargue!'

'Then you'll back Hawthorn up – say she's old enough?'

'The dickens I will! But I won't go out of my way to say that she *isn't*!'

'Bless you. That's settled then!' Julia raised her glass. 'Let's drink to us being nurses – and an end to the war!' Oh, *please*, a speedy end to it, and the troops safely home.

'Amen to that. And I think that tonight we might just spare another lump or two for the fire. Now, where shall you begin your training? Here, in London, or shall you ask Clementina to get you into that hospital of hers? I don't suppose it matters much where you start.'

'Suppose not. What matters, really, is where we end up. And it isn't Aunt Clemmy's hospital, it's her pet charity. She organizes things for it. It's called Denniston

475

House, and Mother visits there. She started last Monday and she reads to the blind soldiers and writes letters for them.

'Mother actually helps at first hand. Aunt Clemmy won't step inside the place if she can help it; wouldn't be seen dead there. Oh, dear! That was a terrible thing to have said. Me and my silly mouth. So sorry . . .'

'Hm. That's one thing you'll have to learn to keep a check on – that sudden Sutton temper of yours. You're going to have to learn what it's like to put your tongue in your cheek and take orders. And you'll have to mind what you say to sick and wounded men. If you don't, Julia, you won't pass your exams, and you can say goodbye to nursing and France for ever.'

'I know that, but I have been a much better person since I met Andrew and I'll try, I really will. Word of a Sutton.'

'Of course you will.' In a rare demonstration of affection, Anne Sutton hugged her niece to her. 'I *know* you will. It's just that it's going to take you a little longer than you thought to get to that husband of yours.'

'By summer, do you think?'

'That's more like it. If all goes well, you could be there by July.'

'And how was London, Julia, my dear?'

'Different, Aunt Clemmy. Gloomy at night and getting drab, somehow. But you'll know that for yourself, having a house there now.'

No use telling her that London seemed drab because Andrew was no longer there. Only Mrs Sparrow, at the Little Britain lodgings, and only ghosts of past lovers in Hyde Park.

'London is – *different*,' Clementina Sutton acknowledged. It was less restrained in some ways, but socially – the socializing she had hoped to find when she bought the

Cheyne Walk house – it was completely lacking. Everyone who was anyone was taken up, one way or another, with the war. Finding a husband, once the most important consideration in a girl's life, now took second place to war work: the licence it had given young ladies to do the most unimaginable things! Even Julia, who'd said on the telephone that she intended to be a VAD nurse. Not content with marrying beneath her, she now seemed set on a course that could only end in disaster.

'I had a letter from Nathan,' Julia smiled. 'It was waiting for me when I got back from London. He's well, though busy. He seemed happy, too.'

'Happy I'm not sure about, but busy – yes, I can well imagine that. It surprises me how the working classes turn to God when they think they are in trouble.'

'So would I, Aunt. If I were in a foxhole,' Julia said with the candid gaze so like that of her mother, 'being shelled and machine-gunned. I'd sure as anything want God in there with me.'

'Tut!' Clementina forced a smile. 'But what was it you said on the telephone about nursing at Denniston House?'

'I believe you know the matron – will you ask her? We want to go nursing, you see, but we must first be probationers and take exams. Aunt Sutton wondered if it might not be best for us to go to one of the London hospitals and use Andrew's lodgings as a base. But after Robert – and with Giles not long gone away – I thought it would be kinder to Mother if we were to start our training hereabouts. The nearest military hospital is Denniston House, so could you ask the matron if she would take us – *please*?'

'But my dear child, I don't know the matron. We speak, of course, when there is some matter of charity to discuss, but I'm not at all sure if I could place myself under an obligation by asking a favour of her. And who, will you tell me, is *we*? Who else is going nursing with you?'

'Hawthorn, our sewing-maid. Her young man is on his way to the Front, she thinks. We both want to do our bit.'

'Hawthorn?' *That* one? The little innocent who had been the cause of so much upset. Hob-nobbing with her betters now. Was there no end to her impudence? And what was Helen thinking about to allow it? 'I see. And does your mama know about it? Has she consented to – '

'*Consented*, Aunt? I am of age and a married woman. I don't need parental approval for anything I do. But since you ask – no, Mother doesn't know that Hawthorn intends to be a nurse, but I'm sure she'll miss her when she goes.'

'Very well. I shall speak to the matron at Denniston House about you both.' Oh my word, yes! Tell her what a little troublemaker she'd be getting if she took in the servant. Or should she maybe just *hint*?

'Thank you, Aunt Clemmy.' Best not mention Hawthorn's age. It would be just like her aunt to tell on her. 'It's really good of you.' She rose from her seat in the window, walking to the sofa-table, picking up Nathan's photograph. 'Doesn't he look handsome in his uniform? I hope he'll soon be sending a photograph to Rowangarth too. Aren't you so very proud of him?'

'I am proud of *both* my sons,' came the instant reply. 'And doubtless Nathan – Elliot, too – will be sending pictures of themselves to your mama. You know,' she looked down at her fingers, almost coyly, 'your uncle and I used to hope that one day you and Nathan – '

'Would marry?' Julia finished. 'I must say he's very dear to me, but we've always been more like brother and sister than cousins. Same with Giles. He and Nathan were almost like twins; born only weeks apart, as well you know. But I didn't even once think of Nathan as a husband. I like him too much – and, that's a stupid thing to say, though you know what I mean!

478

'But I've already taken up too much of your time. Can I telephone the matron and ask her if she will see us? Can I tell her that my aunt will vouch for us both? Can I, please?'

Put like that, Clementina though wryly as she stood at the window, watching her niece pedal her bicycle most expertly up the carriage drive, what chance did she have to refuse?

And maybe, she thought, Julia would have been altogether too much of a tomboy for Nathan, and certainly little use as the wife of an Anglican vicar.

Perhaps, in the penniless doctor, she had found her true match?

27

Julia's brief apprehension about her future as a nurse was quickly gone. Not only was the matron at Denniston House kindly and sympathetic; she had also been trained at St Bartholomew's, where Andrew had worked. The coincidence was an omen, Julia decided, a good omen. She relaxed at once.

'Very well, young ladies,' smiled the white-haired woman who now had Julia's complete trust and affection, 'I think you might do well as probationers, though the matter does not entirely rest with me. You must now meet Sister Tutor. It is she who has the final say. Her standards are high and you will come to realize that being a VAD nurse is much, much more than a patriotic whim.

'It demands complete dedication and can often be distressing. But it is rewarding. The sick and wounded in your care depend on you. Some even think of their nurses as angels. Can you live up to being angels, do you think? More important – can you convince Sister Carbrooke?'

She rose to her feet, holding out a hand to each in turn.

'I'll try my best, Matron,' said Julia breathlessly, 'and thank you.'

'Yes. Thank you, I'm sure.' Alice, overawed, bobbed a curtsey.

'That Sister Carbrooke's going to be an unholy terror,' she said flatly that night as she sat with Cook and Tilda at the kitchen table.

'Ward sisters is all the same.' Jinny Dobb poured hot milk into the cocoa jug. 'Best neither of you upset her or she'll make your lives a misery. Afore she's finished with

480

you, she'll make you wish you'd never joined, and it'll be too late then.'

'No, Jin. Nothing is final till we've done our training. That's when we sign on, Matron told us.'

'Then be careful what you put your name to,' Tilda offered, obliged to warn them they could be signing themselves into white slavery if they weren't careful.

'It'll be all right. Nurses sign for a year – a contract, sort of. When I've done that year, I sign on again if I want to. And if they want me,' she added dubiously.

'Can't say fairer than that.' The pair of them were set on going to France, Cook brooded, and a year might be all they could stand of it if what she'd heard was true. 'So when will you be going?'

'Don't rightly know. We got as far as filling in the forms.' Alice squirmed inside just to think about it – the date of her birth, that was – and how she had added on a year without so much as a blush. 'We had to give the names of two people who would vouch for our good character. In the end, it'll all depend on that, I suppose.'

'Referees, they're called,' Cook obliged. 'And who did you give, then?'

'Her ladyship, and Miss Sutton in London. Miss Julia gave Judge Mounteagle and Doctor James, him having brought her into the world.'

'You can't do better than a lady of title and a judge,' Jin said comfortably, 'and since it isn't likely you'd be daft enough to give names of folk as would say wicked things about you, I reckon you'll be all right. But best I take a look at your hand afore you go, Alice lass, to make sure you're forewarned.'

'Oooh . . .' Tilda beamed, for when Jin was in the mood and the 'fluence running, she would read any palm thrust at her.

'Next full moon.' Jin didn't hold with fortune-telling at any other time. 'I'll give you all a read, if you like.'

481

'Miss Julia as well,' Alice demanded.

'No. *Not* Miss Julia.' Palm reading and such-like was only for the lower orders as far as Jin was concerned. 'And you'd best not mention it in front of Miss Clitherow, neither, or I'll be out on me ear!' With her promotion from bothy to big house, Jin considered she had fallen on her feet. She ate better, despite the shortages, and looking after the gentry was easier than cooking for apprentice lads and washing their shirts and bedding, though God Himself knew she would forsake her life of ease this minute if things could be as they were and the killing ended. For how many of those apprentices would return to Rowangarth, no one knew, and of the lucky ones who did, none would be lads any longer. 'Ah, well. Best be off home. See you all in the morning,' she beamed, throwing her shawl over her head.

They did not ask her if she would be all right on the walk over, nor if she should take the candlelamp to light her way to the end almshouse – Reuben's house it should have been, thought Alice sadly.

'Careful how you go, Jin,' Cook called.

'She'll be all right.' Tilda carried the empty cups to the sinkstone. 'That one can see in the dark, just like a cat.' Like a witch's cat . . .

. . . so you see, my darling. I am now committed. Nothing will stop my becoming a nurse – except my own stupidity, that is, and I intend not to fail. I didn't tell you before because I feared you would forbid it, but on seeing the wards today at Denniston House, I am prepared to risk your disapproval. Those soldiers are terribly wounded – some blinded – and I want very much to care for them. If all goes well, Hawthorn and I will report to the Barracks Hospital at York for two weeks' training and to be given our uniforms. Then we shall return to Denniston House for the rest of our probation.

Perhaps you never saw Denniston, but if you stood on Holdenby Pike, looking towards Pendenys, then a little to your right, you would see the place. It was empty and neglected when war started; now it holds fifty beds. Sleeping accommodation for nurses there is in short supply, so Hawthorn and I will sleep at Rowangarth and bicycle to the hospital every day. I rather imagine that Aunt Clemmy arranged it for us, but it doesn't matter where we sleep.

Please be proud of me, my love? I do so want your approval. And isn't it good for a doctor's wife to be a nurse? Think what a help I shall be to you when the war is over and we are together again . . .

Julia laid down her pen and read carefully what she had written. She had decided not to tell Andrew about her intention to be an ambulance driver. She had thought then that she could be in France in a matter of weeks and present him with her *fait accompli*. But it hadn't turned out like that, and she knew she could not keep quiet about her nursing training for the next six months; nor did she want to.

Tonight, more than ever, I want you with me. I long to sleep in your arms, though the way I feel now, I would settle for a glimpse of your dear face – and perhaps just one kiss . . .

She would. She had no pride left now. She wanted him with a need that thrashed like a pain inside her. Even if he were to send a telegram forbidding it, nothing would change. She had no illusions about nursing now. The tight-lipped Sister Carbrooke had seen to that. The work would be hard and at times dangerous. So be it. It was the price she must pay to be nearer to Andrew, and besides, all at once, caring for the wounded was what she wanted to do; even had she never met Andrew, she would want it. A ward at Denniston House had been her road to Damascus. A young soldier, his eyes bandaged, had put

483

out a hand as they passed and said, 'Nurse?' And Sister had gone to him and taken his searching hand in her own and said softly, 'What is it?'

Nothing to make a fuss about, but Sister's slab face had softened into gentleness even as she spoke, and that one small act of compassion had made her want to weep as she watched; had made her feel, in one blinding second, that to be a nurse was all she had ever wanted.

Goodnight, my dearest dear. I send you all my love – reach out and gather it to you. I want you so very, very much. God keep you safely.

Your Julia.

Jin Dobb was nobody's fool, thought Alice, as she hugged her bed warmer to her. Sister Carbrooke would indeed need to be watched.

'And how old are you, Miss Hawthorn?' Her gimlet eyes had met and challenged Alice's.

'Gone twenty. I'll be of age come June. It's me nose, Sister . . .'

Sister Tutor, they had come to realize before ever the tour of the hospital was half over, was a stickler for cleanliness and a strong believer in carbolic. Carbolic soap, carbolic disinfectant and Keating's carbolic powder for the banishing of fleas, she had stressed.

'Fleas. Some are covered with them when they come to us. Uniforms *alive* with them . . .'

'But, Sister – they come all the way from the trenches without – '

'Without being cleaned up? Ha! A dressing, if they're lucky, is all some of them get! They do what they can at the front,' she had acknowledged, loyal to her own, 'and I'll admit that conditions are improving out there. By summer there'll be more field hospitals – the wounded will get attention more quickly. That's where you'll both be going: if you satisfy me, that is, that you're up to it!'

'A *field* hospital, Sister?' Alice had frowned.

'Tents!' The reply had been derisive. 'Though I understand a lot of them will have been replaced by huts before another winter. Well, there's a limit to the number of houses they can requisition. Got to put the poor men somewhere . . .'

'You mean there are so many wounded they must put them in huts and *tents*?' Julia's disbelief had been genuine.

'I mean just that! You won't just be fighting the enemy – and by that I mean near-hopeless conditions – but you'll have cold and damp to put up with, and likely as not you'll have to tramp the length of a field just to wash yourselves. Are you up to it? Can you stick it?'

'I don't know, Sister,' Julia had whispered. 'But my husband has stuck it for a long time. He can't complain, so why should I?'

She had thrown back the challenge in true Sutton manner, and Alice had been hard put to it not to cry, 'Good for you, Miss Julia!' But instead, she had thought of Tom, wounded and flea-ridden. Tom Dwerryhouse with a dressing – if he were lucky – on a shattered limb, beginning the long, painful journey back to England.

'How do you know all this, Sister?' she had whispered.

'Because I spent a year there.' Sister's eyes had all at once been far away. 'And when my year here is up, I hope to go back.'

'My young man is out there,' Alice had said to no one in particular, because really she was making the most solemn vow of her life.

Somehow she would get to France; get there in spite of her missing year and childlike nose. And when she did, she wouldn't complain about cold or damp or washing in a field, because every wounded soldier she helped nurse would have as much of her caring and compassion as if they were Tom, and she would fetch and carry and scrub and clean and try never to be afraid.

'Is he out there now?'

'Y-yes. In the West Yorkshires. And I'll do my best, Sister, 'cos I reckon if I do, then some other nurse is going to be good to my Tom, if ever he's . . .' Her voice had trailed into silence as she had fought the tears she dared not allow. Just imagine Sister Carbrooke making mincemeat of a weeping nurse! The thought had steadied her; banished all thoughts of self-indulgence. 'If ever he's in need of nursing,' she had finished quietly.

'Where are you, Tom?' she whispered now into the darkness of her room. 'Are you in France?'

Was he there, already being shelled and shot at; in a trench and unable to let her know? A man didn't take pencil and paper and write to his young lady, did he, not in a fox-hole? 'Keep him safe, God,' she pleaded, 'and make me a good nurse and oh, don't ever let them find out I'm not old enough to go to France . . .'

At the dressing-station forward from the rear trenches, Andrew MacMalcolm shrugged into his greatcoat, nodding to his relief. A few yards away waited the motor transport that would take him back to his bed and the sleep he had been praying for.

Sleep. It made life bearable. He struggled on, thinking of blessed sleep. It helped him ignore the stench of putrefying wounds; to shut out the misery. He had become a doctor because of the injustice of his parents' deaths, yet by contrast they had died in the comparative luxury of a clean bed and with a warm handclasp to help their first uneasy steps into death.

Yet, in this hell-hole, many died afraid and without dignity; died impaled on barbed wire out of reach of help.

. . . hanging on the old barbed wire . . .

Words from the marching song drummed in his ears. How could a Tommy bear to sing it? Had they become so immune to all this that to bleed slowly to death in No Man's Land was a relief?

'There are letters for you, Mac,' his relief called as he picked up his bag.

Letters from Julia, from Rowangarth where there was peace and safety and sanity. It was what he was fighting for.

Hands reached down and helped him into the back of the army lorry that would jolt him back to the base hospital and bed.

Yet he *wasn't* fighting for a faraway place in a faraway country; he was fighting, now, to stay alive – it was as simple as that. And he was here because Sarajevo had set alight the hatred of two nations, each for the other, and because Belgium had wanted to remain apart from the fight. And what now the price of their neutrality and the cavalier fashion in which the British Government had pledged to guarantee it. Broken young bodies and sleepless nights; men crying out to die; men crying out to live. Neutrality and hatred at war with each other, and the youth of Europe trapped in the middle of it!

He clenched tightly on his jaws. He was on stand-down now. He'd done his stint and now he could sleep, had earned sleep. He would take off his dirty, bloodstained clothes and fall naked into bed, with Julia's letters beneath his pillow where he could touch them for comfort; letters to read when finally he awoke.

Her name beat inside his head. When things became near unbearable, her name was the only prayer he knew; the only one he could say without bitterness.

He closed his eyes and she was beside him and the wind – and clean wind on the Pike – taking her hair, blowing it like a cloud about her.

'We're here, sir.' An orderly shook his arm. 'You dropped off . . .'

Back at the base hospital, almost four miles behind the front line; back to a bed and sleep and the defiant satisfaction of having survived another three days under fire. Three days nearer to Julia . . .

The world had become grey. A grey, grizzling sky, a grey sea – a sea forbidden to them by enemy submarines. So they had waited three days and two nights, sleeping in a dockside warehouse, eating food cooked in a field kitchen. It was the way it would be when finally he got to France, Tom Dwerryhouse reasoned; best accept it. And here on the dockside he was safe at least from shellbursts and sudden, whining bullets and machine-gunners with nervous fingers.

He hadn't minded the delay. They had finally left England at night on a frighteningly darkened ship; on a trooper painted grey to match the mood of every soldier on board. He had no idea where his regiment would be quartered, he only knew he wanted to be free of the load on his back. And he wanted to be able to write to Alice; bring her nearer. He ached to reach out and touch her. Alice was love and peace and a tip-tilted nose. Wherever she stood was home to him: waiting for her in Brattocks Wood and the lighted, leaded windows of Rowangarth glowing through the darkness. Alice was springtime and green things growing and soft, brown eyes; she was summer in his arms with buttercups in her hair. She was his. He had taken her, claimed her. Now he wanted this war to be over. It was none of his making and, truth known, he didn't want to fight for France – or was it Belgium? He didn't even want to fight for his King, through everyone said that was why he was here.

So why was he here, and burdened like a packhorse with kit; like the dozens and dozens of horses tied in the standings beyond the ammunition sheds – and with as little freedom of choice? He was fighting, he told himself firmly, for Alice. Fighting for the right to get back to her; to wed her and live with her in Keeper's Cottage and, when the time was proper, to have bairns with her – bonny little lasses and a lad to train into keeping, beside him.

He pulled his thoughts back to the greyness. The platoon sergeant was calling out an order and, dammit, he'd missed the half of it.

'. . . and I'm warning you – if there are any marks at all on that card, it'll be torn up. You signs your name and you turns it over and writes the address on the other side. No secret marks or the Censor'll have you shot. And no crosses for kisses. Kisses ain't allowed, neither. When you've filled in your card, hand it to the corporal, and if you haven't a pencil about you, then hard luck, soldier!'

Tom read the card passed down the line to him. It was buff-coloured and, beneath the warning bawled out by the sergeant, several options were printed.

I am quite well
I have been admitted into hospital
I have received your letter dated . . . . .

Tom considered each of the eight printed lines gravely. Finally, he crossed them all through save the first and last. *I am quite well*, and, *Letter follows at first opportunity*. Then he signed his name and number and rank after carefully printing Alice's name and address on the reverse side.

It would be a coldly worded, impersonal card to receive, but she would understand – be grateful, even – to get it.

'Stay safe, bonny lass,' he thought, passing the card back. 'This war can't last much longer . . .'

It couldn't. One big push, everybody was saying, was all it would take. One great battle on land and another at sea. Our navy was the finest in the world. Two good scraps and he'd be back at Rowangarth. Wars cost money and both sides wanted it over and done with now. Stood to sense, didn't it?

Alice. With luck she would have that card in three days, and maybe, when they got to wherever the faceless ones were sending them, letters from home would be waiting for them. Letters from Alice, who loved him . . .

The letter addressed to Mrs Julia MacMalcolm arrived by the first post. She knew what was inside it and hurried to the kitchen, ripping it open as she went.

'It's come, Hawthorn! Where's yours? What does it say?'

'Nothing for me. Nothing at all . . .' Miss Clitherow had sorted the post and shaken her head to Alice's unspoken enquiry. There had been nothing from Tom, and, even though everyone said no news was good news, it didn't help. There had been only two letters since their snatched goodbye; both hurriedly written notes, telling her he loved her, that he would always love her. Postmarked Aldershot, they bore no address, which meant he would soon be moving on. But since then, nothing had come for almost two weeks. 'When do you go, miss?'

'On Monday, the thirty-first. Report to the matron at ten o'clock, it says, and I'm to take only sufficient clothes for one week – underwear and stockings, they probably mean. Until we get our uniform, I suppose.' She read through the printed notice and the dates and remarks added by pen. 'And I'm to be prepared to take a medical examination, upon which, it says, depends my acceptance as a VAD probationer. Are you *sure* there wasn't one for you, Hawthorn?'

'Sure, miss. Nothing. Not from Tom nor the nursing.'

'Lordy! They've found out how old you are!'

'But who would tell them, miss? And I'm not too young to join, surely; just too young to go to France.'

'So you gave your wrong age, eh?' Cook demanded, button-mouthed, when Julia had left. 'What made you do a daft thing like that?'

Alice opened her mouth to protest and was silenced by Cook's raised finger.

'And no back answers, if you please. Don't be telling me it's none of my business and I shouldn't be listening, because this is *my* kitchen and whatever is said in it is *my* business!'

'I know, Mrs Shaw. And I'm sorry – for what I nearly said,' Alice hastened, pink-cheeked. 'But you won't tell on me? Nobody else knows but Miss Julia. I want to get to Tom, see, and if Reuben got to hear about it he'd stop me, I know he would!'

'Bless you, lass, I'll say nowt. You must do what you think best. If it don't bother your conscience, then it don't bother mine. It's funny, though – your letter not arriving with Miss Julia's . . .'

'And nothing from Tom, either. This isn't my lucky day, is it?'

'There's always the twelve o'clock post. Cheer up, lass.'

'Didn't you say you wanted the pantry floor scrubbed, Mrs Shaw? I'll do it if you like.'

She could have it scrubbed from end to end before Jin arrived at half-past. She felt like taking out her worry and frustration on someone or something – her anger at the war, too. Best it should be the pantry floor!

Alice watched for the postman from the sewing-room window: the midday post came to the back door because parcels came second delivery and the back door was the place for parcels. She was downstairs before the bell had stopped dancing on its spring, waiting for Miss Clitherow to sort upstairs mail from below-stairs.

'Hm. Two for her ladyship, two for Mrs MacMalcolm and two for you.' The housekeeper's lips formed one of her rare smiles. 'What you've been waiting for, I think, Hawthorn. Take Miss Julia's, will you? I'll see to her ladyship's.'

'Ooh, thanks, Miss Clitherow.' Alice stared at the strange buff-coloured postcard. 'From Tom. Think it's from France. Go on – you can read it, miss.' She pushed the card into the housekeeper's hand. 'He's well, and a letter follows.' Tom had made the crossing safely. Not like Sir Robert. She sent up a prayer of thanks, then whisked away to find Julia. 'It's come, miss. A letter with the same writing on it as yours – and one from Tom!'

She handed over the pencilled card. She would have liked it to be in ink – more permanent, sort of – but a soldier couldn't cart around an ink bottle and pen, even if he carried most things else on his back.

'There'll be a letter from him soon,' Julia smiled. 'A proper one with an address for you to write to. He's as safe as he can be. Now open the other one and tell me what it says!'

'Same as yours, miss.' Quickly Alice read it through. 'We're going to York together, it seems . . .'

'Let's hope we can stay together, Hawthorn. Now, off you go and tell Mother about it. You know she'd like you to stay here, don't you, even though you'll be giving notice to Miss Clitherow?'

'Yes – but is it right, miss? Don't seem fair that her ladyship has to keep me and get nothing in return. I can just as easy go to Reuben's . . .'

'Do you want to?'

'Not really – oh, Reuben's a nice old gentleman and I'm fond of him, but he's got set in his ways since his wife died. If I can stay on here, I'd help out whenever I could and not be a nuisance . . .'

'That's settled, then. Mother wants you to stay. She's

492

had enough upset in her life lately. Your staying on would help. And besides, you promised Giles you'd keep an eye on Morgan!'

Alice laid down her pen and corked the ink bottle firmly. Another letter to Tom, but this one she would not send to the Richmond address. This she would hold in readiness because soon she would know his new address.

She had not mentioned going to York at the end of the month. Best say nothing until she'd passed her medical and been given her uniform. She would tell him, perhaps, when they were both settled at Denniston House. He wouldn't worry so much when he knew she was with Miss Julia.

She placed her hands to her burning cheeks. Tom in France and Alice Hawthorn a nurse. And if all went well she might be out there near him, come summer. In July. Come buttercup time . . .

28

'Wouldn't you have thought,' said Alice as they walked through the early morning darkness towards the dim lights of the mess hall, 'they'd have built the nurses' quarters nearer the hospital?'

'I suppose the nurses' quarters were an afterthought.' Julia pulled her coat collar around her ears. 'When this place was built, nursing had still to become a respectable profession.'

'Then, not so very long ago, you and me couldn't have been nurses?' Alice gazed at the outline of the tall, gaunt army hospital.

'Goodness, no! Pity the sick before Miss Nightingale's time. In some hospitals, the night nursing was done by any slut of a woman. Sometimes a prostitute, even, would go in off the streets and offer to help, just to get shelter for the night. Nursing has come a long way since the days when anyone could set herself up as a nurse or midwife.'

'Now fancy that!' Miss Julia was very knowledgeable about such things – but then she would be, her being the wife of a doctor. 'So that's why we're so far away.' They were wet already from cold, driving rain, and their shoes squelched with water. Without a doubt, the next two weeks were going to be very uncomfortable. 'Did you manage to get any hot water in the washroom, miss?'

'I did not! We'll have to get there even earlier tomorrow. And I was so cold in the night I couldn't sleep.'

'At least we know where the mess hall is,' Alice gasped as they hurried to six o'clock breakfast and a mug of hot tea. 'And if we get a move on we can make our beds and still be at Sister Tutor's office for seven.'

The mess hall was as gaunt as the building that housed it, the brown-painted walls damp with condensation. They took their cutlery from a basket at the door, then found places at one of the long, bare tables.

'We're a bit late for the porridge,' smiled the nurse who followed them in. 'There'll only be bread and jam left. Take my advice and grab some margarine if you see any: it goes very quickly!'

They breakfasted on bread and jam and exquisitely hot tea, then ran, heads down, back to the nurses' quarters, hoping fervently that things might soon get better, for surely they couldn't get worse.

Their entry yesterday into hospital life had been by way of a door on which was painted, *Nurses. Strictly Private.* A wooden, well-scrubbed staircase led to the rooms and dormitories; the smallest, dreariest room – an attic with a small, grimy skylight – being given to Alice and Julia.

'Oh, my word.' Alice gazed in dismay. Against each wall stood a black iron bed on which lay folded blankets and sheets. Behind the door were two coat-pegs; the floor was as bare as the staircase.

'But where do we put our things?'

'In our cases, miss, it seems; beneath our beds. At least there's a peg for our coats . . .'

'Spartan,' Julia muttered, all at once glad their stay here would be brief. 'And imagine them not letting us out at all?'

No young lady would be allowed to leave the hospital without permission for any reason whatsoever, Matron had read from her list of rules, then asked them if it was perfectly understood. They had murmured that it was.

'It's freezing in here!'

'It's to be expected. Attics are cold in winter and hot in summer,' Alice supplied, making a determined start on the beds. 'It won't be so bad, though. Think of the poor lads in the trenches. At least we aren't up to our ankles in water.'

'Trench-foot,' Julia said. 'Andrew says that's what they get, from having to keep wet boots on for days at a time. And I'm not complaining, Hawthorn, though I'll be glad when we've had our medical and can start being nurses. And I'm glad we're still together. It would be awful having to share with someone I didn't know.'

'There, now.' Alice smoothed the bedspread. 'Looks better already. Would you mind sitting on the other bed so I can see to this one? And don't forget we have to go for our pinafores.'

'Pinafores!' Julia wrinkled her nose. She had so wanted her uniform, instead of which they had been told to tie back their hair, roll up their sleeves and, for the time being, wear the red-cross armband which would be given them at the stores, together with long white aprons and heavy-duty pinafores – scrubbing aprons, Alice supposed they'd be. 'Oh, dear, when do you think we'll get on the wards?'

'Tomorrow, happen. When we've had our medicals . . .'

'It's all a bit daunting, isn't it, when you think how unimportant we are here? Two new, untried VADs who don't even merit a uniform, it seems.'

'Unimportant.' All at once, Alice had missed Rowangarth and the warmth of the kitchen; missed Tilda with her love books, Miss Clitherow's straight back and button mouth, and Reuben and Mrs Shaw. 'We'll have to stick it out here, though, if we're ever to get to France.'

Her bottom lip had trembled with doubt, and she wished, just for a moment, to run like the wind, home to Rowangarth.

Then she thought about Tom and Doctor Andrew, and how dreadful this place must be for Miss Julia, who was used to the softest of beds and a fire in her bedroom, and who wouldn't know what to do with a scrubbing apron if she fell over one.

'Don't worry, miss. We'll be all right. Things are going to seem a lot better in the morning, just you see.'

So now they ran, eyes squinting against the rain, splashing through puddles to Sister Tutor's office.

'Trench-foot!' Julia gasped. 'That's what we'll get. My shoes are soaking!'

'They'll soon dry out if we stuff them with newspaper,' Alice gasped over her shoulder, even though they didn't have a newspaper between them. 'Hurry, miss, do! It's nearly seven!'

'Where have you been?' Sister Tutor glared. 'Hawthorn and MacMalcolm, isn't it? You were told to see me immediately after breakfast, which in this hospital is one minute past seven a.m. You are five minutes late!'

'Yes, Sister.'

'Sorry, Sister.'

'Do you realize how precious the minutes are? I am here to teach nursing, not shepherd ewe-lambs who can't find their way from A to B on time. Do *not* be late again!'

'No, Sister.'

'Sorry, Sister.'

Julia fretted silently inside her; silently, because she learned quickly, and she had been warned never to say anything to Sister Tutor other than 'yes' or 'no' or 'sorry', and only to ask a question when given permission to ask it.

'Your medicals – best get them over with. Don't want you here if you aren't fit. Cut along to the lady doctor in Room 102. Wait until she has written your medical reports, then bring them back to me here at half-past ten. Do *not* read them!'

'She's going to be worse than Sister Carbrooke,' Julia muttered.

'At least she doesn't smell of carbolic.'

'There's a lot to learn in just two weeks,' Alice said soberly. 'It'll take longer than that just to find our way around this place.'

'But we'll learn it. If we don't . . .' Julia pulled a forefinger dramatically across her throat, then knocked firmly on the door of Room 102.

A voice bade them enter. Taking a deep breath, Julia stepped inside. Alice, as was her habit, followed behind.

They had passed their medical, Sister Tutor said, when she had studied the reports placed unread on her desk.

'But be that as it may,' she said severely, 'you have been here for all of a day and a half and done nothing at all. I therefore suggest that you report with your aprons to the staff nurse on Ward 3F. *Now*!'

'We've done it!' Julia exulted when they were out of earshot. 'We've passed! Now we can do some proper nursing!'

'And we'll feel a lot better once they give us our uniforms.'

'We'll get them,' Julia said confidently. 'We'll *earn* them. Do hurry, Hawthorn! Let's not upset Staff Nurse as well!'

Ward 3F was easy to find, Alice thought, once you realized that in the large, main building, all wards lay either side of a wide central corridor, and it was really only a matter of counting. She supposed that, given time, she would find her way around the huge hospital, just as once she had accustomed herself to the corridors and unexpected passageways at Rowangarth.

They walked slowly, peering through open doors into wards with long lines of beds. Everyone was busy; no one took the slightest notice of them.

'How many to each ward, do you think?'

'Dunno, miss. A lot . . .' A lot of beds; a lot of wounded soldiers.

The doors of Ward 3F were closed; there were no sounds of occupancy. Cautiously, Julia peeped inside.

'*Well!*' Alice jerked.

'Empty!' frowned Julia. Empty and echoing and un-friendly, somehow.

'She was having us on,' Alice said dubiously.

'I don't think so.' Julia stepped inside, taking in the high windows, the two-shades-of-green walls, the woodblock floor, urgently in need of cleaning. 'Sister Tutor wouldn't play jokes. Ward 3F. Report to Staff Nurse, she said.'

'You are quite right. Sister Tutor never jokes.'

'Staff Nurse?' They turned, eyes questioning.

'Staff Nurse Smith, and you are indeed in the right place. This is your ward, ladies, and I would like it cleaned. From top to bottom with the exception of the ceiling. That has already been done by men with ladders.'

'*Clean it?*' Julia squeaked.

'Clean it.'

'*From top to bottom?*'

'What is your name?' Staff Nurse demanded.

'I'm Julia MacMalcolm – why?'

'Well, MacMalcolm, you and I will get on a great deal better if you stop repeating everything I say before it becomes an irritating habit! I want this ward cleaned in its entirety. Walls, beds, floor: I'm sorry the floor is in such a mess, but the men who cleaned the ceiling are responsible for that. Then, when you have finished, you will do the same to the sluice-room and to Ward Sister's office here beside the door.'

'But – but *how*?'

'I think she means what with,' Alice – who knew how – supplied.

'In the sluice-room are buckets and scrubbers and

anything else you may need. In Ward Sister's office you will find a gas ring; you can heat your water on that.'

'But how long,' asked Julia, mesmerized, 'is it going to take?'

'You are here for twelve more days, I believe. I sincerely hope it will take less than that! You will be wondering why such thoroughness?'

'Frankly – yes.'

'Well, MacMalcolm, I think you have the right to know. There may be some misinformed nurse who will tell you what you'll catch in doing it. But the plain truth is that we took in a lot of wounded from the fighting at Artois. Unfortunately, there were two typhoid cases amongst them.'

'Typhoid! And we've got to – '

'You don't *have* to do anything, MacMalcolm. You can put on your hat and coat and go back from whence you came, if you wish. There is no danger to yourselves. The entire ward has been fumigated and left to air for almost a month. In the circumstances, Matron feels that now is a good time to clean it thoroughly.

'We cannot know when the next influx of wounded will arrive. We would like it to be ready for occupation. Use washing soda in your water, and disinfectant – and I want everything cleaned. Every bed, locker – *every single thing.*'

'She can't mean it,' Julia wailed when they were alone in the vast, echoing room.

'She means it, all right!'

'But it's *yards* long, and the walls are really high!'

'There are step-ladders in yon' corner – we can use those. We'd best start on the walls first; do things methodical, like. Best push all the beds into the middle of the ward to give us elbow room, then we get on with it.'

'They're doing it on purpose,' Julia hissed, suddenly angry. 'We aren't going to learn anything about nursing

500

here. They are seeing how much we can take – giving us a rough passage!'

'You mean, if we can take all they throw at us and don't complain, they'll send us on to Denniston House?'

'I'm sure that's what they're up to. I suppose things could get quite tricky in France and they want to be sure we're up to it. I'm angry, though. I came here thinking to learn about nursing, and it seems instead I'm to be taught to scrub and clean!'

'I learned to scrub and clean when I was thirteen, Miss Julia. I'm good at it – I'll show you how,' Alice said quietly.

'Oh, God! Hawthorn, I'm sorry! I truly am! I didn't mean . . . Forgive me?'

'It's all right, miss. I know you didn't mean it nastily, and I wasn't meaning to be pert. But if scrubbing is going to be our first step towards France, then scrub we will! So tie on your apron and let's get on with it, or we'll have to stay another week to finish the dratted hole and we don't want that, now do we?' She stared wide-eyed at the task ahead of them. 'Oh my word, no.' She lingered, her fingers on the cluster of pearls on her left hand, then reluctantly slipped it off. Strong disinfectant and washing soda would harm her precious ring; best she wore it around her neck. 'When we get our uniforms we won't be allowed to wear any jewellery at all, 'cept wedding rings.' She unfastened the chain at her neck, slipping the ring on to it to hang with Tom's locket and her mother's wedding ring.

'Let me look.' Julia opened the locket carefully. 'Who is this?'

'It's Tom, miss, when he was young. I'm hoping to have one of him in uniform soon, to put there.'

'And the flower – a buttercup?'

'Aye. He gave me buttercups the day he asked me to be his girl.' Alice's eyes filled with tears. 'I miss him. And I get so afraid . . .'

501

'I know, Hawthorn. I do so know.' Julia's voice was rough with emotion. 'Sometimes I think I'd do anything at all just to see Andrew: lie, cheat – anything.'

'Well, Miss Julia, lying and cheating might do very well,' Alice pulled the back of her hand across her eyes, sniffing loudly, 'but in our present predicament there's only one thing is going to get us to France, and that's scrubbing.

'So let's hang up our white aprons – we aren't going to be doing any nursing in them yet a-while. This lot's going to take us days and days.' Alice knew about such things. 'The sooner we start, the sooner we'll be on our way to Denniston!'

'Hm. We'll have to watch out for Staff Nurse Smith, you know. I'll bet she can spot a speck of dust at twenty paces. Ooh! This apron smells *awful*!'

'That's because it's made of sacking, miss. Scrubbing aprons always are. And don't you worry none about Staff Nurse Smith. When we've finished this ward, she can poke and pry till she's blue in the face and she'll find nowt wrong with it!'

There followed a week the like of which Julia MacMalcolm wished never to live through again – or so she thought at the time: a week of hot, cruel water; of aching arms from reaching high to wash walls; of water, grey with dirt, trickling down her arms. And how she came to hate green; the pale, mawkish green of the upper half of the wall; the sombre olive of the lower.

Within two days her hands were red and swollen, her fingernails broken and pitted with dirt. Had it not been for Hawthorn's ability to tackle the work with sense and method, she'd have run home in tears, Julia acknowledged, in her blacker moods. But as the week wore on, it lifted her heart a little to see other cracked and bleeding hands amongst the newcomers in the mess hall, all of them like herself; too stubborn to give in and ask for lotion to help make the aching soreness bearable.

'We'll see to all the walls first,' Alice had pronounced, sizing up the situation with the aplomb of one already well-versed in such matters. 'Then we'll do the lockers and wipe the bed-frames – and after that, the floors . . .'

The sluice-room they would leave until the end, her common sense decided, for that was where buckets were filled and emptied and, anyway, it was such a little room that half a day would see it finished.

'What would I have done without you, Hawthorn?' Now Julia obeyed orders without question. Now her hands were so swollen that she disliked even to look at them; her knees were bruised from kneeling. Even had her bed been soft, their attic warm and snug, still she would have lain awake contemplating her aching back, her sore knees, her throbbing hands. She had been ready, one night, to give up and go home humbled and disgraced, until she thought of the letter she would have to write to Andrew.

. . . I gave up. After ten days it became so unbearable that I went home. Sorry, but I'm not cut out for nursing.

She could not, would not write that letter! Andrew could not give up; Alice's Tom couldn't pack his bags and buy a first-class ticket to Holdenby Halt! How *dare* she be so weak, so childish! She would go on until her back broke and her knees gave way. And come to think of it, why weren't Hawthorn's hands cracked and bleeding like her own, and her knees swollen?

Tears trickled down her cheeks, and she mopped them with her bed-sheet.

I want you, Andrew. I need you to kiss my hands better and tell me it will be all right. And, darling – I'm not going home. I won't give in . . .

Two days from the end of their cold, wet, hungry stay at

the Barracks Hospital, Julia exulted, 'We've done it – it's all finished! Did you ever see such a difference!'

'Just the sluice-room floor to be scrubbed, then that's it,' Alice smiled, equally proud. Such shining windows, clean furniture and oh, how spotless a floor! 'Now, tell you what, miss; by way of a celebration, kind of, I'll finish off. I'm better at it than you. Just rinse those poor hands under the tap and dab them dry. I reckon you deserve a rest.'

'You're a dear, Hawthorn. I couldn't have kept at it without you, I swear I couldn't.'

'You could, Miss Julia. You'd never have given up.'

'Then don't give up now, MacMalcolm,' said a voice behind them. Staff Nurse Smith, who walked with the stealth of a cat, had appeared again without warning. 'Fill your bucket and take your share of that floor! Hawthorn is not your servant now. Here you are equals, and I want to hear no more "Miss Julias". Is that clear?' she flung as she left in a rustle of starched indignation.

'Miss – I'm sorry,' Alice whispered. 'That was cruel and uncalled for. Don't let her upset you. She's annoyed 'cos we've made such a good job of it – *both* of us. She's poked and peeped and never once found anything wrong. So think on – we'll be leaving here on Friday.' It would be like getting out of the lock-up!

'Yes, we *have* made a good job of it, and up until now I've stood my corner. It's kind of you to offer, but I'll help finish it if you don't mind. If we get a move on, we'll be first in the supper queue!' On hands and knees they grinned at each other across the floor.

'First in the queue it is, Miss Julia!'

'She was right, you know. I hate to admit it, but for once Staff Nurse was right!' Julia pronounced as they scraped clean their rice-pudding dishes.

'Miss?'

504

'There you go again, Hawthorn – and there *I* go too. You mustn't call me Miss, or Miss Julia: we are both nurses – or will be, I hope. You must call me MacMalcolm, or Julia. I shall continue to use your surname if Denniston House demands it, but at all other times you are Alice – is that understood?'

'Oooh, miss, I couldn't. And even if I forced it out, what'll I call you when we're back at Rowangarth? Can you imagine Miss Clitherow standing for it? Can you, eh?'

'But it's different, now. We are nurses; it wouldn't be right for me to tell you what to do, now would it?'

'But you've never told me what to do, miss. Not ever. You and her ladyship both have always *asked* me to do things and thanked me for the doing of them. Not like that Mrs Clementina from the Place. Now she's a real martinet, that one. She's – oooops! Was forgetting she's your aunt. No disrespect, miss, I'm sure . . .'

'No. You've got it wrong. She's not a martinet; she's a bitch. Who else could have spawned Cousin Elliot? And as for poor Uncle Edward – it wouldn't surprise me if one day he didn't give her the slap she deserves. She's been asking for it for years!'

'Don't say things like that, miss! You know you shouldn't!'

'Not in front of the servants, you mean? Alice, can't you at least try? All right, I know we'll both forget sometimes, but it won't be long before we get it right. Say you'll try?'

'I'll try.'

'Good! Then let's get back to 3F and have a last look round. Sister Tutor is coming to check it, remember. Let's make sure we haven't missed anything.'

'Yes, an' we'd better tidy our hair and put on our armbands and white aprons.'

'Come on, then. There might even be some hot water

in the wash-room. And the first thing I'll do when I get back to Rowangarth will be to run a bath – a *hot* bath – and wallow in it until the stink of carbolic is gone!'

'Me, too. Just *think* of it . . .' Just to think that in little more than a day they would be on the train to Holdenby and, if they were lucky, with Matron's recommendation that they were ready to start their training at Denniston House . . .

'I've thought of nothing else, Hawthorn, for the past twelve days. And I shall never, *ever*, forget Ward 3F!'

Probationer Nurses MacMalcolm and Hawthorn stood stiff and straight in clean white pinafores, gazing, unblinking, at the wall opposite as Sister Tutor, followed by Staff Nurse Smith, entered Ward 3F, nodding to them in passing.

For what seemed an age – and was actually a full five minutes – Sister's forefinger searched and poked; her eyes slid to left and right and upwards and downwards. Then, without a word, she turned and walked the length of the echoing ward to where the pair stood, dry-mouthed and shaking.

'Let me see – today is . . .?'

'Wednesday, Sister,' Julia choked.

'And you leave on . . .?'

'Friday,' Alice whispered, bobbing a curtsey from sheer fright.

'Very well. I think you have time to wax and polish the floors and make up the beds. Apart from that, everything is satisfactory. Please draw mattresses and bedding from Stores, Staff Nurse.'

'And tomorrow, Sister,' Staff Nurse Smith murmured, 'what are they to do, if you please?'

'*Do?* They are to report after breakfast to Matron. She will sign requisitions for uniforms, doubtless, and when you are satisfied they are wearing them correctly, you will take them on a tour of the hospital and show them what the inside of a *real* ward is like. After which, you will give each a travel warrant to wherever she is going!'

For just a moment when they were alone, neither was able to speak. Then Julia gave out a great shout of laughter.

'We're in! *Uniforms*, she said!'

'Yes, and did you see Staff Nurse as they left? She smiled! She bloomin'-well *smiled*.'

Alice walked self-consciously down the kitchen stairs, pausing before she opened the door, savouring the moment of her homecoming.

'Cook! Oh, see who's here!' called Tilda. 'It's Alice back and, goodness, come and look at her!'

'Hullo, Mrs Shaw. I haven't missed teatime, have I?'

'Lass! Just look at you in that uniform. Our Alice, a nurse!'

Cook's eyes brimmed over with tears and, so overcome was she, that she sat down in the fireside rocker and, burying her face in her pinafore, sobbed as if her heart was ready to break.

'An angel, that's what, and thank God you're safely home, Alice!'

'But, Mrs Shaw, we've only been to York for two weeks,' Alice whispered, placing an arm around the trembling shoulders. 'And we're both to go to Denniston House for our training, so we won't be going away again for ages and ages. Don't cry over me – *please*?'

'I wasn't crying over you,' Cook sniffed, peering over the hem of her pinafore. 'It – it's because I should've baked cherry scones. I would've, if I'd known. And if a body can't have a weep in her own kitchen when two young lasses come back from the war, then it's a poor carry-on!'

507

'But we haven't been to the war.'

Not yet, that was. Not until summer, when she was – well, twenty-one . . .

'Darling, it's so good to be back.' Julia sat at her mother's feet, gazing into the fire, a *real* fire, vowing that never again would she take one for granted.

'It's good to have you back, though I haven't been too lonely. Two weeks would soon pass, I told myself, and though I am still in black for Robert, Tessa and Letty have called – your aunt Clemmy, too. And I have made several visits to Denniston House. The bravery of those young men is incredible, Julia, and their nurses are devoted and hard-working. It made me proud that my daughter is going to be one of them.

'But goodness! How could I forget? There are letters for you. They all came yesterday. On my desk . . .'

'And all from Andrew,' Julia exulted, scanning the envelopes for the date below the Censor's stamp. 'Goodness! The last one was written only four days ago!' She thrust them into the deep pocket of her dress. 'I'll save them for later,' she smiled. 'When we've had tea, I'll take off this drab old dress and have a lovely long bath, if you don't mind, and read them then.

'Oh, Tilda, you don't know what a delight it will be to drink tea poured from a pot,' she laughed as the housemaid set down a tea tray.

'A *teapot*, miss?' Tilda frowned.

'Yes, indeed. We've been getting our tea from an urn, Tilda. A great hissing thing that gave out the most incredible noises. What has Cook sent?'

'Brown bread and blackcurrant jam, Miss Julia. And she managed a slice of fruit cake – well, it's Christmas cake, really – and she says sorry there are no cherry scones; the oven wasn't right, you see. The coal shortage,' she explained, patiently. 'Cook banks the fire down with wood and slack now, in the afternoons. Affects the ovens . . .'

'I see. Thank Cook for her kind thought, won't you? I do understand. And blackcurrant jam is wonderful. I'll pour.'

Julia smiled, almost purring in the warmth of the blazing logs. 'I dreamed of drinking afternoon tea in the firelight. It was cold at the hospital – the stoves in the wards got the coal and coke.'

'And very right and proper, too. The wounded should get – Julia!' Helen stared, horrified, at her daughter's hands.

'Oh dear. They are a bit of a mess, aren't they? All the scrubbing, I'm afraid, but I'll soon have them healed; I'll have to. Can't do dressings with hands like these – wouldn't be allowed. I'll rub them with glycerine tonight, and in the morning I'll see Doctor James. He'll make me up a lotion for them.'

'But, child, they're so cracked and sore-looking. They must hurt terribly.'

'Not a bit. They're fine. Hawthorn says once they've healed, they'll be all right; I'll have broken them in, sort of. I wasn't the only one there with bleeding hands. The soda and disinfectant in the scrubbing water did it.'

'You must have done a lot of scrubbing to get them in that state,' Helen frowned.

'Quite a bit,' Julia grinned, remembering Ward 3F with near affection and not a little pride. 'Hawthorn showed me how. And you're not to worry. At Denniston it'll be much easier.'

And oh, she exulted, tonight she would sleep in her soft, warm bed. Add to that a hot, scented bath and three letters from Andrew, and the world was all at once wonderful!

'Do you know, darling,' she murmured, 'as Hawthorn and I came down the drive there were snowdrops and aconites out. Drifts of white and gold.'

They had never before looked so beautiful, so welcoming. Soon it would be spring, and then, before they knew it, would come summer, and France . . .

Alice walked carefully, the small candlelamp in one hand and the spaniel's lead in the other. So good to be back; to wrap the safeness of Rowangarth around her, sit in the warmth of the kitchen. And good to see that daft old dog, who had yelped and barked and rushed about with such excitement on seeing her that she'd felt obliged to take him for a walk. As far as Keeper's, that was. To Reuben's cottage and no further; tell him she was back; let him see her in her uniform before she took it off and set about making it fit. She would have all her work cut out to get both uniforms seen to in time for Monday.

To her right, Brattocks Wood stood dark and lonely; to her left, just over the stile, a light shone from Reuben's kitchen window. If only, when she pushed open the door, Tom could be there, just as he'd been that late December afternoon. It was her constant daydream, now. Just to think back to those two lovely hours set her longing for him.

'Tom, my love,' she whispered into the night, 'send me a letter, soon?'

Julia lay blissfully in the bath, scrubbing her fingernails until the ingrained dirt was gone, and with it the nightmare of Ward 3F. This was like old times again; as if she had never been away.

She closed her eyes, letting the water lap her shoulders, thinking back to Andrew's letter, written, unbelievably, only on Monday.

> . . . and I find myself glad and sad you are to be a nurse; sad because my precious girl may have to face danger, but glad because a sea will no longer divide us.

I awoke this morning to the sudden realization that, if you came to France, I might, given luck, be able to telephone you. Just to hear your voice would balance out all else. We could even, with a small miracle, find we are sufficiently near each other to be able, briefly, to meet. One minute would be heaven; one hour – oh, my darling, what could we do in an hour?

Julia laughed softly, placing her hands to her cheeks, wishing he wouldn't write such delightfully sinful letters; glad that he did.

She closed her eyes, hearing his voice. Soon she must step out of this warm luxury, towel herself and dry her hair, but now, her body soft and relaxed, she surrendered herself to the exquisite contemplation of one hour with Andrew. Sixty beautiful minutes; the two of them alone. In bed.

29

Last night, Jinny Dobb had told Alice's fortune, despite Cook's protest that telling fortunes on a Sunday wasn't right. To which Jin had snappily replied, without thought for Mrs Shaw's position, that the moon was right and, anyway, the better the day the better the deed!

So Cook folded her arms across her bosom without further comment, because only a fool would gainsay Jin when the 'fluence was on her.

'Sit under the light, lass.' Jin lifted Alice's hand. 'The right one is the way things are; the left hand the way it was meant to be. Sometimes they tally, other times they're in such conflict that – '

She rose abruptly to pull back the kitchen curtain. Over a puffy bank of silvered cloud, the moon shone high and bright and full.

' – such conflict, that sometimes there's no changing it.'

'So it isn't up to Fate? It isn't all cut and dried for us the day we're born?' Alice's suddenly dry mouth made little clicking sounds as she spoke. 'We can change things?'

'What's in your left hand is Fate – intended. Forewarned, you just might be able to change summat in t'other hand. Hush, now . . .'

She laid Alice's right hand on the table-top, palm up, then gazed long at the other, brows meeting in a frown. Then she placed them side by side, running a forefinger lightly over the pads of her fingertips.

'You kept your teacup dregs? You know what to do?'

Unspeaking, Alice made three circles with the cup she had just drunk from, upturning it into the saucer. Jin took it and shook out the drops left there, her mouth tightening as she did it. Then she turned the cup this way and that, shaking her head, closing her eyes, breathing loudly and deeply.

'Lay your hands on mine,' she said, all at once brisk and businesslike again, 'and look at me, lass, while I talk to you. Now then – there's a lot of nonsense in both hands, but young hands are bound to be frivolous, so it makes no matter. There are tears in your cup and tears in both hands, so you'll straighten your back and take what life throws at you.

'You'll know happiness and you'll have two bairns – one of each. The first will bring sadness, the second one joy. I saw a journey in your cup, though these days that's to be expected. Your going will be in hope, your coming back in sadness.'

Alice looked down at the table-top. No unhappiness, please? Surely Jin knew not to tell her about the bad bits?

'Look at me, Alice Hawthorn, and be thankful that you'll know good health and have a longer life than most, though you'll have a brush with death. Tell me – do you know about the walk through the wood?'

Alice shook her head.

'It's a so-to-speak wood, lass, and a so-to-speak walk through it, if you get my meaning. Anyway, you'll walk through that wood three times and twice you'll take the long, sad path. And you'll come out first with a stick that's crooked and worthless and a second time with one that's weak and frail. But you'll find your straight, stout stave in the end if you've the courage to take that third walk, Alice, and the sense to listen to your heart . . .'

The wood, Jin wasn't meaning Brattocks. The wood she was talking about was Life. Alice frowned. And the so-to-speak sticks must be men, really. A bad one, a sickly one, and one that was straight and true. In the end, he would be – if she were brave enough . . .

'Think on about what I've told you, Alice. Happen now it makes no sense, but it will . . .' Jin stuck out her left palm. 'You seal it with silver. A threepenny-piece will suffice.'

Alice thrust her hand into the pocket of her apron – she'd known about the silver – and took out the shilling she had put there in readiness. Then she laid it on the waiting hand and folded her work-worn fingers over it. 'I thank you,' she said gravely.

'Now then, Mrs Shaw, how about you?' Jin challenged.

'Nay, I think not.' Not on a Sunday, any road. 'Maybe I'll be obliged to you next time.' Next full moon, she calculated, wouldn't fall on a Sunday – this being a leap year.

'Me, Jin? Me now!' Tilda had already seated herself at the table.

'All right, Miss Matilda – and what can I do for you? Is it a rich old man you want from me or a young, lusty one?'

'Both,' Tilda giggled, 'and in that order, if you don't mind!'

'I'll go upstairs now if I may, Mrs Shaw,' Alice whispered. 'I still have a few things to do before morning.'

She had, though really she wanted to think about what Jin had told her; to write it all down before she forgot the half of it.

'Aye, Alice. Away you go.'

Three men in the lass's life. Cook frowned. A nonsense, of course. There was only one man for her, and that was Tom Dwerryhouse: Jin should have known it. Walks through the wood indeed!

Don't you believe the half of it, Matilda Tewk. Jin Dobb's a peculiar one – always was and always will be!

'You'll take a sup of tea with us afore you go home, Jin?'

No matter what had disappeared from larders and store

cupboards, at least Rowangarth had tea, Cook was forced to admit. Two chests of Sutton Premier had safely run the blockade and been delivered by the railway cart as they had been since ever she could remember. Their arrival had smacked of normality in a world gone mad.

Sighing deeply, she set the kettle to boil. She was so tired of this war. Everyone was. So very weary of the wretchedness of it; of food queues and the bleakness of having no hopes to an end of it. But mostly it was the partings, the woundings; the telegrams that brought death in terse, cruel sentences.

'I asked you both if you wanted tea,' she flung testily, but they didn't hear her.

Alice was up and dressed next morning long before she need have been, running her finger round the inside of her bone-stiff collar, wondering if she would ever get used to her uniform. In spite of alterations, the dress was still too long for her liking. A show of ankle meant nothing at all now, yet still a VAD's skirt must decorously tip the back of her flat-heeled shoes.

A long white apron and headdress lay carefully folded in one brown paper bag, her shining-clean ward shoes in another, lest they were splashed with mud on the ride to the hospital.

Last night they had checked the carbide lamps at the fronts of their bicycles, and fitted red-glassed candlelamps to the backs. Lady Helen had insisted on it, the road to Denniston House being little more than a lane.

Now, in less than two hours, they would report to Matron, and Alice wished she hadn't lain sleepless half the night worrying about it and about Jin's solemn prophecies. *Three* men? Tcha! Peculiar, Jin Dobb was! And why, Alice wondered, was her stomach making such noises? Was it hunger or apprehension, or a mixing of each?

She needed her breakfast. Porridge, it would be, eaten

515

without sugar, and butterless toast with a scraping of jam – and be thankful for it, girl! Tom wouldn't be eating his breakfast in a warm kitchen!

'Mornin', nurse,' beamed Cook as Alice pushed open the kitchen door. 'Hurry and sit you down, so's we can make a start.'

Tilda and Jin were smiling, their eyes sliding to Alice's plate and Tom's letter.

'Go on, then. Get it opened!' Tilda laughed. 'Thinking he'd run off with a *mam'sel*, weren't you?'

'Course I wasn't!' She took her knife, carefully slitting open the envelope, shaking with relief.

'France. He's got there. And there's an address I can write to.'

'Where?' Tilda demanded.

'It doesn't say. Just a Field Post Office number. But he'll try to let me know if he can. They've got to be careful what they write.' She folded the letter, slipping it in her pocket. 'I'll read it later,' she murmured as Jin, red-faced from the fire, spooned porridge into plates.

Now was the time to tell him; to let Tom know she was a nurse and to beg him, implore him as he loved her, not to write to Reuben and forbid her going to France.

I'm not meaning to deceive you, Tom. It's just that I want to help win the war – get you home sooner. And I want to be near you, my love . . .

But she couldn't tell him. Not yet.

'Denniston House,' said Julia, 'used to scare the wits out of me. Giles and Nathan always insisted that a witch lived there. They were never apart in those days, and I'd follow them around like a lost dog. They hated it – did their best to get rid of me.

'"We're going Denniston way", was all they'd have to say to send me running back home. There wasn't a witch – just an eccentric old woman.'

'I got a letter from Tom this morning,' Alice offered. 'He's got an address now. It's lovely countryside where he is, and some of the trees already greening up, he says. Well, they would be. It's warmer there. Doing bayonet drill and helping unload transports . . .'

'Doesn't sound as if he's in the trenches, does it? I got one, too. Mine didn't say anything at all! Stop, and I'll show you. It's Andrew's writing on the envelope, but look at what's inside!'

Alice withdrew the picture postcard, turning it over, frowning. 'Not a word on it . . .'

'I know. It's too dark to see, but it says "View of the River Meuse", on it, in French – and the postmark is Reims. That envelope hasn't been anywhere near the Censor. There's a French stamp on it – censored letters don't need stamps.'

'You think he bought that postcard and managed, somehow, to post it?'

'At Reims,' Julia nodded. 'He was probably there on army business, or something. It's his way of telling me where he is. I could never be sure before, and I know he shouldn't have done it – but I'm not going to tell anyone, and besides, I still don't know which regiment he's attached to. Tonight I'll have a good look at the map and see if I can pinpoint where he might be. But we'd better get a move on. Don't want to be late this morning, or Sister'll be furious. And had you realized, Alice, that just around that bend is about to begin the first day of the rest of our war? Exciting, isn't it?'

And one step, one day, nearer to Andrew.

'Where on earth have you been, Julia? I was just about to come and find you. I thought you must have fallen asleep.'

'Good job you didn't, or you'd have found me sitting on the edge of the bath, up to the ankles in cold water! We were run off our feet. They're so short-staffed, Mother. Two nurses in sick quarters with streaming colds, and one on compassionate leave – family bereavement.

'It was the heavy shoes, I think. My feet really hurt. But what has Cook sent up? I'm starving. All we had all day was a cup of tea, one sandwich, and a mug of soup, and taken on our feet, too. How nice to eat off trays tonight, just you and me.'

'There's cold meat and chutney and a pear for pudding. Catchpole says the late croppers are starting to ripen now. And just because today has been special for you, I thought we'd have a glass of wine. Now, tell me all about it!'

'Right from the start? Well, we reported to Sister Carbrooke – the junior nurses call her Sister Car*bolic*! She's a dragon. No "Welcome to the VAD" or anything. She just snorted, "You've come!", then told us how short-staffed they are.

'Because my hands aren't properly healed, I went on the convalescent ward – very few of the men need dressings there – and Hawthorn was sent to help out on the surgical ward. There isn't an operating room at Denniston. The ops are done at York, then sent to Denniston.

'I've got a lovely staff nurse. She's called Ruth Love and the men call her Ruthie behind her back. Before long, most of them will be going on leave, then back to their regiments, but some will be discharged. They are all so very cheerful. Hawthorn said that, even in her ward where some of them are really ill, they never grumble. She said it's because they've got Blighty wounds. Do you know what that is, Mother?'

'Sadly, Julia, I do.'

'Sorry. You work at Denniston, too.'

'If you can call it work,' she shrugged. 'I shall be there tomorrow. I might even be in your ward. Really, it's only doing what I can to help without getting in the way of the real nursing – things like just listening to someone who wants to talk, or reading the papers to a man who has lost his sight. And I write letters for them, too. I feel so fortunate, when I've been there. It makes me count my blessings.'

'Me, too. This morning, Nurse Love asked me to help a man to shave – his right arm was shattered. So I lathered his face – he said he enjoyed that bit – but when I tried to shave him his courage failed. He said he'd make a better job of it with his left hand! I was very relieved. That razor made me nervous.

'Mostly, though, I fetched and carried. Hot water for shaving; helping those who couldn't make it to the wash-room; and I nearly died when Staff asked me to give a man a bath!'

'Oh, *dear* . . .' Helen murmured.

'Oh, it turned out all right, in the end. He was more embarrassed than me, I think. He'd lost a leg, above the knee, and couldn't manage on his own. I think it was the first proper bath he'd had since he was wounded, and he looked so embarrassed. I managed to hide my blushes though. Told him I had brothers of my own, and a husband too. I scrubbed his back, then left him to it. Staff thought it best, I suppose, to throw me in at the deep end, though I'll admit I felt a bit hot under the collar at first.'

'Goodness! I don't think your pa would have liked it if I'd been asked to do anything like that. Do you think Andrew – '

'Andrew's a *doctor*!' Julia laid down her knife and fork with a clatter. 'Oh, hell! I do want him.'

'I know, dear. I know.' Helen reached for her daughter's hand. 'And one morning, I promise you, we'll wake up to peace. One day it will be over. The judge says there's going to be a tremendous showdown before long, on land

519

and at sea. It might be over sooner than any of us dare hope.'

'Then if Judge Mounteagle is right, there'll be a lot of casualties. We're bursting at the seams now, and it's just the same at York.'

She gazed into the fire, remembering Ward 3F, clean and empty and its long rows of waiting beds. Then she shut down her thoughts and arranged her lips into a smile. 'I'm going to be a good nurse, Mother. Andrew will be proud of me, one day.'

'He's proud of you already, I shouldn't wonder. And can I tell you my news now? I needed to tell you this morning, and you weren't there. Now that you are, I'm finding it difficult . . .'

'Giles? They haven't sent him to the Front?'

'No. As far as I know, he's fine. It's Cecilia. This afternoon, I had a letter.'

'So she knows? How did she take it?'

'Very bravely. She thanked me for writing and sent me her love, she said, in my distress; but I think that at the moment she is fighting it – trying to convince herself it will all come right. She goes to church every day to pray, she says, that Robert will be found. She's asking for a miracle, but her faith is so strong, she imagines . . .' Her voice trailed into hopelessness.

'She thinks God will listen to her? And you, Mother; what do you think?'

'There'll be no miracle,' Helen said flatly. 'A woman knows if her son is alive. Robert is not. But I shall write every week to Cecilia. I have such fondness for her. I often think that, when the war is over, I'll go to India. I saw the tea garden – just after your pa and I were married. I should like to see it once more, and meet Cecilia.

'I hope her parents won't try to hustle her into a marriage. She's so brave. Each time she writes I find something more to like about her, yet she will never be my daughter now.'

'Darling, don't be sad.' Her mother was close to tears. 'Try not to think about it. I want your advice.' It was Julia's turn to take her mother's hand. 'Dearest, listen. When we were at the Military Hospital, I got a telling-off because Hawthorn called me Miss Julia. Staff Nurse as good as said it wasn't allowed. She said Hawthorn must call me Julia or MacMalcolm, and I agree with her, though here at Rowangarth it would be an embarrassment to her to try to change things. But if I call her Alice, you'll understand and not think she's being pushy?'

'I understand perfectly, though it might be below-stairs who will condemn Hawthorn, not me. I can't see Miss Clitherow allowing it, can you?' Helen smiled. 'I like the child. She's a good influence on you, and she's fond of you too. Don't worry. Things will even out, given time. Tell me, how was Hawthorn's first day?'

'She didn't say much on the way home. I think the ward she was on was a bit of a shock to her. Her Tom is in France. Seeing those awful wounds would upset her.'

'Poor little Hawthorn. She was so alone when she came to Rowangarth. Then Reuben took her under his wing and she met her young man. She was so happy, yet now she must feel it all slipping away from her. This war has much to answer for, and ordinary people like you and me – and Hawthorn and Cecilia, too – can do very little about it.'

'Don't be sad, Mother.' Julia raised her glass. 'Let's drink to those we love.'

'To our loved ones,' Helen murmured. 'And may God keep them safely . . .'

Alice signed her name to the letter, blotted it carefully, then sighed deeply, glad it was done. Tom knew now – or he would do before so very much longer. And how he would take it heaven only knew, because not only had she told him about being a nurse, but her pen had gone quite mad and she had found herself telling him everything. Now all she could do was hope he wouldn't write at once to Reuben, complaining about her foolishness in telling lies about her age.

She shrugged into her warm coat, then tied a scarf around her head. The moon was still bright; she needed no light tonight. She ran quickly towards Keeper's Cottage, knocking on the door, calling out as she entered.

Reuben was sitting beside the fire, reading yesterday's Sunday paper, passed on to him by Cook.

'Hullo, lass. I hoped you'd come. Sit you down. Morgan not with you?'

'I left him. He's in the winter parlour with her ladyship and Miss Julia, so I didn't bother. I can't stay long, Reuben.'

'Aye. Reckon you'll be tired, though I hope you'll stay long enough to tell me what's bothering you, because something *is*.'

'It is.' No use beating about the bush. 'There's something I've been keeping from Tom.'

'Then put it to rights. Write and tell him now.' As far as Reuben was concerned, the solution was as plain as the nose on your face.

'I have done. I've written him a letter and I want you to post it for me tomorrow. If I don't give it to you now, I'll lose courage and tear it up.'

'And what's in it that's so awful? Found another young man, have you?'

'Reuben – *no*! It's just that I hadn't told him about me being a nurse. I thought he wouldn't like it – that he'd forbid it.'

'But he can't forbid it. You're not wed to him yet.' Reuben folded the paper and dropped it to the floor. 'I can, though, because I'm your guardian. And I haven't, now have I – forbidden it, I mean?'

'No, you haven't.'

'Even though you didn't think to come and mention it to me at the time – as a courtesy, like?'

'I'm sorry. I should have.'

'Ar. So now we've straightened things out, why don't we have a sup of tea?'

Unspeaking, she filled the kettle and set it to boil. Then she took two large cups from the dresser, and the milk jug, and teaspoons from the drawer. Only when she had placed the teapot in the hearth to warm did she say, 'It isn't straightened out.'

'There's more?' He unhooked his reading spectacles, the better to see her.

'There is,' she nodded. 'My age.'

'You'll be twenty, come June – what is there to get het-up about in that?'

'Plenty. I told them I'd be twenty-one next, when I signed for nursing, and they didn't check up on me. I told them,' she rushed on, 'because Miss Julia's going to volunteer for abroad and I want to go too. But I've got to be twenty-one, and – '

'And Tom wouldn't like to think of his girl at the Front? I'm inclined to agree with him, an' all.'

'But I wouldn't be at the front line! They don't have hospitals full of wounded men right at the Front. And they wouldn't send a woman where it wasn't safe.'

'Not deliberately. But danger has a habit of turning up unexpected, like. They drop bombs from aeroplanes now, and the Kaiser has got that great gun – Big Bertha – that can send shells for miles and miles. How safe is safe, will you tell me?'

'You're going to say I can't go?' She didn't weep or pout. If she had, there'd have been an end to it and he'd have said she wasn't to go. But she looked up at him, her brown eyes so beseeching that instead he said nothing.

'You are, aren't you?' she insisted.

'Oh, dear. Do you know, lass, I used once to regret not having bairns of my own – but not any more. Sons go to war – even daughters go.'

'But not me; not Alice Hawthorn?' she whispered.

'It isn't up to me, Alice – not entirely. If the VAD people find out you aren't of age, then that'll be an end to it. They'll tell you to wait for another year, and no begging nor pleading is going to change it.'

'I suppose so,' she choked, like a child admitting to stealing jam.

'But you think you can get away with it?'

'I know I can. If they'd wanted proof of age, they'd have asked for it long since They're desperate for nurses out there, and if I pass my exams they'll be satisfied enough. There are plenty of young men give a wrong age to get to the Front.'

'Aye, and their fathers should be taking their belts off to them, the daft young things – like I should be smacking your bottom now for telling lies to the Government. But I won't.' His face shaped itself into one of his rare smiles. 'You shall go, Alice lass, because I admire your spunk. If the nursing folk don't put a stop to it, then I won't either.'

'Reuben! Not even if Tom writes to you and tells you not to let me?'

'*Especially* if he tells me not to let you. The day is long gone when Reuben Pickering took orders from younglings like Tom!'

'Oh, you lovely man! You *lovely* man!' She threw her arms around him, hugging him tightly. 'Thank you! And I'll be all right. Miss Julia and me'll stay together and I won't do anything to let you down. You'll be proud of me, I promise you will.'

'All right then,' he grunted, unwinding her clinging arms. 'Enough's enough. Let's be having that sup of tea, shall us?'

She was, he thought, as he stood on his doorstep watching her go, a right little charmer. His own lass, had he had one, would have been just like Alice; every bit as sweet and thoughtful and wilful and bonny.

A right little bobby-dazzler, in fact . . .

30

It was all very well for Miss Julia, who'd had a head-start, so to speak, with regard to naked male bodies, her being reared with brothers and having the benefit, if only for a week, of a husband. On the other hand she, Alice, had learned about men from women; from whispered gigglings which ill-prepared her for what Julia took almost for granted. Now, however, after two weeks of bedpans and bed-bottles and rubbing male buttocks with ointment to prevent bed-sores, Alice's embarrassment was less acute.

By comparison, Julia's accomplishments were small: her energies had been focused on her feet coming to terms with her uncomfortable shoes; the healing of her hands; and the ability to manoeuvre patients into and out of a slippery bath with nonchalant ease.

'I feel happier now I know where Andrew is.' Julia, who had minutely examined maps of the Reims area, was as certain as she could be that about forty miles from there – somewhere around Verdun – was where she must hope to be sent when her overseas posting was approved. 'Imagine, if I were out there and he went to Reims again, there'd be a chance we could meet, even for just a little while.'

Oh, my darling, what could we do in an hour . . .

'Wish I knew where Tom was.' Alice pedalled harder to keep within earshot. 'Wouldn't it be grand, miss, if he's ended up in the doctor's part of the line? I've asked him – well, sort of . . .' She couldn't ask it outright. Soldiers were not allowed to say where they were, and their sweethearts should know better than to ask. 'I hinted, though.' She'd done it rather well, she thought.

I miss you, Tom, and I wish I could be with you. I wonder all the time where you are . . .

'He'll find a way. They mostly do.' Julia sighed her relief as they rounded the corner to see Rowangarth gate lodges ahead. 'And as long as we don't talk about it, it's all right.'

DON'T TALK! posters constantly reminded them. There were spies everywhere, sending messages back to Germany. Spies on motor buses and trains; spies dressed as nuns and dockyard workers, people said. Spies were the latest fad, and were talked about all the time. It made a change from those Russians shunting the length of the country and back again. Now women whiled away the long waits in sugar queues and margarine queues, embellishing the latest spy story.

'Do you suppose, miss, that we'll start proper duties tomorrow? Nights . . . ?'

'I don't think so. I heard tell the nurses who had 'flu will be back on the wards, so we'll not be kept quite so busy.'

'We'll have to learn a lot, if we're to pass our exams.'

Alice longed for the chance to do some real nursing. On her first day in the surgical ward, a gangrenous wound had sickened her, made her want to turn away from the sight and stench of it. But instead she had smiled gently into eyes uncannily like Tom's, lifting a dressing from the tray with tweezers, passing it to the nurse who was allowed to perform such tasks.

'We'll pass.' After two weeks, Julia needed to catch up with Alice. Both had learned the layout of the hospital and how best to cope with Sister's rapped commands. Now they were so used to the smell of carbolic they hardly noticed it. 'I'm hoping to get on one of the other wards tomorrow. Nurse Love is a dear, but the men in her ward can do most things for themselves. All I seem to have learned is how properly to make a bed, make hot drinks and serve meals.' And fill and empty baths, of course, and run errands until her feet ached and her ankles swelled. Yet whatever she did, however menial, would take her one day nearer to France. It was all, really, that mattered.

Monday morning was cold; a frosty beginning which pinked cheeks and a wind that brought tears to the eyes. Julia, tapping the weather glass in the hall, had watched the pointer tremble to 'Fair'.

'It'll be a good day.' She sniffed inelegantly. 'I wouldn't be surprised to see some sunshine. I hope Sister lets us work together today. Hey! What's going on?'

Outside Denniston House, all was activity, in the middle of which Nurse Love called orders, heaved kitbags, and shepherded men in hospital blue into motors and trucks.

'Staff!' Leaving their bicycles they ran up the gravelled drive. 'What is it? Can we help?'

'I'll say you can help! Imagine – they told me last night they wanted my ward cleared and cleaned. Look, just give me a hand, will you? The men are being transferred; most on leave, a few to another hospital. I'll explain later.

'Hawthorn – you are to work with MacMalcolm and me today. The 'flu nurses aren't fit for duty yet, Matron says. You know the ward, MacMalcolm. Give any help you can, and see that no one leaves anything behind. They're so eager to be off – can't blame them, I suppose. You, Hawthorn, will make sure that each has his leave pass and travel warrant, then you're to go with them to the station and make sure they can manage to get on their trains.

'Most of them are Jocks, so that'll be the best part of them on the Edinburgh train; the rest you'll have to see to as best you can. The driver will give you a hand, then being you back here afterwards – is that understood?'

528

'Don't worry. I'll manage.' Oh, my goodness! More than thirty men, some on crutches, some with arms in slings, all carrying kit, to be despatched safely on their separate ways.

'Listen, *please*!' Ruth Love held up a hand for silence. 'Nurse Hawthorn and the driver will see you get your trains all right. Do exactly as she tells you and you'll be fine. Off you go, then. Goodbye, and good luck. Enjoy your leaves.'

''Bye, Nursie!'

'So long, Ruthie. Thanks a lot!'

To whistles and cheers, the driver slammed home the tail-board.

'See if you can find any Medical Corps lads on the station, Hawthorn – you just might be lucky. If not, get hold of porters to give you a hand. That lot are like kids let out of school, so don't take any nonsense. Let them know who's in charge.'

'Yes, Staff.' Alice took a deep gulp of air which did nothing at all to stop the giddiness inside her. Imagine! Nurse Hawthorn in charge of a lorry-load of walking wounded?

Oh, my goodness. If Tom could see her now!

'Clear and clean the ward?' Julia put on her apron and starched white cap. 'Why?'

'You might well ask! Be a dear, see if you can get me a slice of bread and a mug of tea? I've been hard at it since five this morning, with no help at all!

'And get something for yourself too,' she added. 'Heaven only knows when we'll find time to eat again! I'd best let Sister know they're all on their way – tell you later what it's about.'

Julia gazed around the ward. Beds lay unmade; locker doors hung open. In the kitchen, the VAD cooks could tell her nothing.

'They don't tell *us*. All I know is they wanted thirty-four breakfasts for six o'clock. Convalescent ward being emptied was all I was told. Is this for Ruth Love?' she demanded, cutting two thick slices. 'She likes the crusts cut off. Have some yourself, if you'd like. I tell you, it's mayhem in this place today, and nobody gives a thought to the cooks!'

'I promise from now on I will. And we'll soon know what's going on,' Julia shrugged, jamming the bread. 'They've got their reasons, I suppose.'

Eyes closed ecstatically, Ruth Love drank thirstily from her mug, then bit deeply into the bread. 'Aaah, that's better. Sorry to give you the run-around, MacMalcolm. Best tell you now what it's all about.

'I didn't know until late last night that they wanted the ward emptied. The clerk was at it into the small hours, writing out leave passes and warrants. There's heavy fighting at the Front; a lot of casualties too. Not just the usual wounded; Gerry's been using some new gas – Lord knows what it was. Pretty awful, though. Phosgene, Sister thinks. It burns out the lungs – they choke to death. That's why there's a panic on; the gas cases must have on-the-spot treatment, so most of the rest are being shipped on to Blighty.'

'I didn't know,' Julia whispered. 'There's been nothing in the papers about fighting . . .'

'Nor will there be, yet. They always seem to keep things back.'

'When did it start?' Her mouth had gone suddenly dry.

'About a week ago, I believe. York Military was on to Matron last night. They are being sent one hundred and fifty wounded without so much as a please or thank you. York can only cope with half, at the very most. The rest they've got to farm out anywhere they can.'

'There must have been very heavy fighting.' Julia recalled

Ward 3F and the forty clean beds they had left behind them.

'There was – *is*; it's still going on. Could go on for weeks.'

'How much time do we have, Staff?'

'I'd like everything ready by noon. They're expecting the hospital train at York early afternoon, but you just can't tell. The lockers must be wiped out, the beds stripped and the waterproofs disinfected. Plenty of carbolic in the water. Then the floor will have to be done, but we'll manage that between us with mops. Did they issue you with a scrubbing apron?'

Did they indeed! Julia's cheeks blazed, just to remember.

'Damn!' she hissed. 'My hands are almost better. Not that I mind scrubbing, Staff,' she added hastily, 'but until my hands are healed, they won't let me near any real nursing.'

'I'll give you some rubber gloves. Go easy with them, mind. They're hard to get hold of.'

'What isn't? Bless you, Ruth – *sorry*!' Too late, she realized. Idiot that she was to use a superior's first name!

'That's all right. I don't mind, but be careful when Sister's around. My, but that was good!' She wiped a crumb from her mouth. 'Down to work, then! Beds first. Blankets folded, sheets and pillow-slips in the laundry basket. No rest for the wicked,' she smiled. 'We'll be casualties ourselves before the day is over.'

'Then bags I the bed nearest the big window,' Julia laughed, all at once feeling affection for the red-haired, hazel-eyed nurse. 'Tell you what, though – I'd rather be here than in Alice's shoes. Wonder how she's coping with that lot?'

Probationer Nurse Hawthorn had coped very well, and now, on her way back to Denniston House, she felt the amazed satisfaction of a job well done.

'Thanks for your help,' she said shyly to the driver at her side. 'I couldn't have managed on my own.'

'Lucky for the pair of us there were all those medical lads around.' He offered a cigarette. 'Smoke?'

'No, thanks.' She watched, fascinated as, one hand on the wheel, he lit his own. Then, inhaling deeply and blowing out smoke through his nostrils, he said, 'Makes you think, dunnit – all them stretcher-bearers and orderlies around? Waiting for a hospital train, if you ask me. Balloon must have gone up again at the Front. You'd have thought the bad weather would've kept things quiet.' He sighed loudly. It could only be a matter of time before he, too, would be sent to France. 'Got a boyfriend, Nurse?'

'I have.' *Nurse*. Alice glowed. She would never get used to the heady title. It lifted her at once from a servant to a somebody. She gave him her brightest smile. 'He's at the Front, though I don't know where. With the West Yorkshires.'

'Infantry, aren't they?'

'Mm. Tom's got his marksman's badge, him being a gamekeeper.'

'Ar.' The driver lapsed into silence. If those Medical Corps lads were waiting for a hospital train, it meant only one thing. Wounded. So many wounded they couldn't cope with them over there. He hoped the little nurse's bloke wasn't among them.

Dipping into his pocket, he wrapped his fingers round the hag stone that lay there. Hag stones were lucky, and you needed all the luck you could get in this bloody war. 'Soon have you back,' he said.

Alice, still a little nervous about riding in motors, gave herself to thinking about the morning. Just as Nurse Love had said she might, she had found orderlies and stretcher-bearers on the station platform. Selecting one with two stripes on his arm, she had explained her predicament, then begged his help – just for a little while, she'd hastened to add. And the wonderful man had let go a whistle that hit the roof with a clatter then bawled, '*Aaghovereeeeere!*' In seconds, she'd had her pick of a dozen orderlies.

'Nah then – this little nurse 'ere has thirty walking wounded and their kit to see on to trains and she needs a hand. Do as she bids you, and no old buck, mind!'

She had managed better than she could have hoped. People could be very nice. It was the war, perhaps, that had made them that way . . .

'My word. You know how to time it!' Julia teased when Alice returned to the ward. 'Just off to find some cocoa. What does this remind you of?' She removed her scrubbing apron, regarding the gloves with near affection. 'I'd have killed for a pair of these on Ward 3F.'

'Hullo, Hawthorn.' Ruth Love tied on a clean, white apron. 'Did you get them away all right?'

'Fine. I had plenty of help at the station. You were right; the Medical Corps lads were there. Hope our lot will manage. It's a long journey to Edinburgh.'

'They'll be all right. They're going home. They'll each help the other. I suppose you're wondering what this is all about, but all I can tell you is that we are filling the ward with non-surgical wounded – leastways, let's hope that's what they are. Matron told Sister they'll most likely have a medical officer with them, which will be just as well, since they're coming to us straight from the Front.

'You're both of you being thrown in at the deep end. You'll see some distressing sights – I know, because I've done a stint out there. But at least you're going to learn sooner than later if you've got the stomach for nursing.

'That's all I can tell you at the moment, except to ask you if you could stay just a little later tonight – only this once? If we could get them settled and perhaps fed, it would be a big help to the night staff. I know you'll be tired after so long a day – but would you?'

They said they would; it was what they were there for, after all. They both had men at the Front; it was the least they could do. And besides, they wanted to.

'Bless you. Now let's get that cocoa – and if we're lucky there'll be bread and jam too. And on your way back, pop into Stores and ask them if the bedshirts are ready. And give them this requisition. It's for rubber gloves and scissors for each of you. Look after them. You won't get any more.'

In the nurses' sitting-room where a jug of hot, milky cocoa waited, Ruth Love flopped into the nearest chair and eased off her shoes.

'If I fall asleep,' she whispered, 'don't wake me. Leave me to sleep and sleep, will you? – for a *week*!'

Matron hung up the telephone receiver with a sigh.

'York?' asked Sister Carbrooke.

'The traffic officer at York station. The first of our ambulances is on its way – about an hour, I think it'll be.'

'Right! I'll see to it.' Sister Tutor was not in the habit of using two words where one would suffice. She had already counted out brown paper sacks and clean bedshirts. Now was the time for sterilizers to be set to boil and dressings prepared and placed in covered trays.

And *why* were the two in sick quarters still unfit for duty – because clearly they were! But it was, she supposed, a case of a fit, reasonably healthy female throwing off influenza far more quickly than an overtired, overworked nurse who most times ate snatched meals and neglected her own health shamefully.

There would be the new probationers, of course, but small help they'd be! Willing, but not a lot of use. See what they'd make of this little lot, she pondered grimly.

'You there – MacMalcolm!' Sister strode into the empty, echoing convalescent ward. 'Can you sterilize instruments; lay out a tray?'

'Yes, Sister.' That, at least, Staff Nurse had found the time to teach her.

'Get on with it, then. And from now on, nurses will wear rubbers over aprons. And I don't want to see one wisp of hair beneath caps,' she said to no one in particular. 'Wear gloves and you – Hawthorn, isn't it? You'll be with me to do the sacks. The minute the first ambulance arrives we are all on stand-to until told otherwise.' And heaven only knew when stand-down would be, she thought as the door banged behind her. And heaven wouldn't tell!

'What did she mean – do the sacks?' Alice demanded of Nurse Love. Wouldn't you just know it, though? Of all the nurses here, Alice Hawthorn had landed herself with Sister Carbrooke.

'Brown paper sacks – for the men's things. They'll be coming to us wearing the uniforms they were wounded in. As soon as they start arriving, close your eyes and you could be at a dressing-station in France. No difference at all, except that it'll be much quieter – and safer – here.

'The wounded, if they are lucky, will have had a dressing placed on their wound – that'll be all. It's going to be exactly as if you were on active service, so learn well. You'll write the man's surname and his number, if you can get it, on the sack in black crayon. His boots, tunic, everything he is wearing, will go into that sack. Don't handle them any more than you need to – some will have lice and fleas on them.

'We can take out personal possessions – paybook, things like that – later. The whole lot will be heat sterilized first – get rid of the beasties. Leave on the man's identification. It will be hanging around his neck and, if he is wearing a wristwatch, leave that on too . . .'

She paused, took a deep breath, then continued in the

same, even voice, as if she had said exactly the same words many times before.

'Then, when the patient has been examined, put him into a bedshirt and, if no one is there to carry him into the ward, put a blanket over him to keep him warm. He'll be in shock, most likely, and cold . . .'

'It's like that at the Front?' Julia whispered.

'No. As I said, it's much safer here. And at the Front, when they're brought in, there's a lot of blood about. At least when we get them, the bleeding should have stopped.'

Julia clenched hard on her jaws and said nothing. Alice asked, 'Where will I find Sister? She didn't tell me.'

'Stretchers are being taken into the stableyard. Go there when you hear the first ambulance arriving.'

'They'll be stripped in the stableyard – *outside*!' Julia gasped.

'Outside,' Ruth Love nodded. 'Just the way it would be in France. Only today it isn't snowing or raining and there'll be no shells whining overhead. And remember what you were told about your caps. Fasten them tightly and tuck your hair well in, or you'll be covered in beasties too.'

They hadn't told them it would be like this, Julia thought dully as the first ambulance turned in at the gates. Thrown in at the deep end? Andrew lived all his life in the deep end and she hadn't realized, until now, how awful it must be.

'They're here,' she whispered. 'Best cut along to the stableyard, Alice love. And don't let old Carbolic frighten you. They do say that somewhere beneath that apron she really does have a heart. Good luck . . .'

'You too, Julia.' Pulling back her shoulders, tilting her chin, Alice went in search of Sister – and the deep end they had promised her.

They would always remember the date and the day and the time. Monday, the last but one day of February, and a nightmare from which there could be no awakening.

The first of the ambulances came slowly up the drive as two o'clock chimed out from the stableyard clock. It bore a red cross back and front and on either side. The driver squinted ahead for potholes; the smallest jolt could send red-hot knives through limbs throbbing with pain, and the four he carried had endured enough.

'Right, lads – Blighty!'

The stretcher-bearer jumped down, lifting the canvas flap. Sister Carbrooke swept Alice with her eyes as the first stretcher was gently laid on the stableyard cobbles. 'All right?'

'Yes, Sister – thank you.'

The soldier's eyes were swathed in bandages. His hand reached out, searching for reassurance.

'You're all right.' Briefly the elderly woman cupped the young face in her hands. Then she leaned closer, saying gently, 'I shall undress you now and put you into a bedshirt. Are you in pain?'

'Not a lot. I can't see though. Can't you take the bandages off?' There was panic in his voice. 'When will I be able to see?'

'The doctor who will examine you will know better than I. The first thing is to get you into a warm bed. Tell me your name.'

'Ward. Bill Ward.'

'And your number?'

Impatiently he gave it, cursing the darkness, stiffening his body as she took off his clothes.

Alice wrote quickly on the bag, then stuffed the uniform inside it. The soldier shook with cold and she was ready with a blanket.

'You know where to take him?'

The orderlies nodded and picked up the stretcher. Alice grasped the helpless, searching hand, squeezing it briefly before tucking it beneath the blanket.

The stableyard was filling with stretchers.

537

'Next?' called Sister.

'Over here!' called an orderly.

Sister walked calmly, ignoring the urgency of the summons. Alice followed with sack and blanket, glancing down, frowning.

The soldier's forehead was marked with a purple cross, and she lifted asking eyes to Sister's.

'That's because he's had morphia,' came the terse explanation. 'Help me, please?'

The soldier moaned incoherently, suspended in half sleep above his pain. His trousers had been almost cut away; his legs and lower abdomen were covered with dressings, held fast by dark, congealed blood.

'He's due another injection in half an hour.' Sister read the label pinned to his jacket.

As if she were handling a new-born child, she removed his tunic and shirt.

A land-mine, she frowned. She had seen many such injuries before. An awful way to die. She lifted the identification disc at his throat, then read out the name and number punched on it.

'You can take him now. Please tell Nurse Love that Sister suggests his dressings aren't changed until after his next injection.'

Alice gathered up the bloodstained, mud-caked garments. She could find no boots. Perhaps someone down the line had taken them off.

Her stomach churned. Forty of them, hadn't they said? She wanted a drink of water; wanted to go home to Mrs Shaw's warm, safe kitchen.

'Go to Matron, Hawthorn,' Sister said quietly. 'Tell her I need help. Two nurses for a couple of hours, if she can spare them. And *walk*!' she said.

Out of sight of the stableyard, Alice picked up her skirts and ran. It was against accepted practice, but she did it instinctively, blindly, as if fleeing from danger.

She wanted not to go back. It was awful there. She had never imagined it could be like that. Not just the wounding, but the filth and degradation and, oh, God! Any one of those wounded could have been Tom!

She hurried into the wash-house, filling her hands with clean, cold water, drinking greedily. Then she pulled her sleeve across her mouth, straightened her cap, and walked quickly back to Sister's side.

'Matron's sending two. And she says that if you want her to . . .'

'We'll manage.' A matron wasn't expected to nurse. She was there to teach, to command, to ensure the smooth running of the hospital and, sometimes, to bear the brunt of higher authority's stupidity.

The brief brightness of the afternoon was fading; a cold, snappy wind blew from the north-east.

'How many more?' Sister rose to her feet, hands in the small of her back.

'One of the drivers says we've got the lot now – for the time being. Says there are about a dozen more following in horse ambulances – the walking wounded.'

Sister stifled a sigh of relief. At least walking wounded would be in better shape – could help themselves a little. She made a small, satisfied sound as two nurses hurried into the yard, then did a quick count.

Twelve more to go. Twelve more paper sacks then maybe, just *maybe*, there would be time for a mug of hot tea before the next ambulance arrived

Alice took the black crayon from her pocket. The sight of two more nurses comforted her, made her feel less alone. Surely, soon, it would be over, then she could lock the sacks in the outhouse and run and be sick in the lavatory pan.

The light was beginning to fade as the last of the stretcher cases was carried to convalescent ward. Without waiting, the orderlies returned the empty stretchers to the ambulances, then headed back to the station. No time to dilly-dally. Another hospital train expected, they said . . .

'Thank you, Nurses.' Matron, appearing in the yard, smiled gently. 'I will be in Nurse Love's ward if you need me, Sister. I want the medical officer to sign requisitions before he goes back to York.

'There is a pot of tea in the sitting-room – I suggest you all take a few minutes' break before the next ambulances get here . . .'

A dozen more men, Alice thought dully, and all of them dirty, tired, their hurriedly applied dressings starting to smell. God – don't let them do this to Tom!

Her hands were dirty and blackened with crayon dust; the parts of her apron not protected by the waterproof she was wearing were wet and soiled. Across her right sleeve was a smear of blood; her starched cuffs would never be clean again.

'Are you all right?' asked a nurse.

'No.' Alice shook her head vehemently. 'Are you?'

'You'll get over it. First time it happened to me, I threw up . . .'

'Where was that?' Alice picked up the last of the paper sacks.

'In London, when I was doing my training. That first big bombing raid. Civilians, they were. You'll harden yourself to it . . .'

'Will I?' Would she ever? Did she want to be hard?

She turned the key in the outhouse door, then took off her soiled apron, rolling it into a ball, pushing it into a paper sack.

'If you don't scrub up quick, they'll have drunk all the tea,' the nurse said.

A mug of hot tea. Alice needed it; needed to wrap her numbed fingers around its warmth. She straightened her cap, pushing in her hair, wondering if she had caught any fleas.

Hot, sweet tea. She hurried to the nurses' sitting-room, fastening on a clean apron as she went.

Best she should forget about being sick. There simply wasn't time!

Cook was waiting up when they got back to Rowangarth, her hair in a long plait, her serviceable dressing-gown covering her nightdress.

'Here you are – goodness gracious! Half-past ten!' she chided fondly. 'Her ladyship is in bed. Will you go up, she says, and say goodnight, Miss Julia? I'll bring you up a tray.'

'Don't bother, Mrs Shaw. If you're making tea, I'll come down and have it with you.'

She didn't want her mother to see her; not like this. All she wanted, truth known, was to creep into bed and weep into her pillow.

'You look all-in, lass,' Cook said to Alice. 'Why did they keep you so late? Fifteen hours – it's over-long.'

'Wounded, Cook. Just dumped on us without so much as a by-your-leave. Nurse Love had to clear her ward – all her patients sent home. I went with them to York and got them on to their trains.

'Then the wounded came. Straight from France. All filthy with mud and their wounds – you should have seen them! There's a big battle going on, Verdun way.'

'Isn't that where Doctor Andrew is?' Cook made a sucking noise through her teeth.

'We think so – and maybe Tom, for all I know.'

Tears, held in check for so long, ran down her cheeks. She lifted her pinafore, buried her face in it – just as Cook always did – and wept.

'Poor bairn. There, there now.' Cook took her, held her. Nobbut a bit of a lass. It wasn't right. 'Come on, now. Dry your eyes. Mustn't let Miss Julia find you like this when she comes down.'

'Sorry.' Alice splashed her face with cold water, dabbing it dry on the roller-towel; taking a deep, shuddering breath, vowing that, no matter what, she mustn't ever allow herself to weep again; not until this war was over. Tears were a luxury no nurse could indulge herself in. 'I'm all right, now. I'm just tired. Will there be hot water for a bath?' Have a bath, Sister had told them, and wash your hair.

'Plenty. Enough for both of you. Now then, will I make some toast before I bank the fire down?'

'You're a good soul, Mrs Shaw. Thanks for all you've done for me.'

'Away with you! I'm proud of my nurses! Say goodnight to Miss Julia for me,' she smiled, pushing in the fire dampers. 'And don't sit up all night talking!'

'Tea?' Alice asked, when Julia returned. 'Cook says goodnight, by the way.'

'Please. A mug. Mother's all right. I didn't tell her too much. Don't want to worry her.'

'But she'll find out. Tomorrow is one of her visiting days!'

'I know. She's going to ring Matron first – doesn't want to get in the way. That isn't dripping toast, is it?'

'Mm. Cook left it for you.'

'Hasn't today been awful?' Eyes closed, Julia bit into the toast. 'I'm glad you were there; I couldn't have got through it if I hadn't known you were feeling just like me. Do you remember one of the first in – he had awful injuries.'

'The one with the morphia cross . . . ?'

'That one. Ruth Love looked at his disc, and saw he was a Catholic. So she sent me to Matron to ask her to get the priest from Creesby. She says he might not live through the night. The medical officer who came with them said she wasn't to try to remove his dressings – just

542

see he wasn't in any pain. It was awful. It's how Andrew has to live, day in, day out . . .'

'I know. I kept wanting to be sick. I couldn't stop thinking about Tom.'

'Andrew's at Verdun amongst all that fighting. That's where he is . . .'

'Where you *think* he is.' Where Tom might be. 'Today is over now. We did our best. And nothing will ever hurt us as badly as today. Remember that.'

They had survived their deep end. They were nurses now. She held out her hand across the table and Julia took it in her own.

'Thanks, Alice. Thank you for understanding . . .'

31

Picardy, thought Tom Dwerryhouse, was a bonny area, not unlike the countryside he had left behind him; fresh and green, bursting eagerly into spring. At the lanesides, wild flowers budded and, in the thickly wooded distance, the land swelled into small hills to remind him of Holdenby Pike and Creesby Fell. Those hills, their platoon sergeant had been at pains to point out, were to be viewed with respect and not respected for their view! They were occupied – and never let them forget it – by an unseen enemy. Into those hills, the Kaiser's lot were entrenched, and behind those hidden dugouts, British intelligence gatherers reported, were batteries of enemy guns of all shapes and sizes, every one of them smugly safe – or so they thought, the sergeant added with a peevish smile and nodding of his head to indicate that he knew something his subordinates did not.

So, between those hills and our own front line must be No Man's Land, Tom considered, though it wasn't at all like he'd been given to expect; what he had actually seen on films at the Picture Palace. No Man's Land should be pitted and scarred; stuck with gaunt, drunken tree stumps and shell-holes and mud. Sealed with coils of vicious wire, No Man's Land should be littered with abandoned guns and carts and dead, swollen horses. That had been his imagining of it, with men shivering in rat-ridden trenches either side of it. Until now, that was.

Thus Picardy, and the beautiful River Somme that wound through it had come as a surprise, a bonus; had even provided clean, dry billets in the shape of a row of empty houses a mile outside the town of Albert.

Albert had been all but flattened, but by the whim or bad aim of the German artillery, the row of seven houses had escaped, though those who lived in them had long ago left.

Tom's billet had a sound roof, a kitchen range made good use of, a wash-house with a deep, wooden sink, and a mangle, left behind in the haste of leaving. No soldier could ask for more.

They had been playing at soldiers ever since their arrival in France; practising bayonet charges, yelling like banshees. It was essential to yell, the corporal stressed, and not until they did it as well as the Jocks would he be satisfied.

They learned to advance under cover of night, following tapes laid there to guide them, all orderly and neat and just as it would be when the time for the big offensive came, because come it would; one great land battle and a meeting of warships in the North Sea to decide once and for ever in favour of Britain and her allies. And that land battle could well be here, most thought, in the area of the Somme. It didn't take a lot of working out, or why the great dumps of hidden ammunition? His platoon had unloaded and carried shells for weeks now, and great stocks of tinned food and hard-tack rations – even fodder, for horses. Fatigues, they called it. It would have been boring had it not been so good to know how well-equipped and well-fed the army of the Somme was to be.

Yet, through that almost peaceful spring, he missed Alice as he had never thought possible. The letters she sent to Richmond had reached him now, and he'd arranged them in order of the postmarks, rationing them against such time as she got his new address. Her letters he read and read again. She was never far from his mind, his buttercup girl. He need only close his eyes to see her face, her smile. He'd been a fool not to insist they be wed. He'd have liked more than anything to have a memory of her dark head on the pillow next to his own, his arms cradling her close.

There was a day he remembered well; a day they played the soldier games the sergeant called manoeuvres. They had advanced through a wood to take an imaginary enemy – two corporals, truth known – by surprise and stealth, with no snapping of twigs or rustling of undergrowth.

Tom was bored by it. He knew better how it was done than most and had let his thoughts wander to another wood and a girl who walked in it. And if he whistled like once he used to, would that daft dog come lolloping up and would Alice be there at the turning of the path?

But that was another place. She wouldn't come, and the pain had gone deep. He'd wanted her so much in that Picardy wood that, when he opened the letter in which she told him she was a nurse, he hadn't thought to feel anything but pride; had even smiled indulgently at her fibbing about her age. She wanted to help win the war, she said; needed to be near him.

Don't forbid me, Tom? I miss you so much. I tell myself that to be in France, knowing that one day I might turn a corner and see you there, is worth all the risk . . .

Alice and Miss Julia both; each would care for the other. By June their probation would be over and they could volunteer for France.

He should have written telling her not to, but instead, because he wanted her till he ached of it, he told her that he loved her and was proud of her. And the sooner, he'd thought, they had their big battles and got this war over with, the sooner he could get her into his bed!

'I need to look at your map of the war, miss.' Alice read Tom's letter yet again, and why Mr Nathan's brother was thought worthy of mention she couldn't for the life of her think. 'Tom's trying to tell me something. There's a bit about Mr Nathan's brother – at the Front . . .'

'Elliot? I don't believe it!'

'His *younger* brother! He saw Nathan Sutton's younger brother in the distance, he says. But he wouldn't say it like that. He'd say he'd seen Albert Sutton, now wouldn't he?'

'But Albert is in America – or he was ten days ago. Mother had a letter from him saying how sorry he was about Robert. Albert wouldn't be in France; his wife would see to that! But we'll look at the map when we get home. Something Tom said rings a bell . . .'

The war map was pinned to Julia's bedroom wall, a Union Jack pin stuck in it at Verdun, and now they searched the entire Western Front.

'Alice, look!' Julia's finger jabbed at the map. '*There*, for heaven's sake! Albert-in-the-distance! Tom must be somewhere near a town called Albert. It's in Picardy. *Miles* away from Andrew.' She took a Union Jack pin, sticking it firmly in Albert.

'Funny old name to give to a place,' Alice frowned.

'No, it's not like we say it. The French pronounce it *Ol-bare*. How clever of him. You lucky thing! It's all quiet there – well away from the fighting. Still, that's got tabs on two of them. Wish I could find where Nathan is. Last I heard was a postcard of the Eiffel Tower – living it up in Paris, the gay dog!'

'*Ol-bare*,' Alice said, red-cheeked with pleasure that Tom was on Julia's wall map – away from the fighting, too. 'Think I'll drop him a line to let him know we've twigged; tell him we're pleased he saw young Sutton. And I'd best write to his mother, too.'

'But be sure not to mention the actual *name* – can't be too careful . . .'

'I won't, miss. And I forgot – Jin washed and starched our aprons and cuffs. I'll iron them and put them to air.' Run off their feet they may be, but Sister expected

547

nothing less than white, immaculately pressed aprons of her nurses.

'You don't have to, Alice. You don't work at Rowangarth now.'

'I still get bed and board, though. I don't like being beholden.'

'All right, if it makes you feel better. But mind you write to Tom, and thanks for doing my ironing.'

Nursing must be doing Julia good, thought Alice, or was it the letter she'd just had and the fact that the doctor was safe and well, in spite of the fighting? Four days ago, that had been. Or could it be that she believed more than ever that one day they would meet?

Please – let them not be sent to the *Eastern* Front.

Giles Sutton watched England fade into the distance, wondering when he would again see those cliffs. He had had a good leave, even though he'd seen precious little of Julia.

His mother, he thought, seemed in good spirits, though she could hide heartbreak with a smile better than anyone he knew. He had spent little time in the library, taking long walks instead, fastening a picture of Rowangarth in his mind to carry away with him. Soft old Morgan had hardly left his side; had rushed around like a creature demented, so pleased had he been to see him; colliding with chairs, sending rugs skittering across the floor.

'Dearest. It's good to be home.' He had folded his mother in his arms, loving the sweet, clean scent of her hair, the perfume that had been a part of her since ever he could remember.

'Am I a disappointment to you, Mother?' They had talked, one day, about Cecilia, and inevitably about children. 'Would you be happier if I were married and had children – a son – of my own?'

'I should be ecstatic, but you are not married, so I don't

548

think about it any more. I used to, when first you went to the army. I wanted a grandson so much. I'd worry about it and about you, Giles, not falling in love. I wanted you to. Loving and being loved is so wonderful that I want you not to miss it.

'But will I tell you something? Not long ago, when I said goodnight to your pa, he seemed to be trying to tell me something from his photograph. So I put out the light and closed my eyes and listened. And he told me not to worry about you; that all my fears would amount to nothing. It was such a comfort.'

'Did you perhaps dream it, Mother?' He had touched her cheek with gentle fingertips. 'Did you want it so much that it came to you as you slept?'

'It wasn't a dream.' She had said it softly, surely. 'You *will* come home, Giles. I know it.' She had been so sure, had waved him on his way with a smile.

He sent his thoughts high and wide. *I am leaving you and all I love most now. I shall think about you always. And if it brings you comfort, hold on tightly to your dream, Mother.*

His eyes blurred with tears and he dashed them impatiently away, reaching for a cigarette, then remembered that to smoke on the upper deck of a troopship at sea was forbidden.

But how could a wife be possible? Where, in this mad world, would he find that woman?

Helen, Edward and Catchpole stood on the terrace, watching as Ellen's husband ploughed up Rowangarth's lawns. The gardener looked on with mixed feelings: a little sadly, because a beautiful lawn was disappearing; yet gladly, because now that there was only himself left to see to things, an acre and a half less grass to cut in the summer pleased him greatly.

'Potatoes,' Helen said firmly, as if trying to convince

549

herself that this was the right thing to do. 'You can't eat grass . . .'

'My father,' Edward Sutton murmured, 'will send down fire and brimstone. He was proud of this lawn – camomile, you know.'

Percy Catchpole brightened visibly. He remembered old Sir Gilbert; a right stickler he'd been. Mind, there had been ten gardeners in the old squire's day; things had changed since twelve-year-old Percy Catchpole had the bluest, numbest hands in the Riding from a winter spent scrubbing plant-pots in ice-cold water.

'I'm sorry, Edward, but growing food is more important.' People were going hungry now – especially the old who hadn't the backbone to stand long hours in food queues.

Catchpole, at a respectful distance, sucked on his empty pipe, watching the nodding plough-horses and the farmer who held them straight and true, wondering how he would manage to supervise the growing, as her ladyship had insisted.

But March was almost gone now, and they could look ahead to warmer days; light nights and happen an end, this year, to the fratching and fighting in France.

'What do you think then, Percy, to the extra hour?' Edward Sutton asked. 'Is it going to help?'

Catchpole snorted. Those dratted fools in London who ordered that every clock in the land be put forward one hour must be out of their minds. Saving an hour of daylight, the Government said. And how, would someone tell him, did you save daylight when what you gained evenings you would lose mornings? According to the seasons, there were so many hours of daylight and darkness; juggling about with them was against nature.

The birds would take no notice of it at all, nor the beasts. Cows wouldn't like being milked earlier nor babies having their breast at the wrong time. An experiment, said the Government, yet one they'd be glad to forget

550

about when all was chaos. It would never work, war or no war.

'Ha!' he snorted, by way of reply.

'You don't agree with it?'

''Tain't natural, Mr Edward.' Agitated, he sucked harder on his pipe. 'Might I be excused, milady? There's a lot to be done.'

'Aren't you just a little sad about it?' Edward demanded when they were alone. 'The lawns, I mean . . .'

'Of course I am. If it weren't Ellen's husband doing the ploughing, I couldn't bear it, in fact.'

Ellen, who had been parlourmaid at Rowangarth in the old days, was now married to one of Helen's tenant farmers. She had returned, once, to help wait at table. Dear Ellen, who remembered John. Such unbelievably green lawns; ploughed over by anyone other than Ellen's husband it would have amounted to sacrilege.

'It's time for coffee,' she murmured, linking her arm in his. 'Come inside and have a cup with me. The house is so empty, now, it echoes. And I want to hear about my nephews, and about Clemmy too.'

'I would like that,' he smiled, seeing the appeal in her eyes. 'I would like that very much indeed.'

Even after all the years, it was always good to go home to Rowangarth.

Catchpole pushed his pipe in his pocket, hurrying back to the kitchen garden. Watching other folk work was all very well, but it didn't do. My, but Rowangarth was a lonely old place now. Sir Giles gone a week past, and even Miss Julia planning on getting into the war.

He clanged shut the iron gate of the kitchen garden, feeling the safety of the nine-feet-high walls. Once that gate was closed behind him, he felt the better for it. His plants didn't know there was a war going on; in a garden, nothing changed.

A robin sang out a challenge from atop the wall; in the corner by the asparagus bed, the first of the pear blossom was white and thick. Was it an omen? Would this year see an end to the madness?

'Now tell me, how is Clemmy?' Helen passed the sugar bowl, though she herself had long since ceased to use it.

'She is well – or I imagine she is. She telephoned two nights ago and I haven't heard since. In London, of course, trying to find wallpaper for the Cheyne Walk house and someone to paste it up for her. The house next door is empty; the bombing has made them move further out into the country. Clemmy says she hopes it won't be taken over as an army billet or for Belgian refugees.'

'And Nathan? Do you know where he is?' Helen refrained from commenting on her sister-in-law's selfishness. 'I had such a lovely letter from Albert a few weeks ago. He seems happy with his Amelia, though it is sad he has given up his British citizenship.'

'His wife wants it, I suppose, if only for the sake of any issue.'

'But I understood Amelia is – well – a little past child-bearing.'

'She hopes, I believe,' Edward smiled. 'And Nathan was in Paris, not long ago, though from the tone of his letters, he's back at the Front now.'

'In the fighting? Andrew is at Verdun, you know – well, Julia thinks he is.'

'I can't be sure, but I think Nathan is nearer to Paris than that. He hasn't mentioned running into Andrew or anyone else he knows. But it's a big battlefield; a very long front line. To meet up with anyone he knew would be unlikely.'

'And Elliot,' Helen asked reluctantly, holding out her

hand for his cup, chiding herself for her lack of charity towards Edward's eldest son.

'He's still in London,' Edward sighed. 'Still at the War Office, though for the life of me I haven't been able to discover what it is he does there.'

'Perhaps it's too secret even for you to be told,' Helen smiled. 'And since Clemmy is away, would you take pity on a lonely woman and stay to luncheon? Julia works from early morning until well past seven. When dinner is over she begs to be excused. She looks so exhausted, poor lamb, yet still she makes time to write to Andrew at least once a day.

'Reuben brought in a young rabbit, yesterday, and Mrs Shaw has such a way them them. Stuffed with thyme and parsley, cooked slowly then cunningly carved, you wouldn't know it from chicken. Do stay?'

'Helen – much as I love you, I ought to refuse. I think it is wrong, now, to eat other people's food. But to think of luncheon cooked by Mrs Shaw corrupts me. Yes, please – I'll stay.'

May had only just gone; the bonniest month in all the year, Cook said. It should have made them feel glad, that time of hawthorn blossom and bluebells and apple trees frothing pink. And in Brattocks Wood, arum and windflowers growing thickly and the wild garlic smelling something awful if you trod on it.

It gladdened Alice's heart to see the first buttercup, growing beside the stile at the edge of the wild garden, and she carefully picked it, laying it in her Bible to send to Tom when it was pressed.

So why, at the ending of that cuckoo-month, when they should have been glad that summer was just around the corner, had there been the most awesome of sea-battles to spoil it; a battle long overdue, mind. One good victory at sea, said the man in the street, and a trouncing at the Front was all we needed to see the Kaiser suing for peace.

So now they'd had their sea-fight, Cook thought, becoming more alarmed with every line she read. The Imperial fleet, said the morning paper, had sailed north from its bases in Bremen and Wilhelmshaven; the Royal Navy had upped anchor from Scapa Flow and steamed to engage them. They met in the Skagerrak – somewhere near Denmark, Tilda said it was, after studying Miss Julia's wall map when she should have been making her bed; met and clashed, big guns blazing.

It seemed a pity, Catchpole said when he brought in the vegetables for Cook, that neither side seemed to have won; not *really* won. Each navy had lost more than a dozen ships, and more men than dare be counted. The Victory of the Skagerrak, the Germans called it; the Battle of Jutland, *our* battle honours, claimed the Admiralty, since the Kaiser's fleet had been first to break off firing and turn tail for home, and *our* ships had chased them most of the way back. Therein lay Britain's claim to victory – and the accepted fact that it would be a long time before the Kaiser's navy ventured out again, having being taught that sabre-rattling in seas considered to be ruled by Britannia was not to be tolerated.

It was the loss of His Majesty's ship *Indefatigable*, though, that finally sent Cook's head into her apron. More than a thousand crew, yet only six survivors. It was hardly to be believed.

'What about Mary's brother?' came Cook's muffled cry. 'Poor, poor lad . . .'

'Mary's brother,' said Tilda who had been left to get on with the breakfasts as best she could, 'is on a mine-sweeper in the Channel – hundreds of miles away,' she retorted scathingly, wishing she had a penny-piece for every tear Cook had wept into that apron.

She sighed deeply, casting a long, loving glance at David-above-the-mantel, and sent up a prayer of thanks he'd had the good sense to join the army.

'You're both to go to Matron's office at half-past ten,' Ruth Love announced when breakfast had been cleared and the medicine trolley done its rounds.

'You know what it'll be about,' Julia said, stacking plates and saucers. 'Wouldn't it be a marvellous birthday present for you, Alice, to know you'd passed with flying colours?'

'Don't even mention it.' Alice was apprehensive. Her handwriting was neat and even, but her spelling left much to the imagination; she would need to have done extra well in her practical examinations to balance things up.

'Why ever not? You're a good nurse and you don't get tired out, like I do.'

'I'm more used to it than you.' Alice worked no more hours at Denniston House than she had done when in service, though being a nurse was more upsetting than ever scrubbing and sewing had been.

'We'll both pass. It's been a good six months; you can't say differently. Remember that awful day when first we started – the forty wounded from Verdun? We managed, didn't we?'

Alice did not deny it; was even secretly proud that every one of those terribly injured soldiers had cheated death, even the boy with the purple cross. They'd be sending him back to civvie street for good soon, Alice thought, wondering if he'd ever discovered he'd been given the last rites. The sight of his wounds had made her want to be sick, Alice remembered. It had been a deep, deep end they'd been thrown into that day.

'Well, you're out of your teen-years now,' Julia smiled.

'*Quiet!*' Alice hissed. 'I'm supposed to be twenty-*one* today. If anyone found out it was my coming-of-age, they'd want to celebrate. I'd feel so ashamed . . .'

'What do you make of Nurse Love?' Julia asked, elbow-deep in suds: VAD probationers at Denniston did all the washing-up, except for pans. 'I mean, she's such a dear person and a marvellous nurse.' Ruth Love hated death; had fought it like a mad thing for the purple-crossed soldier. 'Yet there's a barrier there all the time. And she never talks about herself.'

'She once said she'd done a year in France.'

'I know about that. But what she's never told us is why she came back here when her year was up.'

'Sister came back, too . . .'

'So she did, but there's no mystery there. She got a compassionate posting because her mother was ill.'

'All right, that's fair enough. But what was Ruth's excuse? Is it so awful out there that she couldn't stand any more? Are we going to be afraid, Julia, if we find ourselves in the thick of it? Remember the day the wounded came? Ruth said it was just like that at the Front, 'cept there were no shells.'

'What is it?' Julia dried her hands, taking Alice by the shoulders, turning her round to face her. 'Don't you want to go now? When we've done our training and taken our exams, have you changed your mind?'

'No. Far from it.' Alice shrugged away the hands, reluctant to meet Julia's eyes. 'I want to go; I really do. But I'm no scholar and I mightn't have done well in the written papers. I couldn't bear it if you went without me. I'd die of shame.'

'Listen, you'll pass. I promise you will – word of a Sutton.'

'But you *aren't* a Sutton,' Alice said perversely.

'I was for nearly twenty-two years. And you'd better pass, because I'm not going alone. Chin up! If we hurry with these dishes there'll be time to tidy up for half-past. Please, Alice, cheer up?'

They were walking dry-mouthed across the hall,

hands clenched at their sides, when they saw the notice, VOLUNTEER NURSES WANTED.

'Look – they're asking for nurses for France!' Julia pointed. 'Now wouldn't you say that's a coincidence? It's as if it's meant to be! Come on,' she urged. 'What more do you want?' She knocked on the door with more confidence than she felt, swallowing hard.

'Come!' called Matron.

Alice shuddered visibly; Julia crossed her fingers. 'Word of a Sutton . . .' she whispered as she pushed open the door.

They had done well, Matron said, holding out a hand to each, hoping they would continue with the Voluntary Aid Detachment. They would be most welcome to stay at Denniston House, she said – or did they want, perhaps, to try for a teaching hospital?

'Or had you considered –' she hesitated.

'Volunteering for France? Yes – both of us,' Julia smiled.

'Then think about it carefully, and if you have any doubts at all, talk to me about them. You have both done well. I wouldn't like either of you to be lost to nursing.'

'We passed!' Julia closed the door, leaning against it because her knees were shaking. 'We did it – *you* did it, Alice! Won't Andrew be proud of us when he hears?'

Flushed with triumph, they read through the notice again. Suitable volunteers would be paid twenty pounds per annum, a monthly allowance towards the upkeep of uniform, and all travelling expenses. They would be required to serve for the period of one year, after which their contract could, if desired, be renewed.

'Look who signed whilst we were in Matron's office.'

'Sister and Staff Nurse. Both of them going!'

'Shall we, then? Oh, Ruth's all right, but if we sign does it mean we'll be going with Carbolic?'

'Sister's not half bad,' Alice defended, still giddy with relief. 'She's fair and she's a good nurse. Better the devil we know . . .'

Julia picked up the pencil that hung on a string beside the noticeboard and signed J. H. M. MacMalcolm so firmly that the Mac in her name made a hole in the paper. 'Well?' she said, turning to Alice.

'Give it here!' Alice took the pencil and signed her name with such a flourish that anyone could have been forgiven for forgetting that a little less than five minutes ago she had been shaking like a jelly. 'What's Sister going to say – saddled with the pair of us?'

'Who cares?' Julia laughed triumphantly. She was on her way! What else mattered.

32

So much had happened, so quickly, since that morning in Matron's office. They'd had injections – cholera and typhus; repaired and cleaned their uniforms; written letters.

Don't write again until you hear from me . . .

Goodbye to Brattocks Wood, green-flushed with summer, the evening air sweet-smelling with honeysuckle and wild pink roses; goodbye to the wraith of a girl, wide-eyed with love. She had long gone, and the lover she met there. When they would meet again, and where, she did not know; that they would be different people when they did so was the only thing of which she was sure.

Tonight was Midsummer's Eve. Four days ago, Alice had left her girl-years behind her. By the time July came she would be on her way to France. Just to think of it sent a mixture of excitement and fear churning through her.

Julia MacMalcolm was less apprehensive; had travelled abroad many times. The crossing of the Channel held no fear for her, despite Robert's death. To her, the narrow, submarine-infested strip of water was the last hurdle; to Alice it was a terror to be endured.

Many other things had happened. Portugal had been drawn into the war, our ally now; married men had been called up for service, and six months of fighting at Verdun had ended in stalemate. There had been victories and defeats on both sides, yet the No Man's Land between them was little changed. The Pyrrhic victory both sides claimed had cost a million lives: British, German, French, Austrian. Sons, sweethearts, husbands, fathers. So high a reckoning for so few yards of blood-soaked earth.

Now, the Western Front had lapsed into an uneasy,

waiting silence, most felt along the banks of a river in Picardy, did Alice but know it; a stillness waiting to explode into the fearful roar of a new battle.

Alice called Morgan to her side, walking the length of the wood to the tallest tree. Above he head, rooks cawed lazily home to nest. Eyes closed, she whispered:

Black birds, it's Alice here – Nurse Hawthorn – sewing-maid as used to be to her ladyship. I'm going to France with Miss Julia and Sister Carbrooke and Ruth Love. We're all sticking together.

Heaven only knows what's to be the end of it, but I want to go, to be near Tom. You'll remember Tom – he was keeper here – and I'd like you to know about us, just to keep things straight. I won't be coming this way for a while, but look kindly on Rowangarth and, whatever you do, don't fly away.

The day the rooks left Rowangarth woods would be a sad one. Folk hereabouts knew that if they ceased to nest in Brattocks Wood, nothing but grief for the Suttons would follow. Mind, it had never happened; not in more than three hundred years, but it was what folk believed.

Goodbye, then. I'm going to see Reuben now . . .

'Come in and sit you down,' the elderly keeper smiled. 'The kettle's on the boil – I hoped you'd come afore you went.'

'Hoped? You knew I would!'

The windows and doors were open wide to the summer evening; tobacco smoke mixing with night scents and the smell of burning logs sent an ache of sadness through her.

'I've left everything straight and in order, Reuben. I'm taking Tom's locket and Mam's ring with me; all else doesn't amount to a lot. I've written your name on my trunk.'

'Good heavens to Murgatroyd! What on earth's got into you, lass?'

'Nothing that isn't right and sensible,' she retorted severely. 'And my bank book is at the bottom of the trunk. There's four pounds fifteen shillings in it.' She laughed suddenly. 'Didn't know I was a lady of means, did you?'

'I pray you'll be all right, Alice.' He touched her cheek in a rare gesture of affection. 'You'll be aiming to end up near Tom, I shouldn't wonder?'

'Aye, and Miss Julia wants to get near the doctor. We've had a look at the war map and the only solution is to get a hospital in Paris, half-way between the two of them.'

'Gay Paree,' Reuben frowned. 'You'll have to watch your p's and q's if you end up there.'

'It'll be nearer the Front, Sister says – but not too near,' she hastened.

'That hard-faced Sister woman – you'll both be with her?' Reuben felt greatly relieved.

'Yes, and with Nurse Love an' all. And Sister isn't hard-faced, really. If I was in trouble, I'd rather she were beside me than most I could think of. But promise you won't worry about me? I'll be with Miss Julia and it's likely we'll be staying together. I'd be better pleased if you'd keep an eye on Morgan.'

Affectionately she prodded the spaniel with the toe of her shoe. He snuffled softly in his sleep, then went back to his dreaming.

'I'll see to him. Now then, let's be having that sup of tea, shall us? It'll be a long time afore we have another, I shouldn't wonder.'

'It could be as long as a year,' she said, sad again. 'We sign on for a twelve-month, though we'll get home leave after that, I think.'

She hugged Reuben tightly when she left, patting his back, kissing his cheek.

'I'll not say goodbye,' she smiled, snapping on Morgan's

lead. 'Just so-long, and thanks for not telling on me – when I lied about being old enough for France, I mean. Take care. I'll write the minute we get there. Write back, sometimes, won't you?'

'I'll write, lass.'

He stood at his door, watching the bobbing light of her candlelamp grow smaller in the twilight, then slammed it shut with a cold, seething anger. It was either that or tears – and men couldn't weep. Not even old men . . .

Alice and Julia spent the first night in a hostel in Bloomsbury with a dozen other nurses, all bound for France. Their room had eight beds in it and precious little else. From one of them came a muffled sniffing.

Alice wanted to weep, too, but for what she didn't know. She ought to feel happy. Julia was happy, had hardly been able to wait to get into the motor taxi that was to take them to Holdenby Halt.

From the steps, her ladyship had waved them goodbye, head high, a smile on her lips. She'd done the same, Alice all at once thought, to Robert and Giles – now her daughter was leaving, too.

Miss Clitherow had been there, and Cook and Tilda and Jinny Dobb. Tilda had waved frantically; Cook had plucked at the corners of her apron, ready to weep. Miss Clitherow had smiled; only Jin had stood still and silent.

Catchpole had waited by the gate lodges with wheelbarrow and hoe, pretending to be working there, removing his pipe from his mouth, raising his straw panama as they passed.

They had almost missed Reuben, standing at the fence with his dogs, at the place where the single-track railway ran alongside Brattocks Wood for a few score yards.

'Reuben!' Julia had cried, pulling down the compartment window, waving her hand wildly as the train had slipped out of his sight. 'Did you see him, Alice? How kind of him to be there!'

'Aye,' Alice had sniffed, her voice unsteady. 'Remember when we came back from London that first time? I was happy; you were sad at leaving the doctor. Remember that Tom stood there an' all?' The tears she had kept in a hard lump in her throat had all at once welled up and ran down her cheeks. 'Oh, miss . . .' she had choked.

'Alice – don't cry. Please, *please*, don't cry or I'll think it's all my fault for taking you to France with me. What is it?'

'It's nothing.' Alice had taken a folded handkerchief from her pocket. 'And you aren't taking me to France. I *want* to go. It was just – just . . ' She'd mopped her tears, then taken a deep breath, smiling shakily. '. . . just that I'm leaving home, I suppose.'

And, if she'd admit it, it was also partly because of what Jin Dobb had said that moonlit night she'd told her fortune, and the fact that Jin hadn't smiled when they left. Sober-faced, she'd been; as if she'd remembered – as if she had known something . . .

The sniffing from the far corner of the room stopped. It wasn't any use crying, Alice sighed, though she'd indulged her own tears that morning. Now she lay in an unfamiliar bed in unfamiliar darkness and thought of Tom. Tomorrow they would leave for France; before another day had run, they would have arrived. Monday the third of July would be the start of her new life. Two days journeying nearer to Tom; two days nearer the end of a war that could not, must not, last into another winter.

They had crossed a millpond Channel in a troopship filled with soldiers. Most wore new uniforms; others – a few – had the sad eyes of men returning from leave.

They sailed in convoy with three merchantmen, all supply ships. carrying ammunition and horses, whilst three small warships fussed around them.

'Destroyer escort and two frigates,' said someone who knew about such things.

Laying off, riding at anchor, another trooper waited for a berth. Its upper deck was thick with soldiers, crowding the rails for a first sight of home. They all wore full kit and broad smiles. The destroyer whooped three times in greeting. The homecoming soldiers cheered and waved. The sky was bright and cloudless; the Channel glistened blue-green. Reluctantly, almost, the turbines beneath their feet began to turn and throb; hawsers were released, a last link with England. Ahead, as they nosed slowly out to sea, lay France. Astern, Dover's cliffs shone creamily and ever smaller in the sun.

'Look at Ruth Love,' Julia whispered. 'She seems upset, almost . . .'

'Yes.' Alice had noticed. 'Happen a bit of sea-sickness.'

'On a calm day like this?' On, no. It was something deeper, more secret. Julia knew it. 'I'm glad she's with us, though.'

Above them, seagulls cried; the bows lifted and fell gently. Beneath their feet they had felt the steady throbbing of engines. There was no going back now.

French railway stations, Alice noted, and French trains, were little different from those she had left behind her. Calais terminus could be York, or King's Cross even, had it not been for the strange language.

They carried their cases to the luggage van, then found a compartment with four empty seats. Sister shepherded them inside, determined to keep them together. In a brown paper carrier bag were sandwiches, apples, and two bottles of water for the journey. Sister did not trust foreign water; was wary of anything foreign she could not scrub down, disinfect or sterilize.

When the train left the platform, she lapsed into silence, her face wearing a thank-God-we're-almost-there expression. Ruth Love's face was pale and taut. Perhaps she, too, had not slept.

'You may take off your hats and coats,' Sister murmured as the train gathered speed, hooting, just as English trains hooted, at a river-bridge ahead.

Alice pulled her finger round the inside of her high, starched collar. Not even after six months could she abide the tightness at her neck.

The sun beat down. It would be a hot, uncomfortable journey. Her stockings made her legs itch. She smiled across at Julia, then turned to look out on her first real glimpse of France.

Sister looked around the compartment, ascertained the other occupants were French and therefore would probably not understand English, then said, 'Our destination is Celverte. As far as I know, it's a small place between Abbeville and Amiens.'

They would leave the train at Abbeville, she told them, where transport would be waiting. They would be able to unpack and settle in – get a good night's sleep. Tomorrow they could expect to be on duty.

Ruth Love leaned towards Sister, lowering her voice to a whisper.

'Will we be far from the Front?'

Sister held up ten fingers – twice. '*Miles.*' She never bothered with kilometres. 'Is anyone hungry?'

She passed round sandwiches wrapped in greaseproof paper; took out two tin mugs. The sandwiches were spread with margarine and potted fishpaste.

The French family took out sausages, crusty white bread and wine. The woman sliced the sausages, speared a piece on the end of her knife, and saluted the English women.

'*Bonne chance!*' she smiled.

The heat in the compartment became overpowering; Sister lowered the window. Julia rubbed her hot, itching legs.

Alice eased her collar, gazing out, squinting into the sun. Outside was a France exactly as she had thought it would be. Now they sped through villages of small, brightly painted houses, their shutters closed against the afternoon sun. In each garden, vines showing bunches of small, unripe grapes clung in orderly fashion to wires. In every garden, too, grew clumps of arum lilies, white and waxy, their leaves glossily dark green. They reminded Alice of Mr Catchpole and Rowangarth and Tom.

Tom. She knew from her familiarity with Julia's wall map they would be nearer to him than to the doctor, though she had not remarked on it because doubtless Julia had realized it too.

Celverte She wanted more than anything to arrive there; to unpack her case, take off her dull green cotton frock and shoes and stockings and walk barefoot on a floor of cold linoleum. Then hopefully, she could wash. She felt such discomfort that even one tap dripping cold water would be welcome. whilst a real bath would be complete bliss.

Celverte? If it were only twenty miles from the Front, then surely it was close to Tom who was billeted near Albert? If he hadn't been moved on, that was.

She revised her thoughts. Before even taking off her shoes and stockings she would write to Tom; send him her address It would be like posting a letter in England; he would have it in no time.

More vines, more lilies; cows being driven to be milked. Was it always this hot in France? She leaned back her head and closed her eyes. When she opened them, Ruth was shaking her arm, saying, 'Abbeville. Alice . . .'

Celverte was indeed a village. but so humming with war that Alice was taken aback Transports and ambulances of all kinds were everywhere, crowding the narrow streets outside the railway station, while high above them a chateau stood beautiful in the sun, its windows sparkling.

'That big house on the hill – that's the hospital?' Sister asked, checking her cases.

'One of them,' offered the driver sent to meet them, 'but my orders say you're to go to the school.' The chateau, he said, was more of an emergency place – a clearing-station – and a right shambles it was, so he'd heard. More wounded there than they could cope with; lying all over the place – even in the courtyard, outside.

'Wounded?' Sister snapped, instantly alert. 'From where?'

'From the fighting – where else? Listen . . .'

They stood, breath indrawn, until in a quiet moment they heard a noise like distant thunder, continually rumbling.

'Hear it? That's *their* guns. And they tried to tell us it'd be a walk-over. Such a barrage of shells we were going to put up that there'd be no Germans living, they said, by the time our gunners had finished with them. Walk in, then, the infantry could. Just walk in through the gaps the sappers had made, take the Jerry trenches, then press on to the Belgian border.

'The war'd be over before we knew it, they kept telling us. We'd all of us be back home for Christmas. That's what they told the lads,' the driver said bitterly, 'and the poor sods believed it. But how can you run a war from a desk in London? Why don't they come over here; have a look at what it's really like?'

His face was fiercely indignant; he spat his disgust on to the dust-dry cobbles. 'You're going to be needed here. Get in – I'll take you . . .'

'One moment!' Sister took the man's arm, holding it tightly. 'You're saying that more fighting has broken out? We've been travelling for two days, you see – no newspapers.'

'That's right. Been building up to it for months. Never

seen so much stuff: guns, mortars, flame-throwers, the lot. One big push, they said. One barrage from the artillery like no one had ever known before, then over the top, my handsomes! Brussels and Blighty in time for Christmas!'

'And it wasn't like that?' Tight-lipped, she let go of his arm.

'It flaming wasn't! Our lads went in all right – only the Germans weren't lying dead in their lines like they should have been. Their trenches were empty. The crafty sods had a second line, further back. They must've been laughing like drains, seeing our gunners getting it wrong – everything falling short.

'They waited till our lads were standing there like they were looking for the war, then those machine-gunners just let them have it. Slaughter. Hundreds – *thousands* – of them. The lucky ones are up there.' He pointed to the big house on the hill.

'Get in, Nurses,' Sister said, tight-lipped. 'I think they're going to be glad to see us . . .'

Their quarters looked gaunt from outside. Above the door of the building *Institut des Filles* was chiselled in the stone-work. A girls' school, taken over by the authorities and now a home for nurses. Inside, they were greeted warmly.

'Hullo. I'm the housekeeper.'

Not unlike Miss Clitherow in her dress and bearing, Alice thought, though her smile was wider and brighter.

'You'll be thinking it is unusual to have a housekeeper in quarters like this – but they told me I was too old for nursing, so I came here to look after things. Unpaid, but I hope not unsung. I try to make things a little more comfortable for you all.'

Sister nodded her approval, then excused herself to go in search of the matron; all others followed the housekeeper. Hot and dirty, they lugged cases up the wide, uncovered stairs.

'You'll be in this dormitory. Once, when this was a convent school, it had twelve beds; now, we have improved it a little.'

She swished aside a curtain. 'Each cubicle is curtained to give privacy when required, and you must remember to darken your window at night. We are very near the Front. To show a light after dark is not allowed.

'Outside is a little chapel, for all denominations. Chaplains visit each week. Times are on the noticeboard. Now – each of you take a bed, except –' she studied the list in her hand '– Staff Nurse Love.'

'That's me.' Ruth Love stepped forward.

'Here you are.' She opened the door to a small, partitioned-off room at the top of the dormitory. 'This was once occupied by a nun – I hope you'll be comfortable in it. It's less austere than it once was . . '

'Thank you. I hadn't expected –' Clearly she was surprised. 'Just one thing: are you allowed to tell us where the fighting is?'

'I don't see why not. It began three days ago, and as far as I can tell, it's about twenty-five miles away – in the area of the River Somme.'

The Somme. Albert. Alice closed her eyes, pulling in her breath. Tom was there. She slid back the heavy green curtain that separated her bed from Julia's.

'You heard? Tom's in it now.'

'Yes, and I'm sorry, Alice. But you *are* near him. Just think – he could even be billeted just around the corner!'

'He might . .' Alice was not comforted. even though Julia had been through the same when there'd been fighting at Verdun.

'Cheer up. The first thing we must do is let our men know where we are. What's our address?'

'Care of Voluntary Aid Detachment, General Hospital Sixteen, BEF Two,' Alice recited flatly. 'They told us when we got here . . .'

'Thanks. I forgot.' Julia opened her writing case, carefully printing the address at the top of a sheet of pale blue notepaper. The she wrote,

We have arrived and I love you, love you, love you. Letter follows. J.

'We mustn't seal them down. The Censor has to read them first,' Alice frowned.

'Who cares? Censors are human, aren't they?'

Alice unscrewed the top of her ink bottle, dipping in her pen. Tom might get this letter, she thought, in a couple of days. If he were still near Albert, that was. If he hadn't been among the thousands the machine-gunners had – were *supposed* to have . . .

'Hurry up.' Julia broke into her thoughts. 'I'll take them downstairs. We leave them in the basket in the hall. Then we'll unpack and get our bearings. Supper's in an hour. It'll be all right, just you see. We're hungry and tired. Once we've cleaned ourselves up and had something to eat, things are going to seem a whole lot better.'

'I know. And this is streets ahead of York Military.' At the end of the long, narrow room was a cubicled bath and, beside it, curtained off, two washbasins. 'There might even be hot water.'

'And the housekeeper seems very nice . . .'

'I suppose we'll be at the big house tomorrow.' Alice looked up from her unpacking as Julia returned.

'We might be. But the chateau is only a clearing-station. Seems there's another hospital, just across the field, at the back. Wooden huts, but newly built. We might be there. By the way,' she dropped her voice to a whisper, 'when I passed the end cubicle, Ruth was sitting on her bed. Just sitting, staring. I said hullo to her, but she seemed not to hear. She looks sort of strained, somehow. Do you think she's sorry she came?'

'Don't know.' Alice laid her Bible on the chest beside her bed, the buttercup she was pressing for Tom inside it. 'Maybe we should ask her, though really it isn't any of our business.'

'No, it isn't. Not really . . .'

They spun round, gasping. Staff Nurse stood there and they knew she had heard.

'Look – we didn't mean . . .'

'Only concerned. We do care for you,' Julia whispered.

'I know. And I suppose I'd better tell you and then, if sometimes I seem a little – well, *distant* – you'll understand. And if I didn't hear you just now, Julia, perhaps I was listening to the plane going over . . .'

'A plane? You've been bombed?' Julia offered. 'Oh, sit down, won't you?'

'Not bombed.' Ruth sat on the bed, hands clasped tightly. 'It's James, you see. Have either of you lost anyone?'

Alice shook her head. Julia whispered, 'My brother – last year . . .'

'James was in the Flying Corps – an observer in a spotter plane. I was out here. I'd done my year, was going back to England. James had been promised leave too. Flyers seemed to get it more easily – they needed it . . .'

'And James was – ?' Julia prompted, gently.

'He was shot down, two weeks before.'

'How *awful*,' Alice choked.

'More awful than you know. It's bad enough, being told about it, but I had to find out the hard way.

'I was on duty; the ward was bordering on chaos. They'd sent us some stretcher cases from the dressing-station – all of them in a mess. Then someone said they'd brought in a flyer; there'd been two, they said, only one of them was in the mortuary.

'I went to have a look. A nurse was just pulling the sheet over his face. I asked her if he was dead and she said, "Just this minute. I'll find a couple of orderlies. He was horribly burned . . ."

571

'I pulled back the sheet: God knows why, because all the while there was this voice inside me saying, "It isn't. It won't be . . ." That flyer could have been anybody. His face and hands were awful – unrecognizable. But I knew. They'd taken off some of his uniform, you see, and I could see the strawberry mark on his left arm.

'Then I looked at his identity disc – that hadn't burned, either. J. M. Love. God! I'd been not ten feet away while my husband was dying. Some other nurse had been with him.

'I started to scream. I just stood there, screaming. Then someone slapped me: two of them took me by the arms and ran me outside. Imagine? A staff nurse behaving like that? But I wasn't a nurse at that moment. I was a wife, a widow. Such rage in me . . .'

'Don't!' Julia choked. 'Not while it hurts so badly.'

'Oh, it hurts. It won't ever go away. They sent me back to Blighty to pull myself together – to Denniston House. Both men were buried with indecent haste, but I found his grave before I left. Just a marker on it.'

'You shouldn't have come back, Staff,' Alice said, fighting tears. 'Every time you see an aeroplane – hear one – it's going to bring it all back.'

'No, Hawthorn. It's got to be faced. There won't ever be any peace for me if I don't. Sister knew. She understood. Said I should give it a try – one day at a time.'

'Will it help to tell us how?' Julia asked, gently.

'Oh, the usual. One of theirs – shot them up whilst they were taking off. Bill – James's pilot – was killed instantly. Pity James wasn't. He was hours dying, and what's so awful is that I could have been with him .   '

'We didn't know you'd been married,' Julia said. 'No ring, you see.'

'I took it off. When you are wearing a ring they ask you where your man is – patients, especially '

'Put it back,' Julia whispered. 'Keep faith?'

'I will, MacMalcolm. Just as soon as I can bear to – to admit I'm a widow and that I'll never see my Jamie again.' She rose to her feet. 'Well, best finish my unpacking – I've got four drawers and a wardrobe. Very posh!

'And thank you for listening. This is the first time I've really talked about it – actually said out loud that he's dead. Well, best be off . . .'

'Staff!' Alice cried, making to follow her.

'No! Leave her!' Julia hissed, grasping Alice's arm. 'What she told us took a lot of doing. Let her pull herself together.'

'This is a *terrible* war.'

'I know, Alice. But we'll feel a whole lot better about everything in the morning. And when we wake up, there'll be another night to cross off my calendar. I cross them off, you know. Nights, not days . . .' Nights spent wanting Andrew. 'And we are so very lucky: we're so much nearer to them, now, that there's a fair chance we might be able to see them, even if only for a short while.'

An hour would do . . .

33

Tom Dwerryhouse blinked his eyes rapidly, then relaxed. It hadn't been a movement on the skyline; just a trick of the moonlight. He leaned his rifle carefully beside him, then took a drink from the water-bottle at his side, sliding his eyes left and right.

He was hungry and the biscuit in his pocket was hard. He broke off a piece, tonguing it into his cheek to soften it. All was quiet, still, from Geordie's end. Were they all asleep across No Man's Land? On a night as bright as this, dare they be?

Geordie Marshall hated Germans. They had killed his sister in the bombardment of Hartlepool eighteen months ago, and his anger went deep. Now he found comfort in killing; the dummies on the firing range, even, became objects of his hatred. Tom had seen the look in his eyes; the way his finger caressed the trigger, almost with love. Geordie had not joined the army for his mother's sake, or even for the sake of England. He had become a soldier to avenge the death of a girl called Dorothy. He was at the far end of the village – if village you could call it – now. For so long, Tom had looked across No Man's Land to the distant cluster of ten cottages and a church, standing deserted: the army had moved out those who lived there months ago. Now, since the shelling started, it had become a ruin, the little houses no more than empty walls that in the moonlight looked like great, hollow teeth.

Geordie was in the end cottage; the one with its stone staircase still intact. He'd be at the little landing window, passing his tongue round his lips, squinting into the distance like a green-eyed night cat.

Tom crouched in the shattered belfry of the church. He felt safe behind the thick stone wall; had taken up his watch at a slit-like window high enough to support his rifle, narrow enough to give him protection. Tonight neither he nor the man in the end cottage were sniping. Tonight they kept watch over stretcher-bearers who had slipped out into the wastes between to bring back wounded. No betraying rifle-cracks; only a shot in the air to warn them they had been seen; a shot to alert our artillery – start up a protective barrage from guns already ranged and primed.

Tom prayed the silence would continue. He wanted those fools of men to get out safely, if only because he himself had survived the first awful days of the fighting.

They would be all right, they'd been told before it all began; told so often they had come to believe it.

There'll be nothing moving when our gunners have finished. You'll just go in – take prisoners. Fritz will be glad to surrender – if you can find one of them alive, that is.

Into battle. After almost five months of waiting and time-wasting, it would be good to go in. Then on to Brussels: because that was where they expected to be by Christmas. He'd been put out when they'd called him for special duties – duties Tom called sniping. A sniper waited alone, motionless and hidden, for the slightest movement from the trenches opposite; to keep the enemy always on his guard, make sure no one looked over the top of the sandbags, much less tried to advance. You waited for the *second* glimpse of a grey, steel helmet. You didn't fire first time. The first sighting could be a helmet on the end of a bayonet – a toe in the water, a try-out. Second time you shot the bastard and, if you were Geordie Marshall, you smiled as you did it.

Now, Tom was put out no longer; was grateful, almost, that his special skill had separated him from the slaughter of that first, foolish advance. No Man's Land was no longer a spread of bonny, flower-filled meadows. Tonight it was exactly as he knew it should be: a churn of shell-holes; torn, jagged trees that only seven days ago had flourished green. And only seven days ago there had been cottages in No Man's Land, and a church.

Tonight, they had waited for the brief darkness that came before moonrise – Geordie and himself and a dozen men with stretchers. Conchies, all twelve; men who merited white feathers in civvie street yet were the bravest of the brave. On their arms and steel helmets they wore a red cross, their badge of courage. He'd been proud to go in with them.

Two chaplains were out there, too; one British and a priest to give last rites to the dying and absolution to the dead. Brave men who also refused to carry a gun.

The moon slipped behind a cloud; Tom chewed on the biscuit. There would be hot tea when they got back to the rear trenches.– rum in it, if they were lucky. Surprising how cold a July night could be – or was it fear that chilled him through?

Nathan Sutton, Tom thought, could well be out there, or in some other No Man's Land, every bit as dangerous. Happen that applied to Sir Giles, an' all, not so far down the line.

What would her ladyship think if she knew? God in heaven, but this was a wicked war.

A stone hit the wall at his side. He clicked back the bolt of his rifle, pointing it downward.

'*Tom?*' It was Geordie. 'We're on our way. They reckon they can get back while the moon's hidden. I've got two walking wounded here – can you take one?'

Tom felt the ledge beside him, making sure he had left no signs of his being there, then lowered himself to the ground, stretching his cramped limbs.

'Been out there long?' he asked the soldier. Tom could

hardly see him, but he felt the warm damp of his uniform, smelled the blood.

'Only since afternoon. I hoped they'd come and get me. My arm and leg . . .'

'You're all right now.' Tom wrapped the man's waist round with his arm. 'Hang on to my neck . . .'

The wounded man clung like a dead weight. Their progress was slow. 'Easy, mate . . .' Just as long as the darkness lasted, they could make it. 'Lucky devil. Got yourself a Blighty wound there.'

'Yes – lucky . . .'

Doctors were waiting for them, and orderlies. The stretcher-bearers handed over their burdens and were given tea. Geordie carried two mugs. He felt disappointed – cheated almost. He hadn't fired a shot. A wasted night; not one killing.

'They say we can stand down now.' He offered a cigarette and Tom shook his head. Geordie always offered one, always forgot Tom didn't smoke. 'It's me for my bed. G'night, then . . .'

He slouched off to his billet. Geordie wasn't a smart soldier; didn't snap to attention and salute correctly when addressed by an officer. Geordie's eyes often held contempt for the fancy uniforms of his superiors: dumb insolence, it was called, yet the Tynesider got away with it. He was the best shot in the battalion – better even than the gamekeeper – and he knew it. He'd taken more Germans than most.

'So long,' Tom murmured, hands wrapped round the hot tin mug. At times like this, he tried to stand quietly and apart, emptying himself of the horror of it, and the fear; willing himself back to sanity.

And sanity was a place called Brattocks Wood; a lass called Alice. To think of her was the only way to relax the tension from his limbs. She was on her way here – might even have arrived. What had he been about to let her do it? It was three weeks since her birthday. Twenty now, yet still too young to be here; too young to marry.

He sent his thoughts to her, wherever she was. Only weeks ago they'd been sure it would soon be over. The Germans were cracking and the offensive on the Somme would finish them once and for all. Yet now they knew – that lot in London, an' all – that the enemy was as strong as ever and no one was going anywhere at Christmas.

He wanted, all at once, to weep his frustration at a world gone mad. Instead, he spat with contempt on the ground at his feet. Tears wouldn't bring back the dead, heal wounds, or help blinded eyes to see again.

He looked up at the sky. A soldier could be forgiven for thinking that, at times such as this, God was on *their* side. He drained his mug, hitched his rifle on his shoulder, and made for his billet.

There had been no mail for days. He hoped tonight that there might be a letter from Alice, and that someone might have put it beside his bed space.

When he got back, he was amazed to find there were three: two from England, and one that bore the red stamp and scribbled initials of the Censor.

He opened it with the blade of his pocket knife; he always opened her letters carefully. Partly because he was tidy-minded, but really because he wanted to savour the moment when he dipped his fingers into the envelope and pulled out a sheet of paper she had touched, written on, most likely laid to her lips.

The spray of buttercups fell to the floor. Gently he picked it up, slipping it back into the envelope. He read the address at the top of the page and a shock of pleasure tingled through him.

BEF Two. The Somme area! She was somewhere near; might be so near that –

He shook such thoughts from his head. The area of the

River Somme was large and wide; she could be well out
of his finding.

My darling Tom,
    I am here, safe and well. Write to me soon? Take care.
I love you.

                                          Alice.

'Oh, my lovely lass . . .'

The single candle guttered; the wick sank into a pool
of wax, the flame died. Tom pushed the letters into
his pocket to read tomorrow in the daylight. Alice,
near Albert? To see her, touch her. To hold her, kiss
her . . .

He unlaced his boots, unwound his puttees, then lay
down in the darkness, the straw in his palliasse crackling
beneath him.

He smiled. All at once, God had changed sides.

A few days after their arrival, Julia and Alice were on
duty at the chateau. Make yourselves useful, they were
told. VAD nurses weren't properly trained; there were
things they weren't allowed to do, said the time-served
nurse of the Army Reserve, scathingly. Yet now, when
ambulances brought in the injured in long, slow-moving
convoys, and the walking wounded limped up the hill in
an endless straggle, every nurse was needed.

Alice cut open a mud-caked, bloodstained trouser leg,
carefully easing back the rough khaki cloth, laying on a
dressing, offering a cigarette.

*Don't let them bring Tom in; don't let me see him like
Ruth did . . .*

The sun beat down. Already her apron was soiled:
whoever had thought up this uniform – all bits and pieces
to button on, take off, scrub and starch – hadn't known
what they were about!

'Hawthorn!' She responded quickly to Sister's summons. 'Get this man's jacket off . . .'

This was like the frosty February morning at Denniston, only now there were forty times forty wounded and would be, every day, until the fighting eased.

This morning she had awakened before six – out of habit, she supposed – and, wrapping her night shawl around her, had walked without sound to the washbasins at the end of the room. Neither was in use; weary nurses slept until the last minute possible and, anyway, half the beds were empty, those to whom they belonged counting away the minutes to the end of their night duty.

Breakfast, in the early morning cool, had been good. The porridge had been free of lumps, milk to pour on it plentiful; there had even been a bowl of sugar on the table.

Last night, before she slept, she had written again to Tom, telling him she would be working at the chateau, hoping it would help him locate her, though probably every chateau in Picardy was now a hospital.

A stretcher was carried past her. The man who lay on it had been given morphia, his purple cross a passport to the top of the queue.

'That man,' Sister pointed to a soldier she had satisfied herself was not in need of surgery, 'can have soup. See to it, Hawthorn.'

The man smiled his thanks, then lowered himself to the ground, leaning his back against an ornamental urn; glad, in spite of his pain, to be out of the fighting. Soon, he would sleep in a bed; might even learn he'd got himself a ticket to Blighty.

'Can you manage it all right?' Alice placed the mug of soup on the ground beside him.

He told her he could. He looked almost happy, she thought as she washed her hands in the bucket of disinfectant, shaking them dry, thinking that tonight, when she wrote to Tom again, she would tell him that before long she would be working at the new hospital, just as soon as a ward was ready for their use. Such information would help, for where was there a place with a chateau *and* a newly built hospital? Somehow, bit by bit, he would work out where she was.

'Nurse Hawthorn.'

'Coming, Staff!' A plane droned low overhead; a British one, with red, white and blue roundels. *Their* planes had black crosses on them.

'You want me, Staff?'

'Yes.' Ruth Love took her eyes from the sky. 'Find Sister, will you – ask her if she can spare a minute.'

The soldier at whose side she knelt was feverish, mumbling in delirium. His shoulders and back were covered in bright red pinpoints and the spreadings of a rosy rash.

Alice frowned. She had long ago learned to recognize flea bites, but this was something more. 'Is it . . . ?' Some called it trench fever.

'Typhus, I think. Go find her, will you? And *don't run!*'

Alice had not enjoyed the injections she had been given, but now, Staff's message delivered, she had reason to be glad of the headache, high temperature, and swollen arm she had suffered.

'Want a hand?' She hurried to Julia's side.

'Please. Hold that dressing, will you?'

Julia's hands were so sure, Alice thought as she watched her wind and secure the head bandage. Everything she did oozed confidence. It was, Alice supposed, because of her upbringing. Miss Julia's sort were like that.

'Want to know something?' Julia lit a cigarette then passed it, smiling, to the soldier. 'Rumour has it there'll be a break soon. Soup and bread in the kitchen, about noon. Know where the kitchens are?'

'Yes. This is awful, Julia. All these wounded, I mean.'

They lay around the courtyard, most of them not sufficiently ill even to warrant being carried inside, yet all of them seriously wounded.

'I know. Sister thinks the same. She was muttering about being glad when she got her own ward so she'd know what she was about.' Six huts – wards – at the new hospital were still unfinished. 'I think they're only waiting for the paint to dry and the linoleum to be laid. Wonder if there'll be letters tonight?'

Since their arrival, there had been nothing. They had come away, disappointed, each morning from the letterboard.

'Not if they're in the fighting,' Alice shrugged. 'And look out!'

Sister approached; and caught them gossiping.

'You two!' Sister Carbrooke was smiling. 'Cut along to the kitchens and get something to eat. You've got fifteen minutes . . . And for heaven's sake, clean yourselves up and put on fresh aprons! By the way, my ward is finished. Tomorrow we'll be busy moving in!'

She walked away, still smiling. Like a cat who'd been at the cream, Julia thought or, more exactly, like a sister who'd been given a ward . . .

'Come on,' she grinned. 'Food!'

All at once, they felt inexplicably happier.

That night, there were letters.

'Four!' Alice gasped, sorting through hers for sight of Tom's handwriting; frowning at the postmarks. 'One from Tom's mam, one from Mrs Shaw – and *two* from Tom!'

'And I,' smiled Julia serenely, 'have got one from Giles, one from Mother and three from Andrew!'

'Let's read them over supper,' Alice laughed, wondering which she would open first.

'Best we scrub up before we do anything. Did you know they sent a man into isolation?'

'Yes – typhus. Ruth Love found it.'

'That's fleas for you!' Julia took her spongebag from its hook. 'We'd better have a good look at ourselves, I think.' High on the heady delight of five letters, she let out a shout of laughter. 'I don't know why, but suddenly I got a picture of Aunt Clemmy! What *would* she say if she thought her niece had fleas!'

Alice neither knew nor cared. Tom had written, and the awfulness of the dressing-station was behind them. Even with Sister hovering like a hawk, a ward would be nothing short of heaven. She even looked forward to the smell of carbolic.

Julia pulled back the green curtain that separated their cubicles, then lay on her bed, newly bathed and almost content.

'There are days, Alice, you never forget . . .'

'Mm,' Alice smiled.

'And isn't it amazing – Andrew, I mean. I wondered how on earth I was to let him know where I was. I used Tom's trick about seeing Nathan's younger brother, though I wasn't at all sure if he'd remember what his younger brother is called. Just imagine it all being so simple . . .' He had added it to the bottom of his letter, almost casually.

By the way, darling – don't forget that because of my exalted position in the Medical Corps, I can keep tabs on you. So see that you behave yourself!

'It was his way of telling me he knows where General Hospital Sixteen is! What news from Mrs Shaw?'

'They all seem in the best of spirits. The Pendenys cook swopped her a pound of sugar for a quarter of tea!'

'Wonder how the Place comes to have sugar to spare?' Julia grinned.

'I bet Mrs Clementina had sacks and sacks of it put by when she thought there'd be a war.' Mrs Clementina was like that. 'Anyway, Cook made two sponge cakes with it, so everybody was happy.'

'And Tom?'

'He loves me. How is her ladyship?'

'Mother's fine. Remember McIver – the blind soldier at Denniston? We'll both be pleased to know, she says, that he's got back his sight in one eye. Wonder how the old convalescent ward is doing? We've come a long way since then, haven't we?'

They had, Alice agreed. 'When your contract is up, will you stay out here, Julia?'

'I think so – as long as Andrew is in France. We'll be due leave, then. I wonder if we can spend it here.'

'Might be a bit risky, going to Reims,' Alice cautioned. 'We don't know what it's like there. It could be as badly knocked about as Albert. You might even have to get permission to go there.'

'I realize that. All the same, it's worth thinking about.'

A sudden evening breeze moved the window curtains, bringing with it the scent of blossom. 'Isn't it lovely and cool – and *listen*!'

Alice raised her head. 'Can't hear anything.'

'Exactly! That's just it – they've stopped!'

'No guns.' Suddenly, after firing so constant it had become a part of the background, the guns of neither side could be heard. 'Do you think they've stopped fighting?'

'I don't know, but oh, will you listen to that lovely silence . . .'

As she said, there were days you would never forget.

There were days, Clementina Sutton frowned, when she had had enough, especially of Elliot who was in trouble again – though for the very last time, did he but know it!

This journey to London was totally unnecessary. She had not planned another visit to the house in Cheyne

Walk until the decorators were finished and all the carpets laid. Now she must scurry down there to sort out his most recent misdemeanour, before his father heard of it!

Sometimes, she shuddered, she feared for her eldest son. His schooling had been of the most expensive; his grand tour the most prolonged. Before this irritating war began, she lamented, gazing out at telegraph poles that slid past the window, there had been young girls aplenty, all of them more than eager to exchange maidenhood for motherhood. But now they were getting ideas that could lead to nothing but the undermining of our very society! Married women going out to work was bad enough, but unmarried ladies walking out unchaperoned with skirts above their ankles took some getting used to!

And now – and she wouldn't have believed this had she not seen it with her own eyes – young ladies smoking *in public*, and attending tea dances without an escort; partnering young men to whom they hadn't been introduced!

It was on this subject she intended to speak to Elliot most earnestly. Young women on the loose in London could lead to nothing but trouble; and as for young, lonely wives with husbands at the Front – well, it didn't bear thinking about.

It was the fault of the war, of course. Men taken from their homes, and hastily married women left alone to pick up the pieces of their strange new lives as best they could, created an explosive situation from which nothing but trouble could come – *had* come.

She had always thought, Clementina reflected, that she had managed the matter of Elliot's army service rather well; had secured him a posting to the War Office where, had he been in possession of one iota of the sense he'd been born with, he could have sat out the war and returned to his family unscathed. What was more, she had worked extremely hard to convince her immediate social circle that her eldest son was employed on a project so secret that he simply couldn't be spared for active service in France.

She sighed deeply. Elliot's secret project, it seemed, was the seducing of a young wife whose husband was fighting in France! Aunt Sutton had written in high indignation to tell her so; said the whole of London was talking about it, and that it was only a matter of time before the cuckolded husband received an unsigned letter and up the balloon would go!

Spiteful old maid! Clementina couldn't think why Edward liked her so. Mad as a hatter, of course.

Yet, for all that, Clementina could cheerfully clatter her son's ears for his stupidity, though to stop his allowance would bring him to repentance far more quickly! And that was not all! There was the matter of an unpaid mess bill and a gambling debt to a fellow officer not honoured. Oh, Mary Anne Pendennis, you have much to answer for!

The train began to slow at the approaches to Grantham, and she hoped no one would invade the privacy of the empty compartment she occupied. People these days thought nothing of engaging one in conversation, and it simply did not do – even if they *had* purchased a first-class ticket.

Beatrice, the woman's name was. The daughter of a baronet, married to the second son of a peer, she should have known better than to engage in an affair with an unmarried man, no matter how attractive she found him. She'd set her cap at Elliot, of course. Good looks, of a good family and money – or so he gave the impression – to burn. *Her* money, Clementina thought savagely.

Why couldn't Elliot have been more like his younger brother; been blessed with his sunny nature, his fairness of looks? Why had her firstborn been a direct throwback to the Cornish washerwoman, and why, in spite of all the heartache he caused her, did she love him so much?

Was it because he and she were so alike; would never be totally accepted by the society into which her father's money had bought her? Was Elliot tilting at windmills, just to show he didn't care? And who were they, anyway, those blue-blooded aristocrats whose lineage went back to the Plantagenets and who hadn't a sixpenny-piece to scratch their backsides with?

She understood Elliot's rebellious ways – she really did – and most times she would have been prepared to deal kindly with him. But he was due for a reckoning-up, a jerking in of the reins; after which he usually behaved himself for a six-month at least.

If only her Elliot were married: women would leave him alone then . . .

Clementina hoped her bed would be made up and aired when she arrived. She kept no servants at the London house, only an elderly woman who, grateful for a roof over her head and a fire to sit beside, kept watch over the property in her absence for three shillings and sixpence a week and a daily pint of milk. And a hamperful of cast-offs sent down by carrier, Clementina added. The caretaker did well out of that hamper, she shouldn't wonder, selling off most of it to better-off friends and making a nice little sum with which to buy the gin Clementina supposed she drank. Drink was the downfall of the working classes. It had made them what they were and would ever remain. Mary Anne Pendennis had signed the pledge the moment she'd been able to print her name, and never a drop of liquor had passed her lips; that at least Clementina gave her credit for.

She knew Elliot was in the house. The minute she opened the door the stink of his Turkish cigarettes met her. Why couldn't he smoke cigars? At least they smelled of good breeding. Turkish tobacco made Clementina think of brothels, though for the life of her she couldn't think why.

'*Elliot!*' She gave him the full force of her displeasure. He'd be lolling in the study – the only habitable room in the house – and if he thought he was getting away with this latest carry-on, she hoped the tone of her summons would warn him otherwise.

'Mama, dear! How lovely to see you.'

Oh, but he was handsome in his uniform. She wavered just a little, then snapped, 'And what kind of mess have you got yourself into this time?'

'Mess, Mama? Let me take your coat?'

'*Mess!* With the Beatrice woman. Your Aunt Sutton knows about it, and half of London too. Have you got her into trouble?'

It was the worst, most frequent nightmare of all. Elliot, in Court, cited as co-respondent, and a greasy little man reading intimate details from a tattered notebook. And always in those nightmares, Helen sat beside the divorce judge, smiling sweetly, eating sugared rose petals.

'Trouble?' Elliot's deep brown eyes opened wide, their expression one of hurt. 'I don't know what you mean.'

'Trouble, son. Let me explain. It comes of taking liberties with another man's wife. Is she pregnant?'

'Beatrice is a lady, Mama!'

'Is she, now? So damned ladylike that the minute her husband's back is turned she's in your bed!'

'*Please!*' He had been about to remark upon her crudeness, but thought better of it lest she flew into a rage and threw him out without so much as a penny-piece. 'You've got it wrong, Mama.'

'All right, then! You were in *her* bed!'

Unspeaking, Elliot sized up the situation. His mother's face was chalk-white, her eyes small slits of anger. When she was really angry, the only solution was to throw himself upon her mercy – grovel, if he had to. Because if he didn't settle his mess bill at once he'd be in trouble enough; to renege on a gambling debt was even worse.

Thus far, he'd been able to keep out of the way of Authority at the War Office; had managed to look busy at all times – even to walking the corridors, frowning studiously, with a large brown envelope inscribed OHMS SECRET beneath his arm.

Trouble – even a whiff of it – and Authority could well seek to discover who this officer was and what he did with his time. He could be off to France so fast his feet wouldn't touch the ground!

'I thought you were an officer and a gentleman, Elliot,' Clementina pressed. 'And gentlemen don't play cards with money they haven't got!'

'I'm sorry. I got carried away. I promise I won't let it happen again.'

'*Promise?* Your promises aren't worth the breath you make them with! Now it's me, your mother, you're dealing with; *me*, who'll get you out of trouble, same as always. So stop your play-acting and tell me how much it is you want this time?'

'My mess bill is fifty pounds; I owe Billy Smythe two hundred . . .'

'Now say that again,' she challenged.

'We-e-ll – it's thirty-nine pounds fifteen shillings to the mess steward, and a hundred and fifty to Smythe. And neither will take a cheque. I've already tried.'

'And the woman?'

'I think just a few pounds to Molly will ensure that on any date anyone cares to mention, I was here, all night, *alone*.'

'And who the hell is Molly?'

'The scrubbing-woman you keep in the basement, Mama.'

'The caretaker, don't you mean?'

'Caretaker, then. Though why you don't have staff

here, I don't know. That woman's an embarrassment sometimes, answering the door.'

'That woman comes cheap! And when staff is needed here I bring them down from Pendenys, you know that.' It was more economical to bring down a cook and two or three maids third class by railway than to keep servants here, eating their heads off, their followers having the run of the place the moment she returned to Pendenys Place. 'I'll arrange for you to have a couple of hundred, though as to the caretaker, you'll have to bribe her out of your own pocket if it comes to the worst. *That* kind of trouble you get yourself out of from now on. When you find yourself a suitable wife – or let me find one for you, Elliot – then you'll realize I can be more than generous. But I will *not* pay for your whores, and that is my last word! And you might as well tell me the worst. How far has this scandal gone? Is your Aunt Sutton right? *Are* people talking?'

'Not any longer. I've finished with Beatrice – told her so a while back. I don't think she'll make trouble, but if she does, it's my word against hers.'

'Were you indiscreet, Elliot? Did anyone see you in public?'

'Not that I know of. Don't know why Aunt says people are talking – we mostly came here . . .'

'You did *that*! In *my* bed!'

'Of course not, Mama dear. I wouldn't be so foolish. Sufficient to say that I saw to it Molly kept her mouth shut.'

'Dear, sweet heaven – where will it all end? When are you going to learn sense? You'll drive me to my grave, and that's a fact! Why can't you see how lucky you are, safe in London for the duration? Why must you take such delight in rocking the boat?'

'I don't know,' he whispered contritely, because she was right. He'd gone too far with Beatrice, and if her husband were to hear about it and kick up a fuss, he'd be in the trenches without so much as a by-your-leave.

'Please, son, try to behave yourself. Try to keep out of trouble – be more like Nathan . . .'

'I will. I promise. I truly do.'

'Good,' she said wearily. 'And now, since there's nothing to eat in the house, I suppose we'd better telephone for a taxi and see if we can find somewhere with food to serve.'

'Better than that – I'll drive you! My motor is round the back. I keep it here, didn't you know?' Poor Mama. She really looked tired. Showing her age, these days. Not a patch on Aunt Helen when it came to looks. 'Now off you go and put on something nice and I'll take you to the best little restaurant in London.'

'That will be nice,' she smiled briefly, knowing who would be picking up the bill. 'Very nice indeed . . .'

And oh, *why* did she feel like bursting into tears?

34

Their new ward had smelled of paint, unseasoned timber, and never-before-used cotton bed-covers. Within two hours of moving in, it smelled crisply of carbolic.

'Almost like Denniston House,' Alice sniffed.

'Only tonight, when we go off duty, we'll walk the field path back to quarters instead of pedalling home.'

Home to Rowangarth; to that far-away, creaking old house with the remembered smell of beeswax polish and precious old furniture and the roses that climbed its summer walls.

'They'll be busy getting in the hay,' Alice sighed, though who was left there to scythe it she couldn't for the life of her think.

'Forty-four,' Julia murmured, not to be tempted into nostalgia. 'Everything comes in forty-fours . . .'

Beds, bed-mackintoshes, feeding cups; forty-four trays, bowls, cups, saucers, plates, spoons; and every one to be accounted for before their reliefs took over at duty's end.

'The patients will be moving in tomorrow.' Alice still thrilled to the title of 'nurse', though she and Julia would never be proper nurses like Sister and Ruth Love. They should not even, yet, dress a wound, though no one seemed to complain when there were too many wounded and too few to nurse them.

'I would like everything to be counted, cleaned and in place by the time we go off duty,' said Sister, unable to disguise her satisfaction. 'Tomorrow, all the beds will be filled and we'll begin a week of day duties.' And after that, she told them, a week of night work, though when and how they would get a rest-day she would better know when she had consulted with her opposite number – a sister she had yet to meet. 'It will be good, though, to get into a routine again.'

The near chaos at the chateau had appalled her orderly mind. From now on, with her own ward, things, she thought, grimly satisfied, would be vastly different. Now it was no longer Hut Twenty-four, but Sister Carbrooke's ward.

'And since everything seems in good order, I think that when you, MacMalcolm, and you, Hawthorn, have cleaned the windows, you can take what remains of the afternoon off. I'm sure you have things to catch up on in quarters.'

Hawthorn, she supposed, would spend her hour cleaning and pressing her uniform; MacMalcolm would spend it writing to her husband and Love would –

Sister frowned, unsure. Staff Nurse Love's eyes were still troubled, as if returning to France had awakened memories instead of laying them to rest.

'You, Staff Nurse, will check the contents of the poisons cupboard with me, if you please.'

It would be a long time – if ever – before Ruth Love accepted the death of her husband. She would have to be watched most carefully, Sister decided; for her own good, as well as that of the patients.

Such a terrible war, and the end of it nowhere in sight! How had it been allowed to happen? It made her glad she had been born a woman. Men were so *utterly* stupid!

Sister Carbrooke's ward was not to become a haven of well-ordered tranquillity. Before many hours had run, they were all to realize it was to be little more than an extension of the chateau dressing-station; a staging-post, Sister snorted, between the trenches and a hospital ship to England. Since the Somme fighting began, ten thousand wounded had been disembarked at Southampton alone, a nursing colleague had written, and heaven only knew how many more at other ports. Those who came to Hut Twenty-four had first to be divested of mud-caked uniforms and made as comfortable as possible. Thereafter, medical officers called briefly to assess the order of priority in which they were shipped to England. It made a mockery, Sister mourned, of the profession of nursing. It was, said Julia and Alice, Denniston House stableyard all over again, without the bitter cold.

Ruth Love said little, scanning each khaki uniform for the wings of a flyer; feeling guilt-ridden relief when her fears proved unfounded and she was not to be reminded of another death in another ward in another life, it seemed.

Night duties followed day duties. The distant guns began their barrage again. Hopes of a rest-day faded; it became almost unpatriotic even to think of one. In the midst of such killing, merely to be alive was something to be wondered at.

That night, they trod the well-worn path from huts to quarters without speaking. It was Julia who broke the weary silence.

'Penny for them?'

'I was thinking about home – about buttercups and Brattocks Wood and –' Alice stopped, her voice trembling.

'And Tom,' Julia whispered. 'With me, it's usually Holdenby Pike I think of when things get bad; the feeling that everything up there is clean and untouched and away from the taint of war. And Andrew with me, of course . . .'

'It's far worse for the men,' Alice shrugged.

'I know. It's the only thing that helps me to carry on.' That, and the chance that, around the next corner, she might see him . . .

'It would seem,' said Helen Sutton, 'that Julia is well and happy, though how she manages to be so amazes me.'

594

The Government had been unable to keep back the news of the slaughter around the River Somme. The country was stunned by it. There had even been talk about the shortage of Post Office telegraph boys, so many telegrams of death and wounding were there to deliver.

It would be better now, though. It *must* be better. Lord Kitchener had been replaced as War Minister by Mr Lloyd-George, that forthright Celt who cared little for the conventions of polite society. He thundered instead for the rights of the men at the Front, and mocked the stupidity of some in high command who thought that wars were still fought by gentlemen in pretty uniforms and white gloves.

'Well, my dear Helen, between the new man at the War Office and your precious tanks in action at last, we might soon see an end to the wretched business in France,' Judge Mounteagle said. He had called to collect a small bag of Sutton Premier tea. 'Six of these tanks at the Front, so the papers say. Let's hope they frighten the trousers off the Kaiser!'

Not that they would, he reasoned, but Helen, for some peculiar reason, set great store by their development – stupid, new-fangled machines that they were. Clumsy, too. Still, if they gave the dear lady comfort with all her children at war – and one of them never to return from it – then who was he to tell her they were a flash in the pan and would never catch on! And things had come to a terrible pass when a man had reason to be grateful he was old. Calling all men to the Colours from nineteen to fifty-five now!

'Most grateful for this tea, m'dear,' he smiled. 'Not been able to buy so much as a spoonful lately.'

'We are lucky.' Helen believed in sharing her luck. 'So far, all our tea-chests have reached us safely.' And lucky, too, that by this morning's early delivery there had been letters from Julia, Giles and Nathan. She was proud of her family, but how desperately she wanted them home! 'And do you know, I have a feeling inside me – call it woman's intuition, if you wish – that before next year is all that old, we shall see an end to the war. I truly believe it.'

'Do you realize, Alice, that in just three hours it will be 1917?'

'It's been a funny old twelve-month,' Alice acknowledged.

'A bad one,' Julia shrugged. 'All right, so the fighting seems all but over around the Somme, but it has started up again at Verdun.'

Verdun, where Andrew was stationed, and Tom, too, for all Alice could tell. All she was sure of was that his regiment had left Albert – *I won't be seeing Mr Nathan's brother for a while* had been Tom's first intimation. Then there had been almost two worrying weeks without hearing from him, after which came a letter bearing the mark of a different Censor. *I'm still with Geordie, though our billet is little better than a cowshed, now* . . .

'That's it,' Alice said flatly when the relief of hearing from him had subsided. 'I'm sure of it. Tom *has* been moved.'

'Any idea where?' Julia looked at the watch on her wrist, impatient for the New Year, new hope.

'Ypres or Verdun,' Alice sighed, 'and both of them further away.' She had rounded many corners hoping to see him, but Tom had never been there, even though he'd been so near to Celverte. Now there seemed less chance than ever that they would meet, especially since single men were never given leave – nor married ones, she sighed, glancing across the small kitchen to where Julia was making tea for last rounds.

Last rounds? Not tonight. Hardly any of the patients would sleep, for wasn't the New Year just hours away, and weren't all of them Blighty-bound just as soon as maybe? And by the time their wounds were healed and their blue uniforms exchanged for khaki ones once more, the war would be over!

'They aren't going to settle down,' Ruth said. 'Not until after midnight, anyway. Might as well accept it. Take the mugs round, Julia, and warn them that any New Year rowdiness will be punished by ice-cold bedpans at dawn – only don't let Sister hear you!'

Ruth Love was improving. Some of the tenseness had left her – she had even shown them a photograph of a young nurse and a handsome flyer, taken on their wedding day. Then the shutters had gone down again; she had spoken his name just once since then.

'Today is – would have been – Jamie's birthday,' she said, briefly.

Not a lot, Julia thought, but a beginning. Sufficient that she had told them; been prepared to share her grief. Time was a great healer, said people who knew no better. Time would never heal her own wounds should Andrew be killed, Julia thought fiercely. Nothing would.

'Hey!' Alice snapped her fingers. 'You were miles away! Tell me?'

'Forget it!' Julia's voice was sharp. 'This war *is* going to be over soon, isn't it?'

'It is,' Alice said firmly. 'Didn't we agree not half an hour ago that it would be? So how about us having a drink before we see to the ward? There won't be a lot of time afterwards. I'll take a cup to Sister.'

The ward – Hut Twenty-four – had been decorated for Christmas with flags and trails of greenery, gathered from the lanes outside Celverte. It had been the best Christmas some of the wounded had known for three years. Now they were the lucky ones, awaiting a berth on a hospital

597

ship and Blighty; bloody lovely Blighty! Their pain was as nothing. They were alive, would remain alive until summer at least, when it would all be over! Soon they would cheer in another year, and who amongst them cared if the dragon lady called Sister Carbolic frowned!

Sister Carbrooke said yes, of course she would take the flyer. She always tried to keep one bed empty for extreme emergencies.

Prognosis nil? she frowned at the telephone. Very well. He would die in a haze of morphine and receive just the same care as –

'Nurse Love – there's a patient arriving. Top bed,' she said tersely. 'Will you special him, please?'

The top bed was the only one to have curtains around it; curtains to hide the ceremonial of dying from the rest of the ward who, but for a whim of Fate's choosing finger, could each have lain there.

'Yes, Sister.' Ruth Love pulled back the bed-cover and lit the bedside lamp, drawing the curtains quietly. She was no stranger to death. After the night Jamie died, nothing could pierce the shield she had drawn around her emotions.

The stretcher-bearers carried him in. On his forehead was the purple mark of his suffering; on the label pinned to his collar were the details of his condition and drugs injected. His name was Hans-Rudolf Kliene, his rank *Leutnant*.

'No! Sister, I will not . . .' she choked. 'I will *not* nurse him!' Her eyes were fear-filled, her face paper-white. The young man who lay dying was her enemy – and a flyer! He could even be the one who, not so very long ago, had swooped in low over Jamie's aerodrome and –

'Will *not*?' Sister's voice was low with anger. 'Please step outside the ward, Staff Nurse. And close the door behind you. *Quietly . . .*'

Any other woman would have recognized the threat in that voice; any woman other than Ruth Love who was being ordered to live again her own husband's death.

'Sister – I beg you. It isn't fair – it isn't right to ask it . . .'

'What is right or fair in war, Nurse? What was right or fair about *her* death?' She pointed to the photograph of a nurse called Edith Cavell that hung in the corridor. 'You and I are bound by the ethics of our profession to nurse the sick and the wounded, no matter who they be. We tend them regardless of creed or colour because they need our skills. The boy in there is dying and in his rare moments of lucidity he will know it. He needs the comfort of a handclasp. The young fear death. Help him?'

'Nurse MacMalcolm – can't she special him?' Her voice shook with emotion. 'Please, Sister . . . ?'

'Nurse MacMalcolm can and would, but I am asking you, Ruth. You may refuse and I shall try to understand. But if you do, you will have betrayed not only your profession, but your husband too. It is your choice. Yes or no – quickly! A man is dying!'

'I'm sorry.' Ruth Love lifted her chin. 'Forgive me? I'll go to him . . .'

Hans-Rudolf Kliene had white-blond hair and, had his eyelids not been closed, she knew his eyes, too, would have been the same brilliant blue as Jamie's. He lay, moaning softly, wanting to die yet fearing it, resenting it.

Ruth moved the chair nearer and sat down. He was so young. Jamie had been young, hadn't wanted to go to war. University first, then a house in the country and the life of a veterinary surgeon – only there hadn't been time.

'*Mutter* . . .' The eyelids flickered, and were still again.

Only a boy. He wanted his mother. Tears scalded her eyes and she dashed them angrily away. She was a nurse;

599

she could not weep. God! It was all so unfair! She bent closer, her lips close to his ear.

'*Ja*, Hans?' she said gently.

Taking his hand she held it tightly, then whispering her lips over his cheek she laid them to his closed eyelids. His lips moved in a small smile; his hand relaxed inside hers. She sat quietly for a moment, the hand inside hers warm and fragile and afraid. Her fingers searched his wrist for a pulse beat. His dying had been gentle in the end.

'*Jamie!*' Her cry was harsh with pain. She laid the limp hand to her cheek. She had screamed out her anger at the death of her husband, then locked her grief inside her, so terrible had it been to bear. Now, at the dying of his enemy, this boy so like Jamie, she allowed herself the tears she had been unwilling and unable to shed; that had lain so long in her heart in an ache of bitterness.

'It's all right, Nurse.' Sister reached out, gathering her close, holding her tightly. 'Let it come. Weep for him, for them both . . .'

A long time afterwards, when the joy of a New Year had subsided and Hut Twenty-four was quiet again, Ruth Love stripped the top bed, folded the blankets and drew back the curtains.

She was calm, her eyes dry of tears now. Sister, who missed nothing, saw with sad satisfaction that she was once again wearing her wedding ring.

There was a covering of snow at Holdenby, that New Year's Eve, changing Rowangarth into a picture-postcard house, disguising its shabby comfort with a sparkle of white.

Cook always kept the New Year watch. You had to say goodbye to the twelve-month gone, to be thankful for its blessings, vow to learn from its mistakes. Tonight, as she always did, her ladyship would wait with the sherry decanter and a sup of whisky in an old crystal glass and a man – it was to be Reuben again tonight – would knock loudly on the front door at the first stroke of midnight from the church clock.

'Come in, and welcome.' Agnes Clitherow answered the knocking before the clock had finished its striking.

'I'm come to bring in the New Year,' Reuben said formally, wiping his boots carefully, 'and to wish health and content to all. And the Almighty's blessing on absent ones,' he added, glad the speechifying was over.

'Thank you most warmly, Reuben.' Helen offered her hand. She never called him Pickering, which would have been too demeaning, nor *Mr* Pickering, which wouldn't have suited his position, but Reuben – which was friendly between her and him; special, too.

'Thank you kindly, milady.' Reuben accepted the glass, offering a piece of coal, a salt cellar full to the brim and a crust of bread in return. Then he downed the whisky at a gulp, savouring the bite of it and the warmth, tucking the cigar the housekeeper gave him into his pocket.

'Bid you goodnight, then . . .' He never outstayed his welcome. On the doorstep he replaced his best tweed hat, brought his forefinger respectfully to its brim, then walked briskly down the steps.

'A Happy New Year, Miss Clitherow.' Helen smiled.

'Thank you – and to you, milady.' She bobbed a curtsey. She always curtseyed at certain times of the year, just to keep things straight. 'Are we to go below stairs? I know Cook would appreciate it.'

'Of course.' Nothing must change. Once, in the good days, there had been a party for servants; now they were almost all gone to war and a party would have seemed out of place, even had there been food. 'We must have a glass of sherry.' New Years at Rowangarth were always made welcome.

'May we come in,' Helen peeped round the kitchen door, 'and share your fire?'

'You may, milady, and welcome,' Cook beamed, rising – as did Tilda and Jinny – to her feet.

Agnes Clitherow poured sherry, passing it round. Helen settled herself comfortably in one of the rockers and all sat down again.

'Do you suppose,' Helen pondered, 'that Mr Lloyd-George will make a difference to things, now that he's Prime Minister?'

She shouldn't talk about the war, she knew, but everyone did, if only to comfort each other.

'Oh yes, indeed, milady.' Agnes Clitherow nodded, sipping daintily from her glass.

'And it's a known fact,' beamed Mrs Shaw, 'them Germans is hungrier than we are. They had a poor harvest an' all, this summer.'

'Bread ninepence a loaf.' Jinny Dobb gazed mournfully into her glass. 'How's a soldier's wife with bairns to feed to afford that kind of money, milady?'

'They're hungrier in Germany,' Cook insisted. 'Be thankful for small mercies, Jin. We have tea here, and potatoes; and there's always rabbits. Mr Pickering sees that every household has its fair share!' The sherry was going to her head. It always did, but she didn't care. 'Though it's got to be said it's time for official rationing – fair shares of food at fair prices!'

'I think Mr Lloyd-George will see to that,' murmured Agnes Clitherow. The old guard had done nothing for the war; perhaps the hot-blooded Welshman with the gift of words would do better.

'I worry about Russia,' Helen frowned. 'The Czarina – so foolishly influenced. Her poor son, though – she has so much to worry her . . .'

'That Rasputin,' said Jin, 'is a nasty, evil old man.' Jin could recognize evil; could smell it almost. 'Needs locking up in prison,' – or wherever it was they put mad, meddlesome monks. 'You can't blame the Russian peasants for getting fed up about it.'

'No. But it couldn't happen here.' The housekeeper shot a warning glance across the room. The British working man knew his place. Always would. That was why Britain was great.

'Happen not.' Jin drained her glass and gazed meaningfully at the decanter. The houskeeper replaced the stopper firmly.

'I think,' said Tilda, 'we should drink to our soldiers and nurses, milady, and that next year they'll all be back home.'

Tilda disliked the war. Not for her the high wages of factory work. She hid from it happily at Rowangarth, in spite of the extra tasks thrust upon her.

'Most happily.' Helen raised her glass. 'To my son and daughter and Hawthorn and the doctor. And to my nephews and to Will and Davie and Dwerryhouse. May God keep them safely – and grant us all a Happy New Year.'

They all said Amen to that. There had been one taken already from Rowangarth; they wanted no more. And as for the Almighty taking a hand in things, Jin Dobb thought darkly, it was in the tea-leaves that Mr Lloyd-George, now that he was Prime Minister instead of that Mr Asquith, would make a great difference to the war.

But it was in the stars, she was forced to admit, the war hadn't anywhere near run its course. There were deaths and woundings aplenty yet to come. And terrible rumblings from a far-away country.

Nowhere near over, this war wasn't. Jin *knew* . . .

35

1917

Spring came suddenly to Rowangarth. All at once, the sharpness left the air, the weeping willows on the edge of the wild garden grew green, and the avenue of linden trees began to burst bud.

In Brattocks Wood, celandines glowed like small yellow stars, and violets peeped from beneath their leaves. In and out of the tallest trees in the wood, rooks carried twigs, repairing nests. The worst of winter was over, Reuben noted with satisfaction. Now, the third spring of the war was here, bringing with it a gentleness to compensate for the misery of a cold, hungry winter. It made him hopeful that this year would see an end to the fighting; that Himself-up-there had finally decided who would win this war. Us, Reuben thought, without a doubt!

Helen Sutton stood at her wide-open bedroom window. On a day such as this, anyone could be forgiven for feeling happy. Half-way into March; skies a pale, clear blue and the air so heavy with the scent of green things growing that just to breathe it in made her dizzy. It would be better, too, at the Front; no mud-filled trenches or soldiers keeping watch with frozen fingers.

This morning there was such joy in her heart she knew beyond doubt that all those she loved were safe. This was not a telegram day. Soon, Miss Clitherow would bring her morning tea – Helen never ate breakfast now; her personal contribution to the war effort – and she would be wearing the expression that meant she was bringing letters from France, Helen was sure of it.

She shrugged into her wrap, quickly pinned up her hair, smiling at Helen-in-the-mirror, listening to the measured tread along the passage, waiting for the creak of the floorboard half-way along it.

'Come in, please,' she called. 'Good morning, Miss Clitherow!'

'Milady.' The housekeeper nodded her head. 'There are no letters – well, not from France and –' She hesitated, offering the folded newspaper. 'I think you should see this – well, sooner than later . . .'

She busied herself pouring tea, eyes downcast. Helen read the headlines. They were half an inch high and screamed: CZAR NICHOLAS ABDICATES.

'Oh, dear heaven!' She shook open the paper, ignoring the offered teacup. 'Please don't go, Miss Clitherow.' News such as this she did not wish to read alone. 'You've seen it?'

'Not read it, milady, but Cook has. She could hardly tell it, she was so upset . . .'

'Then it would seem the Czar of Russia has given up his throne – or been dismissed from it. So *awful* . . .'

The King's cousin, forced into ignominy! There had been rumours, of course; undercurrents of discontent in Moscow and St Petersburg, with the Mensheviks and the Bolsheviks at each other's throats for the support of the peasants. *Peasant*. A word long gone in these islands. Here, a peasant was a part of history.

'It couldn't happen here, Miss Clitherow?' Helen's hands shook so much that the paper made little crackling noises.

'Absolutely not, milady. Here, we are a democracy,' said the housekeeper with conviction. 'Now, drink your tea, then I'll have Tilda run your bath. The newspapers always make things sound ten times worse.'

'But what of the Russian troops holding the Eastern front? The Czar was their commander-in-chief.' Who would command them now?

'They'll have it all worked out, be sure of that,' Agnes Clitherow soothed. 'We won't be losing an ally. It's the fault, though, of that monk Rasputin,' she offered in a rare show of opinion. 'Men in holy orders shouldn't meddle in matters of state! He asked to be killed.

'And had you thought, milady, that the Czar has many loyal supporters? The Russian aristocracy will back him, and the Cossacks to a man would die for him. Don't worry. He'll soon be Czar again.'

'Yes. Yes, of course.' Helen picked up her cup, but the tea in it had gone cold and tasted bitter on her tongue. Strange, she pondered, gazing out of the window, that the sun continued to shine and the birds to sing.

But the sun cared nothing for wars or Czars, she shivered, and oh, how lucky those birds who could not read.

'I've said it all along,' muttered Jinny Dobb, 'and there's none present as can contradict me; that Czar of Russia should have put his foot down over his wife and that Rasputin, the mucky old devil. Spiritual adviser, indeed . . .'

'What do you mean?' Cook demanded, sliding her eyes in the direction of Tilda whose ears she considered too innocent for Jin's implications.

'She means,' offered Tilda blithely, 'that he's had carnal knowledge –'

'*Tilda!* You are talking about a Czarina – an Empress!' Cook's cheeks flamed red. 'And where did you hear such a word? *Carnal*, indeed! You don't even know what it means!'

'I heard it plenty when they murdered that Rasputin at New Year. Served him right, folk said. Shouldn't interfere in politics, some said; others said he shouldn't have interfered with the –'

'*That will do!*'

'The lass is right,' defended Jin. 'Was only what folk were saying at the time. And now they'll be thinking it's all going to blow over in Russia; that we'll send troops to help put the Czar back in power. But why should we? Why should one drop of British blood be spilled, just to save a man who treats his subjects like they was dirt? An' I'll tell you something else, Cook. There's worse to come from that quarter of the globe. Jin knows . . .'

'I said that would do, and I meant *do!*' Cook banged the flat of her hand on the table-top. An Emperor having to abdicate was bad enough, without Jin Dobb's prophecies to make it worse. Trouble was, when Jin went into one of her utterances, she was rarely wrong.

'All right,' Jin grumbled. 'I'll shut me mouth. Pity you don't want to hear the good news . . .'

'Good news!' Tilda gasped. 'Is the war going to end?'

'Nay, lass. Not this twelve-month. We shall lose an ally, too: they'll be little help to us now, them Russian soldiers. But we'll gain another friend, and before so very much longer, an' all. One so powerful as will make that Kaiser wish he'd never started the dratted war!'

'Who, then?' Cook asked reluctantly.

But Jinny Dobb, having had the last word, kept her mouth tightly closed on the subject. 'I'll see to the vegetables and peel the potatoes,' she said stubbornly, and not all Tilda's soft-soaping nor Cook's cajoling could draw forth another word.

Julia hurried to Matron's room, a summons which had her worried. Usually, a reprimand from the matron of General Hospital Sixteen was first passed to a sister who passed it to a staff nurse to deliver. Interviews with Matron were so rare – unless you were a sister, of course – that a nurse so summoned shook with trepidation.

'What have you done?' Alice demanded.

'Nothing.' Julia swallowed hard. 'Nothing, truly.'

'Said, then? There's got to be *something* . . .'

Each skirted round what she really thought – that it was news of such seriousness that only Matron could give it.

'I shall never get through the night,' Julia choked. 'I shall worry and worry . . .'

'Have you asked Sister?'

'Of course I have! All I could get out of her was that Matron said that when MacMalcolm came off night duty she would like to see her – see *me*!'

'There you are, then! If it were anything – well, *awful* – she'd be bound to tell you at once. So stop your worrying.'

Julia said she would, but it was a white and shaking nurse who tapped timidly on the door marked 'J. Campbell, Matron'.

'Yes? Who is it then?'

'It's MacMalcolm, Matron. You wish to see me?' Her voice sounded hoarse; she cleared her throat noisily.

'Ah, yes. Sit down, please.'

Julia remained standing. To be invited to sit in Matron's presence meant only bad news to follow. And even had she wanted to, her feet refused to move one step towards the chair.

'To get to the point, Nurse, I have a message from your husband.'

'*From?*' Not *about*! She sat down heavily, grasping the chair seat.

'From Major MacMalcolm. And I have to say at once that I strongly disapprove of army telephone lines being taken up for personal messages,' she said in a rounded

Scottish accent. 'However, on this occasion . . .' She paused to smile – to *smile* – which gave Julia time enough to gasp, 'Major? He's a captain, though . . .'

'Then he's been promoted, girl! On this occasion, and because we are all of us of the same professional calling, I agreed to tell you that he'll be in Paris on army business on Friday next – the 6th. Can you meet him, he asks, at the Gare du Nord between one and two p.m. – in the vicinity of the main entrance? He could not be more specific, timewise, than that.'

'*Meet* him! Oh please, Matron *please*, let me go?' Julia was on her feet again, her heart thumping, her cheeks flushing hotly. 'Friday I'll be sleeping, anyway, and I haven't had a rest-day for six weeks. We haven't seen each other since we –'

'Aye. Since you were married, he told me.'

'More than two years ago.'

'This meeting will only be in passing, as it were. You'll not be getting any time off, Nurse . . .'

'I can go? You'll give me permission to travel, ma'am?'

'On this occasion – yes. But do *not* make habit of it. I can't have my nurses gallivanting off when they should be sleeping after night duty. Be that as it may, there will be an ambulance convoy leaving on that morning for Calais. You may have a ride as far as Amiens with them; from there you can catch a train to Paris. At seven a.m., that will be . . .'

'But I don't come off duty until eight!'

'I am well aware of that, Nurse. However, Sister Carbrooke agreed that you can leave the ward at six-thirty.'

'She *knew*? She knew all along and she never said – never breathed a word!' Tears of utter happiness filled Julia's eyes and she dashed them impatiently away. 'Thank you, ma'am, so very much. And is that all? Can I go now, if you please . . . ?'

'Away with you! And don't shout it all over the place or they'll all be wanting permission to meet their men in Paris!' came the dour parting shot.

Friday April 6th. Spring in Paris. The loveliest time of the whole year. A time for lovers!

Julia picked up her skirts and ran; down the field path, past the farm buildings, up the wooden stairs.

'Alice! Where on earth –' She swished back the green dividing curtains. 'Oh, thank goodness . . .'

'It's all right then!' Alice saw the shining eyes, the flushed cheeks. 'Now sit yourself down. I won't have you spoil it in the telling – because it's good news, isn't it?'

'*Good?*' Julia collapsed on her bed. 'Andrew! In Paris on Friday! He managed to get Matron on the telephone! Round about midday at the railway station I'm meeting him. I can't believe it!'

'Matron said *yes*?'

'Mm. Oh, she tut-tutted a bit about using army telephones and all that, and at first I thought it was some awful April Fool's joke, but –'

'Oh, *hush*, will you! Just take a deep breath and start at the beginning,' Alice beamed. 'I want every word of it, right from start to finish.'

So, just a little more calmly, Julia told it, punctuating each sentence with little happy laughs.

'And all I know for certain is that he'll be in Paris on army business, that we'll be able to have a few hours together and, oh! I forgot – he's a major now! Major MacMalcolm. Sounds good, doesn't it?'

'Sounds *very* good.'

'And listen to this! Carbolic must have known all along what it was all about! She must've, because she told Matron I could go off duty early. Yet not by a wink or a nod did she let on!'

'Sister's an old poker-face.'

'Yes, and I love her!'

'Letter for you, Alice.' Ruth Love had collected the morning mail. 'Nothing for you, Julia – but you can't expect letters *and* telephone messages,' she grinned.

'You knew! You and Sister both!' Julia gasped. 'And neither of you said a word!'

'Indeed not,' Staff Nurse smiled primly, 'and why should we? It's only the bad news that travels fast. Good news gets even better for the keeping. I'm so glad for you, Julia.' She turned quickly and left, and they heard the gentle closing of her cubicle door.

'Poor Ruth,' Julia sighed. 'I have no right to be so happy, have I? Oh, Lordy – I've just thought. Nothing will go wrong this time, will it? Andrew won't have to cancel?'

'Not this time,' Alice said firmly. 'Now we're going to get some breakfast then we're both going to sleep. And no tossing and turning!'

'I'll try not.'

What a lovely, *lovely* morning this was. Julia raised her eyes to the bright April sky.

Thank you, God. Thank you with all my heart for this happiness . . .

Paris had never been so beautiful, nor would ever be again – the entrance to the Gare du Nord station, and the tables outside it, that was.

Ten minutes to one o'clock. The local train had crawled, but here she was, with minutes in hand to savour their meeting, to wonder what she would say, what Andrew would say.

If she turned a little to the right from where she waited she could see a clock. She fixed the minute hand with her eyes and began to count. It took her to seventy before it jerked forward. She slowed down her count and began again.

Five minutes to go. She became impatient with counting, and turned her attention to the motor taxis and cabs drawing up at the entrance. It was them she should be watching. And what was Andrew doing in Paris? Was the Medical Corps moving him on to another theatre of war; to India, even? India would be safer, but did they have VAD nurses there and how was she to get to him? Please – not India?

A flower-seller nearby tied up bunches of violets; a poilu strolled past, his girl on his arm; a one-legged man on crutches rattled his tin at her, begging with his eyes for money. Smiling, she gave him a coin.

One o'clock. Very soon, Andrew would come. Any minute now they would wipe out thirty-one months – almost a thousand nights – of being apart. Soon she would see him, touch him, kiss him . . .

At half-past one she was wondering, panic-stricken, if she had heard Matron aright; if their interview was only in her imagination. Had she got not only the time wrong, but the place and day too? Perhaps she had dreamed the whole thing; an illusion born of her desperate need of him.

There were other entrances; two, perhaps three. Should she try them? Could she find them? Would Andrew do the same? Would they spend the entire afternoon shuttling from entrance to entrance, missing each other by seconds?

She would wait here! If she had got it wrong then Andrew would find her. In desperation she turned to the clock as if God Himself pushed round the minute hand. Between one and two, Matron had said. Oh, *please* don't let her have got it wrong.

She pulled her eyes from the clock, searching the station approaches, the cabs outside it, the flower-seller.

Darling, as you love me, come now! Don't let it all come to nothing, again.

Another cab drew up. She hardly dared look. It was the eleventh she had counted. She smoothed down her coat, straightened her cap again, then looked up.

He was there, crossing the street towards her. *He had come!* Andrew: thinner, taller, more good to look at than ever she could remember from her dreamings.

She whispered his name but no sound came. *Over here, my darling! I'm here!*

He sidestepped a porter's trolley, then turned to see her. For just a second he stopped, as if the sight of her was beyond his believing. Then he smiled, quickening his pace.

'Andrew!' She ran to him, arms outstretched, and they were holding each other close. Cheek on cheek. Not speaking nor kissing. Clinging, desperately reluctant to let go; as if each were afraid that, if they did, the other would vanish like a mirage.

'My darling love.' He was the first to find words. 'It *is* you!'

She pulled herself a little way from him. Her eyes filled with tears and his image blurred.

'Sweetheart!' He tilted her chin and his mouth found hers, and it was their first kiss at Aunt Sutton's house all over again only a million times more lovely.

'I'm sorry,' she whispered as tenderly he dried her eyes, her cheeks. 'I wasn't weeping – just happy . . .'

'Tell me?' he said softly.

'I love you, love you,' she whispered. 'I can't believe any of this.'

'It's happening.' He kissed her again. 'Let me look at you. You're so very beautiful – even in that ridiculous hat.'

'I'm in uniform. This is my walking-out hat.' She pulled it off.

'That's better. You haven't had your hair cut?'

'No. I just pin it up tightly.'

'Never have it cut . . .'

'I won't, I promise. And we're wasting time. It's half a minute since you kissed me . . .'

'I think,' he said eventually, 'you are even more beautiful. Sometimes, when things were bad, I'd blot it all out and see only your face . . .'

'Darling – don't?' She began to weep again, then impatiently pulled her hand across her eyes. 'And we *are* wasting time. I want you to make love to me. Where can we go?'

'Sweetheart, ssssh . . .' He took her face in his hands. 'Not this time. The Reims train leaves in just over an hour and I must be on it. There isn't time, even, to find a room . . .'

'Andrew, *no*!'

'That idiot at HQ – he went on and on. I wanted to yell at him that my wife was waiting!'

'I want you,' she said, stubbornly.

'Darling, listen. There is so much to tell you, let's sit down.' He nodded towards the pavement tables. 'Please?'

'Sorry, Andrew. Just a few days ago I'd have given all I had in the world just to see you walk past the bottom of the lane, yet now I'm complaining. Forgive me?'

He took her arm, finding an empty table. 'Now will you listen to me, woman?' He reached across the table-top, taking her hands in his. 'First – I am now Major MacMalcolm!'

'Matron told me. I should have said congratulations, darling. I'm proud of you, but they won't move you because of it?'

'They will – they *are*. That's why I came to Paris. Oh, I'll still be in France, but going to a hospital which is soon to open, so I've just been told. There are too many wounded being shipped to Blighty who ought to be treated here . . .'

'I know, darling,' she murmured, pouring coffee.

'Of course you do. Well, I shall get surgical experience now, and at a place called Cotterets. It's well behind the lines. No more forward dressing-stations. I've had almost three years of them; it's someone else's turn now.'

'You'll be safer at a base hospital, won't you?'

'Much safer. I can hardly believe my luck. But the best thing about the move is that, if we all work together – each do extra duties for the other – there shouldn't be anything to stop any of us getting time off. Not leave, of course, but it's going to mean that sometimes I shall be able to get away. How will that suit you, wife?'

'It sounds too good to be true,' she murmured, 'especially since I've been bargaining with God for only an *hour*.'

'Two nights, it should be. We'll have to decide which place will suit us best to meet – can't waste time travelling. And I'll go on the leave rota, too, which might eventually give me seven days. We could take a long leave in Paris, then – make it a second honeymoon . . .'

'So we'll be together – *really* together – soon?'

'With a bit of deviousness and a spot of luck – yes.'

'Don't! And keep your voice down. The Fates might hear you! But it doesn't matter where we meet, darling. As long as there's a bed – a big, soft, sinful bed – and oh, my goodness! I've only got uniform with me! I'll write home and ask mother to have some clothes sent out.'

'The blue dress with the white lace collar – that's a must.'

'My wedding dress . . .'

'Aye. The one you were wearing when I asked you to marry me. And be sure she sends a nightgown – the one with the little blue ribbons on it.'

'But *why*?' she teased. 'Whenever I wear it you take it off at once!'

615

'I know. Pity to crease it,' he grinned, 'and you'll never know the delight it gives me, unfastening the ties at the shoulder!'

'Don't talk like that, Andrew. It makes it even worse. I wanted so much for us to be together. I'm a selfish creature but I have such need of you. And here we are, sitting either side of a table, when all I want to do is hold you and touch you and kiss you . . .'

'We'll be together soon. I promise we will.' He dipped into his pocket, leaving coins on the table. 'And I've got an idea. We'll go into the station and – hey! Over there! What's the commotion!' A boy was selling newspapers, and around him men and women snapped them up eagerly. 'Hurry, darling. Let's see what it's about!'

It seemed important; good news, too. Everyone smiling, chattering excitedly in a language he hardly understood.

'Here – your French is better than mine . . .' He passed her the newspaper. 'Something about the USA, isn't it?'

'Oh, my goodness! They're in the war! The United States has come in – on our side! America declared war at one o'clock. Then they seized eighty-seven German ships in American ports! And Cuba and Panama have declared war on Germany, too! I never thought they'd come in with us – after all, it isn't their war. But what a difference it's going to make!'

'Amen to that. But Germany *has* been asking for it – stirring up trouble for the United States in Mexico; breaking off diplomatic relations. And sinking American ships, which were neutral, after all.'

'You could hardly call them neutral, Andrew, when they were bringing food and supplies to British ports.' Her cheeks throbbed; she could hardly believe what she had read.

'I never thought it would happen. Americans of German and Irish origin were so much against them

616

coming into the war. Do you realize what this will mean, Julia?'

'I realize we've lost the Russians and gained the United States – that's *got* to be important,' she frowned.

'Yes, but *think*,' he urged. 'We are weary of the fighting. Three years of it! We've drained ourselves! This will be like a shot in the arm! The Americans are strong and so full of confidence . . .'

'Yes, and I'm glad – relieved. It takes a bit of getting used to, though.'

Why, all at once, was she thinking about Kentucky and Amelia and all the women the length and breadth of that country? Did they want their men to fight? Were American women allowed a say in it?

'Sweetheart! I promise you it's going to shorten this war by *years*.'

'Yes – but will they actually send troops over here, Andrew? Will they fight in the trenches?'

'It's almost certain they will. I'll bet the German High Command is feeling pretty sick at this moment! And look around you – the French are pretty pleased about it!'

The streets around had all at once filled with people; talking, gesturing, shaking hands, hugging. And all of them smiling, laughing.

'I'm pleased, too. I truly am. I'm so relieved I could cry. But, darling, I want us to have children – sons – yet I couldn't bear to have them and love them then see them taken from me to fight some senseless war. Do you realize almost all the world is at war now?'

'Sweetheart, there *won't* be another war. This one will be so terrible to look back on that no one will let it happen again. And it's my bet they'll give the vote to women, once it's all over – if only for what women have done for the war effort. So you'll be able to rise in your monstrous regiments and say, "No more wars!"'

'But do you realize, wife, that we're just about the only two people not jumping for joy?'

He wrapped her in his arms, swinging her off her feet, kissing her soundly.

The flower-seller called, '*Bonne chance, mes enfants!*' as they passed, and Andrew stopped to buy a bunch of violets. 'For you, my darling Julia,' he whispered, 'to remember this day . . .'

'I love you,' she whispered, breathing in the sweet, soft perfume. 'Did you know – Tom gave Alice buttercups – she has some pressed in her Bible. They are her special flower now, and these shall be mine. April violets. I shall keep some of these in my own Bible, and when I want you so much I can't bear it, I shall look at them and remember lovers' meetings.'

'Lovers' meetings *to come*,' he said softly. 'We are so lucky. The worst of our war is over, I know it. Now, let's find the Reims platform and I shall take you in my arms and hold you and kiss you for the rest of the time we have left. A long goodbye, and I don't care who sees us!'

'Not goodbye,' she murmured, her lips close to his cheek. 'We'll say *au revoir* – so long. And it doesn't matter at all who sees us. The French love lovers. They won't care. And, darling – I'll remember this lovely afternoon for the rest of my life.'

'Away with your bother,' he laughed. For the first time since their parting, Andrew MacMalcolm's cautious heart beat with happiness and hope. 'Just be writing to Rowangarth for that nightdress!'

36

June blazed brilliantly. The trenches dried of their mud and the walls, beginning to crumble, were repaired in the lull in the fighting. For lull there seemed to be. Those at the hospital realized it. Nothing official; just the sure knowledge that beds were being filled less quickly.

Alice and Julia walked the field path that connected the hut-wards to the school and convent. Their eyes pricked for want of sleep, even though the night duty had been one of comparative calm. No soldier had called out in a fearsome nightmare; most had slept peacefully. Without the often-present tension, they had carried out morning routine: temperatures, bedpans, washing bowls, tea. Bed-mackintoshes, creased into discomfort in the night, had been smoothed, beds made, the floor mopped. The ward was in perfect order for the day staff who had arrived at five minutes to eight with the breakfast trolley rattling behind them.

'You've forgotten, haven't you?' Julia demanded as they passed the empty farm building once occupied by the convent cows. 'After all the bother it caused you, you've forgotten the date!'

'I haven't,' Alice laughed. 'At three o'clock this morning I remembered it was the twentieth of June!'

'Nineteen-seventeen. It's the *year* that's important. Twenty-one! You are your own woman now. Congratulations!'

They linked hands and did a little jig, then hugged Alice close.

'I'm so glad for you. Now you can marry Tom at the drop of a hat! No more asking permission.'

'Mm. Just to think about it makes me feel giddy. I wonder if there'll be a letter from him. I haven't heard for days.'

'Yes you have, though you didn't know it. There was one for you two days ago. I was going to bring it up to you and then I saw he'd written *Not to be opened until 20 June* on the back of the envelope. So I put it in my locker in case you were tempted.'

'I left it on your bed last night – other letters, too. Come on! Let's run!'

They clattered up the stairs two at a time, then pulled back the cubicle curtains.

'There you are! You didn't think we'd forgotten, did you?'

'Just look!' Tom's letter was there; one from Julia, too. And envelopes from Reuben, Tilda and Tom's mam.

'This is for you from me with dearest love.' Julia held out a small blue box with a jeweller's name in gold letters on the lid. 'I tried to find something to bring with me when we left England – something special. But there was nothing in the shops. So I hope you don't mind these being secondhand, sort of. I thought they'd match your engagement ring. They were Grandmother Whitecliffe's . . .'

Alice opened the box. Pearl ear-drops lay on a tiny cushion of black velvet, glowing creamily.

'Julia! You shouldn't have, but I'm glad you did. They are *beautiful*!'

'Wear them on your wedding day.'

Tears filled Alice's eyes. 'I'm so happy . . .'

'Me, too.' Ever since that April afternoon in Paris. 'Are we too happy, Alice?'

'No. Jinny Dobb always said folk get what they deserve.'

She stopped abruptly. Not today Jin's prophecies! Alice Hawthorn wasn't walking into any wood: not three times; not even once! She had found her straight, stout

620

stave long ago, and now she was old enough to marry him of her own free will.

'Thank you,' she said simply, shyly kissing Julia's cheek. 'And can you give me a couple of minutes? Save me a chair at breakfast? I'll follow you down. Just want to read Tom's letter . . .'

'And have a little weep?'

'Just a little one. And we aren't too happy, Julia. It's just that now it seems our turn has come round. Off you go now!'

They were *not* too happy, she repeated inside her, and the Fates *wouldn't* get jealous. She laid Tom's letter to her cheek.

'I love you, Tom Dwerryhouse,' she whispered. 'Wherever you are, my love, take care . . .'

July came, and with it a starting again of the fighting, which they soon learned from passing drivers was further away, in the region of Ypres.

Tom was at Ypres; he and Geordie Marshall, still together. That morning, before she went on duty, Alice opened the door of the tiny chapel the nuns once used and, kneeling at the altar, she begged God and the Virgin whose face gazed down benignly, to take care of her man.

'And let this war end soon. Please God, let there be a finish to all this senseless killing.'

The war had taken the sweetest years of her youth, yet she would count them as nothing if only Tom could come home safely.

'And *all* our soldiers and sailors and flying men, please? Keep them safe?'

She knew she was asking for a miracle, but still she prayed, because miracles *did* happen.

That same month, Julia and Alice sewed the narrow scarlet bands to their sleeves – a band a VAD nurse was

621

entitled to wear for every year of service. They had signed a new contract, too, for another year's duty in France.

'We're entitled to leave, you know,' Alice snapped off the cotton, gazing proudly at her right sleeve. 'And to a travel warrant, too.'

'I know, but I shan't go home. There's a rest home for nurses at Etaples. Think I might go there instead and sleep for a week. See if I can find a hairdresser, too, and get my hair sorted out. It's grown too long to manage.'

She ached for England; for sight of Rowangarth and all those she loved; longed, too, to be away from the awfulness of the war. But she couldn't go on leave when any day she might hear that Andrew had got time off from duty.

'On that first day at Denniston House,' that first, carbolicky day, 'I never thought I'd stick it for a year. I'm proud of this, you know.' Alice squinted this way and that at the red band, making sure it was straight. 'I feel like an old hand, now.'

'It wasn't Denniston for me – oh, bother! We don't have to sew these things on everything, do we?'

'Only on our frocks. Here – give it to me – I'll sew it on for you.'

'Bless you.' Julia lay back on her bed, hands behind head. 'Not Denniston House. It was the York hospital that nearly finished me. We were about half-way through Ward 3F and I seriously thought about packing my bags . . .'

'Your poor hands – I remember.'

'Not just my hands, Alice. It was my dignity more than anything. Being ordered about as if we were the lowest of the low.'

'We were. Completely useless, as nurses . . .'

'We aren't now, though. We've got a stripe up. Does our red band mean we're lance-corporals?'

'No, it doesn't,' Alice giggled. 'It shows we've got some service in, though.'

'Hmm.' For a while Julia contemplated the ceiling. 'I got a letter from Aunt Sutton this morning and I realize the matter might still be taboo, but I think I should read you some of it.' She pulled open her locker drawer, taking out an envelope. 'Listen to this.

"In case you should hear a garbled version of the latest air-raid on London, this is to let you know I am all right; continuing to do my bit for the FANY whilst still managing to live at home. But for those arrogant sods to come in broad daylight to drop their bombs made me furious at the cheek of it. Suppose it was their way of cocking a snook at all the American troops who have arrived here.

"The raid made quite a mess. Dead horses in the streets – poor dumb creatures – and motors blown sky-high. Rows of houses gone. Hundreds injured and killed. Poor London.

"Figgis was very upset, poor old girl. Had to give her a drop of brandy, but all's well now and they won't try it again, be sure of that."

'Now here comes the bit I thought you should hear.' Julia paused, then said, 'It's Elliot. He's on his way here.

"They have caught up with Elliot at last; even Clemmy wasn't able to do anything about it this time. Scandal, of course. He was his own undoing. Playing around with the wife of an officer serving in the trenches. Stood to reason the husband would hear of it, sooner or later.

"Simply not done, but Elliot will never be the stuff a gentleman is made of, in spite of Clemmy's money. I warned her; told her people were talking. Yesterday she was on the telephone to me, blubbering like an idiot. Not worried about me and Figgis and if we were all right after the raid; not even worried if her London house was still standing. All she could say was that Elliot had arrived at Pendenys with all his kit – on ten days' embarkation leave!

"I tell you, I could have burst my stays laughing at her performance. Mind, I'm sorry any young man has to go to war and, however awful Elliot is, his mother loves him, let's face it. But I am firmly of the opinion that it will do that young man the power of good to get some of the mud of the trenches on his fancy boots!"

'Well?' Julia looked up. 'Thought at least you'd be glad to hear that his womanizing has caught up with him at last, even if it does mean he'll be coming here. I'm not a bit sorry he'll have to do his share of the fighting. Why should Elliot sit it out at the War Office?'

'I don't care one way or the other about the War Office.' Alice's needle jabbed fiercely. 'That was up to him and his conscience. I hope I don't meet up with him, that's all.'

'Alice! You *won't*! Out of all the soldiers in France we're going to run into *him*? When we are both aching and praying for just a glimpse of our own men? The Fates wouldn't be *that* cruel! And even if he were wounded – which heaven forbid,' she added hastily, 'he wouldn't come to us. We don't nurse officers here.'

She laughed, which caused Alice to demand, frowning, what was so very funny about any of it.

'None of it, really. But I just thought that if Cousin Elliot was in one of my beds, I'd take the greatest pleasure in waking him up in the middle of the night and plonking him on an ice-cold bedpan! And I'd so enjoy giving him an injection. *Bang!* in his backside! He'd hit the roof!'

'You know we aren't allowed to give injections,' Alice said crossly.

'I know – but what a thought!'

'I'd rather *not* think about it. And I don't want to talk about it, either. You don't know how much I hate that man – still. He tried to treat me like a street woman!' Even now, she was reluctant to speak his name. 'I wish Morgan had bitten his face, spoiled his good looks. I wish Tom had knocked his teeth out!'

'Alice, lovey! If I'd known – well, I thought you were over it. I'm sorry. I truly am.'

She gathered Alice into her arms, hugging her tightly, laying her cheek on her hair.

'We'll never see him, I know it. It's against all the laws of average. And if it's any comfort to you, Alice, I hate him too. He was a nasty little boy and he's grown into a nasty man. Cheer up, or I'll be sorry I told you.'

'It's all right. I've grown up a bit since the Brattocks Wood affair.' Nursing had taught her a lot – given her a greater respect for herself, too. 'Sorry, Julia. I shouldn't have taken on so. Forget the man. And in case you hadn't noticed, it's suppertime.'

They hurried to the rest-room in search of bedtime bread and jam and mugs of cocoa, each proudly wearing the red mark of a time-served nurse on her sleeve. Tom would be proud of her too.

Her fingers found the locket at her throat and the pearl ring that hung with it. The wedding ring, too, that once belonged to a mother she had never known; the ring Tom would one day place on her finger.

Tom, I need to see you, touch you. Take care, my love.

Ellen's farmer husband cut Rowangarth's hay in return for half the crop, which suited Helen nicely, since they had never replaced the carriage horses the army had commandeered. The mare and her foal had long since been sold, and only the pony remained. The hay crop was no longer of such importance.

Helen breathed in deeply. There wasn't a scent quite like it in all the world. Hay, lying in the fields, almost dry enough to stack, with the scent of high summer on it; the sure promise of winter fodder. Wars began and ended, but haymaking, planting and harvesting went on as it had always done; always would. The seasons did not acknowledge war; the thrush in the far linden tree singing in the early evening cool didn't, either. And the rooks, sensible old creatures, cawed lazily home to roost after a day's scavenging, not knowing about France or that Robert would never come home again.

Or did they know? Some said they did. She shrugged, turning to look at what had once been her lawns. Last year, potatoes; cabbages and turnips growing there this year. Food. It was more important, now, than pretty green grass. Almost everyone felt hunger. Rowangarth managed better than most, though what they had she shared. Tea from India; rabbits, hares and game-birds from the estate; turnips and cabbages from what had been her lawns.

She thought of France. British troops there were better fed, people said. If that were true, then she minded little that here they were sometimes hard put to it to find the next meal. But never again, she vowed, would she take for granted sugar in her tea or butter or good red meat. Or bread. Some days, they had to make do with only one slice. Why, she fretted, did the Government not order rationing – *real*, honest rationing, so that everyone had fair shares and food was not all bought by the rich. Because food was mostly for those who could pay for it. Rumour had it that there was no shortage of butter at Pendenys Place, but that was between Clemmy and her conscience. Poor Clemmy. Elliot gone to the Front now . . .

Helen straightened her shoulders. There were some good things to think about. American troops had brought hope to British soldiers in France, and the King had at last changed his name. Politic, really, especially after what had happened to the Czar, poor foolish man. And you couldn't in all honesty have an English King with so German a name; not Saxe-Coburg-Gotha. Windsor sounded far more British as a surname, although, Helen sighed, she would have better liked it had His Majesty adopted the surname Plantagenet. So romantic, those long-ago medieval kings.

She shivered and pulled her shawl round her. The dew was falling heavily and her feet felt the cold through her flimsy shoes. It was almost dark. Best go inside; sit out another lonely evening with only the creaks and small bumps of an old house settling to rest for company. She had never been so alone, felt so desolate.

A bat swooped above her head and she flinched, then hurried up the garden steps for the safety of her home. Dear, old dependable Rowangarth. Come what may, at least she would always have her house . . .

Tilda waited, arms folded, for the kettle to boil, gazing at the photograph over the fireplace. David, Prince of Wales, beloved of all women for his boyish good looks, adored to distraction by Matilda Tewk. David Windsor, she supposed he was now, though the name Saxe-whatever-it-was had sounded grander. But, like Cook said, you couldn't have a German name now, in England. Even German shopkeepers who had lived in England for ages and taken British nationality before ever the war started, had had their windows smashed and their doors daubed with paint. And anyone who had a dachshund for a pet had to keep them indoors now, for fear of them being kicked on the streets. Even German dogs bore the brunt of British hatred for all things Germanic.

Yes, she conceded, sighing; better in view of what had happened in Russia that the royal family should become a little less foreign-sounding.

'Will you hurry up with that cocoa, Tilda!' Cook snapped. 'There's some of us as wants to go to our beds!'

'Just coming up to the boil, Mrs Shaw.' You didn't back-answer Cook when she had one of her moods on her, and Cook had been in a mood all day. Jin's fault, of course. Jinny Dobb would never learn sense.

'If I have to cook another rabbit or pluck another pheasant, I'll go off my head,' Cook had grumbled. 'Everybody knows that rabbits is vermin.' And out-of-season pheasants were scraggy and didn't taste anything like a bird taken proper in the shooting season.

'Food is food, Mrs Shaw!' Jin had retorted, 'and vermin or not, a rabbit tastes very nice when the butcher hasn't had sight of red meat for nigh on a week. There's some in towns as would give a lot to get their hands on a few of your vermins!'

To which there had been no answer, really, except for Mrs Shaw to retire on her dignity and keep a tight-mouthed silence for the remainder of the day.

It was awkward, though, when you were piggy-in-the-middle, Tilda sighed, longing for days past when there had been food aplenty, cream on Sundays and six house staff to fetch and carry.

'Ready now, Mrs Shaw,' she murmured soothingly, having received a rakish smile of understanding from her beloved. 'I've made it nice and milky for you. Now sit you down and enjoy it. You've had a busy day.'

To which unsolicited sympathy, Cook's eyes filled with tears and she set her chair rocking furiously.

'Thanks, Tilda lass. Oh, if only you knew how weary I am of this war.'

'I do know. We're all of sick and tired of it.'

They were. Just to think of another winter, with not enough coal and houses freezing cold; grey skies and queuing hours for a bit of margarine, a pound or two of flour, and most folk dreading a knock on the door and one of those telegrams.

'Just you drink it up and get yourself off to bed. I'll see to the fire and lock the doors. We'll all feel better in the morning.'

In the morning there might even be something good to read in the newspapers!

'Would you ever have believed it?' demanded Reuben of Percy Catchpole, laying a rabbit on his kitchen table.

'Thank you kindly and believed what?'

The gardener, himself a widower like Reuben, hung the stiff, furry creature on a nail in his pantry, selected a large onion and two carrots to give in exchange, then offered his tobacco pouch.

Reuben accepted a fill for his pipe from it, then settled himself for a chat. 'Why, that Mata Hari woman, though that isn't her real name. Spying for the Jerries and her born in Holland. I thought the Dutch were supposed to be on our side. It only goes to show, Percy, that there's nowt so queer as folk.'

'They're putting her on trial, aren't they? Talk is if they find her guilty, our lot'll shoot her.'

'They can't shoot a woman.'

'Can't they? Them Germans shot Nurse Cavell and all she did was to help some of our soldiers escape.'

'All the same,' Reuben puffed thoughtfully on his pipe, 'it's a terrible thing, even for a German, to shoot a woman. Our lads wouldn't like doing it – if they find that Mata Hari woman guilty, that is.'

'Our lot is soft; too gentlemanly for their own good. They'll let her off!' Catchpole spat derisively into the fire. 'What else did the newspapers have to say today – that was worth reading, I mean?'

629

'Nowt,' said Reuben flatly. 'But it's the Government; won't let them print the half of what happens.'

'It's a poor carry-on,' sighed the elderly gardener gloomily. 'If things get any worse, there'll be trouble here, like in Russia. Mark my words if there isn't!'

'*Nay!*' said Reuben, shocked to the tips of his toes at the thought. Such a thing couldn't happen here, could it? Our soldiers were loyal to King and country. 'Wonder how young Alice is getting on.' Hastily he changed so dangerous a subject. 'Tom Dwerryhouse, too.' Aye, and Sir Giles and Mr Nathan an' all. With things not going so well for us at Ypres, it was a rum do and no mistake. There were times, Reuben sighed, when he was thankful to be old!

Private Tom Dwerryhouse felt a brief, rare peace, but then he always felt that way at stand-down when men from the rear trenches came to relieve them. Two, sometimes three days and nights on duty, rifles at the ready, one foot on the firing step, head down, listening, waiting. Or perhaps, with Geordie, nerves raw, creeping under cover of darkness into No Man's Land, following the dim tape to lead them through a minefield to a high, forward position to snipe: to justify his doubtful title of marksman, earn the few extra shillings that came with it.

Geordie was never so pleased as when ordered out. By now he thought himself indestructible, possessed of a cunning that would see him safely to the end of the war. Of no concern was it to the Tynesider that the war was going better for the enemy in spite of the arrival of the fresh, well-armed, well-dressed American troops. Our side always won, in the end, and the German was yet to be born who could see off Geordie Marshall.

'I'll kill those bliddy fleas,' he said viciously. 'C'mon, Tom lad. Let's get out of these stinking togs . . .'

It was one of the things about war he hated most, Tom acknowledged, unstrapping his ammunition belt, throwing down his cap. It was not the blind obedience to those above him, nor being deprived of a man's right to live his life as he pleased, wed the lass he loved, go to his bed alive and wake up alive. It wasn't even the killing and maiming around him. It was, in truth, the complete loss of his dignity; the foul stink of his body after three days in the forward trenches. Never taking off his clothes, his boots, even. And peeing where he stood. The trenches reeked in summer like middens. It was worse, almost, than winter's mud and slime.

They had been billeted for a time in stables. Now, as the fighting intensified, the army had moved out the farmer and his family, who left, possessions piled on two carts, driving their livestock in front of them, cursing the Boche volubly. It would have been a sad sight were it not for the empty farmhouse, taken possession of at once by grateful soldiers, each man's sleeping space guarded jealously. Their new billet was dry, clean and free of vermin, so that to enter it without delousing themselves, no matter how desperate for sleep, was considered a sin: bodies and uniforms must first be cleaned. There was a well in the farmyard; better still in this blazing July day, a shallow river across the empty pasture.

It was beside this clear, slow-moving river that Tom's platoon had stripped naked, examining underclothes for lice, turning uniforms outside-in, running a candleflame up and down the seams to kill the fat, incubating eggs. They did it with a ritual satisfaction, then plunged naked into the river, soap secured on a string, to wash heads and bodies, splashing like bairns let loose from a sweltering schoolroom.

Then clean, straw-filled palliasses and blessed oblivion, to sleep the clock round, sleep away one of their precious safe days to be awakened only by the ache of hunger in empty bellies.

Three days on stand-to; two days on stand-down; the pattern of a soldier's life with only sometimes the satisfaction of a properly cooked meal over a field-kitchen fire. And letters. News of Alice, of Mam and his sisters and brothers. Strange intrusions from a life almost forgotten and which would never come again, because this war would go on until there wasn't a man left on either side to carry on fighting it.

All at once Tom felt kinship with those in strange, far-away Russia, who had deposed their Czar. It made sense. Those men fought for their motherland, they were told, just as he was fighting for King and country. Only his King hadn't even heard of Tom Dwerryhouse, and his country seemed no longer to care. Only Mam and Alice cared. Alice, walking the daft dog, calling his name. Only there had never been a place called Brattocks Wood, and Rowangarth was all in his imagining.

He held his soap tightly, pulling in his breath, plunging beneath the water, only surfacing when his lungs seemed near to bursting. Then he shook his head and opened his eyes and Geordie was standing beside him, hair sleeked back.

'Come on, bonny lad. Sit yourself on the grass and dry out while I have a fag.' He offered the packet he had hidden on the riverbank.

'No, thanks, mate.' Tom lay down, eyes closed, hands behind his head. 'Shake me if I nod off . . .

His brief, rebellious anger was over. Soon he would return to the billet to blessed, beautiful sleep. And the near certainty of a letter from Alice.

The fourth winter of the war was almost upon them. At home, Britain looked on it with despairing dread. Those who had money spent it on food; those without it tried to blank out their minds to yet another twelve months of war, reminding themselves that they, at least, existed in comparative safety and that soon the Government would bring in a fair-shares-for-all rationing of food. Mr Lloyd-George was a man of the people; he surely must understand.

Leave from the trenches began again for married men. The Flying Corps, no longer a flash in the pan, had been changed in title to the Royal Air Force. Aeroplanes, like tanks, had proved themselves; become a force to be reckoned with.

That winter the armed forces opened their ranks to women volunteers.

'They'll give us the vote after this,' some said. Other women cared only about keeping their children fed and clothed and the day their man would come home. And never, ever, would they let him go to fight another war in another country in strange-sounding places most women couldn't even pronounce! This war must be the one to end all wars, they vowed, or there would be fighting here at home as they fought in Russia now.

Those Russian soldiers knew what they were about, said the man in the street grimly; were leaving the trenches to join the revolutionaries in Petrograd – and let the French and British get on with it! Rather those men should fight for the piece of land Lenin promised them and an end to serfdom. And, as the soldiers returned to their motherland, so the ruling classes left their townhouses, their country estates, sewing jewels into their clothing, taking gold and silver and only things of value they could carry with them; seeking refuge in any country that would take them in. A tiara bought a passage from Lisbon to New York. Their land was useless now.

Some aristocrats stayed behind to join the fight against Bolshevism; to seek out their Czar from wherever he had been imprisoned, get him and his family to safety. Some not of Russian birth rallied to the romanticism of their cause. British battalions were ordered to Russia to fight with them, which angered most people, since King George had done nothing to help his cousin in his peril.

Yet why should he? some reasoned. The foolish Czar and the arrogant Czarina had begged on bended knees for all their troubles, said most, and anyway, the house of Romanov was already doomed by the strange blood disease brought into the family by the Czarina. A woman passed it to her sons. Sons could bleed to death just from a scratch.

There was only one small and doubtful satisfaction in that sad October. Mata Hari, convicted of spying, her appeals against the death sentence refused, faced an Allied firing squad, bringing with it a strange justice.

At least now the unlawful killing of Nurse Cavell had been avenged.

Winter came to Celverte, not with snow, like in England, but a final falling of leaves and frosted morning grass. Alice pulled her night-cape around her and hurried after Julia, who had run ahead to collect the letters she was sure would be there.

'One for me from Andrew and one from Nathan – and one for you, from Tom,' she smiled.

They spread their letters on the table-top, hugging both hands round mugs of hot tea. Soon they would fill bed-warmers, snuggle beneath the sheets, sleep off the fatigue of a busy night. But these minutes between were a precious unwinding. Time to drink the tea they had been longing for all night; to read letters, eat a slice of bread and jam they didn't really want.

'Andrew is well,' Julia announced.

'Tom, too . . .'

'There's a leave rota at the hospital now. This time he says he'll be lucky. Sometime after Christmas, he thinks.' They would give the Christmas leave to men with families, Julia supposed.

'Tom says his platoon found an abandoned cart piled high with wood. They had fires in the farmhouse and washed and dried their clothes.' The letter had been written four days ago. Tom would be back in the forward trenches now.

'Listen to this, Alice! Nathan met Giles last week. He was at a dressing-station, and who should walk past him but my big brother! I'm glad he's all right. Nathan wrote especially to tell me. He's a dear, good man. And, oh my goodness. Nathan met – ' She stopped, her cheeks flushing.

'Met who?' Alice demanded, knowing she had no need to ask.

'Met Elliot. Nathan said he'd been to Calais with a convoy of wounded – chaplains sometimes do, you know – and there on the quayside was Elliot! And would you believe it – Master Elliot has been posted to Paris! To Combined HQ. God! How does that blighter manage it – keeping out of the trenches, I mean? He must have friends in high places!'

'He's got a rich mother who hasn't a shred of conscience,' Alice snapped.

'Yes – well, never mind. Nathan says he has a good idea where I am and hopes, soon, to be seeing me. Which means, I suppose, that he's expecting a posting to these parts.'

'I'll go and get the warmers.' Alice rose to her feet, tucking Tom's letter in her apron pocket. 'There's plenty of hot water in the geyser. I'll fill them . . .'

Damn Elliot Sutton and his luck, though she'd rather he were in Paris; rather he were still in England, truth known. Anywhere but Celverte.

She filled a jug with boiling water, unscrewed the stoppers then, with a steady hand, filled the earthenware bed-warmers.

She was pleased at the steadiness of her hand; glad that Elliot Sutton's name could no longer upset her.

'*Bed!*' she said crisply to Julia.

37

1918

The war that was supposed to have been over in months, began its fourth year. That first Sunday of January was declared a national day of prayer, when women, children and elderly men – for now there were no young men left at home – prayed for an end to the madness.

At home, women with too little food and warmth waited in dread for the telegram that would devastate their lives. The entire country took on a greyness: grey skies, a grey future. It seemed to many women that all hope was gone; many children were too young to remember peace and plenty; had never known childhood.

Air-raids on London increased. In Berlin, the High Command was jubilant. They were winning the war in spite of the intervention of mighty America!

At the Western Front, the tommies and poilus hung on with fatalistic desperation. They had endured it for three years; had become immune to feeling, almost. Now it was less trouble to accept it without resentment, for surely death waited just around the next corner.

Some soldiers began to have strange thoughts. The dead had come back to Mons, hadn't they? Angels had protected them in that first winter of the war, and now, when they so desperately needed help, their comrades, long since dead and buried, returned from the darkness to fight beside them.

Some soldiers said they had seen and talked to men they knew to be dead; others said those ghosts walked in clean boots that made no sound in the squelching mud, nor left a footprint behind them.

At Celverte, nurses worked until they were desperately weary, only to be summoned from sleep by the call of a bugle as an air-raid threatened or a convoy of choking, gasping soldiers was brought in, spitting away lungs poisoned with mustard gas. They died protesting, arms flailing as they fought to breathe.

French civilians, scenting danger, began to leave homes too near the fighting. The Boche was about to start his breakthrough, and poison gas could be carried on the wind. Better homeless than dead.

Then, from out of the greyness, a light shone. Only a penny-candle light, but how it glowed golden with hope. On the sixth of February, women were given the vote. Not the young ones; not those who would be foolish enough to waste it by encouraging women into Parliament, but those who had reached the age of thirty and would have the sense to be guided by the opinions of their menfolk.

Then – and of equal importance to women – official food rationing came at last, passed by an Act of Parliament. Fair shares for all now; no more queuing in the wet and cold. Official food cards, to be distributed at once, would guarantee rations on demand.

'Well now,' Mrs Shaw beamed. 'There's four of us lives in and one who lives out, so we can't count on Jin's card. But according to the paper,' and this morning Cook was prepared to believe that for once the newspapers had got it right, 'we shall have two pounds of sugar, half a pound of margarine, a pound of bacon and red meat enough for two good meals. And half a pound of *butter*!

'Mind, that's between the four of us, but her ladyship has got used to tea without sugar, she says, and she'll let me have her half-pound for baking.'

'And bread is to be rationed an' all, don't forget,' Tilda offered.

Four pounds of bread a week for a woman and child. Two fair-sized loaves, that was – *each* – which was more like it, thought Cook, who had already decided to convert their bread ration into flour and bake her own loaves.

'Sense at last,' she exulted. 'And now we've got the vote, it's up to us to get some women into Parliament.'

A woman would have understood what it was like to be hungry; to stand hours for a loaf and a few scraps of mutton, aye, and with crying bairns clinging to her skirts an' all! Women would have seen to it that food rationing had come sooner.

She sighed contentment and bade Tilda put on the kettle for a sup of tea. Now she might even be able to make cherry scones again – if she could lay hands on a few cherries. February was almost over, spring and warmer days just around the corner; and though nobody was going to get fat on their food cards, at least the poor and the old would have food they could afford.

Happen soon, she thought, crossing her fingers tightly, we might even win this dratted war!

Julia lit a cigarette. Once, she would never have thought to smoke, but she always carried a packet in her pocket to offer to wounded soldiers. 'You wouldn't have a fag on you, Nurse?' She had heard it so often. Now she used them – *needed* them – herself. Many nurses smoked. Cigarettes soothed and comforted and often took the place of the meal they were too busy to eat.

'Want one?' she asked of Alice.

'No thanks. And that's your third since we came off duty.'

'Yes, but I'm worried. Not so long ago, Andrew was hopeful of getting a few days' leave, yet there hasn't been a mention of it in his last two letters. It's ten months since Paris. Something's wrong, I know it.'

'He's busy. You don't have to tell *us* that, now do you?'

'I suppose not. And I'm a spoiled brat for wanting to see him. I should be glad he's alive and not at a clearing-station at the Front. But I've tried counting my blessings and in the end it all boils down to the same thing. I miss him. I want him!'

'I know, love. I've got a man of my own, remember? I'm beginning to forget what he looks like, it's so long since I saw him. Let's go down to the rest-room. Ruth said some new records have arrived for the gramophone. Why don't we find ourselves a cup of tea, then listen to some music?'

'Oh, don't be so patient with me! Just say what's on your mind and tell me I'm a self-centred little beast and give me a good thump!'

'All right! Nurse MacMalcolm is a self-centred little beast and she's too big for me to thump, or I'd do it! Now are you coming downstairs?'

'Yes – and I'm sorry, Alice. If I can't have Andrew, a cup of tea and a spot of jazz is just about the next best thing. You got a letter, didn't you – how is Tom?'

'Fine, I think. It was only a hasty note, though. Said he'd been sent back to the billet and told to get into his best uniform. Going on a special duty. Said he'd write later. I don't know whether to be pleased or worried about it.'

'Special duty,' Julia frowned, throwing her cape around her shoulders against the cold of the early March evening. 'Don't suppose it'll be anything dangerous or he'd not need his good clothes. Probably being sent to some inter-regimental shooting contest or something. Or maybe a special guard duty. They do sometimes pick men out at random.'

'Shooting contest? When there's fighting all along the front line from Ypres to Verdun! They wouldn't be so daft!'

'Want to bet? That lot at HQ don't know the first thing about what it's really like. Or perhaps there's some big-wig from London paying a visit. I wouldn't worry if

I were you. Anything that gets him out of the front line is good.'

'You're right. I tell you this, though. When I get Tom Dwerryhouse safe home from the army – '

'And married!'

' – and married, I'll not let him out of my sight for a minute!'

Special duties? Perhaps they were going to give him a stripe. She wondered if Geordie would be going with him.

'You're to report to Epernay,' the platoon sergeant had said when Tom arrived smartly dressed and breathless at Company HQ. 'Are your boots blacked, lad? Best bib and tucker? There's a motor waiting; you'll pick up another two lads on the way. Got to be there before dark, so get a move on!'

It was all he knew. The sergeant couldn't tell him any more. Dropping a hastily written letter into the post – Alice would worry if the duties turned out to be so special he wasn't able to write – he threw his knapsack into the back of the waiting motor, laid his rifle carefully beside it, then heaved himself inside. Little more than two hours ago he'd been in the firing line; now he was dressed up like a dog's dinner and heading for a jaunt to Epernay where, if his memory still served him, there would be a lot of brass-hats since Brigade Headquarters was stationed there.

He took off his cap and unbuttoned his tunic. What it was all about he had no idea – but then, his was not to reason why . . .

The three marksmen – Tom and two they had collected on the way – arrived at Epernay a little before sundown.

'You're part of the special party are you?' asked the guardroom corporal glumly. 'Best go to the quartermaster's and draw your palliasse and straw. Then go over to the cookhouse and get yourselves something to eat. That's all I know, 'cept that you're to see the RSM at nine. There's your chitties. Enjoy yourselves.'

He slammed three requisitions on the desk-top, then went back to his figuring.

'I'll tell you summat,' remarked one of Tom's new companions, a red-haired soldier with a Leeds accent, 'this is a rum do and no mistake. They tell you nowt around here. What are we supposed to be up to, then?'

Tom neither knew nor cared. He hadn't eaten since morning and the thought of a hot meal drove all else from his mind.

'Happen the RSM knows about it. They'll tell us,' he grinned, 'when they want us to know.'

The regimental sergeant-major did not know, or if he did he kept the knowledge to himself.

Their numbers had risen, now, to a round dozen; all of them privates, all wearing the badge of a marksman.

'You will all get to your beds,' they were told. 'Number Three hut behind sick-bay is empty. Kip down in there. And no sloping off into the town, mind. Epernay is strictly out of bounds.

'Get your heads down, the lot of you. You'll be given a shake at half-past four, after which you will shave and see to it your boots are well-polished. You'll get a hot drink, then you'll be here at five. *Five a.m.*, that is! You'll report to RSM Poole.'

'What are we supposed to be doing, sir?' asked one of the twelve.

'You'll know, all in good time,' came the trite reply. 'Now get yourselves off; and no playing cards into the small hours – do I make myself clear?'

They murmured yes sir, he did, and stood smartly to attention as he rose and left the room.

'It's a queer carry-on,' repeated the red-haired soldier.

'Happen it is,' Tom grinned, 'but I'm not complaining.'

The meat stew was good; the tea that followed it hot and sweet. He had spent two wakeful nights forward of the line with Geordie, now all he wanted to do was sleep. 'Let's find that hut,' he said.

At exactly five in the morning, when the sky to the east lit slowly with pale streaks of gold, they presented themselves at the guardroom asking for RSM Poole. From a billycan they had drunk hot, sweet tea; breakfast, they were told, would be later. A corporal eyed them cagily, counted them, then ordered them into two ranks. A door opened. The RSM walked out. All twelve sloped arms in salute.

'Carry on, Corporal. Issue each man with one round.'

The corporal ordered, 'Stand at ease', then dipped into his pocket, handing out twelve small, slim bullets. His eyes were downcast as if, Tom thought, he had no wish to look at them. Then he gave the order to shoulder arms, and '*Squaaad*, quick march!'

They were brought to a halt at a field a few hundred yards away. They were not the first to arrive. Two horses were tethered by the field gate, an ambulance and a small truck were parked farther down the lane.

'What the 'eck's going on?' the Leeds man demanded.

'No talking in the ranks!' the corporal hissed.

Tom slid his eyes left and right. A chaplain spoke to one of the officers standing a few yards away, then hurried off. The corporal saluted the regimental sergeant-major.

'All present and correct, *sah*!' He stamped his feet, then stood stiffly to attention.

'At ease.' Even the RSM seemed not to want to look at them. 'You'll want to know why you are here. Special duties, you were told, and when you go back to your

643

regiments you'll not speak of this to anyone on pain of severe reprimand!

'You are all marksmen, for which you draw extra pay, I would remind you, and you have been selected for your skill.'

He drew a deep breath, lifted his chin, clasped his hands behind his back and walked the length of their ranks, lips pursed. Then he swung to face them.

'You are here as a firing party. You are required to carry out the execution of a man condemned by his own actions to death by shooting.' He spoke quickly, quietly. 'No man present has the right to refuse to take part,' he added, his eyes narrowing to warning slits.

There was a terrible, stunned silence. No one moved. One of the twelve drew a shuddering breath, then let it out slowly.

'Did you hear me? Do you understand?' the RSM rapped.

His mouth had gone dry. He hadn't wanted this. No man in his right mind wanted it. And why were they all looking at him like that?

He cleared his throat, opened his mouth, shut it again, trap-like. Then he motioned to the corporal to take over, walking quickly to where the officers stood, glad to be away from stares of hatred.

Like automatons the twelve loaded their rifles.

'I don't like this any more than you do,' hissed the corporal.

'Then why the hell are you doing it?' The Leeds man was the first to find words.

'For the same reason as you lot. I can't refuse!'

'Who says we can't?' asked one in the rounded accents of a west country man.

Tom stood still and unspeaking. To his left more had joined the officers and the chaplain; to his right was a wood, the trees in it leafless, still. Ahead, the sky

644

was brightening into morning. Soon, the light would be good enough for them to – to – Almighty God! To shoot a man!

His mouth began to fill with spittle. Sniping, shooting at an enemy at long range was what he was trained for and a part of war. In return, an enemy sniper was entitled to shoot him, were he daft enough to let him. But to shoot a man in cold blood, enemy or not; to take aim and fire at a defenceless man was asking too much of any soldier!

He glanced at the man on his left. At his shoulder he wore the badge of the Durham Light Infantry. He had thick black hair and a thick black moustache. His face was chalk-white; he stared ahead, unblinking.

'You will carry out your orders briskly and without comment.'

It was the corporal again; the bloody corporal!

'When commanded, the first rank of six will kneel, rifle on the ground to his right. The prisoner will be brought in, blindfolded. A white envelope will be pinned to the left of his tunic. You will aim for the envelope. Those in the rank behind will fire first.'

To the left. His heart. Tom swallowed noisily, realizing he stood in the rear rank of six; he would be one of the first to fire.

They couldn't do this! This wasn't war. This was cold-blooded, deliberate killing.

'When the prisoner is brought in, you will observe that to one side of him will be a medical officer. Don't shoot the MO.'

Funny? That's supposed to be funny? White-hot anger thrashed inside Tom.

'After the first command to fire, the medical officer will quickly ascertain if the prisoner has been despatched. If he is dead, the MO will walk away. If, in his opinion, the prisoner is still alive, he will raise his hand and the front

645

rank will rise smartly, take aim, and await the order to fire – which will be quickly given.'

'And what if we *all* miss? What if he's still alive, even then?' It was asked with contempt by the black-haired man.

'Don't get any ideas! If that happens, then an officer who will be standing close by, will take his pistol and . . ' He left the sentence in mid-air.

Tom gritted his teeth. The corporal had done this before, he knew it. He recited the paraphernalia of death exactly as, when a boy, Tom had recited his multiplication tables each morning at school. *I hope you catch the pox, you nasty little sod,. and die slow of it . . .*

'And should that become necessary, you will all be deemed to have disobeyed an order given by a senior officer and you know what'll happen, then . . .'

Tom knew. They all knew. *No man shall disobey an order; shall fall asleep at his post; shall cast away his arms.* The penalty for all three was death; death by firing squad like the poor wretch they would bring in just as soon as the light was good enough.

He looked at his right, wondering if the leaf buds were swelling in Brattocks Wood. Alice used to go there. Once, in another life, she walked the daft dog there, then ran to meet him. *Alice, lass, I'm sorry.* Sorry? He'd never tell her about this day; never admit to anyone they had turned him into an animal.

. . . you will not speak of this to anyone on pain of severe reprimand. Speak of it? He'd be ashamed of this until the day he died.

The regimental sergeant-major returned. With him was one of the two officers. A bit of a lad, dressed up to the nines. His face was pale, his hands tightly clenched in brown leather gloves.

The senior of the officers walked across the field to where a lone tree stood. At his side hung a pistol.

The field gate opened. It was the medical officer. He walked to the opposite side of the tree, stopping a few feet away from it. He did not look up; not even to glance at the captain with the pistol.

Tom's hands were numb with cold and he blew on his right one. He had started to shake. It started at his knees and went right up to his diaphragm. The shaking stopped there and turned to a spasmodic retching. He clenched his teeth, then held his breath to stop the jerking inside him.

A small motor bumped into the field, then drew up beside the tree. Two sergeants jumped out, helping down a man who was already blindfolded. He stumbled and fell and they helped him to his feet. The van drove away, stopping beside two stretcher-bearers. Tom pulled his eyes to the front again. He had to look at the prisoner, beg his forgiveness and – *No*!

They were tying the man to the tree. He was not wearing field grey uniform; was not a German or an Austrian. The man they were going to shoot was a British soldier. Nor was he a man! He was a boy! Even the bloodstained bandage around his head and the black cloth that bound his eyes could not disguise his youth.

'*God in heaven!*' whispered the black-haired soldier. 'What did he do?'

'Cowardice,' the corporal mumbled. 'They give them a shot of morphine, though,' he added, as if in mitigation. 'Or a cup of rum . . .'

The boy lifted his head, turning it from side to side as if to find one last small slit of daylight.

'Squaaaaad . . .'

It was the young officer; the RSM was standing behind him.

Tom jerked his gaze to the boy. His lips were moving. He was trying to pray, to follow the intoning of the chaplain.

'*Aim* . . .'

Aim. Not at that white envelope. There was a quicker way. Deliberately, carefully, Tom squinted down his gun sight. *Sorry, lad* . . .

Six shots rang out, almost as one. The medical officer ran quickly to the sagging body, searching at his neck for a pulse. Then he rose to his feet and walked to where the stretcher-bearers waited.

The kneeling rank rose slowly, dizzily, leaving their rifles where they lay. The stretcher-bearers ran quickly, supporting the lifeless body as the captain with the pistol slashed the ropes. Then gently they lifted the boy on to the stretcher; lifted him with compassion as if he were a small, helpless child.

They walked quickly to the ambulance, slid the stretcher inside it, then pulled across the back flaps. The twelve men stood like statues, watching the ambulance manoeuvre through the field gate.

Tom ran his tongue round his lips. It was finished. Minutes, it had taken. He was glad the stretcher-bearers had been gentle. Conchies, they were, who had shown pity. Like Sir Giles. One of them could have been Giles Sutton.

The man from Leeds broke ranks, running to the hedge to fall vomiting to his knees; the black-haired man hissed, '*Bastards. Bloody bastards* . . .'

'He was only a lad,' one said. 'A bit of a lad. They'd no right . . .We shouldn't have . . .'

Anger took Tom; shook him. Blind with rage he strode to the young officer who had taken off his cap and was mopping his forehead with a white handkerchief.

'Sir!' he rapped. He lifted his rifle into the air, then flung it with all the contempt of his pent-up hatred at his feet. 'With respect, sir, I will *not* do that again!'

He lifted his head high, gazing defiantly into the eyes of his superior.

. . . shall not cast away his arms . . . But it had been all he could think of to do.

'Pick up your rifle, Private,' the young officer said quietly.

'Go on, lad. Pick it up,' said the regimental sergeant-major. 'Don't be a bigger fool than you need . . .'

Alice. Alice who loved him, waiting in Brattocks . . .

He bent and picked it up. He'd made his protest, now he was drained of feeling. He turned and ran towards the wood. He wanted to be sick, too; wanted never to have to look into the eyes of the other eleven again.

'That man there! Return to the ranks!'

Tom's foot hit a sod of grass and he stumbled and fell. He lay there, his burning face in the cold, wet grass. He had plumbed the depths; he despised himself, despised the army and the King and country in whose names he had been ordered to war.

Get up! The voice echoed above his head. *Get up, you fool. Go back . . .*

It's all over now, said the soft voice of reason inside him. *Think of Alice. Think of yourself. You've survived, this far. What's done is done . . .*

He pulled himself to his knees, reaching for his cap. His rifle lay where it had fallen, several feet away, and he walked unsteadily to the bole of a tree to pick it up.

The familiar, screeching whine made him stop. Instinctively he threw himself flat, hands over his head, breath indrawn.

The shell exploded in the field. A barrage! They were being shelled! The Germans – they couldn't be *that* near? Another explosion and another; more and more. A shattering continuous roar.

The earth shook beneath him. He cringed closer to the tree, holding his nose, blowing into it to ease the pain inside his ears as the roaring increased.

There'd be no one left alive; nothing left standing. He hadn't a hope in hell! He turned his face as a shell slammed into the transport that had brought them here, then closed his eyes, wincing as it exploded into flames.

He pressed himself closer to the ground and began to pray. A scream, louder than the first, filled the air around him and he felt the thud as the shell struck.

There was a roaring in his ears. The earth beneath him moved, flew high in a million pieces.

The breath left his body; a pain pierced his head. He cried out as a red mist blotted out his sight. Then the blessed blackness took him . . .

'Will you listen to this!' Julia exulted, waving Andrew's letter. 'Good news at last, he says.' Quickly she scanned the single sheet, then passed it over. 'You read it, Alice. Tell me I'm not dreaming!'

'The lovey-dovey bits too?'

'There aren't any,' Julia said impatiently. 'Go on, read it. He's got five days – well four, plus his sleeping day. He'll be duty night-surgeon that week and,' she did a rapid calculation, 'and we'll be on nights, too. The twenty-second, that is . . .'

'So you'll be able to travel on your sleeping day as well. Julia, love, I'm so pleased for you. Go and see Ruth right away, then she can put in a good word for you with Sister, though they'll have to give you leave. They can't refuse a married woman.'

'Even though we're so busy we none of us know which way to turn?'

'We'll all double-up for you – and what makes you think you're so important, *Norrrrse*, that you can't be done without for a few nights?' Alice giggled, doing an excellent imitation of Matron.

'Oh, I do love you,' Julia sighed. 'I love the whole world – except the Kaiser's lot. You don't think it'll go wrong again?' she whispered, suddenly serious.

'It will *not*. Andrew has got leave – dates, everything – and they won't refuse it to his wife. We'll have to get out your civilian things and press your dresses. You'd better try the blue on and see if you think the hem needs taking up. They're wearing them a lot shorter now.'

'I will. It'll be like old times again. Me meeting Andrew in the park in that dress. Remember?'

'Mm. And you getting married in it . . .'

'And being disappointed in it, too . . .'

'He'll come, this time. That blue frock has been waiting here to be worn for ages. And I'll press your wedding nightgown too. You must take that with you.'

'I must.' Julia's cheeks pinked, thinking how little she would wear it. 'And it'll be your turn next. Who's to know that Tom's special duties won't land him here, right on your doorstep. Goodness! I've just thought – you could get married! Would it be legal, here in France?'

'I don't know.' It was Alice's turn to blush bright red. 'If an English vicar read the service and there were witnesses, I don't see why not . . .'

'On a ship at sea, the captain can marry you – well, that's what I heard.'

'Don't! Please don't! We're tempting Fate. I'd settle for just seeing him, knowing he was all right. All I want is for this war to be over and Tom safe. We didn't know how lucky we were, did we?'

'It seems so long ago, that night in Hyde Park.' Julia's eyes misted over.

'It *is* long ago. Just before my birthday, you both met; nearly *five* years gone!'

'And now I'm going to see him again in – ' She drew a ring around the date on her wall calendar. 'Friday the twenty-second of March. I'll be seeing him in sixteen days!'

651

'Where?' Alice asked, ever practical.

'He didn't say. Once we thought Paris was too far, but now, with the extra day, we could make it there. And Paris in early spring would be wonderful.'

Come to think of it, Paris in freezing mid-winter would have been equally marvellous.

'*Anywhere* will be wonderful. Now mind you tell Ruth about it. And don't be fobbed off. A wife is entitled to leave with her husband, remember.'

'Mmm.' Julia's sigh was long and blissful.

'What news from Rowangarth?' Alice ventured. 'Her ladyship's letter – you haven't read it.'

'Nor have I!' Laughing, Julia slit open the envelope then, 'Oh, my goodness! News, you asked. Aunt Clemmy is a grandmama!'

'She's *what*? Mr Albert?' It *had* to be Albert.

'The very same! Out of the blue, it seems. They kept it a secret because – well, everybody thought Amelia was past child-bearing – anything could have gone wrong.'

'Seems it didn't . . .'

'I think Amelia always secretly hoped – but she has a fine, healthy son, it would seem. Mother says she's green with envy: she does so want a boy for Rowangarth. Aunt Clemmy, it seems, isn't at all sure if she wants to be a grandmother yet.'

'Well, there's nothing she can do about it. She *is*.'

'Yes, officially this time,' Julia giggled wickedly. 'Bet she'll be nagging her Elliot to get married now. Well, there's one thing certain: when some brave woman takes him on, there'll be no shortage of pregnancies, Elliot being what he is.'

'Don't spoil good news by talking about *that* one,' Alice admonished. 'I'm pleased for Albert Sutton and I'll bet his father is pleased, an' all.'

'He is. It was Uncle Edward told Mother about it. Went over to Rowangarth in high good humour, especially to give her the news. But I think Mother wishes it could have been her. When the war is over, Giles really will have to get himself married. I don't know why some girl hasn't snapped him up. He's very good-looking. If he doesn't get on with it, people are going to think he's a pansy.'

'Oh, for shame. He's never that! Nor Nathan Sutton, either. I suppose,' Alice defended, 'they're both slow starters and the pair of them will surprise us all one day. My word, but they say good news always happens in threes and you've had two lots already. Wonder what the third will be?'

'It'll be for you. I've had good news enough for one day. You are due a letter from Tom – there'll be one soon.'

'Yes, and maybe he'll be able to tell me what his special duties were. Mind, if I don't hear for a while I won't worry overmuch. When things are special, sort of, maybe he won't be allowed to write.'

'I agree absolutely. There'll be nothing at all to have worried about, just you see. Our luck is in at the moment.'

'And not before time!' Why, even now, Tom might be so near to Celverte that –

Alice shut off such thoughts firmly. All she wanted was for him to be safe. She could wait.

Take care of yourself, my lovely lad . . .

Elliot Sutton regarded his newly shaved face, his glossy, brilliantine-sleeked hair with satisfaction.

'You've got to admit,' he whispered to his smirking reflection, 'that you were born with the luck of the devil.'

Posted to France. It had struck fear into his guts, and all because of Beatrice and the meddling old biddies – Aunt Sutton had been one of them – who had stirred things up till her husband was bound to hear of it.

He'd been called a cad and a womanizer; his immediate superior at the War Office had read him a solemn warning about not honouring gambling debts, let alone his mess bill. His stock had been pretty low when he had arrived at the Place on embarkation leave, his mother alternating between screaming, floor-pacing anger and drooping depression. She had called him all the nasty things he'd ever heard, and a few he hadn't, then relented, spending a lot of time on the telephone, eyes narrowed, mouth tight as a sprung trap. And she had done it!

Got him a posting to Combined Allied Headquarters in Paris, and though he had been relegated to the meanest, smallest office in the darkest, dreariest room in the whole building, his spirits were on the up again.

Good old Mama! She had a way of getting anything she set her heart on. She could bully and bluster and put the fear of God into anyone who stood in her way. Mama, with one of her moods on her, could put the fear of God into God Himself!

She wasn't a bad old stick, all things considered. A little on the earthy side, sometimes, but who cared about that when her pockets were bottomless?

So now, he thought, when he could wangle a spot of absent-without-leave, he might just look up Nathan, because even from the smallest, darkest office in CAHQ, Paris, he could find at once exactly where, at the Front, any regiment was quartered. Nathan, newly posted to another division, was somewhere in the region of the Somme, it seemed. Giles, too, wasn't all that much further away. It might be rather fun to look him up too; to have Giles salute him and call him Sir! Private Sir Giles Sutton having to stand to attention and tip his cap to his cousin Elliot would help make up for the demeaning position Giles had placed him in when he'd had to make the most grovelling of apologies over the sewing-maid affair.

It would be possible to get near to the front line. Some messages were still delivered by hand, in spite of wireless telegraphy. If it meant seeing Giles, he didn't mind being a messenger boy. And going near enough to the trenches would, he considered, give him place-names to drop when later it was all over and men talked in their clubs about the war.

'Ah, yes – the Somme. I was there in '18. Bad job, that,' he would say, refusing modestly to be drawn further.

He sighed long and deeply and with great satisfaction. Nathan and Giles could wait. At this moment Paris called, and Paris could knock spots off London and Leeds when it came to finding a good time.

He reached for his greatcoat, arranged his cap at a rakish angle, and gave a satisfied smile to the handsome young officer in the mirror.

Be damned if Elliot Sutton didn't always land on his feet!

38

Days that were so deliciously slow-moving for Julia, became increasingly worrying for Alice. Each morning, as Julia crossed off another day on the calendar, Alice came to dread the arrival of the mail and the letter that did not come.

Two weeks without hearing from Tom; almost three since the date of his hastily pencilled note. Just to think of special duties, whatever they might be, made her shake inside, all the while insisting that no news *must* be good news.

In her less bleak moments, she would tell herself it would all come right; that this was the very day on which a platoon of West Yorkshires would come marching down Celverte's main street and Tom with them.

Daydreaming, for all that. Better she should take solace from Julia's joy and her often repeated, 'Your turn next, Alice!' with always the final comforting thought that, since the Kaiser's armies had started a massive attack on all fronts, the army post office seemed the first affected by it, because, in all honesty, no nurse in quarters seemed to be getting her usual quota of letters.

On the Wednesday before Julia was to leave for Paris – for Paris it was to be – all hospital units in the area of the Somme front were put on emergency alert. This meant, amongst other irritating restrictions, that no nurse could leave the vicinity of the hospital without permission, even to walk down the lane into Celverte.

'It's serious,' Ruth Love frowned. 'Gas. They can send it inside shells now.' No longer was an adverse wind their friend. 'And I've heard – though for pity's sake don't

656

tell Julia – that the Germans have made a breakthrough somewhere in the Verdun area.'

'Andrew isn't in the front line now.' Alice spoke with genuine relief, whilst wishing with all her anxious heart she could be as certain of Tom's whereabouts.

'Only two days to go.' Julia began to pack her case. They were working night duties and, though Julia was exhausted at the end of each one, sleep was impossible. She lay, alternately thinking of lovers' meetings and the telegram which would begin, 'Sorry, darling, but – '

I'll never forgive You, God, if You do it to me again. She sent her thoughts high and wide, then relented at once. Poor God, who was blamed for everything these days and thanked for very little. *I'm sorry. It's just that I love him so much. I'm grateful You've kept him safe for all this time. It's just that I couldn't bear it if anything went wrong.*

The next day she folded the blue-ribboned nightdress and laid it in her case. It was an act of defiance, a tilting at Fate. That morning, when they came off duty, she placed the final cross on the calendar.

'There, now. Tomorrow, I'll be on my way to Paris. Oh, Alice, nothing will go wrong . . .?'

'*Nothing* is going to go wrong. You will come off duty and get yourself off to the station. And had you thought, it's almost certain that Andrew is on his way to Paris already. He's got one day extra, remember?'

'Mm. He said he'd spend it finding somewhere for us to stay and getting his uniform sponged and pressed – and a decent haircut. I think he'll have had my letter telling him when I'll be arriving. I hope so . . .'

'Stop your worrying! So he hasn't got the letter? All he's got to do is to ask the times of the trains arriving from Amiens and meet each one. He isn't stupid! Tomorrow you'll see him. You *will*, so for goodness' sake let's find something to eat then get ourselves into bed. I'm so tired, I could weep.'

Alice did not look at the criss-crossed letterboard as they passed it on the way to breakfast. There would be no letter from Tom.

Just one letter, God – a card, even?

'Sorry, nothing for you. Nothing for me either. The mail has gone all to pot,' Julia comforted.

Let Andrew be there tomorrow, God. Let him be on the Paris train this very minute.

'I know. I think things are getting bad, Julia. We are still on emergency alert.' She would be glad to see Julia on her way, if only because of a crawling inside her that refused to go away; a feeling of something being very wrong. It was so strong, it made her afraid.

She clucked irritably. She was getting as bad as daft Jin Dobb. It would be all right! Tomorrow, Julia would catch the early train and there would be a letter from Tom. There *would*!

'Breakfast,' she said firmly. 'Then bed.' Only, like Julia, she wouldn't sleep.

That night, the noise of shellfire was so loud, so near, they were afraid.

'Is it our guns or theirs?' Alice whispered as she did the rounds of the beds with Julia, plumping up pillows, enveloping blanket corners.

'Ours, of course! Got to be!' Julia stopped, frowning, as Ruth Love answered Sister's unspoken summons. 'Did you see that? Ruth almost ran!' No one ran, except in an emergency.

'It's gas,' said Ruth, when they were out of earshot of the beds. 'The shelling we can hear is *theirs*. They're getting nearer. Sister just said there's a big push on. She wants us to fill palliasses: we might have to take in a lot of wounded, bed them down on the floor . . .'

'We'll manage,' Julia whispered. 'I only hope they don't send us gas cases.' There was so little they could do for the victims of mustard gas – save watch them slowly die.

'Best get on with it. I've got the stable key. The straw is in there; we can fill them, then leave them ready in case they're needed.'

The stable was dry, the straw clean. Long before daylight they had filled a dozen palliasses.

'We did well,' said Ruth, relieved that so far there had been no call to use them. When their morning relief arrived a little before eight, the ward was calm, though the sound of gunfire could still be heard.

'This is it, then! You've got half an hour to bathe and change and get to the station. Just think, Julia. In a few more hours you'll be with him!'

'*Hours* . . .' Julia's eyes took on a far-away look. The time had come, and still no telegram had arrived; no letter. Andrew would be in Paris, waiting for her. She wanted to cry; she wanted to laugh. She hugged Alice tightly.

'I know I keep saying it, but your turn will come. And I'll give your love to Andrew. I'll be back on Tuesday – late. You'll have had a letter from Tom by then and there'll be so much to talk about . . .'

'I'm happy for you – you know that?' Alice laid her cheek to Julia's.

'Mm. 'Bye . . .'

'MacMalcolm! You're still here!' Ruth Love pulled back the cubicle curtains impatiently. 'I thought you'd have gone!'

'What is it?' Something wrong, Alice knew it. Ruth's cheeks were bright red, her eyes wide.

'It's stand-to! Didn't you hear the bugle? Day staff to remain on duty in the ward – night staff to go to the chateau!'

'But I'm asleep on my feet!' Alice protested.

'So are we all. But I'm to tell you both to go there at once.'

'*Both?*' Julia's face drained slowly of colour. 'Ruth, I'm going to Paris.'

'Matron said I was to stop you. Heavy casualties. They need all the help they can get.'

'Please?' Julia's voice was little more than a whisper. 'Andrew is waiting for me. Didn't you tell Sister?'

'I did, but you know how it is with her . . .'

'Don't ask me, Ruth! I beg you, don't ask me!'

'I'm asking you nothing. I'm telling you what Sister said, that's all.'

'So you might have missed her . . .?' Alice breathed.

'Exactly!' Ruth picked up the suitcase, thrusting it at Julia. 'So *go*! All right – I was too late – you'd gone. But go to him! *Go*, you little fool . . .'

'Down the back stairs!' Alice hissed. 'Out the back way, past the stables. Run, Julia! *Run!*'

'But – '

'Will you *go*,' Ruth urged. 'Just get out of here! I'll tell her I missed you!'

'I'm sorry.' Still Julia hesitated, eyes troubled. 'The wounded, I mean. I – '

'*Out!*' Ruth yelled.

They stood, breath indrawn, as Julia's footfalls echoed along the narrow staircase passage.

'She's gone. I was too late. When I got there she'd already left, Hawthorn!'

'Yes.' Alice let go her indrawn breath. 'Gone by five minutes. Wait for me, Ruth?' She threw on her nightcape. She ached for bed; to take off her shoes, her stiff collar. 'Things are bad at the Front?'

'Heavy casualties. Come with me to tell Sister I missed Julia, then I'll walk up to the chateau with you.'

'Thanks for what you did. It was good of you.'

'No it wasn't! If Sister ever finds out we'll all be in trouble, so watch what you say!' Ruth snapped. 'And she had to go, Alice. I'd never have forgiven myself if she hadn't.'

'I don't know what you mean . . .'

'No? When it might be the last chance they'll ever have of being together?'

'Don't, Ruth! You're wrong!' Alice's mouth had gone dry; her words came out roughly. 'Say you didn't mean it?'

'I mean that the war isn't going well for us – surely you'd realized that?'

'Yes, I suppose I had.' She'd thought it for a long time, only she hadn't dared to say it. 'But Andrew is going to be all right!'

Tears pricked Alice's eyes; tears of despair and fatigue. *Tom. Where are you?*

Julia leaned back, eyes closed. She was on her way now. The train was an express; no stopping between Amiens and Paris. It would be all right! She pushed all thoughts of guilt from her mind. She was leaving when they needed her, but Andrew came first. She had been so obsessed with want of him she would have gone, even without Ruth's help.

Dear Ruth. Dear, lovely Alice. But they wouldn't regret helping her. Afterwards, when she was back at Celverte, she would work extra hard, do anything asked of her. She would do extra duties, be more kind to Alice on mornings when there were no letters for her. Only let Andrew be waiting at the station and she would never again ask anything of God.

Andrew stood at the barrier, checking his watch with the station clock. The previous train from Amiens had arrived on time, but Julia had not been on it. The one due was already late, but what was a few minutes when it was almost a year since their last kiss?

A ticket collector arrived to take up his position; the train was coming. *Please, my darling, be on this one* . . .

A signal down the line dropped with a thump; he heard the train before he saw it. Then it came into the station, slowly, importantly; hissing and clanking, its brakes squealing, coming to a stop with a final hiss of steam.

There was a long, drawn-out second, then windows dropped, hands reached out for handles. All along the train, doors swung open.

His eyes searched the bobbing heads for her ridiculous cap. She was almost at the barrier before he saw her.

'*Darling!*' He reached for her hand, taking her case, pushing through the waiting crowd.

Then he gathered her in his arms, searching for her mouth, knowing again the exquisite delight of the scent of her soap. the sweet, clean smell of her hair. She felt fragile in his arms.

'You've lost weight, and I love you,' he said eventually.

She looked at him through eyes bright with tears, trying to speak, shaking her head impatiently because the words wouldn't come. She reached up, cupping his face in her hands, mouthing, 'I love you, too.'

'Darling, darling Julia.' He held her to him, resting his cheek on her cap. 'You are here. I can't believe it. I wanted you so much I was afraid something would go wrong.'

'It nearly did.' She took in a calming gulp of air. 'We were on stand-to. Alice and I had just come off night duty. Sister sent Ruth to tell us we were to go to the chateau – it's a dressing-station. I wanted to scream and shout and say I wouldn't, but I just stood there, not believing it.

'Then Ruth told me to go; said she'd tell Sister I'd already left. I ought to feel guilty. I do, I suppose, but I promised in my mind I'd make up for it – and I will!'

'I don't feel guilty being here. I have a wife I love to distraction, and I've been kept from her for more than three years – allowing for the odd hour. I did more than two years in a front-line dressing-station: I think we deserve these few days.'

'They say we get what we deserve,' she laughed shakily, feeling a little less guilty about her flight from quarters. 'And, Andrew – have you found us somewhere to stay?'

'I have indeed!'

'What is it like? It isn't madly expensive is it?'

'Like? It's a room, I suppose. Haven't taken a lot of notice. But it has a splendid bed. Big and soft – I slept in it last night. Bliss.'

'Then take me there this instant. Is it far?'

'Only a few streets away.' He picked up her case, then drew her arm through his, smiling down at her. 'I love you, Julia MacMalcolm – did I tell you?'

The *patronne* at the *pension* was middle-aged and plump, though her smile, when she allowed one, transformed her face completely.

'Ah, monsieur, you are back!' She felt a stab of guilt. 'I am going,' the young soldier had said, 'to meet my wife', and she had thought, may God forgive her, that he was going to find a woman. Not that she could blame him, with the war going so badly. A fighting man, when he had leave, deserved all the comforts he could find.

But the *fille* beside him *was* his wife – there was no disputing it; a woman in love, and that love showing in her smile, her eyes, the way her hand clung to his. And may Our Lady bless them both and grant them a splendid time together!

'The bed was to your liking last night?' she asked solicitously.

'It was absolutely *magnifique*,' Andrew beamed.

'*Le déjeuner* – it is still being served if Monsieur wishes a table?' She returned his smile, handing over the key.

'Thank you but no!' He picked up the case, walked purposefully past the dining-room door and up the stairs. It would not surprise her, thought the *patronne* – and she wasn't often wrong when it came to matters of *amour* – if they stayed upstairs for a very long time!

They proved her suppositions well-founded when they came downstairs, hand in hand, just as the dining-room doors were being opened for the evening meal: he, handsome in his uniform; she looking exquisite in blue. And, *Dieu*! How the colour suited her. It made her positively glow!

'*Bon appétit*,' she beamed as they passed the desk. 'The bed? Did Madame also find it to her liking?'

'Oh, very much to my liking,' Julia laughed, eyes shining with mischief. 'Very, *very* much . . .'

They spent three days which, were the Fates to decide they should be their last together, would compensate for a lifetime of aloneness, Julia thought. The sun shone especially brightly, the flowering trees were at their most beautiful, and the river, when they walked beside it, winked sunshine back at their happiness.

They laughed, drank coffee at pavement tables, walked hand in hand down narrow, unexpected streets, visited the church of the Sacred Heart, leaving a candle for their happiness at the feet of the Virgin.

They made love passionately and often. No one other than themselves existed. Paris was theirs and theirs alone; their happiness wiped out the years apart.

'Will you always love me like this?' Julia asked softly, her hand in his.

'For ever, my darling – if you'll promise never to stop loving *me*.'

'Always, I promise. I can't bear to think we have only one day and one night left.'

'Don't be sad. We shall be so happy, my Julia! It's at times like this when I love you so much I can hardly bear it, that I send my heartfelt thanks to the fat policeman who was the cause of our meeting.'

'And to Alice, who pushed him!' She reached up, clasping her arms around his neck, searching, eyes closed, for his lips, nor caring at all that they stood in view of every passer-by.

'Let's go back to our room,' she whispered, throatily. '*Please?*'

It had been unbelievably easy. It had not even, Elliot Sutton exulted, been necessary to await the call to deliver a message. When no one had entered his small room at Combined Allied Headquarters for two days, when the telephone on the wall had not demanded his attention either, he'd thought, and rightly, that no one knew he was here. That far emboldened, he had taken a large, thick envelope, tied it round with tape, then sealed it all over with blobs of red wax. It could not have looked more secret, more important. Then he wrote: BY SPECIAL MESSENGER, FOR SIGHT ONLY OF GO/C 52ND DIVISION, hoped that such a division existed, placed the envelope in his case, and took a train to Amiens. From there it would be easy to find Celverte, where Julia nursed, and the clearing-station twenty miles away to which Cousin Giles had lately been sent. He was wasting his time, Elliot considered, as he settled himself on the train, being one of a number, when he would have made so excellent a spy. The ease with which he'd obtained the whereabouts of his cousins had amazed him. Small wonder the Allies appeared to be losing the war.

He adjusted the cushion at his neck, then lit a cigarette, considering what his defence would be in the event of his absence being discovered. Having decided the odds against it were in his favour, he turned his attention to more mundane matters.

He must first look up Nathan at Brigade Headquarters at some obscure castle five miles out of Amiens on the Abbeville road. Nathan, always eager to help, would find him a billet for the night, were a bed not available in more salubrious surroundings. After which it would be easy, because of the identification he carried, to obtain transport and a driver and go where the whim took him. Perhaps he would meet none of his family, he shrugged, but no matter. A jaunt near enough to the fighting would relieve the boredom of his existence at CAHQ, though had it not been for Beatrice's stupidity and the wagging tongues of London matrons, his posting would not have been necessary.

Yet Paris was the place to be, though Parisian women were notoriously expensive as well as expecting to be wined and dined at expensive restaurants. Perhaps the brothel women would be easier and cheaper out in the countryside, he mused. He hoped so. His allowance was spent and until April he was living on his army pay.

But something would turn up. It always did. In his case, he could never be sure if it was heaven taking care of the righteous or the devil looking after his own. A bit of both, maybe.

He smiled, stubbed out his cigarette, and closed his eyes.

'Nathan, dear fellow! How good to see you!' Elliot clasped his brother to him. 'My, but you took the devil of a time to find!'

'I can't believe this!' Nathan Sutton's pleasure was genuine and evident. 'What on earth brings you here?'

'Oh – you know. Least said . . .' Elliot tapped his nose with his forefinger in a say-no-more gesture. 'Something to deliver to someone in high places. Took a chance on finding you.'

'And I'm glad you did. How long can you stay?'

'Must be away by morning,' Elliot smiled, still smugly satisfied at the ease with which he had located his brother.

'Then I'm sorry – I'm going up to the line. Almost certain I won't get back before tomorrow afternoon. The troops you see: many like to receive the Sacrament before they – well – go over the top into action, and I am duty chaplain.'

'Bother!' Elliot's smile was easy. 'But I suppose the Lord's work must come first. Never mind. Surely we can have a little time together. When do you leave?'

'In half an hour. My, but it's splendid seeing you. You look so well,' Nathan laughed. 'I'm sorry not having more time, but I'm new here and so far I don't seem able to have sorted out any free time for myself. I plan to look Julia up soon, though. I'm pretty sure she's only four miles from here. A little place called Celverte. There's an enormous chateau – a hospital, now – perched on a hill. It's probably there that she works.

'Still, I can at least introduce you to the adjutant. You'll be welcome to eat here; use my bed tonight, if you'd like. I'll get back as soon as I can, but – '

'Your work takes priority,' Elliot finished smoothly.

'It must, but come with me to the mess. At least we can have a drink together before I leave. And did you know that Giles isn't all that far away? I haven't managed to meet him yet, but I've already written, and I hope it won't be too long before we can fix something up.'

'David and Jonathan – that's what the two of you are. Inseparable,' Elliot teased. 'I might just look him up too.

Got a pass that'll take me past most guardrooms, you know.'

'I wish you would. Stretcher-bearers don't have it very easy, and it's time you patched up your differences. I know he'd be glad to see you – if he isn't on duty, that is. So many of his kind spend long stints at the Front, I'm afraid.

'But let me show you to my room. It is small, yet I have a bed, which is more than the poor beggars at the Front have. I'll introduce you around; I know you'll be welcome.'

They made him very welcome. Elliot said his farewells to his brother, then took advantage of the invitation to dine. The arrangement suited him well. Free bed and board was most opportune at this time, and an evening spent in the mess might be altogether more entertaining than spending it with his earnest, saintly brother. Or, he considered, if the evening promised to be stuffy, with no card-games in the offing, he could always look up Cousin Julia. She just might offer him a welcome; tell him where exactly he could find Giles. There were many possibilities open to him; his visit to the Front – or as near as dammit – might prove most entertaining. He would make up his mind when he had eaten.

He smiled into the small mirror, tweaked his tie straight, then went in search of a meal.

It was something of a shame, Elliot was to think afterwards, that his early welcome so quickly ran thin. It could have been blamed, of course, on the fact that he ate too little and drank too much and quickly became the worse for it. Half a bottle of good red wine and several brandies had taken charge of his tongue. In no time at all, the commanding officer was obliged to ask the adjutant to deliver a message to the padre's brother, reminding him he was a guest, and please to conduct himself accordingly. To which gently whispered words of advice, Elliot had flushed deeply, pushed back his chair noisily, and left the table.

It was simply not done. He knew it, but was powerless to curb his impetuosity. He knew better than to leave before the senior officer present, but Elliot in his cups cared not one jot for tradition or rank or age. He'd be away from here first thing in the morning; to hell with the lot of them!

But first a walk in the evening air to clear his head, then be damned if he wouldn't find himself transport and look up Nurse Julia! Even her thinly veiled disapproval would be better than having to make his apologies, then creep away to his brother's bed. Pulling on his cap, making sure his hip-flask was full, he set off in search of his cousin.

The duty officer in charge of motor transport was young, inexperienced, and easily impressed by Elliot's air of command and the imposing pass that gave him entry into the Paris headquarters.

'Celverte, sir? No – not all that far away. We have a convoy leaving for St Omer: I could arrange to have you dropped off as near as possible, perhaps?'

Elliot thanked him charmingly. He was always charming when things went his way, and in less than half an hour he was travelling in the direction of Celverte.

The driver, beside whom Elliot sat, knew the place well. Very small, but with a large chateau. They would reach the crossroads very soon. From there, it would only be a short walk into the village.

The chateau was easy to find. It stood high and arrogant, dominating the village, a splendid target for a German gunner with a good eye – if they got any nearer, Elliot thought. In the courtyard he waylaid a nurse, asking for Julia MacMalcolm, but she shook her head impatiently.

'No one of that name here,' she snapped, 'though we get them from time to time from Sixteen-General, when we are busy – which we are,' she added.

'Then can you tell me – '

'Over there – through Celverte.' The nurse pointed in the direction of the woods. 'Ask for the convent or the school; the nurses will be there if they're off duty. Huts, the hospital's made up of. You can't miss them.'

'Is it far? Will it take me long?' Elliot demanded, having had exercise enough for one day.

'Depends how quickly you can walk,' she shrugged, turning abruptly, hurrying away.

She had no time to waste on dandily dressed officers with brilliantly polished boots, when another convoy of wounded was expected within the hour. A cup of hot, sweet tea was more to her liking! And he had smelled of drink. Maybe the walk to Sixteen-General would sober him up a bit!

Tuesday. Soon, Julia would be back. Not that she wished it, but Alice had missed her more than she had ever thought possible.

She was tired. Julia's extra hands had been missed, especially since Sister had been unable to find a relief for her.

She walked the field path back to quarters, hoping there might be a letter from Tom. It was three weeks now, and she was getting more and more worried. But Julia should be here by ten tonight; Julia would tell her things would be all right, urge her not to worry.

She stopped briefly at the letterboard, then went at once to the dining-room, pleased at least that in the morning her friend would be beside her at breakfast, still talking about Paris and Andrew and so starry-eyed she'd be not one bit of use on the ward for the whole of the day. Alice took her place at the table beside Ruth Love.

'She'll be back soon, won't she? Do you suppose we'll get any sense out of her?' Ruth grinned.

'I was thinking much the same thing myself.' The soup was hot and thick. Alice had not realized how hungry she was. 'Any news?' she murmured.

'From the Front, you mean? No, though if things had got worse, surely we'd have been warned – to evacuate, I mean.' It would be far from easy, were the German divisions to get nearer, to carry the wounded to safety. 'But cheer up. There's a bit of good news – for you, at least. I put a letter on your bed. Did you find it?'

'I haven't been upstairs yet.' Alice jumped to her feet, hunger forgotten. 'I'll go and get it!'

'There's no hurry!' Ruth called, too late. Poor love. She thought it was from Tom and she was going to be disappointed. The letter had borne an English stamp.

Breathless from running, Alice flung aside the green curtain, then gazed with disappointment at the envelope on her bed.

Not from Tom. Not from anyone she knew. She turned it over and read the name of Tom's sister on the back.

But of course! His family had had news of him! Eagerly she tore open the envelope.

It was a long time before the words stopped swimming in front of her eyes, the floor tilting beneath her feet. She stood in time suspended, trying to sort them into some kind of order, make sense out of them.

. . . and Mam is so beside herself that I am writing to let you know that Tom –

'No! *No!*'

Tom was *not* dead; had *not* been killed in action! At Epernay? There was no such place!

. . . died at Epernay on Tuesday 5 March. I am sorry to be the one to have to give you such terrible news. I hope in time you will bring yourself to forgive me. I share your grief. I loved Tom, too . . .

'*Julia!*' For God's sake, where was Julia! Her cry was raw with terror. She crumpled the letter in her hands, flinging it on the bed. Julia would know what to do; would tell her it was all a mistake. She should be back by now. Why wasn't she here? '*Julia . . .*'

She began to run, blindly, wildly; away from that letter and the cruelty of a world that had caused it to be written. Tom wasn't dead! He *wasn't*!

Her heel caught a hole in the path and she hurtled to the ground, the palms of her hands and her knees taking the brunt of her fall. She stayed there, hugging herself as pain tore through her. Then she pulled herself unsteadily to her feet and looked into the face of Elliot Sutton. Only it wasn't Elliot Sutton and the letter hadn't happened! It was all part of a nightmare and she wanted to awaken from it.

'*Tom!*'

A hand grasped her wrist and held it tightly. She closed her eyes, shutting out a world gone mad.

'Well, if it isn't the little sewing-maid!'

'No! Don't touch me! Tom! Help me, Tom . . .'

'There's no Tom here, my girl,' he laughed. 'And no damn dog, either!'

His words were slurred; his breath smelled of drink. She kicked out wildly, but he held on to her wrist, laughing at her efforts to be free.

Her struggling excited him. He felt a stirring in his loins. Dammit, but she'd be cheaper and cleaner than a whore!

He pulled her towards the building, kicking open the door. In the dimness he could see the straw-filled palliasses. Be blowed if it wasn't all laid on for him; all there for his comfort!

He flung her down, then straddled her, ripping open the bodice of her dress, tearing at it wildly. His mouth covered hers and she bit viciously at his lips then, digging

672

her heels into the soft, shifting straw of the palliasse, she put her weight on them, heaving up her back in an effort to throw him off.

He tore at her skirt. She screamed, '*No. Help me! Someone please help me!*'

His mouth found hers again. His moustache was rough and hurt her lips. She ceased to struggle. It was no use. There would be no awakening from this nightmare.

He thrust into her; viciously, cruelly, laughing triumphantly, throatily, trailing his mouth over her neck, searching for her breasts.

She wanted him to kill her. She wanted to be dead, like Tom. The face above her began to swim as dizziness took her. She closed her eyes and surrendered to the darkness that shifted and slipped before her eyes, blotting out her sight.

Tom. Wait for me . . .

She stirred, opening her eyes. She was alone in the cowshed. It hadn't happened. Elliot Sutton's cruel thrusting had been a part of the nightmare, too.

She rose slowly to her feet, her body throbbing with pain. She put her hands to her breasts, pulling her bodice over them.

'Julia!' She began to run. Please, Julia *must* be there!

She clattered up the stairs, flinging open the dormitory door. Julia had not come. It was Ruth Love who stood at her bedside, the crumpled letter in her hand.

'Alice, I came to look for you. What is it? What have you done to yourself?'

'The letter – you read it?'

'Yes – I'm sorry, but I – '

'It says he's dead, doesn't it? He's dead, isn't he?'

Sobs shook her body. She paced the cubicle like an animal caged.

'Sssssh, now.' Tenderly Ruth took her, cradling her, clucking softly. 'Alice, I *do* understand.'

'Why Tom, Ruth . . .?'

'Why my Jamie? Why any of them?'

'I wish he'd killed me. I wish I were dead, Ruth.' She lifted her eyes skywards. 'Do you hear me, God! You should have let him kill me!'

'*Kill* you? Alice – what has happened?'

It was Julia. She was back! Moaning softly, Alice went into her arms. Over her shoulder, Ruth held up the letter.

Tom, she mouthed. *Killed*.

'Dear God, *no*,' Julia gasped. 'Alice, what did you do?'

She cupped the tear-ravaged face in gentle hands, mopping it with her handkerchief.

'Do? It's all right, Julia. My face is all right. He didn't hit me, this time . . .'

'He?' Julia stared with disbelief at the torn frock, the marks on her neck, her shoulders. '*This* time? *He* did this? Elliot Sutton did it?'

'I ran out. In the stable, it was. I went dizzy, then everything went black. I thought I was dying. I wanted to die!'

'Alice – tell me? Did he? This time, *did* he?'

Mutely, Alice nodded.

'She's been – *raped*? I'm going to find Sister!' Ruth gasped.

'No! Please, Ruth – don't! Not yet. Let's try to get things straight first. She's been through this before, you see. Same man . . .'

'Then we *must* tell Sister. He can't be allowed to get away with it!'

'No, Ruth,' Alice whispered. 'Just leave me alone – please?'

Ruth's eyes met Julia's, questioningly. Julia nodded.

'Very well. I'll be in my room, though, if you want me.'

'Thanks,' Julia whispered as the staff nurse left, pulling the curtains together behind her.

'Now, let's have those clothes off,' Julia said softly, 'and get you into the bath.'

'Yes.' She wanted to wash herself; get rid of the touch and smell and memory of him – scrub her body clean. 'Don't tell, Julia? Don't tell anyone?'

'No, love. I won't tell.'

'And Ruth won't?'

'We'll ask her not to.'

'It was awful, Julia. He hurt me.'

'Sssssh.' Julia undressed her friend as if she were a helpless child; wincing to see the bruises showing already on her body. 'But there shouldn't be any damage done. They say it can't happen – not first time . . .'

'But it wasn't the first time – Tom and me, just the once – you know we did. Oh, God!' The sobs began afresh. 'Julia, I want Tom!'

'Hush now. Tom's going to be all right.'

'Maggie wrote that he's been killed . . .'

'Well he *hasn't*! It's all a mistake. Tom's all right. I know it. He'll have been taken prisoner. Let's run that bath . . .?'

Gently, she slipped Alice's arms into the sleeves of her dressing-gown; tenderly, she guided her down the long room to where the bath stood curtained.

God! Listen to me! I swear on the love I hold for Andrew that Elliot Sutton will answer for this! I swear it!

39

Julia watched over Alice like a hen with an only chick, trying never to leave her too long alone to brood, insisting that Tom had not been killed. Nor was her optimism merely for Alice. She truly believed he was alive; that soon there would be a letter from him.

'I won't even let myself *think* things won't come right for you,' she insisted, again and again. 'Something inside me says it. Don't stop hoping, please?'

Yet Alice had lost hope; lost all faith. There could be no God when that awful thing had been allowed to happen; when she was reeling from the shock of Maggie's letter. That night, she would never forget. Each year she would remember the anniversary of the dying of her happiness.

Then Sister gave them the grave news.

'You are to pack your cases,' she said, sadly. 'Put everything in them you are least likely to need, then push them beneath your beds. It seems we must all be ready to evacuate the hospital at short notice, and since the wounded will take priority over all else, it is up to each nurse to prepare herself as best she can.'

'But how are we to leave – even if the Germans come?' Ruth whispered. 'Most of our wounded now are gas cases – in no fit state to be moved. How can we leave them?'

'There I cannot help you. It will be up to each nurse to search her conscience, then decide whether to stay or to leave. As perhaps you already know, nurses from a forward dressing-station arrived here last night. They were completely without possessions. German troops overran their post, taking our wounded soldiers prisoners, allowing the nurses to go free. Two wanted to stay, but they were made to leave.

'Let us hope the enemy will not reach Celverte. I think we should carry on as best we can, and leave the rest in God's hands. Sometimes, I have found, He does know best.' She cleared her throat noisily, then tilting her chin defiantly she whispered, 'Before we go on duty, shall we say a prayer?'

Stunned, they bowed their heads.

'May God, in the troubled days that lie ahead,' Sister whispered, 'grant to us all at this hospital the serenity to accept the things we cannot change, the courage to change the things we can, and the wisdom to know the difference.

'There now, ladies,' she smiled, almost with relief. 'It is out of our hands now. Shall we collect the breakfasts for the ward, then relieve the night staff?'

'She's one love of an old dragon,' Julia said shakily as she and Alice pushed the breakfast trolley to Hut Twenty-four. 'She and Aunt Sutton would get on like a house on fire. And cheer up, Alice! No one has had a letter in ages. Everything has just gone haywire. I've only had a couple from Andrew since our leave – and that was almost three weeks ago. He writes every day – you know he does – so somewhere in the pipeline are nearly twenty missing letters. Tom is alive, I know it. Do you think I'd be so cruel as to say it if I didn't believe it? Word of a Sutton, I wouldn't.'

'No, you wouldn't. But there's something else.' Alice took a deep, shuddering breath. 'I'm pregnant.'

'*What!*' The trolley stopped with a clattering of cups and plates. 'You can't be!'

'I can. I'm a week overdue.'

'Nonsense!' Shock hit Julia hard in the pit of her stomach. 'It's all the worry: the letter from Maggie;

Elliot doing what he did; all the talk of the Germans advancing . . .'

'It isn't. I'm always regular, no matter what. And when you smoke, it makes me feel sick, and it never did before. I've fallen – I know I have. What am I going to do?' Her voice was thick with tears. 'Where can I go? There's Reuben, but how can I go back to Rowangarth? Folks are going to say that I asked for what I got. The men always stick together, and the women are no better. Where am I to go with my shame?'

'You are going nowhere, that I promise you! Rowangarth is your home, and we'll take care of you if you really are having a baby. And Elliot Sutton isn't going to get away with it!'

'Julia – it'll be my word against his. And what was he doing in Celverte? Who saw him? What proof do I have?' She sighed, despairingly. 'Tom's dead and I wish I were. Perhaps I'll die, having it. Women do . . .'

'Stop it!' Julia's voice was rough with anger. 'Just stop it, will you? You are *not* alone! What we'll do, I don't know, but we're going to think calmly about it. And I'll ask Ruth if there's anything you can take – anything safe, that is – to help bring you on. Ruth's a proper trained nurse. If there's anything at all, she'll know about it.'

'There's nothing to know, Julia. And even if there is, Ruth wouldn't tell us about it. It's against all she's ever been taught as a nurse. She can't help me. Nobody can. And I don't want you to tell Ruth just yet.'

'All right. But I'll help you, I promise. And as for Elliot.' Her eyes narrowed into vicious slits. 'May God help him if you really are pregnant. I'll make him wish he'd never been born.'

'Leave it for now, Julia? And Sister's glaring. Come on – or we'll be in trouble.'

Trouble? She was already in more trouble than she knew what to do with.

Tom – please don't be dead.

It was not long after they had finished duty, after they had eaten a supper they neither wanted nor could taste, that the bugle sounded. Its strident notes sent alarm slicing through those who heard it, for a bugle-alert meant either an air-raid threatened or that off-duty nurses were on stand-to.

'It isn't a raid,' said Ruth, 'but Sister says we can expect a convoy of wounded. They can't cope with them at the chateau, so somehow we've got to fit them in here.'

It was almost with relief they put on clean aprons and fastened on caps, hurrying to what had once been the school yard to wait for the ambulances.

'Where are they from?' Ruth asked of Sister Carbrooke.

'North of Albert, I believe. So far, I think our lines are holding, but with so many wounded, who can tell?'

'How many can we take?'

'I'm not sure. But we can find room for five in Hut Twenty-four. There's the emergency bed and we can put four on the floor. Thank heaven for the palliasses. Can you tell Night Sister where they are?'

There were twelve ambulances. The stretchers were laid in rows on the ground; those of the wounded who could walk were tended at once by nurses; those seriously hurt waited examination by a doctor.

Beside each medical officer walked a nurse with trays of syringes and dressings; another wrote down the names and numbers of the wounded.

Some tried to smile in spite of their pain. They were out of the fighting; little else mattered.

Others lay pale and still, eyes closed. Some would die before morning, their wounds such that it was kinder to let them slip away from their pain in a haze of morphine.

'This man is bleeding badly – can he be found a bed?' a doctor asked.

'There's always a bed kept empty in Hut Twenty-four,' Sister said at once. 'He can have that. How bad is he?'

'I can't say. He's lost a lot of blood. He might make it, though.'

The wounded soldier wore the red cross of a stretcher-bearer on his arm. His face was paper-white, his yellow hair wet with sweat.

'Nurse Hawthorn!' Sister held up a hand. 'Take down this patient's name and number, then show the orderlies the way to our ward. Tell Night Sister he's to have the empty bed – MO's orders.'

Alice dropped to her knees, searching beneath the rough shirt for the discs that hung there. Then she pulled in her breath sharply.

'Sister – can I stay with him? They're going to need all the help they can get tonight in Hut Twenty-four.'

'Why, when you've just done a full duty? You look fit to drop where you stand. *Why*, Hawthorn?'

'Because he's bad, I know it.' Alice dropped her voice to a whisper. 'And if he's going to – to die, he should have someone he knows beside him. I know him well, only don't let Julia hear about it suddenly. Tell her gently? He's her brother, you see.' And Giles Sutton could die, if not from his wounds, then from loss of blood. 'Let me stay with him, Sister?'

The night nurses in Hut Twenty-four laid Giles Sutton on the emergency bed, then pulled the curtains round it. Alice stood at Duty Sister's desk, coughing to gain her attention.

'What is it?'

'Sister Carbrooke said – if it's all right with you, that is – that I could stay and special that patient.' She nodded in the direction of the curtained bed.

'Why?'

'Because you are busy enough and the MO agrees. I'd like to stay. I know him, you see.'

'Your young man, is he? Going to have a fit of hysterics, are you?'

'He isn't my young man, and I'll be all right, Sister. He's Sir Giles Sutton – I used to work for his mother. Best, when he comes round, he should see a face he knows.'

'Think you can manage?' Sister demanded brusquely.

'Yes. He's had an injection. When he needs another, someone else will have to give it to him. Apart from that, I'll be all right.'

'Very well.' She seemed the sensible sort, Night Sister decided. 'Go to him. I'll be in as soon as I've had a word with the MO about him. Bad, is he?'

'They think it was a land-mine.'

'I see.' Land-mines were the very devil. A dirty way of fighting. 'All right. Away with you . . .'

The white-haired sister covered her face with her hands. She had been a nurse more years than she cared to remember, but never had she seen such wanton wasting of good young lives. Once, she had been a midwife. Now every waking day she wondered how many of the boy children she helped to be born were already dead. She rose to her feet as the medical officer came into the ward.

'Good evening, sir,' she said softly, all traces of her despair gone.

'How is he?' Night Sister came to stand beside Alice's chair.

'No change, though he's been stirring as if he's going to come out of it. And I think the dressing has stopped the bleeding. Sister, do you think –' Alice stopped, embarrassed.

'Go on, Nurse. I haven't got all night!'

'Well – when first I was nursing, we had a patient just like this. Another land-mine. He lived, though. Nurse Love was in charge of that ward and she'd whisper in his ear. I think she thought it might help him hang on a bit longer. I'm not meaning to be forward, Sister,' she dropped her eyes to the floor, 'but can I try?'

'Whisper about *what*?' the elderly nurse frowned.

'I could tell him that it's me, Hawthorn, and I could talk about Morgan – that's his dog. I used to take it out for him. And I'd talk about Rowangarth, where he lived. Familiar words might help.'

'They might. It won't hurt to try.' Sister's voice was gentler. Anything that might help save just one young life was worth a try. She turned and left abruptly, swishing the curtains behind her.

Alice reached for Giles's hand, her fingers automatically searching for a pulse. There was the slightest movement in his fingers, as if he knew.

'Sir Giles?' She laid her hand over his. 'When are you going to finish those old books? Morgan needs a run.'

There was a flickering of his eyelids, the slightest moving of his lips as if he had heard her and was trying to speak.

'I'll take Morgan out for you. To Brattocks . . .'

Brattocks. She shouldn't have said that word. She would never see Brattocks again. How could she go back there?

'You're going home, Sir Giles, to Rowangarth. Her ladyship is waiting at the top of the steps. Can you see her?'

Sister parted the curtains, scanning the chart that hung at the foot of the bed. 'No change?'

Alice shook her head, rising to her feet. 'I think he can hear me, though. Just small signs. I'll carry on talking to him.'

'It's probably that he's in need of another injection,' Sister murmured, tight-lipped. 'I'll give him it now. Then I'll stay with him for a while. I've been talking to Sister Carbrooke; we've agreed MacMalcolm should be told. All the wounded have been seen to, found beds. She'll be going off duty soon. Will you tell her, Nurse? Are you up to it?'

'I don't know. I'll try, though. Best it comes from someone close. What am I to tell her, Sister?'

'That he's very ill; that he's being special-nursed. Will she make a fuss, do you think?'

Alice shook her head. 'Her husband is a doctor; she'll be all right.'

'Then will you ask her if she wants me to send for the padre?'

'He's *that* bad?' Alice sucked in her breath sharply.

'I'm afraid so.'

'I'd better hurry.' Alice was cold with shock. 'Can she see him? Can she come back with me?'

'Nurse! You have worked one duty, and half the night too. You'll be expected here as usual in the morning. A few hours' sleep would do you more good.'

'No. I'll stay with him.'

She found Julia in the yard of the school, hugging her cape around her, ready to leave.

'Alice! I haven't seen you for ages – are you all right?'

'Yes – but come inside, will you? There's something Night Sister said I was to tell you.'

'What is it?' Julia's face drained of colour.

'Tonight they brought a soldier in.' Alice turned to close the door behind them, give herself a moment in which to think. 'I've been with him. They took him to our ward – the top bed. He's not so good . . .'

'Who is he?' Julia demanded through clenched teeth.

'Sister says you can come and see him. He's just had another injection, so he's not in pain.'

'Alice – *who*?'

'It's Giles – and wait!' She grasped Julia's arm as she made for the door. 'Sister thinks he's in need of a priest. Will I ask her to send for one?'

'Yes. Yes, of course!' Julia was running, stumbling in the darkness. Then she paused, holding out her hand, taking Alice's in her own. 'I'm sorry you had to tell me. Be with me when I see him?'

'I'm staying with him.'

'But I should do it. I should be with him!'

'You're too close. Sister wouldn't allow it. Just be with him for a while. You'll be near him all day when we go on duty – he's in our ward, don't forget.'

They entered the familiar ward, nodding to the staff nurse, opening the green curtains. Night Sister sat beside the bed, and she rose to her feet as they went in.

'You are his sister?' she asked, tersely.

'Yes. Thank you for letting me know.' Julia bent to touch the white cheek with her lips, saying his name softly.

'Giles, it's Julia.' She turned to Sister, her eyes begging. 'Can I stay for a little while? Alice says you want to send for a priest. I agree. Can I stay until he comes?'

'I don't know if one will get here in time. And I have already sent . . .'

'Thank you,' Julia said gravely. 'And I can stay?'

Sister pursed her lips, then shrugged. 'For a while, perhaps.' She would be all right. Her sort knew how to keep a hold on their feelings.

She left, shaking her head. She hoped a padre would be available. It could well be too late, if he didn't come soon.

One long, sad hour later, the army chaplain came. Julia lifted her head wearily, then flung herself into his arms.

'Nathan! Oh, my dear . . .'

Sister followed close behind, eyebrows questioning.

'They're cousins,' Alice offered. 'The padre and Sir Giles grew up like brothers.'

Sister nodded, accepting the explanation. Nathan moved to the head of the bed, his face taut with pain. 'The Sacrament,' he murmured. 'I'd thought he would . . .'

Sister shook her head.

White-faced, Nathan knelt at the bedside. Julia and Alice sank to their knees. They heard the swishing of the curtains as Sister left, then Nathan softly intoned prayers for those about to die.

'Giles,' he whispered, taking his cousin's hand, holding it to his cheek. 'Why did it have to be you?'

'Can you stay?' Julia whispered. 'Just for a little while?'

Nathan lifted his hand, giving Absolution, signing his forehead with the Cross.

'My dear, dear friend,' he whispered. 'I wish I could have done more . . .'

'You must go?' Julia whispered.

'I'm sorry – yes. But I'll be back as soon as I can. Are you all right, Julia?'

'Yes. But will you pray for us, and for Mother especially?'

'I will.' He kissed her cheek then, nodding his thanks to Night Sister, he left.

When Julia returned, Alice was seated beside the bed once more, Giles's hand in hers.

'I've been talking to him,' she smiled. 'Just softly, about Rowangarth and Morgan – things he knows about.

685

Ruth did it at Denniston, remember? That boy had just the same injuries. We didn't lose him, did we?'

'And you want another miracle?'

'Yes, I do,' Alice said stubbornly, leaning closer.

'Here's that Morgan again, Sir Giles. He's been down to the kitchen, soft-soaping Cook for scraps. We're going to Brattocks, him and me. It's Hawthorn, come to take him to Brattocks . . .'

'It isn't any use.' Julia bit hard into her lip. 'He can't feel pain. We must be grateful for that.'

'Go, Julia. You're upset. I'll stay.' Stay all night, if she had to.

'No. We'll stay together.' She sat down, opposite. 'Dear Giles, who never harmed a soul. Why him, Alice? Is it only the good who die young?'

Her mouth was set traplike and Alice knew she was thinking about Elliot Sutton. And hating him for being alive.

In the morning, when the night nurses left and Sister Carbrooke and Ruth came to take over, Giles Sutton still held on to life. Sister read his chart, frowning.

'One of you must take some rest. You, Hawthorn – go back to quarters. Get some breakfast and a few hours' sleep. I'll send MacMalcolm to wake you at noon. You're neither of you any use to him half asleep. That's an order. I'll give him another injection, then change his dressings. Staff will keep an eye on him.' And on MacMalcolm, too, who looked pale and strained, the smudges beneath her eyes dark against her cheeks.

'I want to stay,' Julia whispered. 'He's my brother. And anyway, Nathan is coming back. I want to see Nathan.'

'The chaplain,' Alice whispered. 'Nathan – their cousin.'

She drew her cape around her shoulders. Her eyes felt dry and full of grit and there was a dull ache inside her. Hungry, she supposed. Tea – that was what she wanted. Hot, sweet tea – and to sleep the clock round.

'Talk to him, remember,' she said, softly.

In the early afternoon, Alice returned to take her place at Giles's bedside, whilst Julia, too tired to protest, touched her brother's cheek gently and allowed Ruth Love to push her towards the door.

Not long afterwards, the duty medical officer stood at the bedside as Sister changed Giles's dressings.

'The bleeding has stopped.' He bent to examine the gaping wound. 'It seems clean. No indication of – ?'

'No gangrene,' she said firmly, anticipating the question.

'Then perhaps, Sister, no more morphine, would you say?'

'I agree, sir.' She could not disguise the triumph in her voice.

'I'll leave you a prescription when I've done my rounds. I didn't think, you know –'

'No.' No one had thought it. MacMalcolm's brother, by the law of averages, was lucky to have seen another day. Only get him through this one, and the next, and they could begin to hope.

Alice wiped Giles's forehead with a cool cloth, then moistened his dry lips, listening to the medical officer's murmurings as he stopped beside each bed in the ward.

'Sister says you are to go, Alice.' Ruth parted the curtains. 'We can manage until the night nurses come on. And as soon as Julia wakes up, tell her that her brother is being taken off morphine. He's being put on a different pain-killer now; one not nearly so drastic. So if she's able to take it in, tell her that's good news, will you?'

'There's hope?'

'It's early days yet . . .'

'Then I'll tell her it's early days yet, but there *is* hope.'

Alice leaned over the bed. 'It's Hawthorn. I'm going now, Sir Giles.' Then her eyes flew wide. 'Look!'

His lips were moving. He was trying to speak.

Ruth took the feeding cup, easing the spout between his lips. Carefully she tilted it; weakly he sucked on it, then swallowed the cool water slowly, gratefully. Then his eyes opened and he looked around him in bewilderment.

'*Hawthorn?*' he whispered.

'It's Hawthorn,' she smiled, eyes wet with sudden, happy tears. 'I've been in Brattocks Wood with Morgan!'

'Julia!' Asleep or not, this news was too important to keep. 'Listen! Giles is –'

'What is it?' Julia sat upright, eyes blinking, still half asleep. '*Giles?*' She made to get out of bed, but Alice pushed her back.

'Good news! He's to have no more morphine. He's on a milder pain-killer now!'

'But that's good. It *is*!'

'Yes, an' Ruth said especially to tell you. Said it's early days yet, but –'

'But there's a chance? He's going to be all right!' Julia covered her face with her hands and wept.

'Hush, now. Stop that noise!' Alice lifted the sheet corner, mopping Julia's eyes. 'Get yourself dressed and go over. He might have drifted off again, but he took a drink of water, and he spoke.'

'He was lucid? What did he say?'

'Clear as a bell, it was. He saw me and said my name,' Alice choked.

The agony of her own troubles faded a little and she smiled tremulously. Giles Sutton was going to get well. He *was*!

Back to night duties again, and so far, the Somme line had held. Giles, too weak yet to be sent to England, improved a little each day. Nathan was a constant visitor; Sister, though she tried not to show it, became fond of the softly spoken young man who had been wounded in No Man's Land, trying to bring help to those unable to help themselves.

'They spoil me outrageously,' he smiled to Nathan. 'Julia, of course, cannot nurse me, but Hawthorn is a dear creature, and they both pop in for a talk when Sister's back is turned. They tell me I shall soon be leaving for England, though I shall miss being here.'

'I have written to Aunt Helen, Giles; told her to try not to worry. Heaven only knows how long it will take to get to her, but at least she'll know at first hand that you are getting well and that we are all together here. I long to see Holdenby.' Nathan's eyes spanned the miles to the little railway station and the hills behind it.

'I shall be discharged, they tell me.' Giles fidgeted with his bed-cover. 'I haven't told this to anyone yet; the MO only sprang it on me yesterday, but I'm a poor creature, it seems. I've been a fool, Nathan. Mother was right. I should have found myself a wife.'

'But you can't fall in love to order, old chum! When you get back home, a hero, they'll be falling over themselves to flirt with you.'

'No! Mother knew, you know. After Robert was killed she would talk about grandchildren. But what she really wanted was a boy, for Rowangarth. Now it's too late, though it seems I'm going to make it. I'll always be a bit of a weakling; never one hundred per cent. . .'

'Nor will a lot of men.'

'I know. I've got a lot to be thankful for. At least I have my lungs and my eyesight. But, Nathan, the MO was as certain as he can be that I'll never father a child. It's going to break Mother's heart.'

'It won't, Giles. She'll be so relieved to have you out of the army she won't care. I'll bet Julia agrees with what I say, too. I'm sorry though; desperately sorry.'

'Thanks. Julia doesn't know, by the way. I'll tell her, of course, but she isn't going to like the title leaving Rowangarth. You know how she feels about that? She won't want it to pass to Elliot when I've snuffed it. She can't abide him. I mentioned his name only yesterday and she bit my head off.'

'Elliot isn't everybody's cup of tea,' Nathan grinned, 'but one day he'll mend his ways. Perhaps the love of a good woman, as they say, might well be the making of him.'

'Elliot isn't interested in *good* women,' Giles murmured, his eyes mischievous. 'But I shall tell Julia, next time she pops her head through the curtains. And I'm thankful to be out of the war, Nathan. I did my best – now I can't wait to be home again. How are things going, by the way? I suppose the fighting is as bad as ever?'

'It is. And the Germans are by no means finished. One good push, just one breakthrough and –' He shrugged eloquently. 'The war could go either way, you realize that, don't you?'

'I do, yet sometimes I think I wouldn't care who won it, if only the killing would stop.'

'We'll win,' Nathan said quietly, sadly. 'But what a price we'll have paid.'

Alice was eating breakfast when someone called, 'Hawthorn! Young man to see you!'

'*Me?*' She jumped to her feet, heart thumping. 'Where?'

'At the front door. A soldier. Off you go, then!'

'Oh, God, *Tom*!' She began to run. It was him. It *was*! Julia had been right all along!

She ran down the hall, flinging wide the door. 'Tom?'

690

The soldier turned. His hair was fair, his eyes bright blue; at his shoulder he wore the insignia of the West Yorkshire Regiment.

'Nurse Alice Hawthorn?' he said. 'I'm Geordie Marshall. Tom was my mate . . .'

Despair took her, held her. She wanted to smile, to hold out her hand, ask for news of Tom. Instead, she stood there, unspeaking, wanting to fall to her knees and beat the floor with her fists. For just a few seconds, it had been Tom. She wished Geordie hadn't come because she knew what he would tell her.

'I haven't got long,' he said, gently. 'We're on our way to Ypres. The lads are covering for me, but I can't stay. Tom had got it worked out where you were, and I took a chance on it – finding you, giving you some of his things.'

'It's true, then? Tom is really –' She couldn't say the word.

'He was sent on special duties. That's all I know for sure. But I did hear he was in a motor transport that got hit by a shell. At Epernay, it was. All the blokes in it – gone. But he wouldn't have known any pain. Not like some . . .'

'It's good of you to come.' She held out her hand. 'He wrote about you in his letters.'

'Aye. I miss him. We were a good team. When they came to collect his things, I got in there quick. I've brought you his Testament. He usually had it in his top pocket – we all do. Daft, I suppose. They're supposed to stop a bullet. But even if he'd remembered to take it with him, it wouldn't have helped him a lot.

'I've brought the letters you wrote him. Been carrying them around with me for ages. They meant a lot to him.'

He handed them to her awkwardly and she smiled and thanked him, reaching up to kiss his cheek.

'I'll have to be off,' he murmured.

'Yes. Thank you, Geordie. God keep you . . .'

She watched him walk away, then break into a run. She laid the Testament to her cheek and something fluttered to the ground at her feet.

She bent to pick up a spray of buttercups. It was as if he were saying goodbye to her.

Tom, my love, what's to become of me . . . ?

40

'So you see, Sis, that's the way it is.' Julia sat at her brother's bedside, his hand in hers. 'I dilly-dallied, left it too late. There'll be no sons, now, for Rowangarth. But at least Mother will have grandchildren to fuss over – yours and Andrew's.'

'But are you sure?' The enormity of his words hit her like a slap. 'Doctors can be wrong. How could he make such a snap diagnosis? I shall write to Andrew – he'll know of the best specialist in London.'

Write to Andrew? Much good would it do her. No one got letters these days. You just had to write them and post them and hope.

'I think the MO is right, but it seems I shall live. There are millions who'll never be so lucky.'

Julia drew in her breath sharply. Had Giles not survived that awful first night, his title would already have passed to Pendenys, to Uncle Edward. She didn't mind that; Uncle Edward was a Garth Sutton. But for it to go one day to Elliot made her cold with fury. This war, dammit, would have handed to Aunt Clemmy on a plate what her father's money had failed to do: obtain a knighthood for the Pendenys Suttons.

'Yes, lucky,' she hastened, suddenly ashamed. And was a title really so important? When Giles had pulled through, did it matter?

Yes, it did! It damn well did! She'd rather it went to the first tinker who knocked on the door than to Elliot. Elliot Sutton was evil; a changeling. If only some land-mine had taken *his* manhood . . .

'You are right, old love.' She lifted his hand to her

cheek. 'Just to survive this war is a small miracle but oh, it's so ironic. You will never father a child; Alice is carrying a baby she doesn't want. It's a strange old world, isn't it?'

'*Alice?* Our Hawthorn? But that's awful – Dwerryhouse being killed, I mean. What will she do now?'

'God knows.' Despair trembled on Julia's words. 'And it isn't Tom's child. She'd have wanted it if it had been. It's Elliot's,' she finished bitterly.

'You mean – *again*?' Giles's cheeks flushed crimson.

'Again. Only this time Reuben wasn't there, or Morgan or Dwerryhouse. Alice was out of her mind with grief that night; didn't know what to do. I hadn't got back from Paris, and she'd just had a letter telling her that Tom had been killed. There was no one to turn to. She ran blindly, she said – literally bumped into Elliot Sutton. And he'd been drinking. Life can be rotten, can't it? He'll deny it, of course; swear he was never near Celverte!'

'Poor little Hawthorn. I feel so disgusted, so angry.'

'Don't we all? Ruth Love wanted him found, but Alice begged her not to. It was bad enough that time in Brattocks; all Rowangarth knowing about it. I think she didn't want to face it again. But she'll have to, now, because she's as sure as she can be that the worst has happened. And only Ruth and I know about it, so don't say anything, will you?'

'You know I won't. But it makes me feel so useless having to lie here, too shot-up to do anything about it,' he said, bitterly. 'How can we help her?'

'I don't know. She's worried sick. Losing Tom has been bad enough and now this. She has no parents to go to – Rowangarth is all she's got. But I'm going to ask Aunt Sutton to have her. No one need know then. I know Aunt will take her in. She doesn't like Elliot either.'

Eyes closed, Giles lay back on his pillows, wanting more than anything to thrash his cousin half to death.

'Giles! I haven't upset you? I'm sorry! I shouldn't have told you, but it just slipped out. I don't know what to do for the best. I'm so fond of her, you see . . .'

'It's all right, Sis. I am upset, but not in the way you think. I'm glad you've told me and I want to help. Best I talk to Nathan about it – she wouldn't mind Nathan knowing? When do you think he'll be here again?'

'Tomorrow morning. He's holding early Communion in the ·chapel. I intend going, when I come off duty. Shall I ask him to look in on you?' And whatever God was about, she thought despairingly, at least He had sent Nathan to them.

'Would you? And don't worry. We'll help Hawthorn. Nathan will know what to do. Off you go now. That's Sister calling for you!'

'Sure you're all right?' Hurriedly, Julia rose to her feet.

'I'm fine. Just let me think . . .'

'I talked to Julia after Communion,' Nathan said, sitting down at Giles's bedside. 'She asked me to look in on you. Desperately urgent, she said.'

'That's my awful sister for you, but I do want to talk to you. Can you spare me a little time? It's advice I want.'

'Be only too glad, you know that.'

'And you'll hear me out? You won't tell me I'm half out of my mind?'

'Army chaplains have to be good listeners. I won't interrupt.'

'I've been awake half the night thinking about it, and I know I'm right. But it's all up to you, really. Tell me, Nathan; can you marry people?'

'*Marry* – yes, of course . . .'

'Here in France?'

'I suppose so: if there were witnesses, I don't see why not. I don't know about the reading of the banns, though, but out here, on wartime emergency footing, sort of, I don't know they'd be all that necessary. But why do you ask – though I know you're going to tell me.'

And Giles told him, holding nothing back, about Tom's death and Alice and Elliot and Alice having to bear the shame of it alone – she innocent, too.

'Elliot is a Sutton – your brother, Nathan. Alice carries a Sutton child and we are in part responsible for what has happened,' Giles finished.

'Responsible – yes. And God forgive my brother and his ways. I'm deeply ashamed.' Nathan shook his head, wearily. 'And Hawthorn: one sorrow on top of another. What can I do to help her? Find a good home for the child when it's born, perhaps?'

'No. I've already found that. You might though, on my behalf, give your brother the hiding of his life. I would, and gladly, if I weren't so weak still. But if your calling prevents such a thing, then at least help by marrying us – Hawthorn and me.'

'*Marrying* . . .?'

'That's what I said.'

'But, Giles, had you thought? Has the girl thought? She might be unhappy as your wife, as lady of a house where once she had been a – an employee. And there is no snobbery in my reasoning,' he added, hastily. 'I'm only thinking of her.'

'So am I, and her shame as a mother unmarried. And I'm thinking of my mother, too. I can't father a child, Nathan, yet Hawthorn has a babe in need of a father. And Rowangarth has need of a son, or –'

'Or Elliot will one day inherit?'

696

'Yes. Not only the title, but Rowangarth too. A knighthood is Aunt Clemmy's dearest wish for him; he would like it, too, yet it's the one thing she has never been able to give him. I'm sorry to be so blunt, but you know it's true.'

'It's a thought that pleases me.' Nathan's smile bore out his words. 'Mind, the child could be a girl . . .'

'It's slightly better odds it will be a boy. I've heard that more boys are being born now than girls. Nature's way of compensating for this war. Can you marry us, Nathan?'

'I'd have to go into the legalities of it, but I see no reason why not. An English service said by an English priest and with witnesses . . .'

'Bless you, Nathan! I'll talk it over with Julia. She'll agree with me, I know it. I can take it there's probably nothing to stand in the way of it then – except Hawthorn. She knows nothing of this.'

'Then you'd do well to consider she might want nothing of it. She's a straight, sensible girl, what I know of her. She might thank you kindly, and refuse!'

'She might, but I hope not. I want her to say yes. It would make so many people happy: the child would grow up without the stigma of illegitimacy; marriage would protect Hawthorn and ease my own conscience. And, best of all I think, Mother might have her boy for Rowangarth.'

'Or a granddaughter, don't forget?'

'I won't; but at least I'll have tried. Do you think the deceit is justified? As a priest, do you?'

'As a priest, no. As Elliot's brother, *yes*! But talk to Julia first. Heaven only knows she's a bossy, self-opinionated love of a girl, but in this she'll talk sense!'

She would, Giles thought. If it were entirely left to his sister, she would most likely push him to the chapel in a bathchair *tomorrow*! Julia would back him, but what of Hawthorn?

*   *   *

'Had you thought, you idiot,' Julia demanded of her brother, 'that it's perfect in every way but for two things. Not only must Alice agree, but the dates must too! A baby, from start to finish, takes about nine months; yours would be born in *seven* – from the date of your marriage, that is.

'When were you wounded? The middle of April, wasn't it? And you are going to marry Alice after you'd received wounds that made you – well, you know – and have a seven-month baby into the bargain; because that's what everyone would have to believe it was!'

'Doc. James would help with the dates . . .'

'Yes. I think he would but, even so, you'd have to tell people you were married in March – or earlier. Would you be prepared to do that, for Mother's sake, because she must never know it isn't your child?'

'I'd do it. And since I can't give Elliot a hiding for what he's done, I think what I propose is the next best thing. Mind, Elliot must never know either.'

'He might put two and two together, Giles. He's a devious swine.'

'What? Say publicly that Alice's child isn't mine because on the twenty-sixth of March *he* raped her. Because that's when it was. Nathan told me. Elliot *was* here. He slept in Nathan's bed that night – made a fool of himself in the mess, too. It all adds up. That's why this time Elliot can do nothing about it!'

'There's still Alice, remember?'

'You mean she wouldn't fit in? And why not?'

'I'm not saying that at all. I care for Alice a lot. I once said if I could have had a sister, I'd have chosen her. I'd be happy for her to be my sister-in-law.

'But there's Tom. She'll never love you, Giles; not like she loved him. No man will ever take his place. It would have to be a loveless marriage; oh – not *loveless*! She cares for you; she always has. But you know what I mean?'

'Only too well. And I accepted that when I was told I was unlikely ever to father a child . . .'

'Oh, dammit! That was an awful thing for me to say! I'm a fool! Forgive me, Giles?' Tears glittered in her eyes.

'It's all right, Sis. But you do see why I'm so desperate to have Hawthorn's child for my own, for Rowangarth? And I care for her too. I always have.'

'Then are you going to ask her, or shall I sound her out? And remember, she might want to wait the war out to see if Tom comes back.'

'I accept that, and I'd like more than anything for him to be alive – a prisoner. But I don't think he is.'

'Then I'll talk to her; see if I think there's a chance she'll say yes?'

'I'd be grateful. It could be made to work, I'm sure it could.'

'All right. I'll do a bit of fishing, but you do your own proposing, don't forget. I practically proposed to Andrew; I'm not going to make a habit of it!'

'You are an extremely nice lady, Mrs MacMalcolm – did you know that?' he said softly, a smile softening his pale gaunt face.

It was good, Julia thought, to see him smile. She hoped with all her heart that Alice would say yes.

As they left the ward that morning, cold with fatigue, Julia said, 'I had quite a long chat with Giles last night, when Sister was out of the ward.'

'Mm. It's good – if there's anything good about being wounded, I mean – that he ended up with us. Even Sister and Ruth know Rowangarth and her ladyship from her hospital-visiting at Denniston.'

'Yes – and Aunt Clemmy, too! But he was lucky, though he's such a dear person that he deserves to be in our ward. You like him, don't you?'

'You know I do – always did. He's a lovely gentleman.'

'So would you marry him?'

'*Julia!*' Alice stopped in her tracks. 'That's a cruel thing to say. It's Tom I love, only –' She hid her face in her hands, taking deep, gulping breaths, fighting the sobs that writhed in her throat. '– only he's never coming back. He'd have stood by me, though. Tom would have married me.'

'If they hadn't hanged him first for beating Elliot to death. Giles said he would've thrashed Elliot if he could.'

'You told him, Julia? How *could* you?'

'Giles is going to have to know. Everyone is. Sooner or later, it's going to show. And Giles is on your side, Alice. But let's get in to breakfast. We'll find ourselves a quiet spot and talk about it. I was serious, you see, when I asked if you'd marry him . . .'

'No!' Alice shook her head violently.

'I see. Giles not good enough for you? You don't want me for a sister?'

'Don't talk so dáft,' Alice flung. 'Tom isn't coming back. Geordie Marshall confirmed it, as good as. I'll have to learn to live with what happened. And don't think I wouldn't want to marry some decent man who'd accept the child and not hold it over me that I was no better than I ought to be . . .'

'No better? God, Alice, you were *raped*! But just think. Giles wants a son for Rowangarth; you need a father for your child –'

'Not for my child, Julia. It isn't *my child*. It's something lying inside me like a great *sin*!'

'Oh, love, I'm sorry.' Julia grasped her friend's hand, squeezing it tightly. 'Let's get something to eat. And hear me out – please?'

'No, Julia. Sir Giles is a gentleman born. I'm a servant. There's nothing more to be said.'

'Isn't there? Oh, but there *is*, and you'll listen, Alice! Now – do we talk?'

That night, when Sister was taking her usual ten-minute tea-break with Night Sister in Hut Twenty-three, Julia whispered, '*Now*, Alice! He's not asleep. I just looked in. Talk to him?'

For the first time, Alice felt embarrassment as she pulled aside the cubicle curtains, then slowly, carefully, pulled them together again.

'Sir Giles?' she breathed

'Mm?'

'Are you in any pain?' she demanded, taking his wrist, checking his pulse.

'Not too bad. Anxious, though . . .'

As if to put off the question she knew he would ask, Alice ordered, 'Open, please,' then placed a thermometer in his mouth.

'It won't do, Hawthorn.' Giles removed the impediment. 'Julia says you've had a good long chat . . .'

'Yes.' Her eyes were fixed steadily on the chart she held. 'And?'

'I've given it some thought – no! I've thought about little else since breakfast – and perhaps, if we mind our p's and q's, some good might come of it. Only how I'm going to go home to Rowangarth afterwards, I don't know.'

'You agree, then?' he said softly.

'Yes, I thank you. Mind – I'm not doing it lightly, and there'll be a lot to be sorted out one way or another, but I think it's up to us both to make the best of a bad job, though the way my luck is running it won't be the boy you want, but twin girls!'

'Oh, dear – we sound so awkward, don't we? And never once the most important word. Do you suppose we could start again, at the beginning? Hawthorn, will you marry me?'

'Yes, sir, thank you. I will – with reservations, that is.'

'Reservations accepted – and you won't have to worry about *that*,' he said, so softly she could hardly hear him. 'And do you think we might be a little less formal? Could you bring yourself to call me Giles, do you think?'

'I'll try. It'll come after a while, I shouldn't wonder. I felt awkward with Julia at first, but now – well – it isn't any bother. Now, are you going to let me take your temperature or is Sister going to come back and find us chatting together as if I've got all the time in the world, which I haven't! Open your mouth, please – and Sir Giles, I do thank you.'

It was, Giles Sutton thought as he lay awake into the small hours of the morning, the most peculiar proposal – and acceptance – of marriage ever. Poor Hawthorn. She had been so embarrassed, yet there had been relief in her eyes and gratitude, though it was he who should be grateful. And he *must* learn to call her Alice. Alice Sutton. Lady Alice – oh, hell! Had she grasped the full significance of it, he wondered. Would a title sit heavily on those thin shoulders?

Poor little Alice. He'd do his best for her and no one – absolutely no one – would be allowed to treat her with anything less than her position deserved.

And Mother – what of her? Should he write to her now, or should he wait? Soon he would be fit enough to make the journey back to an English hospital. No private soldier was allowed his own nurse to accompany him, even if she were his wife. Alice would have to return to Rowangarth alone; by the time she did, his mother would have had time to get over the shock of their marriage. For shock it would be.

There were so many ifs; so very many buts. Here, wide-eyed and with nothing else to do but think, he was only too well aware of them. Would Alice, when she'd had time to think about them too, call the wedding off? And where, he thought in sudden cold panic, were they to find a shop with wedding rings to sell?

He closed his eyes, pretending to sleep, as the curtains at the foot of his bed parted. Then a voice said softly, 'I know you are awake. I'll bring you in a drink if you'd like. And don't worry. We'll manage, somehow . . .'

Alice. Practical as ever. And dammit, they *would* manage!

One week later and with Sister Carbrooke – who'd had to be told or how else were they to get Giles to the chapel? – and Ruth Love as witnesses, Nathan Sutton joined together till death did them part, his cousin Giles and Alice Hawthorn.

'You're all right?' Julia had whispered as they washed and dressed. 'Even though this isn't how you'd hoped it would be?'

Alice looked pale and tired, a condition which couldn't be entirely blamed on a night duty more hectic than usual.

'I'm fine.' She took a long look into the wall mirror, unfastening the chain at her neck as she did so, taking from it the wedding ring with which her own mother had been married. 'Will you give this to Giles – unless there's going to be a best man, that is?'

'No. Just you and him and me, and Nathan marrying you and dear old Carbolic and Ruth to sign the certificate afterwards – make it all legal and above board. You *are* happy about it, Alice?' she demanded. 'And you needn't worry; no one here will know about it, and we can trust Sister. She was just a bit annoyed that we hadn't told her about – well, what happened that night.'

'I know. I only hope it's going to be all right at Rowangarth.'

'When mother goes to visit Giles in hospital and hears what he has to tell her, she'll be giddy with happiness.'

'Even though it might be a girl? Even though she might find out it's Elliot Sutton's? It might be black dark, like him.'

'But you've got dark hair too, Alice. A son often favours his mother. And she won't ever find out it isn't Giles's child, even if we have to lie through our teeth for the rest of our lives. You aren't having second thoughts?'

'No.' Alice shook her head. 'It's just that –'

'That it should have been Tom? I understand. But we've agreed to make the best of a bad job, so shall we pick up Ruth and Sister? It's almost time.'

'Yes. And thanks, Julia. And no one will find out?'

'They won't – not here, anyway. Everyone thinks it's a special Communion – thanks for Giles's recovery. A family Communion, sort of. And, Alice – I'm glad I'm getting a sister. When this war is over, we'll visit each other and talk about our children, and –'

'We will, Julia.'

And Tom, my lovely lad, forgive me? And try to understand?

'So!' said Sister. 'Your husband is on his way home! Before so very much longer he'll be a civilian, with the medal he deserves if there's any sense left in the British army. But why you aren't going too, I don't know. In your condition it would have been easy to get your release. We might even have been able to get you on the same hospital ship.'

'I want to stay, Sister, if it's all right with you. In just a few weeks I'll have done another year and my contract will come up for renewal. I'll just not sign on again. It'll be a lot simpler to do it that way. And if I don't have to apply for release on grounds of pregnancy – well, the

less who know, the better. Besides, I'm not showing yet.
I can work a little longer, surely? And you need every
pair of hands you can get.'

She wanted to stay; she wanted to leave. She didn't
want to part from Julia; she dreaded returning to Rowangarth. Lady Alice, indeed! It was enough to make Jin
Dobb's cat laugh! Putting off the moment, she was.

'Work? You'll have to remember to be very careful when
you are lifting – if at all. I shall see that MacMalcolm
keeps an eye on you.'

'She's at it already, Sister. Don't do this! Stop doing
that! It's a wonder the entire hospital hasn't found out.
You'll never tell, will you?'

'You know I won't. Sir Giles deserves a son – a child,
and a child born in wedlock belongs to the marriage.
He's a fine young man. He'll never be fully fit, you
understand, but he should do well enough. It's you I
worry about.'

'I'll be all right, Sister. I'll manage. And one way or
another, it won't be all that long before Julia's home.'
In a rare burst of insubordination she reached up to
kiss Sister's cheek. 'Can I go now? They're busy on
the ward.'

'Yes, indeed! Be off with you!'

Sister Carbrooke dabbed her eyes and blew her nose
loudly. *Damn* this war! And damn the fools who let it
start and the idiots who didn't seem to be doing half
enough to help our soldiers win it!

And thank goodness young Hawthorn – *Sutton* – would
be on her way home to England soon. A pregnant nurse
in all this mayhem was something she could well do
without!

Alice stood at the ship's rail, hugging her coat around
her, determined to stand there, in spite of the cold wind
from the sea, until the coast of France could no longer

be seen. She worried about Julia; about Andrew too. She worried about the hospital at Celverte and all the patients and nurses there.

The Germans were advancing – there was no denying it. Balanced now as the fighting was, one stroke of good or bad luck could give victory to either side. And Julia was there, separated from Andrew and hardly a letter from him recently.

We've been together so long, Julia. Ever since that night in Hyde Park we've been close. We are sisters now.

Yet she didn't know how her ladyship had taken it; didn't know how Giles was doing because there had been no letters for anyone from anywhere. She hoped Giles was getting better quickly. It was summer now; the days were warm and long. He'd be able to spend time sitting quietly in the sun; help him forget the nightmare he'd been through. He might even have gone home now to Rowangarth, and Morgan licking him and fussing and slobbering all over him.

The ship's engines began to throb. The gap between the ship and the quayside widened.

Goodbye, France. Take care, all of you. I wish I could have stayed there, right up until the end . . .

She gripped the rail tightly. France was little more than a grey blur now: somewhere beyond that long, flat streak of coastline a war was being fought to the bitter end, and young men were being killed every second of every minute.

Goodbye, Tom, my lovely lad. I'm going home to Rowangarth. I shall see Reuben again and that daft dog and I'll take him walks like I used to, in Brattocks. But you won't be there. You'll never whistle me and I'll never again run to you.

There would be buttercups now, at Rowangarth. The pastures would be yellow over with them.

I don't know where you are, Tom, where they have laid you. But one day I'll find you, stand beside you. And when I come, my darling, I'll bring you buttercups, so you'll know I have been . . .

41

Alice sat in the waiting-room at Holdenby Halt, cases and bags at her feet. She had given the stationmaster a sixpenny-piece, asking that he telephone Rowangarth, tell them she was here.

She was tired. The slow, late-night crossing had been without incident, but the turmoil inside her had prevented sleep. She was in need of food, too, to stop the rumblings inside her and the empty ache that went with them.

She thought back to the long, lonely train journey north, and England so heartbreakingly dear, slipping past the window.

At York, the Holdenby train stood at a side platform, letting out puffs of smoke, little hisses of steam, ready to leave. A few more miles more and she would be home – but to what? Perhaps it would be better if she sat here for ever and people became so used to her being there that they treated her as part of the furniture, and dusted and polished her every day.

The door opened. The stationmaster lifted his top hat.

'I did the telephoning. They're coming to fetch you, miss.'

He was looking at her strangely, doubtless thinking her face was familiar, yet not knowing who this Nurse Sutton was. A porter loaded her luggage on to a trolley. He was too old to be working, but there were no young men left now.

'I'm to tell you Sir Giles is on his way, miss. Is there owt you need?'

'No, thank you.' She smiled because he, too, gazed at

her questioningly. She would have to get used to such looks.

Her fingers twisted on her lap, making her aware of her wedding ring. Married, yet not married; wanting Tom still. She was glad Giles was coming to meet her; it could only mean he was getting stronger.

She had no way of knowing. Seven weeks married and only two letters: one hurriedly written on arriving in England; the other giving the address of the London hospital to which he'd been sent. It told her that the situation on the Western Front had not improved – for the Allies, that was. Shifting positions, small advances and counter-attacks did nothing to help the army deliver letters. And letters were so precious; so necessary to those over there.

She closed her eyes, thinking of Julia and Ruth and Sister, hoping they hadn't been overrun, that the Allied lines were holding. Celverte was so near, now, to the fighting. She should be glad to be away from it, but she wasn't. Hut Twenty-four, with all its dangers, was better by far than what might await her here.

From the minute she'd left Celverte she had felt lonely and alone. She wanted, *needed*, to be back there.

'Alice!' Giles stood in the doorway, a walking-stick in either hand. 'No crutches, you see!' He swayed awkwardly towards her, then kissed her cheek.

'You shouldn't have come,' she said, all at once shy.

'I wanted to. When the station telephoned, I rang Pendenys. Aunt Clemmy is in London so I knew Uncle Edward would offer a car. I persuaded Mother to wait at home – told her I could manage all right. I've got to talk to you first, you see.'

The porter pushed the trolley ahead of them. Alice took one of Giles's sticks. 'Put your arm round my shoulder, it's better that way. Take it slowly,' she murmured, still the nurse.

Pendenys had sent their biggest, shiniest car. The driver opened the door, helped Giles in, then covered his knees with a rug

'They treat me like a wounded hero,' he murmured, reaching to close the glass panel between the front and back seats. 'I came because I've got to tell you,' he said softly as, slowly, majestically, they left the station yard.

'It's her ladyship, isn't it?' Alice choked. 'She's upset.'

'She is *not*. She's as pleased as can be. Only Mother knows, and Aunt Sutton. Mother's longing to tell everyone. but I asked her not to – not yet. I told her all about it; said the baby was the result of one brief loving.'

'*Loving*, Giles?'

'Yes. You and me, I said. Just the once, before I was – injured . . .'

'But why? She'll think I'm – *common*.'

'No! Exactly the opposite! She said it was as if it had been meant to be. I told her, you see, that I met you the night you'd heard Tom had been killed. That *I* met you, Alice – not Elliot. I told her I held you, comforted you and – well, it happened . . .'

'But you shouldn't have. I don't know what to think.' She shook her head, bewildered.

'Then don't think – not anything. Especially don't think about Elliot. You and I – *we* got the child. Can you accept that, Alice? You were upset, needing comfort; I forgot myself and –'

'We're deceiving her. It isn't right.'

'It *is*. And we knew we'd have to tell some lies. But she doesn't care that I lost my head. She even said it would be a special child because love children are always particularly beautiful. She refuses to be anything but glad about it. She's happy – truly. Some good has come of it, after all.

'She came to visit me in hospital in London – stayed with Aunt Sutton whilst she was there. I'm afraid Aunt

Sutton knows; Mother just had to tell her. Aunt is delighted, but sworn to secrecy – about the baby, that is.

'Did you get any of my letters, by the way? I'm officially a civilian now. And in case you hear it from someone else, I've been recommended for the Military Medal.'

'Giles! I'm so pleased! Yours was a special kind of bravery – and don't try to say it wasn't. I was there, remember? And I didn't get your letters; only two telling me you'd made it back.'

'Letters still not getting through? Things must still be bad.'

'They are. People here at home don't realize how bad. Things are being kept back. The papers aren't allowed to print the half of it. But I won't say anything to her ladyship. Julia's still out there, and Andrew, remember.'

'Well, she's got you and me to fuss over now. And her precious grandchild. But you agree with me – telling her that it was the result of a slip, kind of? It's better than the way it really was. I want her to think the baby is mine. It's what Nathan would call a permissible untruth.'

'I'll admit it's better than what Julia suggested – trying to tell people we were married before we really were so it wouldn't have to be a seven-month baby.'

'My sister is a great one for her spot of drama. The way I told it sounds far more believable.'

'With you taking the blame for what Elliot Sutton did.'

'And taking his child for my own, don't forget. So no more talk about him. Let's try to make this a happy day, Alice?'

'All right. You don't think he heard any of what we said?' She nodded towards the driver who was steering the car through the lodge gates.

'No. We whispered, and anyway, I think he's a bit hard of hearing. Probably why Aunt Clemmy engaged

711

him in the first place. Chin up? Look! There's Mother waiting at the door. I knew she would be!'

'You are a good man, Giles Sutton. I'm grateful to you, and I'll try my best – I promise.'

She stared ahead, chin high. And it would have been all right – it really would – if a dog hadn't dashed out to join them; a big, daft lovable spaniel.

Does this creature belong to you . . .?

'Alice, my dear, don't cry! Please don't cry.'

Her ladyship, hugging her, kissing her, and the familiar sweet smell of her special soap so easy to recall.

'I'm sorry.' Alice dabbed her eyes, took a deep, calming breath. 'Only it's so long since I went away – so good to be back.'

'And it is so good to have you home. Come inside, child. You look exhausted.'

Over his mother's shoulder, Giles smiled. It was going to be all right, Alice insisted silently. Only Brattocks Wood to face now, and Reuben. Reuben wouldn't ask any questions, point any fingers, and the rooks kept secrets. There'd only be the ghost of a lost love to face . . .

Miss Clitherow stood in the hall at the foot of the staircase, hands clasped in front of her, a half-smile on her lips.

Nothing had changed.

Alice was sent at once to bed. She had been travelling for twenty-four hours, and with very little food, it would seem, Helen Sutton told the housekeeper. First something light to eat, then sleep.

'You must not overtire yourself,' Helen smiled, offering daintily cut sandwiches and a glass of cool milk. 'In your condition,' she settled herself on the bed, 'you must have peace and quiet. No visitors at all until tomorrow.'

'My *condition*, milady –' Alice whispered. 'What must you think of me – of us?' She dropped her eyes to fingers

712

nervously plucking at the bed-cover. 'I want to say I'm very sorry . . .'

'Sorry, my dear good girl? Sorry you are giving me what I have wanted for so long! It didn't help at all when Clemmy told me Albert had a son; now, soon, I shall announce my own grandchild!'

'But the way of its getting – don't think too badly of it?'

'The way of my grandchild's getting is nobody's business but yours and Giles's. The fact that he chose to tell me was only to explain Dwerryhouse's death – and I was so sad to hear about it. But I do understand – and I thank God that He didn't create any of us entirely perfect, or where would the baby have been now? There wouldn't have been one, Alice. Giles would never have had a son – or daughter,' she added hastily. 'Just remember that I adored Giles's father; that I know how easily the act of love can happen.

'Julia, too, I am glad to say, knows just such a happiness.' Her eyes took on a remembering sadness, then she said, 'How is Julia? How was she when you left her?'

'She was fine, milady. She'd finished her second year, just as I had. I wanted her not to sign another contract. I begged her to come home with me, but she would have none of it. Andrew is out there and she wants to be as near to him as she can. They had a lovely three days together, in Paris. She looked so happy when she got back.'

But only for a while, milady. When she got back I was there, beside myself, weeping, half out of my mind.

'Julia made a good choice, you know Andrew will be a splendid husband – when finally this war allows him to be. Some say the fighting is going badly for us, that we aren't being told the truth about what it is really like in France. Are they right, Alice?'

'That I can't say.' Not for anything would she add to her ladyship's worries. 'I only know about my part of the war. We were always busy at the hospital. It was like another little world, all wrapped in cotton wool and bandaged round to keep everything else out. You learned to live from duty to duty, and always the wounded must come first, no matter what.

'So I can't tell you how things really are – except that at one time letters came quite quickly and regular, like. Lately though, hardly any mail was getting through.'

'I'd noticed that myself . . .'

'But it'll be all right,' Alice hastened. 'Since the doctor got to be a major he was sent to a hospital much further away from the fighting. Julia's ever so thankful he's away from the front line now. And nurses would be moved out at once if they were threatened. Don't you worry none. They'll both of them be home soon, milady.'

'I do so hope they are. Thank you for those words of comfort, Alice. It's going to be such a joy, having you and Giles to fuss over and spoil. I've been so lonely. And, my dear, do you think you could remember not to call me milady? It is you who must be called that. *You* are Lady Sutton now.'

'Aye. It bothers me.'

'Then you mustn't let it. And will you remember that I am your mother now?'

'Oh, I couldn't!' Not calling her ladyship 'Mother'. 'Oh, my word no!'

'Then perhaps you could make a start with "Mother-in-law"? I suppose, really, that's what I am. And in time you might try "Mother", or even "dearest", which is what Giles mostly calls me. Will you, Alice?'

'I'll try.' It had been strange, at first, using Julia's name – or calling her MacMalcolm.

Faraway days at the York hospital: that huge, empty, dirty ward, and Julia's poor chapped hands. Then Denniston

714

House and France and being able to sew two years' service on uniform sleeves. Five years of being friends, being together – until two days ago, that was.

'I don't want you to go, Alice. What will I do without you?' Julia had whispered.

They had held each other tightly as if it were the last time each would see and hold and touch the other; as if there was to be no more laughter together or whispered secrets or shared tears.

'Come home with me, Julia? Two years out here is more than enough.'

'No! Oh, I long to see Rowangarth. Sometimes I ache for its sanity and safeness. But Andrew is here and I must be near him. Just think – the door at the top of the ward might open and in he could walk, demanding to know where his wife was. She couldn't be in England, could she?'

'No. I'll give your love to Rowangarth, though.'

The honeysuckle and foxgloves would be flowering when she got back; buttercups, too. Tom had picked buttercups. Tom was there now, in Brattocks. She had only to take Morgan's lead, cross the wild garden, climb the stile. Then Tom would whistle and she would run to him . . .

'Alice?' Gently Helen touched the hand lying so child-like on the bed-cover. 'Bless the girl – she's asleep already.'

She bent to kiss the pale cheek. Alice had thickened at her waist, her breasts were fuller; signs of the child she carried – Giles's child. But her hands, her arms, her once-bonny face, were all painfully thin.

It was the fault of the war. Its horror even reached out to touch young girls who by rights should have been home with their mothers with nothing more to worry them than which hair ribbons to wear that morning.

'Welcome home.' Helen tiptoed across the room.

'Don't worry now, Alice. I shall take care of you – and the baby.' She raised her eyes to the sky. 'And thank you, God, with all my heart. Thank you for this day . .'

'I am extremely put out, Edward.' Clementina Sutton paced the floor, heels tapping. 'I ordered the car to meet me. You knew I needed the Rolls-Royce at York at five.'

'Yes, but it was out; I'd offered it to Giles, so I sent you another. He had to go to Holdenby. And I really don't see why you can't change trains at York – it's only a cockstride to the Place from Holdenby station.'

'I dislike the local train; you know I do. It is slow and dirty and often there are no decent seats on it.'

'That is because there is so little demand, locally, for first-class travel. But why are you so agitated, my dear? I asked you not to go to London. There is always the risk of an air-raid and you always come back upset these days.'

'Then don't blame me! Blame this awful war that parts a mother from her sons and causes shortages and restrictions and –'

'I think our soldiers in the trenches would be happy to take on your shortages and restrictions, Clemmy.' Her husband's retort was touched with reproof. 'And why did you hare off to London without so much as a word when there was really no need?'

'There was *every* need! I heard from Molly that things are happening next door.'

'Molly?'

'Of course *Molly*! You know of her! The basement woman at Cheyne Walk, the one who caretakes! She wrote to me.'

'You said next door was empty,' Edward reasoned gently. 'Has someone broken in – done damage?'

'No, but I was right! As soon as I got there –'

Signs not of occupation, exactly; curtains at the windows, though. Heavy curtains. And a tall strange man with a thick beard appearing from the basement area, marching glowering around the house, disappearing again. Not so much a caretaker like herself, Molly had confided in awed tones; more of a *keeper*. Most likely they'd got someone locked up in the attic like in that novel. And not English. Molly had heard the bearded one shouting at a stray dog, chasing it away, slamming the gates shut. Swearing, he'd seemed to be, though she hadn't understood one word of it. But not French, she was sure of that. She'd have recognized swearing if it had been in French.

'I always knew it, Edward, from the minute next door moved out when the air-raids began! Refugees! "There'll be refugees in that house next door, mark my words if there isn't!" I said, and I was right!'

'But don't you feel some small compassion for them, Clemmy? To have had to leave their homes; not knowing whether they are still standing, probably leaving most of what they had behind them.'

'Why should I? Did I start the war, Edward? *Did* I? Oh, no, it was *them* started it. Molly said those people next door aren't like us; aren't even Europeans, if you ask me! But there'll be no more trouble. I've seen to that!'

'I wasn't aware there had been any,' Edward frowned.

'No, and there won't be now. I've had a carpenter in. He has built an eight-foot fence all round the back. That should keep them out!'

'And your daylight too. But are you sure the refugees want to invade the back garden?'

'Those peculiar people will invade anything, if the mood takes them. It's why this war started; why it has lasted almost four years. *Four* years it'll be, come August, and the end of it nowhere in sight! I swear my nerves are in shreds! And why did Giles need the car? Are they so down-at-heel at the Garth that they can't buy a motor?'

'You know how Helen feels about motors, though I fear she's going to have to acknowledge their existence soon. They are here to stay. When the war is over, they'll be much in demand.' Change the subject. Refugees upset Clemmy; especially refugees living next door. 'It wouldn't surprise me if they don't turn out a small motor most people can afford – just as Mr Ford does, over in America.'

'A *people's* car?' Clementina's eyebrows rose. Every Tom, Dick and Harry on the roads, honking and tooting? Trippers all over the place? Oh, but she hoped not! 'And what did Giles need with our motor when he's still supposed to be an invalid?'

'Giles *is* an invalid and will always be so. He's been given a medal because of it. And he needed the car to meet his wife at Holdenby. She was returning from France, where she was a nurse.'

'Ha! And that's another thing! Why was I the last to hear of it? Why wasn't I told? Had to get it secondhand from Aunt Sutton last night that Giles had married a nurse! Don't gawp, Edward. Kept it quiet, didn't they? How long have you known?'

'Since Giles was discharged from hospital, about a week ago.'

'And it didn't occur to you to tell me?'

'You were in London.'

'So didn't you think to pick up the telephone?'

'No. I imagined – quite rightly, it seems – that you would hear of it from Aunt Sutton.'

'Hm. Well . . . I shall call on Helen in the morning! What else do you know about it? You'll have been to Rowangarth, I take it?'

'I have. Helen told me Giles is discharged on medical

718

grounds; a civilian now. Oh, and there was a letter from Nathan this morning. I read it, then left it on your desk.'

'How long did it take to get here?'

'About three weeks. At the time of writing he was well. He said he'd met Elliot, though they hadn't had much time together. But read it for yourself.'

Edward reached for his jacket. A walk was indicated, for when Clemmy read Nathan's letter – read that Giles's wife was the pretty little sewing-maid from Rowangarth and that Nathan himself had married them in the chapel of a convent in France, they would hear her dismay as far away as Creesby! He hadn't been married to Clemmy all these years not to know that. And be blowed if he wasn't going to go over to the Garth tomorrow with her and wish the youngsters well; congratulate Giles on his medal.

Strange, though, that Helen hadn't thought to mention the wedding until recently, Edward frowned, or even put an announcement in the papers. But likely Giles hadn't been able to tell her, being wounded so soon afterwards; and anyway, it seemed to have been a quiet affair. Rather nice to think Nathan had married Giles and his lady – Alice, wasn't she called?

Clemmy wouldn't like it, mind; had called the poor girl all manner of names after the Brattocks Wood affair, even though Elliot had been entirely to blame for it and deserved all he'd got. But that was forgotten now, and rightly so, he thought gratefully.

Quietly he crossed the huge, echoing hall and slipped out of a side door. Poor Clemmy. Got herself into such tizzies; mostly over nothing, too.

He breathed deeply on the soft evening air until his lungs were full to bursting, then made for the hills. A walk to the top of Holdenby Pike was exactly what he needed.

* * *

Alice awoke, threw on a shawl, then tiptoed to the attic room that once had been her own. Closing the door quietly, she switched on the light, blinking in its sudden glare.

She ran a forefinger, Sister Carbrooke fashion, along the dressing-table top. Everything was clean, exactly as it had been more than two years ago. Her trunk stood beneath the slope of the ceiling still; slippers, hand-knitted by Tilda, lay beneath the bedside chair. She pushed her bare feet into them and their warm softness gave her comfort.

What now to wear? Her uniform had accommodated her swelling figure; the white apron, tied less tightly at her waist, disguised her swelling breasts. She had been a slip of a thing when she and Julia left for France; thinner than she'd ever been with all the running about there had been at Denniston House.

Now her best grey costume wouldn't go near her, she frowned, taking it from the wardrobe. She had always thought to wear it to her wedding, but there would be no wedding, now – not to Tom. She would never see him again and she didn't know why she was allowing herself even to think of him when such foolish indulgences sent white-hot pains slicing through her. And it were best she should remember she was married to Giles now, and be thankful for it, though she'd never be his wife; not really a wife.

She returned the costume to its hook, then quietly opened a drawer, lifting out the black cardigan her lady-ship had given her at the end of her mourning for Sir John. It had been a little on the large side, but far too good to refuse. Now, unbuttoned, it would disguise her thickening figure, and it wouldn't take her long to ease out the waistband of one of her skirts, move the buttons on her best blouse.

Carefully she crept down the back stairs, walking softly

to the sewing-room, closing the door with hardly a click. Someone had been using the sewing-machine. It was threaded with black cotton; a pair of sharp-pointed scissors lay beside it.

She began to snip at the waistband, resisting the urge to stand at the window, look down at the bothy. But no one lived there, now. Davie and Will and Tom had all gone and the garden apprentices and improvers. How many would return, and would Jin go back there to care for them when they did?

Tom wasn't coming back. She hugged herself tightly, fighting back tears. She was Lady Sutton now, and she would have to learn to act as Lady Helen acted and not allow herself to burst into tears like some foolish housemaid.

But she *was* a housemaid; under-housemaid, before she'd taken over the sewing. Glad of the scrubbing and cleaning an' all; to be away from Aunt Bella and learn to laugh and have second helpings and fall in love.

Leave me, Tom? Leave me be? I'll always love you. It isn't possible for me to love again. I'll be a good wife to Giles; he'll need nursing for the rest of his days. But never think, Tom, that I shall forget you, or that every leaf on every tree in Brattocks won't whisper your name to me, nor every buttercup that ever grows won't remind me of what I lost.

She sniffed, pulling the sleeve of her nightdress across her eyes; taking a shuddering gulp of air, pulling it down into her stomach. Then she glanced up sharply.

'Tilda!'

'Ooooh! I heard someone – I never thought . . .' She dropped her eyes to her shoes, embarrassed.

'Tilda, it's good to see you! So long, isn't it? Two years . . .'

'Yes, milady.' Tilda bobbed a curtsey, eyes still lowered.

'Tilda – *no*! Don't do that! I'm home again!'

'Home. Aye, but to upstairs. We've got to watch ourselves. Miss Clitherow said so. You're a milady now.'

'But not here? Not in the sewing-room, Tilda? I suppose it's going to take some getting used to – me being married.'

'Married to the *gentry*.'

'Tom was – Tom died . . .'

'Aye, so he did. Him and millions of others.' She said it with condescension as if, partly, to excuse Alice's haste in finding herself another man to love.

'Tilda, *please*? Oh, I know things will have to be different, but you and me were friends. In the sewing-room, can't we be Tilda and Alice? It's going to be lonely here, for me . . .'

'You've got Sir Giles, milady. And might I be excused? There's the fire to see to for breakfast. And to save time, will I bring yours to your room? The hens are laying well, now; it's boiled eggs this morning.'

'Thank you. I won't have an egg. Just a little bread and marmalade. I'll be giving my food card to Miss Clitherow. They gave me one when I left France. I'm not a nurse any longer. I get civilian rations now.'

Her words hung on the air, a silent appeal for understanding, but they were wasted on the housemaid.

'Will you take it in the morning-room or your bedroom, milady?'

'Neither, thank you. I'll have my breakfast here, in the sewing-room, Tilda.'

She smiled, trying to do it as Lady Helen would have done, and the effort hurt her lips. Teeth clenched tightly, she returned to her sewing.

After breakfast, and when she had made sure Giles was comfortable, she would take Morgan and walk the long way through Brattocks; visit Reuben. Reuben would understand that it was Alice come to see him and not milady. She would have to learn to walk again in Brattocks, lean on the rearing-field gate, aye, and even look at the buttercups she knew would be growing golden in the pasture this very day; learn to do it all again. Without Tom.

She felt a sudden upsurge of nausea and hoped that Tilda wouldn't be long in coming. Dry bread, Ruth had told her, or a plain biscuit, often helped relieve morning sickness.

Where are you, Ruth? And you, Julia?

She glanced at the mantel-clock, still ticking away as if the years between had never happened.

Day duty, that's what. Just getting dressed, they would be, then off to breakfast and to collect the trolley for Hut Twenty-four.

Who would be sleeping in her bed, now; sharing the curtained bed-space with Julia, folding her uniform into the drawers that Alice Hawthorn had once used?

I miss you, Julia. I wish the letters came more quickly. I need to hear from you. And it isn't any of Alice Hawthorn's business who sleeps in her bed in the schoolhouse because Alice Hawthorn is gone. She ceased to live and breathe one night in March. The twenty-sixth of March, if you want to be exact. A little after half-past eight. On a straw-filled palliasse in the shed where the nuns once kept their milk cows. That was when Alice Hawthorn ceased to be – she and Tom Dwerryhouse both.

So get on with letting that skirt out, Milady Sutton, or the whole of the Riding is going to know you are pregnant with a bairn you don't want . . .

'Come in,' she said sharply, in answer to Tilda's knock.

Alice cast a practised eye on the thermometer, let go of Giles's wrist.

'You'll do,' she smiled, 'though you shouldn't have met me yesterday. It was more tiring than you thought, wasn't it?'

'Yes, Nurse,' Giles smiled. 'I'll admit it, but every day I'm a little better; I know it.'

'I'm bound to agree there's a lot more to recommend you than the poor soul they brought into Hut Twenty-four that night,' Alice sighed. 'And there's still the best of the summer ahead of you. Peace and quiet and sunshine are great healers. By Christmas, when Julia and Andrew might be home –'

'And the baby born –'

'Aye. By then, you'll be stronger in every way. Your just being here is a miracle.'

'I know it, Alice. I remember so much about it. That awful explosion that made me feel as if I were blind and deaf and dumb for a moment. Then lying there, wondering if I were dead.'

'Don't, Giles. It's over – a bad dream.'

'It won't ever be over. And I want to tell you about it because that miracle very nearly didn't happen. I remember lying there, wanting to die, wanting to live. Then someone came for me.'

'Like you so often crawled out into No Man's Land to bring some other soldier to safety, Giles.'

'I felt a jab. I knew what they were giving me, Alice, that I would soon feel a kind of peace; floating above my body, not caring. The darkness came then and I seemed to slip in and out of it. A part of me wanted to let go – to die; the other part of me couldn't, because there was a voice in my head. It wouldn't go away. I tried not to listen to it, but it kept calling me back to Rowangarth; all the time insisting that Rowangarth needed me.

'It was your voice I heard, and I know it was your hand, holding mine so tightly that I couldn't float away. It *was* you, wasn't it? It was you wouldn't let me die that night?'

'We were all willing you to live, not only me. I just sat with you, talked to you, that's all. Julia would have, but

724

Sister said she wasn't to. Nathan came that night – did you know that? He prayed for you and blessed you.'

'So many good friends . . .' Then he smiled, his eyes bright with mischief. 'Do you think I might sit in the conservatory? It's such a lovely morning and, that way, I can hide behind the plants when Aunt Clemmy comes. And you don't have to be there,' he hastened, seeing the look of alarm that widened her eyes. 'Mother wants all the glory this morning – if you'll agree to her telling people about the baby now? She wants to. Can she, Alice?'

'Aye. It's all right. Folk'll have to know sooner or later. She can tell them it'll be a Christmas baby.'

'And will it?'

'I'm not sure, but Christmas will suffice for now. And I'd like to go to Keeper's – see Reuben. He'll know I'm back. Wouldn't be right if I didn't.'

'Good idea. Take Morgan with you. He'll take care of you. Mother will understand – and, Alice . . .' He grasped her hand, holding it tightly. 'Thank you for making Mother so happy. We won't regret what we did, I promise you.'

'What *we* did? We got married, that was all.'

'I know. But thanks all the same.'

'It's me should thank you. I hate him, you know. I'll hate him as long as I live. You said yesterday you were taking Elliot's child. Well, you aren't. I give it to you gladly, for I don't want it.'

'Alice! Please, *no*? You'll love it when it's born!'

'I won't. I try not to look at my body, Giles. It's getting ugly and it'll get uglier. It's a nightmare I've got inside me, not a child – so you'll understand how grateful I am to you and her ladyship. And if you could bear with me, try not to let my bitterness spoil things for you? You want this child; if it wasn't for that, I couldn't go on living.'

725

'Poor little Alice. Off you go and see Reuben – tell him about it. Reuben will understand.'

'I shall tell him the truth, Giles. He'll say nothing; he'll keep it a secret. But Julia knows and Ruth Love knows and Nathan, too. It's only right I should tell Reuben. For my sake, he'll never tell.'

'I know he won't, and I agree he should know. So come on, Nurse Sutton. Give me a hand to the conservatory, then be off with you, into that lovely sunshine. Reuben makes a mashing of tea round about this time, if I'm not mistaken.'

'You are a kind man.' Fleetingly she laid her lips to his cheek. 'And I hope it's a boy. About time you had a little of your own goodness back.' She smiled fleetingly, picking up his walking-sticks. 'Let's disappear before Mrs Clementina arrives . . .'

Reuben's kettle was indeed on the hob, and when Morgan burst into his kitchen, did a wild circuit, then skittered out again, he knew it would be Alice he would see, walking up his path. He held wide his arms, his pale eyes dimming with tears.

'Lass!' He held her to him, his unshaven cheek rough on hers. 'Eh, lovey, but I've missed you. Come on in and tell me if it's right that the nurse young Giles wedded in France was our little Alice. I couldn't believe it when I heard.'

'It's true. I did write, telling you, three weeks ago, but the letters haven't been getting through. Perhaps it'll arrive soon.'

'It's all right. I'm only teasing. I'm that glad to see you I'd forgive you anything.'

He took the teapot from the mantel, setting it to warm.

'Then will you forgive me for having a baby, Reuben, because I am.' Best say it quickly.

'A babbie,' Reuben gasped. 'Giles's, or Tom's?'

'Bless you for not saying "Are you sure?"' Alice laughed shakily. 'And it belongs to neither. It was the night I heard about Tom – that he'd been killed. There was no one I could tell about it: Julia was in Paris with Andrew. I just ran and ran, crying all the time. Then I met up with Elliot Sutton.

'I thought he was a part of the nightmare, but he wasn't.

'I had to tell you, Reuben. Only me and Giles know about it, and Julia, and Nathan Sutton who married us. Giles won't ever have a child – his injuries, you see – that's why he married me. And you're not to say a word to anyone about that either. Her ladyship thinks the child is Giles's, and that's the way it'll always have to be. You'll never tell?'

'Eh, lass.' Reuben shook his head sadly, sitting down heavily. 'I swear that if that arrogant young swine was to walk through that door, I'd take a gun to him!'

'No you wouldn't. Elliot Sutton was so drunk the night it happened that I doubt he even knew it was me he – he –'

'Aye, lovey. Aye. Best we try to forget about it. Some good came of it. Her ladyship'll get her grandchild, after all. Let's hope you give her a lad. It would make up for losing one son to the war and the other being sent back only half a man.'

'But say you won't *tell*?' Alice insisted.

'You know I won't! When's it due, then?'

'Round about Christmas.'

'Well now. Christmas is a nice time to have a babbie born. And what you told me is forgotten already. Only I'll not forget about Elliot Sutton. I'll bide my time, lass, but I'll do him a mischief if ever I can.'

'Forget him – and can I stay with you for a while? Her ladyship has been bursting to tell folk about her grandchild, and this morning she's going to. She'll be telling that Mrs Clementina and I can just imagine the sneer on that woman's face when she finds out it's me that's having it.'

'And you as is Lady Sutton now. That'll not please her, either. Does it please you, lass?'

'No, Reuben. I'd rather have lived here at Keeper's with Tom, but I've got to count my blessings. Giles wanted a son; I have one that I didn't want to conceive. It seemed the right thing to do – for us to marry. If Tom hadn't been killed I'd have told him, hoped he'd have stood by me.'

'He would have, lass. But then –' Reuben rubbed his chin reflectively. 'If Tom hadn't been killed you'd not have run out all upset and straight into Elliot Sutton's path. It's a queer carry-on, and no mistake. Treating you all right, are they?'

'Aye. Her ladyship is so pleased. This morning she kept giving little smiles and I knew she was thinking about the baby and that Mrs Sutton from Pendenys was coming and how she couldn't wait to tell her.

'But Miss Clitherow is polite – too polite – and when I wanted to talk to Tilda Tewk she went all uppity on me and reminded me of my position. I haven't seen Mrs Shaw yet, nor Jin Dobb. I hope they'll take it a bit better. If they knew the truth of it, they'd be on my side.'

'But you can't tell them the truth, Alice, so you'd best stop fretting about it. And *I'm* pleased for you, no matter who fathered that babbie. And, like you say, happen Elliot Sutton doesn't remember it happened.'

'And he'll never know, will he, Reuben?'

'Not from me he won't, so let's have that tea. And Lady Sutton or not, you'll sup out of the same mug as Alice did!'

'You're an old love, Reuben,' she choked, blinking away a tear. 'I hoped you'd understand – and about Tom, too.'

'Aye, well, it's a funny old world we're living in.' Reuben blew his nose noisily. 'And I'm here, don't forget, if things get a bit too much for you. If you want to unburden, I'll listen. And I'll never ask you anything you don't think fit to tell. So don't fret none, eh lass?'

'Thank you, Reuben,' she said softly.

She had never loved him more.

42

July, and the enemy armies almost at Reims, driving further on to a place on the map called Epernay. And all along the front line, heavy attacks at Vimy and Ypres and the Somme and nearer to Celverte than they had ever been.

Was Julia still there, Alice fretted, laying aside the newspaper. Had General Hospital Sixteen been evacuated or had it been overrun?

There had been one letter only, written a month ago. Fighting lines could change overnight, Alice knew. The letter, though Lady Helen had opened it with relief, did not guarantee Julia's safety, nor that of the wounded in her care.

The Germans did not kill babies nor rape nuns – that was a nonsense put out by men in small back rooms to whip up hatred for the enemy – but a screaming shell was no respecter of persons. One only could wipe out the ward on which Julia worked.

Why didn't you come home with me, Julia? Why must you stay there so stubbornly Sutton when you have done all and more than is required of you?

But would Alice Hawthorn have even considered returning to England? Would she have given up, given in, left Tom in the trenches when well she could have stayed – to meet him, perhaps, at the turning of a corner?

But she was no longer that girl, and Alice Sutton was pregnant, and pregnant women were of no use on the Western Front. And it wasn't a pregnancy, it was a punishment, and when her labour began, every pain would be inflicted by Elliot Sutton, and the child would nurse at her breasts with *his* mouth. It would live and thrive because of who had fathered it, but maybe she would die at the birthing? She sometimes hoped she would.

She jumped, clucking, to her feet. There was so little to do, save eat as many of the right things as were available to a woman in her condition, take gentle exercise, keep her mind peaceful and her thoughts beautiful, Doctor James had stressed, so her child might be perfectly born.

Julia! I want to come back to Celverte! I want this nightmare never to have happened. I want to be Alice Hawthorn again and Tom still alive!

Damn this war and damn the German who wiped out Tom's life as if it were of no consequence! And she was sick and tired of being a sewing-maid with a title that insisted she was a lady!

They would be having tea-break downstairs – she would go and share their pot, sit at the table as she had always done! They couldn't refuse her; wasn't she Lady Sutton now? If she insisted, surely they would allow her back?

She heard Cook's sobbing before ever she pushed open the kitchen door; heard the agitated rocking of the fireside chair.

'Mrs Shaw – what's wrong?'

'This whole world is wrong. It's gone mad; *mad*, I say,' came the muffled cries from the depths of her apron.

'Tell me?' Alice laid an arm around the quivering shoulders.

'You haven't read the papers, then? Surely you've seen it?'

'I know the Germans are advancing, but they can be thrown back just as easily,' she comforted.

'But what about that poor King of Russia, eh? How could they do it? And his bairns an' all . . .'

Alice picked up the newspaper from where it had been flung. It was a special edition; four pages only, printed later than the one she had just read.

RUSSIAN ROYAL FAMILY MURDERED, blazed the headlines. *At a house in Ekaterinburg, Nicholas II, Czar of all the Russias, his Consort and children were put to death by a Bolshevik firing squad on or about Tuesday 16 July . . .*

'It can't be true, Mrs Shaw,' Alice whispered. 'They couldn't kill their Czar. The papers have got it wrong again.'

'They've done it, all right, and him crowned and anointed. And what harm did that sick little lad of his ever do to anybody, aye, and them Grand Duchesses, too?' Cook was a Royalist through and through, extending her respect to the Czar even though his soldiers hadn't done all that well for us in the fighting and taken themselves off when we'd needed them most. 'If it can happen there it can happen here. If we don't win something, soon, there'll be revolution on our streets an' all, and the gentry stood up against a wall and shot! They had a revolution in France – now Russia. Who's to say it won't – '

'Of course it won't happen here. This is England, Mrs Shaw. It could *not* happen to us. Come on, now – dry your eyes. I'll put the kettle on and we'll all have a cup and a chat, just like it used to be. I haven't seen hide nor hair of you since I came home. Let's pretend, shall we, that this war never happened and that Bess and Mary will be coming down soon for a – '

'But it *has* happened.' All at once, Cook was on her feet, taking the kettle from Alice's hand. 'Bess and Mary are gone and you can't turn back the clock. It isn't right you should come down here, supping tea with servants!'

Breathing deeply, defiantly, she dabbed at her eyes with her apron corner.

'But it's *me*, Alice!'

'No. You went away Alice and you've come back her ladyship. I'd like it if you'd go or Miss Clitherow'll find you here and it'll be me and Tilda and Jin what gets the sharp edge of her tongue!'

'No!' Alice wanted to cry that they wouldn't; that Miss Clitherow could not say her nay if she wanted to drink tea in her own kitchen!

But it wasn't her kitchen. It was Lady Helen's and ever would be, and you didn't make a silk purse from a sow's ear, though try telling that to the straight-laced Agnes Clitherow who was the worst snob in the Riding. And upstairs and below-stairs didn't mix. Giles Sutton wouldn't have looked at her twice had he been choosing a wife as he should have; wouldn't even have considered her, but for the bairn he so desperately needed.

Yet she *was* Lady Sutton, and though Doctor James and Mrs Effie had been kindness itself, and Mr Lane and Mrs Letty – aye, and Lady Tessa an' all – they'd only done it from genteel politeness, and because she carried her ladyship's precious grandchild.

And how was she to rear that child when it was born – she who knew nothing of the ways of the gentry? Would she be allowed to take over its upbringing? Wouldn't it be best, once it was all over, if she were to go; vanish as if Alice Hawthorn had never been; leave them their child and find some place to start afresh, alone?

'I'm sorry.' She backed towards the door. 'I wouldn't want to get any of you into trouble. I didn't think, Mrs Shaw. I won't come down here again; please forgive me.'

'Nay – oh, that's not what I mean!' Cook's face flushed red. 'You are mistress of this house, now – or could be if you wanted to. And by right, an' all.' The plump, elderly woman looked down at her anxiously twisting fingers. 'But what I'm trying to say is that you aren't one of us any longer. You are Sir Giles's wife, and we've all got to remember it. And that's an order from Miss Clitherow.'

'What have I ever done to Miss Clitherow to deserve this?' Alice choked.

'Nothing, I suppose – and everything.' Cook lifted her head, gazing into Alice's eyes. 'I'd appreciate it if you'd bear in mind what I've just said. With respect, that is, and remembering the fondness I've always had for you. I'm mistress in this kitchen, but your place is upstairs now. It has to be said . . .'

Alice turned and, closing the door quietly behind her, walked slowly up the wooden stairs. Cook was right. She didn't belong below stairs now, any more than the saying of the wedding service and the ring she wore meant that all at once she was as good as her betters.

Best she should run away – but where to? Who in all of this world wanted her?

She crossed the hall, sped down the stone steps outside the sturdy front door, and made for Keeper's Cottage. Reuben knew; he would understand. She could pour out her unhappiness to him; weep until there were no tears left in her.

Then he would take a clean handkerchief from the top, left-hand drawer, mop her eyes, and send her back to where she now belonged.

I want to die when this bairn is born, God, and You'd be doing me a service if You'd let me!

And for shame, Alice Hawthorn! For shame to think such dreadful things when there are young men fighting with their last breath to stay alive. At this very minute, there were at least two score of them, in Hut Twenty-four and oh, Julia, how I wish I could turn back the clock . . .

The tide of the war began to turn. High summer had seen an Allied counter-offensive on the Western Front, though the newspapers were not allowed to print the entire truth for fear of raising hopes too high. Then, to Cook's great joy, it began to be cautiously admitted that the enemy had not only been halted but pushed back, in places. She read and reread the newspapers now, sure as ever she could be that by Christmas it would all be over. The lads would be home and there'd be all the flour and sugar and butter that any cook could ever want and she would roast the biggest piece of sirloin that dratted oven could accommodate!

'I think,' said Helen, 'that our little baby might well be born into a world at peace, Alice. And we must never let such a terrible thing happen again. We have the vote now. We must use it!'

'*You* have the vote, Mother-in-law.' Alice shifted uncomfortably in her chair. 'And please don't set your hopes too high on a boy? It might just as easy be a girl.'

'Does it matter? It will be *my* grandchild. Clemmy doesn't know how lucky she is, yet she rarely talks about that little boy in Kentucky.'

'Sebastian,' Alice murmured. 'An unusual name.'

'Yes. He's starting to talk. In Albert's last letter he said the little one calls himself Bas. Do you know, Albert's marriage was one of convenience – no one tried to deny it. There were hurtful remarks, too, from some quarters. Yet now he seems so very happy. I think he will bring his wife and son to England when the war ends. Clemmy hasn't met her daughter-in-law and – '

The conservatory door opened and a red-cheeked Tilda offered a salver with a flourish nothing short of triumphant.

'Milady! Did you ever see so many letters? Eight, and nearly all from France. Miss Clitherow says it's a good sign.'

'Two for you, Alice, and oh! six for me. Thank you, Tilda.'

Helen rewarded her housemaid with a brilliant smile, sending her back to the kitchen on a cloud of contentment, she being the one to have brought such good news.

'Mine are from Julia.' Alice tilted the envelopes, the better to see the postmark. 'Written some time ago, but to get so many at once – it's got to mean that things are getting better over there.'

'Mine are from Nathan, Andrew and Julia – and one from India, from Cecilia. Such a feast. Let's read them, then exchange news?'

'Would you mind if I shared mine with Giles?' Alice worried about him. What little she knew about nursing confirmed that his return to full health would never be. For the rest of his life, Giles would have good days and bad days; might never walk again without the help of sticks.

It was because of this, and because of his goodness, that she was able to show her affection in small ways: by never leaving him alone for too long; by anticipating his periods of silence that indicated pain he was reluctant to admit to; by talking about the child she carried, though it pained her to do it.

'I shall claim a father's right and choose the name if we have a son.'

Already the child she carried was his own – Rowangarth's – yet to her it was still a child of rape, conceived on the day she had learned of Tom's death.

'I have letters,' she smiled, 'from Julia. And Mother-in-law has six.' She settled herself at his side. This was one of his good days; he should be outside, she frowned. Already it was August: the warm days, soon, would grow less.

'And I have two. Tilda brought them to me. One from Julia and one from Nathan. He asks after your health, by the way.'

'He's a kind man. I think if he were here, he'd want you outside in the sunshine. They're cutting the wheat. Why don't I take you there?'

Every grain of corn was precious; the harvest had never before been so important.

'No. You mustn't push my chair now.'

'But from here to the field isn't far, though if you really want to go, I can ask Reuben to give a hand.'

'Do you think he might, Alice? I'd like to go out.'

'Then you shall!'

Reuben was not at Keeper's; Morgan sniffed him out at the far end of the wood, looking up into the tallest trees.

'Now then, Alice lass.' His smile was one of pleasure. 'Summat I can do for you?'

'Yes, there is.' She could be herself in Reuben's company, and she smiled happily. 'I want you to help me push Giles to the ten-acre field. He'd like to watch the harvesting, but won't let me take him there.'

'Nor must you.' He bent to fondle the spaniel's ears. 'What time shall it be?'

'About two, if you can spare a couple of hours.'

'Time is what I've got plenty of, these days. No rearing, no growers to see to; no shoots like there used to be. Just showing myself from time to time to warn the poachers off – though there's little in the way of game-birds to take now. That old war has a lot to answer for.'

'That it has, Reuben – I should know. But tell me – what do you find so interesting about those trees?'

'Trees? Why do you ask?' His reply was too sharp. 'A keeper has to have his eyes everywhere, you should know that.'

'Then tell me – where are the rooks? Because that's why you haven't had your eyes off those elms all the time I've been here.' She said it lightly, yet all the time knowing she should have known better than to ask. '*I* haven't heard them, come to think of it, these few nights past . . .' She liked the rooks in Brattocks Wood; they were a part of Rowangarth, with their lazy, sunset cawing as they settled to roost. They were her friends, keepers of her secrets, and if they ever left . . . 'And do you believe what folks say, Reuben – that if those birds ever leave Brattocks sorrow will strike the Suttons?'

'Who's been telling you nonsense like that? Jin Dobb, was it, the daft old biddy?'

'No one told me; I think I've known it all along. And they aren't there, Reuben. They've gone.'

'Happen not at this moment. They'll be out, foraging. They'll be back.'

'They *must* come back. They can't go, Reuben . . .'

'Lass! Stop your fretting. It's nowt but a nonsense. Rooks are canny birds; have better instincts than humans. And those elms are old; rooks know when a tree might blow down. Like as not they're just flying round, looking for a safer place to nest,' he comforted.

'The elms aren't old. Sir John had them planted, the same year as him and her ladyship were wed. You told me so. They're good for fifty years yet. And the rooks *have* gone . . .'

'Will you give over nattering? All that talk is superstition. They'll be back, I tell you. Now, about this afternoon. I'll be up at the house after dinner and we'll take Sir Giles round the back way – no steps, round the back. I reckon we might go by way of the garden. Percy'd like to see him; might appreciate a visit. Us'll have a rare afternoon, Alice, if you think the master's up to it.'

'He's grand today, though other times I know he's in pain. What do you think to him, Reuben?'

'He's no worse'n he was when he comed home. Better, in fact. He looked right badly the day they brought him back to Rowangarth. And he's a better colour now,' he added for good measure. Reuben set great store by colour. A body was either a good colour or a bad colour; healthy or ill. As simple as that.

'We'll make it a good afternoon, Reuben – not let him tire himself?'

'Us will, lass.' An outing would do Alice good an' all;

her looking that pinched and tired sometimes, and dark rings under her eyes that had never been there before. 'Come on, then.' He offered his arm. 'Let's walk back nice and gentle and forget those rooks, the daft old things.'

She smiled up into his eyes. 'I've forgotten them already. I'm not superstitious.'

But she *hadn't* – and she *was* . . .

By early September, when the harvest stubble had been ploughed in and a nip in the air warned of autumn, it became certain the war was going in favour of the Allies. French, American and British troops pushed the enemy out of France, then began the slow liberation of Belgium.

By the end of the month, Bulgaria sued for peace and, soon after, came reluctant offers of co-operation from the German High Command. Austria surrendered, and Turkey; it was becoming almost too much to bear.

Cook could not so much as open a newspaper, and Tilda was obliged to read the news to a Cook terrified it would all come to nothing; that the Germans would produce some fearful weapon even more deadly than Big Bertha and the awful business would begin all over again.

In November, the Kaiser abdicated his throne and fled his country. The Allies had won the war. Nothing, now, could stop them! Weeks – *days*, even – and it would all be over. No more killing; no more sacrificing young lives to the god of Teutonic arrogance. Lovers would love again; fathers see children for the first time. No more trenches, lice, the stench of death.

At daybreak on the eleventh of November 1918, all fighting ceased. At eleven o'clock, an armistice was signed. *It was over!* Telephone lines sang the news all over Britain; church bells rang out, motor horns blared, women banged tin trays with wooden spoons; many a pan on many a hob boiled dry from neglect.

'Helen!' It was Edward, telephoning. 'We are opening champagne! Come over?'

'Can't! We are opening it too! Oh, Edward, I can't stop weeping, it's so wonderful!'

In towns and cities, work came to a standstill, and men and women from shops and factories and offices spilled out on to the streets, dancing, hugging, laughing, singing. At noon, Big Ben chimed out for the first time in years and the King and Queen stood on the balcony at Buckingham Palace, Queen Mary waving a Union Jack, would you believe!

'I've taken the liberty, milady . . .' Miss Clitherow emerged from the cellar carrying a bottle of champagne

'Miss Clitherow! *One* bottle? For shame!' Helen laughed. The housekeeper disappeared to return, flushed and triumphant, with two more.

'Tilda – be a dear, good girl and find Reuben and Catchpole, will you? We must all celebrate!'

Crystal glasses, unused since Julia's wedding, were quickly polished; corks popped, champagne fizzed and spilled.

'Alice, darling – it's *over*!' Helen hugged her son's wife, kissing her soundly. 'I knew we'd have a peacetime baby; I *knew* it!'

Over. Alice took her place at Giles's side. Helen held up her hand.

'Please – everyone . . . Shall we first thank God it is all over and remember those who are still away from us and,' her voice fell to a whisper, 'those who will never come home.'

Giles reached for Alice's hand, holding it tightly 'Over,' he said softly. 'No more killing . . .'

'And Julia and Andrew home for Christmas,' Alice murmured. She would like to have Julia beside her when her time came. Julia would understand.

'Let's try to be happy today, Alice. You and I – we

know how it was over there – but let's try not to think too deeply about *anything* . . .'

He raised his glass to Agnes Clitherow, who smiled back broadly, tilting her glass with her little finger genteelly raised, whilst on the bottom step of the great staircase from which Sutton ancestors gazed down, Jinny Dobb lapped contentedly at her glass, not at all sure she could ever quite take to champagne, but appreciating the feeling it gave to her. It was why she had been obliged to sit down, truth known.

Cook drained her glass and thought happily about pounds and pounds of butter, sugar by the sackful, dinner parties every week. Tilda shared her dreams with David, who had been in the fighting – well, *near* it – even though he needn't have bothered.

Percy Catchpole regarded his daft little glass balefully, wishing it were a pint tankard and full of ale; Reuben gazed over to Brattocks to the almshouse he'd waited four long years to move into, hoping that Jin Dobb would shift herself sharpish and be off back to the bothy, where she rightly belonged. He looked over to where Alice stood, giving her a smile and a nod to let her know that he, too, was remembering.

'I can't stop weeping,' Helen laughed, taking a fresh handkerchief, dabbing happily at her eyes. 'And Julia will be home and Andrew and oh, Miss Clitherow, pour yourself another glass, *do*!'

It was a good day; a day four years too long in coming. There would be no work done today at Rowangarth; no rhyme or reason in anything anyone did, but who cared? It was over! *It was over!*

That night, when Giles slept, Alice walked in slippered feet to the sewing-room. Every light in every window made Rowangarth a blaze of light, but the bothy, locked and silent, stood dark and apart.

. . . those who will never come home. Her hand reached for the locket at her throat.

It's over, Tom. When we thought we'd lost, almost, the war turned round on itself and we won! I want you to know there won't ever be a day I don't think of you and send you my love and want you till it hurts.

I'm all right now. Giles will look after me and the child, when it is born. And one day I shall find you, Tom. And I'll bring you buttercups, like I promised . . .

Alice was the first to see Julia. She was crossing the cow pasture, hands in pockets, head down, as if she had walked from Holdenby.

Frowning, she reached for her shawl, then ran quickly down the back stairs. How like her! How exactly like Julia to arrive, not in the carriage or the station cab or even in one of Pendenys's cars. No! She must savour the moment; leave her luggage at the station, then walk the last miles home in the crisp cold of an early December afternoon.

'Julia! My dear, you're back!' Alice ran, arms wide, then stopped in her tracks. 'Julia – what is it? What's wrong? And what on earth made you want to walk? You're blue with cold!'

Julia's eyes sought those of her friend. They were dull; dark with pain. 'Cold? Yes, it *is* cold,' she murmured as if the thought had only just occurred to her.

'Julia:' Alice's voice was low with concern. 'Tell me what's wrong? You look awful. Have you been ill? Have you caught this 'flu that's about? Hurry, let's get you to bed; then we'll call Doctor James.'

'Alice – listen, please? I haven't told anyone. I was waiting to tell *you* . . .'

'Tell me?' Alice tried to speak but no sound came; just the moving of her lips. 'Tell me what, Julia?'

'Andrew. Dead . . .'

'No! Oh God, *no!*'

Julia nodded, her face a mask, then the words tumbled out in a rush of pain.

'Ruth Love first told us. It was over! The whole ward went mad. I'd never felt so happy. Then, just before we went off duty, someone brought me a telegram. On the sixth of November, it had happened – and I'd thought he was safe . . .'

'He isn't dead! He can't be! Come home?' Alice held out her hand. It would be all right, once they were home.

'Home? Dear God – how am I to tell Mother? How am I to face people? This pain inside me – it won't go away . . .'

'*Come home?*' Alice pulled Julia's arm into her own. 'We'll go in by the back door. There's a fire in the winter parlour. Mother-in-law is out. There'll be nobody but us – only please, Julia, don't look at me like that?' It was as if she were dead with only the fierce pain that blazed in her eyes to show she lived and breathed.

And please let it not be true, God? Let there have been some foolish, careless mistake? Not Andrew? Not Julia's love taken, too?

'On the sixth, the telegram said. He was up at the front line. He shouldn't have been there. I went to his hospital. I wouldn't believe it – had to find out for myself. Just walked out of the ward. I didn't care . . .'

'And?' Alice opened the back door, closing it quietly.

'He would have been all right, Alice. Four years he'd kept alive, and then a toothache got him. A bad tooth it was, not a bullet!' Her voice rose to a wail of torment as if her agony, once released, must have its terrible way.

'Sssssh.' Alice closed the parlour door, turning the key. She wanted no one here; no one but her and Julia. 'A bad tooth?'

'They told me at the hospital. One of the young doctors at a dressing-station at the Front had a raging toothache. Driving him mad. One of the stretcher-bearers brought back the message: could someone at the hospital give him something to take back with him to ease the poor man's pain, he said; something to put in the tooth to numb it. And Andrew said he could do better than that.

'He wasn't on duty, so he went back with the ambulance; said he'd take out the tooth, then put a dressing in it. Only he didn't. He never got there. The ambulance drove into a minefield – one of our own minefields, left behind in the advance, and unmarked. Four of them killed. Two stretcher-bearers, the driver and Andrew. My husband died because someone had an aching tooth . . .'

'There now, there, there . . .' Alice gathered the shaking body to her. 'Let it come, love? Alice understands . . .'

Tears ran silently down her cheeks as her friend, her sister, cried out her grief in great, tearing sobs.

'They gave me his things at the hospital – his instruments and clothes – and transport back to Celverte. I told Sister I was going home. I was so full of rage, of disgust. Ruth wanted me to cry, but I couldn't. Sister went to see Matron. They knew I'd be no more use to them, so they sent me home on sick leave . . .'

'But where have you been till now?' Alice brushed away her tears with an impatient hand.

'I went to Little Britain. D'you know, I thought I'd find him there, but there was only Sparrow. I slept in our bed. All London seemed happy and I hated them for it.

'Then I made myself open one of his cases. I suppose I needed to find something there – some sort of goodbye to convince me it really was true. Then I knew it was. There was his uniform in that case – the one he'd been wearing when it happened. They hadn't the decency to keep it from me. The front of his jacket and his shirt and vest – all blood-soaked and ripped. That mine must have torn his heart out. So what do I do now, Alice? Shall I go to Brattocks – tell it to the rooks? Do they bring dead lovers back?'

'The rooks have left, Julia . . .'

'Gone? Left Rowangarth? So it's sorrow to the Suttons, then. Which one of us is next?' She closed her eyes, shaking her head. 'Alice, I'm sorry! I shouldn't have said that – not to you, the way you are.' She looked at the swollen body as if seeing it clearly for the first time. 'Please, love, I'm sorry. And you *do* know. You've been through all this. How do you bear it? Is it going to get any better for me?'

'I don't know, Julia. I only know I shall never forgive those who allowed that war to happen. Let them that want a war fight it themselves, I say. They've taken your brother and your man – my Tom, too – and sent Giles home a poor wreck. Jin Dobb knows how to ill-wish, some say. I wish with all my heart I could do it.'

'Bear with me, Alice? When it gets too much to bear, be kind?'

'I shall be here, always. And your mother – she knows how it is, too.'

'Yes – but oh, Alice, less than a week and Andrew would have made it home. And there'll be no children now, for me.'

'Then you shall share this one – show me how it should be reared. I don't know the ways of the gentry, Julia – I need you, too.' She dropped awkwardly to her knees, unlacing Julia's shoes, placing them in the hearth. 'Your stockings are soaking an' all. Take them off. Your feet are like blocks of ice.' She took off her shawl, wrapping it round them. 'I'll build up the fire – stay by it, warm yourself. That's the pony and trap – your mother is back. Best leave it to me, to tell her . . .'

She turned the key in the lock, then closed the door behind her, doing it slowly to put off the moment. Her heart ached dully – not with grief, but with blind, passionate hatred for those who had caused the war, fuelled it uncaringly with young lives.

745

Perhaps you didn't have to learn how to ill-wish. Maybe it was there inside you all along and all you had to do was hate.

She did not know. All she was certain of was that Helen was smiling and waving, calling out to her to walk carefully on the stableyard cobbles – and that she, Alice, must tell her that Andrew wasn't coming home.

43

'I'm glad to have met you.' Alice stood at the open front door, saying goodbye to the midwife. 'It was thoughtful of Doctor James to send you.'

'I think it was two birds with one stone, Lady Sutton. The doctor is run off his feet with 'flu – an epidemic now – and he wanted me to look in on you. I shall be with him when your time comes, assisting . . .'

'This influenza – is it really bad?' Alice frowned.

'I'm afraid so. As if we hadn't had enough with the war – now people have more to worry about. A lot have no resistance to it – been undernourished for years, you see. But you are not to worry.' She believed in keeping mothers-to-be serene. 'Take a little gentle exercise when the weather allows, and keep away from anyone sniffing or sneezing, and you'll do nicely.'

Against all her instincts, Alice thought about Elliot Sutton, wondering how soon he would return to Pendenys Place.

Not yet, she hoped. She wouldn't want to think of him so near when her labour began. People said you forgot your labour when you held your child, but she wouldn't want to hold it; it would be like touching *him*. She shivered, visibly.

'You aren't worrying, Lady Sutton?' The nurse was quick to notice the worried frown. 'Believe me, if birthing was that awful, this world would be full of only children. I shall tell Doctor James you are a healthy young lady and that all is well. And don't fret. I am just a telephone call away,' she beamed.

Alice closed the door, walking carefully across the

hall, avoiding rugs that might slide beneath her feet, having care for small objects underfoot she was not able to see now. She was so big, so ugly.

'That was the midwife, come to check up on me.' She opened the library door, smiling at Giles who lifted his head from the book on his knee. 'Doctor James is busy with 'flu visits; I was warned to keep away from sniffles and sneezes.'

'And the baby?'

'Fine. She seemed well pleased. Doctor James puts great trust in her.'

'I'll be glad when it is over.'

'So shall I.' She threw back her head, forcing a laugh. 'Do you know – I swear I haven't seen my feet for over a week!'

'Poor little Hawthorn.' He took her hand and held it to his cheek. 'I'm grateful to you.'

'And me to you, so let's hear no more of your thanks. But I do so miss Julia. I wish she hadn't gone back to London. She says she wants to end the lease on Andrew's lodgings, but she doesn't really. She just wants to be near him. If she had given it a little time, waited until spring, I could have gone, too – helped her through it.

'I was there the night she met Andrew, you know. It would be better if I could be with her when finally she says goodbye to him: one day she must let him go.'

'I think she'll never get over it, Alice.'

'Maybe not – but at least the pain gets less bad. In time, she'll be able to call him back without hurting inside.'

'You know how it is, don't you?'

'I know. Life can be very unfair. And you deserved better than this, Giles, but I'll try, always, to do what I can to help you.'

'We'll have to lean on each other.'

'We'll do that. And I'll build up the fire, then perhaps we could have tea together.' She felt such pity for him, such gratitude, that she cupped his face in her hands, gentling his forehead with her lips.

'That was to say thank you,' she whispered, pink-cheeked. 'For everything.'

The first Christmas of peace was quiet at Rowangarth; subdued, almost. Food rationing had not miraculously disappeared with the signing of the armistice, nor shortages ended. Julia became a shadow, a wraith of the loved and loving woman she had been, taking long walks to the top of the Pike, returning exhausted, eyes dark with pain and red-rimmed from weeping.

'I didn't give up the lease on Little Britain,' she confided on her return from London. 'I meant to, but I couldn't. It would have been like a betrayal. Sparrow will take care of the place still, and I shall use it whenever I go to London.'

'You'd do far better to stay at Aunt Sutton's,' Alice urged. 'Think of the expense of keeping the lodgings going – and empty, most times.'

'The army gives me a widow's allowance,' she said, tight-lipped 'Let that pay for it. And did you know that Figgis has left Aunt Sutton; gone to her sister in Bristol. She's too old to work now. Aunt misses her, but she plans to spend as much time as she can in France, now it's possible for her to travel there again.

'She can't wait to get back to her Camargue, see how her friends there fared during the war. She plans to go for New Year Did I ever tell you she's left her house to me?'

'No. It's kind of her, though. One day you'll be able to have a home of your own if the mood takes you; later, when things get easier for you, that is.'

'Things won't get easier, and I don't want a home if Andrew isn't in it with me,' she shrugged, her voice flat with indifference.

'Julia, I do know what it's like. Let me share it with you?' If only she would rage and weep and slam doors like the Julia of old would have done, it might be the first step along the road to acceptance. But she was like a woman in a dream; a half-alive creature with wide, troubled eyes in a face pinched with pain. And all the time getting thinner, more pale. 'And please don't go back to London just yet? The baby – it could happen any day now. I want you, *need* you, with me.'

'I'll be here – but there'll be Doc. James and the nurse. You'll be all right.'

'But, Julia, it's you I shall need, *really* need. And there's something else – ' she hesitated.

'Mm?'

'Listen, please!' She was away with her dreams again. In Paris, was it, or Hyde Park, with Andrew? 'Giles didn't sleep, last night. And his temperature is up.'

'How do you know? Did you take it?'

'No, but it's up. His forehead was burning. Take a look – see what you think, will you?'

Julia removed the thermometer from her brother's mouth, read it quickly, then passed it to Alice, reaching for his wrist.

'It's up – just a little,' she murmured. 'Feel a bit off, do you?'

Up a *little*? Alice read and read again the thin line that showed an unacceptable high. Her eyes met Julia's. *I told you so.*

'Any chest pains – tightness?' Julia was the nurse again, her cool hand on his forehead.

'No – *yes*! Oh, I don't know! It's just that I've had a bad night . . .'

'You should have rung your bell: I'd have heard you,' Alice scolded.

'You need your rest.'

'It wouldn't have mattered. I'm not sleeping too well, these nights. And Julia would have come . . .'

'Of course I would. And if you aren't improved by tonight, I'll have Doc. James call. So let's make you comfortable. I think we might start with a wash down, and dry sheets.'

Alice rang the bedside bell, grateful that something had taken Julia's interest; worried that Giles should be the cause of it.

'Julia, you *can't*!' Giles whispered. 'My sister, I mean, undressing me . . .'

'Idiot! I've given more bed-baths, rubbed more male buttocks than you'll ever imagine. And done far worse!'

There was the glimmer of a smile in her eyes, in her voice. It was like a snatch of sunshine on a grey day, and Alice latched on to it gratefully.

'We were the terrors of Hut Twenty-four, weren't we, Julia? Brave men trembled at our approach.'

'No. That was Sister Carbrooke.'

The moment soon passed; the sudden smile was gone when out of earshot Julia whispered, 'I'm going to phone Richard James at once. Giles says he's cold, yet he's wringing with sweat. Where is Mother?'

'Gone to Denniston; but she must be told as soon as she comes back. I think Giles has caught 'flu. He's got all the symptoms.'

'But how could he? He hasn't been out of the house since before Christmas.'

'It's 'flu,' Alice insisted. 'The doctor should see him, straight away.'

Richard was out, Effie James told Julia flatly. 'He was up half the night, now he's trying to catch up on house calls. If he rings in, I'll get him to you at once, but it could be ages before he's back. This influenza is serious, Julia; you don't think it's that, with Giles?'

'I don't know what to think, but Alice is certain it is. Can you treat it as urgent, Effie? I'm worried. His temperature is too high.'

'The doctor's on his way,' Julia said brightly, closing the door behind her. 'I'll just clear up in here. Aspirin and plenty of water to drink,' she said lightly to Alice, who had pulled a chair to the bedside. 'I'll see what I can find in Andrew's bag.'

On his way? He could be hours, Julia frowned, collecting sheets and towels, carrying out the water bowl. And Alice was right. Giles, somehow, had caught 'flu, and Effie James said people were dying of it. What, she demanded silently, bitterly, had Rowangarth done to deserve such punishment? Robert, Andrew – Alice, even. And now Giles, bright-eyed with fever, and God only knew when Richard James would get here.

Andrew, where are you? Andrew would have known what to do, made it all come right. And may hell damn toothache into eternity!

'It's influenza,' Richard James told Helen, who had waited downstairs. 'I'm sorry to have been so long coming, but half the Riding is down with it. Five deaths, too – a vicious strain; either that, or people are so frail after four years of war they have nothing to fight it with . . .'

'What more can we do?' There was fear in Helen's voice.

'Nothing that hasn't already been done. All the fluids he can take . . . There'll be a crisis, though with two nurses in the house, Giles is luckier than most. I don't know which way to turn. And my own nurse is laid up too.'

'The midwife? But she was here recently. Is it she who brought the germ into the house?'

'No, Helen, it is not. She, poor soul, fell on the ice yesterday. Her arm is broken, and a badly bruised nurse with an arm in a sling isn't a lot of use to me, I'm afraid. And I'm sorry to be the bringer of such bad news, but – '

'I'm sure Giles will be fine.' Helen tilted her chin. 'When will crisis time come, do you think?' The crisis, people called it, when a fever reached its height; when a strong person survived it and a sickly one did not.

'I should say in about twenty-four hours. This influenza isn't like other diseases. There is no known medicine to fight it with. It's all a question of waiting and hoping – and praying, Helen my dear. I'd send Effie to you, but I need her at the surgery. I'm sorry, but – '

'I understand. You have all your other patients to think about.' And with most of the young doctors still not released from army service, Richard must surely be hard put to it to cope with the sudden epidemic. 'Thank you for coming. We'll take every care, between us.'

'And keep an eye on Alice. By rights she shouldn't be in that sickroom.'

'No! Of course not!' Helen took the stairs in a panic. How thoughtless of her to let Alice near Giles. Her labour could start any day, any hour; the midwife with a broken arm and Richard not knowing which way to turn!

'Alice, I think you should go to your room – have a rest,' Helen said, closing the door behind her. 'I will sit with Giles – you mustn't overtire yourself.' *And oh, my dear, you must not catch influenza. Not now when your time is so near.*

'I'm all right, Mother-in-law. I was a nurse, don't forget? Often we worked so hard we didn't take off our shoes for days at a time.'

'But you were not carrying a child then.'

'I shall stay with him,' Alice insisted. 'Julia is resting; she will take the night duty. We must try to get his temperature down; cool drinks, cold cloths – anything to fight the fever. And pray for him, dearest? He hasn't got his strength back, yet, after his wounds. Prayers do get answered, I know it.'

'Alice! I'm not being a fuss-pot. Richard James said you shouldn't be in here.'

'I'm sure the doctor means well, but he must not order me out of my husband's room,' Alice said softly, returning to take her place at the bedside. 'I'm sorry to disobey him – and you, too, mother-in-law – but I will stay, until Julia takes over. And I need cold water and more cloths. And drinking-water, too. Will you ask they be brought up, please?'

'Alice – I *beg* you . . .?'

Unspeaking, Alice shook her head and, taking Giles's hand in her own, laid it to her cheek. And wasn't it too late? She and Julia had been in the sickroom for most of the day. No use, now, to start worrying . . .

Julia built up the fire, pulled back the curtains, staring out into the night.

'Poor Giles.'

She looked down at her brother's flushed face. His eyes were closed, but he wasn't sleeping. How could he, when his breathing was so laboured, his temperature so high?

Richard James had called again, white-faced with fatigue, had shaken his head at the questioning in Julia's eyes, then turned to leave.

'Perhaps I had better look in on Alice, if she is awake?' he murmured. 'Just to make sure all is well.'

'Mother checked up on her half an hour ago. Her light was out; she seemed to be sleeping . . .'

'I shall be out on calls half the night, but I will ring Effie every time I'm near a telephone. I will come at once if I am needed here.'

'Look, I know it couldn't happen at a worse time – the midwife laid up too,' Julia said softly, 'but if anything starts, Mother will sit with Giles and I'll take care of Alice. We'll manage till you can get here. We've been together a long time, she and I. She trusts me.'

'Yes – well . . .' He picked up his hat and gloves, wrapped his muffler round his neck. 'Best be off. I'll call again in the morning – if not before,' he added, his thoughts with the woman upstairs whose time was so near.

He sighed loudly. It was going to be a long, weary night.

Alice awoke suddenly to the certain knowledge that her labour had started. She reached for the light-pull over her bed, blinking her eyes, focusing them on the clock. Three in the morning; an ungodly hour, when a night nurse's body screamed for sleep.

She shivered, reaching for her night shawl, pulling on her slippers. No need to fuss yet, though she'd better tell Julia.

She walked quietly along the passage towards the welcome strip of light that shone beneath Giles's door.

'Are you awake?' she said softly, pushing it open.

'Hullo, love,' Julia smiled. 'Can't sleep . . .?'

'I woke up. I think it's started.'

'Pains? Are they bad? How often?' Julia was instantly alert.

'Not bad at all, honestly. More like niggles. I'm all right. Knew you'd be awake – just wanted to be near someone, that's all.'

'You're sure?'

'Absolutely certain. And now that I've told you,

it'll probably stop. How is Giles?' Alice laid her hand on his forehead, pulling it sharply away. 'He – he's burning . . .'

'He's delirious, too – rambling about the war. I phoned Doc. James. Effie, poor love, sounded worn out. Said he was out on a call but should be back soon. When he comes, we'll tell him it's started, shall we – just to be on the safe side?'

'If you want to. But it's nothing I can't cope with yet. Like I said – '

'Forgive me, milady, but is anything the matter?' The housekeeper stood in the open doorway, her hair down her back, a shawl clutched around her. 'I heard footsteps outside my door.'

'I'm sorry, it was me. Did I wake you?'

'No, milady, I couldn't sleep. Been tossing half the night. How is Sir Giles?'

'Poorly, I'm afraid,' Julia said softly. 'I've sent for Doctor James.'

'Then I shall dress, and put up my hair. I'll let him in when he comes. And I think I'll stir up the kitchen fire – set a kettle to boil.'

'Would you, Miss Clitherow? I'd appreciate a cup of tea,' Julia smiled.

'Then I'll make a large pot and we can all have one. Won't be long, Miss Julia, milady . . .' She was gone, quickly, silently.

'Good old Clitherow. She can be a pain sometimes,' Julia smiled, 'but she's all right underneath.'

'Wish she wouldn't call me milady.'

'Sorry, Alice, you're stuck with it, I'm afraid. But are you sure you are all right – *really* all right?'

'Fine. And it might turn out to be nothing that a good hot cup of tea won't take care of.'

It might, but it wouldn't; not when she was six days past her time . . .

* * *

Richard James laid aside his stethoscope, then confirmed Julia's fears. The crisis time of Giles's illness had begun. Within the span of twenty-four hours, they would know the worst – or the best.

'It is so awful,' Julia fretted. 'Such advances in the war; the best brains of the country finding better and more deadly ways to kill, but no one thinks to look for something to help fight a fever.'

'One day they will, be sure of it,' the doctor shrugged. 'So many advances, even since my student days . . .'

'One day – but not tonight. Nothing to help Giles,' Julia accepted bitterly. 'And I think Alice's pains have started.'

'Oh, dear.' It was all he could think of to say.

'Not pains,' Alice insisted, 'but there's – well – *something* . . .'

'Then you must go back to bed at once!'

'I will, later.' When the waters broke, she would. She knew about such things. Didn't she once help Sister deliver the baby of a refugee? A small, roadside miracle, it had seemed. A noisy one, but quite wonderful. And the look on the face of the father when –

No remembering! This is *now*, Alice Sutton. Soon your own child will come bawling into the world, but there'll be no joy of it . . .

By late afternoon, Alice's pains could no longer be brushed aside. Helen Sutton had taken her place at her son's bedside; Julia mopped Alice's face and Miss Clitherow and Tilda hovered within earshot of either room.

In the corner, made up with dainty sheets and blankets, stood the cot used by all Helen's children. Alice tried not to look at it. A prettily draped cot should have been a comfort, a joy; a promise that soon she would hold her child to her.

But she didn't want to hold it, to love it. She wanted

Tom's child and Tom pacing the floor downstairs. She had imagined it so often in her dreamings. Their first bairn; born in springtime and a whole world of happiness theirs just for the taking. She had been so sure.

'I think I'm going to be sick, Julia.'

'*Sick?*' Without panic, Julia reached for a basin.

'No. Maybe not. But I feel – *peculiar*.'

'How – *peculiar*?'

'I don't know. My head hurts and I'm so hot. Can you take the blankets off?'

Julia lifted the sheet, bellying it out to make a rush of air. 'That better?' There had been no blankets on the bed. And Alice was right: she was too hot, and she shouldn't be. 'Won't be a minute,' she said softly, reaching for the bell-push. 'I won't leave you   .'

She opened the door and stood there, waiting. Her ring was answered at once.

'Miss Julia?' Tilda stood there, wide-eyed and breathless from running

'Ask Miss Clitherow to telephone Doctor James at once,' she said softly, urgently. 'Tell her I don't care what he's doing – he must come, *now*. Tell him it's Lady Alice. She's in labour, and I think she's got 'flu!'

'Ooooh, miss   .' Tilda clattered down the stairs, heart bumping. Sir Giles was badly – maybe couldn't last the night out – and now Alice.

'Miss Clitherow, ma'am!' she yelled.

Alice's child was born in a scream of pain. Her body hurt, her head ached blindingly and there was a tightness in her chest that prevented her, almost, from drawing breath.

There had been a moment, minutes ago, when she had wanted to give in to the pain; to close her eyes and slip high and away, over Brattocks and up and up towards a sun that shone brilliantly

'Push, will you! One more push, Alice . . .'

Julia, urging her, holding her hands so tightly she couldn't get free, fly to Tom.

'Alice – *try*. One more push . . .'

And then there was peace. This was dying, a release from pain. Yet why was she on fire, her whole body burning? Was it hell she was going to? Had they judged her already, and must she pay, now, for her sin?

'Alice, love, it's all right!' She heard a mewling, a baby crying. 'You have a fine son! It's all over. We have a boy!' Julia laughing, crying.

Go away, Julia. Go, and take my sin with you. I want to go to Tom.

She tried to breathe deeply, but the pain inside her was too great. She let go a little gasp, then darkness came. Sweet, gentle darkness.

'I'll see to her now.' Richard James threw off his coat and began washing his hands. 'Sorry   '

He tied, then cut the cord that bound mother and child; then, swaddling the baby in a towel, cleaning out the little mouth, he whispered, 'Take him to Giles. Don't go in. Tell him he has a son. Let him hear him!'

Eyes bright with tears, Julia sped to her brother's room, flinging open the door.

'Giles! Can you hear me?' she called.

'It's over?' Helen sprang to her feet. 'She's all right?'

'I mustn't come in, but tell Giles? Tell him he has a fine son – and Sutton fair! The image of Uncle Edward!'

Briefly, Helen closed her eyes against tears of relief and joy, grasping her son's hand.

'Giles, can you hear me? You have a son – a fine son to get well for!'

His eyes opened, his hand stirred in that of his mother. His lips moved in the gentlest of smiles.

'A son!' Helen exulted.

* * *

Julia stood at the window of Alice's bedroom, her heart beating with pain, watching the slow, black procession that carried her brother away from her.

Poor, broken Giles; too weak from his wounds, still, to fight back.

She was glad she must remain here, take care of Alice and the baby; Alice who tossed and muttered in delirium, and the little one, so hungry, so sick.

No milk had come to Alice's breasts; the fault of the influenza. Giles was dead; Rowangarth's son must live at all costs.

Yet he could not feed. They had searched, but no wet nurse could be found; no woman with breast milk to spare for a baby who vomited back the cow's milk they gave him. He sucked at the bottle hungrily, but it was all no use.

The last coach of the funeral procession was lost to her sight as it rounded the bend in the drive.

'Goodbye, Giles,' she whispered. 'You were too good a soul for this world, but your son will live, I swear it. And I'll watch over him and love him always, I promise you.'

Rowangarth was deserted, save for herself and Jinny Dobb. Jin watched over the baby in the warmth of the kitchen; she, Julia, sat with Alice until her mother returned. Outside the skies were grey, the January wind bitter from the east.

Andrew, I need you so. Our lovely world has gone mad. We are being punished for I know not what. The rooks have deserted us and Alice is sick. The baby can't feed. He's losing weight and crying with hunger. What am I to do, my darling? Help us, please?

Jin Dobb could stand it no longer. She had offered to mind the bairn because she detested funerals and especially the burying of a young man on a day so bleak as this. But the bairn had cried solid for half an hour and not even her little finger in his mouth to suck on had silenced him for long.

The mite was not just hungry; he was slowly starving. First Sir Giles and now his bairn; a little scrap with a title already to hang on him, but no name. Alice must choose the name, Miss Julia had insisted, yet Alice wasn't capable of thought at the moment. Fighting that 'flu, and her weak from a long labour because the doctor hadn't been able to get there in time to be of much help.

But that was men the whole world over, she thought bitterly, pacing the floor yet again, patting the little back, stiff with anger. Never there when you needed them. And no use giving the bairn more water It only gave him gripes. It was sustenance he needed; something his little belly could keep a hold of and not throw back. Cow's milk for a new-born babbie, indeed! They hadn't the sense they were born with. For two pins she'd go upstairs and tell Miss Julia now!

Wrapping the baby tightly, she mounted the stairs with determination, knocking on the sickroom door.

'I'm come to tell you, ma'am, that this bairn is fading slow and I can't stand by and see it!'

'I know, Jin; I know! And don't bring him in here. We've enough on our plate already.'

'Then if I might suggest – ' and if someone didn't do something soon, the lass would keel over and go the same way as Alice on the bed over there – 'that it isn't milk from a cow this babbie needs.'

'Then tell me,' Julia flung, her face red with anger and frustration. 'Just tell me, and if I have to go to the ends of the earth to get it, I will!'

'Nay. No need to put yourself out. Soon as they gets back from the churchyard I can get it from my sister for you. He'll keep it down, or I'm a Dutchman!'

'Keep *what* down?'

'Goat's milk, that's what. And proved times over. My sister never could feed a babbie – not with breast milk – so she brung hers up with the help of a nanny goat; though much good it did her, them lying dead in a foreign country and begging your pardon, Miss Julia, for reminding you of such sorrow.'

'Tell me,' Julia urged, 'can you bring some milk and how will I give it to him?'

'Well, you make it weak at first, it being so rich. One measure of milk and two measures of good fresh water – and sugar for energy, of course. That's what my sister did and fine young men they growed into and never a suck of mother's milk did they ever have!'

'Then you'll get me some? You think it's worth a try?'

'The state this babbie's in, anything's worth a try. He'll either keep it down or he'll throw it back. We'll soon know.'

She stuck her finger into his mouth and he sucked on it eagerly. Then he turned his head in anger, crying out again.

'We'll try it, Jin. And bear with me? Give him some more water – keep him quiet. I'll take him from you once Mother is back.'

She would try anything. Rowangarth's child must not die. She loved him already; loved the way his fingers clung and his cheeks went into tiny hollows as he sucked down his bottle milk. And she loved him because he was Sutton fair; so like her uncle and not a trace of the blackness of the man who had fathered him. Mary Anne Pendennis's darkness had skipped a generation, and Alice had borne a child that was a true Sutton.

Now Elliot would never know about his son; never suspect. He would see his child grow into manhood and envy Rowangarth their fine young heir. Because he *would* grow into manhood: somehow she would find sustenance for him, even if she had to hawk the streets in desperation for some woman with breast milk to spare. She would beg for it on her knees.

But they would try Jin's way first. The little one could only vomit it back. She closed the door on the crying child, returning to the bed, taking Alice's hands in her own.

'Don't go! Not you too. Giles has gone and our baby is sick – I can't go on, Alice, if you don't get well. You are all I have left now. Please, *please* don't leave me?'

The frail hand in hers stirred; there was a moving of the head on the pillow. Alice's eyes opened, blinking, looking questioningly about her.

'*Alice!* Alice, it's Julia!'

'Drink?' Her lips formed the word, but no sound came.

'Yes! Oh, yes!' Julia reached for the feeding-cup, holding it to the dry, cracked lips. Alice sucked weakly at first, then greedily. Then she smiled.

'I'm not leaving,' she whispered.

'You're going to be all right, Alice! You *are*.'

'Feel dreadful. How long . . .?'

'You've been ill – very ill. For four days. But the baby – well, we managed between us, didn't we; though Doc. James got here in the end.'

Alice turned her head on the pillow. Somewhere, in her dark, giddy floatings, she knew there was a baby, a boy, safely born; but she had tried to run from it; not to touch it, touch Elliot.

'Did I – did I *say* anything?'

'No. No names, though you yelled something awful at times. I'll bring the baby to you as soon as Doc. James says it's safe, but there's something I've got to tell you first.' There was no easy way to say it so she whispered, 'Giles. He was too weak. It beat him in the end . . .'

'Did he know?' Alice closed her eyes, her mouth set tightly against the sudden choke of tears in her throat.

'He knew. I stood in the doorway so he could hear his son crying. He smiled, Alice.'

'Yes.' She didn't want to open her eyes again. She wanted to rest here and not have to see the baby.

'They took Giles to the church at two. It'll be over now.'

'Poor, dear man,' Alice murmured. 'I wanted to die, too. I didn't want to hang on. I wanted to be with Tom.'

'I know, love; I know. Do you think I haven't thought things like that too? But there's a child to bring up now. I love him already, Alice. You'll love him as well.'

'I don't want to see him. Don't bring him in here?'

'Sssh. You're weak and hungry. When they all get back, I'll ask Cook to make you some pobs. Pobs will slip down nicely, won't it? And Mother will be so glad you are on the mend.'

Alice closed her eyes. It was no use. So Julia loved the child – let her, then. She, Alice, wanted nothing of it; not Elliot Sutton's child. Even to touch it would be impossible.

'I want to go to sleep,' she whispered.

When the mourners had left Rowangarth, Helen Sutton let down her guard. The war was over, ah yes, but today it had claimed another life. Both her sons taken and the son-in-law who had been so unbelievably like John. Now Alice lay ill: she, who had braved the dangers of nursing in France, lay in delirium, struck down by the epidemic sent to torment more these already tormented islands.

Black again. No sooner out of mourning than back into it; and the child whose coming had raised her flagging spirits now daily becoming more sickly.

She must get out of this house of widows, she thought desperately; walk the anger and bewilderment out of her whilst the daylight lasted.

She stood at the top of the steps, Morgan beside her,

determined to follow where he led – anywhere, save to the sickroom where Alice lay so ill and from where she could hear the crying of a hungry child.

The spaniel, who had been neglected of late, made for the wild garden stile with the joy of a captive released. He had had little petting or spoiling, and been dismissed from the kitchen each time he poked his nose around the door. Yet there was one place left and he made for it, nose down, yelping with joy.

'If it isn't that daft dog Morgan.' Reuben stroked the head of the creature who sat on his doorstep, eyes beseeching. 'And her ladyship. Taking him out, are you? I'd be careful in the wood, milady. It's muddy underfoot.'

'I think rather that he's taking me, Reuben.' Helen sighed deeply. 'Though truth known I need to be out of the house. I can't even bring myself to go and see how Alice is . . .'

'Don't take on, milady. Things aren't all bad.'

'No? Alice so ill and the baby sickening still? He can't feed. So robust a child born, yet now he can't keep milk down.'

'Oh, dear. Your ladyship is in a worse state than Russia,' Reuben chuckled. 'And since I'm in my best suit still, it might be fitting if I walked with you through the wood. It's slape underfoot; don't want you to fall over.'

He took a crust from his pocket, offering it to the spaniel who swallowed it greedily. By rights he shouldn't be talking to her ladyship in so familiar a fashion, but it was clear she was in need of comfort. A body could take only so much, and she was at the far end of her tether, poor sad woman. He crooked his arm gallantly, tipping his hat, bowing his head in deference.

'If you would please take my arm, milady, there's something I want you to see. You'll mind what folks have always said about the rooks over the years?'

'That if ever they should leave Rowangarth, then sorrow would follow? I know. Sir John believed it too, Reuben. And they left, suddenly – and what has happened since? More sorrow, when we might have expected some happiness. Giles taken, Alice so ill and the child – ' She stopped, shaking her head, fighting back tears. Then she slipped her hand through the crook of Reuben's arm. 'What is it, then, that I must see?'

'Come with me. And don't you worry none.'

'How can you say that, today of all days? And Alice and the baby getting no better . . .'

'Milady – I was upset, too. Couldn't get the worry of it out of my mind, till this morning. See now, up there.' He pointed to the elms, the tallest trees in the wood. 'Look, and listen.'

Above the topmost branches, birds wheeled and dived. Black birds, cawing loudly, slipping in and out of the leafless branches.

'I heard them yesterday, milady, but I couldn't see them; thought I was dreaming. Then this morning I looked again and there they were – just a pair of them, but nesting; carrying twigs like they do to repair old nests. So count, milady. How many do you see now?'

'Several. At least six.'

'Three pairs, maybe more. Them old rooks is back. There'll be no more sorrow now. I reckon the bad luck has run its course. Nothing lasts, milady – good luck nor bad – but Rowangarth has had more'n its share of bad luck. Things are going to pick up now.'

'I shouldn't believe this, Reuben.' She smiled up at him, eyes bright. 'It's superstitious nonsense and we shouldn't take any notice of it.'

'No more we should, milady,' he chuckled. 'But I'm right glad to see them back – and mending them nests as if they intend staying.'

'And so am I, Reuben. Oh, so am I!'

Jin Dobb said she couldn't wait for teatime. Got things to do more important than bread and jam; an errand for Miss Julia. She'd be back in about half an hour, she called over her shoulder, breathless to be gone.

She returned with a milk can which she deposited on the cold slab in the pantry, then made for the housekeeper's sitting-room.

'Will you tell Mrs MacMalcolm that Jin has got what she wanted for the babbie, and if she'll come below stairs with a feeding bottle, I'll be glad to oblige.'

'I'm to say *what*?' The thin eyebrows rose.

'Just say *goat's milk*,' Jin snapped, impatient to be about the business in hand. 'She'll know what I'm on about!'

She had the mixture prepared in a well-scalded jug when Julia appeared in the kitchen, a red-faced child cradled in her arm, a feeding bottle in her hand.

'You're sure?' she asked anxiously.

'Sure as I can be. Us'll soon know, Miss Julia,' she sighed, filling the bottle.

The baby stopped crying, pulled the offered teat into his mouth, and began to suck hungrily. Then he closed his eyes, taking the feed more gently, making little smacking noises with his lips, stopping, sometimes, to rest.

The bottle emptied with a squeaking of air; Julia removed the teat from the puckered, milky mouth.

'There now, miss. Pat his back – gentle like. See what comes up.' Only wind, Jin hoped, but they'd soon know.

Julia rubbed the little back with gentle, circular movements; the tiny head lolled against her arm. Ten perfect toes, touched by the fire glow, spread themselves fanlike in its warmth. His eyes opened briefly, his mouth contorted.

'Ah, bless the little love – he's smiling at us,' Cook sighed.

'Smiling be blowed,' said Jin derisively. ''Em can't do that for weeks. That's wind he's trying to get up. Rub careful, Miss Julia.'

Wind – *flatulence* – it was indeed. It came in two resounding burps, to the delight of those who watched.

'There now,' Jin smiled proudly. 'If he'd been going to throw that feed back, it'd have been then. He'll keep it down now. Just see if he doesn't!'

'You think so?' Julia whispered. Her eyes were bright, her cheeks flushed from the heat of the kitchen fire. A smile tilted her lips and she looked, for just a moment, Tilda thought, like the Miss Julia of old.

'I think,' Jin said, 'that the little fellow is going to do all right on that old nanny's milk. Oh my word, yes!'

'He's nodding off,' Cook whispered, rising from the chair by the fire. 'Would you like to sit there, miss, and rock him?'

'No thank you,' Julia smiled. 'You shall get him to sleep for me. I need a cup of tea. Shall you set the kettle to boil, Tilda, and will the rations run to a slice of bread and jam? I don't think I have eaten for days.'

'Spare it and gladly.' Cook nestled the baby to her. 'It's just like when you was a little lass, come down to my kitchen for jam sandwiches.'

'Then can I eat it here with you – a celebration, sort of? Alice is much improved, you see. Her fever is gone. Mother is back from her walk, sitting with her now and looking so relieved.'

'Then thanks be,' Cook sighed. 'I was getting to think there was a curse on this house.'

'Not any longer,' Julia smiled; not when the rooks had come back to Brattocks Wood. 'I think some good things will happen to us now.'

Not that she really believed such nonsense; she never had – even as a child – but if it made her mother happy, then who was she to scoff? Or to question the wisdom of those old black birds?

44

1919

'You will *have* to go out,' said Julia flatly. 'Today is so lovely.'

It was a rare February afternoon, with a silver-blue sky trailed with fat white clouds, and everything touched to life by a pale gold sun.

'I'd rather not. You go. Take the child.'

'Listen! You had a bad confinement and 'flu – of course you feel frail. But that was weeks ago! We could tuck the babe up warm in the perambulator – you could push. And that's another thing. His birth must be registered. All right! I know things were upside down here when he was born, but I want him named.'

'Giles said he would name a son; I was to choose for a girl . . .'

'Alice – why are you so listless, so uninterested?' Julia flung, impatiently. 'You aren't trying. It's as if you don't want to get well. You call your son *the child* . . .' Julia was worried. Things had to be brought into the open.

'He *isn't* my son,' Alice countered defiantly. 'He's Rowangarth's. He belonged to the Suttons the minute Giles married me.' It had been a silent bargain she'd made with the Madonna in that little chapel – and with Tom.

'Please, can't we try to make the best of things? We both lost the man we loved . . .'

'I was fond of Giles, an' all!'

'I know you were. But we understand each other; we are sisters now. There is a little boy to be brought up and you are his mother!'

'*You* are that, Julia!' she flung in a rare blaze of anger.

'I thought I'd died, I really did. After all the pain there was a lovely floating feeling and a long, warm passage to walk down – all echoes, it was. I wanted to get to the end of it. Tom was waiting for me; I know he was.'

'Well, I didn't let you die – neither you nor your child!' Julia flamed; the Julia of old. 'And do you think I didn't want to die? Do you imagine your love for Tom was any greater than mine for Andrew? You sit there in a dream. Once, just *once,* you've held the baby, and you gave him back to me so quickly it was as if you didn't want to touch him!'

'I was afraid I would drop him, he wriggled so.' Alice walked to the window, staring out. It seemed, she thought dully, that the world was coming alive out there; waking after a four-year nightmare.

She looked across to the wild garden. There would be hazel catkins, fluffily gold, and pussy-willows, round and soft like palest moleskin. And beyond, in Brattocks Wood, would be the scent of the earth awakening and buds swelling and wild snowdrops beneath the trees.

Yet no matter how often she walked there or stood beneath the tallest elms, Tom would never come; would never whistle her; stand there, arms wide.

They had been lovers; why hadn't that one coupling made a child? Why had it happened on a straw-stuffed palliasse in a cowshed?

Evil, evil, *evil*! She could not love a child of so cruel a getting. Julia adored him; had taken him to herself. He had been born when she yearned for someone to love, ached for Andrew's child in her arms.

'You are more his mother than I shall ever be,' she said softly, sadly. 'The child must be reared by one of his own kind – not by a sewing-maid. You and he are bonded. I give him to you as I gave him to Giles.

'And you are right. You must register his birth. I would like him to be called Andrew Robert Giles – can you bear it, him being Andrew? Call him Drew, if it hurts . . .'

'It doesn't hurt. I am pleased and proud. And Drew shall be his pet-name until he is shortened and breeched – till he's a real little boy. Sir Andrew Sutton . . .' She gathered Alice to her. 'Come out into this lovely afternoon, please try? You have been so long away from us. I want you back, Alice Hawthorn. I want us to be as we were.'

'We can't be. Those days are gone. But we'll have to make the best of a bad job, I'll grant you that.'

'Then come out? I'll go and get Drew – tuck him in all snug.'

'No! A walk round the garden, if you'll give me your arm – but just you and me?'

'Very well. Put on some thick shoes and a coat and muffler . . .'

Julia watched her go, acknowledging the wisdom of her words. Things would never, could never be the same again. They could neither of them turn back the clock, return to yesterday. But the pale sun of February promised that spring was just around the corner and, please God, a new, brave beginning.

'Andrew,' she smiled softly. 'Andrew Sutton . . .'

The first of March: days were lengthening and daffodils grew in thick drifts in the wild garden. Most of the married soldiers were back home now, and the single ones impatient to follow. King and country had no use for armies now. They cost money to feed and house; the sooner they were demobilized, the better.

Will Stubbs returned to the stables, horses still his first love; and if her ladyship would trust him with the buying of a decent pair for the carriage, he'd said, he'd be glad to oblige. Horses came cheaply now, the army no longer needing them.

Motors were the rage now, he stressed. He had learned

to drive during his last months in the army, and knew enough about internal combustion engines to look after any motor in his care, he'd hinted.

He had smiled at Alice, glad to see her again, advancing with hand outstretched until he remembered.

'Mornin', milady,' he said instead, hand at his side.

'Will! So good to see you safe and sound!' She had offered her own hand, smiling gently, hoping he wouldn't ask about Tom.

Jinny Dobb left Rowangarth kitchen at about the same time. The bothy was to be opened again and needed a good bottoming, she declared, bucket and scrubber at the ready. It would be good to care for the garden boys again; move out of the almshouse and let Reuben move in.

'Mother isn't going to replace Reuben when he retires, and he agrees,' Julia confided. 'He'd like to be out of Keeper's as soon as he can. He feels he'd be better replaced by a woodman: there'll be no more shoots here; not until Drew is old enough. Reuben says we can worry about stocking up with game when the time comes.'

'And the woodman – he'll have Keeper's?' Alice murmured.

'Mm. He can keep an eye on the wild game and see to the trees and hedges at the same time.'

Alice was glad about that. She hadn't wanted a new, young keeper living in a house she should have shared with Tom.

'I think the child should learn to shoot – handle a gun properly – though Giles wouldn't have wanted it,' Alice shrugged. 'But there's time enough for that . . .'

Alice was slowly regaining her health, taking walks with Morgan, most times to Reuben's cottage. She felt at home there; had no need to watch what she said or the way in which she said it; could be Alice Hawthorn from the minute she stepped over his threshold.

Her first real test had been the child's christening.

Never had she been so thankful that Rowangarth was in mourning. Because of it, the ceremony had been simple, with no celebration afterwards.

Julia, as godmother, carried the child to the font, announcing his names proudly; Nathan, at Pendenys on leave, stood at her side, a godfather. Alice felt safe with the two of them there, who knew her secret and would keep it always.

Andrew Robert Giles Sutton cried lustily at his christening, which pleased his grandmother to dwell upon as she held him tightly to her on the carriage ride home.

'I like a child to cry at the font,' she smiled fondly. 'It cries the devil out of them, you know.'

Edward and Clementina Sutton called briefly to drink the health of the child; Clementina reluctantly acknowledging her nephew's wife, asking archly after *Lady* Alice's health.

'I am much improved, I thank you, ma'am,' Alice replied softly, exactly as Lady Helen would have done. And such magnanimity she could afford in her relief that Elliot Sutton had not been there.

'Awaiting his demobilization; having a gay old time in Paris, I shouldn't wonder,' Clementina said fondly as she took her leave, telling Helen what a beautiful grandson she had and how lucky she was to have him so close.

'I have only photographs of my Sebastian,' she sighed, even though she wasn't remotely interested in her youngest son's boy. She wanted Elliot married; needed him to give her the grandson to whom Pendenys Place would one day pass.

'I think, Alice, she would like to see Elliot married,' Helen murmured as the motor bore them back to Pendenys. 'Elliot should have a son.'

'My thoughts exactly, Mother-in-law.'

And she, Alice, had that Sutton-fair son. And she

hoped, when Elliot Sutton married, that he fathered a dozen bairns – and never a boy amongst them!

'Where,' demanded Helen, closing the door behind her, 'is my grandson? Julia surely hasn't made off with him again? She is becoming quite bossy about him. You must put your foot down, Alice!'

'She and Nathan are wheeling him round the garden; they have a lot to talk about. They haven't met, remember, since Giles and I were married.'

'Nor have they. Nathan is such a dear soul. He'll be missing Giles, too.'

'He will. And don't scold Julia for the way she feels about the child, Mother-in-law. He was born when she needed someone to love; he gave her something to live for. She laughs, now. We must be grateful for that.'

'She and Nathan,' Helen frowned. 'You don't think – one day, perhaps . . .'

'One day, maybe, but not yet. Not for a long time. After Andrew, any other man would be second-best. You of all women know that.'

'I do.' Then frowning, she said hesitantly, 'Alice, I know there is a strangeness between you and little Drew: it often happens, Richard assures me. You suffered shock and the trauma of war; you had a far from easy delivery, then succumbed to influenza. It would not be unnatural in the circumstances, he says, for a mother to seem to reject her child for a while. Nature, he says, sorts it all out in the end.'

'Yes, thank you for understanding. Things will come right, I'm sure of it. At the moment, Julia's need of him is greater than mine; she thinks of him as Andrew's son; and it doesn't matter to a young baby,' Alice hastened, 'who loves him and feeds him and cuddles him. Leave him with Julia for the time being?'

'You have a wise head on those young shoulders.' Helen kissed her daughter-in-law tenderly. 'And I am lucky to have you. We shall stay here together, the three of us, and comfort each other.'

'And rear a spoiled little boy between us if we aren't careful,' Alice warned.

'May heaven forbid!' Helen laughed with delight. 'One Elliot in the Sutton clan is enough, surely!'

'More than enough.' Alice matched her mood to the moment of laughter, though her heart was sad because of the sin that would never be far from her innermost conscience.

Much more than enough, and may you never need to know the truth, dearest lady, of your grandson's getting . . .

Mary Strong returned to Rowangarth a week after the christening. Having received three proposals, she had weighed up the pros and cons of marriage, and turned all her suitors down to return to her position as parlourmaid to her ladyship as she had left it: a spinster.

The factory in which she worked for most of the war years had closed with amazing speed once the need for shells ended, and she had returned to her parents' home to take a well-earned rest and allow the pink and white of her complexion to return.

Bess, chaperoned by an elderly aunt, had already moved in with her young man above the shop in which he sold tobacco, newspapers and periodicals and, when the sugar situation again allowed it, boiled sweets, chocolates and toffees. Bess Thompson had done very well for herself, she not minding the squint in his right eye that had kept him out of the army, and him not caring that she looked as yellow as a Chinaman. It was all most upsetting, thought Tilda, who hadn't had one offer in any shape or form.

'I shall be moving out afore so very much longer,' Reuben told Alice. 'Lady Day, the new man should've started, but he'll not be coming till the first of April. Seems a decent young chap, the woodsman. Got a wife and bairn – came with good references. That housekeeper woman showed them to me; asked my advice.'

'I shall miss you not being at Keeper's, though you won't be far away, in the almshouse.'

'I'll be glad to go. I've made a start, sorting things. I had it in mind to get myself out a few days before – give the man's wife time to get the place to her liking. You wouldn't care to give me a hand – pack things into boxes . . .?'

'I'll have some tea-chests sent over and a few old newspapers, if you like. And you know I'll come.' Tomorrow would be best; just one year since Tom was killed, since Elliot Sutton thrust into her with as little feeling as a dog taking a bitch on the street.

She covered her face with her hands, shutting out the memory, angered she could allow such crudeness into her head.

'What is it, lass? Tell old Reuben?'

'It's just that – ' She took a shuddering breath, tilting her chin as her ladyship would have done. 'Just that tomorrow is the day I heard that Tom was killed. A year, it'll be. And – '

'And the day you happened on young Sutton,' he finished. 'Well, just you arrange to have tomorrow at Keeper's. Miss Julia will have the bairn, won't she?'

'She has him all the time, Reuben. Won't even consider a nursemaid. He's hers, as far as I'm concerned. She loves him like her own – like I shall never be able to, God forgive me. But it's best, that way. He'll get his bringing up from one of his own kind. I'll come to Keeper's tomorrow – and gladly.'

'Aye. Then if you feel like a little weep, or having a talk about it, I'll be near. So shall us have a sup of tea? Have you got the time?'

She had time. She had all the time in the world.

'I would like, Miss Clitherow, to borrow a bucket and scrubber,' Alice said to the housekeeper who had come to see what her ladyship was doing in the broom pantry.

'*A bucket and scrubber?*' Her words were a question that demanded an answer.

'Reuben moves out of Keeper's soon. There may be floors that need a scrub.'

'But, milady – *you* cannot! Tilda must do it!'

'Miss Clitherow, *I* wish to help Cousin Reuben, and I will be taking a bucket, floorcloth, scrubber and – ' with unnecessary force she sliced a piece of soap from the end of a long yellow block – '*and* a piece of primrose soap!'

She threw them one by one into the bucket with a clatter, then marched up the wooden stairs. She crossed the great hall, shaking with dismay at her outburst, and opened the door of the bedroom beneath the eaves. There she took out her cotton housedress, a pinafore and a scrubbing apron, and drat Miss Clitherow and her snobbish eyebrows! And be blowed if Alice Sutton couldn't still scrub a floor with the best in the Riding!

Her anger had gone by the time she reached Reuben's cottage; anger that in truth had helped rid her of the feeling of doom that wrapped her round the moment she opened her eyes that morning; would help her, if she scrubbed hard enough, to forget the awfulness of today, this first anniversary of her sorrow.

'Are you there, Reuben?' Strangely, the door was locked and she peered through the window, relieved to hear footsteps crossing the kitchen flags.

'You forgot to unbolt the door,' she said accusingly, taking off her coat, hanging it on the clothes peg. 'I'm dressed for scrubbing, if there's any to be done. Did the tea-chests come?'

'Aye. Will Stubbs left them last night, but lass – ' He grasped her arm, eyes troubled. 'There's something I must tell you afore anything else. Sit you down. Kettle's about boiling – a sup of tea first, eh?'

'Yes, please. But what – '

Her eyes lit on the kitchen table. Milk and sugar had been laid there, and three mugs.

'You're expecting someone?' She held her hands to the fire.

'Not expecting, exactly.' His back was towards her; she was unable to read the expression on his face, but there was no mistaking the agitation in his voice.

'What is it, Reuben? Is someone coming?'

'No. Someone's comed. And best you sit down.' He laid his hands on her shoulders, pushing her into the chair. Then he walked to the staircase door, opening it, holding it wide, saying not a word.

A man was sitting on the stairs. Alice jumped to her feet, taking a step towards him, not seeing the bucket she had left there, knocking it over with a clatter. The noise of it filled the room sharply, the echoes hanging there strangely menacing.

The man rose to his feet, walking carefully down the three remaining stairs, and stepped into the light.

He was tall; his eyes were blue – so blue you had to notice them – and his short-cut hair was Viking-fair.

She blinked her eyes, the better to see him; the floor tilted beneath her. She cried out for Reuben and felt his hands hard on her elbows.

There was a churning inside her, a shaking she could not control. Her lips moved, but only the whispering of his name came from them.

Tom? Tom Dwerryhouse . . .

'Sit down, lass.'

Reuben's voice, echoing above her head; Reuben, guiding her to a chair, helping her into it.

Her hands gripped the wooden arms until her knuckles showed white. It was Tom! It *was*!

She rose, swaying, watching as he closed the staircase door. Then she stumbled towards him. 'Tom. Tom, bonny lad! Say something so I'll know it's you?' She held wide her arms, laughing, weeping.

Unspeaking, he looked at her as if she were someone he knew but whose name he had forgotten, taking a step away from her, placing the table between them. Then slowly he brought his finger to his forelock; did it unsmiling, his face a blank.

'Bid you good day, milady,' he said.

'There's no call for that, lad,' Reuben said sharply. 'I told you how it was; told you she wed, now . . .'

'And what else, Reuben?' Her eyes were wide with fear. This was a nightmare. The man she loved – had never stopped loving – could not have hurt her more had he slapped her. 'What else did you tell him?'

'Nowt, 'cept you had a babbie and that Sir Giles has been dead these three months. What else is there to tell?'

'You must be proud of your son, Lady Sutton,' Tom offered. His words were clipped, acid-tipped.

'Reuben,' Alice choked. 'Can you leave us?'

'I'd intended doing that – let you talk things over. But I'm not so sure now that I will, or you'll be fratching and fighting and I won't have that! I warned you, Tom. You knew the way it was before ever she got here.'

'I want you to go – please, Reuben?' she whispered. 'And there'll be no cross words.'

Unspeaking, Reuben fixed his gaze on the younger man.

'There won't be,' Tom said quietly. 'Give us an hour, will you?'

'Slip the bolt when I'm gone.' Reuben reached for his shotgun. 'If anybody knocks, don't answer.'

'If you say not,' Alice whispered, 'though why?' She picked up the teapot with hands that shook. Her mouth had gone dry; her voice sounded peculiar when she tried to speak. 'Why the bolt, Tom? And where have you been till now?'

'I'll tell you, if you'll tell me why you got yourself wed and pregnant within weeks of my being killed – leastways that's how it seemed, the way Reuben told it.'

'Geordie Marshall came to see me – he was passing through Celverte. He told me he'd heard there were twelve of you in a transport, blown up by a shell. Best I didn't hope, he said.'

'And does it give you a grand feeling, being Lady Sutton?' His mouth was set traplike, as if every word he spoke came out only with the greatest effort.

'No, it doesn't. And I need a cup of tea – you, too?'

'Please.'

He was standing too close; his nearness set her heart beating. Every woman's instinct told her to fling her arms around him as once she had done, searching for his mouth, eyes closed, lips parted. She wanted to say, 'I love you.'

'What else did Reuben tell you?' she said instead, pouring milk into the mugs, her hand shaking so much it slopped on to the table-top.

'He said you'd been wed to Giles Sutton in France and that you'd had a boy.'

'And that Giles died the night it was born? Did he tell you I'm a widow?'

'He did, though much good it did me to hear it. That bairn has bound you to Rowangarth: you're one of them now.'

'I'm Alice,' she whispered. 'I never forgot you; used to talk to you with my heart. I thought you'd been killed, Tom. Maggie and Geordie said so.'

She passed him a mug, pulling out a chair, sitting at the table. He moved a step to sit down opposite.

'Are you going to tell me? Were you taken prisoner? It's a year today since I knew. It's why I'm here. I wanted Reuben to help me through it.'

'He told me that an' all, yet none of it rings true. What are you keeping back?'

'Say my name, Tom? Say *Alice*. Or is it so awful to you that you can't bear to hear it?'

Her face was paper-white, her eyes wide with pain, and he hated himself for hurting her because all through that year it had only been thoughts of her that had kept him going; thinking how it would be when they met.

'Your tongue's got sharp, milady.'

'Happen. And as for ringing true – I'll admit if I sat where you are sitting now, I'd not be satisfied with half a story. But it concerns other people; people I couldn't hurt. There are things I can never tell you.'

'Not if I tell you where I was?'

'Not even . . .' Her eyes begged understanding. 'I'm asking you, though. Where were you, Tom? Tell me?'

'I went home, to see Mam. Only Mam died in January of the 'flu.'

'I'm sorry.' She truly was. 'And before that?'

'Before I got back to Blighty, you mean?'

Silently Alice nodded.

'I was on a farm, about fifteen miles from the Front. I spent the last year of the war there. Safe. I wasn't killed like they said; I wasn't taken prisoner. I was a deserter. I still am.' There. He'd said it!

'*Deserter* . . .? No, Tom! Not you!'

'*Me*! And don't think it was cowardice. Going out into No Man's Land sniping – that was a part of the war – getting Jerry before he got me. But taking cold aim; snuffing out a bit of a lad accused of cowardice was a different matter. Taking life like that was murder, and

782

I had to do it – all of us had to – or we'd every one of us been shot. They could shoot you for disobeying an order, did you know that? Once, a platoon down the line from us refused to take any more of it; said they wouldn't go over the top to be gunned down. They stood their ground when the order was given, so an officer picked out two of them; shot them as an example to the others. One of *our* officers did that.' He stopped, shaking his head. 'I wasn't a coward, though.'

'Tom – I'd never think you had been. I was there, don't forget. I saw men with terrible injuries. I cut filthy stinking uniforms off wounded men. I had to clean men of lice and fleas; stand by and watch them die of mustard gas. And not just spitting up their lungs – their faces burned by it, and their eyes. Don't tell *me* about that war! If you deserted I can understand why. But it was those special duties, wasn't it?'

'Aye.' He looked down at his hands, ashamed still. 'You'll never know how special! Do you really want to know?' he flung, bitterly. 'I was one of a firing party. They made an executioner of me!'

'Tell me, Tom.' She reached out over the table, but he pulled his hands away.

'It was at Epernay. One morning, early on. He was one of our own – a lad too young even to have been in the fighting.'

And so he told her; haltingly at first, then the words came out as if he'd waited for nothing more than to cleanse his soul. Tom had a sin too.

'That's how it was,' he finished. 'Like stepping into hell. I tell you, the only men there with any compassion were the stretcher-bearers – conscientious objectors – white-feather men. They lifted him gently, like he was a new-born bairn.'

'Giles was a stretcher-bearer, Tom. I wonder if Andrew was ever called to an – an *execution* . . .'

'I hope not. He was a decent man. But there'd have been no need for the doctor that morning at Epernay. They told us to aim for the white envelope on his tunic. I aimed straight between his eyes. I suppose if there's to be any salve for my conscience, it's that. I did it clean, and quick. I couldn't trust the other five, you see. They were shaking, useless, when they found what those special duties meant. If they'd missed . . .' Still he refused to meet her eyes. 'Do you despise me for what I did?'

'No. I went to France a girl, wanting to be near her young man. I came home a woman who'd seen things, experienced things, no one should have to endure.'

'And *I* came home a murderer. Can you wonder I deserted?'

She shook her head, then whispered, 'What then? Where did you go?'

'There was a terrible silence when it was over – none of us could believe what we'd done. Then I went wild. I knew what I intended doing could get me shot like the lad they'd just carried away, but there was such rage in me.

'I walked over to the officer who'd given the order to fire, and I flung my rifle at him. Everybody there was in a bad way, and I got away with it. I just walked away from them all, into the wood: I remember thinking it was like Brattocks. And then the shelling started – Jerry, giving us all he'd got. I thought I'd copped one, thought I was dead. The last thing I saw was the transport I should have been in – a direct hit. Eleven of them, just wiped out. They must've thought I was in there too . . .'

'Go on,' she urged.

'I woke up. It must have been afternoon. It had been just another bonny place before the shelling started, but the tree they'd tied that lad to was blown out of the earth, and the wood was like something out of No Man's Land. Trees splintered, the earth churned and pitted. And not a sound.

'I was like a man in a dream. I picked my rifle up – it was caked with mud – and I started walking. I thought that before long I'd meet up with some of our lot, but I didn't. It was getting dark when I realized I'd been walking away from the front line, not back to it.'

'I'm glad, Tom, that you walked into that wood. You'd really have been killed, if you hadn't. That protest you made saved your life,' Alice comforted. 'Perhaps God saw that act of pity, and remembered it . . .'

She ached to touch him, hold him to her, tell him everything would be all right. But the man who had come back was a stranger.

'There was a farm,' he said. 'It was so peaceful I wondered if I really was dead. I had a drink of water from a well, then I went into the barn and slept. And I knew that when I woke up, I wasn't going back to the front line. No more fighting. I swore on that dead lad's life I'd never fire another shot.'

Alice shook her head, not able to speak, dashing away her tears impatiently.

'Don't weep, lass. That war wasn't worth anybody's tears.'

'No, it wasn't. But where did you hide, Tom?'

'I went no further. I awoke and this little lass was standing there – not a bit frightened.

'Hullo. Have you come to help Papa?' she asked me, and I told her I had.

'Seems her father was sick and the farm work wasn't getting done. He'd been kicked by a horse – hurt bad. She spoke English, that little lass – Chantal, her name was.

'She took me into the farmhouse. Her mother looked at me old-fashioned, then started gabbling in French.

'Maman says if we take you in we'll have big trouble,' the lass said. But she made me understand that if I pretended to be shell-shocked and not able to speak so folk wouldn't know I was English and a deserter, I was welcome to stay if I would work.

'They needed me, you see – they didn't have a lot of choice. Chantal told me I must be their cousin who'd been wounded – badly shell-shocked – and couldn't speak or hear. The farmer agreed to it; I began to think I'd be all right. All I had to do was keep my mouth shut and act daft. And it wasn't hard. Anyone who came would jabber away in French to me. I didn't have to act gormless – I couldn't understand a word of it.'

'And no one ever suspected?'

'No. People felt pity for me, I think – a poor poilu shocked out of his mind. And it was an out-of-the-way place; they didn't have many visitors. I hid my uniform and my rifle and wore old clothes they gave me. Henri, the farmer was, and his wife was called Louise. I learned a bit of French and Chantal's English improved a lot. When Henri got better they kept me on.

'Then one day Louise went into the village; she told me when she came back that the war was over. Did I want to stay? they asked me, and I told them I'd bide my time, wait till something turned up . . .'

'So how did you get back – get away with it?' She fidgeted with her mug, not looking at him.

'My chance came three weeks ago. Chantal said there were a lot of soldiers – *Ingleesh Tommees,* she called them – in the village. Said they were marching and had put up tents for the night. Not three miles away, near where Chantal went to school.

'I knew I'd never have a better chance. I got out my uniform, polished my buttons and badges, and said goodbye. I set off before it was light – found the camp just about six o'clock. They'd got their tents taken down, ready to move off. There was a queue for breakfast at the field kitchen. I just joined it.'

'And you got away with it?'

'I did. Nobody took a lot of notice of me. They were all going back to Blighty for demob, I found out. There were all kinds there. Jocks, King's Own Yorkshires, Artillery lads. Nobody knew anybody and no one cared. They were going home!

'The southern regiments separated at Dover and went to Aldershot. The northerners were taken to Catterick. I needn't have worried. All I had to do was slip camp when it got dark, and walk home. Mind, I'll admit I'd been expecting all along to get found out. I had no kit with me, you see – just my rifle – so I decided if they challenged me I'd tell them my stuff was still in camp, back at Albert; that I was going home on compassionate leave because Mam was very ill.'

'And when you got home she – '

'She'd been dead two months. I felt ashamed.'

Alice pushed back her chair, walking to the window, staring out, seeing nothing. She didn't believe anything of this morning. In just sixty seconds from now, she would awaken to the sound of Tilda's knock and the pulling open of her bedroom curtains; would know it had all been a dream.

'So what will you do, Tom?'

'Do? I'm officially dead. They reckon there'll be a pardon for deserters, but not yet. I told them at home what I've just told you, then said I was coming to Rowangarth to find you. They said they hadn't heard from you in months.'

'Well, you've found me, so can I ask just one question?' She turned to face him, cheeks flushed. 'Why couldn't you have written? All the time you were on that farm you could have found a way to let me know. Andrew did it. He sent a postcard of Reims cathedral to Julia; just posted it without the Censors seeing it. You could have sent a card. The little girl would have posted it. You needn't have put your name on it, I'd have known.'

'It would have been too risky. Best I didn't go into the village, they said. If I'd been caught, Henri and Louise would have been in trouble, and I'd have been shot for desertion. And can I ask *you* one question? Why didn't you wait for me – at least till the war was over?'

'Life is full of whys and if-onlys, Tom. I can only say I'm sorry. What are we to do?' she whispered.

'*We? Do?* You and me aren't doing anything. It's too late. There's a baby – a Sutton child – between us. You won't leave your bairn and they wouldn't let you take him away. Sir Andrew, isn't he?'

'Called for Julia's husband. And that wasn't exactly what I meant. I was trying to ask how I can help you.'

'But of course! I got it wrong!' Anger showed briefly in his eyes, then he said, 'There's a job for me down south. It's a long story, but it was offered me by a bloke I met up with again at home. Up north on business, he was. Hadn't been in the army – had a lame foot that kept him out. So he'd got himself started on war contracts: supplies, buying and selling. Ended up a very rich man and wanting to give jobs to ex-soldiers – ease his conscience, I reckon, because he'd done so well out of the war.

'Seems he's just bought an estate in Hampshire. There's a head keeper's job there for me. All I have to do is send him references from my past two employers. I've got one – it was given me before I came to Rowangarth; all I want is one from her ladyship. But how do I tell her I'm not dead, nor ever was? How do you tell a woman who's lost both her sons to the war you are a deserter – much less ask for a reference?'

'You don't. I'll talk to Julia. She'll understand.'

'Tell her? Not likely!'

'Tom! She'll understand when she knows what made you do it. She hates that war too. Andrew was killed just days before it ended. Will you let me ask her?'

'I don't have a lot of choice, do I?'

'You don't. And Tom – say my name? Say, "I forgive you – *Alice*!" '

'Alice. Alice, bonny lass, I forgive you, though I wish you'd tell me what I'm to forgive you for; what is so enormous that you can't trust me with it like I've just trusted you?'

'It isn't possible for me to tell you, Tom. I want you to forgive me for not waiting, though. There was a reason for it, but I can't tell you.'

'All right. I'll forgive you – if you'll say you understand my not writing?'

'I do. I know how it was out there. Oh, Tom.' Tears came afresh to her eyes and she hugged herself tightly against the ache inside her. 'I used to have daydreams – they kept me going – about you and me meeting. One day I'd walk in Brattocks and you'd be there – that one was my favourite. And in that dream you'd tell me the war had never happened; and always in my dreamings, you picked me a buttercup.'

'I'll come back as soon as I can, and I'll bring your Testament with me. It's written inside it that your mam gave it to you when you left for the army. You'll want it back.'

'I'd like to have it, especially now she's – gone.'

'And the buttercup that's pressed inside it – do you want that too?'

For only a second he hesitated, then he said softly – said it like the Tom she knew and loved would have – 'Bring me the buttercup an' all, Alice.'

'You're staying with Reuben?'

'For tonight . . .'

'Best Julia gives you the reference. Her handwriting is better'n mine. But if she won't, then I'll do it – on Rowangarth notepaper. You won't go? You'll wait, till morning?'

'I'll wait, Alice.'

'Then tell me just one thing more? How did you get such a job, land on your feet like that when there are men back from the army – aye, and with medals to show for it – selling bootlaces on the streets?'

'Dad knew him from way back. He owed my father a favour. And I haven't got the job. It all depends on that reference. Men like him don't give jobs without checking up, even when it's for old times' sake.'

'I'll get it,' Alice whispered, wondering if he knew how much she wanted him to hold her, kiss her. 'And I'll not forget your little Bible.'

'Be careful what you say, Alice?'

He stood at the kitchen window, watching her go, wondering why he'd been such a fool; why he hadn't held her close like he'd wanted – like her eyes had begged him to. And kissed her, just the once.

He turned to the fire, raking it, laying on logs. He'd have liked to go out, take a walk in Brattocks Wood, but best he shouldn't; best no one saw him. There was no amnesty, yet, for deserters.

He sat in the fireside rocker and closed his eyes, thinking about her. He'd expected her, after what Reuben told him, to be dressed real smart, but she hadn't been. Just like she always was, in her cotton dress and pinafore; as if the war had never happened and she was sewing-maid at Rowangarth still. But those days were gone, and tomorrow, before it got light, he'd take himself off and out of her life. And regret coming here for the rest of his days – seeing her again. Because she was bonnier than ever he'd remembered, and he loved her every bit as much as when they had said goodbye that winter afternoon at the station. More, if it were possible, now that he knew he'd lost her.

45

'Thank heaven you're here!' Alice burst into the nursery, breathless from running.

'Where else do you expect me to be,' Julia demanded, 'when my sister leaves me to cope with babies and burpings and bottles and – '

'Julia! This is serious! I don't know how to tell you.'

'What is it? Is something wrong at Keeper's?'

'No! Oh, *yes*! Put that child down, and *listen*!'

'Hold your horses and I'll take him down to Mother. And I didn't expect you back yet. Just told Cook there'd only be two for luncheon.'

'Will you *go*!'

'All right!' She snatched up a shawl, wrapping the baby in it. Something *was* wrong. 'Won't be a minute . . .'

'Now tell me.' Alice was still pacing the floor when Julia returned.

'Well, I – ' Alice drew a shuddering breath, all at once tongue-tied. How was she to tell it to Julia, whose husband would never come home? 'I – oh – it's Tom! He's at Keeper's. And I'm sorry, but there's just no other way to tell you.'

'Tom Dwerryhouse? *Your* Tom? *Alive?*'

Mutely, Alice nodded.

'But *how*? A prisoner, was he? Are you sure?'

'I'm sure.' Alice closed her eyes. She wanted to laugh, to cry. She wanted not to hurt Julia; wanted it to be exactly like in her dreamings, with the clock turned back to those blissful days before the war. She began to shake, then the tears came again, and deep, jerking sobs. 'Can you imagine it, Julia? Can you?'

'I imagine it all the time – about Andrew, that is.'

'Of course you do, and that's why it's so awful, telling you. Yet I'm glad.'

'And I'm glad for you; I truly am. But I'll ring for tea. You look as if you need a cup. And have a cigarette? They're very soothing . . .'

'No, thanks.' She turned to stare out of the window as Mary opened the door. Not for anything could she be seen in this state: hair disarranged, cheeks red from running, wearing an old cotton housedress and apron. Because Mary *would* notice. She always had. Straight down to the kitchen with the news, and what-did-they-make-of-that? Not that she cared. Not for herself. It was Tom she worried about.

'Tom's a deserter,' she gasped, the minute Mary closed the door behind her. 'He wasn't killed. Those special duties he was sent on . . .'

'Alice, go to your room! Change your dress and put your hair up properly – quickly, before Mary comes back!'

'Didn't you hear me? I said that Tom was a – '

'I heard you! But calm yourself, then you can tell me.'

In a daze, Alice went through the motions of washing her face and pinning up her hair. She was wearing a skirt and blouse when she met Mary, walking along the passage.

'Thank you. I'll take it in,' Alice smiled. She was learning never to be forward; never to be Alice of old; never to risk a snub.

'Milady . . .' Mary opened the nursery door for her, then closed it again softly.

'That's better,' Julia smiled. 'I'll pour. And I'm having a cigarette, if you don't mind.'

Alice shook her head, then started her pacing again, teacup ignored.

'You aren't taking this seriously, Julia. You haven't heard one word I've said.'

'Oh, but I have. And as for taking it seriously – well, it took me just the time you were out to realize we could be in quite a mess.'

'Why, for goodness' sake?'

'Because you'll be going to him, won't you – and there's Drew to think about. Legally he's yours.'

'But I'm not going anywhere! Tom made it plain he didn't want me. He mellowed a bit, but at first there was such anger in him it was as if he'd slapped me. And he was right. I should have waited for him.'

'Did you tell him why you hadn't?'

'How could I? But he told me where he had been – *he* trusted *me*. I said I'd have to tell you and he agreed that I must. He didn't do anything bad, Julia. Giles would have agreed with him, if he'd been here. Will you let me tell you? There's only you and me can help him. Will you give him a fair hearing?'

'You know I will. Just drink your tea, then begin at the beginning.'

So Alice told it; every smallest detail; every word remembered. About the special duties and the soldier condemned to die and him too young ever to have been in the fighting. Poured out every word, her eyes begging absolution for Tom.

'And that's it,' she finished, hands to her blazing cheeks, taking a gulp of tea gone cold in the cup. 'I'll give him a reference if you can't bring yourself to do it – but it would be better in your hand and, besides, I don't know what to say.'

'You would tell nothing but the truth, Alice: that Thomas Dwerryhouse was employed at Rowangarth for three years before joining the army; that he had always given satisfactory service, and could be well recommended for the position of head keeper. And then you would sign it *Alice Sutton*. Simple.

'But I'll do it for you – sign your name too. And you

are right. Giles would have agreed with Tom. He hated any killing, and to have to do it in cold blood . . .'

'You understand, then? You don't condemn Tom for a coward?'

'A coward doesn't throw down his rifle and risk a firing squad. Your Tom was brave to do that.'

'He isn't my Tom – not any longer. We can't turn back the clock. But he's alive, and I'm thankful for that.'

'I don't understand you.' Julia stubbed out her cigarette. 'Do you imagine anything would keep me from Andrew – little Drew, even? Look, love – why don't we tell Mother? She would understand. She loved Pa just as I loved Andrew; just as I know you love Tom. She would tell you to go to him.'

'Happen she would, but what would folk think if I was to leave the child? Yet he's Rowangarth's son. Giles took him when he wed me. He isn't mine and I can't love him. I know that to your way of thinking he's the child that you and Andrew never had, and you can love him because you helped him to be born and found milk for him when he was hungry. But you aren't *me*! You weren't in the nuns' stable; didn't have to endure what I did!

'And do we tell your mother the truth, Julia – that I can leave the child because he's Elliot's? She was willing to accept the story Giles told her – could understand it, even. But to tell her now I could give up the child because I hate the man who fathered him – would she forgive the lies we'd told her?'

'But we *won't* tell her! She knows it is Tom you really loved; that it was easy to seek comfort in a moment of terrible grief. She thinks Drew was meant to be; sent to comfort *her*. To tell her the truth would be cruel. There are times when it is better to lie . . .'

'You're telling me to go to Tom. Will you also tell me what people would think of a woman who left her child?'

'But it's nothing to do with *people,* though we could tell them you've gone to France with Aunt Sutton because you haven't picked up as you should have done after Drew's birth. Richard James would confirm it. He's said it often enough. That would do, to be going on with. Think about it, Alice, though if I were in your shoes I'd be packing my cases now.'

'I can't believe this – not any of it. I'd expected you not to understand, to be angry about what Tom did. Is it that you want me to go? Do you want the child for yourself, Julia, and me out of the way?'

'Alice Sutton, what a goose you are! Of course I want the child. At first, I had to keep him alive – not for me, but for Mother and for Rowangarth too. And then I realized I had someone to love. Not in the way I loved Andrew – that will never happen to me again. But there was someone who needed me – can you blame me?

'And I don't want you out of the way. You are special to me, Alice. You were there the night Andrew and I met. When you go, *if* you go, there'll be a part of me goes with you. But can't you see I want *someone* to be happy; for something good to have come out of that dreadful war!'

'You mean it, don't you? You honestly want me to be happy.' Alice took out her handkerchief, making no effort to stop the sudden tears.

'Alice! Stop your boo-hooing! I'll write that reference and you must take it at once. And while you are gone, I'll tell Mother all about it. She will agree with me – and with what Tom did, too. But tell me just one thing more? Tell me you believe me when I say I care so much for you that I want you to go? Because I do.'

'I believe you. But here we are, making plans – what are we to do if Tom is so hurt he won't ever forgive me? We're taking it for granted he wants me?'

'Don't be an idiot,' Julia flung. 'I'll go and write

that reference for you. Are you *sure* you won't have a cigarette; you're shaking all over?'

Alice sped to Keeper's Cottage, the reference in her hand, Morgan straining on his lead. She wanted to laugh and cry, both at the same time. Big, lovely, happy tears. Julia had understood and so would her mother-in-law. And it were best the child be brought up amongst his own kind. Julia would be a good mother; make sure he never wanted for love. Panting for breath, she pushed open the door.

'Reuben? Tom? I'm back, and see who's with me?'

She stopped, looking around her, trying not to notice the sadness, the pity, in the old man's eyes.

'Reuben?' She snatched at her breath, running into the little front parlour, flinging wide the door. 'Where is Tom? What has happened?'

'He's gone, lass. I'm sorry. I begged him to stay, say goodbye, decent like, but he'd have none of it.'

'But I've brought his reference, his Testament.'

'He asked that I send them on. He's away down south, he says – will tell that man the reference is being sent by post. It isn't unusual for them to be sent that way.'

'Where is he, Reuben – at the station?'

'Nay, lass – he'll be half-way to York now. Had it in mind to get the afternoon train south, if he could. He had his cases with him, ready to go. You'll not catch him.'

'He didn't want me.' Alice sat heavily in the chair at the fireside, holding her hands to the warmth. 'He didn't give me a chance to explain – tell him I wanted to be with him. He only knows half the story, Reuben.'

'Aye, an' it's a shame. If I hadn't given my word, I'd have told him.'

'Maybe it's as well he never knew the truth. God knows what he might have done; blamed Elliot Sutton for coming between him and me. Knowing Tom, he'd likely have gone looking for him, done him an injury. Tom has a terrible temper on him when he's roused. Best he never knew.'

'So that's what you think, is it?' He picked up the envelope she had laid on the table, reading the words, *To Whom It May Concern.* 'That's Miss Julia's writing. Did she do it, then?'

'Yes, and gladly. I told her everything and she said I should go to Tom; leave the child with her and be damned to what people might think.'

'And so you should. Us as knows the whole truth of it would wish you well, Alice. Now you leave those things with me – I'll post them on. I said I would.'

'You know where he is? Where am I to find him?'

'Easy.' He reached behind the tea caddy. 'He left me his address. You know where he is now. Seems he decided to leave the choice to you.'

'You mean I should swallow my pride and go to him?'

'One of you has to – best it's you, Alice. Tom made the first move: let you know where he'll be. He was hurt bad. And there's no room for pride in loving. Must an old man tell you that?'

Alice met up with Jin Dobb at the stile. She was carrying the can she brought twice a day now, filled with milk for the child.

'Now then,' Jin greeted her. 'And where are you off to in such a rush? And haven't you something to tell me?'

'Tell, Jin? What about?'

'You've forgotten, haven't you; forgotten what I said that night before you went off nursing?'

'When you told my fortune, you mean? But wasn't that just a bit of fun?' Alice chose her words with care. You never knew quite where you were with Jin Dobb.

'It wasn't fun, not the way I saw it, and you'd do well to think back!'

'I remember you said I'd have two children. Small hope of that now,' Alice admitted, warily.

'I told you there were tears for you, and I told you you'd know happiness and have two bairns. One would come in sadness; the other would bring joy. And nothing has changed. There's another bairn for you.'

'Don't, Jin! There's times I'm afraid of what you say. You said I'd have a brush with death – I remember you telling me that.'

'And you did an' all, when that babbie was born!'

'Yes,' Alice said quietly. 'But what are you trying to say? Is there something more I should know?'

'Not *know*. Remember, more like. I told you about a wood; an imaginary wood. I told you you'd walk three times through it, and twice sadly. I don't know about the crooked stick I said you'd find, an' I don't want to. But I know who the weak and frail stick was. Do you get my meaning, Alice Hawthorn?'

'I do, Jin.' They were standing at the stile, unwilling to climb over it. 'There's another walk for me?'

'You know there is. I said you'd have your straight, stout stave – if you had the courage to take that third walk, and the sense to listen to your heart . . .'

'You told me that, I'll not deny it.'

'Then if you won't listen to me, why aren't you listening to your heart? Where has your courage gone? Are you going to lose him a second time, just because you can't see the wood for the trees?'

'Now see here, I don't know what you are on about!' Alice swallowed hard but it did nothing to stop the wild pulse in her throat, nor calm the panic that thrashed inside her. 'Tell me? Lose him a second time? Lose *who*?'

'Tom Dwerryhouse – who else? He's here, an' you know

it. I saw him this morning afore it was hardly light, going into Reuben's house. And don't try to deny it – you who looks like she don't know whether she's coming or going!'

'Jin, don't tell? He shouldn't have been here. Please, Jin . . .?'

'Course I won't tell if you say I'm not to. But it was him I saw, wasn't it?'

'It was, and he's gone. He just came for something.'

'He came for Alice Hawthorn, and well she knows it! Foolish woman you, to let him go!'

'He was a prisoner,' Alice gasped. 'Nobody was told.'

''Tis none of my business where he was, and I'll hold my tongue about seeing him, if that's what's upsetting you. But think on about what old Jin told you!'

She climbed the stile, hurrying towards the house with never a backward glance.

Think on, Jin had said, and Reuben too. And she *had* thought!

She turned on her heel, hurrying back the way she had come; past Keeper's Cottage, along the winding path to the edge of the wood where the rooks had built their nests again.

Black birds, it's Alice – Alice Hawthorn, as was – and I'm come to tell you that Tom is safe; he wasn't killed, like they said. And I want you to know I'm going to him, and nothing shall stop me! I don't know when it will be, but I'll come and see you before I go – say goodbye . . .

May, and the hawthorn blossom smelling bitter-sweet on the hedgerows, and the first of the buttercups flowering in the cow pasture. This was the time to go: six years on from the time of their first meeting was when it must be.

She had said her goodbye to Reuben, weeping bitterly at their parting. 'I don't want to leave you. You've always been here when I needed you – come live with me and Tom?'

'Nay, lass. The young and the old don't mix. Write me letters so I'll know how you are, and if I think you're needed here, I'll send for you – the little lad, I mean . . .'

'Bless you – though Julia would let me know. And it would only be if something legal cropped up – me being his mother, like. But I don't want to think this is goodbye. Come and stay with us, Reuben, for a holiday?'

'All that way? How's an old man like me to go travelling all those miles; me, that's never set foot outside the Riding?'

'But you'd be fine! I've been to France, remember, and thought nothing of it. Julia would see you on to the London train at York – you know she would – and I'd be at King's Cross to meet you. Say you'll come? Promise me hand on heart you will?'

'We-e-e-ll – happen I might. I'll think about it, though long train rides cost good money, remember!'

'But I'd send you the fare, you stubborn old thing!' Alice laughed. 'Wouldn't seeing you be worth a few shillings?'

'I'd like to think it would,' he smiled, 'but you'll need every penny you can lay hands on, once you're wed.'

'*If* we're wed! Tom mightn't want me.'

'Happen he mightn't – but if I'm any judge, he will. A man has his pride, though, and till he knows the truth of how it was, then it's you must go to him.'

'I know that. And I *can* afford your fare, Reuben. Remember I once told you I had nearly five pounds in my penny bank when I left to go nursing? Well, they paid us twenty pounds a year when we were in France, and I hardly touched any of it. And there is Giles's money. Oh, I know that what he owned will go to the child – all of Rowangarth and the tea, in India – but when I came

800

home he made me an allowance. My own money, he said it was, for clothes and fripperies, he said. And since I've never been one to waste money on fripperies, and needed few clothes as I was either pregnant or in black, I've got quite a lot of money. I've got enough,' she rushed on, 'to buy me a little cottage of my own, if the worst happens. If Tom doesn't want me, then I'll send to Rowangarth for my things and set up on my own, taking in sewing. I'll manage.'

'Lass, lass – he *will* want you. He's never stopped wanting you nor you him, but I'd be careful if I were you, not to let him know about all that money you have – leastways not what Sir Giles put into your pocket. Tom's so cussed proud that sometimes I could shake him – if I were young enough and daft enough to try it. Keep that brass for a rainy day, eh?'

'I will, Reuben – though now you'll be able to come to see us without having to fret overmuch about where the fare is coming from. And you *will* come? I couldn't bear it if – if . . .'

She threw herself into his arms, not wanting to leave him, because in leaving him she was leaving Julia, and Mother-in-law, and Brattocks Wood, and everything and everyone she had loved these years past.

'Don't take on, lovey. Old Reuben won't forget you. And when you've got saved up for a bed in the spare room, then I'll come and see you – I promise. I'm not so old I can't get myself on and off a train.'

He held her until her weeping stopped, patting her back, making little hushing sounds, telling her she'd once have given most of what was left of her life just to see Tom, yet now she was weeping because very soon she would be with him for the rest of her days.

She had walked back to Rowangarth sadly, slowly too, to give herself time to pull herself together; to tell herself how lucky she was, how easy it had been.

Mother-in-law had smoothed the way for her, letting it be known that Lady Alice was to stay for a time with Aunt Sutton, a change of air and surroundings being considered beneficial by Doctor James. It had been accepted without question too, except by Jin Dobb, who had smiled secretly because she liked knowing something others did not.

Now the time to leave had come and Julia was to drive her to the station in the pony and cart. Alice was taking just one case: the rest of her things she left behind in the little attic bedroom to be sent on later, because she was afraid to tempt Fate.

'Don't worry,' Julia had smiled. 'He'll be there, waiting.'

'I'm not so sure.' Courage it would need, Jin had said, to take a third walk through that so-to-speak wood, and courage she had in plenty, but listening to her heart, her foolish, uncertain heart, was altogether another matter.

Go! it told her most times; *stay*! it said, others. She had not heard from Tom, though Reuben seemed to know he was settled comfortably, and liking the south, though stubbornly he told her precious little else.

This then was her last walk in Brattocks Wood. She had thanked the rooks for keeping her secrets, and said goodbye, and now she must say goodbye to the child; to the bonny little boy with Sutton-fair hair, and eyes already changing from blue to grey; to the colour Sir John's had been, and Andrew's. Sad that one day he would come to realize his real mother had abandoned him, and him never to know the real truth of it. He lay in his cot in the nursery. He smiled a lot now, and gave out little chuckles when something pleased him. He looked up, smiling broadly, when she took his hand in her own.

'I'm come to say goodbye, and to wish you well, child. You have a good aunt and a fine inheritance in Rowangarth.

Julia will love you always – your grandmother, too – and there will be Nathan to guide you when it's a man's advice you need. I'm sorry I couldn't love you, and that you'll always believe it was Giles who fathered you. For those things I ask your forgiveness.'

She touched his cheek gently and he smiled again, chubby arms waving. 'I'm going to Tom. This life is not for me. Once, I coveted orchids but now I know I'm a buttercup girl.

'Goodbye, little Sir Andrew. Your aunt Julia will write to me, let me know how you are. Grow up decent and true – Sutton-true – for her.'

She turned abruptly, closing the door quietly, walking down the stairs for the last time.

'Can I come in, Mother-in-law?' she whispered, standing hesitantly in the doorway of the little winter parlour.

'It's time to go already, Alice?'

'Yes. Julia has gone to get the pony and cart.'

'I would so like to come to the station with you – wave you goodbye.'

'No, dearest. We agreed it was best you shouldn't.' She was near to tears. One more kind word and she would weep like a baby. 'I want to thank you for being so good to me, so kind.'

'And I want to thank you for Drew, Alice; for letting us keep him. You must always stay in touch. You are Drew's mother – his legal guardian still. There might be decisions only you can make – you know that?'

'You shall always know where I am – even if Tom doesn't want me.'

'I don't want you to go, child. You have been such a joy to me. If ever you need a shoulder, I am here. But your Tom wants you, is waiting for you, I'm sure of it. Be happy together. You deserve to be.'

'Bless you.' Her voice was little more than a whisper. 'And will you remember me not as Alice Sutton – proud though I've been to bear the name – but as Hawthorn, who did your sewing and was glad to do it.'

She went into Helen's open arms, wanting to go, wanting to stay; wanting, all at once, to be the Alice who had come here with all she owned in a brown paper carrier bag.

Gently she laid her lips to Helen's cheek, then walked, head high, to the door. There she paused, and turned.

'Goodbye, milady.' She made a deep, slow curtsey, head bowed, and in that moment she was a sewing-maid again.

'Goodbye, my very dear Hawthorn. God bless you and keep you.'

'I put something in your case,' Julia said as they stood on the platform at the little station. 'It's to remember me by – I want you to have it.'

'You shouldn't have. You gave me Morgan – he's enough. I'll never be far away from Rowangarth, with him to remind me.'

'Giles would have wanted you to have him.'

'Aye.' Alice wanted the train to come. If it didn't arrive soon her courage would fail her, no matter what Jinny Dobb had said. 'You'll write?' Already her eyes were bright with tears she had vowed not to shed.

'All the time.' Julia was weeping too.

'Please don't cry. And you know how I dislike being waved goodbye? Why don't you go now?' Alice pleaded. 'Give me a hug and a kiss, and promise never to forget me, then go – *please?*'

They stood, arms clasped, cheek upon cheek. 'I won't forget you.' Julia turned, then walked quickly away, head high, shoulders stiff.

Down the track, the train hooted. In just half a minute it would unload passengers and mailbags then return to York.

Alice dabbed her eyes, breathing deeply to help calm

804

the turmoil, the awful ache inside her. The engine came to a stop, hissing and clanking and making altogether too much noise for so small and unimportant a train. She held Morgan's lead tightly, picking up her case.

Only one passenger alighted, and already a porter was piling his luggage on to a trolley. He had many cases and bags, and wore the uniform of a guards officer. He was tall, and dark, and spoke to the porter in too loud a voice.

Morgan stiffened, then gave a yelp of anger. The lead slipped from Alice's fingers.

'Come back! Come here!'

She hurried to where the spaniel crouched, teeth bared in a snarl, at the feet of the loud-mouthed man.

'Well, well, well. If it isn't the little sewing-maid,' the voice softly mocked. 'Tut! I beg your pardon. It's the young widow Sutton! Good afternoon, your ladyship!'

The dark eyes, the too-familiar smile, mocked her. The man took a step away from Morgan, still giving out low, warning growls.

Alice picked up the lead, inclining her head exactly as her ladyship would have done, clenching her hands so he wouldn't know how they shook, looking down at her shoes so he might not see the fear in her eyes.

'Mr Sutton,' she said gravely, picking up her case, walking past him as though her heart were not thudding nor her hands cold with sweat. 'Good day to you.'

She stepped on to the train, closing the compartment door, pulling on the leather strap to close the window, strangely glad she had come face to face with Elliot Sutton. Had she felt any doubts about that third walk through the wood, they were gone the instant she saw him.

Outwardly she had acquitted herself well; inside, in spite of the silent, screaming panic, she was grateful he would be the last to use her title; for where she was going, no one would ever hear of it.

The train pulled slowly away from the platform, gathering speed as it passed the far end of Brattocks Wood, where once Tom had stood to welcome her home from London.

She dabbed her eyes dry, calmer now. Alone in the compartment, she took a tiny key from her purse, and unlocked her case, curious to know what Julia had left inside for her. She lifted the tissue paper that covered it.

She remembered it well. Every stitch by hand; sewn with affection for a November bride – for a woman with love in her eyes who carried creamy white orchids, and wore a blue dress.

'Goodbye, Julia.' She lifted the silk nightdress to her cheek. They had shared too much happiness, too many tears ever to forget. 'Thank you for giving me something so precious.'

Alice rounded the bend in the lane and stopped, breath indrawn, gazing at the house standing alone in the trees. Taking in every detail with one sweeping glance, she walked nearer until she could read the words Head Keeper, painted in faded letters on the five-barred gate.

The red-brick cottage stood neglected, as if no one had passed this way for years, let alone lived there. She closed her eyes, seeing the doors brightly green again, the windows painted freshly white, and polished too – for surely they hadn't been cleaned in years!

The house stood surrounded by beech trees, their newly-opened leaves pale green and silky, bluebells growing thickly beneath them. She stood, hands possessively on the gate, loving the neglected house, wanting to clean it, care for it, live in it for ever. Timidly she lifted the iron knocker, bringing it down three times, listening to its echo inside.

It was empty. No one lived there and the realization saddened her. She had so wanted this to be Tom's house – hers and Tom's – had seen it briefly, mentally, as it should be, could be.

Unwilling to leave just yet, she made her way to the back, for wasn't it a fact that no one in the country ever knocked on front doors. The one at the back was the one friends and visitors used; the front one was opened only for funerals, weddings and christenings – and when the vicar called.

Hope rose afresh inside her. A milk can had been left on the doorstep, a flat stone holding down the lid. Someone lived here; someone who kept labrador pups in the brick kennels to her left. They yapped excitedly as Morgan stopped, sniffed, growled a warning, then went snuffling on his way, tail wagging, nose down.

All at once she knew this was Tom's house and that his door would not be locked. She squinted through the uncurtained window at what was surely the kitchen of a man living alone; a man who piled unwashed pans and dishes into the stone sink. She knocked on the door then turned the knob, calling, 'Tom? Tom Dwerryhouse?'

A rocking chair stood to the right of a cooking range that hadn't had a shining in years, though a fire was laid in the grate with kindling and logs, ready to be lit.

She looked around her for some familiar object to finally establish that this was the house she sought. There was no rug at the hearth; the floor was in need of sweeping and scrubbing. A single chair stood beneath the whitewood table; one chair, where there ought to be a pair. It looked so lonely and alone, that tears rose in a knot in her throat. Then, as her eyes swept the walls, the mantelshelf, she knew without doubt that this was where Tom lived. She reached to take down the photograph of a smiling young girl wearing the uniform of a nurse.

To Tom with all my love. Alice.

He had not destroyed it as he might have done; he had kept it, hopefully loving her still, though his cussed pride had prevented him from writing and telling her so. And she loved him, and would tell him so; beg him not to send her away. She would even, she decided in a rush of grateful relief, tell him the truth of it all, though she had vowed never to do so. But now they had found each other again, nothing must stand in the way of their love. There must be no deceits, no suspicions, nor words left unspoken between them. She owed him the truth; best he should know so their new beginning should be free from doubt.

She looked at the mantel-clock, checking it with the watch pinned to her blouse. Soon he should return for his midday break. Taking off her hat and shawl, she laid them on the chair, then walked slowly, quietly, up the uncovered stairs.

There, she found three bedrooms; two of them small and empty; the third large and light. In it stood an unmade bed; beside it a chair with a candlestick on it. Hung on a hook behind the door was Tom's best keeping suit – the one he had been measured for in York so long ago. She touched it gently, lovingly, then returned to the bed. Turning the mattress, plumping the pillows, she quickly made it, then returned to the kitchen to wait.

The pantry door stood open, demanding her inspection. In it a rabbit hung from a hook; behind the door stood a sack of potatoes. On a plate, covered with a bowl, lay butter, margarine and cheese in small amounts; one man's rations for a week.

She closed her eyes, in her mind seeing clean-scrubbed shelves filled with jams, pickles, bottled fruit and apple pies, brown from the oven, set to cool on the slate slab.

'Tom, lad, when did you last have a decent meal?' she asked of no one in particular, checking the time again.

Suppose he didn't come home until nightfall? He could be at the far end of the estate, bread and cheese in his game bag, and a bottle of cold tea. She would wait half an hour, she decided – exactly half an hour – then return to her lodgings and unpack her case. First, though, she would leave a note to tell him where to find her – if he wanted to find her.

She opened drawers, but could find no paper on which to write; no pencil, no ink bottle, nor pen. Then all at once she remembered there was another way to tell him.

. . . and when I find you, my darling, I'll bring you buttercups, so you'll know I have been . . .

A vow made long ago to a dead lover, only he hadn't died and he still loved her – oh, please, he still loved her? She would leave something better than a pencilled note; something only she could have left there – something only he would understand.

Taking the chipped glass vase from the mantel, she filled it with water at the backyard pump, then set it on the table.

'Sorry, Morgan.' She tied the spaniel's lead to the boot scraper at the door. 'Good dog – stay!'

She heard the excited barking as she left the field, a bouquet of buttercups in her hand. The garden gate she had closed behind her stood open, and she stopped, all at once unable to move.

He was standing on the doorstep, Morgan's lead in his hand and his eyes were the blue that made you notice them, and he was every bit as tall and fair and good to look at.

'Does this creature belong to you?' He asked it gravely, softly, because his throat had gone peculiar. He could hardly say the words because she looked so beautiful; eyes big and brown and anxious, a tendril of hair trailing her cheek.

'He does,' she whispered. 'Once, he belonged to Sir Giles, but he's mine now. And he isn't a creature. He's

809

called Morgan, and I won't let him upset the game-birds.'
She stood there, one hand on the gate, still wanting him,
begging him silently to let her back into his heart.

'You came, Alice.'

'Did you think I wouldn't?'

'I don't know, but I wanted you to.'

He held wide his arms then, and she went into them
thankfully, joyfully, letting the flowers fall, spilling them
at their feet.

'Why didn't you write, Tom – tell me so?' She felt
the roughness of his jacket against her cheek; the years
between rolled away and they were in Brattocks Wood
again, and she a slip of a lass, not old enough to wed him.

'It wouldn't have been right. That's why I left Reuben's
house without saying goodbye; the choice had to be
yours.' He laid his cheek to hers, loving her, needing
her. 'You'll be staying?'

'Aye. I've got lodgings in the village for six weeks.'
Three weeks to establish her name on the parish register;
three weeks for the calling of the banns.

'I was feared you wouldn't come,' he whispered.

'Darling.' She strained closer, his nearness sending an
ache of wanting tearing through her. 'Do you remember
I once said there is a time and a place for everything, and
that our time would come: it was the night you went away
to Richmond, to the army. This isn't the place I thought
it would be, but this is our day, and our time has come.

'And, Tom – I want to tell you. I said that morning at
Reuben's that I never would, never could, but it's only
right you should know why I didn't wait – why I married
Giles. And when I tell you, will you try to understand,
and happen forgive me?'

He pushed her a little way from him, marvelling at the
magnitude of his love for her, wondering how he had
endured so long without her.

'Forgive? That I won't, bonny lass, because I took a

solemn oath that if ever you came to me I would never ask. I'd take you as you were, I vowed, as the woman I loved – *love* – and wouldn't care what had come between us. Whatever it was, I don't want to know. It's you I want. Is the bairn at Rowangarth still? Do you want him here with you?'

'No, Tom. He's with her ladyship. He belongs there. He's a Sutton; Rowangarth will be his one day. Best he's with his own kind. And Julia loves him so. He's all she has now.

'But one day I *will* tell you how I could leave him behind me; explain how it was so you'll understand everything that seems not to make sense now. And since you are taking me on trust, I'll make you a promise, Tom Dwerryhouse. When I hold our firstborn in my arms, then you shall know – every last word of it. Will that satisfy you?'

'If that's the way you want it. It seems there'll be no peace till you've told it, sweetheart, so I reckon the sooner I wed you the sooner I shall know – if know I must.'

He looked down then, seeing the buttercups scattered at their feet, and he bent to gather them up, giving them to her.

'I see you've been picking flowers,' he smiled.

'For you – so you'd know who it was had left them.' She stepped inside the house, put the bouquet in the vase, then turning to him said, 'Kiss me, Tom – please?'

He tilted her chin with his forefinger, and laid his mouth gently on hers.

'I love you, Alice. Don't leave me again?'

'Never. I promise.' She reached on tiptoe, trailing her lips across his cheek, his chin, searching, eyes closed, for his mouth. And with that kiss yesterday was banished, and tomorrow was a delight still to come. 'I love you, too,' she whispered. 'I never stopped loving you.'

Through the open door a shaft of sunlight touched the buttercups and turned them into a shimmer of gold, and from the meadow a skylark flew high into the sky, trilling out a love song in notes of silver; but they did not hear it.